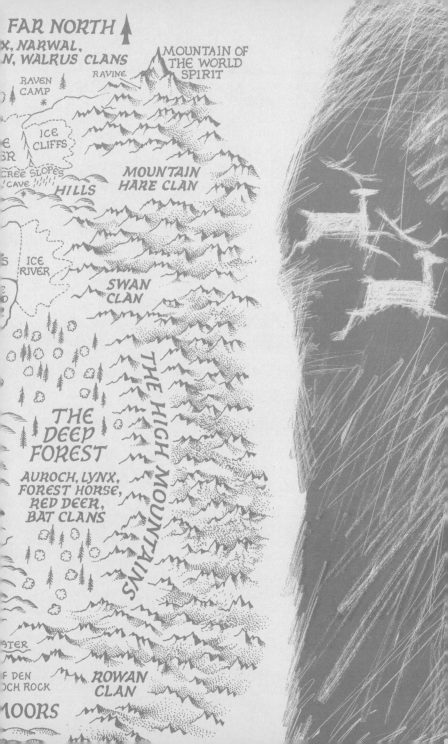

CHRONICLES of ANCIENT DARKNESS

OMNIBUS

3 books in 1

WOLF BROTHER ⊼ SPIRIT WALKER ⊼ SOUL EATER

'*Wolf Brother* . . . is the kind of story you dream of reading and all too rarely find . . . The descriptions of an ancient world . . . are wonderful. The vivid prose leaps off the page.' *The Times*

'It is comforting to read a book that provides one with the feeling that the author has served his or her work with the level of devoted precision that is apparent in *Spirit Walker*. Every little detail or snippet of description is well calculated and elegantly handled by Michelle Paver ... the perfect concoction of action and narrative is what make the book so attractive . . . a first-class story' *Saturday Telegraph*

'the third of the consistently superb *Chronicles of Ancient Darkness* novels, [*Soul Eater*] is meticulously realised' Amanda Craig, *The Times*

'crackles with atmosphere' Julia Eccleshare, *Guardian*

Also by Michelle Paver

Outcast
Oath Breaker
Ghost Hunter
(from August 2009)

Visit Michelle Paver's website at
www.michellepaver.com

and meet other readers of the
Chronicles of Ancient Darkness series
at the official worldwide fan site, www.torak.info

CHRONICLES OF ANCIENT DARKNESS

OMNIBUS

WOLF BROTHER ⚹ SPIRIT WALKER ⚹ SOUL EATER

MICHELLE PAVER

Orion
Children's Books

This omnibus edition first published in Great Britain in 2008
by Orion Children's Books
This paperback edition first published in Great Britain in 2009
by Orion Children's Books
a division of the Orion Publishing Group Ltd
Orion House
5 Upper St Martin's Lane
London WC2H 9EA
An Hachette UK Company

3 5 7 9 10 8 6 4 2

Originally published in three separate volumes:
Wolf Brother
First published in Great Britain in 2004
Spirit Walker
First published in Great Britain in 2005
Soul Eater
First published in Great Britain in 2006
All by Orion Children's Books

A catalogue record for this book is available from the British Library
Printed in Great Britain by Clays Ltd, St Ives plc

ISBN 978 1 84255 775 4

CONTENTS

WOLF BROTHER

ONE

Torak woke with a jolt from a sleep he'd never meant to have.

The fire had burned low. He crouched in the fragile shell of light and peered into the looming blackness of the Forest. He couldn't see anything. Couldn't hear anything. Had it come back? Was it out there now, watching him with its hot, murderous eyes?

He felt hollow and cold. He knew that he badly needed food, and that his arm hurt, and his eyes were scratchy with tiredness, but he couldn't really *feel* it. All night he'd guarded the wreck of the spruce bough shelter, and watched his father bleed. How could this be happening?

Only yesterday – *yesterday* – they'd pitched camp in the blue autumn dusk. Torak had made a joke, and his father was laughing. Then the Forest exploded. Ravens screamed. Pines cracked. And out of the dark beneath the trees surged a deeper darkness: a huge rampaging menace in bear form.

Suddenly death was upon them. A frenzy of claws. A welter of sound to make the ears bleed. In a heartbeat, the creature had smashed their shelter to splinters. In a heartbeat, it had ripped a ragged wound in his father's side. Then it was gone, melting into the Forest as silently as mist.

But what kind of bear *stalks* men – then vanishes without making the kill? What kind of bear plays with its prey?

And where was it now?

Torak couldn't see beyond the firelight, but he knew that the clearing, too, was a wreck of snapped saplings and trampled bracken. He smelt pine-blood and clawed earth. He heard the soft, sad bubbling of the stream thirty paces away. The bear could be anywhere.

Beside him, his father moaned. Slowly he opened his eyes and looked at his son without recognition.

Torak's heart clenched. 'It – it's me,' he stammered. 'How do you feel?'

Pain convulsed his father's lean brown face. His cheeks were tinged with grey, making the clan-tattoos stand out lividly. Sweat matted his long dark hair.

His wound was so deep that as Torak clumsily stanched it with beard-moss, he saw his father's guts glistening in the firelight. He had to grit his teeth to keep from retching. He hoped Fa didn't notice – but of course he did. Fa was a hunter. He noticed everything.

'Torak . . . ' he breathed. His hand reached out, his hot fingers clinging to Torak's as eagerly as a child. Torak swallowed. Sons clutch their fathers' hands; not the other way around.

He tried to be practical: to be a man instead of a boy. 'I've still got some yarrow leaves,' he said, fumbling for his medicine pouch with his free hand. 'Maybe that'll stop the –'

'Keep it. You're bleeding too.'

'Doesn't hurt,' lied Torak. The bear had thrown him against a birch tree, bruising his ribs and gashing his left forearm.

'Torak – leave. Now. Before it comes back.'

Torak stared at him. He opened his mouth but no sound came.

'You must,' said his father.

'No. *No.* I can't –'

'Torak – I'm dying. I'll be dead by sunrise.'

Torak gripped the medicine pouch. There was a roaring in his ears. 'Fa –'

'Give me – what I need for the Death Journey. Then get your things.'

The Death Journey. No. No.

But his father's face was stern. 'My bow,' he said. 'Three arrows. You – keep the rest. Where I'm going – hunting's easy.'

There was a tear in the knee of Torak's buckskin leggings. He dug his thumbnail into the flesh. It hurt. He forced himself to concentrate on that.

'Food,' gasped his father. 'The dried meat. You – take it all.'

Torak's knee had started to bleed. He kept digging. He tried not to picture his father on the Death Journey. He tried not to picture himself alone in the Forest. He was only twelve summers old. He couldn't survive on his own. He didn't know how.

'Torak! Move!'

Blinking furiously, Torak reached for his father's weapons and laid them by his side. He divided up the arrows, pricking his fingers on the sharp flint points. Then he shouldered his quiver and bow, and scrabbled in the wreckage for his small black basalt axe. His hazelwood pack had been smashed in the attack; he'd have to cram everything else into his jerkin, or tie it to his belt.

He reached for his reindeer-hide sleeping-sack.

'Take mine,' murmured his father. 'You never did – repair yours. And – swap knives.'

Torak was aghast. 'Not your knife! You'll need it!'

'You'll need it more. And – it'll be good to have something of yours on the Death Journey.'

'Fa, please. Don't – '

In the Forest, a twig snapped.

Torak spun round.

The darkness was absolute. Everywhere he looked the shadows were bear-shaped.

No wind.

No birdsong.

Just the crackle of the fire and the thud of his heart. The Forest itself was holding its breath.

His father licked the sweat from his lips. 'It's not here yet,' he said. 'Soon. It will come for me soon . . . Quick. The knives.'

Torak didn't want to swap knives. That would make it final. But his father was watching him with an intensity that allowed no refusal.

Clenching his jaw so hard that it hurt, Torak took his own knife and put it into Fa's hand. Then he untied the buckskin sheath from his father's belt. Fa's knife was beautiful and deadly, with a blade of banded blue slate shaped like a willow leaf, and a haft of red deer antler that was bound with elk sinew for a better grip. As Torak looked down at it, the truth hit him. He was getting ready for a life without Fa. 'I'm not leaving you!' he cried. 'I'll fight it, I – '

'No! No-one can fight this bear!'

4

Ravens flew up from the trees.

Torak forgot to breathe.

'Listen to me,' hissed his father. 'A bear – any bear – is the strongest hunter in the Forest. You know that. But this bear – *much* stronger.'

Torak felt the hairs on his arms rise. Looking down into his father's eyes, he saw the tiny scarlet veins, and at the centres, the fathomless dark. 'What do you mean?' he whispered. 'What – '

'It is – possessed.' His father's face was grim; he didn't seem like Fa any more. 'Some – demon – from the Otherworld – has entered it and made it evil.'

An ember spat. The dark trees leaned closer to listen.

'A *demon*?' said Torak.

His father shut his eyes, mustering his strength. 'It lives only to kill,' he said at last. 'With each kill – its power will grow. It will slaughter – everything. The prey. The clans. All will die. The Forest will die . . . ' he broke off. 'In one moon – it will be too late. The demon – too strong.'

'One moon? But what – '

'Think, Torak! When the red eye is highest in the night sky, that's when demons are strongest. You know this. That's when the bear will be – invincible.' He fought for breath. In the firelight, Torak saw the pulse beating in his throat. So faint: as if it might stop at any moment. 'I need you – to swear something,' said Fa.

'Anything.'

Fa swallowed. 'Head north. Many daywalks. Find – the Mountain – of the World Spirit.'

Torak stared at him. *What?*

His father's eyes opened, and he gazed into the branches overhead, as if he saw things there that no-one else could. 'Find it,' he said again. 'It's the only hope.'

'But – no-one's ever found it. No-one can.'

'You can.'

'How? I don't – '

'Your guide – will find you.'

Torak was bewildered. Never before had his father talked like this. He was a practical man; a hunter. 'I don't understand any of this!' he cried. 'What guide? Why must I find the Mountain? Will I be safe there? Is that it? Safe from the bear?'

Slowly, Fa's gaze left the sky and came to rest on his son's face. He looked as if he was wondering how much more Torak could take. 'Ah, you're too young,' he said. 'I thought I had more time. So much I haven't told you. Don't – don't hate me for that later.'

Torak looked at him in horror. Then he leapt to his feet. 'I can't do this on my own. Shouldn't I try to find – '

'No!' said his father with startling force. 'All your life I've kept you apart. Even – from our own Wolf Clan. Stay away from men! If they find out – what you can do . . . '

'What do you mean? I don't – '

'No time,' his father cut in. 'Now swear. On my knife. Swear that you will find the Mountain, or die trying.'

Torak bit his lip hard. East through the trees, a grey light was growing. Not yet, he thought in panic. *Please* not yet.

'Swear,' hissed his father.

Torak knelt and picked up the knife. It was heavy: a man's knife, too big for him. Awkwardly he touched it to the wound on his forearm. Then he put it to his shoulder, where the strip of wolf fur, his clan-creature, was sewn to his jerkin. In an unsteady voice he took his oath. 'I swear, by my blood on this blade, and by each of my three souls – that I will find the Mountain of the World Spirit. Or die trying.'

His father breathed out. 'Good. Good. Now. Put the Death Marks on me. Hurry. The bear – not far off.'

Torak felt the salty sting of tears. Angrily he brushed them away. 'I haven't got any ochre,' he mumbled.

'Take – mine.'

In a blur, Torak found the little antler-tine medicine horn that had been his mother's. In a blur, he yanked out the black oak stopper, and shook some of the red ochre into his palm.

Suddenly he stopped. 'I can't.'

'You can. For me.'

Torak spat into his palm and made a sticky paste of the ochre, the dark-red blood of the earth, then he drew the small circles on his father's skin that would help the souls recognise each other and stay together after death.

First, as gently as he could, he removed his father's beaver-hide boots, and drew a circle on each heel to mark the name-soul. Then he drew another circle over the heart, to mark the clan-soul. This wasn't easy, as his father's chest was scarred from an old wound, so Torak only managed a lopsided oval. He hoped that would be good enough.

Last, he made the most important mark of all: a circle on the forehead to mark the Nanuak, the world-soul. By the time he'd finished he was swallowing tears.

'Better,' murmured his father. But Torak saw with a clutch of terror that the pulse in his throat was fainter.

'You can't die!' Torak burst out.

His father gazed at him with pain and longing.

'Fa, I'm not leaving you, I – '

'Torak. You swore an oath.' Again he closed his eyes. 'Now. You – keep the medicine horn. I don't need it any more. Take your things. Fetch me water from the river. Then – go.'

I will *not* cry, Torak told himself as he rolled up his father's sleeping-sack and tied it across his back; jammed his axe into his belt; stuffed his medicine pouch into his jerkin.

He got to his feet and cast about for the waterskin. It was ripped to shreds. He'd have to bring water in a dock leaf. He was about to go when his father murmured his name.

Torak turned. 'Yes, Fa?'

'Remember. When you're hunting, look behind you. I – always tell you.' He forced a smile. 'You always – forget. Look behind you. Yes?'

Torak nodded. He tried to smile back. Then he blundered through the wet bracken towards the stream.

The light was growing, and the air smelt fresh and sweet. Around him the trees were bleeding: oozing golden pine-blood from the slashes the bear had inflicted. Some of the tree-spirits were moaning quietly in the dawn breeze.

Torak reached the stream, where mist floated above the bracken, and willows trailed their fingers in the cold water. Glancing quickly around, he snatched a dock leaf and moved forwards, his boots sinking into the soft red mud.

He froze.

Beside his right boot was the track of a bear. A front paw: twice the size of his own head, and so fresh that he could see the points where the long, vicious claws had bitten deep into the mud.

Look behind you, Torak.

He spun round.

Willows. Alder. Fir.

No bear.

A raven flew down onto a nearby bough, making him jump. The bird folded its stiff black wings and fixed him with a beady eye. Then it jerked its head, croaked once, and flew away.

Torak stared in the direction it had seemed to indicate.

Dark yew. Dripping spruce. Dense. Impenetrable.

But deep within – no more than ten paces away – a stir of branches. Something was in there. Something huge.

He tried to keep his panicky thoughts from skittering away, but his mind had gone white.

The thing about a bear, his father always said, *is that it can move as silently as breath. It could be watching you from ten paces away, and you'd never know. Against a bear you have no defences. You can't run faster. You can't climb higher. You can't fight it on your own. All you can do is learn its ways, and try to persuade it that you're neither threat nor prey.*

Torak forced himself to stay still. Don't run. Don't run. Maybe it doesn't know you're here.

A low hiss. Again the branches stirred.

He heard the stealthy rustle as the creature moved towards the shelter: towards his father. He waited in rigid silence as it passed. Coward! he shouted inside his head. You let it go without even trying to save Fa!

But what could you do? said the small part of his mind that could still think straight. Fa knew this would happen. That's why he sent you for water. He knew it was coming for him . . .

'Torak!' came his father's wild cry. '*Run!*'

Crows burst from the trees. A roar shook the Forest – on and on till Torak's head was splitting.

'*Fa!*' he screamed.

'*Run!*'

Again the Forest shook. Again came his father's cry. Then suddenly it broke off.

Torak jammed his fist in his mouth.

Through the trees, he glimpsed a great dark shadow in the wreck of the shelter.

He turned and ran.

Two

Torak crashed through alder thickets and sank to his knees in bogs. Birch trees whispered of his passing. Silently he begged them not to tell the bear.

The wound in his arm burned, and with each breath his bruised ribs ached savagely, but he didn't dare stop. The Forest was full of eyes. He pictured the bear coming after him. He ran on.

He startled a young boar grubbing up pignuts, and grunted a quick apology to ward off an attack. The boar gave an ill-tempered snort and let him pass.

A wolverine snarled at him to stay *away*, and he snarled back as fiercely as he could, because wolverines only listen to threats. The wolverine decided he meant it, and shot up a tree.

To the east, the sky was wolf grey. Thunder growled. In the stormy light, the trees were a brilliant green. Rain in the mountains, thought Torak numbly. Watch out for flash floods.

He forced himself to think of that – to push away the horror. It didn't work. He ran on.

At last, he had to stop for breath. He collapsed against an oak tree. As he raised his head to stare at the shifting green leaves, the tree murmured secrets to itself, shutting him out.

For the first time in his life he was truly alone. He didn't feel part of the Forest any more. He felt as if his world-soul had snapped its link to all other living things: tree and bird, hunter and prey, river and rock. Nothing in the whole world knew how he felt. Nothing wanted to know.

The pain in his arm wrenched him back from his thoughts. From his medicine pouch he took his last scrap of birch bast, and roughly bandaged the wound. Then he pushed himself off the tree trunk and looked around.

He'd grown up in this part of the Forest. Every slope, every glade was familiar. In the valley to the west was the Redwater: too shallow for canoes, but good fishing in spring, when the salmon come up from the Sea. To the east, all the way to the edge of the Deep Forest, lay the vast sunlit woods where the prey grow fat in autumn, and berries and nuts are plentiful. To the south were the moors where the reindeer eat moss in winter.

Fa said that the best thing about this part of the Forest was that so few people came here. Maybe the odd party of Willow Clan from the west by the Sea, or Viper Clan up from the south, but they never stayed long. They simply passed through, hunting freely as everyone did in the Forest, and unaware that Torak and Fa hunted here too.

Torak had never questioned that before. It was how he'd always lived: alone with Fa, away from the clans. Now, though, he longed for people. He wanted to shout, to yell for help.

But Fa had warned him to stay away from them.

Besides, shouting might draw the bear.

The bear.

Panic rose in his throat. He pushed it down. He took a deep breath and started to run again, more steadily this time, heading north.

As he ran, he picked up signs of prey. Elk tracks. Auroch droppings. The sound of a forest horse moving through the bracken. The bear hadn't frightened them away. At least, not yet.

So had his father been wrong? Had his wits been wandering at the end?

'Your fa's mad!' the children had taunted Torak five summers before, when he and Fa had journeyed to the sea-shore for the clan meet. It was Torak's first ever clan meet, and it had been a disaster. Fa had never taken him again.

'They say he swallowed the breath of a ghost,' the children had sneered. 'That's why he left his clan and lives on his own.'

Torak had been furious. He would've fought them all if his father hadn't come along and hauled him off. 'Torak, ignore them,' Fa had laughed. 'They don't know what they're saying.'

He'd been right, of course.

But was he right about the bear?

Up ahead, the trees opened into a clearing. Torak stumbled into the sun – and into a stench of rottenness.

He lurched to a halt.

The forest horses lay where the bear had tossed them like broken playthings. No scavenger had dared feed on them. Not even the flies would touch them.

They looked like no bear kill Torak had ever seen. When

a normal bear feeds, it peels back the hide of its prey and takes the innards and hind parts, then caches the rest for later. Like any other hunter, it wastes nothing. But this bear had ripped no more than a single bite from each carcass. It hadn't killed from hunger. It had killed for fun.

At Torak's feet lay a dead foal, its small hooves still crusted with river clay from its final drink. His gorge rose. What kind of creature slaughters an entire herd? What kind of creature kills for pleasure?

He remembered the bear's eyes, glimpsed for one appalling heartbeat. He'd never seen such eyes. Behind them lay nothing but endless rage and a hatred of all living things. The hot, churning chaos of the Otherworld.

Of course his father was right. This wasn't a bear. It was a demon. It would kill and kill until the Forest was dead.

No-one can fight this bear, his father had said. Did that mean the Forest was doomed? And why did he, Torak, have to find the Mountain of the World Spirit? The Mountain that no-one had ever seen?

His father's voice echoed in his mind. *Your guide will find you.*

How? When?

Torak left the glade and plunged back into the shadows beneath the trees. Once again he began to run.

He ran for ever. He ran till he could no longer feel his legs. But at last he reached a long, wooded slope and had to stop: doubled up, chest heaving.

Suddenly he was ravenous. He fumbled for his food pouch – and groaned in disgust. It was empty. Too late, he remembered the neat bundles of dried deer meat, forgotten at the shelter.

Torak, you fool! Messing things up on your first day alone! Alone.

It wasn't possible. How could Fa be gone? Gone for ever?

Gradually he became aware of a faint mewing sound coming from the other side of the hill.

There it was again. Some young animal crying for its mother.

His heart leapt. Oh, thank the Spirit! An easy kill. His belly tightened at the thought of fresh meat. He didn't care what it was. He was so hungry he could eat a bat.

Torak dropped to the ground and crept through the birch trees to the top of the hill.

He looked down into a narrow gully through which ran a small, swift river. He recognised it: the Fastwater. Further west, he and Fa often camped in summer to gather lime bark for rope-making; but this part looked unfamiliar. Then he realised why.

Some time before, a flash flood had come roaring down from the mountains. The waters had since subsided, leaving a mess of wet undergrowth and grass-strewn saplings. They'd also destroyed a wolf den on the other side of the gully. There, below a big red boulder shaped like a sleeping auroch, lay two drowned wolves like sodden fur cloaks. Three dead cubs floated in a puddle.

The fourth sat beside them, shivering.

The wolf cub looked about three moons old. It was thin and wet, and was complaining softly to itself in a low, continuous whimper.

Torak flinched. Without warning, the sound had brought a startling vision to his mind. Black fur. Warm darkness. Rich, fatty milk. The Mother licking him clean. The scratch of tiny claws and nudge of small, cold noses. Fluffy cubs clambering over him: the newest cub in the litter.

The vision was as vivid as a lightning flash. What did it mean?

His hand tightened on his father's knife. It doesn't matter what it means, he told himself. Visions won't keep you alive. If you don't eat that cub, you'll be too weak to hunt. And you're allowed to kill your clan-creature to keep from starving. You know that.

The cub raised its head and gave a bewildered yowl.

Torak listened to it — *and understood.*

In some strange way that he couldn't begin to fathom, he recognised the high, wavering sounds. His mind knew their shapes. He remembered them.

This isn't possible, he thought.

He listened to the cub's yowls. He felt them drop into his mind.

Why won't you play with me? the cub was asking its dead pack. *What have I done now?*

On and on it went. As Torak listened, something awakened in him. His neck muscles tensed. Deep in his throat he felt a response beginning. He fought the urge to put back his head and howl.

What was happening? He didn't feel like Torak any more. Not boy, not son, not member of the Wolf Clan – or not *only* those things. Some part of him was wolf.

A breeze sprang up, chilling his skin.

At the same moment, the wolf cub stopped yowling and jerked round to face him. Its eyes were unfocused, but its large ears were pricked, and it was snuffing the air. It had smelt him.

Torak looked down at the small anxious cub, and hardened his heart.

He drew the knife from his belt and started down the slope.

THREE

The wolf cub did not *at all* understand what was going on. He'd been exploring the rise above the Den when the Fast Wet had come roaring through, and now his mother and father and pack-brothers were lying in the mud – *and they were ignoring him.*

Since long before the Light he'd been nosing them and biting their tails – but they still didn't move. They didn't make a sound, and they smelt strange: like prey. Not the prey that runs away, but the Not-Breath kind: the kind that gets eaten.

The cub was cold, wet, and very hungry. Many times he'd licked his mother's muzzle to ask her please to sick up some food for him to eat, but she didn't stir. What had he done wrong this time?

He knew that he was the naughtiest cub in the litter. He was always being scolded, but he couldn't help it. He just loved trying new things. So it seemed a bit unfair that now, when he was staying by the Den like a good cub, nobody even noticed.

He padded to the edge of the puddle where his pack-brothers lay, and lapped up some of the Still Wet. It tasted bad.

He ate some grass and a couple of spiders.

He wondered what to do next.

He began to feel scared. He put back his head and howled. Howling cheered him up a bit, because it reminded him of all the good howls he'd had with the pack.

Mid-howl, he stopped. He smelt wolf.

He spun round, wobbling a little from hunger. He swivelled his ears and sniffed. Yes. *Wolf.* He could hear it coming noisily down the slope on the other side of the Fast Wet. He smelt that it was male, half-grown, and not one of the pack.

But there was something odd about it. It smelt of wolf, but also of not-wolf. It smelt of reindeer and red deer and beaver, and fresh blood – and something else: a new smell that he hadn't yet learnt.

This was very odd. Unless – *unless* – it meant that the not-wolf wolf was actually a wolf who'd eaten lots of different prey, and was now bringing the cub some food!

Shivering with eagerness, the cub wagged his tail and yipped a noisy welcome.

For a moment the strange wolf stopped. Then it moved forwards again. The cub couldn't see it very clearly because his eyes weren't nearly as sharp as his nose and ears, but as it splashed across the Fast Wet, he made out that this was a *very* strange wolf indeed.

It walked on its hind legs. The fur on its head was black, and so long that it reached right down to its shoulders. And strangest of all – *it had no tail!*

Yet it *sounded* wolf. It was making a low, friendly yip-and-yowl which sounded a bit like *it's all right, I'm a friend*. This was reassuring, even if it did keep missing out the highest yips.

But something was wrong. Beneath the friendliness there was a tense note. And although the strange wolf was smiling, the cub could tell it didn't really mean it.

The cub's welcome changed to a whimper. *Are you hunting me? Why?*

No, no, came the friendly but not-friendly yip-and-yowl.

Then the strange wolf stopped yip-and-yowling and advanced in frightening silence.

Too weak to run, the cub backed away.

The strange wolf lunged, grabbed the cub by the scruff, and lifted him high.

Weakly, the cub wagged his tail to fend off an attack.

The strange wolf lifted its other forepaw and pressed a huge claw against the cub's belly.

The cub yelped. Grinning in terror, he whipped his tail between his legs.

But the strange wolf was frightened too. Its forepaws were shaking, and it was gulping and baring its teeth. The cub sensed loneliness and uncertainty and pain.

Suddenly, the strange wolf took another gulp, and jerked its great claw away from the cub's belly. Then it sat down heavily in the mud, and clutched the cub to its chest.

The cub's terror vanished. Through the strange furless hide that smelt more of not-wolf than wolf, he could hear a comforting thump-thump, like the sound he heard when he clambered on top of his father for a nap.

The cub wriggled out of the strange wolf's grip, put his forepaws on its chest, and stood on his hind legs. He began to lick the strange wolf's muzzle.

Angrily, the strange wolf pushed him away, and he fell

backwards. Undeterred, he righted himself and sat gazing up at the strange wolf.

Such an odd, flat, furless face! The lips weren't black, like a proper wolf's, but pale; and the ears were pale too – *and they didn't move at all.* But the eyes were silver-grey and full of light: the eyes of a wolf.

The cub felt better than he had since the Fast Wet had come. He'd found a new pack-brother.

Torak was furious with himself. Why hadn't he killed the cub? Now what was he going to eat?

The cub jabbed its nose into his bruised ribs, making him yelp. 'Get off!' he shouted, kicking it away. 'I don't want you! Understand? You're no use! Go a*way*!'

He didn't even attempt that in wolf talk, because he'd realised that he didn't actually speak it very well. He only knew the simpler gestures and some of the sound-shapes. But the cub picked up his meaning well enough. It trotted off a few paces, then sat down and looked at him hopefully, sweeping the ground with its tail.

Torak got to his feet – and the world tilted sickeningly. He had to eat soon.

He cast around the riverbank for food, but saw only the dead wolves, and they smelt too bad even to think about. Hopelessness washed over him. The sun was getting low. What should he do? Camp here? But what about the bear? Had it finished with Fa, and come after him?

Something twisted painfully in his chest. Don't think about Fa. Think what to do. If the bear had followed you, it would've got you by now. So maybe you'll be safe here – at least for tonight.

The wolf carcasses were too heavy to drag away, so he decided to camp further upstream. First, though, he would use one of the carcasses to bait a deadfall, in the hope of trapping something to eat overnight.

It was a struggle to set the trap: to prop up a flat rock on a stick, then slot in another stick crossways to act as a trigger. If he was lucky, a fox might come along in the night and bring down the rock. It wouldn't make good eating, but it'd be better than nothing.

He'd just finished when the cub trotted over and gave the deadfall an inquisitive sniff. Torak grabbed its muzzle and slammed it to the ground. 'No!' he said firmly. 'You stay away!'

The cub shook itself and retired with an offended air.

Better offended than dead, thought Torak.

He knew he'd been unfair: he should've growled first to warn the cub to stay away, and only muzzle-grabbed if it hadn't listened. But he was too tired to worry about that.

Besides, why had he bothered to warn it at all? What did he care if it wobbled along in the night and got squashed? What did he care if he could understand it, or why? What use was that?

He stood up, and his knees nearly gave way. Forget about the cub. Find something to eat.

He forced himself to climb the slope behind the big red rock to look for cloudberries. Only when he got there did he remember that cloudberries grow on moors and marshes, not in birchwoods, and that it was too late in the year for them anyway.

He noticed that in certain spots the ground was littered with woodgrouse droppings, so he set some snares of twisted grass: two near the ground, and two on the sort of low branch that woodgrouse sometimes run along – taking care to hide the snares with leaves so that the woodgrouse wouldn't spot them. Then he went back to the river.

He knew he was too unsteady to try spearing a fish, so instead he set up a line of bramble-thorn fishing-hooks baited with water-snails. Then he started up river to look for berries and roots.

For a while the cub followed him; then it sat down and mewed at him to come back. It didn't want to leave its pack.

Good, thought Torak. You stay there. I don't want you pestering me.

As he searched, the sun sank lower. The air grew sharp. His jerkin glistened with the misty breath of the Forest. He had a hazy thought that he should be building a shelter instead of looking for food, but he pushed it away.

At last he found a handful of crowberries, and gulped them down. Then some late lingonberries; a couple of snails; a clutch of yellow bog-mushrooms – a bit maggoty, but not too bad.

It was nearly dusk when he got lucky and found a clump of pignuts. With a sharp stick he dug down carefully, following the winding stems to the small, knobbly root. He chewed the first one: it tasted sweet and nutty, but was barely a mouthful. After much exhausting digging, he grubbed up four more, ate two, and stuffed two in his jerkin for later.

With food inside him, a little strength returned to his limbs, but his mind was still strangely unclear. What do I do next? he wondered. Why is it so hard to think?

Shelter. That's it. Then fire. Then sleep.

The cub was waiting for him in the clearing. Shivering and yipping with delight, it threw itself at him with a big wolf smile. It didn't just wrinkle its muzzle and draw back its lips; it smiled with its whole body. It slicked back its ears and tilted its head to one side; it waved its tail and waggled its forepaws, and made great twisting leaps in the air.

Watching it made Torak giddy, so he ignored it. Besides, he needed to build a shelter.

He looked around for deadwood, but the flood had washed most of it away. He'd have to cut down some saplings, if he still had the strength.

Pulling his axe from his belt, he went over to a clump of birch and put his hand on the smallest. He muttered a quick warning to the tree's spirit to find another home fast, then started to chop.

The effort made his head swim. The cut on his forearm throbbed savagely. He forced himself to keep chopping.

He was in an endless dark tunnel of chopping and stripping branches and more chopping. But when his arms had turned to water and he could chop no more, he saw with alarm that he'd only managed to cut down two spindly birch saplings and a puny little spruce.

They'd have to do.

He lashed the saplings together with a split spruce root to make a low, rickety lean-to; then he covered it on three sides with spruce boughs, and dragged in a few more to lie on.

It was pretty hopeless, but it'd have to do. He didn't have the strength to rain-proof it with leafmould. If it rained, he'd have to trust his sleeping-sack to keep him dry, and pray that the river spirit didn't send another flood, because he'd built too close to the water.

Munching another pignut, he scanned the clearing for firewood. But he'd only just swallowed the pignut when his belly heaved, and he spewed it up again.

The cub yipped with delight and gulped down the sick.

Why did I do that? thought Torak. Did I eat a bad mushroom?

But it didn't feel like a bad mushroom. It felt like something else. He was sweating and shivering, and although there was nothing left in his belly to throw up, he still felt sick.

A horrible suspicion gripped him. He unwound the bandage on his forearm – and fear settled on him like an icy fog. The wound was a swollen, angry red. It smelt bad. He could feel the heat coming off it. When he touched it, pain flared.

A sob rose in his chest. He was exhausted, hungry and frightened, and he desperately wanted Fa. And now he had a new enemy.

Fever.

FOUR

Torak had to make a fire. It was a race between him and the fever. The prize was his life.

He fumbled at his belt for his tinder pouch. His hands shook as he took out some wisps of shredded birch bark, and he kept dropping his flint and missing his strike-fire. He was snarling with frustration when he finally got a spark to take.

By the time he had a fire going, he was shivering uncontrollably, and hardly felt the heat of the flames. Noises boomed unnaturally loud: the gurgle of the river, the hoo-hoo of an owl; the famished yipping of that infuriating cub. Why couldn't it leave him alone?

He staggered to the river for water. Just in time, he remembered what Fa said about not leaning over too far. *When you're ill, never catch sight of your name-soul in the water. Seeing it makes you dizzy. You might fall in and drown.*

With his eyes shut, he drank his fill, then stumbled back

to the shelter. He longed for rest, but he knew that he had to see to his arm, or he wouldn't stand a chance.

He took some dried willow bark from his medicine pouch and chewed it, gagging on its gritty bitterness. He smeared the paste on his forearm, then bound up the wound again with the birch-bast bandage. The pain was so bad that he nearly passed out. It was all he could do to kick off his boots and crawl into his sleeping-sack. The cub tried to clamber in too. He pushed it away.

Dully, teeth chattering, he watched the cub pad over to the fire and study it curiously. It extended one large grey paw and patted the flames – then leapt back with an outraged yelp.

'That'll teach you,' muttered Torak.

The cub shook itself and bounded off into the gloom.

Torak curled into a ball, cradling his throbbing arm and thinking bitterly what a mess he'd made of things.

All his life he'd lived in the Forest with Fa, pitching camp for a night or two, then moving on. He knew the rules. *Never skimp on your shelter. Never use more effort than you need when gathering food. Never leave it too late to pitch camp.*

His first day on his own, and he'd broken every one. It was frightening. Like forgetting how to walk.

With his good hand he touched his clan-tattoos, tracing the pair of fine dotted lines that followed each cheekbone. Fa had given them to him when he was seven, rubbing bearberry juice into the pierced skin. You don't deserve them, Torak told himself. If you die, it'll be your own fault.

Again the grief twisted in his chest. Never in his life had he slept alone. Never without Fa. For the first time, there was no goodnight touch of the rough, gentle hand. No familiar smell of buckskin and sweat.

Torak's eyes began to sting. He screwed them shut, and

slid down into evil dreams.

He is wading knee-deep in moss, struggling to escape the bear. His father's screams ring in his ears. The bear is coming for him.

He tries to run, but he only sinks deeper into the moss. It sucks him down. His father is screaming.

The bear's eyes burn with the lethal fire of the Otherworld – the demon fire. It rears on its hind legs: a towering menace, unimaginably huge. Its great jaws gape as it roars its hatred to the moon . . .

Torak woke with a cry.

The last of the bear's roars were echoing through the Forest. They weren't a dream. They were real.

Torak held his breath. He saw the blue moonlight through the gaps in his shelter. He saw that the fire was nearly out. He felt his heart pounding.

Again the Forest shook. The trees tensed to listen. But this time Torak realised that the roars were far away: many daywalks to the west. Slowly he breathed out.

At the mouth of the shelter, the cub sat watching him. Its slanted eyes were a strange, dark gold. Amber, thought Torak, remembering the little seal amulet that Fa had worn on a thong around his neck.

He found that oddly reassuring. At least he wasn't alone.

As his heartbeats returned to normal, the pain of his fever came surging back. It crisped his skin. His skull felt ready to burst. He struggled to get more willow bark from his medicine pouch, but dropped it, and couldn't find it again in the half-darkness. He dragged another branch onto the fire, then lay back, gasping.

He couldn't get those roars out of his head. Where was the bear now? The glade of dead horses had been north of the stream where it had attacked Fa, but now the bear seemed to be in the west. Would it keep heading west? Or had it caught Torak's scent, and turned back? How long before it got here, and found him lying helpless and sick?

A calm, steady voice seemed to whisper in his mind: almost as if Fa were with him. *If the bear does come, the cub will warn you. Remember, Torak: a wolf's nose is so keen that he can smell the breath of a fish. His ears are so sharp that he can hear the clouds pass.*

Yes, thought Torak, the cub will warn me. That's something. I want to die with my eyes open, facing the bear like a man. Like Fa.

Somewhere very far off, a dog barked. Not a wolf, but a dog.

Torak frowned. Dogs meant people, and there were no people in this part of the Forest.

Were there?

He sank into darkness. Back into the clutches of the bear.

FIVE

It was nearly dark when Torak woke up. He'd slept all day. He felt weak and ragingly thirsty, but his wound was cooler and much less sore. The fever was gone.

So was the cub.

Torak was surprised to find himself wondering if it was all right. Why should he care? The cub was nothing to him.

He stumbled to the river and drank, then woke the slumbering fire with more wood. The effort left him trembling. He rested, and ate the last pignut and some sorrel leaves he'd found by the riverbank. They were tough and very sour, but strengthening.

Still the cub didn't come.

He thought about trying to summon it with a howl. But if it came, it would only ask for food. Besides, howling might attract the bear. So instead he pulled on his boots and went to check the traps.

The fish-hooks were empty except for one, which held

the bones of a small fish, neatly nibbled clean. He was luckier with the snares. One held a woodgrouse, struggling feebly. *Meat.*

Muttering a quick thank you to the bird's spirit, Torak snapped its neck, slit its belly and gulped the warm liver down raw. It tasted bitter and slimy, but he was too famished to care.

Feeling slightly steadier, he tied the bird to his belt, and went to check the deadfall.

To his relief, it contained no dead cub. The cub was sitting by its mother, prodding her stinking carcass with one paw. At Torak's approach, it started towards him, then looked back at the she-wolf, yipping indignantly. It wanted Torak to sort things out.

Torak sighed. How could he explain about death when he didn't understand it himself?

'Come on,' he said, not bothering to speak wolf.

The cub's large ears swivelled to catch the sound.

'There's nothing here,' Torak said impatiently. 'Let's go.'

Back at the shelter, he plucked and spitted the woodgrouse, and set it to roast over the fire. The cub lunged for it.

Torak grabbed the cub's muzzle and slammed it to the ground. *No!* he growled. *It's mine!*

The cub lay obediently still, thumping its tail. When Torak released its muzzle, it rolled onto its back, baring its pale fluffy belly, and gave him a silent grin of apology. Then it scampered off to a safe distance, head politely lowered.

Torak nodded, satisfied. The cub had to learn that *he* was the lead wolf, or there'd be endless trouble in the future.

What future? he thought with a scowl. His future didn't include the cub.

The smell of roast meat drove all other thoughts away. Fat sizzled on the fire. His mouth watered. Quickly, he twisted one leg off the woodgrouse and tucked it into the fork of a birch tree as an offering for his clan guardian; then he settled down to eat.

It was the best thing he'd ever tasted. He sucked every shred of meat and fat off the bones, and crunched up every morsel of crisp, salty skin. He forced himself to ignore the great amber eyes that watched every bite.

When he'd finished, he wiped his mouth on the back of his hand. The cub followed every move.

Torak blew out a long breath. 'Oh, all *right*,' he muttered. He tore the remaining foot off the carcass and tossed it over.

The cub crunched it up in moments. Then it looked at Torak hopefully.

'I haven't got any more,' he told it.

The cub yipped impatiently and glanced at the carcass in his hands.

He'd picked the bones clean, but they'd still make needles, fish-hooks and broth; although without a cooking-skin, he couldn't make any broth.

Sensing that he might be storing up trouble for himself, he tossed half the carcass to the cub.

The cub demolished it in its powerful jaws, then curled up and went instantly to sleep: a gently heaving ball of hot grey fur.

Torak wanted to sleep too, but he knew that he couldn't. As night fell and the cold came on, he sat staring into the fire. Now that he'd shaken off the fever and eaten some meat, he could think clearly at last.

He thought of the glade of dead horses, and the bear's demon-haunted eyes. *It is possessed*, Fa had said. *Some demon has entered it and made it evil.*

But what actually *is* a demon? Torak wondered. He didn't know. He only knew that demons hate all living things, and sometimes escape from the Otherworld, rising out of the ground to cause sickness and havoc.

As he thought about this, he realised that although he knew quite a lot about hunters and prey: about lynxes and wolverines, aurochs and horses and deer, he knew very little about the other creatures of the Forest.

He only knew that clan guardians watch over campsites, and that ghosts moan in leafless trees on stormy nights, forever seeking the clans they have lost. He knew that the Hidden People live inside rocks and rivers, just as the clans live in shelters, and that they seem beautiful until they turn their backs, which are hollow as rotten trees.

As for the World Spirit who sends the rain and snow and prey – about that, Torak knew least of all. Until now he'd never even thought about it. It was too remote: an unimaginably powerful spirit who lived far away on its Mountain; a spirit whom no-one had ever seen, but who was said to walk by summer as a man with the antlers of a deer, and by winter as a woman with bare red willow branches for hair.

Torak bowed his head to his knees. The weight of his oath to Fa pressed down on him like a rock.

Suddenly, the cub sprang up with a tense grunt.

Torak leapt to his feet.

The cub's eyes were fixed on the darkness: ears rigid, hackles raised. Then it hurtled out of the firelight and disappeared.

Torak stood very still with his hand on Fa's knife. He felt the trees watching him. He heard them whispering to each other.

Somewhere not far off, a robin began to sing its plaintive night song. The cub reappeared: hackles down, muzzle soft and smiling slightly.

Torak relaxed his grip on the knife. Whatever was out there had either gone, or wasn't a threat. If the bear had been close, that robin wouldn't be singing. He knew that much.

He sat down again.

You've got to find the Mountain of the World Spirit within the next moon, he told himself. That's what Fa said. *When the red eye is highest . . . that's when demons are strongest. You know this.*

Yes I do know it, thought Torak. I know about the red eye. I've seen it.

Every autumn, the great bull Auroch – the most powerful demon in the Otherworld – escapes into the night sky. At first he has his head down, pawing the earth, so that only the starry gleam of his shoulder can be seen. But as winter comes on, he rises and grows stronger. That's when you see his glittering horns and his bloodshot red eye. The red star of winter.

And in the Moon of Red Willow he rides highest, and evil is strongest. That's when the demons walk. *That's when the bear will be invincible.*

Glancing up through the branches, Torak saw the cold glint of stars. On the eastern horizon, just above the distant blackness of the High Mountains, he found it: the starry shoulder of the Great Auroch.

It was now the end of the Moon of Roaring Stags. In the next moon, the Blackthorn Moon, the red eye would appear, and the power of the bear would grow stronger. By the Moon of Red Willow, it would be invincible.

Head north, Fa had said. *Many daywalks.*

Torak didn't want to go further north. That would take him out of the small patch of the Forest that he knew, and into the unknown. And yet – Fa must have believed that he stood a chance, or he wouldn't have made him swear.

He reached for a stick and poked the embers.

He knew that the High Mountains were far in the east, beyond the Deep Forest, and that they curved from north to south, arching out of the Forest like the spine of an enormous whale. And he knew that the World Spirit was said to live in the northernmost mountain. But no-one had ever got close to it, for the Spirit always beat them back with howling blizzards and treacherous rockfalls.

All day, Torak had been fleeing north, but he was still only level with the southernmost roots of the High Mountains. He had no idea how he was going to get so far on his own. He was still weak from the fever, and in no state to start a journey.

So don't, he thought. Don't make the same mistake twice: don't panic and nearly kill yourself out of sheer stupidity. Stay here for another day or so. Get stronger. Then start.

Making a decision made him feel a little better.

He put more sticks on the fire, and saw to his surprise that the cub was watching him. Its eyes were steady and quite un-cub-like: the eyes of a wolf.

Once again, Fa's voice echoed in his memory. *The eyes of a wolf aren't like those of any other creature – except those of a man. Wolves are our closest brothers, Torak, and it shows in their eyes. The only difference is the colour. Theirs are golden, while ours are grey. But the wolf doesn't see that, because his world doesn't have colours. Only silvers and greys.*

Torak had asked how he knew that, but Fa had smiled and shaken his head, saying he'd explain when Torak was older. There were lots of things he'd been going to explain when Torak was older.

Torak scowled and rubbed his face.

The cub was still watching him.

Already it had something of the beauty of a full-grown wolf: the slender pale-grey muzzle; large silver ears with their edging of black; elegant, dark-rimmed eyes.

Those eyes. As clear as sunlight in spring-water . . .

Suddenly, Torak had the strangest sense that the cub knew what he was thinking.

More than any other hunters in the Forest, Fa whispered in his mind, *wolves are like us. They hunt in packs. They enjoy talking and playing. They have a fierce love for their mates and cubs. And each wolf works hard for the good of the pack.*

Torak sat upright. Was that what Fa was trying to tell him?

Your guide will find you.

Could it be that the cub was his guide?

He decided to put it to the test. Clearing his throat, he got down on his hands and knees. He didn't know how to say 'mountain' in wolf talk, so he guessed: gesturing with his head and asking – in the low, intense yip-and-yowl which forms part of wolf talk – if the cub knew the way.

The cub swivelled its ears and looked at him, then glanced politely away, because in wolf talk, to stare too hard is a threat. Then it stood up, stretched, and lazily swung its tail.

Nothing in its movements told Torak that it had understood his question. It was simply a cub again.

Or was it?

Could he really have imagined that look?

SIX

It was many Lights and Darks since Tall Tailless had come. At first he'd slept all the time, but now he was being more of a normal wolf. When he felt sad, he went quiet. When he was angry, he snarled. He liked playing tag with a bit of hare-skin, and when the cub pounced on him he rolled on the ground, making odd yip-and-yowls which the cub guessed was his way of laughing.

Sometimes Tall Tailless would join the cub in a howl, and they'd sing their feelings to the Forest. Tall Tailless's howl was rough and not very tuneful, but full of feeling.

The rest of his talk was the same: rough but expressive. Of course he didn't have a tail, and couldn't move his ears or fluff up his fur, or hit the high yips. But he usually made himself understood.

So in many ways, he was just like any other wolf.

Although not in everything. Poor Tall Tailless could hardly smell or hear at all, and during the Dark he liked to stare at the Bright Beast-that-Bites-Hot. Sometimes he took his hind paws *right off*, and one terrible time, even his pelt. Strangest of all, he slept for *ages*. He didn't seem to know that a wolf should only ever sleep in snatches, and must get up often, stretching and turning, so that he's ready for anything.

The cub tried to teach Tall Tailless to wake up more often, by nudging him and biting his ears. Instead of being grateful, Tall Tailless just got very, very cross. In the end the cub let him sleep; and next Light, Tall Tailless got up after a stupidly long sleep, in an extremely bad mood. Well what did he expect, if he wouldn't let his pack-brother wake him up?

Today, though, Tall Tailless had woken up before the Light, and in a very different mood. The cub sensed his nervousness.

Curiously, the cub watched Tall Tailless set off along the pack-trail that went up-Wet. A hunt?

The cub bounded after him, then yipped at him to stop. This wasn't a hunt. And Tall Tailless was going the wrong way.

It wasn't just that he was following the Fast Wet, which the cub now hated and feared more than anything. This was the wrong way because – because it wasn't the right way. The right way was over the hill, then on for many Lights and Darks.

The cub didn't know how he knew this, but he felt it inside: a faint, deep pull – like the pull of the Den when he'd strayed too far; only fainter, because it was coming from so far away.

Up ahead, Tall Tailless strode along unaware.

The cub gave a low, warning 'Uff!' – like his mother used to when she wanted them back in the Den *now*.

Tall Tailless turned round. He asked something in his

own talk. It sounded like 'Whatisit?'

'Uff!' snapped the cub. He trotted to the foot of the hill and stared at the right trail. Then he glanced at Tall Tailless, then back to the trail. *Not that way. This way.*

Impatiently, Tall Tailless repeated his question. The cub waited for him to catch on.

Tall Tailless scratched his head. He said something else in tailless talk. Then he started back towards the cub.

Torak watched Wolf's body tense.

Wolf's ears flicked forwards. His black nose twitched. Torak followed his gaze. He couldn't see anything through the tangle of hazel and willowherb, but he knew that the buck was in there, because Wolf knew it, and Torak had learned to trust Wolf.

Wolf glanced up at Torak, his amber eyes grazing the boy's. Then his gaze returned to the Forest.

Silently, Torak broke off a head of grass and split it with his thumbnail, letting the fine seeds float away on the breeze. Good. They were still downwind of the buck: it wouldn't catch their scent. And before setting out, Torak had, as always, masked his smell by smearing his skin with wood-ash.

Without a sound, he drew an arrow from his quiver and fitted it to his bow. It was only a small roe buck, but if he could bring it down, it would be the first big kill he'd ever made on his own. He needed it. Prey was much scarcer than it should be at this time of year.

The cub's head sank low.

Torak crouched.

Together they crept forward.

38

They'd been tracking the buck all day. All day, Torak had followed its trail of bitten-off twigs and cloven prints: trying to feel what it was feeling; guessing where it would go next.

To track prey, you must first learn to know it as you would a brother. What it eats, and when and how; where it rests; how it moves. Fa had taught Torak well. He knew how to track. He knew that you must stop often to listen: to open your senses to what the Forest is telling you . . .

Right now, he knew that the roe buck was tiring. Earlier in the day, the cleaves of each small hoof-print had been deep and splayed, which meant it had been galloping. Now the cleaves were lighter and closer together: it had slowed to a walk.

It must be hungry, because it hadn't had time to graze; and thirsty, because it had kept to the safety of the deep thickets, where there was no water.

Torak glanced about for signs of a stream. West through the hazel, about thirty paces off the trail, he glimpsed a clump of alders. Alders only grow near water. That was where the buck must be heading.

Softly, he and the cub moved through the undergrowth. Cupping his hand to his ear, he caught a faint ripple of water.

Suddenly, Wolf froze: ears rammed forwards, one forepaw raised.

Yes. There. Through the alders. The buck stooping to drink.

Carefully Torak took aim.

The buck raised its head, water dripping from its muzzle.

Torak watched it snuff the air and fluff out its pale rump fur in alarm. Another heartbeat and it would be gone. He loosed his arrow.

It thudded into the buck's ribs just behind the shoulder. With a graceful shudder, the buck folded its knees and sank to the ground.

Torak gave a shout and pushed through the undergrowth towards it. Wolf raced him and easily won, but then pulled back to let Torak catch up. The cub was learning to respect the lead wolf.

Panting, Torak stood over the buck. Its ribs were still heaving, but death was near. Its three souls were getting ready to leave.

Torak swallowed. Now he had to do what he'd seen Fa do countless times. But for him it would be the first time, and he had to get it right.

Kneeling beside the buck, he put out his hand and gently stroked its rough, sweaty cheek. The buck lay quiet under his palm.

'You did well,' Torak told it. His voice sounded awkward. 'You were brave and clever, and you kept going all day. I promise to keep the pact with the World Spirit, and treat you with respect. Now go in peace.'

He watched death glaze the great dark eye.

He felt grateful to the buck, but also proud. This was his first big kill. Wherever Fa was on the Death Journey, he would be pleased.

Torak turned to Wolf and put his head on one side, wrinkling his nose and baring his teeth in a wolf smile. *Well done, thank you.*

Wolf pounced on Torak, nearly knocking him over. Torak laughed and gave him a handful of blackberries from his food pouch. Wolf snuffled them up.

It had been seven days since they'd set out from the Fastwater, and still there was no sign of the bear. No tracks. No fur snagged on brambles. No more Forest-shaking roars.

Something was wrong, though. At this time of year, the Forest should be echoing with the bellows of rutting red deer, and the clash of their antlers as they fought for females. But all was silence. It was as if the Forest was slowly emptying; the prey fleeing from the unseen menace.

In seven days the only creatures Torak had encountered were birds and voles – and once, with heart-stopping suddenness, a hunting party: three men, two women and a dog. Luckily, he'd managed to slip away before they saw him. *Stay away from men*, Fa had warned. *If they find out what you can do . . .*

Torak didn't know what that meant, but he knew Fa was right. He'd grown up away from people; he wanted nothing to do with them. Besides, he had Wolf now. With every day that passed, they understood each other better.

Torak was coming to know that wolf talk is a complex blend of gestures, looks, smells and sounds. The gestures can be with the muzzle, ears, paws, tail, shoulders, fur, or the whole body. Many are very subtle: the merest tilt or twitch. Most do not involve sound. By now, Torak knew quite a lot of them, although it wasn't as if he'd had to learn them. It felt more as though he was remembering them.

Still, there was one thing he knew he'd never be able to master, because he wasn't a wolf. This was what he'd taken to calling 'wolf sense': the cub's uncanny knack of sensing his thoughts and moods.

Wolf had his own moods, too. Sometimes he was the cub, with a puppyish love of berries and an inability to keep still: like the time he'd wriggled incessantly when Torak had held a naming rite for him, then licked off all the red alder juice daubed on his paws. Unlike Torak, who'd been nervous about performing so important a rite, Wolf had seemed unimpressed: merely impatient for it to be over.

At other times, though, he was the guide: mysteriously sure of the way they must take. But if Torak tried to ask him about that, he never gave much of an answer. *I just know.* That was all.

Right now, Wolf wasn't being the guide. He was being the cub. His muzzle was purple with blackberry juice, and he was yipping insistently for more.

Torak laughed and batted him away. 'No more! I've got work to do.'

Wolf shook himself and smiled, then went off to have a sleep.

It took Torak two full days to butcher the carcass. He'd made the buck a promise, and he had to keep it by not wasting a thing. That was the age-old pact between the hunters and the World Spirit. Hunters must treat prey with respect, and in return the Spirit would send more prey.

It was a daunting task. It takes many summers of practice to use prey well. Torak didn't make a very good job of it, but he did his best.

First, he slit the deer's belly and cut a slip of the liver for the clan guardian. The rest of the liver he cut into strips and set to dry. Then he relented and cut off a bit for Wolf, who slurped it up.

Next, Torak skinned the carcass, scraping the hide clean of flesh with his antler scraper. He washed the hide in water mixed with crumbled oak bark to loosen the hairs, then stretched it between two saplings – well out of Wolf's leaping-range. Then he scraped off the hairs – inexpertly, making several holes – and softened the hide by rubbing it with mashed deer brain. After a final round of soaking and drying, he had a reasonable skin of rawhide for rope and fishing-lines.

While the hide was drying, he cut the meat into thin

strips and hung them over a smoky birchwood fire. When they were dry, he pounded them between two stones to make them thinner, then rolled them into small, tight bundles. The meat was delicious. One little piece would last him half a day.

The innards he washed, soaked in oak-bark water, and draped over a juniper bush to dry. The stomach would make a waterskin; the bladder a spare tinder pouch; the guts would store nuts. The lungs were Wolf's share – although not yet. Torak would chew them at daymeals and nightmeals, then spit them out for the cub. But as he had no cooking-skin for making glue, he let Wolf have the hooves straightaway. The cub played with them tirelessly before crunching them to bits.

Next, Torak washed the long back sinews he'd saved from the butchering, pounded them flat, then teased out the narrow fibres for thread: drying them and rubbing them in fat to make them supple. They weren't nearly as smooth or even as the thread his father used to make, but they'd do. And they were so tough that they'd outlast any clothes he sewed with them.

Finally, he scraped the antlers and the long bones clean, and tied them into a bundle for splintering later into fish-hooks, needles and arrowheads.

It was late on the second day by the time he'd finished. He sat by the fire, pleasantly full of meat, whittling a whistle from a piece of grouse bone. He needed some way of summoning the cub when it was off on one of its solitary journeys: some way quieter than a howl. That hunting party might still be about. He couldn't risk any more howling.

He finished whittling, and gave the whistle a try. To his dismay, it made no sound. Fa had carved countless whistles just like this one, and they'd always made a clear, bird-like chirp. Why didn't his?

Frustrated, Torak tried again, blowing as hard as he could. Still no sound. But to his surprise, Wolf leapt up as if he'd been stung by a hornet.

Torak glanced from the startled cub to the whistle. Once more he blew on it.

Again no sound. This time Wolf gave a brief snarl, then a whine, to show that he was a bit annoyed, but didn't want to go too far and offend Torak.

Torak said sorry by gently scratching under Wolf's muzzle, and the cub slumped down. His expression made it clear: Torak shouldn't call unless he meant something by it.

Next day dawned fine and bright, and as they set off again, Torak's spirits rose.

It was twelve days since the bear had killed Fa. In that time Torak had fought hunger and conquered fever, found Wolf, and made his first big kill. He'd also made plenty of mistakes. But he was still alive.

He pictured his father on the journey to the Land of the Dead – the land where arrows are plentiful, and the hunt never fails. At least, thought Torak, he has his weapons with him, and my knife for company. And all that dried meat. That blunted the edge of his grief a little.

Torak knew that the loss of his father would never leave him – that he'd carry it in his chest all his life, like a stone. This morning the stone didn't feel quite so heavy. He'd survived so far, and his father would be proud.

He felt almost happy as he pushed through the undergrowth on the sun-dappled forest path. A couple of thrushes squabbled overhead. The fat, happy cub kept close to his side, his bushy silver tail held high.

Fat, happy and careless.

Torak heard a twig snap behind him just as a large hand grabbed him by the jerkin and yanked him off his feet.

SEVEN

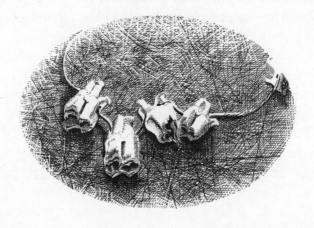

Three hunters. Three lethal flint weapons. All aimed at him.

Torak's mind whirled. He couldn't move. Couldn't see Wolf.

The man gripping his jerkin was enormous. His russet beard was a bird's nest tangle; one cheek was pulled downwards by an ugly scar, and whatever had bitten him had taken off one ear. In his free hand he held a flint-edged knife, its point jabbed under Torak's jaw.

Beside him stood a tall young man, and a girl about Torak's own age. Both had dark-red hair, smooth, pitiless faces, and flint arrows trained on his heart.

He tried to swallow. He hoped he didn't look as scared as he felt. 'Let me go,' he gasped. He took a swing at the big man and missed.

The big man grunted. 'So here's our thief!' He hoisted Torak higher – chokingly high.

'I'm not – a thief!' coughed Torak, snatching at his throat.

'He's lying,' the young man said coldly.

'You took our roe buck,' said the girl. To the big man she said, 'Oslak, I think you're choking him.'

Oslak set Torak on his feet. But he didn't loosen his hold, and his knife stayed at Torak's throat.

Carefully, the girl replaced her arrow in her quiver, and shouldered her bow. The young man did not. From the gleam in his eyes, it was clear that he was enjoying himself. He wouldn't hesitate to shoot.

Torak coughed and rubbed his throat, surreptitiously reaching for his knife.

'I'll take that,' said Oslak. Still gripping Torak, he relieved him of his weapons and tossed them to the girl.

She studied Fa's knife curiously. 'Did you steal this too?'

'No!' said Torak. 'It – it was my father's.'

Clearly they didn't believe him.

He looked at the girl. 'You said I took your buck. How could it be yours?'

'This is our part of the Forest,' said the young man.

Torak was puzzled. 'What do you mean? The Forest doesn't belong to anyone – '

'It does now,' snapped the young man. 'It was agreed at the clan meet. Because of . . . ' he broke off with a scowl. 'What matters is that you took our prey. That means death.'

Torak broke out in a sweat. *Death?* How could taking a roe buck mean death?

His mouth was so dry that he could hardly speak. 'If – if it's the buck you're after,' he said, 'take it and let me go. It's in my pack. I haven't eaten much.'

Oslak and the girl exchanged glances, but the young man tossed his head in scorn. 'It isn't that simple. You're my captive. Oslak, tie his hands. We're taking him to Fin-Kedinn.'

'Where's that?' asked Torak.

'It's not a place,' said Oslak, 'it's a man.'

'Don't you know anything?' sneered the girl.

'Fin-Kedinn is my uncle,' said the young man, drawing himself up. 'He's the leader of our clan. I am Hord, his brother's son.'

'What clan? Where are you taking me?'

They did not reply.

Oslak gave him a shove that knocked him to his knees. As he struggled to his feet, he glanced over his shoulder – and saw to his horror that Wolf had trotted back to look for him. He stood uncertainly some twenty paces away, snuffing the strangers' scent.

They hadn't spotted him. What would they do if they did? Presumably even they respected the ancient law which forbade the killing of another hunter. But what if they chased Wolf away? Torak pictured him lost in the Forest. Hungry. Howling.

To warn Wolf to stay out of sight, he gave a low, urgent 'uff'. *Danger!*

Oslak nearly fell over him in surprise. 'What did you say?'

'Uff!' said Torak again. To his dismay, Wolf didn't retreat. Instead, he put back his ears and raced straight for Torak.

'What's this?' muttered Oslak. He reached down and grabbed Wolf by the hackles.

Wolf wriggled and snarled as he dangled from the huge red hand.

'Let him go!' shouted Torak, struggling. 'Let him go or I'll kill you!'

Oslak and the girl burst out laughing.

'Let him *go*! He's not doing you any harm!'

'Just chase it away and let's go,' said Hord irritably.

'No!' yelled Torak. 'He's my gui – no!'

The girl threw him a suspicious look. 'He's your what?'

'He's with me,' muttered Torak. He knew he mustn't reveal his search for the Mountain, or that he could talk to Wolf.

'Come on, Renn,' snarled Hord. 'We're wasting time.'

But Renn was still staring at Torak. She turned to Oslak. 'Give it to me.' From her pack she pulled a buckskin bag into which she shoved the cub, drawing the neck tightly shut. As she shouldered the wriggling, yowling bag, she told Torak, 'You'd better come quietly, or I'll bash him against a tree.'

Torak glared at her. She probably wouldn't do it, but she'd just ensured his obedience far more effectively than either Oslak or Hord.

Oslak gave Torak another push, and they started along a deer-track, heading north-west.

The rawhide bindings were tight, and Torak's wrists began to hurt. Well let them, he thought. He was furious with himself. *Look behind you*, his father had said. He hadn't, and now he was paying for it – and so was Wolf. No more muffled yowls were coming from the bag. Was he suffocating? Already dead?

Torak begged Renn to open the bag and let in some air.

'No need,' she said without turning round. 'I just felt it wriggle.'

Torak set his teeth and stumbled on. He had to find some way to escape.

Oslak was behind him, but Hord was right in front. He looked about nineteen, well-built and handsome. He also seemed both arrogant and uneasy: desperate to be first, but scared that he'd only ever come second. His clothes were finely made and colourful, his jerkin and leggings stitched in braided sinew dyed red, and edged in some kind of birdskin stained green. On his chest he wore a magnificent necklace of red deer teeth.

Torak was mystified. Why would a hunter want so much colour? And that necklace clinked, which was the last thing you needed.

Renn resembled Hord in feature, and Torak wondered if they were brother and sister, although Renn was younger by four or five summers. Her clan-tattoos – three fine blue-black bars on her cheekbones – showed clearly on her pale skin, giving her a sharp, mistrustful look. Torak didn't think he'd be asking her for help.

Her buckskin jerkin and leggings were scruffy, but her bow and quiver were beautiful, the arrows deftly fletched with owl feathers for silent flight. On the first two fingers of her left hand, she wore leather finger-guards, and strapped to her right forearm was a wrist-guard of polished green slate. Torak guessed that such wrist-guards were worn by people who lived for their bows. That's what matters to her, he thought. Not fine clothes, like Hord.

But what clan was she? Sewn to the left side of her jerkin – and those of Hord and Oslak – was their clan-creature skin: a strip of black feathers. Swan? Eagle? The feathers were too tattered. Torak couldn't tell.

They walked all morning without stopping for food or water: crossing boggy valleys choked with chattering aspen; climbing hills darkened by ever-wakeful pines. As Torak passed beneath, the trees sighed mournfully, as if already lamenting his death.

Clouds obscured the sun, and he lost his bearings. They came to a slope where the Forest floor was bumpy with the waist-high nests of wood-ants. As wood-ants only build by the south side of trees, Torak worked out that they were heading west.

At last they paused at a brook to drink.

'We're much too slow,' growled Hord. 'We've got a whole valley to cross before we reach the Windriver.'

Torak pricked up his ears. Maybe he'd overhear something useful . . .

Renn sensed he was listening. 'The Windriver,' she told him slowly, as if talking to a baby, 'is to the west, in the next valley. It's where we camp in autumn. And a couple of daywalks to the north is the Widewater, where we camp in summer. For the salmon. They're fish. Maybe you've heard of them.'

Torak felt himself reddening. But he knew now where they were heading: his captors' autumn camp. It sounded bad. A camp would mean more people, and less chance of escape.

As they walked, the sun sank lower, and Torak's captors became edgy, pausing often to listen and look about them. He guessed that they knew about the bear. Maybe that was why they'd adopted the unheard-of measure of 'owning' prey. Because it was getting scarce; the bear was frightening it away.

They descended into a big valley of oak, ash and pine, and soon reached a wide silver river. This must be the Windriver.

Suddenly Torak smelt woodsmoke. They were nearing the camp.

EIGHT

As the four of them crossed the river by a wooden walkway, Torak stared down at the sliding water and thought about jumping in. His hands were tied. He'd drown. Besides, he couldn't leave Wolf.

About ten paces downstream, the trees opened into a clearing. Torak smelt pine-smoke and fresh blood. He saw four big reindeer-hide shelters unlike any he'd ever seen, and a bewildering number of people: all hard at work, and as yet unaware of him. With a clarity born of fear, he took in every detail.

On the riverbank two men were skinning a boar strung from a tree. Having already slit the belly, they'd sheathed their knives and were peeling off the hide by hand, to avoid tearing it. Both were bare-chested, and wore fish-skin aprons over their leggings. They looked terrifyingly strong, with raised zigzag scars on their muscled arms. From the carcass, blood dripped slowly into a birch-bark pail.

In the shallows, two girls in buckskin tunics giggled as they rinsed the boar's guts, while three small children solemnly made mud-cakes and studded them with sycamore wings. Two sleek hide canoes were drawn up out of the water. The ground around them glittered with fish-scales. A couple of large dogs prowled for scraps.

In the middle of the clearing, near a pinewood long-fire, a group of women sat on willow-branch mats, talking quietly as they shelled hazelnuts and picked over a basket of juniper berries. None of them looked anything like Hord or Renn; Torak wondered briefly if, like him, they'd lost their parents.

A little apart from them, an old woman was heading arrows: slotting needle-fine flakes of flint into the shafts, then gluing them in place with a paste of pine-blood and beeswax. A round bone amulet etched with a spiral was sewn to the breast of her jerkin. From the amulet, Torak knew she must be the clan Mage. Fa had told him about Mages: people who can heal sickness, and dream where the prey is and what the weather will do. This old woman looked as if she could do far more dangerous things than that.

By the fire, a pretty girl leaned over a cooking-skin. Steam crinkled her hair as she used a forked stick to drop in red-hot stones. The meaty smell of whatever was cooking made Torak's mouth water.

Near her, an older man knelt to spit a couple of hares. Like Hord, he had reddish-brown hair and a short red beard, but there the resemblance ended. His face had an arresting stillness, and a strength that made Torak think of carved sandstone. Torak forgot about the cooking smell. He knew, without being told, that this man wielded power.

Oslak untied the bindings and pushed Torak into the clearing. The dogs leapt up, barking ferociously. The old woman made a slicing motion with her palm, and they subsided into growls. Everyone stared at Torak. Everyone except the man by the fire, who went on calmly spitting the hares. Only when he'd finished did he rub off his hands in the dust and rise to his feet, waiting in silence for them to approach.

The pretty girl glanced at Hord and smiled shyly. 'We saved you some broth,' she said.

Torak guessed that either she was his mate, or wanted to be.

Renn turned and rolled her eyes at Hord. 'Dyrati saved you some broth,' she mocked.

Definitely his sister, thought Torak.

Hord ignored them both, and went to talk to the man by the fire. Quickly, he related what had happened. Torak noticed that he made it sound as if he, not Oslak had caught 'the thief'. Oslak didn't seem to mind, but Renn flashed her brother a sour glance.

Meanwhile, the dogs had scented Wolf. Hackles bristling, they advanced on Renn.

'Back!' she ordered. They obeyed. Renn ducked into the nearest shelter and emerged with a coil of wovenbark rope. She tied one end round the neck of the bag containing Wolf, tossed the other over the branch of an oak tree, and hoisted the bag high: well out of the dogs' reach.

And out of mine, realised Torak. Now even if he got the chance to escape, he couldn't. Not without Wolf.

Renn caught his eye and gave him a wry grin.

He scowled back. Inside, he was sick with fear.

Hord had finished talking. The man by the fire nodded once, and waited for Oslak to push Torak towards him. His eyes were an intense, unblinking blue: vividly alive in that impenetrable face. Torak found it hard to look into them for long – and even harder to look away.

'What is your name?' said the man in a voice that was somehow more frightening for being so quiet.

Torak licked his lips. 'Torak. – What's yours?' But he thought he already knew.

It was Hord who answered. 'He is Fin-Kedinn. Leader of the Raven Clan. And you, you miserable little runt, should learn more respect – '

Fin-Kedinn silenced Hord with a look, then turned to Torak. 'What clan are you?'

Torak raised his chin. 'Wolf.'

'Well there's a surprise,' remarked Renn, and several people laughed.

Fin-Kedinn wasn't one of them. His burning blue eyes never left Torak's face. 'What are you doing in this part of the Forest?'

'Heading north,' said Torak.

'I told him it belongs to us now,' Hord put in quickly.

'How could I know that?' said Torak. 'I wasn't at the clan meet.'

'Why not?' said Fin-Kedinn.

Torak did not reply.

The Raven Leader's eyes drilled into his. 'Where are the rest of your clan?'

'I don't know,' said Torak truthfully. 'I've never lived with them. I live – lived – with my father.'

'Where is he?'

'Dead. He was – killed by a bear.'

A hiss ran through the watchers. Some glanced fearfully over their shoulders; others touched their clan-creature skins, or made the sign of the hand to ward off evil. The old woman left her arrows and came towards them.

No emotion showed in Fin-Kedinn's face. 'Who was your father?'

Torak swallowed. He knew – and so must Fin-Kedinn – that it is forbidden to speak a dead person's name for five summers after they die. Instead they can only be referred to by naming their parents. Fa had hardly ever talked about his family, but Torak knew their names, and where they'd come from. Fa's mother had been Seal Clan; his father had been Wolf Clan. Torak named them both.

Recognition is one of the hardest expressions to conceal. Not even Fin-Kedinn could hide it completely.

He knew Fa, thought Torak, aghast. But how? Fa never mentioned him, or the Raven Clan. What does this mean?

He watched Fin-Kedinn run his thumb slowly across his bottom lip. It was impossible to tell whether Torak's father had been his best friend or his deadliest enemy.

At last Fin-Kedinn spoke. 'Share out the boy's things between everyone,' he told Oslak. 'Then take him downstream and kill him.'

NINE

Torak's knees buckled.

'Wh – at?' he gasped. 'I didn't even know the buck was yours! How can I be guilty if I didn't know?'

'It's the law,' said Fin-Kedinn.

'Why? *Why*? Because you say so?'

'Because the clans say so.'

Oslak put a heavy hand on Torak's shoulder.

'No!' cried Torak. 'Listen! You say it's the law, but – there's another law, isn't there?' He caught his breath. 'Trial by combat. We – we fight for it.' He wasn't sure if he'd got that right – Fa had only mentioned it once, when he was teaching him the law of the clans – but Fin-Kedinn's eyes narrowed.

'I'm right, aren't I?' Torak insisted, forcing himself to give the Raven Leader stare for stare. 'You don't know for sure if I'm guilty, because you don't know whether I actually *knew* the buck was yours. So we fight. You and me.' He swallowed. 'If I win, I'm innocent. I live. I mean, me and the wolf. If I lose – we die.'

Some of the men were chuckling. A woman tapped her brow, shaking her head.

'I don't fight boys,' said Fin-Kedinn.

'But he's right, isn't he?' said Renn. 'It's the oldest law of all. He has the right to fight.'

Hord stepped forward. 'I'll fight him. I'm closer to him in age. It'll be fairer.'

'Not by much,' Renn said drily.

She was leaning against the tree from which Wolf was suspended. Torak saw that she'd loosened the neck of the bag a little, so that Wolf's head was poking out. He looked bedraggled, but was gazing curiously down at the two dogs slavering beneath him.

'What do you say, Fin-Kedinn?' said the Mage. 'The boy's right. Let them fight.'

Fin-Kedinn met the old woman's eyes, and for a moment there seemed to be a battle of wills between them. Slowly, he nodded.

Relief washed over Torak.

Everyone seemed to be excited by the prospect of a fight. They talked in huddles, stamping their feet, their breath steaming in the chill evening air.

Oslak tossed Torak his father's knife. 'You'll need that. And a spear and an arm-guard.'

'A what?' asked Torak.

The big man scratched the scar where his ear had been. 'You know how to fight, don't you?'

'No,' said Torak.

Oslak rolled his eyes. He went off to the nearest shelter, and returned with an ashwood spear tipped with a vicious basalt point, and what seemed to be a length of triple-thickness reindeer hide.

Torak took the spear uncertainly, and watched in puzzlement as Oslak strapped the toughened hide round his right forearm for him. It felt as heavy and unwieldy as a haunch of deer meat. He wondered what he was supposed to do with it.

Oslak nodded at the bandage on Torak's other arm, and grimaced. 'Seems like the odds are against you.'

Just a bit, thought Torak.

When he'd suggested a fight, he'd had in mind a wrestling-bout, with maybe some knife-play thrown in: the sort of thing he and Fa used to practise quite often, but just for fun. Clearly, to the Ravens, a fight meant something else. Torak wondered if there were special rules, and whether it would look weak to ask.

Fin-Kedinn prodded the fire, making sparks fly. Torak watched him through a shimmer of heat haze.

'There's only one rule,' said Fin-Kedinn, as if he'd guessed Torak's thoughts. 'You can't use fire. Do you understand?' His eyes caught and held Torak's.

Torak nodded distractedly. Not using fire was the least of his worries. Behind Fin-Kedinn, he could see Hord having his arm-guard strapped on. He had taken off his jerkin. He looked enormous, and frighteningly strong. Torak decided against taking off his own jerkin. No need to emphasise the contrast.

He untied everything from his belt and laid it in a pile on the ground. Then he wound a length of wovengrass twine round his forehead to keep his hair out of his eyes. His hands were slippery with sweat. He stooped and rubbed them in the dust.

Someone touched his shoulder, making him jump.

It was Renn. She was holding out a birch-bark beaker.

He took it gratefully and drank. To his surprise, it was elderberry juice: tart and strengthening.

Renn saw his surprise and shrugged. 'Hord's had a drink. It's only fair.' She pointed to a pail by the fire. 'There's water when you need it.'

Torak handed back the beaker. 'I don't think it'll last that long.'

She hesitated. 'Who knows?'

A hush fell. The watchers formed a ring round the edge of the clearing, with Torak and Hord in the middle, near the fire. There were no formalities. The fight was on.

Warily, they circled each other.

For all his size, Hord moved with the grace of a lynx, flexing his knees and repositioning his fingers on knife and spear. His face was taut, but a small smile played about his lips. He loved being the centre of attention.

Torak didn't. His heart was hammering against his ribs. Dimly, he could hear the watchers shouting encouragement to Hord, but their voices were muffled, as if he were underwater.

Hord's spear lunged for his chest, and he dodged just in time. He felt the sweat start out on his forehead.

Torak tried the same move, hoping it didn't look like copying.

'Copying won't get you very far,' called Renn.

Torak's face burned.

He and Hord were moving faster now. In places, the ground was slimy with boar's blood. Torak slipped and nearly went down.

He knew he couldn't hope to win by force. He'd have to use his wits. The trouble was, he only knew two fighting tricks, and he hadn't practised them more than a few times.

Here goes, he thought recklessly. He jabbed his spear at

Hord's throat. As expected, Hord's hide-arm rose to block it. Torak tried a quick undercut to the belly, but Hord parried it with alarming ease, and Torak's spear slid harmlessly off his arm-guard.

He knew that one, thought Torak. With every move, it was becoming obvious that Hord was a seasoned fighter.

'Come on, Hord,' yelled a man. 'Give him a red skin!'

'Give me time,' Hord called back with a curl of his lip.

A ripple of laughter.

Torak tried his second trick. Feigning total incompetence, which wasn't hard, he hit out wildly, tempting Hord with a glimpse of his unprotected chest. Hord took the bait, but as his spear came in to strike, Torak's guard-arm swung across to meet it. Hord's spearpoint sank into the thick hide guard, nearly knocking Torak off his feet, but Torak managed to keep to his plan by twisting his guard-arm sharply upwards. Hord's spear-shaft snapped in two. The watchers groaned. Hord staggered back without a spear.

Torak was astonished. He hadn't expected it to work.

Hord recovered swiftly. Lunging forwards, he jabbed his knife into Torak's spear-hand. Torak cried out as the flint bit between finger and thumb. He lost his footing and dropped his spear. Hord lunged again. Torak only just managed to roll away in time and scramble to his feet.

Now they were both spearless. Both down to knives.

To gain some breathing space, Torak dodged behind the fire. His chest was heaving, and his wounded hand throbbed. Sweat was pouring down his sides. He bitterly regretted not copying Hord and taking off his jerkin.

'Hurry up, Hord,' yelled a woman. 'Finish him off!'

'Come on, Hord!' shouted a man. 'Is this what they taught you in the Deep Forest?'

By now, though, not all shouts were for Hord. There was a smattering of encouragement for Torak, although he guessed it was less genuine support than pleased surprise that he was lasting longer than expected.

He knew it wouldn't be much longer. He was tiring rapidly, and he'd run out of tricks. Hord was taking control.

Sorry, Wolf, he told the cub silently. I don't think we're going to get out of this.

From the corner of his eye, he glimpsed Wolf high in the tree. He was wriggling and yowling in a haze of steamy breath. *What's happening?* he was asking. *Why won't you come and free me?*

Torak leapt aside to avoid a knife-slash across his throat. Concentrate, he told himself grimly. Forget about Wolf.

And yet – something was nagging him: something about Wolf. What was it?

He glanced at Wolf yowling in the tree, his breath steaming . . .

'You can't use fire,' Fin-Kedinn had said . . .

Suddenly Torak's mind flooded clear and he knew what to do. Jabbing and feinting, he edged sideways, putting the fire between them once more.

'Hiding again?' taunted Hord.

Torak jerked his head at the birch-bark water pail. 'I want a drink. All right?'

'If you must. *Boy.*'

Keeping his eyes on Hord, Torak squatted, and cupped water to drink. He did it slowly, to make Hord think he was up to something with the water pail, and to distract attention from the cooking-skin bubbling by the fire.

It worked. Hord stepped closer to the fire, looming over it to intimidate Torak.

'You want a drink too?' said Torak, still squatting.

Hord snorted his contempt.

Suddenly, Torak lashed out – but at the cooking-skin. Jabbing his knife into the tough hide, he upended it, and sent boiling broth pouring onto the white-hot embers. Hissing clouds of steam billowed into Hord's face.

The watchers gasped. Torak seized his chance and jabbed at his opponent's wrist. Blinded, Hord howled in pain and dropped his knife. Torak kicked it away, then threw himself on Hord, knocking him to the ground.

As Hord lay winded, Torak straddled his chest and knelt on his arms to pin them down. For one roaring heartbeat his sight misted red, and he knew the urge to kill. He grabbed a handful of dark-red hair and bashed Hord's head once against the earth.

Then he felt strong hands on his shoulders, pulling him off. 'It's over,' said Fin-Kedinn behind him.

Torak struggled in his grip. Hord sprang up and scrambled for his knife. Panting and glaring, they faced each other.

'I said it's *over*,' snapped Fin-Kedinn.

Chaos erupted among the watchers. They didn't think it was over at all. 'He cheated! He used fire!'

'No, he won fairly enough!'

'Who's to say? They'll have to fight it out again!'

Both Torak and Hord looked appalled at that.

'The boy won,' said Fin-Kedinn, releasing his grip on Torak.

Torak shook himself and wiped the sweat from his face as he watched Hord re-sheathing his knife. Hord was furious, though whether with himself or with Torak it was impossible to tell. Dyrati put her hand on his arm but he shook it off angrily, and pushed his way through the others, disappearing into one of the shelters.

Now that the blood-lust had left him, Torak felt shaky and sick. He sheathed his knife and looked round for his things. Then he saw Fin-Kedinn watching him.

'You broke the rule,' the Raven Leader said calmly. 'You used fire.'

'No I didn't,' said Torak. He sounded a lot more confident than he felt. 'I didn't use fire. I used steam.'

'I would have preferred it,' said Fin-Kedinn, 'if you'd used water instead of broth. That was a waste of good food.'

Torak did not reply.

Fin-Kedinn studied him, and for a moment there was a gleam of humour in his blue eyes.

Oslak pushed through to them, with the bag containing Wolf in his arms. 'Here's that cub of yours!' he boomed, tossing the bag at Torak with a force that made him stagger.

Wolf squirmed and licked Torak's chin and told him how awful it had been, all at once. Torak wanted to say something comforting, but stopped himself. It would be stupid to slip up now.

'The law's the law,' Fin-Kedinn said briskly. 'You won. You're free to go.'

'No!' A girl's voice rang out, and all heads turned. It was Renn. 'You can't let him go!' she cried, running forward.

'He just has,' retorted Torak. 'You heard him. I'm free.'

Renn spoke to her uncle. 'We can't let him go. This is too important. He might be . . . ' she drew Fin-Kedinn aside, whispering urgently.

Torak couldn't make out what she was saying, but to his dismay, others drew closer to listen. The Mage scowled and nodded. Even Hord emerged from the shelter, and when he heard what they were saying he gave Torak a strange, wary stare.

Fin-Kedinn studied Renn thoughtfully. 'Are you sure about this?'

'I don't *know*,' she said. 'Maybe he is. Maybe he isn't. We need time to find out.'

Fin-Kedinn stroked his beard. 'What makes you suspect –'

'The way he defeated Hord. And I found this in his things.' She held out her palm, and Torak saw his little grouse-bone whistle. 'What do you use it for?' she asked him.

'For calling the cub,' he replied.

She blew on it, and Wolf twisted in his arms. A shiver of un-ease ran through the crowd. Renn and Fin-Kedinn exchanged glances. 'It doesn't make any noise,' she said accusingly.

Torak did not reply. He realised with a jolt that her eyes were not light-blue like her brother's, but black: black as a peat pool. He wondered if she was a Mage, too.

She turned to Fin-Kedinn. 'We can't let him go till we know for sure.'

'She's right,' said the Mage. 'You know what it says as well as I do. Everyone does.'

'What *what* says?' pleaded Torak. 'Fin-Kedinn, we had a pact! We agreed that if I won the fight, me and Wolf would go free!'

'No,' said Fin-Kedinn, 'we agreed that you would live. And so you shall. At least, for now. Oslak, tie him up again.'

'*No!*' shouted Torak.

Renn raised her chin. 'You said your father was killed by a bear. We know about that bear. Some of us have even seen it.'

Beside her, Hord shuddered and began to gnaw his thumbnail.

'About a moon ago it came,' Renn went on quietly. 'Like a shadow it darkened the Forest, killing wantonly; even killing other hunters. Wolves. A lynx. It was as if – as if it was searching for something.' She paused. 'Then thirteen days ago it disappeared. A runner from the Boar Clan tracked it south. We thought it had gone. We gave thanks to our clan guardian.' She swallowed. 'Now it's back. Yesterday our scouts returned from the west. They'd found many kills, right down to the Sea. The Whale Clan told them that three days ago, it took a child.'

Torak licked his lips. 'What's this got to do with me?'

'There's a Prophecy in our clan,' said Renn as if he hadn't spoken. '*A Shadow attacks the Forest. None can stand against it.*' She broke off, frowning.

The Mage took up her words. '*Then comes the Listener. He fights with air, and speaks with silence.*' Her gaze fell on the whistle in Renn's hand.

Everyone was silent, watching Torak.

'I'm not your Listener,' he said.

'We think you might be,' replied the Mage.

Torak thought about the Prophecy. *The Listener fights with air* . . . He had done just that: he had used steam. 'What – happens to him?' he asked in a low voice. 'What happens to the Listener in the Prophecy?' But he had a terrible feeling that he already knew.

The silence in the clearing grew more intense. Torak looked from the frightened faces around him to the flint knife at Oslak's belt. He looked at the glistening carcass of the boar hanging from the tree; at its dark blood trickling into the pail beneath. He felt Fin-Kedinn's eyes on him, and turned to face the burning blue gaze.

'*The Listener,*' quoted Fin-Kedinn, '*Gives his heart's blood to the Mountain. And the Shadow is crushed.*'

His heart's blood.
Under the tree, the blood dripped softly into the basin.
Drip, drip, drip.

TEN

'What are you going to do to me?' said Torak as Oslak tied his wrists behind his back and then to the roofpost. 'What are you going to do?'

'You'll know soon enough,' said Oslak. 'Fin-Kedinn wants it settled by dawn.'

Dawn, thought Torak.

Over his shoulder, he watched Oslak tying a reluctant Wolf to the same roofpost on a short rawhide leash.

His teeth began to chatter. 'Who decides what happens to me? Why can't I be there to defend myself? Who are all those people by the fire?'

'Ow!' exclaimed Oslak, sucking a bitten finger. 'Fin-Kedinn sent runners to call a clan meet about the bear. Now they're deciding about you too.'

Torak peered at the figures hunched about the long-fire: twenty or thirty men and women, their faces starkly lit by the flames. He didn't give much for his chances.

Dawn. Somehow, before dawn, he had to get out of here.

But how? He was sitting in a shelter, tied to a roofpost, without weapons or pack; and even if he got free, the camp was heavily guarded. Now that darkness had fallen, a ring of fires had sprung up around it, and men with spears and birch-bark horns were keeping watch. Fin-Kedinn was taking no chances with the bear.

Oslak yanked off Torak's boots and tied his ankles together, then left, taking the boots with him.

Torak couldn't hear what they were saying at the clan meet, but at least he could see them, thanks to the odd construction of the Raven shelter. Its reindeer-hide roof sloped sharply down behind him, but in front there was no wall at all: only a cross-beam, which seemed to deflect the smoke from the small fire that crackled just in front, but trapped the warmth inside.

Straining to make out what was going on, Torak saw people rising one by one to speak. A broad-shouldered man holding an enormous throwing-axe. A woman with long nut-brown hair, one lock at the temple matted with red ochre. A wild-eyed girl whose skull was weirdly plastered with yellow clay to give it the roughness of oak bark.

He couldn't see Fin-Kedinn, but a little apart from the others, the Mage crouched in the dust, watching a large glossy raven. The bird stalked fearlessly up and down, uttering the occasional harsh 'cark!'

Torak wondered if it was the clan guardian. What was it telling her? How to sacrifice him? Whether to gut him like a salmon, or spit him like a hare? He'd never heard of clans sacrificing people, except long in the past, in the bad times after the Great Wave. But then, he'd never heard of the Raven Clan either.

'Fin-Kedinn wants it decided by dawn . . . The Listener gives his heart's blood to the Mountain . . .'

Had Fa known about the Prophecy? He couldn't have done. He wouldn't have sent his own son to his death.

And yet – he'd made Torak swear to find the Mountain. He'd said, *Don't hate me later.*

Later. When you find out.

The cub's rasping tongue on his wrists brought him back to the present. Wolf liked the taste of the rawhide. Torak felt a surge of hope. If Wolf could be made to bite instead of lick . . .

Even as Torak was wondering how to put that in wolf talk, a man rose from the long-fire and crossed the clearing towards him. It was Hord.

Frantically, Torak growled at Wolf to *stop*. He was too hungry to notice, and went on licking.

Hord wasn't interested in Wolf, though. He stood by the smaller fire in front of the doorway, gnawing his thumbnail and glaring at Torak. 'You're not the Listener,' he snarled, 'you can't be.'

'Tell that to the others,' retorted Torak.

'We don't need a *boy* to help us kill the bear. We can do it ourselves. *I* can do it. I'll save the clans.'

'You wouldn't stand a chance,' said Torak. He felt Wolf starting to nibble the rawhide with his sharp front teeth, and kept very still so as not to put him off. He prayed that Hord wouldn't look behind him, and see what Wolf was doing.

But Hord seemed too agitated to notice. He paced back and forth, then turned on Torak. 'You've seen it, haven't you? You've seen the bear.'

Torak was startled. 'Of course I've seen it. It killed my father.'

Hord cast a furtive glance over his shoulder. 'I've seen it too.'

'Where? When?'

Hord flinched, as if warding off a blow. 'I was in the south. With the Red Deer Clan. I was learning Magecraft. Saeunn,' he nodded at the old woman talking to the raven, 'our Mage, she wanted me to go.' Again he tore at his thumbnail, which had started to bleed. 'I was there when the bear was caught. I – I saw it made.'

Torak stared at him. 'Made? What do you mean?'

But Hord had gone.

Middle-night passed, the dying moon rose, and still the clan meet went on. Still Wolf licked and nibbled at the rawhide. But Oslak had tied the knots securely, and Wolf couldn't seem to get his jaws around them. Don't stop, Torak begged him silently. *Please* don't stop.

He was too scared to be hungry, but he felt bruised and stiff from the fight with Hord, and his shoulders ached from being tied up for so long. Even if Wolf managed to gnaw through the bindings, he wasn't sure that he'd have the strength to run away, or slip through the guards.

He kept thinking about what Hord had said. 'I saw it made . . .'

There was something else, too. Hord had been with the Red Deer Clan, and Torak's mother had been Red Deer. He'd never known her, she'd died when he was little; but if the Ravens were friendly with her clan, then maybe he could persuade them to let him go . . .

Outside, boots scuffed the dust. Quick. They mustn't catch Wolf at his wrists.

Torak just had time for a swift warning 'Uff!' – which luckily Wolf obeyed – before Renn appeared in the doorway, chewing a leg of roast hare.

Her sharp eyes took in Wolf sitting innocently behind him, then fixed on Torak – who stared back, willing her not to come any closer.

He jerked his head at the clan meet and asked if any Wolf Clan were present.

She shook her head. 'Not many Wolf Clan left these days. So you're not going to be rescued, if that's what you're thinking.'

Torak did not reply. He'd just pulled at the rope around his wrists, and felt it give a little. It was beginning to stretch, as rawhide does when it gets wet. If only Renn would go away.

She stayed exactly where she was. 'No Wolf Clan,' she said with her mouth full, 'but plenty of others. Yellow Clayhead over there is from the Auroch Clan. They're Deep Forest people; they pray a lot. That's how they think we should deal with the bear, by praying to the World Spirit. The man with the axe is Boar Clan. He wants to make a fire-wall to drive the bear towards the Sea. The woman with the earthblood in her hair is Red Deer. Not sure what she thinks. With them it's hard to tell.'

Torak wondered why she was talking so much. What did she want?

Whatever it was, he decided to go along with it, to keep her attention away from Wolf. He said, 'My mother was Red Deer. Maybe that woman over there is my bone kin. Maybe – '

'She says not. She's not going to help you.'

He thought for a moment. 'Your clan are friendly with the Red Deer, aren't they? Your brother said he learnt

Magecraft with them.'

'So?'

'He – he told me he saw the bear "made". What did he mean?'

She gave him her narrow, mistrustful stare.

'I need to know,' said Torak. 'It killed my father.'

Renn studied the hare's leg. 'Hord was fostered with them. You know about fostering, don't you?' Her voice held a touch of scorn. 'It's when you stay with another clan for a while, to make friends, and maybe find a mate.'

'I've heard of it,' said Torak. Behind him, he felt Wolf snuffling at his wrists again. He tried to bat him away with his fingers, but it didn't work. Not now, he thought. Please not now.

'He was with them for nine moons,' said Renn, taking another bite. 'They're the best at Magecraft in the Forest. That's why he went.' Her mouth curled humourlessly. 'Hord likes to be the best.' Then she frowned. 'What's that cub doing?'

'Nothing,' Torak said too quickly. To Wolf he said in a stilted voice, 'Go away. Go away.'

Wolf, of course, ignored him.

Torak turned back to Renn. 'What happened next?'

Another look. 'Why are you asking?'

'Why are you talking to me?'

Her face closed. She was as good at keeping things back as Fin-Kedinn.

Thoughtfully she picked a shred of hare from between her teeth. 'Hord hadn't been with the Red Deer long,' she said, 'when a stranger came to their camp. A wanderer from the Willow Clan, crippled by a hunting accident. Or so he said. The Red Deer took him in. But he – ,' she hesitated, and suddenly looked younger and much less confident. 'He betrayed them. He wasn't just a wanderer, he knew Magecraft. He made a secret place in the woods, and conjured a demon. Trapped it in the body of a bear.' She paused. 'Hord found out. By then it was too late.'

Beyond the shelter, the shadows seemed to have deepened. Out in the Forest, a fox screamed.

'*Why?*' said Torak. 'Why did he do it, this – wanderer?'

Renn shook her head. 'Who knows? Maybe to have a creature to do his bidding? But it went wrong.' The firelight glinted in her dark eyes. 'Once the demon got inside the bear, it was too strong. It broke free. Killed three people before the Red Deer could drive it away. By then the crippled wanderer had disappeared.'

Torak was silent. The only sounds were the trees whispering in the night breeze, and the rasp of Wolf's tongue as he licked the rawhide.

Wolf accidentally caught Torak's skin in his teeth. Without thinking, Torak turned and gave him a sharp warning growl.

Instantly Wolf leapt back and apologised with a grin.

Renn gasped. 'You can *talk* to him!'

'No!' cried Torak. 'No, you're wrong –'

'I *saw* you!' Her face was paler than ever. 'So it's true. The Prophecy is true. You *are* the Listener.'

'No!'

'What were you saying to him? What were you plotting?'

'I've told you, I can't –'

'I won't give you the chance,' she whispered. 'I won't let you plot against us. Neither will Fin-Kedinn.' Drawing her knife, she cut Wolf's leash, scooped him up in her arms, and raced across the clearing towards the clan meet.

'Come back!' yelled Torak. Furiously he yanked at the bindings, but they held fast. Wolf hadn't had time to bite them through.

Terror washed over him. He'd put all his hopes in Wolf, and now Wolf was gone. Dawn was not far off. Already the birds were stirring in the trees.

Again he tugged at the bindings round his wrists. Again they held tight.

Across the clearing, Fin-Kedinn and the old woman called Saeunn rose to their feet and started towards him.

ELEVEN

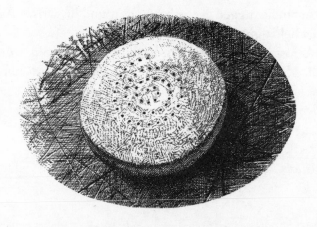

'How much do you know?' said Fin-Kedinn.

'Nothing,' said Torak, eyeing the jagged bone knife at the Raven Leader's belt. 'Are you going to sacrifice me?'

Fin-Kedinn did not reply. He and Saeunn crouched at either side of the doorway, watching him. He felt like prey.

Behind his back, he scrabbled around for something – anything – that he could use to cut the rawhide. His fingers found only a willow-branch mat: smooth and useless.

'How much do you know?' Fin-Kedinn said again.

Torak took a deep breath. 'I am not your Listener,' he said as steadily as he could. 'I can't be. I've never even heard of the Prophecy.' And yet, he wondered, why was Renn so certain? What does speaking wolf talk have to do with it?

Fin-Kedinn turned away. His face was as unreadable as ever, but Torak saw his hand tighten on his knife.

Saeunn leaned forwards and peered into Torak's eyes. In

the firelight, he saw her closely. He'd never encountered anyone so old. Through her scant white hair, her scalp gleamed like polished bone. Her face was sharp as a bird's. Age had scorched away all kindly feelings to leave only the fierce raven essence.

'According to Renn,' she said harshly, 'you can talk to the wolf. That's part of the Prophecy. The part we didn't tell you.'

Torak stared at her. 'Renn's wrong,' he said. 'I can't – '

'Don't lie to us,' said Fin-Kedinn without turning his head.

Torak swallowed.

Again he groped behind him. This time – yes! A tiny flake of flint, no bigger than his thumbnail: probably dropped by someone sharpening a knife. His fingers closed over it. If only Fin-Kedinn and Saeunn would return to the clan meet, he might be able to cut himself free. Then he could find wherever Renn had taken Wolf, and dodge between the guards and . . .

His spirits sank. He'd need a lot of luck to manage all that.

'Shall I tell you,' said Saeunn, '*why* you can talk to the wolf?'

'Saeunn, what's the use?' said Fin-Kedinn. 'We're wasting time – '

'He must be told,' said the old woman. She fell silent. Then, with one yellow, claw-like finger, she touched the amulet at her breast, and began tracing the spiral.

Torak watched her talon going round and round. He started to feel dizzy.

'Many summers ago,' said the Raven Mage, 'your father and mother left their clan. They went to hide from their enemies. Far, far away in the Deep Forest, among the green souls of the talking trees.' Still her talon traced the spiral: drawing Torak down into the past.

'Three moons after you were born,' Saeunn went on, 'your mother died.'

Fin-Kedinn got up, crossed his arms over his chest, and stood staring out into the darkness.

Torak blinked, as if waking from a dream.

Saeunn didn't even glance at Fin-Kedinn. Her attention was fixed on Torak. 'You were only an infant,' she said. 'Your father couldn't feed you. Usually when that happens, the father smothers his child, to spare it a slow death from starvation. But your father found another way. A she-wolf with a litter. He put you in her den.'

Torak struggled to take it in.

'Three moons you were with her in the den. Three moons to learn the wolf talk.'

Torak gripped the flint flake so hard that it dug into his palm. He could feel that Saeunn was telling the truth. This was why he could talk to Wolf. This was why he'd had that vision when he'd found the den. The squirming cubs. The rich, fatty milk . . .

How could Saeunn possibly know?

'No,' he said. 'This is a trap. You couldn't know this. You weren't there.'

'Your father told me,' said Saeunn.

'He can't have done. We never went near people –'

'Oh, but you did once. Five summers ago. Don't you remember? The clan meet by the Sea.'

Torak's pulse began to race.

'Your father went there to find me. To tell me about you.' Her talon came to rest at the heart of the spiral. 'You are not like others,' she said in her raven's croak. 'You *are* the Listener.'

Again Torak's grip on the flint tightened. 'I – I can't be. I don't understand.'

'Of course he doesn't,' said Fin-Kedinn over his shoulder. He turned to Torak. 'Your father told you nothing about who you are. That's right, isn't it?'

Torak nodded.

The Raven Leader was silent for a moment. His face was still, but Torak sensed a battle raging beneath his mask-like features. 'There is only one thing you need to know,' said Fin-Kedinn. 'It's this. It is not by chance that the bear attacked your father. It's *because* of him that it came into being.'

Torak's heart missed a beat. 'Because of my father?'

'Fin-Kedinn –' warned Saeunn.

The Raven Leader shot her a sharp glance. 'You said he should know. Now I'm telling him.'

'But,' said Torak, 'it was the crippled wanderer who –'

'The crippled wanderer,' cut in Fin-Kedinn, 'was your father's sworn enemy.'

Torak shrank back against the roofpost. 'My father didn't have enemies.'

The Raven Leader's eyes glinted dangerously. 'Your father wasn't just some hunter from the Wolf Clan. He was the Wolf Clan Mage.'

Torak forgot to breathe.

'He didn't tell you that either, did he?' said Fin-Kedinn. 'Oh yes, he was the Wolf Mage. And it's because of him that this – *creature* – is rampaging through the Forest –'

'No,' whispered Torak. 'That isn't true.'

'He kept you ignorant of everything, didn't he?'

'Fin-Kedinn,' said Saeunn, 'he was trying to protect –'

'Yes, and look at the result!' Fin-Kedinn rounded on her. 'A half-grown boy who knows nothing! Yet you ask me to believe that he is the only one who can – ' He stopped short, shaking his head.

There was a taut silence. Fin-Kedinn took a deep breath. 'The man who created the bear,' he told Torak quietly, 'did it for a single purpose. He created the bear to kill your father.'

The sky was lightening in the east when Torak finally cut the rope round his wrists with the flake of flint. There was no time to lose. Fin-Kedinn had just gone back to the clan meet with Saeunn, where they were locked in heated argument with the others. At any moment they might reach a decision and come to get him.

It was an effort to saw through the binding at his ankles. His head was reeling. 'Your father put you in the den of a she-wolf . . . He was the Wolf Mage . . . He was murdered . . . '

The flake of flint was slippery with sweat. He dropped it. Fumbled for it again. At last the binding was cut. He flexed his ankles – and nearly cried out in pain. His legs burned from being cramped for so long.

Worse than that was the pain in his heart. Fa had been murdered. Murdered by the crippled wanderer, who had created the demon bear with the sole aim of hunting him down . . .

It wasn't possible. There had to be some mistake.

And yet, deep down, Torak knew it was true. He remembered the grimness in Fa's face as he lay dying. *It will come for me soon*, he had said. He had known what his enemy had done. He had known why the bear had been created.

It was too much to take in. Torak felt as if everything

80

he'd ever known had been swept away: as if he stood on day-old ice, watching the cracks spreading like lightning beneath his feet.

The pain in his legs wrenched him back to the present. He tried to rub some feeling into them. His bare feet were cold, but there was nothing he could do. He hadn't been able to see where Oslak had taken his boots.

Somehow, without being spotted, he had to get out of the shelter, across to the hazel bushes at the edge of the clearing. Somehow, he had to evade the guards.

He couldn't do it. He'd be seen. If only he could find some way to distract them . . .

At the far end of the camp, a lonely yowl rose into the misty morning air. *Where are you?* cried Wolf. *Why did you leave me this time?*

Torak froze. He heard the camp dogs taking up the howl. He saw people leaping up from the clan meet and running to investigate. He knew that Wolf had given him his chance.

He had to act fast. Quickly, he edged out of the shelter and dived into the shadows behind the hazel bushes. He knew what he had to do – and he hated it.

He had to leave Wolf behind.

TWELVE

Cold air burned Torak's throat as he tore through a willow thicket towards the river. Stones bloodied his bare feet. He hardly noticed.

Thanks to Wolf, he'd got out of the camp unseen, but not for long. Behind him came a deep, echoing boom. Birch-bark horns were sounding the alarm. He heard men shouting, dogs baying. The Ravens were coming after him.

Brambles snagged his leggings as he skidded over the riverbank and splashed down into a bed of tall reeds. Knee-deep in icy black mud, he clamped his hand over his mouth to stop his steamy breath betraying him.

Fortunately, he was downwind of his pursuers, but the sweat was pouring off him, and he was still clutching the rawhide rope from his ankles; the dogs would easily pick up his scent. He didn't know whether to toss it away or keep it in case he needed it.

Confusion swirled in his head like an angry river. He had no boots, no pack, no weapons – and nothing with which to make any more, apart from the knowledge in his head and the skill in his hands. If he managed to escape, what then?

Suddenly, above the horns, he heard a yowl. *Where are you?*

At the sound, Torak's doubts cleared. He couldn't leave Wolf. He had to rescue him.

He wished there was some way he could howl back – *I'm coming. Don't be afraid, I haven't abandoned you* – but of course there wasn't. The yowling went on.

His feet were freezing. He had to get out of the river or he'd be too numb to run. He thought fast.

The Ravens would expect him to head north, because that was where he'd said he was going when they'd captured him; so he decided to do exactly that – at least for a while – and then double back to the camp, and find some way of reaching Wolf, hoping that the Ravens would be tricked into continuing north.

Further downstream, a branch snapped.

Torak wheeled round.

A soft splash. A muttered curse.

He peered through the reeds.

About fifty paces downstream, two men were stealing down the bank towards the reed-bed. They moved carefully, intent on hunting him. One held a bow that was taller than Torak, with an arrow already fitted to the string; the other gripped a basalt throwing-axe.

It had been a mistake to hide in the reed-bed. If he stayed where he was, they'd find him; if he tried to swim the river he'd be seen, and speared like a pike. He had to get back into the cover of the Forest.

As quietly as he could, he started clambering up the bank. It was thick with willows which gave good cover, but very steep. Red earth crumbled beneath him. If he fell back into the river, they'd hear the splash . . .

Pebbles trickled into the water as he clawed at the dirt. Luckily the booming of the birch-bark horns masked the noise, and the men didn't hear.

Chest heaving, he made it to the top. Now to head north. The sky was overcast, so he couldn't get his bearings from the sun, but since the river flowed west, he knew that if he kept it directly behind him, he'd be heading roughly north.

He set off through a thick wood of aspen and beech, taking care to trail the rawhide behind him so as to leave a good strong scent.

A furious baying erupted behind him, terrifyingly close. He'd trailed the rope too soon. Already the dogs had picked up his scent.

In panic he scrambled up the nearest tree – a spindly aspen – and had just managed to screw the rawhide into a ball and throw it as far as he could towards the river when a massive red dog burst through the brambles.

It cast about beneath Torak's tree, loops of spit swinging from its jaws. Then it picked up the scent of the rawhide, and raced off in pursuit.

'There!' came a shout from downstream. 'One of the dogs has found the trail!'

Three men ran beneath Torak's aspen, panting as they struggled to catch up with the dog. Torak clung to the tree trunk. If one of them looked up . . .

They pushed on and disappeared. Moments later, Torak heard faint splashes. They must be searching the reeds.

He waited in case more followed, then jumped down from the tree.

He ran north through the aspens, putting some distance between himself and the river, then skidded to a halt. It was time to turn east and head back towards the camp – provided he could find some way of putting the dogs off his trail.

Desperately he looked round for something to mask his scent. Deer droppings? No good: the dogs would still chase after him. Yarrow leaves? Maybe. Their strong, nutty smell should be powerful enough to mask his sweat.

At the foot of a beech tree, he found a pile of wolverine droppings: twisted, hairy, and so foul-smelling that they made his eyes water. Much better. Gagging on the stench, he smeared his feet, shins and hands. Wolverines are about the same size as badgers, but they'll fight anything that moves, and they usually win. The dogs probably wouldn't risk an encounter.

The booming of the horns suddenly cut off.

The silence beat at his ears. With a clutch of terror he realised that Wolf's yowls had also ceased. Was he all right? Surely – surely the Ravens wouldn't dare harm him?

Torak fought his way through the undergrowth towards the camp. The ground rose, and the river ran swiftly between tumbled boulders slippery with moss.

Ahead, smoke curled into the heavy grey sky. He must be getting close. He crouched, straining for sounds of pursuit above the rushing water. With every breath, he expected to hear the thwang of a bowstring; to feel an arrow slicing between his shoulder blades.

Nothing. Maybe they'd fallen for his trick, and were following his trail north.

Through the trees, something big and domed rose into

sight. Torak lurched to a halt. He guessed what it was, and hoped he was wrong.

Like a huge toad, the mound squatted above him. It was a head taller than him, and thickly covered with moss and blueberry scrub. Behind it stood two smaller mounds, and around them loomed a dense thicket of yews and ivy-choked holly trees.

Torak hung back, wondering what to do. Once, he and Fa had come across mounds like these. This must be the Raven Clan's bone-ground: the place where they laid the bones of their Dead.

His way to the camp – to Wolf – lay through the bone-ground. But would he dare? He wasn't Raven Clan. He couldn't venture into another clan's bone-ground without angering their ancestors . . .

Mist floated in the hollows between the mounds, where the pale, ghostly skeletons of hemlock reared above his head, and the purple stalks of dying willowherb released their eerily drifting down. All around stood the dark, listening trees: trees that stayed green all winter, that never slept. In the branches of the tallest yew perched three ravens, watching him. He wondered which one was the clan guardian.

A baying of dogs behind him.

He was caught in a trap. Clever Fin-Kedinn: throwing his net wide, then tightening it around the quarry.

Torak had nowhere to go. The river was too fast to swim, and if he climbed a tree, the ravens would tell the hunters where he was, and he'd be dropped like a shot squirrel. If he burrowed into the thicket, the dogs would drag him out like a weasel.

He turned to face his pursuers. He had nothing with which to defend himself; not even a rock.

He edged backwards – straight into the largest mound. He stifled a cry. He was caught between the living and the dead.

Something grabbed him from behind and dragged him down into darkness.

THIRTEEN

'Don't move,' breathed a voice in Torak's ear, 'don't make a sound, and *don't touch the bones!*'

Torak couldn't even see the bones; he couldn't see anything. He was huddled in rotten-smelling blackness with a knife pressed to his throat.

He gritted his teeth to stop them chattering. Around him, he sensed the chill weight of earth, and the massed and mouldering bones of the Raven Dead. He prayed that all the souls would be far away on the Death Journey. But what if some had been left behind?

He had to get out of here. In the first shock of being caught, he'd heard a scraping of stone, as if his captor were sealing the mound. Now, as his eyes adjusted to the dark, he made out a faint edge of light. Whatever had been dragged across the entrance didn't seem to be a perfect fit.

He was thinking about making a run for it when he heard voices outside. Faint, but coming closer.

Torak tensed. So did his captor.

The crunch and rustle drew nearer, then halted about three paces away. 'He'd never dare come here,' said a man's hushed, frightened voice.

'He might,' whispered a woman. 'He's different. You saw the way he won against Hord. Who knows what he'd do?'

Torak heard the squelch of moss. His foot twitched – and in the darkness, something clinked. He winced.

'Sh!' said the woman. 'I heard something!'

Torak held his breath. His captor's knife pressed harder.

'Cark!' A raven's cry echoed through the trees.

'The guardian doesn't want us here,' muttered the woman. 'We should go. You're right. The boy wouldn't dare.'

Sick with relief, Torak listened to them move away.

After a while he tried to shift position, but the knife-point stopped him. 'Stay still!' hissed his captor.

He recognised that voice. It was Renn. *Renn?*

'You stink,' she whispered.

He tried to turn his head, but again the knife stopped him. 'It's to keep the dogs away,' he whispered back.

'They'd never come here anyway, they're not allowed.'

Torak thought for a moment. 'How did you know I'd be coming this way? And why – '

'I didn't. Now be quiet. They might come back.'

After a cold, cramped wait that seemed to last for ever, Renn gave him a kick and told him to move. He thought about trying to overpower her, but decided against it. If there was a struggle, they would disturb the bones. Instead, he heaved aside the slate slab which blocked the entrance, and crawled into the daylight. The mounds were deserted. Even the ravens had gone.

Renn came after him, backing out on hands and knees and dragging two hazelwood packs – one of them his own.

Perplexed, he crouched in the willowherb and watched her go back inside, emerging with two rolled up sleeping-sacks, two quivers and bows – both wrapped in salmon-skin against the damp – and a buckskin bag that was wriggling furiously.

'Wolf!' cried Torak.

'*Quiet!*' Renn darted a wary glance in the direction of the camp.

Torak wrenched open the bag and Wolf shot out, sweaty and bedraggled. He took one sniff and would have fled if Torak hadn't grabbed him and assured him in low half-barks that it really was him, and not some murderous wolverine. Wolf broke into a big wolf smile, wagging his hindquarters and nibble-greeting Torak rapturously under the chin.

'Hurry up,' said Renn behind him.

'Coming,' snapped Torak. Grabbing handfuls of dew-soaked moss, he wiped off the worst of the dung, then yanked on his boots. Renn had had the foresight to bring them too.

As he turned to reach for his pack, he saw to his astonishment that she had fitted an arrow to her bow and was training it on him. She'd also slung his own bow and quiver over her shoulder, and stuck his axe and knife in her belt.

'What are you doing?' he said. 'I thought you were helping me.'

She looked at him in disgust. 'Why would I help you? The only thing I'm helping is my clan.'

'Then why didn't you give me away just now?'

'Because I intend to make sure that you get to the Mountain of the World Spirit. If I didn't make you, you wouldn't even try. You'd just turn tail and run. Because you're a coward.'

Torak gasped. 'A *coward*?'

'A coward, a liar and a thief. You stole our roe buck, you tricked Hord into losing the fight, and you lied about not being the Listener. Then you ran away. Now for the last time, move!'

With Renn's arrow at his back and her accusation burning in his ears, Torak headed west downriver, keeping to the willows for cover, and carrying Wolf in his arms to prevent his pads leaving a scent trail for the dogs.

Amazingly, there were no sounds of pursuit. Torak found that even more disturbing than the birch-bark horns.

Renn set a fast pace, and he stumbled often. He was tired and hungry, while she was rested and fed; that would make getting away from her more difficult. But she was smaller than him, and he thought he could probably overpower her before she did too much damage with that bow.

The question was, when? For the moment, she seemed genuinely keen to evade the Ravens, guiding him along little twisting deer-paths that clung to the best cover. He decided to wait till they were further from the camp. But her insult rankled.

'I'm not a coward,' he said over his shoulder as they followed the river into a shady oak wood, and the threat of pursuit seemed to lessen.

'Then why did you run away from our camp?'

'They were going to sacrifice me!'

'They hadn't decided that yet. That's why they were arguing.'

'So what should I have done? Waited to find out?'

'The Prophecy,' Renn said coldly, 'could mean two different things. If you hadn't run away, you would have learnt that.'

'And I suppose you're going to tell me,' said Torak, 'because you know everything.'

She heaved a sigh. 'The Prophecy could mean that we sacrifice you and give your blood to the Mountain – and by doing so, destroy the bear. That's what Hord thinks it means. He wants to kill you, so that *he* can take your blood to the Mountain.' She paused. 'Saeunn thinks it means something else: that only you can find the Mountain, and destroy the bear.'

Torak turned and stared at her. 'Me. Destroy the bear.'

She looked him up and down. 'I know, it doesn't seem possible. But Saeunn's sure of it. So am I. The Listener must find the Mountain of the World Spirit – and then, with the Spirit's help, he must destroy the bear.'

Torak blinked. It couldn't be. They'd got it wrong.

'Why must you go on denying it?' Renn said angrily. 'You *are* the Listener. You know you are. You fought with air, just as the Prophecy says. You spoke with silence: that whistle. And the very first words of the Prophecy say that the Listener can talk to the other hunters in the Forest – and you *can* talk to them, because your father put you in a wolf den when you were small.'

Torak narrowed his eyes. 'How do you know about that?'

'Because I listened,' she said.

They followed the river west. As he walked, Torak heard the soft piping of bullfinches eating the brambles; a nuthatch tapping a branch for grubs. With all these birds around, the bear couldn't be anywhere close . . .

Suddenly, Wolf pricked his ears and twitched his whiskers.

'Down!' hissed Torak, pulling Renn with him.

Moments later, two dugout canoes slid past. Torak had a good view of the one closest to him. The man who paddled it had short brown hair cut in a fringe on the brow. He wore a stiff hide mantle across his broad shoulders, and a boar's tusk on a thong at his breast. A black slate throwing-axe lay on his knees. Like his companion in the other canoe, he was scanning the banks as he sliced the water with powerful strokes. It was only too clear what he was seeking.

'Boar Clan,' whispered Renn in Torak's ear. 'Fin-Kedinn must have got them to help search for us.'

Torak was instantly suspicious. 'How did they know we'd come this way? Did you leave them some kind of trail?'

She rolled her eyes. 'Why would I do that?'

'For all I know, you're leading me to some other clan, to be sacrificed.'

'Or maybe,' she said wearily, 'those Boar Clan were passing this way because their autumn camp is downstream, and –' She stopped. 'How did you know they were coming?'

'I didn't. Wolf told me.'

She looked startled – then alarmed. 'You really can talk to him, can't you?'

He did not reply.

She stood up, struggling to overcome her unease. 'They've gone. It's time we headed north.' She replaced her arrow in her quiver and slung her bow over her shoulder, and for a moment Torak thought she was having a change of heart. Then she drew her knife and jabbed at him to get moving.

They reached a streamlet that tumbled out of a rocky gorge, and started to climb. Torak began to feel dizzy with tiredness. He hadn't slept the night before, and hadn't eaten for over a day.

At last he couldn't go another step, and sank to his knees. Wolf jumped out of his arms, falling over his paws in his eagerness to reach the water.

'What are you doing?' cried Renn. 'We can't stop here!'

'We just did,' snarled Torak. He grabbed a handful of soapwort leaves, mashed them in water, and washed off the last of the wolverine dung. Then he bent and drank his fill.

Feeling a lot better, he rummaged in his pack for one of the rolls of dried roe buck that he'd prepared – what seemed like moons ago. After biting off a piece and tossing it to Wolf, he began to eat. It tasted wonderful. Already he could feel the deer's strength coursing through him.

Renn hesitated, then unslung her pack and knelt, but still with her knife trained on Torak. Plunging one hand into her pack, she brought out three thin, reddish-brown cakes. She held one out to him.

He took it and bit off a small fragment. It tasted rich and salty, with an aromatic tang.

'Dried salmon,' said Renn with her mouth full. 'We pound it with deer fat and juniper berries. It stays good all winter.'

To his surprise, she held out a salmon cake to Wolf.

He pointedly ignored it.

Renn hesitated, then gave the cake to Torak. He rubbed it between his palms to mask her scent with his, then offered it to Wolf, who gulped it down.

Renn tried not to show her hurt. 'So?' she said with a shrug. 'I know he doesn't like me.'

'That's because you keep shoving him in bags,' said Torak.

'Only for his own good.'

'He doesn't know that.'

94

'Can't you tell him?'

'There's no way of saying it in wolf talk.' He took another bite of salmon cake. Then he asked something that had been bothering him. 'Why did you bring him?'

'What?'

'Wolf. You got him out of the camp. It can't have been easy. Why?'

She paused. 'You seem to need him. I don't know why. But I thought it might be important.'

He was tempted to tell her that Wolf was his guide, but checked himself. He didn't trust her. She'd been useful for helping him evade the Ravens, but that didn't change the fact that she'd taken his weapons and called him a coward. And she still had her knife pointed straight at him.

The gorge got steeper. Torak judged it safe to let Wolf walk, and the cub plodded before him with drooping tail. Wolf didn't like the climb any more than Torak.

Around mid-afternoon, they reached a ridge overlooking a broad, wooded valley. Through the trees, Torak caught the faraway glitter of a river.

'That's the Widewater,' said Renn. 'It's the biggest river in this part of the Forest. It flows down from the ice rivers in the High Mountains and makes Lake Axehead, then goes over the Thunder Falls and on to the Sea. We camp down there in early summer for the salmon. Sometimes, if the wind's in the east, you can hear the Falls . . . ' her voice trailed off.

Torak guessed that she was wondering how her clan would punish her for helping their captive escape. If she hadn't called him a coward, he might have felt sorry for her.

'We'll cut across the valley,' she said more briskly. 'It should be easy to ford the river where those meadows are. Then we can head north –'

'No,' said Torak suddenly. He pointed at Wolf. The cub had found an elk trail that wound into a wood of tall spruce dripping with beard-moss. He was waiting for them to follow.

'That way,' said Torak. 'Up the valley. Not across it.'

'But that's east. If we head east, we'll reach the High Mountains too soon. That'll make going north much harder.'

'Which way will Fin-Kedinn go?' said Torak.

'West for a while along the trails, then north.'

'Well, then. Heading east sounds like a good idea.'

She frowned. 'Is this some kind of trick?'

'Look,' he said. 'We're heading east because Wolf says we should. He knows the way.'

'What? What do you mean?'

'I mean,' he said quietly, 'that he knows the way to the Mountain.'

She stared at him. Then she snorted. 'That little cub?'

Torak nodded.

'I don't believe you.'

'I don't care,' said Torak.

Wolf *hated* the female tailless.

He'd hated her from the first moment he'd smelt her, as she pointed the Long-Claw-that-Flies at his pack-brother. What a thing to do. As if Tall Tailless was some kind of prey!

After that, the female tailless had done terrible things. She'd wrenched Wolf away from Tall Tailless, and pushed him into a strange, airless Den, where he was bumped around so much that he'd been sick.

Even worse was the way she behaved towards Tall Tailless. Didn't she know that he was the lead wolf? She was so sharp and disrespectful when she yipped at him in tailless talk. Why didn't Tall Tailless just snarl and chase her away?

Now, as Wolf trotted along the trail, he was relieved to hear that she was several strides behind. Good. She should stay away.

He paused to munch some lingonberries at the side of the trail, spat out a bad one, and moved on, feeling the dry earth beneath his pads, and the warmth of the Hot Bright Eye on his back. He raised his muzzle to catch the scents wafting from the valley: some jays and a few stale elk droppings; several storm-broken spruce; lots of willowherb and withered blueberries. All were good, interesting smells; but beneath them was the cold, terrifying scent of the Fast Wet.

Fear snapped at Wolf afresh. Somehow, he and Tall Tailless had to get across the Fast Wet. The crossing place was still many lopes ahead, but already Wolf could hear it roaring. It was so loud that soon even his poor, half-deaf pack-brother would hear it.

There was danger ahead, and Wolf longed to turn back, but he knew that he couldn't. The Pull was getting stronger: the Pull that was like the Den-pull, but not.

Suddenly, Wolf caught another scent. He flared his nostrils to take it in. His ears went back.

This was bad. *Bad bad bad.*

Wolf spun round and raced back towards Tall Tailless.

FOURTEEN

'What is it?' whispered Renn, staring at the terrified cub.

'I don't know,' murmured Torak. His skin began to prickle. He couldn't hear any birds.

Renn took his knife from her belt and tossed it over to him.

He caught it with a nod.

'We should turn back,' she said.

'We can't. This is the way to the Mountain.'

Wolf's amber eyes were dark with fear. He padded slowly forwards: head down, hackles raised.

Torak and Renn followed as quietly as they could. Junipers snagged their boots. Beard-moss trailed thin fingers against their faces. The trees were utterly still: waiting to see what would happen.

'Maybe it isn't . . .' said Renn. 'I mean, it could be a lynx. Or a wolverine.'

Torak didn't believe that any more than she did.

They rounded a bend and came to a fallen birch that was bleeding from deep claw-marks gouged in its bark.

Neither spoke. Both knew that bears sometimes claw at trees to mark their range, or frighten off other hunters.

Wolf approached the birch for a better sniff. Torak followed – then gave a sigh of relief. 'Badger.'

'Are you sure?' said Renn.

'The scratches are smaller than a bear's, and there's mud on the bark.' He circled the tree. 'It got its front claws clogged with earth, digging for worms. Stopped here to scrape them clean. Went back to its sett. That way . . . ' he waved a hand east.

'How do you know all that?' said Renn. 'Did Wolf tell you?'

'No. The Forest did.' He caught her puzzled glance. 'A while back I saw a robin with some badger hairs in its beak. It came from the east.' He shrugged.

'You're good at tracking, aren't you?'

'Fa was better.'

'Well you're better than me,' said Renn. She didn't sound envious; she was merely acknowledging a fact. 'But why would a badger have frightened Wolf?'

'I don't think it did,' said Torak. 'I think it was something else.'

She took his axe, bow and quiver, and held them out. 'Here. You'd better take these.'

They crept up the trail. Wolf went first, Torak next, scanning for signs, and Renn last, straining to see through the trees.

They'd gone another fifty paces when Torak stopped so abruptly that she walked into him.

The young beech tree was still moaning, but it hadn't

long to live. The bear had reared on its hind legs to vent its fury: snapping off the entire top of the tree, ripping away the bark in long bleeding tatters, and slashing deep gouges high on the trunk. Terrifyingly high. If Renn had stood on Torak's shoulders, she wouldn't have been able to reach the lowest claw-mark.

'No bear could be that enormous,' she whispered.

Torak did not reply. He was back in the blue autumn dusk, helping Fa to pitch camp. Torak had made a joke, and Fa was laughing. Then the Forest exploded. Ravens screamed. Pines cracked. And out of the dark beneath the trees surged a deeper darkness . . .

'It's old,' said Renn.

'What?' said Torak.

She gestured at the trunk. 'The tree-blood has hardened. Look, it's almost black.'

He studied the tree. She was right. The bear had clawed the bark at least two days before.

But he couldn't share Renn's relief. She didn't know the worst of it.

With each kill, Fa had said, *its power will grow . . . When the red eye is highest . . . the bear will be invincible.*

Here was the proof. On the night when the bear had attacked, it had been huge. But not this huge.

'It's getting bigger,' he said.

'*What?*' said Renn.

Torak told her what Fa had said.

'But – that's not even a moon away.'

'I know.'

A few paces off the trail, he found three long black hairs

snagged on a twig at about head height. He stepped back sharply. 'It went that way.' He pointed down into the valley. 'See how the branches have sprung back in a slightly different pattern.'

But that didn't reassure him. The bear could have returned by another trail.

Then, from deep in the undergrowth, came the sharp 'tak tak' of a wren.

Torak breathed out. 'I don't think it's anywhere close. Otherwise that wren wouldn't be calling.'

As night fell, they made a shelter of bent hazel saplings and leafmould by a muddy stream. Holly trees gave a pretence of cover, and they lit a small fire and ate a few slips of dried meat. They didn't dare risk the salmon cakes; the bear would have smelt them from many daywalks away.

It was a cold night, and Torak sat hunched in his sleeping-sack, listening to the faint, faraway roar that Renn said was the Thunder Falls.

Why had Fa never told him about the Prophecy? Why was he the Listener? What did it mean?

Beside him, Wolf slept with ears twitching. Renn sat watching a beetle clamber down from the firewood.

Torak now knew that he could trust her. She'd risked a lot to help him, and he couldn't have escaped without her. It was a new feeling, having someone on his side. He said, 'I need to tell you something.'

Renn reached for a twig, and helped the beetle off a branch.

'Before he died,' said Torak, 'my father made me swear an oath. To find the Mountain, or die trying.' He paused. 'I don't know why he made me swear. But I did. And I'll do my best.'

She nodded, and he saw that for the first time she truly

believed him. 'There's something I've got to tell you, too,' she said. 'It's about the Prophecy.' Frowning, she turned the twig in her fingers. 'When – if – you find the Mountain, you can't just ask the Spirit for help. You've got to prove that you're worthy. Saeunn told me last night. She said that when the crippled wanderer made the bear, he broke the pact, because he made a creature that kills without purpose. He angered the World Spirit. It'll take a great deal to get it to help.'

Torak tried to swallow. 'What will it take?'

She met his eyes. 'You've got to bring it the three strongest pieces of the Nanuak.'

Torak looked at her blankly.

'Saeunn says that the Nanuak is like a great river that never ends. Every living thing has a part of it inside them. Hunters, prey, rocks, trees. Sometimes a special part of it forms, like foam on the river. When it does, it's incredibly powerful.' She hesitated. 'That's what you've got to find. If you don't, the World Spirit won't help you. And then you'll never destroy the bear.'

Torak caught his breath. 'Three pieces of the Nanuak,' he said hoarsely. 'What are they? How do I find them?'

'Nobody knows. All we have is a riddle.' She shut her eyes, and recited,

> 'Deepest of all, the drowned sight.
> Oldest of all, the stone bite.
> Coldest of all, the darkest light.'

A breeze sprang up. The holly trees gave a prickly murmur.

'What does it mean?' said Torak.

Renn opened her eyes. 'Nobody knows.'

He bowed his head to his knees. 'So I've got to find a

mountain that nobody's ever seen. And work out the answer to a riddle that nobody's ever solved. And kill a bear that nobody can fight.'

Renn sucked in her breath. 'You've got to try.'

Torak was silent. Then he said, 'Why did Saeunn tell you all this? Why you?'

'I never wanted her to, she just did. She thinks I should be a Mage when I'm grown.'

'Don't you want to be?'

'No! But I suppose – maybe there's a purpose in these things. If she hadn't told me, I wouldn't have been able to tell you.'

Another silence. Then Renn wriggled out of her sleeping-sack. 'I'll take our packs outside. We don't want the food smell to draw the bear.'

When she'd gone, Torak curled up on his side and lost himself in the fiery heart of the embers. Around him, the Forest creaked in its sleep, dreaming its deep green dreams. He thought of the thousands and thousands of tree-souls thronging the darkness: waiting for him, and him alone, to deliver them from the bear.

He thought of the golden birch and the scarlet rowan, and the brilliant green oaks. He thought of the teeming prey; of the lakes and rivers full of fish; of all the different kinds of wood and bark and stone that were there for the taking if you knew where to look. The Forest had everything you could ever want. Until now he'd never realised how much he loved it.

If the bear could not be destroyed, all this would be lost.

Wolf leapt up and went off on one of his nightly hunts. Renn returned, got into her sleeping-sack without a word, and fell asleep. Torak went on staring into the fire.

'There's a purpose in these things,' Renn had said. In a

strange way, that gave him strength. He *was* the Listener. He had sworn to find the Mountain. The Forest needed him. He would do his best.

He slept fitfully. He dreamed that Fa was alive again, but instead of a face, he had a blank white stone. *I am not Fa. I am the Wolf Mage* . . .

Torak woke with a start.

He felt Wolf's breath on his face, then the downy brush of the cub's whiskers on his eyelids, and the needle-fine grooming-nibbles on his cheeks and throat.

He licked the cub's muzzle, and Wolf nuzzled his chin, then settled against him with a 'humph'.

'We should have crossed lower down,' said Renn as they craned their necks at the Thunder Falls.

Torak wiped the spray from his face, and wondered how anything in the Forest could be this angry.

All day they'd been following the calm green Widewater upstream. But now, as it thundered over a sheer wall of rock, it was appalling in its fury. Before it, the whole Forest seemed to stand and stare.

'We should have crossed lower down,' Renn said again.

'We would've been seen,' said Torak. 'Those meadows were too exposed. Besides, Wolf wanted to stay on this side.'

Renn pursed her lips. 'If he's the guide, then where is he?'

'He hates fast water. His pack was drowned in a flood. But he'll be back when we've found a way to get above the falls.'

'Mm,' said Renn, unconvinced. Like Torak, she'd slept badly, and she'd been moody all morning. Neither of them had mentioned the riddle.

Eventually, they found a deer track that wound up the side of the falls. It was steep and muddy, and by the time they reached the top they were exhausted and soaked in spray. Wolf was waiting for them: sitting beneath a birch tree a safe distance from the Widewater, shaking with fear.

'Where to now?' panted Renn.

Torak was watching Wolf. 'We follow the river till he tells us to cross.'

'Can you swim?' asked Renn.

He nodded. 'Can you?'

'Yes. Can Wolf?'

'I don't think so.'

They started upstream, pushing through brambles and tangled rowan and birch. It was a cold, overcast day, and the wind scattered birch leaves onto the river like small amber arrowheads. Wolf trotted with his ears flat back. The river ran fast and smooth on its way to the falls.

They hadn't gone far when Wolf began to run up and down the bank, mewing. Torak could feel his fear. He turned to Renn. 'He wants to cross, but he's frightened.'

'The brambles are too thick here,' said Renn. 'What about further up by those rocks?'

The rocks were smooth and splashed with treacherous-looking moss, but they reared a good half-forearm out of the water. They might provide a way across.

Torak nodded.

'I'll go first,' said Renn, pulling off her boots and tying them to her pack, then rolling up her leggings. She found a stick for balance, and slung her pack over one shoulder, so that it wouldn't drag her down if she fell in. Her quiver and bow she carried in the other hand, high above her head.

She looked scared as she approached the water. But she

made it across without faltering – until the final rock, when she had to leap for the bank, and ended up grabbing a willow branch to haul herself up.

Torak left his pack and weapons on the bank, and pulled off his boots. He would carry Wolf across, then return for his things. 'Come on, Wolf,' he said encouragingly. Then he said it in wolf talk, hunkering down on his haunches and making low, reassuring mewing noises.

Wolf shot under a juniper bush and refused to come out.

'Put him in your pack!' shouted Renn from the other side. 'It's the only way you'll get him across!'

'If I did that,' yelled Torak, 'he'd never trust me again!'

He sat down in the moss on the edge of the bank. Then he yawned and stretched, to show Wolf how relaxed he was.

After a while, Wolf emerged from the juniper and came to sit beside him.

Again Torak yawned.

Wolf glanced at him, then gave a huge yawn that ended in a whine.

Slowly, Torak got to his feet and picked Wolf up in his arms, murmuring softly in wolf talk.

The rocks felt ice-cold and slippery under Torak's bare feet. In his arms, Wolf started shivering with terror.

On the far bank, Renn held onto a birch sapling with one hand, and leaned towards them. 'That's it,' she shouted above the thunder of the falls, 'you're nearly there!'

Wolf's claws dug into Torak's jerkin.

'Last rock!' shouted Renn. 'I'll grab him . . . '

A wave slapped into the rock, splashing them with freezing water. Wolf's courage broke. Twisting frantically out of Torak's grip, he leapt for the bank, landing with his hind legs in the water and his forepaws clawing at the bank.

Renn leaned down and caught him by the scruff. 'I've got him!' she yelled.

Torak overbalanced and crashed into the river.

FIFTEEN

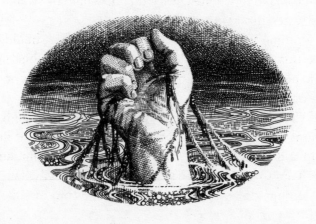

Torak came up spluttering with cold, fighting the river. He was a strong swimmer, so he wasn't too worried. He'd grab that branch jutting from the bank . . .

The next one, then.

Behind him, he heard Renn shouting his name as she tore through the brambles, and Wolf's urgent barks. It occurred to him that the brambles must be very thick, as Renn and Wolf were dropping further and further behind.

The river punched him in the back, smashing him limp as a wet leaf against a rock. He went under.

He kicked his way to the surface, and was shocked to see how far he'd been carried. He couldn't hear Renn or Wolf any more, and the waterfall was sliding closer with astonishing speed, drowning all voices but its own.

His jerkin and leggings were dragging him down. The cold had deadened his limbs to sticks of bone and flesh, working without feeling to keep his head above the surface. He couldn't see anything except white-foam waves and a blur of willows. Then even that disappeared as he went under again.

It came to him quite clearly that he would be swept over the waterfall and killed.

No time for fear. Just a distant anger that it should end like this. Poor Wolf. Who's going to look after him now? And poor Renn. Let's hope she doesn't find the body, it'll be a mess.

Death boomed at him. A rainbow flashed through the spume and spray . . . then the waves smoothed out like a skin and suddenly there was no more river in front, and it was hard to breathe as he went over. Death reached up and pulled him down, and it was shining and smooth, like the moment of falling asleep . . .

Over and over he fell, water filling his mouth, his nose, his ears. The river swallowed him whole: he was inside it and it roared through him, this pounding power of water. Somehow he surfaced, gulping air. Then it pulled him down again into its swirling green depths.

The roar of the river faded. Lights flashed in his head. He sank. The water turned from blue to dark-green to black. He was languid and frozen past feeling. He longed to give up and sleep.

He became aware of a faint, bubbling laughter. Hair like green waterweed trailed across his throat. Cruel faces leered at him with merciless white eyes.

Come to us! called the Hidden People of the river. *Let your souls float free of that dull, heavy flesh!*

He felt sick, as if his guts were being pulled loose.

See, see! laughed the Hidden People. *How swiftly his souls begin to drift free! How eagerly they come to us!*

Torak turned over and over like a dead fish. The Hidden

109

People were right. It would be so easy to leave his body and let them roll him for ever in their cold embrace . . .

Wolf's desperate yowl cut through to him.

Torak opened his eyes. Silver bubbles streamed through the dark as the Hidden People fled.

Again Wolf called to him.

Wolf needed him. There was something they had to do together.

Flailing his numb stick-limbs, he began to fight his way back towards the surface. The green grew brighter. The light drew him . . .

He'd nearly reached it when something made him look down – and he saw them. Far below, two blind white eyes staring up at him.

What were they? River pearls? The eyes of one of the Hidden People?

The Prophecy. The riddle. *'Deepest of all, the drowned sight.'*

His chest was bursting. If he didn't get air soon, he would die. But if he didn't swim down now and grasp those eyes – whatever they were – he would lose them for ever.

He doubled over and kicked with all his might, pushing himself down.

The cold made his eyes ache, but he didn't dare shut them. Closer and closer he swam . . . he reached out towards the bottom – he grasped a handful of icy mud. He had them! No way to make sure – the mud was swirling thick around him, and he couldn't risk opening his fist in case they slipped free – but he could feel the weight of them dragging him down. He twisted round and kicked back towards the light.

But his strength was failing, and he rose with agonising slowness, hampered by his sodden clothes. More lights flashed in his head. More watery laughter. *Too late,*

whispered the Hidden People. *You'll never reach the light now!*
Stay here with us, boy with the drifting souls. Stay here for ever . . .

Something grabbed his leg and pulled him down.

He kicked. Couldn't get free. Something was gripping his legging just above the ankle. He twisted round to wrench himself free, but the grip held tight. He tried to draw his knife from its sheath, but he'd tightened the strap around the hilt before starting the crossing, and he couldn't get it loose.

Anger boiled up inside him. Get away from me! he shouted inside his head. You can't have me – and you can't have the Nanuak!

Fury lent him strength and he kicked out savagely. The grip on his leg broke. Something gave a gurgling howl and sank into darkness. Torak shot upwards.

He exploded from the water, gulping great chestfuls of air. Through the glare of the sun he glimpsed a sheet of green river, and an overhanging branch approaching him fast. With his free hand he reached for it – and missed. Pain exploded in his head.

He knew that he hadn't been knocked out. He could still feel the slap of the river, and hear his rasping breath – but his eyes were open and staring, and he couldn't see.

Panic seized him. Not blind, he thought. No, no *please*, not blind.

SIXTEEN

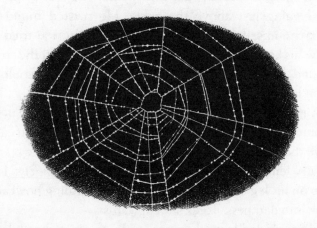

The female tailless was whimpering and waving her forepaws, so Wolf left her and hurtled down the track.

When he smelt Tall Tailless among the willows, he began to whimper too. His pack-brother was slumped over a log, half in the Wet. He smelt strongly of blood, and wasn't moving at all.

Wolf licked his cold cheek, but Tall Tailless didn't stir. Was he Not-Breath? Wolf put up his muzzle and howled.

A clumsy crashing announced the female tailless. Wolf leapt to defend his pack-brother, but she pushed him away, hooked her forepaws under Tall Tailless's shoulders, and hauled him out of the Wet.

Despite himself, Wolf was impressed.

He watched as she put her forepaws on Tall Tailless's chest and pressed down hard. Tall Tailless began to cough! Tall Tailless had breath again!

But just as Wolf was jumping onto his pack-brother to

snuffle-lick his muzzle, he was batted away again! Heedless of Wolf's warning growls, the female pulled Tall Tailless to his legs and they staggered up the bank. Tall Tailless kept blundering into hazel bushes, as if he couldn't see.

Watchfully, Wolf walked beside them, relaxing a little when they reached a Den a good distance from the Fast Wet: a proper Den, not a small, airless one.

Still the female wouldn't let Wolf near his pack-brother. Snarling, Wolf slammed her with his body. Instead of moving away, she picked up a stick and threw it out of the Den, pointing at it and then at Wolf.

Wolf ignored her and turned back to Tall Tailless, who was trying to tug off his pelt. Finally, Tall Tailless had only the long dark fur on his head. He lay curled on his side with his eyes shut, shaking with cold. His poor furless underpelt was no use at all.

Wolf leant against him to warm him up, while the female tailless quickly brought to life the Bright Beast-that-Bites-Hot. Tall Tailless moved closer to the warmth, and Wolf watched anxiously in case he got his paws bitten.

That was when Wolf noticed that one of Tall Tailless's forepaws held something that was giving off a strange glow.

Wolf sniffed at it – and backed away. It smelt of hunter and prey and Fast Wet and tree, all chewed up together; and from it came a high, thin humming: so high that Wolf could only just catch it.

Wolf was frightened. He knew that he was in the presence of something very, very strong.

羊羊

Torak huddled in his sleeping-sack, shivering uncontrollably. His head was on fire and his whole body felt like one big bruise, but worst of all, he couldn't see. *Blind, blind*, thudded his heart.

Above the crackle of the fire he heard Renn muttering angrily. 'Were you *trying* to get yourself killed?'

'What?' he said, but it came out as a mumble, because his mouth was thick with the salty sweetness of blood.

'You'd nearly reached the surface,' said Renn, pressing what felt like cobwebs to his forehead, 'then you turned round and swam, deliberately swam, back down again!'

He realised that she didn't know about the Nanuak. But his fist was so cold that he couldn't unclench it to show her.

He felt Wolf's hot tongue on his face. A chink of light appeared. Then a big black nose. Torak's spirits soared. 'I cad thee!' he said.

'What?' snapped Renn. 'Well of course you can see! You cut your forehead when you hit that branch, and the blood got in your eyes. Scalp wounds bleed a lot. Didn't you know that?'

Torak was so relieved that he would have laughed if his teeth hadn't been chattering so violently.

He saw that they were in a small cave with earth walls. A birchwood fire was burning fiercely, and already his sodden clothes, hanging from tree roots jutting through the ceiling, were beginning to steam. The thunder of the falls was loud, and from its sound, and the view of treetops at the cave mouth, he guessed they must be some way up the side of the valley. He couldn't remember getting there. Renn must have dragged him. He wondered how she'd managed it.

She was kneeling beside him looking shaken. 'You've been very, very lucky,' she said. 'Now hold still.' From her medicine pouch she took some dried yarrow leaves, and crumbled them in her palm. Then, having picked off the cobwebs, she pressed the yarrow leaves to his forehead. They stuck tight to the wound in an instant scab.

Torak shut his eyes and listened to the never-ending fury of the falls. Wolf crawled into the sleeping-sack with him, wriggling till he got comfortable. He felt gloriously furry and warm as he licked Torak's shoulder. Torak licked his muzzle in reply.

When he awoke, he wasn't shivering any more, and he was still clutching the Nanuak. He could feel its weight in his fist.

Wolf was nosing about in the back of the cave, and Renn was sorting herbs in her lap. Torak's pack, boots, quiver and bow were neatly piled behind her. He realised that to retrieve them she must have crossed the river again. Twice.

'Renn,' he said.

'What,' she said without looking up. From her tone, he could tell that she was still cross.

'You got me out of the river. You got me all the way up here. You even fetched my things. I can't imagine . . . I mean, that was brave.'

She did not reply.

'Renn,' he said again.

'*What.*'

'I had to swim down. I had to.'

'Why?'

Awkwardly, he brought out the hand that held the Nanuak, and unclenched his fingers.

As soon as he did, the fire seemed to sink. Shadows leapt on the cave walls. The air seemed to crackle, like the moment after a lightning strike.

Wolf stopped nosing and gave a warning grunt. Renn went very still.

The river eyes lay in Torak's palm in a nest of green mud,

glowing faintly, like the moon on a misty night.

As he gazed at them, Torak felt an echo of the sickness that had tugged at him at the bottom of the river. 'This is it, isn't it?' he said. '"*Deepest of all, the drowned sight.*" The first part of the Nanuak.'

The colour had drained from Renn's face. 'Don't – move,' she said, and scrambled out of the cave, returning soon after with a bunch of scarlet rowan leaves.

'Lucky there's mud on your hand,' she said. 'You mustn't let it touch your skin. It might suck out your own part of the world-soul.'

'Is that what was happening?' he murmured. 'In the river I was beginning to feel – dizzy.' He told her about the Hidden People.

She looked horrified. 'How did you *dare*? If they'd caught you . . .' She made the sign of the hand to ward off evil. 'I can't believe you've just been sleeping with it in your fist. There's no time to lose.'

Bringing out a little black pouch from inside her jerkin, she stuffed it with the rowan leaves. 'The leaves should protect us,' she said, 'and the pouch should help too, it's ravenskin.' Grasping Torak's wrist, she tipped the river eyes into the pouch and drew the neck tight.

As soon as the Nanuak was hidden, the flames grew, and the shadows shrank. The air in the cave stopped crackling.

Torak felt as if a weight had been taken from him. He watched Wolf pad over and lie down beside Renn with his muzzle between his paws, gazing at the pouch on her lap, and whining softly.

'D'you think he can smell it?' she asked.

'Or maybe hear it,' said Torak. 'I don't know.'

Renn shivered. 'Just as long as nothing else can, too.'

SEVENTEEN

Torak woke at dawn feeling stiff and sore. But he could move all four limbs, and nothing felt broken, so he decided he was better.

Renn was kneeling at the mouth of the cave, trying to feed Wolf a handful of crowberries. She was frowning with concentration as she held out her hand. Wolf edged cautiously forwards – then jerked back again. At last he decided he could trust her, and snuffled up the berries. Renn laughed as his whiskers tickled her palm.

She caught Torak looking and stopped laughing, embarrassed to be seen making friends with the cub. 'How do you feel?' she asked.

'Better.'

'You don't look it. You'll need to rest for at least a day.' She got to her feet. 'I'm going hunting. We should keep the dried food for when we need it.'

Torak sat up painfully. 'I'm coming too.'

'No you're not, you should rest –'

'But my clothes are dry, and I need to move around.' He didn't tell her the real reason, which was that he hated caves. He and Fa used to shelter in them sometimes, but Torak always ended up outside. It felt all wrong to be sleeping between solid walls, cut off from the wind and the Forest. It felt like being swallowed.

Renn sighed. 'Promise that as soon as we make a kill, you'll come back here and rest.'

Torak promised.

Getting dressed hurt more than he'd expected, and by the time he'd finished, his eyes were watering. To his relief, Renn didn't notice, as she was preparing for the hunt. She combed her hair with an ashwood comb carved like a raven's claw, then tied it back in a horsetail and stuck in an owl feather for hunting luck. Next, she smeared ash on her skin to mask her scent, and oiled her bow with a couple of crushed hazelnuts, chanting: 'May the clan guardian fly with me and make the hunt successful.'

Torak was surprised. 'We prepare for hunting in the same way. Except we say, "May the clan guardian *run* with me". And we don't oil our bows every time.'

'That's just something I do,' said Renn. Lovingly she held it up so that the oiled wood gleamed. 'Fin-Kedinn made it for me when I was seven, just after Fa was killed. It's yewwood, seasoned for four summers. Sapwood on its back for stretch, heartwood on its belly for strength. He made the quiver, too. Wove the wicker himself, and let me choose the decoration. A zigzag band of red and white willow.'

She paused, and her face became shadowed as she remembered. 'I never knew my mother, Fa was everything. When he was killed, I was crying so hard. Then Fin-Kedinn came, and I hit him with my fists. He didn't move. Just stood there like an oak tree, letting me hit him. Then he said, "He was my brother. I will look after you." And I knew that he would.' She scowled, sucking in her lips.

Torak knew that she was missing her uncle, and probably worrying about him too, as he tracked her through the bear-haunted Forest. To give her time, he made his own preparations and gathered his weapons. Then he said, 'Come on. Let's go hunting.'

She nodded once, then shouldered her quiver.

It was a bright, cold morning, and the Forest had never looked so beautiful. Scarlet rowan trees and golden birch blazed like flame against the dark-green spruce. Blueberry bushes glittered with thousands of tiny, frost-spangled spiders' webs. Frozen moss crunched underfoot. A pair of inquisitive magpies followed them from tree to tree, bickering. The bear must be far away.

Unfortunately, Torak didn't get long to enjoy it. Around mid-morning, Wolf startled a clutch of willow grouse, who shot skywards with indignant gobbles. The birds flew fast and into the sun, so Torak didn't even bother taking aim, knowing he'd never hit one. To his astonishment, Renn nocked an arrow and let fly, and a willow grouse thudded into the moss.

Torak's jaw dropped. 'How did you manage that?'

Renn reddened. 'Well. I practise a lot.'

'But – I've never seen shooting that good. Are you the best in your clan?'

She looked uncomfortable.

'Is there anyone better?

'Um. Not really.' Still embarrassed, she waded off through the blueberry bushes to retrieve the grouse. 'Here.' She flashed him her sharp-toothed grin. 'Remember your

119

promise? Now you've got to go back and rest.'

Torak took the grouse. If he'd known she was such a good shot, he'd never have promised.

When Renn returned to the cave, they had a feast. From the hooting of a young owl, they knew that the bear was far away; and Renn judged that they'd come far enough east to have escaped the Ravens. Besides, they needed hot food.

Renn wrapped two small pieces of grouse in dock leaves and left them for the clan guardians, while Torak moved the fire to the mouth of the cave, as he was determined not to spend another night inside. Half-filling Renn's cooking-skin with water, he hung it by the fire; then, using a split branch, he dropped in red-hot stones to heat it up, and added the plucked and jointed willow grouse. Soon he was stirring a fragrant stew flavoured with crow garlic and big, fleshy wood-mushrooms.

They ate most of the meat, leaving a little for daymeal, and sopped up the juices with hawkbit roots baked in the embers. After that came a wonderful mash that Renn made of late lingonberries and hazelnuts, and finally some beechnuts, which they burst by the fire and peeled to get at the small, rich nuts inside.

By the time he'd finished, Torak felt as if he need never eat again. He settled down by the fire to mend the rip in his leggings where the Hidden People had grabbed him. Renn sat some way off, trimming the flights on her arrows, and Wolf lay between them licking his paws clean, having swiftly despatched the joint of grouse that Torak had saved for him.

For a while there was a companionable silence, and Torak felt contented, even hopeful. After all, he'd found the first piece of the Nanuak. That must count for something.

Suddenly, Wolf leapt to his feet and raced out of the firelight. Moments later he returned, circling the fire and making agitated little grunt-whines.

'What is it?' whispered Renn.

Torak was on his feet, watching Wolf. He shook his head. 'I can't make it out. "Kill smell. Old kill. Move." Something like that.'

They stared into the darkness.

'We shouldn't have lit a fire,' said Renn.

'Too late now,' said Torak.

Wolf stopped the grunt-whines and raised his muzzle, gazing skywards.

Torak looked up – and the remains of his good humour vanished. To the east, above the distant blackness of the High Mountains, the red eye of the Great Auroch glared down at them. It was impossible to miss: a vicious crimson, throbbing with malice. Torak couldn't take his eyes from it. He could feel its power: sending strength to the bear, sapping his own will of hope and resolve.

'What chance do we have against the bear?' he said. 'I mean, really, what chance do we have?'

'I don't know,' said Renn.

'How are we going to find the other two pieces of the Nanuak? *"Oldest of all, the stone bite. Coldest of all, the darkest light."* What does that even mean?'

Renn did not reply.

At last he dragged his gaze from the sky, and sat down by the fire. The red eye seemed to glare at him even from the embers.

Behind him, Renn stirred. 'Look, Torak, it's the First Tree!'

He raised his head.

The eye had been blotted out. Instead, a silent, ever-

121

changing green glow filled the sky. Now a vast swathe of light twisted in a voiceless wind; then the swathe vanished, and shimmering pale-green waves rippled across the stars. The First Tree stretched for ever, shining its miraculous fire upon the Forest.

As Torak gazed at it, a spark of hope re-kindled. He'd always loved watching the First Tree on frosty nights, while Fa told the story of the Beginning. The First Tree meant good luck in hunting; maybe it would bring luck to him, too.

'I think it's a good sign,' said Renn as if she'd heard his thoughts. 'I've been wondering. Was it really luck that you found the Nanuak? I mean, why did you fall into the very part of the river where it lay? I don't think that was by chance. I think – you were meant to find it.'

He threw her a questioning glance.

'Maybe,' she said slowly, 'the Nanuak was *put* in your way, but then it was up to you to decide what to do about it. When you saw it at the bottom of the river, you *could* have decided it was too dangerous to try for. But you didn't. You risked your life to get it. Maybe – that was part of the test.'

It was a good thought, and it made Torak feel a little better. He fell asleep watching the silent green boughs of the First Tree, while Wolf sped out of the cave on some mysterious errand of his own.

$$\text{丰丰}$$

Wolf left the Den and loped up to the ridge above the valley to catch the smell on the wind: a powerful smell of rotten prey like a very old kill – except that it moved.

As he ran, Wolf felt with joy how his pads were toughening, his limbs getting stronger with every Dark that passed. He loved to run, and he wished that Tall Tailless did too. But at times his pack-brother could be terribly slow.

As Wolf neared the ridge, he heard the roar of the Thundering Wet, and the sound of a hare feeding in the next valley. Overhead, he saw the Bright White Eye with her many little cubs. It was all as it should be. Except for that smell.

At the top of the ridge he lifted his muzzle to catch the scent-laden winds, and again he caught it: quite close, and coming closer. Racing back into the valley, he soon found it: the strange, shuffling thing that smelt so rotten.

He got near enough to observe it clearly in the dark, although he was careful not to let it know that he was near. To his surprise he found that it was not an old kill after all. It had breath and claws, and it moved in an odd shambling walk, growling to itself while the spit trailed from its muzzle.

What puzzled Wolf most was that he couldn't catch what it was feeling. Its mind seemed broken; scattered like old bones. Wolf had never sensed such a thing before.

He watched it make its way up the slope towards the Den where the tailless were sleeping. It prowled closer . . .

Just as Wolf was about to attack, it shook itself and shambled away. But through the tangle of its broken thoughts, Wolf sensed that it would be back.

EIGHTEEN

The fog stole up on them like a thief in the night. When Torak crawled stiffly from his sleeping-sack, the valley below had disappeared. The Breath of the World Spirit had swallowed it whole.

He yawned. Wolf had woken him often in the night, racing about and uttering urgent half-barks: *kill smell – watch*. It didn't make sense. Every time Torak went to look, there was nothing but a stink of carrion and an uneasy feeling of being watched.

'Maybe he just hates fog,' said Renn grumpily as she rolled up her sleeping-sack. 'I know I do. In fog, nothing's what it seems.'

'I don't think it's that,' said Torak, watching Wolf snuffing the air.

'Well what is it, then?'

'I don't know. It's as if something's out there. Not the bear. Not the Ravens. Something else.'

'What do you mean?'

'I told you, I don't know. But we should be on our guard.' Thoughtfully, he put more wood on the fire to heat up the rest of the stew for daymeal.

With an anxious frown, Renn counted their arrows. 'Twenty between us. Not nearly enough. Do you know how to knap flint?'

Torak shook his head. 'My hands aren't strong enough. Fa was going to teach me next summer. What about you?'

'The same. We'll have to be careful. There's no telling how far it is to the Mountain. And we'll need more meat.'

'Maybe we'll catch something today.'

'In this fog?'

She was right. The fog was so thick that they couldn't see Wolf five paces ahead. It was the kind that the clans call the smoke-frost: an icy breath that descends from the High Mountains at the start of winter, blackening berries and sending small creatures scuttling for their burrows.

Wolf led them along an auroch trail that wound north up the side of the valley: a chilly climb through frost-brittle bracken. The fog muffled sounds and made distances hard to judge. Trees loomed with alarming suddenness. Once they shot a reindeer, only to find that they'd hit a log. That meant a frustrating struggle to dig out the arrowheads, which they couldn't afford to lose. Twice, Torak thought he saw a figure in the undergrowth, but when he ran to look, he found nothing.

It took all morning to climb the ridge, and all afternoon to scramble down into the next valley, where a silent pine forest guarded a slumbering river.

'Do you realise,' said Renn as they huddled in a hasty shelter after a cheerless nightmeal, 'that we haven't seen a single reindeer? They should be everywhere by now.'

'I've been thinking that too,' said Torak. Like Renn, he knew that the snow on the fells should be driving the herds into the Forest, to grow fat on moss and mushrooms. Sometimes they ate so many mushrooms that they even tasted of them.

'What will the clans do if the reindeer don't come?' said Renn.

Torak didn't answer. Reindeer meant survival: meat, bedding and clothes.

He wondered what he was going to do for winter clothes. Renn had had the foresight to put hers on before she'd left the Raven camp, but she hadn't been able to steal any for him, so all he had was his summer buckskin: not nearly as warm as the furry parka and leggings which he and Fa made every autumn.

Even if they did find prey, there'd be no time to make clothes. Beyond the fog, the red eye of the Great Auroch was climbing ever higher.

Torak shut his eyes to push the thought away, and eventually fell into an uneasy sleep. But whenever he awoke in the night, he caught that strange carrion stink.

Next morning dawned colder and foggier than ever, and even Wolf seemed dejected as he led them upstream. They reached a fallen oak bridging the river, and crawled over it on their hands and knees. Soon afterwards, the trail forked. To the left, it wound into a valley of misty beech trees; to the right, it disappeared up a dank gully, its steep sides an uninviting jumble of moss-covered boulders.

To their dismay, Wolf took the right-hand trail.

'That can't be right!' cried Renn. 'The Mountain's in the north! Why is he forever going east?'

Torak shook his head. 'It feels wrong to me too. But he seems sure.'

Renn snorted. She was clearly having doubts again.

Looking at Wolf waiting patiently, Torak felt a twinge of guilt. The cub wasn't even four moons old. At this age, he should be playing by his den, not traipsing over hills. 'I think,' he said, 'we ought to trust him.'

'Mm,' murmured Renn.

Hoisting their packs higher on their aching shoulders, they entered the gully.

They hadn't gone ten paces before they knew that it didn't want them. Towering spruce trees warned them back with arms spread wide. A boulder crashed in front of them; another struck the path just behind Renn. The stink of carrion grew stronger. But if it came from a kill-site, it was a strange one, for they heard no ravens.

The fog closed in until they could barely see two paces ahead. All they could hear was the drip, drip, of mist on the bracken, and the gurgle of a stream rushing between fern-choked banks. Torak began to see bear shapes in the fog. He watched Wolf for the least sign of alarm, but the cub plodded along, unafraid.

At midday – or what felt like midday – they halted for a rest. Wolf slumped down, panting, and Renn shrugged off her pack. Her face was pinched, her hair soaking. 'I saw some reeds back there. I'm going to plait myself a hood.' Hanging their quivers and bows on a branch, she moved off through the ferns. Wolf heaved himself up and padded after her.

Torak squatted at the edge of the stream to refill the waterskins. It wasn't long before he heard Renn coming back. 'That was quick,' he said.

'*Out!*' bellowed a voice behind him. 'Out of the Walker's Valley or the Walker slits throats!'

Torak spun round and found himself staring up at an unbelievably filthy man towering over him with a knife.

In an instant he took in a ruined face as rough as tree bark; waist-length hair matted with filth; a rancid cape of slimy yellow reeds. And at last the carrion stink was explained, for around the man's neck hung a pigeon's softly rotting carcass.

In fact, everything about him seemed to be rotting: from his empty, festering eye socket to his toothless black gums, and his shattered nose, from which hung a loop of greenish-yellow slime. 'Out!' he bellowed, waving a green slate knife. 'Narik and the Walker say out!'

Quickly, Torak put both fists over his heart in the sign of friendship. 'Please – we come as friends. We mean you no harm –'

'But they already did harm!' roared the man. 'They bring it with them to the beautiful valley! All night the Walker watches! All night he waits to see if they will bring harm to his valley!'

'What harm?' Torak said desperately. 'We didn't mean it!'

There was a stirring in the bracken and Wolf threw himself at Torak. Torak clutched the cub close, and felt the small heart hammering.

The man didn't notice. He'd heard Renn creeping up behind him. 'Sneaking up, is she?' he snarled, lurching round and waving his knife in her face.

Renn dodged backwards, but that only made him angrier.

'Does she want them in the water?' he cried, snatching their bows and quivers from the branch and holding them out over the stream. 'Does she want to see them swim, the pretty arrows and the shiny, shiny bows?'

Mute with horror, Renn shook her head.

'Then they drop knives and axes quick, or in they go!'

They both knew that they didn't have a choice, so they tossed their remaining weapons at his feet, and he stowed them swiftly under his cape.

'What do you want us to do?' said Torak, his heart hammering as fast as Wolf's.

'Get *out*!' roared the man. 'The Walker *told* them! *Narik* told them! And the anger of Narik is terrible!'

Both Renn and Torak looked round for Narik, whoever he was, but saw only wet trees and fog.

'We are getting out,' said Renn, eyeing her bow in the enormous fist.

'Not *up* the Valley! Out!' He gestured to the side of the gully.

'But – we can't go up there,' said Renn, 'it's too steep – '

'No more tricks!' bellowed the Walker, and hurled her quiver into the stream.

She screamed and leapt after it, but Torak grabbed her arm. 'It's too late,' he told her. 'It's gone.' The stream was deeper and faster than it looked. Her beloved quiver had disappeared.

Renn turned on the Walker. 'We were doing what you said! You didn't have to do that!'

'Oh yes he did,' said the Walker with a toothless black grin. 'Now they know he means it!'

'Come on, Renn,' said Torak. 'Let's do as he says.'

Furiously, Renn picked up her pack.

If their journey had been hard before, this was worse. The Walker strode behind them, forcing them almost at a run up a rocky elk trail that at times had them climbing on their hands and knees. Renn went in front, stony-faced, grieving for her quiver. Wolf soon began to lag behind.

Torak turned to help him, but the Walker sliced the air a finger's breadth from his face. 'On!' he shouted.

'I just want to carry – '

'On!'

Renn cut in. 'You're Otter Clan, aren't you? I recognise your tattoos.'

The Walker glared at her.

Torak seized his chance and hoisted the flagging cub in his arms.

'*Was* Otter Clan,' muttered the Walker, clawing his neck, where the crusted skin was tattooed with wavy blue-green lines.

'Why did you leave them?' asked Renn, who seemed to be making a supreme effort to forget about her quiver and befriend him, in order to keep them alive.

'Didn't *leave*,' said the Walker. 'Otters leave *him*.' Twisting a wing off the pigeon, he sucked it between his toothless gums, taking in with it a generous loop of slime.

Torak swayed. Renn turned pale green.

'The Walker was making spearheads,' he said through a rancid mouthful, 'and the flint flies at him and bites him in the head.' He gave a bark of laughter, spraying them both. 'Bits of him going bad, getting sewn up, going bad again. In the end his eye pops right out, and a raven eats it. Ha! Ravens like eyes.'

Then his face crumpled, and he pounded his head with his fist. 'Ach, but the hurts, the hurts! All the voices howling, the souls fighting in his head! That's why the Otters chase him away!'

Renn swallowed. 'One of my clan lost an eye the same way,' she said. 'My clan is friendly with the Otters. We – we mean you no harm.'

'Maybe,' said the Walker, removing a bone from his mouth and stowing it carefully inside his cape. 'But they still bring it with them.' All of a sudden, he halted and scanned the slopes. 'But the Walker was forgetting. Narik asks him for hazelnuts! Now where did the hazel trees go?'

Torak hefted Wolf higher in his arms. 'The harm you think we bring,' he said. 'Do you mean – '

'They know what he means,' said the Walker. 'The bear demon, the demon bear. And the Walker *told* him not to summon it!'

Torak stopped. 'Told who? Do you mean – the crippled wanderer? The one who made the bear?'

A jab of the knife reminded him to keep moving. 'The crippled one, yes of course! The wise one, always after the demons to do his bidding.' Another bark of laughter. 'But the Wolf boy doesn't know about demons, does he? Doesn't even know what they are! Ah yes, the Walker can always tell.'

Renn looked surprised. Torak avoided her eyes.

'The Walker knows about them,' the man went on, still scanning the slopes for hazel trees. 'Oh yes. Before the flint bit him, he was a wise man himself. He knew that if you die and lose your name-soul, then you're a ghost, and you forget who you are. The Walker always feels sorry for ghosts. But if you lose your *clan*-soul, then what's left is a demon.'

Leaning forwards, he engulfed Torak in a blast of rank breath. 'Think about that, Wolf boy. No clan-soul, and you're a demon. The raw power of the Nanuak, but with no clan feeling to tame it; just the rage that something's been taken from you. That's why they hate the living.'

Torak knew the Walker was telling the truth. He'd seen

that hatred himself. It had killed his father. 'What about the crippled one?' he asked hoarsely. 'The one who caught the demon and trapped it in the bear? What was his name?'

'Ah,' said the Walker, gesturing at Torak to move on. 'So *wise*, so *clever*. To start with, he only wants the little demons, the slitherers and the scurriers. But they're never strong enough for him, he always wants more. So then he calls up the biters and the hunters. Still not enough.' He grinned, giving Torak another blast of carrion breath. 'In the end,' he whispered, 'he summons – an *elemental*.'

Renn gasped.

Torak was mystified. 'What's that?'

The Walker laughed. 'Ah, she knows! The Raven girl knows!'

Renn met Torak's eyes. Her own were very dark. 'The stronger the souls, the stronger the demon.' She licked her lips. 'An elemental comes into being when something hugely powerful dies – something like a waterfall or an ice river – and its souls are scattered. An elemental is the strongest demon of all.'

Wolf wriggled out of Torak's arms and disappeared into the ferns. An elemental, Torak thought dazedly.

But this talk of demons was upsetting the Walker all over again. 'Ach, how they hate the living!' he moaned, rocking from side to side. 'Too bright, too bright, all the shiny, shiny souls! Hurts! Hurts! It's *their fault*, the Wolf boy and the Raven girl! They bring it with them to the Walker's beautiful valley!'

'But we're nearly out of your valley,' said Renn.

'Yes, look,' said Torak, 'we're nearly at the top – '.

The Walker would not be calmed. 'Why do they do it?' he shouted. 'Why? The Walker never did them any harm!' Brandishing their bows above his head, he gripped them at both ends, as if to break them in two.

That was too much for Renn. 'Don't you *dare*!' she shouted. 'Don't you *dare* hurt my bow!'

'Back!' roared the Walker, 'or he snaps them like twigs!'

'Put them *down*!' yelled Renn, leaping at him and trying in vain to reach her bow.

Torak had to act fast. Quickly he opened his food pouch, then held out his palm. 'Hazelnuts!' he cried. 'Hazelnuts for Narik!'

The effect was immediate. 'Hazelnuts,' murmured the Walker. Dropping their bows on the stones, he snatched the nuts from Torak's hand and squatted on his haunches. Then he pulled a rock from his cape and began cracking them. 'Hm, nice and sweet. Narik will be pleased.'

Quietly, Renn retrieved the bows and brushed off the wet. She offered Torak his, but he didn't take it. He was staring at the rock which the Walker was using to crack the nuts. 'Who is Narik?' he said, keen to keep the Walker talking so that he could get a closer look. 'Is he your friend?'

'The Walker can see him plain enough,' he muttered. 'Why can't the Wolf boy? Something wrong with his eyes?' Plunging his hand into his cape, he drew out a mangy brown mouse. It was clutching half a hazelnut in its paws, and looked up peevishly at being interrupted.

Torak blinked. The mouse sneezed and went back to its meal.

Tenderly, the Walker stroked the small, humped back with his grimy finger. 'Ah, the Walker's fosterling.'

The rock lay discarded on the ground. It was about the size of Torak's hand: a sharp, curved claw – made of gleaming black stone.

Where there's a stone claw, might there also be a stone tooth? Torak glanced at Renn. She'd seen it too. And from her expression, she'd had the same thought. *'Oldest of all, the stone bite.'* The second part of the Nanuak.

'That stone,' Torak said carefully. 'Would the Walker tell me where he got it?'

The Walker raised his head, dazed from stroking his mouse. Then his face convulsed. 'Stone mouth,' he said. 'Long time, bad time. He's hiding. Otters have thrown him out, but he's not yet found his beautiful valley.'

Again Torak and Renn exchanged glances. Did they dare risk another outburst?

'The stone creature,' said Torak. 'Does it have stone teeth inside the stone mouth?'

'Of course!' snarled the Walker. 'Or how could it eat?'

'Where can we find it?' asked Renn.

'The Walker *said*! In the stone mouth!'

'And where is the creature with the stone mouth?'

Suddenly, the Walker's face went slack, and he looked very tired. 'Bad place,' he whispered. 'Very bad. The killing earth that gulps and swallows. The Watchers everywhere. They see you, but you don't see them. Not till it's too late.'

'Tell us how to find it,' said Torak.

NINETEEN

'How can you have a stone creature, anyway?' said Renn crossly. She'd been in a bad mood ever since losing her quiver.

'I don't know,' said Torak for the tenth time.

'And what kind of creature? Boar? Lynx? We should've asked.'

'He probably wouldn't have told us.'

Renn put her hands on her hips, shaking her head. 'We've done everything he said. We've walked for two whole days. Crossed three valleys. Followed the stream he mentioned. Still nothing. I think he was just trying to get rid of us.'

The same thought had occurred to Torak, but he wasn't going to admit it. In two days, the fog hadn't lifted. It felt wrong. Everything about this place felt wrong.

After some persuasion, the Walker had returned the rest of their weapons, and sent them on their way. Following his directions, they'd left the 'stream at the foot of the stony grey hill', and were climbing the trail that snaked towards the top. It had a bleak, menacing feel. Stunted birches loomed out of the fog. Here and there they saw the gleam of naked rock, where the hill had been rubbed raw. The only sound was the hammer-like 'chack-chack' of a woodpecker warning rivals away.

'He doesn't want us here,' said Renn. 'Maybe we've come the wrong way.'

'If we had, Wolf would have told us.'

Renn looked doubtful. 'Do you still believe that?'

'Yes,' said Torak, 'I do. After all, if he hadn't led us to the Walker's valley, we wouldn't have seen the stone claw, and then we wouldn't have known anything about a stone tooth.'

'Maybe. But I still think we've come too far east. We're getting too close to the High Mountains.'

'How can you tell, when we can't see ten paces ahead?'

'I can feel it. That freezing air? It's coming off the ice river.'

Torak stopped and stared at her. 'What ice river?'

'The one at the foot of the mountains.'

Torak set his teeth. He was getting tired of being the one who didn't know things.

They climbed on in silence, and soon even the woodpecker was left behind. Torak became uneasily aware of the noise they were making: the creak of his pack, the rattle of pebbles as Renn struggled ahead. He could feel the rocks listening, the twisted trees silently warning him back.

Suddenly, Renn turned and clattered down towards him. 'We got it wrong!' she panted, her eyes wide and scared.

'What do you mean?'

'The Walker never said it was a stone *creature*! *We* were the

ones who said that. He only ever said it was a stone *mouth!*'
Grabbing his arm, she dragged him up the hill.

The ground levelled out and the trail ended. Torak came
to a dead halt in the swirling fog. As he took in what lay
ahead, dread settled inside him.

A rockface towered above them, grey as a thundercloud.
At its foot, guarded by a solitary yew tree, was a cavern of
darkness like a silent scream: a gaping stone mouth.

革丰

'We can't go in there,' said Renn.

'We – I – have to,' said Torak. 'This is the stone mouth
the Walker was talking about. It's where he found the stone
claw. It's where I might find the stone tooth.'

Close up, the cave mouth was smaller than he'd first
thought: a shadowy half-circle no higher than his shoulder.
He put his hand on the stone lip and bent to peer inside.

'Be careful,' warned Renn.

The cave floor sloped away steeply. Cold flowed from it:
an acrid uprush of air like the breath of some ancient
creature that has never seen the sun.

'Bad place,' the Walker had said. 'Very bad place. The
killing earth that gulps and swallows. The Watchers
everywhere.'

'Don't move your hand,' said Renn beside him.

Glancing up, he saw with a start that his fingers were a
hair's breadth away from a large splayed hand that had
been hammer-etched deep into the stone. He snatched his
own away.

'It's a warning,' whispered Renn. 'You see the three bars
above the middle finger? Those are lines of power, warding
off evil.' She leaned closer. 'It's old. Very old. We can't go

in. There's something down there.'

'What?' asked Torak. 'What's down there?'

She shook her head. 'I don't know. Maybe a doorway to the Otherworld. It must be bad, for someone to have carved that hand.'

Torak thought about that. 'I don't think I have a choice. I'll go. You stay here.'

'No! If you go, I'm going too –'

'Wolf can't come with me, he couldn't take the smell. You stay here with him. If I need help, I'll call.'

It took a while, but the more he argued, the more he convinced himself too.

He got ready by laying his bow and quiver under the yew tree along with his pack, sleeping-sack and waterskin, then unhooking his axe from his belt. Only his knife would be any use in the dark. Finally, he cut a rawhide leash for the cub. Wolf wriggled and snapped until Torak managed to explain that he had to stay with Renn, who settled the matter by producing a handful of dried lingonberries from her food pouch. But Torak couldn't find a way to tell Wolf that he'd be coming back. Wolf talk didn't seem to deal with the future.

Renn gave him a sprig of rowan for protection, and one of her salmon-skin mittens on a cord. 'Remember,' she said, 'if you find the stone tooth, don't touch it with your bare hands. And you'd better let me have the pouch with the river eyes.'

She was right. There was no telling what might happen if he took the Nanuak into the cave.

With an odd sense of giving up an unwelcome burden, Torak handed her the ravenskin pouch, and she tied it to her belt. Wolf watched what was happening with ears swivelling: as if, thought Torak, the pouch were making some kind of noise.

'You'll need light,' said Renn, glad to be doing something
practical. From her pack she brought out two rushlights:
the peeled pith of rushes that had been soaked in deer fat,
then dried in the sun. With her strike-fire, she lit a curl of
juniper bark tinder, and one of the rushlights flared into
life: a bright, clear, comforting flame. Torak felt hugely
grateful.

'If you need help,' she said, kneeling and hugging Wolf
to stop herself shivering, 'shout. We'll come running.'

Torak nodded. Then he stooped and entered the stone
mouth.

He groped for the wall. It felt slimy, like dead flesh.

He shuffled forward, feeling the way with his feet. The
rushlight trembled and shrank to a glimmer. The stench
wafted up from the darkness, stinging his nostrils.

After several halting steps, he came up against stone.
The cave mouth had narrowed to a gullet: he'd have to turn
sideways to get through. Shutting his eyes, he edged in. It
felt as if he was being swallowed. He couldn't breathe. He
kept thinking of the weight of the rockface pressing in on
him . . .

The air cooled. He was still in a tunnel, but it was wider,
and twisted sharply to the right. Glancing back, he saw
that the daylight had vanished, and with it, Renn and Wolf.

The stink got stronger as he followed the tunnel, hearing
nothing but his own breathing, seeing nothing but
glimpses of glistening red stone.

A sudden chill to his left, and he nearly lost his footing.
Pebbles rattled, then dropped into silence.

The left-hand wall had vanished. He was standing on a narrow ledge jutting out over darkness. From far below came an echoing 'plink' of water. One slip and he'd be over the edge.

Another bend – this time to the left – and a rock beneath his foot tilted. With a cry he grabbed for a handhold, righting himself just in time.

At the sound of his cry, something stirred.

He froze.

'Torak?' Renn's voice sounded far away.

He didn't dare call out. Whatever had moved had gone still again: but it was a horrible, waiting stillness. It knew he was there. 'The Watchers everywhere. They see you, but you don't see them. Not till it's too late.'

He forced himself to go on. Down, always down. The stink came at him in waves. *Breathe through your mouth*, said a voice in his head. That was what he and Fa used to do when they came upon a stinking kill-site or a bat-infested cave. He tried it, and the stench became bearable, although it still caught at his eyes and throat.

Abruptly the ground levelled out, and he felt space opening up around him. A dim light had to be coming from somewhere, because he made out a vast, shadowy cavern. The fumes were almost overwhelming. He was in the dripping, reeking bowels of the earth.

The ledge he was standing on ended, and the floor beyond it was weirdly humped. In the middle of the cavern, a great, flat-topped stone gleamed like black ice. It looked as if it had stood untouched for thousands of winters. Even from twenty paces away, Torak could feel its power.

This was where the Walker had found his stone claw. This was the reason for the warning hand at the cave mouth. This was what the Watchers guarded: a door to the Otherworld.

Torak couldn't take another step. It was like the times when he awoke so heavy with sleep that to stir even a finger seemed impossible.

To steady himself, he put his free hand on the hilt of his knife. The sinew binding felt faintly warm, giving him the courage to step down onto the cave floor.

As he did, he cried out in disgust. The floor sank beneath his boot: a noisome softness sucking him down. 'The killing earth that gulps and swallows . . .'

His cry rang round the walls, and far above him he heard a stealthy movement. Something dark detached itself from the roof and swooped towards him.

There was nowhere to hide, nowhere to run. The softness sucked at his boots like wet sand. A foetid downrush, and the thing was on him: greasy fur clogging his mouth and nose, sharp claws tearing at his hair. Snarling with horror, he beat at the silent attacker.

At last it lifted away with a leathery 'thwap'. But he knew that it wasn't vanquished. The Watcher had merely come to find out what he was. Once it knew, it had left.

But what was it? A bat? A demon? How many more were there?

Torak floundered on. Halfway to the stone, he stumbled and fell. The stink was unbearable. He wallowed in choking blackness, he couldn't see, couldn't think. Even the rushlight turned black – a black flame flaring above him . . .

He staggered to his feet, shaking himself free like a swimmer gasping for air. His mind steadied. The black flame burned yellow again.

He reached the stone. On its ancient smoothness, six

stone claws had been arranged in a spiral, with a gap where the Walker had snatched the seventh. At the centre lay a single black stone tooth.

'Oldest of all, the stone bite.' The second part of the Nanuak.

Sweat slid down his spine. He wondered what power he would unleash if he touched it.

He stretched out his hand, then snatched it back, remembering Renn's warning. 'Don't touch the Nanuak with your bare hands.'

Where was the mitten? He must have dropped it.

With the rushlight he cast around, plunging his hand into the stinking mounds. Again the dizziness mounted. Again the flame darkened . . .

Just in time, he found the mitten, tied to his belt. Yanking it on, he reached for the tooth.

The rushlight glimmered on the cave wall behind the stone – and lit the gleam of thousands of eyes.

With his hand poised above the tooth, he moved the flame slowly to and fro. It caught the liquid gleam of eyes. The walls were swarming with Watchers. Wherever the light touched, they rippled and heaved like a maggot-riddled carcass. If he took the tooth, they would come for him.

Suddenly, everything happened at once.

From far above came Wolf's sharp urgent bark.

Renn screamed. 'Torak! It's coming!'

The Watchers exploded around him.

The rushlight went out.

Something struck him in the back and he fell forward onto the stone.

Again Renn screamed. 'Torak! *The bear!*'

TWENTY

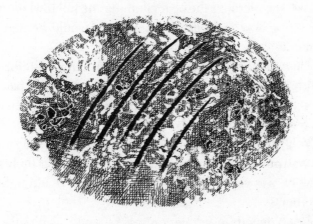

Clutching Torak's quiver, Renn raced to the edge of the trail and tripped on a tree root, spilling arrows in the dirt. Panic bubbled in her throat. What to do? What to do?

Only moments before, she'd been pacing up and down, while a flock of greenfinches tore at the yew tree's juicy pink berries, and Wolf tugged on the leash, uttering bark-growls which Torak would have understood, but she just found worrying.

Then the finches had fled in a twittering cloud, and she'd glanced down the hill. A gap in the fog had given her a clear view: she'd seen the stream rushing past a clump of spruce, and a big dark boulder hunched beside them. Then the boulder had moved.

Frozen in horror, she'd watched the bear rear up on its hind legs, towering over the spruce. The great head swung as it tasted the air. It caught her scent and dropped to all fours.

That was when she'd run to the cave and screamed a warning to Torak – and got nothing back but echoes.

Now, as the fog closed in again and she fumbled for the arrows, she pictured the bear climbing the hill towards her. She knew how fast bears can move: it would be here in moments.

The rockface was too steep for her to climb; besides, she couldn't leave Wolf. That left the cave, but every part of her screamed not to go inside. They'd be caught like hares in a trap, they'd never get out.

Wolf's desperate tugging on the leash broke her panic. He was pulling her towards the cave – and in a flash she knew he was right. Torak was inside. They would fight it together.

She plunged in, dragging packs and sleeping-sacks behind her. The darkness blinded her. She ran into solid rock, hitting her head.

After a breathless search she worked out that the cave narrowed sharply to a slit. Wolf was already through, tugging at her to follow. She turned and edged sideways – quickly, quickly – then dropped to her knees and reached through the gap to drag the gear in after her.

As she yanked in packs and bows and quiver, she felt a flicker of hope. Maybe the gap was too narrow for the bear? Maybe they could hold out . . .

Her waterskin was wrenched from her hand with a force that slammed her against the gap and sent pain shooting through her shoulder. In a daze she scrambled sideways into a hollow, yanking Wolf with her.

The bear couldn't have moved that fast, she thought numbly.

A deep growl reverberated through the cave. Her skin crawled.

It can't get through the gap, she told herself. Stay still. Stay very, very still.

From deep within the cave came a cry. 'Renn!'

Was Torak calling for help, or was he coming to help her? She couldn't tell. Couldn't call out. Couldn't do anything but cower with Wolf in the hollow, knowing she was too close to the gap – just two paces away – yet powerless to move. Some force was keeping her there. She couldn't take her eyes from that narrow slit of daylight.

The daylight turned black.

Knowing it was the worst thing to do, Renn leaned forward and peered through the gap. The blood roared in her head. A nightmare glimpse of dark fur flickering in an unfelt wind; a flash of long cruel claws glistening with black blood.

A roar shook the cave. Moaning, Renn jammed her fists against her ears as the roar battered through her, on and on till she thought her skull would crack . . .

Silence: as shocking as the roar. Taking her fists from her ears, she heard a whisper of dust. Wolf panting. Nothing else.

Slowly, appalled at what she was doing, she crawled towards the slit, pulling the reluctant cub with her.

She saw daylight again. Grey rockface. The yew tree with a scattering of berries beneath. No bear.

A shuddering growl: so close that she heard the wet champ of jaws, smelt the reek of slaughter. Then the daylight was blotted out, and an eye held hers. Blacker than basalt, yet churning with fire, it drew her – it *wanted* her.

She tilted forwards.

Wolf wrenched her back, breaking the spell so that she

shrank out of the way just as the deadly claws sliced the
earth where she'd been kneeling.

Again the bear roared. Again she cowered in the hollow.
Then she heard new sounds: the clatter of rocks, the
groans of a dying tree. In its fury, the bear was clawing at
the mouth of the cave, uprooting the yew and tearing it
apart.

Whimpering, she pressed herself into the hollow.

Against her shoulder, the rock moved. With a cry she
jumped back.

From the other side, she heard stones shattering, and
earth being flung aside with lethal intent. She realised what
was happening. The rock that formed this side of the gap
was not, as she had thought, a part of the cave itself, but
merely a tongue of stone that jutted from the earth floor.
The bear was clawing at its roots: digging them out like
wood-ants from a nest.

Sweat streamed off her. She stared at Wolf.

With a shock, she saw that he was cub no longer. His
head was down, his eyes fixed on the thing beyond the slit.
His black lips were peeled back in a snarl, baring
formidable white fangs.

Something hardened inside her. 'Not like wood-ants,'
she whispered. The sound of her voice gave her courage.

She untied the leash to give Wolf his freedom: maybe he
could escape, even if she and Torak could not. Then she
groped for her bow. The touch of the cool, smooth yew
gave her strength. She got to her feet.

Concentrate on the target, she told herself,
remembering the many lessons Fin-Kedinn had given her.
That's the most important thing. You must concentrate so
hard that you burn a hole in the target . . . And keep your
draw arm relaxed, don't tense up. The force comes from

146

your back, not from your arm . . .

'Fourteen arrows,' she said. 'I should be able to put in a few of them before it gets me.'

She stepped out from the hollow and took up position.

Torak tore at the Watchers swarming over him.

Claws snagged his face and hair. Foul wings stifled his mouth and nose. Somehow he managed to pull on Renn's mitten and reach for the stone tooth. It was heavier than he'd expected. He wrenched off the mitten with the tooth inside, and shoved it into the neck of his jerkin.

'Renn!' he yelled as he pushed himself off the stone. His cry was deadened by leathery wings.

He struck out through the stench – but with the rushlight gone, he couldn't even see his hands in front of his face.

Faint and far above came Wolf's frenzied yowls: *Where are you? Danger! Danger!*

He waded towards the sound with the Watchers swarming over him, pushing him down into the stink.

Terrible images thronged his head. Wolf and Renn lying dead – just like Fa. *Why* had he made them stay up there where it was 'safe', when all the time that was where the true danger lay?

Raging inwardly, he drew his knife from its sheath and slashed at the Watchers. They seemed to lift to avoid the blade. 'Oh, so you're scared of it, are you?' he shouted. 'Well here's some more!' He slashed at them – and again they lifted, a dark cloud just out of reach. The hilt grew hot in his hand. Snarling, he ploughed on through the stink.

He barked his shins on solid rock. He'd reached the

ledge. 'I'm coming!' he shouted, pulling himself out and starting up the slope.

A roar shook the cave, beating him to his knees. The Watchers rose in a cloud and vanished.

The silence after the last echo had died was worse. Torak became aware of rock beneath his knees, the stone tooth throbbing inside his jerkin. He struggled to his feet and ran up the ledge. It was steep – so steep. Why was there no sound from above? What was happening up there?

On and on he climbed till his knees ached and the breath seared his throat. Then he rounded the last bend and the daylight blinded him.

The cave mouth was five paces away, and wider than he remembered. The gap he'd squeezed through on his descent had been wrenched open, and before it stood Renn, a small, upright figure, incredibly brave, taking aim with her last arrow at the thing looming over her.

For a heartbeat, Torak was back with Fa on the night of the attack, transfixed by the malice of those demon-haunted eyes . . .

'No!' he shouted.

Renn loosed her arrow. The bear batted it away with one sweep of its claws. But just as it was about to move in for the kill, Wolf leapt from the shadows – leapt not at the bear, but at Renn. With a single snap of his powerful jaws, Wolf tore the ravenskin pouch from her belt – knocking her off her feet, out of reach of the bear – then sped out of the cave. The bear lashed out, gouging the earth a hand's breadth from where the cub had been.

'Wolf!' shouted Torak, throwing himself forwards.

With the pouch in his jaws, Wolf disappeared into the fog. The bear swung round with terrifying agility and raced after him.

'*Wolf!*' Torak shouted again.

The fog engulfed them, leaving the empty hillside mocking him. The bear was gone. So was Wolf.

TWENTY-ONE

Where are you? Torak's desolate howl echoed off the rockface.

Where are you? the hills howled back at him.

The old pain was opening up in his chest. First Fa, now Wolf. Please, not Wolf...

Renn stood blinking at the mouth of the cave.

'*Why* did you let him off the leash?' he cried.

She swayed. 'I had to. Had to set him free.'

With a cry, Torak started rooting around in the wreckage.

'What are you doing?' said Renn.

'Looking for my pack. I'm going after Wolf.'

'But it'll be dark soon!'

'So we just sit here and wait?'

'No! We salvage our gear, we build a shelter and a fire. *Then* we wait. We wait for Wolf to find us.'

Torak bit back a retort. For the first time, he noticed that

Renn was shaking. She had a bloody scrape down one cheek, and a bruise the size of a pigeon's egg coming up over the other eye.

He felt ashamed. She'd faced the bear. She'd even had the courage to shoot at it. He shouldn't have shouted. 'I'm sorry,' he said. 'I didn't mean . . . You're right. I can't track him in the dark.'

Renn sat down heavily on a boulder. 'I had no idea what it would be like,' she said. 'I never thought it would be so . . . ' She covered her mouth with both hands.

Torak unearthed an arrow from the rubble. The shaft was snapped in two. 'Did you hit it?' he asked.

'I don't know. I don't think it matters. Arrows can't bring it down.' She shook her head. 'One moment it was after me, and the next, it was after Wolf. Why?'

He tossed away the broken arrowshaft. 'Does that matter?'

'Maybe.' She glanced at him. 'Did you get the stone tooth?'

He'd almost forgotten about it. Now, as he reached inside his jerkin and brought out the mitten, he just wanted to be rid of it. Because of the Nanuak, Wolf might be dead. No more grooming-nibbles in the morning; no more uproarious games of hide and hunt . . . Torak bit his knuckle, fighting his fear. He couldn't lose Wolf.

Renn took the mitten and turned it in her fingers. 'We've got the second part of the Nanuak,' she said thoughtfully, 'and lost the first. But why did Wolf take it?'

With an effort, Torak forced his mind to what she was saying. Something flickered in his memory. 'Do you remember,' he said, 'when I found the river eyes – it was as if Wolf could hear them. Or sense them in some way.'

Renn frowned. 'You think – the bear can too?'

"'All the shiny shiny souls,'" he murmured. 'That's what the Walker said. Demons hate the living, they hate the brightness of the souls.'

'And if the souls of ordinary creatures are too bright,' said Renn, getting to her feet and beginning to pace, 'then how much brighter – more dazzling – must the Nanuak be!'

'That's why it attacked you, because you had the river eyes –

'And that's why Wolf took the pouch. Because he *knew*. Because –,' she stopped pacing and stared at Torak. 'Because he was luring the bear away from us. Oh, Torak. He saved our lives.'

Torak stumbled to the edge of the trail. The fog was clearing at last, and below him, the vastness of the Forest marched away into the west. What chance did Wolf have out there, alone against the bear?

'Wolves are cleverer than bears,' said Renn.

'He's just a cub, Renn. He's not even four moons old.'

'But he's also the guide. If anyone can find a way, he can.'

Wolf raced between the beech trees, the wind at his tail and the shining, singing ravenskin gripped tight in his jaws.

Far away, he heard the lonely howl of Tall Tailless.

Wolf longed to howl back, but he couldn't. The wind was gusting the demon's scent towards him. He smelt its rage and its terrible hunger; he heard its tireless breath. Strongest of all, he sensed its hatred: hatred for him and for the thing he bore.

But Wolf knew with a fierce, bright joy that it would never catch him. The demon was fast, but he was faster.

He no longer felt like a cub who must wait for the poor,

slow taillesses to catch up. He was a *wolf* – racing between the trees in the swift wolf-lope that goes on for ever. He revelled in the strength of his legs and the stretch of his back; in the suppleness that let him turn at full speed on a single paw. Oh no, the demon would never catch him!

Wolf paused to drink at a noisy little Wet, dropping the ravenskin for a moment. Then he snatched it up and settled back into his stride, climbing higher towards the Great White Cold that he'd only ever smelt in his sleeps.

A fresh scent drove that from his head: he was entering the range of a pack of stranger wolves. Every few paces, he passed their scent-markings. He must be careful. If they caught him, they might attack. When he needed to spill his scent, he waited till he reached another little Fast Wet, and spilt into that, instead of marking a tree. His scent would wash away, and neither the stranger wolves nor the demon would smell him.

The Dark came. Wolf loved the Dark. In it, smells and sounds were sharper, but he could see almost as well as in the Light.

Far ahead, the stranger pack began its evening howl. That made Wolf sad. He remembered how joyfully his pack used to howl; how keenly they greeted each other after their sleeps. The snuffle-licking and the rubbing of scents against each other; the smiling and playing as they encouraged one another for the hunt.

Quite suddenly, as Wolf thought of his pack, he began to tire. He felt each pad strike the rocks as never before. He felt an ache running up his legs. He began to hurt.

Fear gnawed at him. He could not go on for ever. He could not go on much further at all. He was far from Tall Tailless, and crossing the range of a stranger pack. And the demon was tracking him relentlessly through the Dark.

Torak dragged what remained of their gear into the yew branch shelter, then kicked at the fire, sending sparks shooting skywards. This waiting was terrible. He'd been howling since dusk. He knew that he risked drawing the bear, but Wolf was more important. Where was he?

It was a cold, starry night, and even without looking up, he could feel the red eye of the Great Auroch glaring down at him. Relishing his turmoil.

Renn emerged from the darkness, bearing an armful of leaves and bark.

'You were a long time,' Torak said curtly.

'I needed the right things. No sign of Wolf?'

He shook his head.

Renn knelt by the fire and tipped her load on to the ground. 'When I was looking for these, I heard horns. Birch-bark horns.'

Torak was horrified. 'What? Where?'

She nodded towards the west. 'Long way away.'

'Was it – Fin-Kedinn?'

Again she nodded.

Torak shut his eyes. 'I thought he'd have given up by now.'

'He doesn't give up,' said Renn. There was a hint of pride in her voice which irritated him. 'Have you forgotten,' he said, 'that he wanted to kill me? *"The Listener gives his heart's blood to the Mountain"*?'

She rounded on him. 'Of course I haven't forgotten! But I'm worried about them! If the bear isn't up here, then it's down there, where they are. Why else would Fin-Kedinn blow the horn?'

Torak felt bad. Renn was worried, and so was he. Fighting didn't help.

From his belt he untied the little grouse-bone whistle he'd made when he'd first found Wolf. 'Here.' He held it out. 'Now you can call Wolf too.'

She looked at him in surprise. 'Thanks.'

There was a silence. Torak asked her why she needed the herbs.

'For the stone tooth. We've got to find some way of hiding it from the bear. If we don't, it'll track us down.'

Like it's tracking Wolf, thought Torak. The ache in his chest deepened. 'If the rowan leaves and the pouch couldn't hide the river eyes,' he said, 'why do you think bark and wormwood can do any better?'

'Because I'm going to use them for something stronger.' She chewed her lip. 'I've been trying to remember exactly what Saeunn does. She's always trying to teach me Magecraft, and I'm always going hunting instead. I wish I'd listened.'

'You're lucky there's something you can do,' muttered Torak.

'But what if I get it wrong?'

He didn't answer. He could feel the red eye mocking him. Even if Wolf did find a way back, he'd be bringing the bear with him, drawn by the river eyes. And the only way Wolf could shake off the bear would be by losing the river eyes – which would mean there'd be no chance of destroying the bear.

There had to be a way out; but Torak couldn't see it.

Wolf was tiring fast. There was no way out.

By now, the demon had fallen too far behind to be able to sense the ravenskin, but it was still tracking him by scent, and it would go on tracking him. When at last he slowed, as his aching paws longed to, it would catch him.

The stranger pack had long since ended their howl and gone hunting, far away in the Mountains. Wolf missed their voices. He felt truly alone.

The wind turned, and he caught a new scent. Reindeer. Wolf had never hunted reindeer, but he knew the scent well, for his mother used to bring him the branches that grow from reindeers' heads, with the hide hanging off in delicious, chewable tatters. Now, as he smelt the herd in the next valley, the blood-urge put new strength in his limbs, and hope leapt within him. If he could reach them . . .

As he heaved himself up the slope, the thunder of many hooves drew nearer. Suddenly the great prey burst upon him, galloping with their branched heads high and their huge hooves splayed, as they flowed between the beech trees like an unstoppable Fast Wet.

Wolf turned on one paw and leapt among them, and they towered over him as he plunged into their musky scent. A bull charged, and Wolf dodged the head-branches. A cow snorted at him to stay away from her calf, and he ducked beneath her to escape her pounding hooves. But soon the herd sensed that he wasn't hunting them, and forgot about him. He ran up the valley: his scent swallowed up by that of the herd.

They left the beeches and ran through a spruce forest. The rocks became bigger, the trees smaller; then the trees were left behind entirely as they streamed out onto a stony flatness like nothing he'd ever known.

By the smell on the wind, Wolf knew this flatness

stretched for many lopes into the Dark, and that beyond it lay the Great White Cold. What was it? He didn't know. But somewhere beyond lay the thing that had called to him from his first Den, pulling him on . . .

Far behind him, the demon bellowed. It had lost his scent! In delight, Wolf tossed the ravenskin high in the air and caught it with a snap.

After a time, another noise reached him. Very faint, but unmistakable: the high, flat call that Tall Tailless made when he put the bird-bone to his muzzle!

Then another, even more beloved sound: Tall Tailless himself, howling for him! The best sound in the Forest!

The reindeer ran on, but Wolf knew that he had to turn back and head into the Forest again. It was not yet time to reach the Great White Cold and what lay beyond; he had to go back and fetch Tall Tailless.

TWENTY-TWO

Renn was huddled in her sleeping-sack, thinking about getting up, when Torak appeared at the entrance to the shelter, making her jump.

'Time we got started,' he said, crouching by the fire and handing her a strip of dried deer meat. From the shadows under his eyes, she guessed that he hadn't slept any better than she had.

She sat up and took a half-hearted bite of her daymeal. The scrape on her cheek felt hot, and the bruise above her eye hurt. But worse than that was the creeping dread. It wasn't only the nearness of the cave, or terror of the bear. It was something else: something she didn't want to think about.

'I found the trail,' said Torak, cutting across her thoughts.

She stopped in mid-chew. 'Which way did they go?'

'West, round the other side of the hill, then down into a beech wood.' He reached out and stirred the fire, his thin face sharp with anxiety. 'The bear was right behind him.'

Renn pictured Wolf racing through the Forest with the bear closing in. 'Torak,' she said, 'you do realise that when we track Wolf, we'll also be tracking the bear?'

'Yes.'

'If we catch up with it –'

'I know,' he broke in, 'but I'm sick of waiting. We've waited all night, and still nothing. We've got to go and find him. At least, I've got to. You can stay here –'

'No! Of course I'm coming with you! I was only saying.' She looked at the salmon-skin mitten hanging from the roofpost.

'Do you think it'll work?' said Torak, following her gaze.

'I don't know.'

The charm had sounded so clever when she'd explained it to him yesterday. 'When someone gets ill,' she'd said, feeling quite important, 'it's usually because they've eaten something bad. But sometimes it's because their souls have been lured away by demons. The sick souls need to be rescued. I've seen Saeunn do it lots of times. She ties little fish-hooks to her fingertips to help her catch the sick souls; then she takes a special potion to loosen her own souls, so that they can leave her body and find the –'

'What's this got to do with the Nanuak?'

'I'm about to tell you,' she'd said with a quelling look. 'To find them, Saeunn has to hide her *own* souls from the demons.'

'Ah. So if you do what she does, you can hide the Nanuak from the bear?'

'I think so, yes. To disguise herself she smears her face with wormwood and earthblood, then puts on a mask of rowan bark tied with hairs from each member of the clan. That's what I'm going to do. Well, in a way.'

After that, she'd made a little box of folded rowan bark, and smeared it with wormwood and red ochre. Then she'd put the stone tooth inside, and tied it up with locks of her own and Torak's hair.

It had been a relief to be doing something instead of worrying about Wolf, and she'd felt proud of herself. But now, in the freezing dawn, doubts crowded in. After all, what did she know about Magecraft?

'Come on,' said Torak, jumping up. 'The tracking's good. Light's nice and low.'

Renn peered out of the shelter. 'What about the bear? It might have lost Wolf's scent and come back for us.'

'I don't think so,' he said. 'I think it's still after Wolf.'

Somehow, that didn't make her feel any better.

'What's wrong?' said Torak.

She sighed. What she wanted to say was: 'I'm really, *really* missing my clan; I'm terrified that Fin-Kedinn will never forgive me for helping you escape; I think we're mad to be deliberately tracking the bear; I've got a horrible feeling that we're going to end up at the one place I don't ever want to go; and I'm worried that I shouldn't even *be* here, because unlike you, I'm not the Listener and I'm not in the Prophecy, I'm just Renn. But it's no use saying any of this, because all you can think about is finding Wolf.' So in the end she simply said, 'Nothing. Nothing's wrong.'

Torak threw her a disbelieving look and started stamping out the fire.

All morning, they followed the trail through the beech wood and then through a spruce forest, turning north east and steadily climbing. As always, Renn was unsettled by

Torak's skill at tracking. He seemed to go into a trance, scanning the land with endless patience, and often finding some tiny sign that most full-grown hunters would have missed.

It was mid-afternoon and the light was beginning to fail when he stopped.

'What is it?' asked Renn.

'Sh! I thought I heard something.' He cupped his hand to his ear. 'There! Do you hear it?'

She shook her head.

His face broke into a grin. 'It's Wolf!'

'Are you sure?'

'I'd know his howl anywhere. Come on, he's up that way!' He pointed east.

Renn's heart sank. Not east, she thought. Please not east.

As Torak followed the sound, the ground got stonier, and the trees shrank to waist-high birch and willow.

'Are you sure he's here?' said Renn. 'If we keep going, we'll end up on the fells.'

Torak hadn't heard her; he was running ahead. He disappeared behind a boulder, and a few moments later she heard him excitedly yelling her name.

She raced up the slope and rounded the boulder into the teeth of an icy north wind. She staggered back. They had reached the very edge of the Forest. The edge of the fells.

Before her stretched a vast treeless waste, where heather and dwarf willow hugged the ground in a vain attempt to avoid the wind; where small peat-brown lakes shivered amid tossing marsh grass. Far in the distance, a treacherous scree slope towered above the fells, and beyond it rose the High Mountains. But between the scree slope and the Mountains, glimpsed only as a white glitter, lay what Renn had been dreading.

Torak, of course, was unaware of all that. 'Renn!' he shouted, the wind whipping his voice away. 'Over here!'

Dragging her gaze back, she saw that he was kneeling on the bank of a narrow stream. Wolf lay beside him, eyes closed, the ravenskin pouch at his head.

'He's alive!' cried Torak, burying his face in the wet grey fur. Wolf opened one eye and feebly thumped his tail. Renn stumbled through the heather towards them.

'He's exhausted,' said Torak without looking up, 'and soaking wet. He's been running in the stream to throw the bear off the scent. That was clever, wasn't it?'

Renn glanced around her fearfully. 'But did it work?'

'Oh yes,' said Torak. 'Look at all the marsh pipits. They wouldn't be here if the bear was near.'

Wishing she could share his confidence, Renn knelt and fumbled in her pack for a salmon cake to give to Wolf. She was rewarded with another, slightly stronger, tail-thump.

It was wonderful to see Wolf again, but she felt oddly cut off. Too much else was crowding in on her; too much that Torak didn't know about.

She picked up the ravenskin pouch and loosened its neck to check inside. The river eyes were still in their nest of rowan leaves.

'Yes, take it,' said Torak, lifting Wolf in his arms and laying him gently on a patch of soft marsh grass. 'We need to hide it from the bear right away.'

Renn untied the rowan-bark box that held the stone tooth, and tipped in the river eyes; then she refastened the box, put it back in the pouch, and tied it to her belt.

'He'll be all right now,' said Torak, stooping to give the cub's muzzle an affectionate lick. 'We can make a shelter over there in the lee of that slope. Build a fire, let him rest.'

'Not here,' said Renn quickly. 'We should get back to the

Forest.' Out on this windswept fell, she felt exposed, like a caterpillar dangling on a thread.

'Better if we stay here,' said Torak. He pointed north towards the scree slope and the white glitter. 'That's the fastest way to the Mountain.'

Renn's belly tightened. 'What? What are you talking about?'

'Wolf told me. That's where we've got to go.'

'But – we can't go up there.'

'Why not?'

'Because that's the ice river!'

Torak and Wolf looked at her in surprise, and she found herself facing two pairs of wolf eyes: one amber, one light-grey. It made her feel very left out.

'But Renn,' said Torak patiently, 'that's the shortest way to the Mountain.'

'I don't care!' She tried to think up some reason that he'd accept. 'We've still got to find the third piece of the Nanuak, remember? *Coldest of all, the darkest light.*' We're not going to find it up there, are we? It'll be cold all right, but there's nothing up there!' Nothing but death, she added to herself.

'You saw the red eye last night,' said Torak. 'It's getting higher. We've only got a few days – '

'Aren't you listening?' she shouted. 'We cannot cross the ice river!'

'Yes we can,' he replied with terrifying calm. 'We'll find a way.'

'How? We've got one waterskin and four arrows between us! *Four arrows!* And winter's coming, and you've only got summer clothes!'

He looked at her thoughtfully. 'That's not why you don't want to go up there.'

She leapt to her feet and stalked off, then marched back again. She said, 'My father died on an ice river just like that one.'

The wind hissed sadly over the fells. Torak looked down at Wolf, then back to her.

'It was a snowfall,' she said. 'He was on the ice river beyond Lake Axehead. Half an ice cliff came down on him. They only found his body in the spring. Saeunn had to do a special rite to get his souls together.'

'I'm sorry,' said Torak. 'I didn't – '

'I'm not telling you so that you'll be sorry for me,' she cut in. 'I'm telling you so that you'll understand. He was a strong, experienced hunter who *knew* the mountains – and still the ice river killed him. What hope – what chance – do you think we'd have?'

TWENTY-THREE

'Be very, *very* quiet,' whispered Renn. 'Any sudden noise and it might wake up.'

Torak craned his neck at the ice cliffs towering over them. He'd seen ice before, but nothing like this. Not these knife-sharp crags and gaping gullies, these icicles taller than trees. It was as if a great, overarching wave had been frozen by one touch of the World Spirit's finger. And yet, when he'd caught sight of the cliffs from the scree slope, they'd seemed just a wrinkle in the vast, tumbled river of ice.

After letting Wolf rest for a day by the lake, they'd plodded over the marshes and up the scree, where they'd camped in a hollow that had given scant shelter from the wind. There had been no sign of the bear. Perhaps the masking charm had worked; or perhaps, as Renn pointed out, the bear was in the west, wreaking havoc among the clans.

Next morning, they'd climbed the flank of the ice river and started north.

It was madness to walk beneath the ice cliffs when at any moment a snowfall might obliterate them, but they had no choice. The way to the west was blocked by a torrent of meltwater that had carved a deep blue gully.

It was impossible to move quietly. The snow was crisp, and their boots crunched loudly. Torak's new reed cape crackled like dead leaves; even his breath sounded deafening. All around, he heard weird creaks and echoing groans: the ice river murmuring in its sleep. It didn't sound as if it would take much to waken it.

Strangely, that didn't seem to bother Wolf. He *loved* the snow: pouncing on it and tossing lumps of ice high in the air, then skidding to a halt to listen to lemmings and snow-voles burrowing under the surface.

Now he stopped to sniff at an ice chunk, and patted it with one paw. When it didn't respond, he went down on his forepaws and asked it to play, whining invitingly.

'Sh!' hissed Torak, forgetting to speak wolf.

'Sh!' hissed Renn up ahead.

Desperate to quieten Wolf, Torak pretended to spot some distant prey, by standing very still and staring intently.

Wolf copied him. But when he caught no scent or sound, he twitched his whiskers and glanced at Torak. *Where is it? Where's the prey?*

Torak stretched and yawned. *No prey.*

What? Then why are we hunting?

Just be quiet!

Wolf gave a small, aggrieved whine.

'Come *on*!' whispered Renn. 'We've got to get across before nightfall!'

166

It was freezing in the shadow of the ice cliffs. They'd done what they could while camping by the lake: stuffing their boots with marsh grass, making mittens and caps from Renn's salmon skin and the rest of the rawhide, and a cape for Torak from bunches of reeds tied with marsh grass, then stitched with sinew. But it wasn't nearly enough.

Their supplies were getting low, too: one waterskin and only enough dried salmon and deer meat for a couple of days. Torak could imagine what Fa would say. *A journey in snow is no game, Torak. If you think it is, you'll end up dead.*

He was painfully aware that he didn't actually know much about snow. As Renn had said with her usual unflinching accuracy, 'All I know is that it makes tracking a lot easier, it's good for snowballs, and if you get caught in a snowstorm you're supposed to dig yourself a snow cave and wait till it stops. But that's all I know.'

The snow deepened, and soon they were wading up to their thighs. Wolf dropped behind, cleverly letting Torak break the trail so that he could trot in his footsteps.

'I hope he knows the way,' said Renn, keeping her voice down. 'I've never been this far north.'

'Has anyone?' said Torak.

She raised her eyebrows. 'Well, yes. The Ice clans. But they live out on the plains, not on the ice river.'

'The Ice clans?'

'The White Foxes. The Ptarmigans. The Narwals. But surely you – '

'No,' he said wearily, 'I don't. I don't even – '

Behind him, Wolf gave an urgent grunt.

Torak turned to see the cub leaping for cover beneath an arch of solid ice. He glanced up. 'Look out!' he cried, grabbing Renn and yanking her under the arch.

An ear-splitting crack – and they were overwhelmed by

roaring whiteness. Ice thundered around them, smashing into the snow, exploding in lethal shards. Huddled under the arch, Torak prayed that it wouldn't collapse. If it did, they'd be splattered over the snow like crushed lingonberries . . .

The ice-fall ended as abruptly as it had begun.

Torak blew out a long breath. Now all he could hear was the soft settling of snow.

'Why did it stop?' hissed Renn.

He shook his head. 'Maybe it was just turning over in its sleep.'

Renn stared at the ice piled around them. 'If it wasn't for Wolf, we'd be under that right now.' She was pale, and her clan-tattoos showed up lividly. Torak guessed that she was thinking of her father.

Wolf stood up and shook himself, scattering them with wet snow. He trotted a few paces, took a long sniff, and waited for them to join him.

'Come on,' said Torak. 'I think it's safe.'

'*Safe?*' muttered Renn.

As the day wore on and the sun travelled west through a cloudless sky, puddles of meltwater appeared in the snow, more intensely blue than anything Torak had ever seen. It grew steadily warmer. Around mid-afternoon, the sun struck the cliffs, and in the blink of an eye, the freezing shadows turned to a stark white glare. Soon Torak was sweating under his reed cape.

'Here,' said Renn, handing him a strip of birch bast. 'Cut slits in this and tie it round your eyes. Otherwise you'll go snow-blind.'

'I thought you'd never been this far north.'

'I haven't, but Fin-Kedinn has. He told me about it.'

It made Torak uneasy to be peering through a narrow

slit, when he needed to be on his guard – when every so often a slab of snow or a giant icicle thudded down from the cliffs. As they trudged on, he noticed that Renn was lagging behind. That had never happened before. Usually she was faster than he was.

Waiting for her to catch up, he was startled to see that her lips had a bluish tinge. He asked if she was all right.

She shook her head, bending over with her hands on her knees. 'It's been coming on all day,' she said. 'I feel – drained. I think – I think it's the Nanuak.'

Torak felt guilty. He'd been concentrating so hard on not waking the ice river that he'd forgotten that all this time she'd been carrying the ravenskin pouch. 'Give it to me,' he said. 'We'll take turns.'

She nodded. 'But I'll carry the waterskin. That's only fair.'

They swapped. Torak tied the pouch to his belt, while Renn looked over her shoulder at how far they'd come. 'Much too slow,' she said. 'If we don't make it across by nightfall . . .'

She didn't need to add the rest. Torak pictured them digging a snow cave and cowering in darkness, while the ice river heaved and groaned around them. He said, 'Do you think we've got enough firewood?'

Again Renn shook her head.

Before heading for the scree slope, they'd each gathered a faggot of firewood, and prepared a little piece of fire to bring with them. To do this, they'd cut a small chunk of the horsehoof mushroom that grows on dead birch trees, and set fire to it, then blown it out so that it was just smouldering. Then they'd rolled it in birch bark, pierced the bark a few times to let the fire breathe, and plugged the roll with beard-moss to keep it asleep. The fire could be carried all day, slumbering quietly, but ready to be woken with tinder and breath when they needed it.

Torak judged that they had enough firewood to last for maybe a night. If a storm blew up and they had to dig in for days, they would freeze.

They trudged on, and soon Torak understood why the Nanuak had tired Renn. Already he could feel it weighing him down.

Suddenly Renn stopped, yanking the birch bast away from her eyes. 'Where's the stream gone?' she breathed.

'What?' said Torak.

'The meltwater! I've just noticed. That gully's gone. Do you think that means we can get out from under the cliffs?'

Taking off his own birch bast, Torak squinted at the snow. He couldn't see for the glare. 'I can still hear it,' he said, moving forwards to investigate. 'Maybe it's just sunk further under the –'

He got no warning. No crack of ice, no 'whump' of collapsing snow. One moment he was walking, the next, he was falling into nothingness.

TWENTY-FOUR

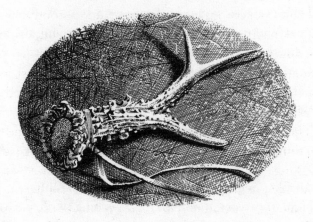

Torak jarred his knee so painfully that he cried out. 'Torak!' whispered Renn from above. 'Are you all right?'

'I – think so,' he replied. But he wasn't. He'd fallen down an ice hole. Only a tiny ledge had stopped him tumbling to his death.

In the gloom he saw that the hole was narrow – he could touch its sides with his outstretched hands – but fathomless. Far below, he heard the rush of the meltwater torrent. He was *inside* the ice river. How was he going to get out?

Renn and Wolf were peering down at him. They must be about three paces above. It might as well be thirty. 'Now we know where the meltwater went,' he said, struggling to stay calm.

'You're not *that* far down,' said Renn, trying to encourage him. 'At least you've still got your pack.'

'And my bow,' he replied, hoping he didn't sound too scared. 'And the Nanuak.' The pouch was still securely tied to his belt. *The Nanuak*, he thought in horror.

What if he couldn't get out? He'd be stuck down here, and the Nanuak would be stuck with him. Without the Nanuak, there would be no chance of destroying the bear. The entire Forest would be doomed: doomed because he hadn't watched his step . . .

'Torak?' whispered Renn. 'Are you all right?'

He tried to say yes, but it came out as a croak.

'Not too loud!' breathed Renn. 'It might send down another snowfall – or – or close up the hole with you inside . . . '

'Thanks,' he muttered, 'I hadn't thought of that.'

'Here, try to catch hold of this.' Leaning perilously over the edge, she dangled her axe head first, with the shaft strap wound around her wrist.

'You couldn't take my weight,' he told her. 'I'd pull you down, we'd both fall . . . '

'Fall, fall,' echoed the ice around him.

'Is there any way you can climb out?' said Renn, beginning to sound shaky.

'Probably. If I had the claws of a wolverine.'

'Claws, claws,' sang the ice.

That gave Torak an idea.

Slowly, terrified of slipping off the ledge, he unhitched his pack from one shoulder and checked that he still had the roe buck antlers. He did. They were short, and their roots had jagged edges. If he could tie one to each wrist and grip the tines, he might be able to use the roots as ice picks to claw his way out.

'What are you going to do?' asked Renn.

'You'll see,' he said. He didn't have time to explain. The

ledge was getting slippery beneath his boots, and his knee was hurting.

Leaving the antlers in his pack until he needed them, he took his axe from his belt. 'I've got to cut notches in the ice,' he called to Renn. 'I just hope the ice river doesn't feel it.'

She did not reply. Of course it would feel it. But what choice did he have?

The first axe-blow sent splinters of ice rattling into the chasm. Even if the ice river didn't feel that, it must have heard it.

Clenching his teeth, Torak forced himself to strike another blow. More shards crashed down, the echoes rumbling on and on.

The ice was hard, and he didn't dare swing his axe for fear of toppling off the ledge, but after much anxious chipping he managed four notches at staggered intervals as high as he could reach, with about a forearm's length between each one. They were frighteningly shallow – no deeper than his thumb-joint – and he had no idea if they'd hold. If he put his weight on one, it might give way, taking him with it.

Shoving his axe back in his belt, he took off his mittens and felt in his pack for the antlers and the last strips of rawhide. His fingers were clumsy with cold, and tying the antlers to his wrists was infuriatingly difficult. At last, using his teeth to tighten the knots, he managed it.

With his right hand he reached for the notch above his head, and dug deep with the jagged edge of the antler. It bit and held. With his left foot, he felt for the first foothold, just a little higher than the ledge. He found it and stepped onto it.

His pack was pulling him backwards into the ice hole. Desperately he leaned forward, pressing his face into the ice – and regained his balance.

Wolf yipped at him to hurry. Snow showered down into his hair.

'Stay *back!*' Renn hissed at the cub.

Torak heard sounds of a scuffle – more snow trickled down – then Wolf gave a peevish growl.

'Just a bit further,' said Renn. *'Don't look down.'*

Too late. Torak had just done so, and caught a sickening glimpse of the void below.

He reached for the next handhold, and missed, snapping off a crust of ice that nearly took him with it. He fought for the handhold – and the antler bit just in time.

Slowly, slowly, he bent his right leg and found the next foothold, about a forearm higher than the one he'd stepped onto with his left. But as he heaved himself onto it, his knee began to shake.

Oh, very clever, Torak, he told himself. You've just put all your weight on the wrong leg – the one you hurt in the fall! 'My knee's going,' he gasped. 'I can't – '

'Yes you can,' urged Renn. 'Reach for that last handhold, I'll grab you . . .'

His shoulders were burning; his pack felt as if it was filled with rocks. He gave a huge push and his knee buckled. Then a hand grabbed the shoulder strap of his pack and he was half-pulled, half-pushed out of the hole.

Torak and Renn lay panting at the edge of the ice hole. Then they heaved themselves up, staggered away from the ice cliffs, and collapsed in a drift of powdery snow. Wolf thought it a huge game, and pranced round them with a big wolf smile.

Renn gave way to panicky laughter. 'That was *far* too close! Next time, look where you're going!'

'I'll try!' panted Torak. He lay on his back, letting the

breeze waft snow over his cheeks. High in the sky, thin white clouds were stacking up like petals. He'd never seen anything so beautiful.

Behind him, Wolf was clawing at something in the ice.

'What have you got there?' said Torak.

But Wolf had freed his prize and was tossing it high and catching it in his jaws, in one of his favourite games. He leapt to catch it in mid-air, gave it a couple of chews, then bounded over and spat it out on Torak's face. Another favourite game. 'Ow!' said Torak. 'Watch what you're doing!' Then he saw what it was. It was about the size of a small fist: brown, furry and oddly flattened, probably by an ice-fall. The look of outrage on its little face struck Torak as inexpressibly funny.

'What is it?' said Renn, taking a pull at the waterskin.

He felt laughter welling up inside him. 'A frozen lemming.'

Renn burst out laughing, spraying water all over the ice.

'Squashed flat,' gasped Torak, rolling around in the snow. 'You should see its face! So – *surprised!*'

'No, don't!' cried Renn, clutching her sides.

They laughed till it hurt, while Wolf pranced around with a joyful rocking gait, tossing and catching the frozen lemming. At last he tossed it extravagantly high, made a spectacular twisting leap, and swallowed it in one gulp. Then he decided he was hot, and flopped into a pool of meltwater to cool down.

Renn sat up, wiping her eyes. 'Does he ever just *fetch* things, instead of throwing them in your face?'

Torak shook his head. 'I've tried asking him. He never does.'

He got to his feet. It was turning colder. The wind had strengthened, and powdery snow was streaming over the ground like smoke. The petal-like clouds had completely covered the sun.

'Look,' said Renn beside him. She was pointing east.

He glanced round and saw clouds boiling up over the ice cliffs. 'Oh, no,' he murmured.

'Oh, yes,' said Renn. She had to raise her voice above the wind. 'A snowstorm.'

The ice river had woken up. And it was angry.

TWENTY-FIVE

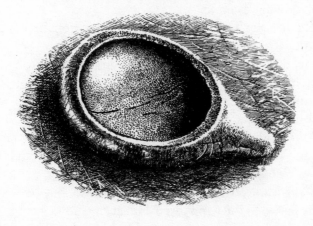

The fury of the ice river broke upon them with terrifying force.

Torak had to lean into the blast just to stay standing, and clutch his cape to stop it being ripped away. Through the streaming snow, he saw Renn pushing forwards with all her strength; Wolf staggering sideways, his eyes slitted against the wind. The ice river had them in its grip and it wasn't letting go. It howled till Torak's ears ached, and scoured his face with flying ice; it spun him round till he could no longer see Renn, or Wolf, or even his own boots. At any moment it might hurl him into an ice hole . . .

Through the swirling whiteness he caught sight of a dark pillar. A rock? A snowdrift? Could it be that they'd finally reached the edge of the ice river?

Renn grabbed his arm. 'We can't go on!' she shouted. 'We've got to dig in and wait till it's over!'

'Not yet!' he yelled. 'Look! We're nearly there!'

He battled on towards the pillar. It shattered and blew apart. It was nothing but a snow cloud: the ice river's vicious trick. He turned to Renn. 'You're right! We've got to dig a snow cave!'

But Renn was gone.

'Renn! *Renn!*' The ice river tore her name from his lips and whirled it away into the gathering dusk.

He dropped to his knees and groped for Wolf. His mitten found fur, and he clutched the cub. Wolf was casting around for Renn's scent. But what could even a wolf pick up in this?

Amazingly, Wolf pricked his ears and stared straight ahead. Torak thought he saw a figure gliding through the snow. '*Renn!*'

Wolf leapt after it, and Torak followed, but he hadn't gone far when the wind threw him against solid ice. He fell back, nearly crushing the cub. He'd blundered into what looked like an ice hill. In its side was a hole just big enough to crawl through. A snow cave? Surely Renn wouldn't have had time to dig one so quickly?

With one bound, Wolf disappeared inside. After a moment's hesitation, Torak followed.

The clamour of the ice river died down as he crawled into the darkness. With ice-caked mittens he felt out his surroundings. A low roof, so low that he had to crouch on hands and knees; a slab of ice by the entrance hole. Someone must have cut it for a door. But who?

'Renn?' he called.

No reply.

He pushed the slab across the hole, and the stillness closed in around him. He could hear Wolf licking the snow from his paws; ice sliding from his own shoulders.

He put out his hand, and Wolf gave a warning growl.

Torak snatched his hand away. The hairs on the back of his neck began to prickle. Renn wasn't in here – but something was. Something that waited in the dark. 'Who's there?' he said.

The icy blackness seemed to tense.

Wrenching off his mittens with his teeth, he whipped out his knife. *'Who's there?'*

Still no answer. He groped for one of Renn's rushlights. His fingers were so cold that he dropped his tinder pouch. It took forever to find it again; to hit the flint against the strike-fire, and shower sparks on the little pile of yew bark shavings in his hand, but at last the rushlight flared.

He cried out. He forgot about the ice river, he even forgot about Renn.

Almost touching his knee lay a man.

He was dead.

Torak flattened himself against the ice wall. If Wolf hadn't warned him, he would have touched the corpse – and to touch the dead is to risk terrible danger. When the souls leave the body, they can be angry, confused, or simply unwilling to embark on the Death Journey. If one of the living strays too close, the disembodied souls may try to possess it, or follow it home.

All this rushed through Torak's mind as he stared at the dead man.

His lips looked chiselled from ice; his flesh was waxen yellow. Snow had drifted into his nostrils in a cruel parody of breath, but his ice-filmed eyes were open, staring at something Torak couldn't see: something that was cradled in the crook of his dead arm.

Wolf seemed unafraid, even drawn to the corpse. He lay with his muzzle between his paws, gazing at it steadily.

The dead man had worn his long brown hair loose, except for a single lock at the temple, matted with red ochre. Torak thought of the Red Deer woman at Fin-Kedinn's clan meet; she'd worn her hair the same way. Had this man been of the same clan? The same clan as Torak's own mother?

He felt the stirrings of pity. What was the man's name? What had he been seeking out here, and how had he died?

Then Torak saw that on the brown forehead, a shaky circle had been daubed in red ochre. The thick winter parka had been wrenched open, and another circle drawn on the breastbone. Torak guessed that if he were reckless enough to remove the heavy, furred boots, he'd find a similar mark on each heel. Death Marks. The man must have felt death coming for him, and put on his own marks so that his souls would stay together after he died. That must be why he'd left the slab ajar too: to set the souls free.

'You were brave,' said Torak out loud. 'You didn't flinch from death.' He remembered the figure he'd glimpsed in the snow. Had that been one of the souls setting out on its final journey? Could you see souls? Torak didn't know.

'Be at peace,' he told the corpse. 'May your souls find their rest, and stay together.' He bowed his head for his dead kinsman.

Wolf sat up, pricking his ears at the corpse. Torak was startled. Wolf seemed to be listening.

Torak leaned closer.

The dead man gazed calmly at the thing cradled in his arm. But when Torak saw what it was, he was even more puzzled. It was an ordinary lamp: a smooth oval of red sandstone about half the size of his palm, with a shallow bowl to hold the fish oil, and a groove for the wick of twisted beard-moss. The wick had long since burned away, and all that remained of the oil was a faint greyish stain.

Beside him, Wolf gave a high, soft whine. His hackles were up but he didn't seem frightened. That whine had been – a greeting.

Torak frowned. Wolf had acted like that before. In the cave below the Thunder Falls.

His eyes returned to the dead man. He pictured his final moments: curled in the snow, watching the small, bright flame as his own life flickered and sank . . .

Suddenly, Torak knew. *'Coldest of all, the darkest light.'* The darkest light is the last light a man sees before he dies.

He had found the third piece of the Nanuak.

Gripping the rushlight in one hand, Torak untied the ravenskin pouch with the other, and tipped the box into the snow.

'Uff!' warned Wolf.

Torak slipped off the hair cord and lifted the lid. The river eyes stared blindly up at him, nestled in the curve of the black stone tooth. There was just enough room beside them for the lamp: almost, he thought, as if Renn had known how big to make the box.

With numb fingers he pulled on one mitten and leaned over the dead man – being careful not to touch him – and lifted the lamp clear. It was only when he'd got it safely boxed and back in the pouch that he realised he'd been holding his breath.

It was time to go and find Renn. Quickly he tied the pouch to his belt. But as he turned to push the slab aside, something made him stop.

He had all three pieces of the Nanuak. Here, in this

snow cave, where he was safe.

'If you get caught in a snowstorm,' Renn had said, 'you dig yourself a snow cave and wait till it stops.' If he ignored that now – if he braved the wrath of the ice river to look for her – he probably wouldn't survive. The Nanuak would be buried with him. The entire Forest would be doomed.

If he didn't, Renn might die.

Torak sat back on his heels. Wolf watched him intently, his amber eyes quite un-cub-like.

The rushlight wavered in Torak's hand. He couldn't just leave her. She was his friend. But could he – should he – risk the Forest to save her?

As never before, he longed for Fa. Fa would know what to do . . .

But Fa isn't here, he told himself. *You've* got to decide. You, Torak. By yourself.

Wolf tilted his head to one side, waiting to see what Torak would do.

TWENTY-SIX

'Torak!' yelled Renn at the top of her voice. 'Torak! Wolf! Where are you!'

She was alone in the storm. They could be three paces away and she'd never see them. They could have fallen down an ice hole and she'd never hear the screams.

The wind tossed her into a drift, and she choked on snow. One of her mittens slipped off, and the ice river blew it away. '*No!*' she shouted, beating the snow with her fists. 'No, no, no!'

On her hands and knees, she crawled into the wind. Stay calm. Find solid snow. Dig in.

After an endless struggle, she hit a snow hill. The wind had packed it hard, but not so hard that it was solid ice. Wrenching her axe from her belt, she began hacking a hole.

Torak's probably doing the same thing, she told herself. By the Spirit, I hope so.

With surprising speed, she hacked out a hollow just big enough to take herself and her pack, if she curled up small. The digging warmed her, but she could no longer feel her mittenless hand.

Crawling in backwards, she piled the scooped-out chunks in the entrance hole, walling herself up in the freezing darkness. Her breath soon melted the ice that caked her clothes, and she began to shake. As her eyes adjusted to the gloom, she saw that her mittenless fingers were white and hard. She tried to flex them, but they didn't move.

She knew about frostbite: the Boar Clan Leader's son, Aki, had lost three toes to it last winter. If she didn't warm up her fingers soon, they'd turn black and die; then she'd have to cut them off, or she would die too. Desperately, she blew on them, then shoved her hand inside her jerkin, under her armpit. The hand felt heavy and cold; no longer part of her.

Fresh terrors arose. Would she die alone, like her father? Would she never see Fin-Kedinn again? Where were Torak and Wolf? Even if they survived, how would she find them?

Pulling off her remaining mitten, she fumbled at her neck for the grouse-bone whistle that Torak had given her. She blew hard. It made no sound. Was she doing it right? Would Wolf be able to hear it? Maybe it only worked for Torak. Maybe you had to be the Listener.

She blew till she felt giddy and sick. They won't come, she thought. They'll have dug in long ago. If they're still alive.

The whistle tasted salty. Was that the grouse bone, or was she crying? No point crying, she told herself. Screwing her eyes shut, she went on blowing.

She awoke to find herself floating in beautiful heat. The

snow was as warm and soft as reindeer skins. She snuggled into it, so drowsy that she couldn't even lift her eyelids . . . much too drowsy to crawl into her sleeping-sack . . .

Voices dragged her awake. Fin-Kedinn and Saeunn had come to visit her.

I wish they'd let me sleep, she thought hazily.

Her brother was sneering, as he always did. 'Why did she make it so small? Why can't she ever do things properly?'

'Hord, that's not true,' said Fin-Kedinn. 'She did her best.'

'Still,' said Saeunn, 'she could have made a better door.'

'I was too tired,' mumbled Renn.

Just then, the door blew open, scattering ice all over her. 'Shut the door!' she protested.

One of the camp dogs jumped on top of her, showering her with snow, and nudging his cold nose under her chin. She batted him away. 'Bad dog! Go 'way!'

'Wake up, Renn!' Torak shouted in her ear.

'I'm *asleep*,' murmured Renn, burying her face in the snow.

'No you're not!' shouted Torak. He was longing for sleep himself, but first he had to make room for him and Wolf, and waken Renn. If she fell asleep now, it would be for ever. 'Renn, come *on!*' He grabbed her shoulders and shook her. 'Wake up!'

'Leave me alone,' she said. 'I'm fine.'

But she wasn't. Her face was blotched and inflamed by the flying ice, her eyes almost swollen shut. The fingers of her right hand were hard and waxy, unnervingly like those of the Red Deer corpse.

As Torak hacked at the snow, he wondered how much

longer she would have lasted if Wolf hadn't found her; and how much longer he and Wolf would have lasted if they hadn't found her snow cave. Torak was nearly worn out; he'd never have had the strength to start one afresh.

Of the three of them, Wolf was holding up the best. His fur was so thick that the snow lay on top of it without even melting. One good shake, and the snow flew off, showering them all.

Swaying with exhaustion, Torak finished enlarging the snow cave, and walled up the entrance again, leaving a gap at the top to let out the smoke from the fire he'd promised himself. Then he knelt beside Renn, and after several attempts, dragged her sleeping-sack out from behind her. 'Get into this,' he growled.

She kicked it away.

Scooping snow between his frozen fists, he rubbed it into her face and hands.

'Ow!' she yelped.

'Wake up or I'll kill you,' he snarled.

'You *are* killing me,' she snapped.

Knowing he had to make a fire soon, he rubbed his own hands in the snow, then tried to warm them in his armpits. As feeling returned, so did pain. 'Ow,' he moaned. 'Ow, ow, it hurts.'

'What did you say?' said Renn, sitting up and banging her head on the ceiling.

'Nothing.'

'Yes you did, you were talking to yourself.'

'*I* was talking to myself? You were chatting to your entire clan!'

'I was not,' she retorted indignantly.

'You were,' he said with a grin. She was waking up at last. He'd never been so glad to be having an argument.

Somehow, between them, they managed to make a fire. Fire needs warmth as well as air, so they used some of their firewood to make a little platform to keep the rest off the snow – and this time, instead of fumbling with his strike-fire, Torak remembered the fire-roll in his pack. At first the fire in the birch-bark roll refused to wake up, even when he blew on it coaxingly, and Renn fed it morsels of tinder warmed in her hands. Eventually it flared, rewarding their efforts with a small but cheering blaze.

With dripping hair and chattering teeth, they huddled over it, moaning as it thawed their hands and blistered their faces. But the flames gave them comfort greater than heat. Every night of their lives they'd gone to sleep to that crackling hiss and that bittersweet tang of woodsmoke. The fire was a little piece of the Forest.

Torak found his last roll of dried deer meat and shared it between the three of them. Renn gave him the waterskin. He hadn't known he was thirsty, but as he took a long drink, he felt strength returning.

'How did you find me?' Renn asked.

'I didn't,' he replied. 'Wolf did. I don't know how.'

She considered that. 'I think I do.' She showed him the grouse-bone whistle.

Torak thought of her blowing that silent whistle in the dark. He wondered what it had been like, all alone. At least he'd had Wolf.

He told her about the Red Deer corpse, and finding the third part of the Nanuak. He didn't mention the awful moment when he'd considered not trying to find her. He felt too ashamed.

'A stone lamp,' murmured Renn. 'I wouldn't have thought of that.'

'Do you want to see it?'

She shook her head. After a while she said, 'If it had been me, I'd have thought twice about leaving the snow cave. You were risking the Nanuak.'

Torak was silent. Then he said, 'I did think twice. I thought about staying, and not going to look for you.'

She went quiet. 'Well,' she said. 'I'd have done the same.'

Torak didn't know if he felt better or worse for telling her. 'But what would you have *done?*' he asked. 'Would you have stayed? Or gone to look for me?'

Renn wiped her nose on the back of her hand. Then she flashed him her sharp-toothed grin. 'Who knows? But maybe – it was another kind of test? Not whether you could find the third piece of the Nanuak. But whether you could risk it for a friend.'

‡‡

Torak awoke to a hushed blue glow. He didn't know where he was.

'Storm's over,' said Renn. 'And I've got a crick in my neck.'

So had Torak. Huddled in his sleeping-sack, he turned to face her.

Her eyes were no longer swollen, but her face was red and peeling. When she smiled, it obviously hurt. 'Ow!' she croaked. 'We survived!'

He grinned back, then wished he hadn't. His face felt as if it had been scrubbed with sand. He probably looked just like Renn. 'Now all we've got to do is get off the ice river,' he said.

Wolf was whining to be let out. Torak groped for his axe and hacked a hole. Light streamed in, and Wolf shot out. Torak crawled after him.

He emerged into a glittering world of snow hills and

wind-carved ridges. The sky was intensely blue, as if it had been washed clean. The stillness was absolute. The ice river had gone back to sleep.

Without warning, Wolf pounced on him, knocking him into a snowdrift. Before he could get up, Wolf leapt onto his chest, grinning and wagging his tail. Laughing, Torak lunged for him, but Wolf dodged out of his reach, then spun round in mid-air and bowed down with his tail curled over his back. *Let's play!*

Torak went down on his forearms. *Come on then!*

Wolf launched himself at Torak, and together they rolled over and over, Wolf play-biting and tearing at Torak's hair, and Torak muzzle-grabbing and tugging at his scruff. Finally, Torak tossed a snowball high, and Wolf made one of his amazing twisting leaps and snapped it up, landing in a snowdrift, and surfacing with a neat pile of snow on top of his nose.

As Torak struggled breathlessly to his feet, he heard Renn making her way out of the snow cave. 'I hope,' she yawned, 'it's not too far to the Forest. What happened to your cape?'

He was about to tell her that the storm had ripped it away, when he turned – and forgot about the cape.

East beyond the snow cave – beyond the ice river itself – the High Mountains were terrifyingly close.

For many days the fog had hidden them; then yesterday the ice cliffs had loomed so close that nothing could be seen beyond them. Now, in the clear, cold light, the Mountains ate up the sky.

Torak reeled. For the first time in his life, they weren't just a distant darkness on the eastern horizon. He stood at their very roots: craning his neck at vast, swooping ice-faces, at black peaks that pierced the clouds. He felt their power and menace. They were the abode of spirits. Not of men.

Somewhere among them, he thought, lies the Mountain of the World Spirit. The Mountain I swore to find.

TWENTY-SEVEN

The red eye was rising. Torak had only a few days to find the Mountain.

Even if he found it, what then? What did he actually have to *do* with the Nanuak? How would he ever destroy the bear?

Renn crunched through the snow to stand beside him. 'Come on,' she said. 'We've got to get off the ice river, back to the Forest.'

At that moment, Wolf gave a start, and ran to the top of a snow ridge, turning his ears towards the foothills.

'What is it?' whispered Renn. 'What's he heard?'

Then Torak heard it too: voices far away in the Mountains, weaving together in the wild, ever-changing song of the wolf pack.

Wolf flung back his head, pointed his muzzle to the sky, and howled. *I'm here! I'm here!*

Torak was astonished. Why was he howling to a strange

pack? Lone wolves don't do that. They try to avoid strange wolves.

With a whine, he asked Wolf to come to him – but Wolf stayed where he was: eyes slitted, black lips curled over his teeth as he poured out his song. Torak noticed that he was looking much less puppyish. His legs were longer, and he was growing a mantle of thick black fur around his shoulders. Even his howl was losing its cub-like wobble.

'What's he telling them?' asked Renn.

Torak swallowed. 'He's telling them where he is.'

'And what are they saying?'

Torak listened, never taking his eyes off Wolf. 'They're talking to two of their pack: scouts who've gone down onto the fells to seek reindeer. It sounds–,' he paused. 'Yes, they've found a small herd. The scouts are telling the others where it is, and that they should howl with their muzzles in the snow.'

'Why? What for?'

'It's a trick wolves do sometimes, so the reindeer think they're further away than they really are.'

Renn looked uneasy. 'You can tell all that?'

He shrugged.

She dug at the snow with her heel. 'I don't like it when you talk wolf. It feels strange.'

'I don't like it when Wolf talks to other wolves,' said Torak. 'That feels strange, too.'

Renn asked him what he meant, but he didn't reply. It was too painful to put into words. He was beginning to realise that although he knew wolf talk, he was not, and never would be, truly *wolf*. In some ways, he would always be apart from the cub.

Wolf stopped howling, and trotted down from the ridge. Torak knelt and put his arm around him. He felt the fine light bones beneath the dense winter fur; the fierce beat of a loyal heart. As he bent to take in the cub's sweet-grass scent, Wolf licked his cheek, then gently pressed his forehead against Torak's own.

Torak shut his eyes tight. *Never leave me*, he wanted to tell Wolf. But he didn't know how to say it.

They started north.

It was an exhausting trudge. The storm had packed the snow into frozen ridges, with thigh-deep troughs in between. Mindful of ice holes, they prodded the snow in front of them with arrows, which slowed them down even more. Always they felt the Mountains watching them, waiting to see if they would fail.

By noon they'd made little progress, and were still within sight of the snow cave. Then they encountered a new obstacle: a wall of ice. It was too steep to climb, and too hard to cut through. Another of the ice river's savage jokes.

Renn said she'd investigate while Torak waited with the cub. He was glad of the rest: the ravenskin pouch was weighing him down. 'Watch out for ice holes,' he warned, watching anxiously as she peered into a crack between two of the tallest fangs of ice.

'It looks as if there might be a way through,' she called. Unslinging her pack, she squeezed in, then disappeared.

Torak was about to go after her when she stuck out her head. 'Oh Torak, come and see! We've done it! We've done it!'

Wolf leapt after her. Torak took off his pack and followed them in. He hated edging through the crack – it reminded him of the cave – but when he got to the other side, he gasped.

He was looking down at a torrent of jumbled ice like a frozen waterfall. Below it stretched a long slope of snowy boulders, and beyond that, scarcely a pebble's throw away, and shimmering in its white winter mantle, lay the Forest.

'I never thought I'd see it again,' said Renn fervently.

Wolf raised his muzzle to catch the smells, then glanced back at Torak and wagged his tail.

Torak couldn't speak. He hadn't known how much it had hurt – actually hurt – to be out of the Forest. They'd only spent three nights away, but it felt like moons.

By mid-afternoon, they'd clambered off the last ice ridge and started zigzagging down the slope. The shadows were turning violet. Pine trees beckoned with snow-heavy boughs. It was a huge relief to get in among them, out of sight of the Mountains. But the stillness was unnerving.

'It can't be the bear,' whispered Renn. 'There was no sign of it on the ice river. And if it had gone round by the valleys, it would've taken days.'

Torak glanced at Wolf. His ears were back, but his hackles were down. 'I don't think it's close,' he said. 'But it isn't far, either.'

'Look at this,' said Renn, pointing at the snow beneath a juniper tree. 'Bird tracks.'

Torak stooped to examine them. 'A raven. Walking, not hopping. That means it wasn't frightened. And there was a squirrel here, too.' He pointed to a scattering of cones at the base of a pine tree, each one gnawed to the core like an apple. 'And hare tracks. Quite fresh. I can still see some fur marks.'

'If they're fresh, that's a good sign,' said Renn.

'Mm.' Torak peered into the gloom. 'But that isn't.'

The auroch lay on his side like a great brown boulder. In life he'd stood taller than the tallest man, and the span of his gleaming black horns had been almost as wide. But the bear had slashed open his belly, leaving him in a churned-up mess of crimson snow.

Torak gazed down at the great ruined beast, and felt a surge of anger. Despite their size, aurochs are gentle creatures who only use their horns to fight for mates, or defend their young. This blunt-nosed bull had not deserved such a brutal death.

His carcass hadn't even fed the other creatures of the Forest. No foxes or pine martens had gone near it; no ravens had feasted here. Nothing would touch the prey of the bear.

'Uff,' said Wolf, running about in circles with his hackles up.

Stay back, warned Torak. The light was fading, but he could still make out the bear tracks, and he didn't want Wolf touching them.

'It doesn't look like a fresh kill,' said Renn. 'That's something, isn't it?'

Torak studied the carcass, careful to avoid touching the tracks. He prodded it with a stick, then nodded. 'Frozen solid. A day or so at least.'

Behind him, Wolf growled.

Torak wondered why he was so agitated, when the kill wasn't fresh.

'Somehow,' said Renn, 'I thought we'd be safer now that we're back in the Forest. I thought – '

But Torak never found out what she thought. Suddenly the snow beneath the trees erupted, and several tall, white-clad figures surrounded them.

Too late, Torak realised that Wolf had not been growling

at the auroch – but at these silent assailants. *Look behind you, Torak.* He'd forgotten. Again.

Drawing his knife in one hand and his axe in the other, he edged towards Renn, who'd already nocked an arrow to her bow. Wolf sped into the shadows. Back to back, Torak and Renn faced a bristling circle of arrows.

The tallest of the white-clad figures stepped forward and threw back his hood. In the dusk, his dark-red hair looked almost black. 'Got you at last,' said Hord.

TWENTY-EIGHT

'Why are you doing this?' cried Renn. 'He's trying to help us! You can't treat him like an outcast!'

'Watch me,' said Hord, dragging Torak through the snow.

Torak fought to stay on his feet, but it wasn't easy with his hands tied behind his back. There was no hope of escape: he was surrounded by Oslak and four sturdy Raven men.

'Faster!' urged Hord. 'We've got to reach camp before dark!' 'But he's the *Listener*!' said Renn. 'I can prove it!' She pointed at the ravenskin pouch at Torak's waist. 'He found all three pieces of the Nanuak!'

'Did he,' muttered Hord. Without breaking stride, he drew his knife and cut the pouch from Torak's belt. 'Well now it's mine.'

'What are you doing?' cried Renn. 'Give it back!'

'Hold your tongue!' snapped Hord.

'Why should I? Who says you can –'

Hord slapped her. It was a hard blow across the face, and she went flying, landing in a heap.

Oslak growled a protest but Hord warned him back. He was breathing hard as he watched Renn sitting up. 'You're no longer my sister,' he spat. 'We thought you were dead when we found your quiver in the stream. Fin-Kedinn didn't speak for three days, but *I* didn't grieve. I was glad. You betrayed your clan, and you shamed me. I wish you *were* dead.'

Renn put a trembling hand to her lip. It was bleeding. A red weal was coming up on her cheek.

'You shouldn't have hit her,' said Torak.

Hord turned on him. 'Keep out of this!'

Torak looked hard at Hord – and was shocked by the change in him. Instead of the stocky young man he'd fought less than a moon ago, he was facing a gaunt shadow. Hord's eyes were raw from sleeplessness, and the hand that clutched the Nanuak had no fingernails: just oozing sores. Something was eating him up from inside.

'Stop staring at me,' he snarled.

'Hord,' said Oslak, 'we've got to keep moving. The bear . . .'

Hord wheeled round, his eyes straining to pierce the darkness. 'The bear, the bear,' he muttered, as if the very thought hurt.

'Come, Renn.' Oslak leaned down and offered his hand. 'We'll soon have a poultice on that. Camp's not far.'

Renn ignored him, and got unaided to her feet.

Glancing up the trail, Torak caught an orange flicker in the deepening dusk. Nearer, in the shadows beneath a young spruce, a pair of amber eyes.

His heart turned over. If Hord saw Wolf, there was no

knowing what he might do . . .

Luckily, Renn had everyone's attention. 'Is my brother Clan Leader now?' she demanded. 'Do you follow him instead of Fin-Kedinn?'

The men hung their heads.

'It's not that simple,' said Oslak. 'The bear attacked three days ago. It killed – ' his voice cracked. 'It killed two of us.'

The blood drained from Renn's face. She drew closer to Oslak, whose brow and cheekbones were marked with grey river clay.

Torak didn't know what the marks meant, but when Renn saw them she gasped. 'No,' she whispered, touching Oslak's hand.

The big man nodded and turned away.

'What about Fin-Kedinn?' Renn said shrilly. 'Is he – '

'Badly wounded,' said Hord. 'If he dies, I *will* be Leader. I'll make sure of it.'

Renn clapped her hands to her mouth and raced off towards the camp.

'Renn!' shouted Oslak. 'Come back!'

'Let her go,' said Hord.

When she'd gone, Torak felt utterly alone. He didn't even know the names of the other Raven men. 'Oslak,' he begged, 'make Hord give me back the Nanuak! It's our only hope. You know that.'

Oslak started to speak, but Hord cut in. 'Your part in this is finished,' he told Torak. '*I* will take the Nanuak to the Mountain! *I* will offer the blood of the Listener to save my people!'

Wolf was so frightened that he wanted to howl. How could

he help his pack-brother? Why was everything so chewed up?

As he followed the full-grown taillesses through the Bright Soft Cold, he struggled against the hunger gnawing his belly, and the muzzle-watering smell of the lemmings just a pounce away. He fought against the Pull that was now so strong that he felt it all the time, and the fear of the demon he scented on the wind. He turned his ears from the distant howls of the stranger pack: the pack that didn't sound like strangers any more, but faraway kin . . .

He had to ignore it all. His pack-brother was in danger. Wolf sensed his pain and fear. He sensed, too, the anger of the full-growns, and *their* fear. They were scared of Tall Tailless.

The wind changed, and Wolf caught a wave of scents from the great Den of the taillesses. Sounds and smells overwhelmed him. *Bad, bad, bad!* His courage failed. Whimpering, he shot under a fallen tree.

The Den meant terrible danger. It was huge and complicated, with angry dogs who didn't listen, and many of the Bright Beasts-that-Bite-Hot. Worst of all were the taillesses themselves. They couldn't hear or smell much, but they made up for it by doing clever things with their forepaws, and sending the Long-Claw-that-Flies-Far to bite the prey.

Wolf didn't know whether to run or stay.

To help himself think, he chewed a branch, then a chunk of the Bright Soft Cold. He ran in circles. Nothing worked. He longed for the strange sureness that sometimes came to him and told him what to do. It didn't come. It had flown like a raven into the Up.

What must he *do*?

Torak blamed himself. Because of his carelessness he'd lost the Nanuak. It was all his fault. Around him the snow-laden trees cast blue moon-shadows across the trail. 'Your fault,' they seemed to be telling him.

'Faster,' said Hord, jabbing him in the back.

The Ravens had camped in a clearing by a mountain stream. At the heart of the clearing, a long-fire of three pine logs glowed orange. Clustered around it were the clan's sloping shelters, then a ring of smaller fires and spiked pits, guarded by men with spears. It looked as if the entire clan had come north.

Hord ran ahead while Torak waited with Oslak by one of the shelters. He saw Renn, and his spirits rose. She was kneeling at the mouth of a shelter on the other side of the clearing, talking urgently. She didn't see him.

People were huddled around the long-fire. The air was thick with fear. According to Oslak, scouts had found signs of the bear only two valleys away. 'It's getting stronger,' he said. 'Tearing up the Forest as if – as if it's seeking something.'

Torak started to shiver. Hord's forced march had kept him warm, but now, in his summer buckskin, he was freezing. He hoped they wouldn't think he was scared.

Oslak untied his wrists and put his hand on his shoulder to guide him into the clearing. Torak forgot about the cold as he stumbled into the glare of the long-fire, and a buzz of voices like a hive of angry bees.

He saw Saeunn, cross-legged on a pile of reindeer hides with the ravenskin pouch in her lap; Hord beside her, gnawing his thumb; Dyrati watching Hord, her face strained.

Silence fell. People made way for four men bearing Fin-Kedinn on an auroch-hide litter. The Raven Leader's face was drawn, and his left leg was bandaged in soft bindings blotched with blood. His face contracted slightly as the men set him down by the long-fire. It was the only sign he gave of being in pain.

Renn appeared, rolling a chunk of pine log. She put it behind Fin-Kedinn for him to lean against, then curled up beside him on a reindeer skin. She didn't look at Torak, but kept her eyes on the fire.

Oslak nudged him in the back, and he took a few halting steps closer to the litter.

The Raven Leader caught his gaze and held it, and Torak felt a rush of relief. The blue eyes were as intense and unreadable as ever. Hord would have to wait a while longer to be Clan Leader.

'When we first found this boy,' said Fin-Kedinn, his voice ringing clear, 'we didn't know who, or what, he was. Since then, he has found the three pieces of the Nanuak. He has saved the life of one of our own.' He paused. 'I have no more doubts. He is the Listener. The question is, do we let him take the Nanuak to the Mountain? A boy, on his own? Or do we send our strongest hunter: a full-grown man with a far greater chance against the bear?'

Hord stopped gnawing his thumb and squared his shoulders. Torak's heart sank.

'Time is short,' said Fin-Kedinn, glancing at the night sky where the Great Auroch blazed. 'In a few days, the bear will be too strong to overcome. We can't call a clan meet, there's no time. I must decide this now, for all the clans.' The only sound was the hiss and crackle of the fire. The Ravens were hanging on every word.

'There are many among us,' Fin-Kedinn went on, 'who say it would be madness to trust our fate to a boy.'

Hord leapt to his feet. 'It *would* be madness! *I'm* the strongest! Let me go to the Mountain and save my people!'

'You're not the Listener,' said Torak.

'What about the rest of the Prophecy?' said Saeunn in her raven's croak. '"*The Listener gives his heart's blood to the Mountain.*" Could you do that?'

Torak took a breath. 'If that's what it takes.'

'But there's another way!' cried Hord. 'We kill him now, and I take his blood to the Mountain! At least then we stand a chance!'

A murmur of approval from the Ravens.

Fin-Kedinn raised a hand for silence, then spoke to Torak. 'You used to deny that you were the Listener. Why so keen now?'

Torak raised his chin. 'The bear killed my father. That's what it was made to do.'

'This is greater than vengeance!' sneered Hord.

'It's greater than vanity, too,' Torak retorted. He spoke to Fin-Kedinn. 'I don't care about being "the saviour of my people". What people? I've never even met my own clan. But I swore to my father that I'd find the Mountain. I swore an oath.'

'We're wasting time!' said Hord. 'Give me the Nanuak and I will do it!'

'How?' said a quiet voice.

It was Renn.

'How will you find the Mountain?' she asked.

Hord hesitated.

Renn stood up. 'It's said to be the furthest peak at the northernmost end of the High Mountains. Well, here we are, at the northernmost end of the High Mountains. So where is it?' She spread her hands. 'I don't know.' She turned to Hord. 'Do you?'

He ground his teeth.

She spoke to Saeunn. 'Do you? No. And you're the Mage.' She faced Fin-Kedinn. 'Do you?'

'No,' he answered.

Renn pointed at Torak. 'Not even he knows where it is, and he's the Listener.' She paused. 'But somebody knows.' She looked directly at Torak, her eyes drilling into his.

He caught her meaning. Clever Renn, he thought. Just so long as it works . . .

He put his hands to his lips and howled.

The Ravens gasped. The camp dogs leapt into uproar.

Again Torak howled.

Suddenly, a streak of grey sped across the clearing and crashed into him.

People muttered and pointed; the dogs went wild until men shooed them away. A small child laughed.

Torak knelt and buried his face in Wolf's fur. Then he gave the cub's muzzle a grateful lick. It had taken enormous courage for Wolf to answer his call.

As the uproar subsided, Torak raised his head. 'Only Wolf can find the Mountain,' he told Fin-Kedinn. 'He got us this far. It's only because of him that we found the Nanuak.'

The Raven Leader ran a hand over his dark-red beard.

'Give me back the Nanuak,' pleaded Torak. 'Let me take it to the World Spirit. It's our only chance.'

The fire crackled and spat. Snow thudded off a nearby spruce. The Ravens waited for their Leader's decision.

At last Fin-Kedinn spoke. 'We'll give you food and clothing for the journey. When do you leave?'

Torak breathed out.

Renn gave him a curt nod.

Hord shouted a protest, but Fin-Kedinn silenced him with a glance. Again he spoke to Torak. 'When do you leave?'

Torak swallowed. 'Um. Tomorrow?'

TWENTY-NINE

Tomorrow, Torak and Wolf would set out into the bear-haunted Forest – and Torak had no idea what he was going to do.

Even if they reached the Mountain, what next? Should he simply leave the Nanuak on the ground? Ask the World Spirit to destroy the bear? Try to fight it on his own?

'Do you want new boots, or do we mend yours?' snapped Oslak's mate, who was measuring him for winter clothes.

'What?' he said.

'Boots,' repeated the woman. She had tired eyes, and river clay markings on her cheeks – and she was furious with him. He didn't know why.

He said, 'I'm used to my boots. Could you maybe –'

'Mend them?' She snorted. 'I think I can manage that!'

'Thank you,' Torak said humbly. He glanced at Wolf, who was cowering in the corner with his ears back.

Oslak's mate snatched a length of sinew and spun Torak round to measure his shoulders. 'Oh, it'll fit all right,' she muttered. 'Well sit down, sit down!'

Torak sat, and watched her tying knots to mark the measurements. Her eyes were moist, and she was blinking rapidly. She caught him looking. 'What are you staring at?'

'Nothing,' he replied. 'Should I take off my clothes?'

'Not unless you want to freeze. You'll have the new things by dawn. Now give me the boots.'

He did, and she eyed them as if they were a pair of rotting salmon. 'More holes than a fishing net,' she said. It was a relief when she bustled out of the shelter.

She hadn't been gone long when Renn came in. Wolf padded over and licked her fingers. She scratched him behind the ears.

Torak wanted to thank her for standing up for him, but he wasn't sure how to start. The silence lengthened.

'How'd you get on with Vedna?' Renn said abruptly.

'Vedna? Oh. Oslak's mate? I don't think she likes me.'

'It's not that. It's your new clothes. She was making them for her son. Now she's got to finish them for you.'

'Her son?'

'Killed by the bear.'

'Oh.' Poor Vedna, he thought. Poor Oslak. And that explained the river clay. It must be the Raven way of mourning.

The bruise on Renn's cheek had turned purple; he asked if it hurt. She shook her head. He guessed that she was ashamed of what her brother had done.

'What about Fin-Kedinn?' he said. 'How bad is his leg?'

'Bad. Bone-deep. But no sign of the blackening sickness.'

'That's good.' He hesitated. 'Was he – very angry with you?'

'Yes. But that's not why I'm here.'

'So why are you here?'

'Tomorrow. I'm coming with you.'

Torak bit his lip. 'I think it has to be just me and Wolf.'

She glared at him. 'Why?'

'I don't know. I just do.'

'That's stupid.'

'Maybe. But that's how it is.'

'You sound like Fin-Kedinn.'

'That's another reason. He'd never allow it.'

'Since when did I let that stop me?'

He grinned.

She didn't grin back. Looking thunderous, she moved to the fire at the entrance to the shelter. 'You're to eat nightmeal with him,' she said. 'It's an honour. In case you didn't know.'

Torak swallowed. He was scared of Fin-Kedinn, but in a strange way, he also wanted his approval. Eating nightmeal with him sounded unnerving. 'Will you be there too?' he asked.

'No.'

'Oh.'

Another silence. Then she relented. 'If you like, I'll keep Wolf with me. Best not to leave him alone with the dogs.'

'Thanks.'

She nodded. Then she saw his bare feet. 'I'll see if I can find you a pair of boots.'

Some time later, Torak made his way to Fin-Kedinn's shelter, stumbling in his borrowed boots, which were much too big.

He found the Raven Leader in heated talk with Saeunn, but they stopped when he came in. Saeunn looked fierce.

Fin-Kedinn's face gave nothing away.

Torak sat cross-legged on a reindeer skin. He couldn't see any food, but people were busy at cooking-skins by the long-fire. He wondered how soon they would eat. And what he was doing here.

'I've told you what I think,' said Saeunn.

'So you have,' Fin-Kedinn said evenly.

They made no attempt to include Torak, which left him free to study Fin-Kedinn's shelter. It was no grander than the others, and from the roofpost hung the usual hunter's gear; but the string of the great yew bow was broken, and the white reindeer-hide parka was spattered with dried blood: stark reminders that the Raven Leader had faced the bear, and survived.

Suddenly, Torak noticed a man watching him from the shadows. He had short brown hair and dark, wizened features.

'This is Krukoslik,' said Fin-Kedinn, 'of the Mountain Hare Clan.'

The man put both fists over his heart and bowed his head.

Torak did the same.

'Krukoslik knows these parts better than anyone,' said Fin-Kedinn. 'Talk to him before you set out. If nothing else, he'll give you a few hints on surviving the Mountains. I wasn't impressed by the state you were in when we caught you. No winter clothes, one waterskin and no food. Your father taught you better than that.'

Torak caught his breath. 'So you did know him?'

Saeunn bristled, but Fin-Kedinn quelled her with a glance. 'Yes,' he said. 'I knew him. There was a time when he was my best friend.'

Angrily, Saeunn turned away.

Torak felt himself getting angry, too. 'If you were his best friend, why did you sentence me to death? Why did you let me fight Hord? Why did you keep me tied up while the clan meet decided whether to sacrifice me?'

'To see what you were made of,' Fin-Kedinn said calmly. 'You're no good to anyone if you can't use your wits.' He paused. 'If you remember, I didn't keep you under close guard. I even let you have the wolf cub with you.'

Torak thought about that. 'You mean – you were testing me?'

Fin-Kedinn did not reply.

Two men came over from the main fire, carrying four steaming birchwood bowls.

'Eat,' said Krukoslik, handing one to Torak.

Fin-Kedinn tossed over a horn spoon, and for a while Torak forgot about everything as he dug in hungrily. It was a thin broth made from boiled elk hooves and a few slivers of dried deer heart, bulked up with rowanberries and the tough, tasteless tree-mushroom that the clans call auroch's ears. With it, they had a single flatcake of roasted acorn meal: very bitter, but not too bad once it was broken up and mashed into the broth.

'I'm sorry we can't do better,' said Fin-Kedinn, 'but prey is scarce.' It was the only reference he made to the bear.

Torak was too hungry to care. Only when he'd licked his bowl did he notice that Fin-Kedinn and Saeunn had hardly touched theirs. Saeunn took them back to the cooking-skin, then returned to her place. Krukoslik hung his spoon on his belt, and went to kneel by the small fire at the entrance to the shelter, where he murmured a brief prayer of thanks.

Torak had never seen anyone like him. He wore a bulky robe of brown reindeer hide that hung all the way to his calves, and a broad belt of red buckskin. His clan skin was a mantle of hare fur over the shoulders, dyed a fiery red, and his clan-tattoo was a red zigzag band across the forehead. On his breast hung a finger-long shard of smoky rock crystal.

He saw Torak looking at it, and smiled. 'Smoke is the breath of the Fire Spirit. Mountain clans worship fire above all else.'

Torak remembered the comfort the fire had given him and Renn in the snow cave. 'I can understand that,' he said.

Krukoslik's smile broadened.

With nightmeal over, Fin-Kedinn asked the others to leave so that he could speak to Torak alone. Krukoslik stood up and bowed. Saeunn gave an angry hiss and swept from the shelter.

Torak wondered what was coming next.

'Saeunn,' said Fin-Kedinn, 'doesn't think you should be told any more. She thinks it would distract you tomorrow.'

'Any more about what?' asked Torak.

'About what you want to know.'

Torak considered that. 'I want to know everything.'

'Not possible. Try again.'

Torak picked at a tear in the knee of his leggings. 'Why me? Why am I the Listener?'

Fin-Kedinn stroked his beard. 'That is a long story.'

'Is it because of my father? Because he was the Wolf Mage? The enemy of the crippled wanderer, who made the bear?'

'That is – part of it.'

'But who was he? Why were they enemies? Fa never even mentioned him.'

211

With a stick, the Raven Leader stirred the fire, and Torak saw the lines of pain deepen on either side of his mouth. Without turning his head, Fin-Kedinn said, 'Did your father ever mention the Soul-Eaters?'

Torak was puzzled. 'No. I've never heard of them.'

'Then you must be the only one in the Forest who hasn't.' Fin-Kedinn fell silent, the firelight etching his face with shadow. 'The Soul-Eaters,' he went on, 'were seven Mages, each from a different clan. In the beginning, they were not evil. They helped their clans. Each had his own particular skill. One was subtle as a snake, always delving into the lore of herbs and potions. One was strong as an oak; he wished to know the minds of trees. Another had thoughts that flew swifter than a bat. She loved to enchant small creatures to do her bidding. One was proud and far-seeking, fascinated by demons, always trying to control them. They say that another could summon the Dead.' Again he stirred the fire.

When he did not continue, Torak mustered his courage. 'That's only five. You said – there were seven.'

Fin-Kedinn ignored him. 'Many winters ago, they banded together in secret. At first they called themselves the Healers. Deceived themselves into believing that they wished only to do good; to cure sickness, guard against demons.' His mouth twisted contemptuously. 'Soon they drifted into evil, warped by their hunger for power.'

Torak's fingers tightened on his knee. 'Why were they called Soul-Eaters?' he asked, scarcely moving his lips. 'Did they really eat souls?'

'Who knows? People were frightened, and when people are frightened, rumour becomes truth.' His face became distant as he remembered. 'Above all things, the Soul-Eaters wanted power. That's what they lived for. To rule the

212

Forest. To force everyone in it to do their bidding. Then, thirteen winters ago, something happened that shattered their power.'

'What?' whispered Torak. 'What happened?'

Fin-Kedinn sighed. 'All you need to know is that there was a great fire, and the Soul-Eaters were scattered. Some were badly wounded. All went into hiding. We thought the threat had gone for ever. We were wrong.' He snapped the stick in two and threw it on the fire. 'The man you call the crippled wanderer – the man who created the bear – he was one of them.'

'A *Soul-Eater*?'

'I knew as soon as Hord told me about him. Only a Soul-Eater could have trapped so great a demon.' He met Torak's eyes. 'Your father was his enemy. He was the sworn enemy of all the Soul-Eaters.'

Torak couldn't look away from the intense blue gaze. 'He never told me anything.'

'He had reasons. Your father–,' he said. 'Your father did many wrong things in his life. But he did all he could to stop the Soul-Eaters. That's why they killed him. It's also why he brought you up apart. So that they'd never know you even existed.'

Torak stared at him. '*Me*? Why?'

Fin-Kedinn wasn't listening. Once again, he was watching the flames. 'It doesn't seem possible,' he murmured. 'Nobody ever suspected there was a son. Not even me.'

'But – Saeunn knew. Fa told her, five summers ago at the clan meet by the Sea. Didn't she – '

'No,' said Fin-Kedinn. 'She never told me.'

'I don't understand,' said Torak. 'Why couldn't the Soul-Eaters know about me? What's wrong with me?'

Fin-Kedinn studied his face. 'Nothing. They mustn't

213

know about you because . . . ' He shook his head, as if there was too much to tell. 'Because one day you might be able to stop them.'

Torak was aghast. '*Me*? How?'

'I don't know. I only know that if they find out about you, they'll come after you.' Once more his eyes held Torak's. 'This is what Saeunn didn't want you to know. And it's what I believe you *must* know. If you live – if you succeed in destroying the bear – it won't be the end. The Soul-Eaters will find out who did it. They'll know you exist. Sooner or later, they'll come after you.'

An ember cracked.

Torak jumped. 'You mean – even if I survive tomorrow, I'll be running all my life.'

'I didn't say that. You can run or you can fight. There's always a choice.'

Torak looked up at the blood-spattered parka. Hord was right: this was a fight for men, not for boys. 'Why did Fa never tell me anything?' he said.

'Your father knew what he was doing,' said Fin-Kedinn. 'He did some bad things. Some things for which I'll never forgive him. But with you, I think he did the right thing.'

Torak couldn't speak.

'Ask yourself this, Torak. Why does the Prophecy speak of "the Listener"? Why not "the Talker" or the "Seer"?'

Torak shook his head.

'Because the most important quality in a hunter is to *be* a listener. To listen to what the wind and the trees are telling you. To listen to what other hunters and prey are saying about the Forest. That's the gift your father gave you. He didn't teach you Magecraft, or the story of the clans. He taught you to hunt. To use your wits.' He paused. 'If you are to succeed tomorrow, that's how you'll do it. By using your wits.'

It was after middle-night, but still Torak sat by the long-fire in the clearing, staring at the looming blackness of the High Mountains.

He was alone. Wolf had gone off on his nightly wanderings, and the only signs of life in the camp were the silent Ravens guarding the defences, and the rumble of snores from Oslak's shelter.

Torak longed to waken Renn and tell her everything. But he didn't know where she was sleeping. Besides, he wasn't sure that he could bring himself to tell her about Fa – about the bad things Fin-Kedinn said he had done.

'If you survive it won't be the end . . . the Soul-Eaters will come after you . . . You can run or you can fight. There's always a choice . . . '

Terrible images whirled in his head like a snowstorm. The bear's murderous eyes. The Soul-Eaters, like half-glimpsed shadows in a bad dream. Fa's face as he lay dying.

To chase them away, he stood up and began to pace. He forced himself to think.

He had no idea what he was going to do tomorrow, but he knew that Fin-Kedinn was right. If he was to stand a chance against the bear, it would be by using his wits. The World Spirit would only help him if he tried to help himself.

Once again, he ran through the lines of the Prophecy. *The Listener fights with air and speaks with silence . . . The Listener fights with air . . . '*

The glimmerings of an idea began to nag at him.

THIRTY

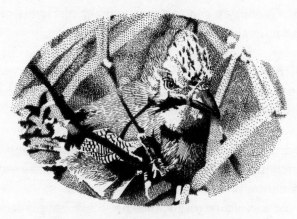

Torak's fingers were shaking so much that he couldn't get the stopper off his medicine horn.

Why had he left this to the last moment? Now Wolf was padding restlessly up and down outside the shelter, and the Ravens were waiting to see him off, and he still couldn't get the stopper off the –

'Want some help?' said Renn from the doorway. Her face was pale, her eyes shadowed.

Torak passed her the medicine horn, and she yanked out the black oak stopper with her teeth. 'What's this for?' she asked, handing it back.

'Death Marks,' he said, not looking at her.

She gasped. 'Like the man on the ice river?'

He nodded.

'But he knew he was going to die. You might survive – '

'You don't know that. I don't want to risk my souls getting separated. I don't want to risk becoming a demon.'

She stooped to stroke Wolf's ears. 'You're right.'

Torak glanced past her into the clearing, where the dark-blue dawn was breaking. During the night, clouds had rolled down from the Mountains, covering the Forest in thick snow. He wondered if that would help or hinder him.

He tipped some red ochre onto his palm, and spat on it. But his mouth was too dry, and he couldn't make a paste.

Renn leaned over and spat into his palm. Then she scooped up some snow, warmed it in her hands, and added that.

'Thanks,' he muttered. Shakily, he daubed circles on his heels, breastbone and forehead. As he finished the one on his forehead, he shut his eyes. The last time he'd done this had been for Fa.

Wolf pressed against him, rubbing his scent into the new leggings. He put his paw on Torak's forearm. *I'm with you.*

Torak bent and nosed his muzzle. *I know.*

'Here,' said Renn, holding out the ravenskin pouch. 'I added more wormwood, and checked with Saeunn. The masking charm should work. The bear won't sense the Nanuak.'

Torak tied the pouch to his belt. Already, he could feel the Death Marks stiffening on his skin.

'You'd better take this, too.' Renn was holding out a little bundle wrapped in birch bast.

'What is it?'

She looked startled. 'What you asked for. What I sat up most of the night making.'

He was appalled. He'd almost forgotten. If he'd left without it, what would have become of his plan?

'I've put in some purifying herbs as well,' said Renn.

'Why?'

'Well. If – if you kill the bear, you'll be unclean. I mean,

217

it's still a bear, still another hunter, even if there is a demon inside. You'll need to purify yourself.'

How like Renn to think ahead. How reassuring that she thought he had a chance.

Wolf gave an impatient whine, and Torak took a deep breath. Time to go.

As they started across the clearing, Torak remembered the medicine horn left behind in the shelter, and ran back for it. As he came out, opening his medicine pouch with trembling fingers, the horn slipped from his grasp.

It was Fin-Kedinn who picked it up.

The Raven Leader was on crutches. As he studied the medicine horn in his hand, the blood drained from his face. 'This was your mother's,' he said.

Torak blinked. 'How did you know?'

Fin-Kedinn was silent. He handed it back. 'Don't ever lose it.'

Torak stowed the horn in his pouch. That seemed an odd thing to say, given where he was headed. As he was turning to go, Fin-Kedinn called him back. 'Torak –'

'Yes?'

'If you survive, there's a place for you here with us. If you want it.'

Torak was too surprised to speak. By the time he'd recovered, the Raven Leader was moving away, his face as unyielding as ever.

The High Mountains were rimmed with gold as Torak crunched through the snow towards the Ravens. Oslak handed him his sleeping-sack and waterskin, Renn his axe, quiver and bow. Surprisingly, Hord helped him on with his pack. He looked haggard, but seemed to have accepted that he wasn't the one who would be seeking the Mountain.

Saeunn made the sign of the hand over Torak, and then over Wolf. 'May the guardian fly with you both.'

'And run with you, too,' said Renn, trying to smile.

Torak gave her a brief nod. He just wanted to be gone.

The Ravens watched in silence as he started through the snow, with Wolf trotting in his tracks.

He did not look back.

丰丰

The Forest was hushed, but as Wolf took the lead, he seemed eager and unafraid. Torak plodded behind him, his breath steaming. It was very cold, but thanks to Vedna, he didn't feel it. While he was sleeping, she'd left the new things in his shelter. An under-jerkin of duckskin with the breast feathers soft against the skin; a hooded parka and leggings of warm winter reindeer hide; hare fur mittens on a thong threaded through the sleeves; and his old boots, deftly patched with tough reindeer shin-hide, lined with pine marten fur, and with bands of dogfish skin sewn to the outer soles to improve the grip.

Vedna had even unpicked his clan skin from his old jerkin, and sewn it to the parka. The band of wolf fur was tattered and filthy, but very precious. It had been prepared by Fa.

Wolf swerved to investigate something, and Torak was instantly alert. A squirrel's tracks: tiny and hand-like. Torak followed the trail as it hopped along between snow-covered juniper bushes, then broke into long, startled leaps and disappeared up a pine tree.

Torak threw back his hood and stared about him.

The Forest was utterly still. Whatever had frightened the squirrel had gone. But Torak was angry with himself. He should have spotted those tracks, too. Stay alert.

A jay followed them from tree to tree as they pushed on. The sun rose in a cloudless sky. Soon Torak was panting as he laboured knee-deep in dazzling new snow. He'd decided against snowshoes: they'd make walking easier, but slow him down if he had to move fast.

Wolf fared better, as his narrow chest cut the snow like a canoe slicing water. By mid-morning, though, even he was tiring. The land was climbing steadily, as Krukoslik had said it would. 'My grandfather once got close to the Mountain,' he'd explained when Torak had woken him in the night. 'So close that he could feel it. From here, you follow the stream north, and the land climbs till you're in the shadow of the High Mountains. Around midday, you reach a lightning-struck spruce at the mouth of a ravine. The ravine is steep: too steep to climb. But there's a trail that clings to its western side – '

'What kind of trail?' Torak had asked. 'Who made it?'

'Nobody knows. Just take it. That lightning tree – it has power to protect. It guards the trail from evil. Maybe it will protect you, too.'

'What then? Where do I go then?'

Krukoslik had spread his hands. 'You follow the trail. Somewhere, at the end of the ravine, lies the Mountain.'

'How far?'

'Nobody knows. My grandfather didn't get far before the Spirit stopped him. The Spirit always stops them. Maybe – maybe you will be different.'

Maybe, thought Torak, trudging through the snow.

If his plan worked – if the World Spirit answered his plea – the bear would be destroyed and the Forest would survive. If not, there would be no second chances. For him or the Forest.

In front of him, Wolf raised his head and sniffed. His hackles were up. What had he sensed?

A few paces on, Torak noticed that the snow had been brushed off the tips of the branches at about shoulder height. Then he found a juniper sapling with several twigs raggedly bitten off. 'Red deer,' he murmured.

A jumble of tracks confirmed it. By the look of them it was a single deer, probably a buck: they don't pick up their feet as high as hinds do, and Torak saw drag marks in the snow.

But if it was only a deer, why were Wolf's hackles up?

Torak looked round. He could feel the Forest holding its breath.

The bear tracks leapt out at him from the snow.

He hadn't seen them before because they were so widely spaced, but now he made out the signs of the buck's panicky leap down the slope below, with the bear tracks racing after it. The length of stride was horrifying.

Struggling for calm, Torak forced himself to study the trail. The bear had been going at a gallop, as the pattern of prints was reversed, with the man-shaped hind tracks in front of the broader front tracks. Each one was three times the size of his own head.

They're fresh, he thought, but the edges are slightly rounding over. Although in this sun that wouldn't take long . . .

Wolf jumped over the tracks, keen to press on.

Torak followed more slowly. Every bush and boulder took on bear form.

As they toiled up the slope, Wolf became more and more excited: bounding ahead, then doubling back for Torak and urging him on with little grunt-whines. Perhaps at last they were nearing the Mountain. Perhaps that was why

Wolf was eager rather than frightened. Torak wished he could share that eagerness, but all he could feel was the weight of the Nanuak at his belt, and the menace of the bear.

A distant roar split the Forest.

The jay gave a squawk and flew away.

Torak gripped the hilt of his knife so hard that it hurt. How close? Where was it? He couldn't tell.

Wolf was waiting for him to catch up: hackles raised, but tail held high. His meaning was clear. *Not yet.*

As Torak waded through the snow, he wondered what had happened to the bear's own souls. After all, as Renn had said, it was still a bear; once it must have hunted salmon and browsed on berries, and slumbered through the winter. Were its souls still inside its body, with the demon? Trapped, terrified?

He rounded a boulder – and there was the lightning-struck spruce.

His spirits quailed.

Above him, the High Mountains swept skywards, blindingly white. The ravine cut through them like a knife-slash. On and on it wound into the Mountains, its end lost in impenetrable cloud. A narrow trail clung to its western side, snaking up from where Torak stood. Who had made the trail? For what purpose? Who would dare set foot on it, and venture into that haunted place?

Suddenly, the clouds at the end of the ravine parted, and Torak saw what lay beyond. Storm clouds writhed about its flanks; a deep, windless cold flowed from its summit; unimaginably high, it pierced the sky: the Mountain of the World Spirit.

Torak shut his eyes, but he could still feel the power of the Spirit forcing him to his knees. He could feel its anger.

The Soul-Eaters had conjured a demon from the Otherworld; they had loosed a monster on the Forest. They had broken the pact. Why should the Spirit help the clans, when some among them had been so wicked?

Torak bowed his head. He couldn't go on. He didn't belong here. This was the haunt of spirits, not of men.

When he opened his eyes, the Mountain was gone, once more shrouded in clouds.

Torak sat back on his heels. I can't do it, he thought. I can't go up there.

Wolf sat in front of him, his tear-shaped eyes as pure as water. *Yes you can. I'm with you.*

Torak shook his head.

Wolf gazed steadily back at him.

Torak thought of Renn and Finn-Kedinn and the Ravens, and of all the other clans that he didn't even know about. He thought of the countless lives in the Forest. He thought of Fa: not Fa as he lay dying in the wreck of their shelter, but Fa as he'd been just before the bear attacked: laughing at the joke Torak had made.

Grief rose in his chest. He drew his knife from its sheath, and slipped off his mitten to lay his hand on the cold blue slate. 'You can't stop now,' he said out loud. 'You swore an oath. To Fa.'

He unslung his quiver and bow and laid them against the tree. Then he did the same with his pack, his sleeping-sack, waterskin and axe. He wouldn't need them; just his knife, the Nanuak in the ravenskin pouch, and Renn's little birch-bast bundle in his medicine pouch.

With a last glance at the Forest, he followed Wolf up the trail.

THIRTY-ONE

As soon as Torak set foot on the trail, the cold grew intense. The breath crackled in his nostrils. His eyelashes stuck together. The Spirit was warning him back.

The ice under his boots was brittle, and each step rang out across the ravine. Wolf's soft paws made no sound. He turned and waited for Torak to catch up: his muzzle relaxed, his tail wagging faintly. It was as if he was glad to be here.

Panting, Torak drew level with him. The trail was so narrow that they only just had room to stand side by side. Torak glanced down – and wished he hadn't. Already, the bottom of the ravine was far below.

They climbed higher. The sun cleared the other side of the ravine, and the glare became blinding. The ice turned treacherous. When Torak stepped too close to the edge of the trail, the ice crumbled, and he nearly went over.

About forty paces ahead, the trail widened slightly beneath a rocky overhang. It was too shallow to make a cave: merely a hollow where the black basalt of the ravine's side showed through. At the sight of it, Torak's spirits lifted. He'd been hoping for some kind of shelter. He would need it if his plan –

Beside him, Wolf tensed.

He was looking down into the ravine, his ears forwards, every hair on his back standing up.

Shading his eyes, Torak peered over the edge. Nothing. Black tree-trunks. Snow-covered boulders. Puzzled, he turned to go – and the bear appeared suddenly, as bears do. First a movement at the bottom of the ravine – then there it was.

Even from this distance – fifty, sixty paces below him – it was enormous. As Torak stood rooted to the spot, it swayed from side to side, casting for a scent.

It didn't find one. Torak was too high up. The bear didn't know he was here. He watched it turn and move off down the ravine, towards the Forest.

Now he had to do the unthinkable. He had to lure it back.

There was only one sure way of doing that. He slipped off his mittens and blew on his fingers to warm them; then he unfastened the ravenskin pouch from his belt. Untying the hair cord that bound it, he opened the rowan-bark box, and the Nanuak stared up at him. The river eyes, the stone tooth, the lamp.

Wolf gave a low grunt-whine.

Torak licked his cold-cracked lips. From his medicine pouch, he took Renn's little birch-bast bundle. He stuffed the purifying herbs and birch-bast wrapping into the neck of his parka, and looked down at what Renn had made for him in the night. A small pouch of knotted wovengrass: the mesh so fine that it would hold even the river eyes, but let the light of the Nanuak shine out; the light that Torak couldn't see, but the bear could.

Taking care not to touch the Nanuak with his bare hands, he tipped the lamp, the stone tooth and the river eyes into the wovengrass pouch. Then he drew it shut, and looped its long drawstring over his head. He was wearing the Nanuak unmasked on his chest.

Wolf's eyes threw back a faint, shimmering gold light: the light of the Nanuak. If Wolf could see it, so could the demon. Torak was counting on it.

He turned to face the bear. It was some distance down the ravine, moving effortlessly through the snow.

'Here it is,' said Torak, keeping his voice low so as not to anger the World Spirit. 'This is what you're after: the brightest of those bright souls that you hate so much – that you long to snuff out for ever. Come for it now.'

The bear halted. A ripple ran through its massive shoulder-hump. The great head swung round. The bear turned and began moving back towards Torak.

A fierce exultation surged through him. This monster had killed Fa. Ever since then, he'd been on the run. Now he wasn't running any more. He was fighting back.

It was faster than Torak expected; soon it was beneath him. Man-fashion, it rose on its hind legs. Although Torak stood fifty paces above, he saw it as clearly as if he could reach out and touch it.

It raised its head and met his eyes – and he forgot about the Spirit, he forgot about his oath to Fa. He was not standing on an icy mountain trail, he was back in the Forest. From the ruined shelter came Fa's wild cry. *Torak! Run!*

He couldn't move. He wanted to run – to race up the trail to the overhang, as he knew he must – but he could not. The demon was draining his will – pulling him down, down . . .

Wolf snarled.

Torak tore himself free and staggered up the trail. Staring into those eyes had been like staring at the sun: their green-edged image stayed stamped on his mind.

He heard the cracking of ice as the bear began to claw its way up the side of the ravine. He pictured it climbing with lethal ease. He had to reach the overhang, or he wouldn't stand a chance.

Wolf loped up the trail. Torak slipped and went down on one knee. Struggled to his feet. Glanced over the edge. The bear had climbed a third of the way.

He ran on. He reached the overhang and threw himself into the rocky hollow, bent double, fighting for breath. Now for the rest of his plan: now to call on the Spirit for help.

Forcing himself upright, he filled his chest with air, put back his head and *howled*.

Wolf took up the howl, and their piercing cries buffeted the ravine – back and forth, back and forth through the Mountains. *World Spirit,* howled Torak, *I bring you the Nanuak! Hear me! Send your power to crush the demon from the Forest!*

Below him, he heard the bear getting closer . . . ice clattering into the ravine.

On and on he howled until his ribs ached. *World Spirit, hear my plea . . .*

Nothing happened.

Torak stopped howling. Horror washed over him. The World Spirit had not answered his plea. The bear was coming for him . . .

Suddenly he realised that Wolf, too, had stopped howling.

Look behind you, Torak.

He turned to see Hord's axe swinging towards him.

THIRTY-TWO

Torak dodged, and the axe hissed past his ear, splintering the ice where he'd been standing.

Hord wrenched it free. 'Give me the Nanuak!' he cried. '*I have to take it to the Mountain!*'

'Get away from me!' said Torak.

From the edge of the ravine came a grinding of ice. The bear was nearing the top.

Hord's haggard face twisted in pain. Torak could barely imagine how he'd brought himself to track them through the demon-haunted Forest; to brave the wrath of the Spirit by venturing up the trail. '*Give me the Nanuak,*' repeated Hord.

Wolf advanced on him, his whole body a shuddering snarl. He was no longer a cub; he was a ferocious young wolf defending his pack-brother.

Hord ignored him. 'I *will* have it! It's my fault this is happening! *I* have to make it end!'

Suddenly, Torak understood. 'It was you,' he said. 'You were there when the bear was made. You were with the Red Deer Clan. You helped the crippled Soul-Eater trap the demon.'

'I didn't *know*!' protested Hord. 'He said he needed a bear – I caught a young one. I never knew what he meant to do!'

Then several things happened at once. Hord swung his axe at Torak's throat. Torak ducked. Wolf sprang at Hord, sinking his teeth into his wrist. Hord bellowed and dropped his axe, but with his free fist rained blows on Wolf's unprotected head.

'No!' yelled Torak, drawing his knife and launching himself at Hord. Hord seized Wolf by the scruff and threw him against the basalt, then twisted round and lunged for the Nanuak swinging from Torak's neck.

Torak jerked out of reach. Hord went for his legs, throwing him backwards onto the ice. But as Torak went down, he tore the pouch from his neck and hurled it up the trail, out of Hord's reach. Wolf righted himself with a shake and leapt for the pouch, catching it in mid-air, but landing perilously close to the edge of the ravine.

'Wolf!' cried Torak, struggling beneath Hord, who was straddling his chest, and kneeling on his arms.

Wolf's hind paws scrabbled wildly at the edge. From just below him came a menacing growl – then the bear's black claws sliced the air, narrowly missing Wolf's paws . . .

Wolf gave a tremendous heave and regained the trail. But then, for the first time ever, he decided to *return* something Torak had thrown, and bounded towards him with the Nanuak in his jaws.

Hord strained to reach the pouch. Torak wrested one hand free and dragged his arm away. If only his knife-arm wasn't pinned under Hord's knee . . .

An unearthly roar shook the ravine. In horror, Torak watched the bear rise above the edge of the trail.

And in that final moment, as the bear towered above them, as Wolf paused with the Nanuak in his jaws – in that final moment as Torak struggled with Hord, the true meaning of the Prophecy broke upon him. *'The Listener gives his heart's blood to the Mountain.'*

His heart's blood.

Wolf.

No! he cried inside his head.

But he knew what he had to do. Out loud he shouted to Wolf, 'Take it to the Mountain! Uff! Uff! Uff!'

Wolf's golden gaze met his.

'Uff!' gasped Torak. His eyes stung.

Wolf turned and raced up the trail towards the Mountain.

Hord snarled with fury and staggered after him – but he slipped and toppled backwards, screaming, into the arms of the bear.

Torak scrambled to his feet. Hord was still screaming. Torak had to help him . . .

From high above came a deafening crack.

The trail shook. Torak was thrown to his knees.

The crack swelled to a grinding roar. He threw himself beneath the overhang – and an instant later, down came the rushing, rampaging, killing snow, obliterating Hord, obliterating the bear – sending them howling down into death.

The World Spirit had heard Torak's plea.

The last thing Torak saw was Wolf, the Nanuak still in his jaws, racing under the thundering snow towards the Mountain. *'Wolf!'* he shouted. Then the whole world turned white.

Torak never knew how long he crouched against the rockface, with his eyes tight shut.

At last he became aware that the thundering had turned to echoes – and that the echoes were getting fainter. The World Spirit was striding away into the Mountains.

The sound of its footsteps faded to a hiss of settling snow . . .

Then a whisper . . .

Then – silence.

Torak opened his eyes.

He could see out across the ravine. He was not buried alive. The World Spirit had passed over the overhang, and let him live. But where was Wolf?

He got to his feet and stumbled to the edge of the trail. The dead cold had gone. He saw the Mountains through a haze of settling snow. Below him, the ravine had disappeared under a chaos of ice and rock. Buried beneath it lay Hord and the bear.

Hord had paid with his life. The bear was an empty husk, for the Spirit had banished the demon to the Otherworld. Perhaps the bear's own souls would now be at peace, after their long imprisonment with the demon.

Torak had fulfilled his oath to Fa. He had given the Nanuak to the World Spirit – and the Spirit had destroyed the bear.

He knew that, but he couldn't feel it. All he could feel was the ache in his chest. Where was Wolf? Had he reached the Mountain before the snow came down? Or did he too lie buried under the ice?

'*Please* be alive,' murmured Torak. 'Please. I'll never ask anything again.'

A breeze lifted his hair, but brought no answer.

A young crow flew over the Mountains, cawing and sky-dancing with the joy of flight. From the east came a thunder of hooves. Torak knew what that meant. It meant that the reindeer were coming down from the fells. The Forest was returning to life.

Turning, he saw that the way to the south remained open; he would be able to find his way back to Renn and Fin-Kedinn and the Ravens.

Then from the north – beyond the torrent of ice that blocked the trail, behind the clouds that hid the Mountain of the World Spirit – a wolf howled.

It was not the high, wobbly yowl of a cub, but the pure, heart-wrenching song of a young wolf. And yet it was still unmistakeably Wolf.

The pain in Torak's chest broke loose and lifted free.

As he listened to the music of Wolf's song, more wolf-voices joined it: weaving in and out, but never drowning that one clear, well-loved voice. Wolf was not alone.

Torak's eyes blurred with tears. He understood. Wolf was howling a farewell. He wasn't coming back.

The howling ceased. Torak bowed his head. 'But he's alive,' he said out loud. 'That's what matters. He is alive.'

He longed to howl a reply: to tell Wolf that it was not for ever; that one day, he would find some way for them to be together. But he couldn't think how to say it, because in wolf talk there is no future.

Instead, he said it in his own speech. He knew that Wolf wouldn't understand, but he also knew that he was making the promise to himself as much as to Wolf.

'Some day,' he called, and his voice rang through the radiant air, 'some day we will be together. We will hunt together in the Forest. Together–' his voice broke. 'I *promise*. My brother, the wolf.'

No answer came back. But Torak had not expected one. He had made his promise.

He stooped for a handful of snow to cool his burning face. It felt good. He scooped up some more, and rubbed the Death Mark from his forehead.

Then he turned and started back towards the Forest.

SPIRIT WALKER

THE FOREST →

CRAG
↓
THE
ROCK

THE SEAL ISLANDS

ONE

The auroch appeared quite suddenly from the trees on the other side of the stream.

One moment Torak was gazing at sun-dappled willows – the next, there she was. She stood taller than the tallest man, and her great curving horns could have skewered a bear. If she charged, he was in trouble.

By bad luck, he was upwind of her. He held his breath as he watched her twitch her blunt black muzzle to taste his scent. She snorted. Pawed the earth with one massive hoof.

Then he saw the calf peering from the bracken, and his belly turned over. Aurochs are gentle creatures – *except* when they have calves.

Without a sound, Torak drew back into the shade. If he didn't startle her, maybe she wouldn't charge.

Again the auroch snorted, and raked the ferns with her horns. At last she seemed to decide that he wasn't hunting her after all, and slumped down in the mud to have a wallow.

Torak blew out a long breath.

The calf wobbled towards its mother, slipped, bleated, and fell over. The cow auroch raised her head and nosed it to its feet, then lay back to enjoy herself.

Crouching behind a juniper bush, Torak wondered what to do. Fin-Kedinn, the Clan Leader, had sent him to retrieve a bundle of willow bark that had been soaking in the stream; he didn't want to return to camp without it. Neither did he want to get trampled by an auroch.

He decided to wait for her to leave.

It was a hot day at the beginning of the Moon of No Dark, and the Forest was drowsy with sun. The trees echoed with birdsong; a warm south-easterly breeze carried the sweetness of lime blossom. After a while, Torak's heartbeats slowed. He heard a clutch of young greenfinches squealing for food in a hazel thicket. He watched a viper basking on a rock. He tried to fix his thoughts on that, but as so often happened, they drifted to Wolf.

Wolf would be nearly full-grown by now, but he'd been a cub when Torak had known him: falling over his paws, and pestering Torak for lingonberries . . .

Don't think about Wolf, Torak told himself fiercely. He's gone. He's never coming back, never. Think about the auroch, or the viper, or –

That was when he saw the hunter.

He was on this side of the water, twenty paces downstream, but downwind of the auroch. The shade was too deep to make out his face, but Torak saw that like him, he wore a sleeveless buckskin jerkin and knee-length leggings, with light rawhide boots. Unlike Torak, he wore a boar tusk on a thong around his neck. Boar Clan.

Ordinarily, Torak would have been reassured. The Boars

were fairly friendly with the Raven Clan, with whom he'd been living for the past six moons. But there was something very wrong about this hunter. He moved with an awkward, lurching gait, his head lolling from side to side. *And he was stalking the auroch.* Two slate throwing-axes were stuck in his belt – and as Torak watched in disbelief, he pulled one out and hefted it in his hand.

Was he mad? No man hunts an auroch on his own. An auroch is the biggest, strongest prey in the Forest. To attack one on your own is asking to be killed.

The auroch, happily unaware, grunted and rubbed deeper into the mud, relishing the relief from the troublesome midges. Her calf nosed a clump of willowherb, waiting for her to finish.

Torak rose to his feet and warned the hunter with urgent slicing motions of his palm: *Danger! Go back!*

The hunter didn't see him. Flexing his brawny arm, he took aim – and hurled the axe.

It whistled through the air and thudded into the ground a hand's breadth from the calf.

The calf fled. Its mother gave an outraged bellow and lumbered to her feet, casting about for the attacker. But the hunter was still downwind; she didn't catch his scent.

Incredibly, he was reaching for his second axe.

'*No!*' Torak whispered hoarsely. 'You'll only hurt her and get us both killed!'

The hunter wrenched the axe from his belt.

Torak thought swiftly. If the axe found its mark, the auroch would be unstoppable. But if she was startled instead of wounded, maybe she would merely make a mock charge, and flee with her calf. He had to get her out of range of that axe, fast.

Taking a deep breath, he jumped up and down, waving

241

his arms and yelling 'Over here! Over here!'

It worked – in a way. The auroch gave a furious bellow and charged at Torak – and the axe hit the mud where she'd stood a heartbeat before. As she splashed towards Torak, he threw himself behind an oak tree.

No time to climb it – she was almost upon him. He heard her grunt as she heaved herself up the bank – he felt her heat on the other side of the tree-trunk . . .

At the last moment she swerved, flicking up her tail and blundering off into the Forest, her calf galloping after her.

The silence when she'd gone was deafening.

Sweat poured down Torak's face as he leaned against the oak.

The hunter stood with his head down, rocking from side to side.

'What were you *doing?*' panted Torak. 'We could've been killed!'

The hunter did not reply. Lurching across the stream, he retrieved his axes and stuck them in his belt, then shambled back again. Torak still couldn't see his face, but he took in the hunter's muscled limbs and jagged slate knife. If it came to a fight, he'd lose. He was just a boy, not even thirteen summers old.

Suddenly the hunter stumbled against a beech tree and began to retch.

Torak forgot his alarm and ran to help him.

The hunter was on hands and knees, spewing up yellow slime. His back arched – he gave a convulsive heave – and spat out something slippery and dark, the size of a child's fist. It looked – it looked like *hair*.

A gust of wind stirred the branches, and in a shaft of sunlight Torak saw him clearly for the first time.

The sick man had yanked handfuls of hair from his scalp

and beard, leaving patches of raw, oozing flesh. His face was crusted with thick honey-coloured scabs like birch canker. Slime bubbled in his throat as he spat out the last of the hair – then sat back on his heels, and began scratching a rash of blisters on his forearm.

Torak edged backwards, his hand moving to his clan-creature skin: the strip of wolf fur sewn to his jerkin. What *was* this?

Renn would know. 'Fevers,' she'd once told him, 'are most common around Midsummer, because that's when the worms of sickness have longest to work: creeping out of the swamps during the white nights when the sun never sleeps.' But if this was a fever, it was unlike any Torak had ever seen.

He wondered what he could do. All he had was some coltsfoot in his medicine pouch. 'Let me help you,' he said shakily, 'I have some . . . Ah no, stop! You're hurting yourself!'

The man was still scratching, baring his teeth as people do when the itching is so unbearable that they'd rather turn it into outright pain. All at once, he dug in his fingernails and savaged the blisters, leaving a swathe of bloody flesh.

'Don't!' cried Torak.

With a snarl the man sprang at him, pinning him down.

Torak stared up into a mass of crusted sores, into two dull eyes filmed with pus. 'Don't – hurt me!' he gasped. 'My name – is Torak! I'm – Wolf Clan, I –'

The man leaned closer. '*It – is– coming,*' he hissed in a blast of putrid breath.

Torak tried to swallow. 'What – is?'

The cankered face twisted in terror. 'Can't you see?' he whispered, flecking Torak with yellow spit. '*It is coming!* It will take us all!'

He staggered to his feet, swaying and squinting at the sun. Then he crashed through the trees as if all the demons of the Otherworld were after him.

Torak raised himself on one elbow, breathing hard.

The birds had fallen silent.

The Forest looked on, appalled.

Slowly, Torak stood up. He felt the wind veering round to the east, turning chill. A shiver ran through the trees. They began to murmur to one another. Torak wished he knew what they were saying. But he knew what they were feeling, because he felt it too: something rising and blowing through the Forest.

It is coming.

Sickness.

Torak ran to fetch his quiver and bow. No time to retrieve the willow bark. He had to get back to camp, and warn the Ravens.

TWO

'Where's Fin-Kedinn?' cried Torak when he reached the Raven camp.

'In the next valley,' said a man gutting salmon, 'gathering dogwood for arrowshafts.'

'What about Saeunn? Where's the Mage?'

'Casting the bones,' said a girl threading fish-heads on sinew. 'She's on the Rock, you'd better wait till she comes down.'

Torak ground his teeth in frustration. There was the Raven Mage perched high on the Guardian Rock: a small, bird-like figure scowling at the bones, while beside her the clan guardian folded its stiff black wings and uttered a harsh 'cark!'

Who else could he tell?

Renn was out hunting. Oslak, whose shelter he shared, was nowhere in sight. By the smoking-racks he spotted

Sialot and Poi, the Raven boys closest to him in age – but they were the last ones he'd approach; they didn't like him because he was an outsider. Everyone else was too busy getting in the salmon to listen to some wild tale about a sick man in the Forest. And as Torak looked about, he almost began to doubt it himself. Everything seemed so normal.

The Ravens had built their camp where the Widewater crashes out of a shadowy gorge and thunders past the Rock, then over the rapids. It was up these rapids that the salmon fought their way each summer on their mysterious journey from the Sea to the Mountains. Always they were driven back by the fury of the river, and always they tried again, hurtling through the foaming chaos in twisting, shining leaps – until they died of exhaustion, or reached the calmer waters beyond the gorge, or were speared by the Ravens.

To catch them, the clan sank poles in the riverbed, and spanned the Widewater with a wicker walkway just strong enough to support a few fishermen with spears. It was skilled work, and anyone falling in risked crippling injury or worse, for the river was relentless, and the rocks jutting from the rapids as sharp as broken teeth. But the prize was great.

The Ravens' shelters stood empty; everybody was at the smoking-racks, getting in the day's haul before it spoiled. Men, women and children scraped off scales and gutted fish, while others sliced strips of orange flesh from the bones, leaving them joined at the tail for easy hanging on the racks. Sialot and Poi pounded juniper berries, which would be mixed with the dried, shredded meat to keep it sweet – or mask its taste if it was not.

Nothing was wasted. The skins would be cured and fashioned into waterproof tinder pouches; the eyes and bones would make glue; the livers and roe would provide a delicacy at nightmeal, and an offering for the guardian and the spirits of the salmon.

Elsewhere in the Forest, other clans camped by other rivers to take part in the bounty. Boar Clan, Willow, Otter, Viper. And where the people did not camp, other hunters came: bears, lynx, eagles, wolves. All celebrating the running of the salmon, which gave them new strength after the rigours of winter.

This was how it had always been since the Beginning. Surely, thought Torak, one sick man couldn't change all that.

Then he remembered the cankered face and the pus-filmed eyes.

At that moment, Oslak emerged from their shelter, and Torak's heart leapt. Oslak would know what to do.

But to his astonishment, Oslak hardly listened as he blurted out his story, seeming more engrossed in re-tying the binding on his fishing spear. 'You say the man was Boar Clan,' he said, frowning and scratching the back of his hand. 'Well then, his Mage will take care of him. Here.' He tossed Torak the spear. 'Get down to the stepping stones and let me see you take a salmon.'

Torak was bewildered. 'But Oslak –'

'Go on, go!' snapped Oslak.

Torak gave a start. It was unlike Oslak to get cross. In fact, it never happened. He was a huge, gentle man with a tangled beard and a slightly alarming face, having lost one ear and a chunk of cheek in a misunderstanding with a wolverine. It was just like him not to blame the wolverine. 'My fault,' he'd say if anyone asked. 'I gave her a fright.'

That was Oslak. He and his mate Vedna had been the first to offer Torak a place in their shelter when he came to live with the Ravens, and they'd always been kind to him. But Oslak was also the strongest man in the clan, so Torak made no further protest, and took the spear.

As he did, he saw something that stopped him dead. The back of Oslak's hand was covered in blisters.

'What's – that on your hand?' he said.

'Midge bites,' said Oslak, scratching harder. 'Worst I've ever had. Kept me awake all night.'

'They don't look like midge bites,' said Torak. 'Do they – hurt?'

Oslak was still scratching. 'Strange. Feels as if my name-soul's leaking out. But that can't be, can it?' He peered at Torak as if the light hurt, and his face was fearful and childlike.

Torak swallowed. 'I don't think you can lose your name-soul through a cut; only through your mouth, if you're dreaming, or – sick.' He paused. 'Are you sick?'

'Sick? Why would I be sick?' A shiver shook his whole body. 'But I can't hold onto my souls.'

Torak's hand tightened on the spear. 'I'll fetch Saeunn.'

Oslak scowled. 'I don't need Saeunn! Now go!' Suddenly he wasn't Oslak any more. He was a big man looming over Torak, clenching his fists.

Then he seemed to come to himself. 'Just – leave me be, eh? Go on. Thull's waiting.'

'All right, Oslak,' said Torak as levelly as he could.

He was halfway to the river's edge when he turned and looked back.

Oslak was still scratching. 'Leaking *out*,' he muttered. Then he went inside the shelter – and Torak saw the raw patch behind his remaining ear where the hair had been yanked out; the thick honey-coloured scab, like birch canker.

Torak felt a coldness settle inside him.

He raced down to the stepping stones, where Oslak's younger brother squatted to clean his knife. 'Thull!' he cried. 'I think Oslak's sick!'

His tale came out in a breathless jumble, and Thull wasn't impressed. 'Torak, those are midge bites. It happens every summer, they drive him mad.'

'It isn't midges,' said Torak.

'Well, he's fine now,' said Thull, pointing at the walkway.

Sure enough, there was Oslak, crouching with a spear – and on the end of it, a wriggling salmon.

Biting his lip, Torak glanced about. It all seemed so *normal*. Children played with glittering handfuls of fish-scales. Reckless young ravens teased the dogs by pecking their tails. Thull's son Dari, five summers old, splashed in the shallows with the pine-cone auroch which Oslak had made for him.

Filled with misgiving, Torak clutched his spear and waded in.

The stepping stones were four boulders between the walkway and the rapids where beginners learned to keep their balance. Thull pointed to the first stone, but Torak made his way precariously to the fourth, placing himself midriver, and downstream from Oslak. He didn't know what he expected; only that he had to keep watch.

'Keep your eyes on the salmon,' shouted Thull from the bank, 'not on the water!'

Torak found that impossible. The rocks were slippery with lichen, and around him the green water boiled, with now and then a silver flash of salmon. The fishing spear was long and heavy, making it hard to balance. It had two barbed antler prongs for gripping and holding the fish – *if* Torak caught any, which he hadn't in all previous attempts.

When he'd lived with his father, he'd only fished with a hook and line. With a spear, as Sialot never tired of remarking, he was as clumsy as a child of seven summers.

He forced himself to concentrate. Stabbed with his spear. Missed. Nearly toppled in.

'Let them get *past* you before taking aim!' yelled Thull. 'Catch them on their way down, when they're tired!'

Torak tried again. Again he missed.

From the smoking-racks came a hoot of laughter. Torak's face flamed. Sialot was enjoying this.

'Better!' called Thull with more kindness than truth. 'Keep at it! I'll come back later.' He went off to feed the fires, leaving Dari in the shallows, crooning to his auroch.

For a while Torak forgot everything as he strove to catch a fish without either dropping the spear or falling in. Soon he was soaked in spray. And the river was *angry*. Every so often it hurled a huge wave against his rock.

Suddenly he heard a shout from the walkway. He jerked up his head – then breathed out in relief.

Oslak had speared another salmon. With one blow he killed it, then knelt to pull it off the spear.

He's all right, Torak told himself.

As he watched, Oslak scratched his hand. Then he reached behind his ear and clawed at the scab.

The salmon slithered off the walkway. Oslak bared his teeth, wrenched off the scab – and ate it.

Torak recoiled and nearly fell in.

The sun went behind a cloud. The water turned black. The discarded salmon slid past, glaring at him with a dull dead eye.

He shot a glance at the shallows.

Dari was gone.

Another cry from upriver.

He turned.

Dari was on the walkway, tottering towards his uncle – who wasn't warning him back, but *beckoning*.

'Come to me, Dari!' he shouted, his face distorted by a horrible eagerness. 'Come to me! I won't let them take our souls!'

THREE

On the banks, none of the Ravens had seen what was happening. Torak had to do something.

As he stood on the stepping stone gripping his spear, he saw two people emerge from different parts of the Forest.

From the east came Renn, her beloved bow in one hand, a brace of woodpigeons in the other.

From downriver came Fin-Kedinn, limping slightly and leaning on his staff, with a bundle of dogwood sticks over one shoulder.

In a heartbeat both grasped what was happening, and quietly set down their loads.

To stop Oslak noticing them, Torak called out to him. 'Oslak, what's wrong? Tell me. Maybe I can help.'

'Nobody can *help*!' shouted Oslak. 'My souls are leaking out! Being *eaten*!'

Now people turned to stare. Dari's mother leapt forward with a cry. Thull held her back. Oslak's mate Vedna jammed her knuckles in her mouth. On the Rock, Saeunn stood motionless.

Renn had reached the walkway – but despite his limp, Fin-Kedinn was there before her. Silently he handed her his staff.

'Who's eating your souls?' Torak called to Oslak.

'The *fish*!' Yellow froth flew from Oslak's lips. '*Teeth*! Sharp teeth!' He pointed to where the thrashing salmon endlessly broke and re-made his name-soul.

Torak felt a twinge of fear. That happened to everyone's name-soul if you leaned over the river, and it didn't do any harm – *unless* you were sick, when it could make you so dizzy that you fell in.

'Soon it will be gone,' moaned Oslak, 'and I will be nothing but a ghost! Come, Dari! The river wants us!'

The child hesitated – then moved towards him, clutching the pine-cone auroch to his chest.

Torak risked a glance at Fin-Kedinn.

The Raven Leader's face was still as carved sandstone. Putting a forefinger to his lips, he caught Torak's eye. *You're between them and the rapids. Catch them.*

Torak nodded, bracing himself on the rock. His feet were numb with cold. His arms were beginning to shake.

At last Dari reached Oslak, who tossed away his spear and snatched him up. The wicker sagged dangerously.

'Oslak,' called Fin-Kedinn. His voice was low, but somehow he made himself heard above the rapids. 'Come back to the bank.'

'Get *away*!' screamed Oslak.

Torak saw to his horror that Oslak had tied a wovenbark rope to the poles supporting the end of the walkway: one hard pull, and the whole structure would go crashing down, taking him and Dari with it.

Torak couldn't bear it. 'Oslak, this is me, Torak! Don't . . . '

Oslak turned on him. 'Who are you to tell me what to do? You're not one of us! You're a cuckoo! Eating our food, taking our shelter! I've heard you sneaking into the Forest to howl for your wolf! We've all heard you! Why don't you give up? He's never coming back!'

Renn flinched in sympathy, but Torak didn't move. He'd seen what Oslak had not: Fin-Kedinn limping onto the walkway.

At that moment Oslak swayed, and the wicker rocked.

Dari's mouth went square, and he began to howl.

Fin-Kedinn stood firm. 'Oslak,' he called.

Oslak lurched backwards. 'Stay *away*!'

Fin-Kedinn raised his hands to reassure him that he wasn't coming any closer. Then, as the clan watched in taut silence, he sat cross-legged on the wicker. He was six paces from the bank, and if Oslak pulled the rope, the walkway would collapse; but he looked as calm as if he were sitting by the fire. 'Oslak,' he said. 'The clan chose me for Leader to keep it safe. You know that.'

Oslak licked his lips.

'And I will,' said Fin-Kedinn. 'I will keep you safe. But put Dari down. Let him come to me. Let me take him to his mother.'

Oslak's face went slack.

'Put him down,' repeated Fin-Kedinn. 'It's time for his nightmeal . . . '

The power of his voice began to work. Slowly Oslak unwound the boy's arms from his neck and lowered him onto the wicker.

Dari gazed up at him as if seeking permission, then

turned and crawled towards Fin-Kedinn.

Fin-Kedinn shifted onto one knee and reached for him.

The pine-cone auroch slipped from Dari's fist and into the water. With a squeal Dari grabbed for it. Fin-Kedinn caught him by the jerkin and swept him into his arms.

On the bank, the Ravens breathed out.

Torak's knees sagged. He watched the Raven Leader rise and edge sideways towards the bank. When he drew near, Thull grabbed Dari and held him tight.

On the walkway, Oslak stood like a stunned auroch. The rope slipped from his hand as he gazed at the churning water. Silently Fin-Kedinn went back for him and took him by the shoulders, speaking in words no-one else could hear.

Oslak's body slumped, and he let Fin-Kedinn lead him to the bank – where men seized him and forced him down. He seemed puzzled, as if unsure how he'd got there.

Torak found his way to the shallows, dropped his spear in the sand, and began to shake.

'Are you all right?' said Renn. Her dark-red hair was wet with spray, her face so pale that her clan-tattoos were three dark stripes on her cheeks.

He nodded. But he knew she wasn't fooled.

Further up the bank, Fin-Kedinn was speaking to Saeunn, who'd climbed down from the Rock. 'What's wrong with him?' he said as the clan gathered around them.

The Raven Mage shook her head. 'His souls are fighting within him.'

'So it's some kind of madness,' said Fin-Kedinn.

'Maybe,' replied Saeunn. 'But not a kind I've ever seen.'

'I have,' said Torak. Quickly he told them about the Boar Clan hunter.

As the Mage listened, her face grew grim. She was the oldest in the clan by many winters. Age had blasted her,

255

polishing her scalp to the colour of old bone, sharpening her features to something more raven than woman. 'I saw it in the bones,' she rasped. 'A message. "It is coming."'

'There's something else,' said Renn. 'When I was hunting, I met a party of Willow Clan. One of them was sick. Sores. Madness. Terrible fear.' Her eyes were dark as peat pools as she turned to Saeunn. 'The Willow Clan Mage sends you word. He too has been reading the bones, and for three days they've told him one thing, over and over. "It is coming."'

People made the sign of the hand to ward off evil. Others touched their clan-creature skins: the strips of glossy black feathers sewn to their jerkins.

Etan, an eager young hunter, stepped forwards, his face perplexed. 'I left Bera on the hill, checking the deadfalls. She had blisters on her hands. Like Oslak's. I did wrong to leave her, didn't I?'

Fin-Kedinn shook his head. His face was unreadable as he stroked his dark-red beard, but Torak sensed that his thoughts were racing.

Swiftly the Raven Leader gave orders. 'Thull, Etan. Get some men and build a shelter in the lime wood, out of sight of camp. Take Oslak there and keep him under guard. Vedna, you're not to go near him. I'm sorry, but there's no other way.' He turned to Saeunn, and his blue eyes blazed. 'Middle-night. A healing rite. Find out what's causing this.'

FOUR

The Mage's apprentice took an auroch-horn ladle and scooped hot ash from the fire. She poured it, still smoking, into her naked palm.

Torak gasped.

The apprentice didn't even wince.

At her feet Oslak clawed the dust, but the bindings held fast. He was strapped to a horse-hide litter, awaiting the final charm. Bera had already undergone it, and was back in the sickness shelter: screaming, sicker than ever.

The Raven Mage and her apprentice had tried everything. The Mage had daubed the sick ones' tongues with earthblood to draw out the madness. She had tied fish-hooks to her fingers and gone into a trance to snare their drifting souls. She'd shrouded them in juniper smoke to chase away the worms of sickness. Nothing had worked.

Now a hush fell on the Ravens as she prepared for the final charm. Firelight flickered on their anxious faces.

It was a hot, clear night, with a gibbous moon riding high above the Forest. The wind had dropped, but the air was full of noises. The creak of the smoking-racks. The caws of the ravens in the gorge. The roar of the rapids.

The Mage stepped towards the litter, her bony arms reaching to the moon. In one hand she gripped her amulet; in the other, a red flint arrow.

Torak darted a glance at the Mage's apprentice, but her face was a blank mask of river clay. She didn't look like Renn any more.

'*Fire to cleanse the name-soul,*' chanted Saeunn, circling the litter.

Renn squatted beside Oslak and trickled hot ash onto his naked feet. He moaned, and bit his lips till they bled.

'*Fire to cleanse the clan-soul . . .*'

Renn poured ash over his heart.

'*Fire to cleanse the world-soul.*'

Renn smeared ash on his forehead.

'*Burn, sickness, burn . . .*'

Oslak screamed with fury, and spattered the Mage with bloody foam.

A ripple of dismay ran through the clan. The charm wasn't working.

Torak held his breath. Behind him the Forest stilled. Even the alders had ceased their fluttering to await the outcome.

He watched Saeunn touch the arrow to Oslak's chest, tracing a spiral. '*Come, sickness,*' she croaked. '*Out of the marrow – into the bone. Out of the bone – into the flesh . . .*'

Suddenly Torak clutched his belly in pain. As the Mage chanted the words, something sharp had twisted inside him.

Slowly she drew the spiral over Oslak's heart. '*Out of the flesh – into the skin. Out of the skin – into the arrow . . . '*

Again that pain, as if her words were tugging at his insides . . . Is this the sickness? he thought. Is this how it starts?

A firm hand gripped his shoulder. Fin-Kedinn stood beside him, watching the Mage.

'Out of the arrow –' cried Saeunn, rising to her feet *'– and into the fire!'* She plunged the arrow into the embers.

Green flames shot skywards.

Oslak screamed.

The Ravens hissed.

Saeunn's arms dropped to her sides.

The spell had failed.

Torak clutched his belly and fought waves of blackness.

Suddenly, a dark shape flew into the firelight. It was the clan guardian, heading straight for him. He tried to duck, but Fin-Kedinn held him steady. Just in time, the raven swerved. It was angry: its clan was under attack. Torak had no idea why it had flown at him.

He tried to catch Renn's eye, but she was kneeling by Oslak, peering at the marks he'd clawed in the dust.

Twisting out of Fin-Kedinn's grip, Torak ran – between the watchers, out of the camp, and into the Forest.

He reached a moonlit glade and collapsed against an ash tree. The giddiness came again. He doubled up and began to retch.

An owl hooted.

Torak raised his head and stared at the cold stars glinting through the black leaves of the ash tree. He slid to the ground with his head in his hands.

The dizziness had subsided, but he was still shaking. He felt frightened and alone. He couldn't even tell Renn about this. She was his friend, but she was also the Mage's apprentice. She mustn't know. No-one must know. If he was sick, he'd rather die alone in the Forest than strapped to a litter.

Then a terrible suspicion took hold of him. *They are eating my souls*, Oslak had said. Was that the rambling of a madman, or did it hide a kernel of truth?

Shutting his eyes, he tried to lose himself in the night sounds. The warble of a blackbird. The wheezy cries of the fledgling robins in the undergrowth.

All his life, Torak had roamed the hills and valleys with his father, keeping separate from the clans. The creatures of the Forest had been his companions. He hadn't missed people. It was hard, living with the Ravens. So many faces. So little time alone. He didn't belong. Their ways were too different from how he'd lived with Fa.

And he missed Wolf so much.

It had been after Fa was killed that he'd found the cub. For two moons they'd hunted together in the Forest, and faced terrible dangers. At times Wolf had been like any other cub, getting in the way, and poking his muzzle into everything. At others he was the guide, with a mysterious certainty in his amber eyes. But always he was a pack-brother. Being without him hurt.

Often, Torak had thought about going in search of him; but deep down he knew he'd never find the Mountain again. As Renn had said with her usual bluntness, 'Last winter was different. But now? No, Torak, I don't think so.'

'I know that,' he'd replied, 'but if I keep howling, maybe Wolf will find me.'

In six moons, Wolf had not found him. Torak had tried

telling himself that that was a *good* sign: it meant Wolf must be happy with his new pack. But somehow, that hurt most of all. Had Wolf forgotten him?

Faint and far away, voices floated on the wind.

Torak sat up.

It was a wolf pack. Howling to celebrate a kill.

Torak forgot his dizziness – forgot everything – as the wolf song flowed over him like a river.

He made out the deep, strong voices of the lead wolves; the lighter howls of the rest of the pack, weaving respectfully around them; the cubs' wobbly yowls as they tried to join in. But the one voice that he longed to hear was not among them.

He had known that it would not be. Wolf – *his* Wolf – ran with a pack far to the north. The wolves he heard now were in the east, in the hills bordering the Deep Forest.

But he still had to try. Shutting his eyes, he cupped his hands to his mouth and howled a greeting.

Instantly the wolves' voices tightened.

Where do you hunt, lone wolf? howled the lead female. Sharp. Commanding.

Many lopes from you, Torak replied. *Tell me. Is there – sickness in your range?*

He wasn't certain he'd got that right, and sure enough, the wolves didn't seem to understand.

Our range is a good range! they howled, offended. *The best range in the Forest!*

He hadn't really expected them to grasp his meaning. His knowledge of wolf talk was not precise, his ability to express himself even less so. And yet, he thought with a pang, Wolf would have understood.

Abruptly, the wolf song ceased.

Torak opened his eyes. He was back in the moonlit glade

among the dark ferns and the ghostly meadowsweet. He felt as if he'd woken from a dream.

A shallow thrumming of wingbeats, and he turned to see a cuckoo on a snag, staring at him with a yellow-ringed eye.

He remembered Oslak's sneer. *You're not one of us! You're a cuckoo!* The rambling of a madman, but with a kernel of truth. The cuckoo gave a squawk and flew off. Something had startled it.

Noiselessly Torak rose to his feet. His hand crept to his knife.

In the bright moonlight, the glade seemed empty.

A short way to the east, a stream flowed into the Widewater. Quietly he searched the bank for tracks. He found none; nor any hairs caught on twigs, or subtly displaced branches.

But someone was here. He could feel it.

He raised his head and stared into the beech tree above him.

A creature glared down at him. Small. Malevolent. Hair like dead grass, and a face of leaves.

He saw it for an instant. Then a gust of wind stirred the branches and it was gone.

That was how Renn found him: standing rigid with his knife in his hand, staring upwards.

'What's wrong?' she said. 'Why did you run away? Are you – did you eat something bad?' She didn't want to voice her fear that he might have the sickness.

'I'm all right,' he replied – which clearly wasn't true. His hand shook as he sheathed his knife.

'Your lips have gone grey,' said Renn.

'I'm all right,' he said again.

As he sat beneath the beech tree, she glanced at his hands, but couldn't see any blisters. She tried not to show her relief. 'Maybe a bad mushroom?' she suggested.

'The Hidden People,' he cut in. 'What do they look like?'

'What? But you know as well as I do. They look like us, except when they turn their backs, they're rotten –'

'Their faces, what about their faces?'

'I told you, like us! Why? What's this about?'

He shook his head. 'I thought I saw something. I thought – maybe it's the Hidden People who are causing the sickness.'

'No,' said Renn. 'I don't think it is.' She dreaded having to tell him what she'd learned at the healing rite. It wasn't fair. After everything he'd done last winter . . .

To put it off, she went to the stream and washed the clay from her face, then chipped away the thick layer on her palms which had allowed her to carry the hot ash without getting burned. Then she grabbed a clump of wet moss and took it back for Torak. 'Put this to your forehead. It'll make you feel better.'

Sitting in the ferns beside him, she shook some hazelnuts from her food pouch and began cracking them on a stone. She offered one to Torak, but he declined. She sensed that neither of them wanted to talk about the sickness, but both were thinking of it.

Torak asked how she'd found him.

She snorted. 'I may not speak wolf talk, but I'd know your howl anywhere.' She paused. 'Still no word of him?'

'No,' he said shortly.

She ate another nut.

Torak said, 'The healing rite. It didn't help, did it?'

'If anything, it made things worse. Oslak and Bera seem to think the whole clan's against them.' She frowned. 'Saeunn says she's heard of sicknesses like this in the deep past, after the Great Wave. Whole clans died out. The Roe Deer. The Beaver Clan. She says there may have been a cure long ago, but it was lost. She says – it's a sickness rooted in fear. That it *grows* fear. As trees grow leaves.'

'Like leaves on a tree,' murmured Torak. He reached for a stick and began peeling off the bark. 'Where does it come from?'

She couldn't put it off any longer. She had to tell him. 'Do you remember,' she began reluctantly, 'what Oslak said on the walkway?'

His fingers tightened on the stick. 'I've been thinking that too. "Eating my souls . . ."' He swallowed. 'Soul-Eaters.'

The birds stopped singing. The dark trees tensed.

'Is that what you mean?' said Torak. 'Do you think the Soul-Eaters have something to do with the sickness?'

Renn hesitated. 'Maybe. Don't you?'

He leapt to his feet and paced, dragging the stick over the bracken. 'I don't know. I don't even know who they are.'

'Torak –'

'All I *know*,' he said with sudden fierceness, 'is that they were Mages who went bad. All I *know* is that my father was their enemy – although he never told me anything.' He slashed at the bracken. 'All I *know* is that something happened that broke their power, and people thought they were gone, but they weren't. And last summer –' he faltered, 'last summer, a crippled Soul-Eater made the bear that killed Fa.'

Savagely he stabbed the earth. Then he threw away the stick. 'But maybe you're wrong, Renn, maybe they didn't –'

'Torak – no. Listen to me. Oslak scratched a sign in the dust. A three-pronged fork for snaring souls. The mark of the Soul-Eaters.'

FIVE

The Soul-Eaters.

They were woven into his destiny, and yet he knew so little about them. All he knew was that there were seven: each from a different clan, each warped by their hunger for power.

Down by the river, a vixen screamed. In the shelter, Vedna tossed and turned, worrying about her mate. Torak lay in his sleeping-sack, thinking of the evil that could send a sickness to ravage the clans.

To rule the Forest . . .

But no-one could do that. No-one could conquer the trees, or stop the prey from following the ancient rhythms of the moon. No-one could tell the hunters where to hunt.

When at last he slept, his dreams were haunted. He crouched on a dark hillside, frozen in horror as a faceless Soul-Eater crawled towards him. He scrambled back. His hand met a scaly softness that wriggled and bit. He tried to run. Tree-roots coiled clammily about his ankles. A winged shadow swooped with a leathery *thwap*. The Soul-Eaters were upon him, and their malice beat at him like flame . . .

He woke.

It was dawn. The breath of the Forest misted the trees. He knew what he had to do.

'Is Oslak any better?' he asked Vedna as he left the shelter.

'The same,' she said. Her eyes were red, but the glare she gave him warded off sympathy.

He said, 'I need to talk to Fin-Kedinn. Have you seen him?'

'He's downriver. But you leave him be.'

He ignored her.

Already the camp was busy. Men and women crouched on the walkway with spears, while others woke the fires for daymeal. In the distance came the 'tock! tock!' of hammer on stone. Everyone was trying not to think about Oslak and Bera, tied up in the sickness shelter.

Torak followed the path downstream: past the rapids, and round a bend which took him out of sight of the camp. Here the Widewater flowed less turbulently, and the salmon were fleeting silver darts in the deep green water.

Fin-Kedinn sat on a boulder by the river's edge, making a knife. His tools lay beside him: hammer-stones, shapers, beaker of black, boiled pine-blood. Already a small pile of needle-sharp stone flakes nestled in moss at his feet.

As Torak approached, his heart began to pound. He admired the Raven Leader, but was scared of him too. Fin-Kedinn had taken him in after Fa was killed, but he'd never offered to foster him. There was a remoteness about him, as if he'd decided not to let Torak get too close.

Clenching his fists, Torak stood on the bank. 'I need to talk to you,' he said.

'Then talk,' said Fin-Kedinn without looking up.

Torak swallowed. 'The Soul-Eaters. They sent the sickness. It's my destiny to fight them. So that's what I'm going to do.'

Fin-Kedinn went on studying a round, buff-coloured stone the size of his fist. It was a Sea egg: a rarity in the Forest. The Ravens used mostly slate, antler or bone for their weapons, because flint – in the form of Sea eggs – was found only on the coast, where the Sea clans traded them for horn and salmon skins.

Frustrated, Torak tried again. 'I have to stop them. To put an end to this!'

'How?' said Fin-Kedinn. 'You don't know where they are. None of us does.' With his hammer-stone he tapped the Sea egg, checking from the sound that the flint was free from flaws.

Torak flinched. That 'tock! tock!' brought back painful memories. He'd grown up to the sound of Fa knapping stone by the fire. It had made him feel safe. How wrong he had been.

He said, 'Renn told me there have been powerful sicknesses like this in the past – but also a cure. So maybe –'

'That's what I've spent all night trying to find out,' said Fin-Kedinn. 'There's a rumour that one of the Deep Forest Mages knows a cure.'

'Where?' cried Torak. 'How do we get it?'

Fin-Kedinn struck the Sea egg a hard blow which took the top clean off. Inside, the flint was the colour of dark honey, threaded with scarlet. 'Not so fast,' he told Torak. 'Think first. Impatience can get you killed.'

Torak threw himself down on the bank, and tore at the grass.

Using a small antler club, Fin-Kedinn struck flakes off

the core, deftly controlling their size by the speed and slant of the blow. *Tock! Tock!* went the hammer, telling Torak to wait.

Eventually, Fin-Kedinn spoke. 'In the night, an Otter woman came in a canoe. Two of them have fallen sick.'

Torak went cold. The Otter Clan lived far in the east, on the shores of Lake Axehead. 'Then it's everywhere,' he said. 'I have to get to the Deep Forest. If there's even a chance . . .'

Fin-Kedinn sighed.

'Who else could you send?' said Torak. 'You're needed here. Saeunn's too old for the journey. Everyone else has to guard the sick, or hunt, or catch salmon.'

Fin-Kedinn chose a thumb-length antler shaper, and sharpened a flint flake with delicate grinding motions. 'The people of the Deep Forest rarely concern themselves with us. Why do you think they'd help?'

'That's why it should be me!' insisted Torak. 'My mother was Red Deer Clan! I'm their bone kin, they'd have to listen to me!' But he'd never known his mother, who had died when he was born, and he spoke with more assurance than he felt.

A muscle worked in Fin-Kedinn's jaw as he took up the haft of the knife: a length of reindeer shin-bone with a groove in it to take the flint. Dipping a sharpened flake in pine-blood, he slotted it into the bone. 'Has it not occurred to you,' he said, 'that this might be exactly what the Soul-Eaters want?' He raised his head, and his blue eyes burned with such intensity that Torak dropped his gaze. 'Last winter after you fought the bear, I forbade anyone to speak of it outside the clan. You know this.'

Torak nodded.

'Because of that, the only thing the Soul-Eaters know is that someone in the Forest has power. *They do not know who.*'

He paused. 'They don't know who, Torak. Nor do they know the nature of that power. None of us does.'

Torak caught his breath. Fin-Kedinn's words echoed what Fa had said as he lay dying. *All my life I've kept you apart . . . Stay away from men, Torak! If they find out what you can do . . .*

But *what* could he do? For a time he'd thought Fa had meant his ability to speak wolf; but from what Fin-Kedinn had said, there had to be more.

'This sickness,' said the Raven Leader, 'it could be a trick: the Soul-Eaters' way of forcing you into the open.'

'But even if it is, I can't just do nothing. I have to help Oslak. I can't stand it seeing him like this!'

The hard face softened. 'I know. Neither can I.'

There was silence while Fin-Kedinn slotted in more flint, and Torak stared across the river. The sun had risen above the trees, and the water was dazzling. Squinting, he made out a heron on the far bank; a raven wading after scraps of salmon.

The blade was complete: about a hand long, and as jagged and sharp as a wolverine's jaw. To finish it, Fin-Kedinn wound finely split pine root around the haft to make a warm, sure grip. 'Now,' he said. 'Show me your knife.'

Torak frowned. 'What?'

'You heard. Show it to me.'

Puzzled, Torak unsheathed the knife which had been his father's, and handed it over.

It had a beautiful leaf-shaped blade of blue slate, and an antler haft bound with elk sinew. Fa had told him that the blade was of Seal Clan making. Fa's mother had been a Seal, and she'd given it to him when he'd reached manhood; he'd fitted the hilt himself. As he lay dying, he had given the knife to Torak. Torak was very proud of it.

But as the Raven Leader handled it, he shook his head. 'Too heavy for a boy. A Mage's knife, made for ceremony.' He handed it back. 'He was always too casual about such things.'

Torak longed for him to say more, but he didn't. Instead he set the new knife across his forefinger, appraising it with a critical eye. It lay level, perfectly balanced.

Beautiful, thought Torak.

The Raven Leader flipped it round, caught it by the blade, and held it out. 'Take it. I made it for you.'

After a moment's astonishment, Torak took it.

Fin-Kedinn cut short his thanks. 'From now on,' he said, rising to his feet with the aid of his staff, 'keep your father's knife hidden. Your mother's medicine horn, too. If anyone asks about your parents, don't speak of them.'

'I don't understand,' said Torak.

But Fin-Kedinn wasn't listening. He'd gone still, staring at the river.

Torak shaded his eyes with his hand, but couldn't see much for the glare. Only the heron on the far bank, and a log in midstream, sliding downriver.

In the camp, a woman began to keen: a tearing sound that rose above the rapids and chilled Torak's blood.

Men and women came running down the trail.

Torak gasped.

That wasn't a log floating downriver.

It was Oslak.

SIX

Oslak had taken no chances. He'd gnawed through his bindings, slipped out of the sickness shelter, and climbed the Guardian Rock. Then he'd thrown himself off.

The fall had probably killed him. At least – Torak hoped so. He couldn't bear to think of him being alive when he'd hit the rapids.

The Raven camp was stunned into silence when he reached it. Vedna had stopped keening, and stood stony-faced, watching the men bring the body on a litter. They took great care not to touch it with their bare hands. No-one wanted to risk angering the dead man's souls, which were still in the camp.

As they set down the litter by Oslak's shelter, Saeunn crouched beside it, and – with her finger protected by a leather guard – daubed the Death Marks in red ochre on the body, to help the souls stay together on their journey. Soon the Ravens would carry him into the Forest. It was vital that this was done swiftly, so that his souls would not be tempted to stay in camp.

Fin-Kedinn stood a little apart, his face a mask of granite. He betrayed no grief as he gave orders to double the watch on Bera, and to empty Oslak's shelter of all but his belongings, which would be burnt when it was put to the fire. But Torak could tell that he was taking it hard. The Raven Leader had told Oslak that he would keep him safe. He would not easily forgive himself for having failed.

Guilt.

Torak felt it too, weighing him down.

Well, the time for doing nothing was over. When the Ravens took the body into the Forest, he would stay behind, not being part of the clan – and that would be his chance to slip away: to make for the Deep Forest, and seek the cure.

But first there was something he had to do.

As the rites began and women fetched clay for the mourning marks, he made his way quietly to the foot of the Guardian Rock. If his suspicion was right – if the creature with the face of leaves had anything to do with Oslak's death – then it might have left tracks.

The Guardian Rock was almost sheer on the side which faced the river, but on its eastern side it was more like a steep hill, which could be climbed if one was careful. Many feet had trampled the mud at its base, and some had tracked mud up this eastern flank.

The message in the mud was confused, but Torak made out a faint line of narrow, day-old prints: that was Saeunn, climbing to the top. He saw paw-marks criss-crossed by sharp little four-toed prints: that was a dog scampering up, and being teased by a raven. And over there, a man's prints. Torak saw only the toes and the balls of the feet. Oslak had been running as fast as he could.

A lump rose in Torak's throat. He forced it down. Grieve later, when you're on your way.

Slowly he followed Oslak's tracks up the rock.

Oslak had dislodged pebbles and moss as he ran. At one point he'd slipped, grazing himself: here was a tiny smear of blood. Then he'd run on.

He was running as fast as he could, thought Torak. As if all the demons of the Otherworld were after him.

At the top, Torak found what he'd been dreading. Another set of prints: much smaller than Oslak's. They were faint, but he saw enough to know that whatever had made them had not been running – but standing: standing quite still, a short way back from the edge. Watching Oslak leap to his death.

The footprints were small, like those of a child of maybe eight or nine summers.

Except that this print had claws.

{{image: two rune-like symbols}}

The clan was getting ready to leave when Torak found Renn by the long-fire, grinding earthblood for the burial rites.

Her face was streaked with river clay – the Raven way of mourning – but tears had cut runnels down her cheeks. Torak had never seen her cry. As he approached, she blinked hard.

'Renn,' he said, squatting beside her and speaking softly so as not to be overheard, 'there's something I've got to tell you. I went up the Guardian Rock, I –'

'What were you doing up there?'

'I found tracks.'

Saeunn called to Renn from across the clearing. 'Come! We're leaving!'

'There's something in the camp,' Torak said urgently. 'I saw it!'

Again the Raven Mage summoned Renn.

'Torak, I've got to go!' she said. Pouring the ground ochre into her medicine pouch, she got to her feet. 'We won't be gone long. Tell me when I get back. Show me the tracks.'

Torak nodded, but didn't meet her eyes. He wouldn't be here when she got back. And he couldn't tell her he was going, because she'd try to stop him, or insist on coming too. He couldn't let her do that. If Fin-Kedinn was right, if there was even a chance that he was walking into a Soul-Eater trap, he wasn't going to risk her life as well as his own.

'I'm sorry you can't come too,' said Renn, making him feel worse. Then she ran to take her place at the head of the clan beside her uncle, Fin-Kedinn.

The Ravens moved off, and Torak watched them go. He knew that they would carry Oslak's body a good distance from the camp before building the Death Platform: a low rack of rowan branches on which they would lay the corpse, facing upriver. Like the salmon, Oslak's souls would make their final journey upstream, towards the High Mountains.

The rites at the Death Platform would be brief, and after saying farewell, the clan would leave his body to the Forest. As he'd fed on its creatures in life, so they would feed on him in death. Three moons later, Vedna would gather his bones and take them to the Raven bone-ground. But for the next five summers, neither she nor anyone else would speak his name out loud. This was strict clan law: to prevent the dead man's souls from troubling the living.

Standing in the clearing, Torak watched till they were gone. When the last Raven had been swallowed by the

Forest, the camp felt eerily lonely. Only the dogs remained to guard the salmon.

Quickly, Torak ran to fetch his things. He crammed his light wicker pack with his few belongings: cooking-skin, medicine pouch, tinder pouch, fish-hooks; his quiver and bow, his rolled-up sleeping-sack; Fa's knife, wrapped in rawhide; his mother's medicine horn. As he stuck his small basalt axe in his belt, he tried not to think of the last time he'd been forced to pack in a hurry. It had been last autumn, as Fa lay dying.

Torak's hand tightened on the hilt of the knife Fin-Kedinn had made for him. It was lighter and easier to use than his father's; but nothing would ever replace Fa's knife.

Don't think about that now, he told himself. Just get out of here before they come back. And this time, don't forget food.

After what had happened to Oslak, he couldn't face salmon: not the smoked meat, nor the Ravens' flat cakes of dried flesh pounded with juniper berries. Instead he cut some strips of elk meat hanging from the rafters in Thull's shelter. They'd keep him going till he reached the Deep Forest.

But how long would that take? Three days? Five? He didn't know. He'd never been near it, and had only encountered two Deep Forest people: a silent Red Deer woman with earthblood in her hair, and a wild-eyed Auroch girl, her scalp weirdly caked in yellow clay. Neither had shown any interest in him, and despite what he'd told Fin-Kedinn, he didn't expect much of a welcome.

On his way out of camp, he passed the Leader's shelter – and that was when it hit him. He was leaving the Ravens, perhaps for good.

First you lost Fa, then Wolf. Now Oslak, and Fin-Kedinn and Renn . . .

It was dark inside the shelter. Fin-Kedinn's corner was neat and spare, but Renn's was a mess: her sleeping-sack crumpled and littered with arrows she hadn't finished fletching. She would be furious that he'd gone without her, and there was no way of saying goodbye.

He had an idea. Outside the shelter he found a flat white pebble. Running to the nearest alder tree, he muttered a thanks to its spirit, cut off a strip of bark, and chewed. Spitting the red mix of saliva and tree-blood into his palm, he painted his clan-tattoo on the stone: two dotted lines, one with a break in the middle. The break wasn't part of the tattoo, it was a small scar on his cheek, but when Renn saw it she would know it was from him.

As he finished making the sign, he stopped. His finger was stained red with alder juice: the same juice he'd used last autumn, in Wolf's naming rite. He'd daubed it on the cub's paws, and been exasperated when Wolf kept licking it off.

'*Don't* think about Wolf!' he cried aloud. 'Don't think about any of them!'

The empty camp mocked him silently. *You're on your own now, Torak.*

Hurriedly he shoved the pebble under Renn's sleeping-sack, then ran into the sunlight.

The Forest was full of birdsong, and achingly beautiful. He could take no joy in it.

Shouldering his bow, he turned east, and started for the Deep Forest.

SEVEN

S orrow ran with Wolf like an unseen pack-brother.
He missed Tall Tailless. He longed for his odd, furless
face and his wavering howl; for the strange, breathless yip-
and-yowl which was his way of laughing.

Many times Wolf had loped off alone to howl for him.
Many times he'd run in circles, wondering what to do. He
was caught between the Pull of the Mountain, and the Pull
of his pack-brother.

The other wolves – the wolves of his new pack – were
puzzled. *You have us now! And you're not yet full-grown, you have
much to learn! You don't know how to hunt the great prey, how would
you survive on your own? Stay here with us!*

They were a strong, close pack, and there had been
times when he'd been happy on the Thunderer's Mountain.
They'd played uproarious games of hunt-the-lemming;
they'd leapt into lakes to frighten ducks. But the other

278

wolves did not understand.

Wolf was thinking of this as he raced to his favourite ridge to catch the smells wafting from the Forest.

The Forest was many lopes away, but he caught the muzzle-watering scent of a newborn fawn, and the sharp smell of tree-blood oozing from a wind-snapped spruce. He heard the slow sucking sound of a boar turning over in its wallow, and the squeak of an otter cub falling off a branch. He longed to be in the Forest with Tall Tailless.

But how could he ever go back?

It wasn't only the thought of leaving his pack which stopped him. It was the Thunderer. The Thunderer would never let him go.

The Thunderer could attack at any time: even now, when the Up was bright and clear, and there was no sign of its angry breath. It could flatten the Forest with storms, and send down the Bright Beast-That-Bites-Hot to blast trees, rocks, wolves. It was all-powerful. Wolf knew that better than most, because it had taken his pack when he was a cub.

He'd gone off to explore, and when he'd come back, the Den had been gone. His whole pack – mother, father, pack-brothers – had lain wet and cold and Not-Breath in the mud. The Thunderer hadn't needed to come close to destroy them. It had sent the Fast Wet roaring down from the Mountains.

Wolf had been lonely and frightened, and *very* hungry. Then Tall Tailless had come. Tall Tailless had shared his kills with him, and let him curl up on top of him to sleep. He had howled with him, and played tag with bits of hide. Tall Tailless had become his pack-brother.

Tall Tailless was a wolf, of course, anyone could smell that; but he wasn't a normal wolf. The fur on his head was long and dark, but the rest of him was without fur, and instead had a loose overpelt – *which he could take off*. His face was flat, and his poor little teeth were hopelessly blunt; and strangest of all, he had no tail.

But he *sounded* wolf, even if he never hit the high yips. And his eyes were true wolf eyes: pale grey, and full of light. Above all, he had the heart and spirit of a wolf.

As Wolf stood on the ridge, sadness filled his chest. He put up his muzzle and howled.

That was when the new smell hit his nose.

Not hunter or prey; not tree or earth or Fast Wet or stone. This was bad. Something bad, blowing through the Forest.

Wolf whimpered with anxiety. His pack-brother was down there in the badness.

Suddenly everything was clear. The Thunderer might come after him, but Wolf couldn't let that stop him any longer. Tall Tailless needed him.

Wolf leapt down from the ridge, and started for the Forest.

He ran for two Darks and Lights, keeping the Mountains at his tail, and heading for where the Hot Bright Eye sinks down to sleep.

Fear snapped at his hindpaws.

He feared the anger of the stranger wolves whose ranges he crossed; if they caught him, they might tear him to pieces.

He feared the wrath of the Thunderer.

But worse than that, he feared for his pack-brother.

As he ran, the smell grew stronger. Something stalked the Forest.

Tirelessly Wolf wove between the trees, seeking the taillesses. Some of their packs smelt like boar, some like otter, but the one he sought smelt like raven. That was the pack Tall Tailless had joined.

At last he found it, on the banks of a furious Fast Wet.

As he'd expected, nobody knew he was here. That was one of the odd things about taillesses. Although in many ways they were like true wolves – being clever and brave, with a fondness for talking and playing, and a fierce love for their pack – they couldn't smell *at all*, and they were practically deaf. So Wolf went unobserved as he roamed the edge of the Den, seeking his pack-brother.

He couldn't find him.

It had rained the previous Light, and many scents had been washed away; but if Tall Tailless had been here, Wolf would have smelt him.

Then he caught the scent of the lead wolf, who sat by the Bright Beast-that-Bites-Hot, as taillesses love to do. Beside him crouched the half-grown female who was pack-sister to Tall Tailless. She was speaking to the lead wolf in the yip-and-yowl of tailless talk, and she sounded both angry and sad.

Wolf sensed that the female was worried about Tall Tailless.

Running up and down, Wolf sought his pack-brother. He found a big bare patch that smelt of new ash; and some strange, straight trees from which hung many fish. He paused only to gulp down a few before heading back into the Forest to seek Tall Tailless.

Maybe his pack-brother had gone hunting. Yes, that must be it. And he couldn't have gone far, because like all taillesses, he ran on his hind legs, which made him slow.

But though Wolf searched and searched, he found nothing.

The awful truth crashed down on him like a falling tree.

Tall Tailless was gone.

EIGHT

To avoid meeting the Ravens, Torak stayed off the clan paths and kept to the hidden deer trails that wound up the Widewater valley.

The prey soon sensed that he wasn't hunting them, and relaxed. An elk munched willowherb as he passed. Forest horses flicked up their tails and cantered into the trees, then turned to stare till he was gone. Two boar sows and their fat, fluffy piglets raised their snouts to watch him go by.

The new leaves were still crinkled from the bud, and letting in plenty of sunlight. He made good speed. Like all Forest people he travelled light, carrying only what he needed for hunting, fire-making and sleep.

All his life he'd wandered the Forest with Fa, pitching camp for a night or so, then moving on. Always moving on. That had been the hardest part about living with the Ravens. They only broke camp every three or four moons.

And there were so many of them! Twenty-eight men, women, and children. And babies. Until last winter, Torak had never even seen one of those. 'Why can't it walk?' he'd asked Renn. 'What does it *do* all day?' She'd laughed so much she'd fallen over.

At the time, that had made him cross. Now it made him miss them all the more.

He left the valley of the Widewater south of the Thunder Falls, and headed east into the next valley. There he had a brief encounter with two Willow Clan hunters in dugout canoes. To his relief they were in a hurry, and didn't ask where he was going, pausing only to give him a warning before heading downriver.

'A sick man escaped from our camp last night,' said one. 'If you hear howling, run. He doesn't know he's a man any more.'

The other shook his head grimly. 'This sickness. Where did it come from? It's as if the very breath of summer is poisoned.'

As mid-afternoon wore on, Torak began to feel watched.

Many times he stopped to listen, but he never heard anyone, and whenever he doubled back, he found nothing. And yet – the follower was there. He could sense it. As the shadows lengthened, he pictured madmen roaming the Forest, small malevolent creatures with sharp claws and faces of leaves.

He pitched camp near a noisy river where the damselflies were blue darts of light, and the midges nearly ate him alive until he rubbed himself with wormwood juice.

It was the first time in six moons that he'd slept on his own in the Forest, and he took care to choose the right spot. Flat ground, high enough above the river to avoid flash floods, and away from ant-nests and obvious prey trails; and no overhanging deadwood or storm-weakened trees to fall on him in the night.

After the Ravens' reindeer-hide shelters, he was keen to get back to the way he'd lived with Fa, so he built a shelter of living trees. He found three beech saplings and bent them inwards, lashing them together with pine root to make a snug sleeping-space. This he thatched with fallen branches, and covered with leafmould, weighing that down with more branches. In the morning he would untie the saplings, and they would spring back unharmed.

After making a mattress of last autumn's crunchy beech mast, he dragged his gear inside. The shelter had a rich, earthy tang. 'A good smell,' he said out loud. His voice sounded uneasy and forced.

It was a warm night with a southerly breeze, so he made only a small fire, walling it in with stones to stop it escaping into the Forest, and waking it up with his strike-fire and a handful of birch-bark tinder.

He remembered nights with Fa when they'd sat over the embers, wondering about this mysterious, life-giving creature who was such a good friend to the clans. What did the fire dream of as it slept inside the trees? Where did it go when it died?

For the first time, too, he thought of the bone kin he might soon encounter. Maybe with the Red Deer Clan he would feel that he belonged. After all, if things had been different, he could have *been* Red Deer. When he was born, his mother could have named him for her own clan, rather than Fa's; and then he would have grown up in the Deep Forest, and Fa might not have been killed, and he would never have met Wolf . . .

It was too much to think about. He went off to find food.

He dug up some sweet orchid roots and baked them in the embers, and made a hot mash of goosefoot leaves flavoured with crow garlic. It tasted good, but he wasn't hungry. He decided to keep it for daymeal.

He was hanging his cooking-skin in a tree out of the way of foragers, when a cry echoed through the Forest.

He froze.

It was not the yowl of a vixen, or a lynx seeking a mate. It was a man. Or something that had once been a man. Far in the west, by the sound of it.

With a creeping sense of dread, Torak watched the light between the trees begin to fail. Midsummer was not far off, so the night would be brief. Just long enough for his spirits to falter.

Dusk deepened, and still the Forest rang with the chatter of thrushes and the raucous laughter of woodpeckers. The birds would sing all night. He was glad of the company.

He thought of the Ravens sitting round their long-fire. The smell of woodsmoke and baked salmon; Oslak's rumbling laugh . . .

The very breath of summer is poisoned.

Quickly he unrolled his sleeping-sack, crawled in and laid his weapons by his side. A moment ago he'd been wide awake. Now he was exhausted.

He slept.

Shrill laughter tore through his dreams. Hazily he became aware of a loud groaning – both familiar and deadly . . .

He was alert in an instant. It was the sound of a falling tree – *and it was falling his way.*

His sleeping-sack was twisted round his legs, he couldn't get free. Wriggling like a caterpillar, he squirmed through the entrance hole. Struggled to his feet – hopped – fell –

narrowly missed the fire – and threw himself sideways into the ferns just as the tree crashed onto the shelter.

Sparks shot upwards. Dark branches swayed and came to rest.

Torak lay among the ferns: heart pounding, sweat chilling his skin. He'd checked for storm-weakened trees, he knew he had. Besides, there was hardly any wind.

That laughter. Malevolent, yet horribly childlike. It hadn't been only in his dreams.

Not daring to move, he waited till he was sure that nothing else was coming down. Then he went to inspect the ruins of the shelter.

A young ash had fallen across it, killing the three saplings and trapping his gear inside. With luck he could salvage the gear, which – by firelight at least – appeared undamaged. But if he hadn't woken when he had, he would have been killed.

And yet – if the Follower had wanted to kill him, why warn him by laughing? It was as if it was playing with him. Putting him in danger, to see what he would do.

The fire was still burning. With a glowing brand in one hand and his knife in the other, he took a look at the ash tree.

He found axe-marks. Small, crude blows. But effective.

This was odd, though. No tracks on the ground. No sign that someone had braced themselves to hack at the tree.

Again he swept the ground with firelight. Nothing. Maybe he'd missed something, but he didn't think so. The one thing he knew about was tracking.

With his finger he touched the oozing tree-blood. It was thickening. That meant the tree-trunk had been cut some time before, then pushed over while he slept.

He frowned. It's impossible to fell a tree in silence. Why hadn't he heard anything?

Then it came to him. He'd filled his waterskin at the river – which had drowned out other sounds.

As he stood there amid the dark and dying trees, he wished Wolf was with him. Nothing would get past Wolf. His ears were so keen that he could hear the clouds pass. His nose was so sharp that he could smell the breath of a fish.

But Wolf isn't here, Torak told himself savagely. He's far away on the Mountain.

For the first time in six moons, he couldn't howl for his lost friend. He didn't like to think of who – or what – might answer his call.

It was past middle-night by the time he'd salvaged his gear and built another shelter, and he was numb with fatigue. He was also uneasily aware that he'd caused the deaths of three saplings. He could feel their souls hanging in the air around him: wistful, bewildered, unable to understand why they'd been robbed of their chance of becoming trees.

It's your fault, the older trees seemed to whisper. *You bring evil with you . . .*

This time, he didn't risk getting into his sleeping-sack. Instead he woke the fire, and sat in his new shelter with the reindeer hide around his shoulders and his axe on his knees. He didn't want sleep. He just wanted dawn to come . . .

He awoke with a start. Again he had that feeling of being watched – but this time it was different. There was a smell in the air: hot, strong and familiar, a little like hedge mustard, although his sleep-fuddled mind couldn't place it.

Then he saw the gleam of eyes on the other side of the

fire. His hand tightened on his axe. 'Who are you?' he said hoarsely.

The creature grunted.

'Who are you?' Torak repeated.

It moved into the light.

Torak tensed.

A boar. An enormous male, fully two paces from snout to tail, and heavier than three sturdy men. Its large, furry brown ears were pricked, and its small clever eyes met Torak's warily.

Torak forced himself to stay calm. Boars don't usually attack unless they're wounded or defending their young; but an angry boar can move as fast as a deer, and is invincible.

'I mean you no harm,' he told the boar, knowing it wouldn't understand, but hoping his tone would carry his meaning.

The large ears twitched. Firelight gleamed on its yellow tusks. Then the boar gave an irritable grunt, lowered its massive head, and started rooting around in the wreck of the shelter.

All it wanted to do was eat. Summer is a lean time for boars, with last autumn's berries and acorns long gone. No wonder it was busy grubbing up roots, beetles, worms; anything it could find.

The boar took no more notice of Torak, and after a while, he got into his sleeping-sack and curled up, listening to the comforting sound of snuffling. His new companion was gruff and none too friendly, but welcome all the same. Boars have keen senses. While it stayed close, no sick man or malevolent Follower could get near him.

But soon it would be gone.

As Torak stared into the red heart of the embers, he

wondered if Fin-Kedinn had been right; if he'd let himself be tricked into leaving the Ravens. Maybe whoever – whatever – was after him had got him exactly where it wanted. Alone in the Forest.

Whoever it was, they'd been busy in the night.

It was raining when Torak crawled out of the shelter. The boar had gone, the fire was cold, and someone had rolled away the stones and smoothed out the ashes. Someone had taken Torak's arrows – had crept inside the shelter while he slept, withdrawn them from the quiver by his head, and planted them in the ash to make a pattern.

Torak recognised it at once. The three-pronged mark of the Soul-Eaters.

He went down on one knee and yanked out an arrow.

'All right,' he said aloud as he got to his feet. 'I know you're clever, and I know you're good at sneaking up on me. But you're a coward if you don't come out and face me right now!'

No-one emerged from the dripping undergrowth.

'Coward!' shouted Torak.

The Forest waited.

His voice echoed through the trees.

'What do you want? Come out and face me! *What do you want?*'

Rain pattered on the leaves and ran silently down his face. His only answer was the rattle of a woodpecker far away.

The morning passed, and still it rained. Torak liked the rain: it kept him cool, and the midges away. His spirits rose as he crossed two more valleys. The feeling of being watched lessened. He heard no more demented howls.

Maybe that was because the boar was keeping him company. He didn't see it, but he kept finding traces of its presence. Big patches of churned-up earth where it had rooted for food. A muddy wallow beside a much-rubbed oak tree, where it had had a good scratch after taking a bath.

Torak found this reassuring. He had a new friend. He wondered how old the boar was, and if it was the father of the piglets he'd seen the previous day.

As the afternoon wore on, their paths crossed. They drank at the same stream, and rested in the same drowsy glade. Once, as they were both searching for wood-mushrooms, the boar gave a tetchy grunt and chased Torak away, then stamped on the mushroom he'd been about to eat. When Torak went to look, he saw why. It wasn't a wood-mushroom at all, but a poisonous lookalike, as its bruised red flesh showed. In the boar's bad-tempered way, it had been warning him to be more careful.

Next morning it was still raining, and the Forest slumbered beneath a mantle of cloud. But as Torak trudged further east, he realised that it wasn't only the clouds that were shutting out the light. The Forest itself was growing darker.

He was used to the Open Forest, where the trees let in plenty of sun, and the undergrowth is usually fairly light; but now he had reached the hills which guarded the Deep Forest. Towering oaks reared before him with mighty limbs spread wide to ward him back. The undergrowth was taller than he was: dense stands of black yew and poisonous hemlock. The sky was hidden by an impenetrable canopy of leaves.

There had been no sign of the boar all day, and Torak missed him. He began to fear not only what followed him, but what lay ahead.

He thought of the tales his father had told him. *In the Deep Forest, Torak, things are different. The trees are more watchful; the clans more suspicious. If you ever venture in, be careful. And remember that in summer, the World Spirit walks in the deep valleys, as a tall man with the antlers of a deer . . .*

In the late afternoon, with the rain still falling, Torak paused at a stream to rest. Hanging his gear on a holly tree, he went to refill his waterskin.

In the mud he found fresh tracks. The boar had been here before him, and recently: the tracks were sharp, their dewclaws deeply indented. It was good to know that his friend was close. As he knelt to fill the waterskin, he caught the familiar mustardy scent, and grinned. 'I was wondering where you'd gone.'

On the other side of the stream, the bracken parted – and there was the boar.

Something was wrong. The coarse brown fur was matted with sweat. The small eyes were dull, and rimmed with red.

Torak let fall the waterskin and backed away.

The boar gave a squeal of rage.

And charged.

NINE

Torak leapt for the nearest tree as the boar crashed towards him.

Panic lent him strength. He caught at a branch and hauled himself up, swinging his legs out of reach as the tusks gouged the trunk where his foot had been.

The tree shuddered. Torak clawed bark.

Hooking his leg over the branch, he hoisted himself into the fork. He wasn't even two paces above the boar, but he couldn't go any higher, the tree was too spindly. He'd lost his boots, and his feet were slippery with mud; he clutched branches to steady himself. One broke with a crack. The boar threw up its head and glared.

The brown eyes that had been so steady and wise were bulging and bloodshot. Something had happened to turn it into a monster. That reminded him horribly of Oslak.

'But I'm your *friend*,' he whispered.

The boar gave a wheezy roar and thundered off into the Forest.

When it did not come back, Torak blew out a shaky breath. But he knew it was too soon to climb down. Boars are cunning; they know how to lie low. This one could be anywhere.

His legs were cramped, and as he shifted position, pain shot through his right calf. Glancing down, he was startled to see that it wasn't mud which had made him slip, but blood. The boar's tusk had caught him on the calf, but in the shock of the attack he hadn't felt it. Nothing he could do about it now.

The rain eased, and the sun came out. Around him he saw holly and oak trees, with an undergrowth of bracken and foamy meadowsweet. It all looked so peaceful.

The boar's mustardy scent hung in the air. It could be five paces away and he'd never know it. Not till it was too late.

Below him a redstart alighted on a clump of burdock, scattering raindrops. He thought, it wouldn't have come if the boar were near.

To make sure, he drew his knife, and with a quick apology to the willow's spirit, lopped off a small branch and tossed it down.

The redstart flew off. The bracken exploded.

Clasping the tree, Torak watched the boar savage the branch he'd let fall: tusking and trampling it to a mess of pulped fibres. If he'd jumped down, that would have been him.

The boar tossed the shredded stick into the bracken, wheeled round and lowered its head. Then it threw itself against the tree.

Its shoulder hit the trunk like a boulder thudding to earth. Willow leaves fell like rain. Grimly, Torak clung on.

Again the boar struck.

And again.

And again.

In a flood of panic, Torak saw what it was doing. It was trying to knock down the tree.

And it could do it, too, because – he realised with mounting horror – he'd climbed the wrong tree. Instead of the sturdy oaks and hollies which could have withstood a rampaging boar, he'd chosen a slender willow with a trunk only slightly thicker than he was.

Oh, very clever, Torak, he snarled inside his head.

Another thud – and this time, a loud splintering. Below him, a wound gaped in the bark. He saw pinkish-brown wood, and glistening tree-blood . . .

Do something. Fast.

The nearest oak was *maybe* within reach, if he edged along this branch –

He jerked back. Don't even try. The branch might look strong, but it'd take never his weight. This tree was a crack willow, and its wood was notoriously brittle. So not only had he picked the *smallest* tree within reach, but also the most fragile.

With startling suddenness, the boar stopped. Torak found its silence almost more terrifying than its rage.

He knew that this would be a fight to the death – and that he would probably lose. His axe, bow and arrows hung neatly on the holly, two paces out of reach.

Hope drained out of him like water into sand. There was no way out. He was going to die.

Without knowing what he was doing, he put his hands to his lips and howled. *Wolf! Where are you? Help me!*

No answer came to him on the wind. Wolf was far away on the Mountain.

And this part of the Forest seemed empty of people. No-one would hear his cry and come to his aid.

Howling made him feel vulnerable, but in a strange way it also gave him strength. You are a member of the Wolf Clan, he told himself. You are not going to die like a squirrel up a tree.

Swiftly, before doubts set in, he cut a switch of willow a bit longer than his arm, and stripped it of side-branches. He squared off the tip, then split its end lengthways to make a tight, springy fork. The distance to his weapons was about two paces. Maybe – *maybe* – he could use the forked stick to hook the thong at the end of his axe, and lift it off the holly.

Beneath him, steam rose from the boar's sweat-blackened hide as it followed his every move.

Luckily, the willow branch which extended closest to the holly was also the sturdiest. Torak edged along it as far as he dared, holding the forked stick at full stretch.

It didn't reach far enough.

He edged back again. Whipping off his rawhide belt, he looped it round the willow trunk, knotted it, and grasped its free end. That let him lean out further.

This time – yes! He hooked the forked stick through the axe-handle loop, and slowly lifted it off the holly branch.

The axe was heavy. The forked stick bent – and Torak watched helplessly as the axe slid off the end and thudded into the mud.

The boar squealed, hooked its tusks under the shaft, and tossed it into the bracken.

Torak could not allow himself to be disheartened. Still at full stretch, he moved the forked stick towards his bow. Gently, *gently* he eased it under the bowstring. The bow was much lighter than the axe – merely a strip of yew wood strung with sinew – and he lifted it easily off the branch.

As soon as he had the bow slung over his shoulder, hope surged through him. 'You see that?' he shouted at the boar. 'You didn't think I could do it, did you?'

Now for the arrows. Still gripping his belt, Torak strained to reach his quiver with the forked stick. He hooked it. It was light, a wovengrass cone, but as he drew it towards him it tilted, and arrows spilled into the mud. He jerked the quiver towards him – just in time to save the last three.

For a moment he felt ridiculously pleased. 'Three arrows!' he yelled.

Three arrows. To kill a full-grown boar. That would be like trying to fell a bull elk with a bunch of flowers.

The boar snorted and resumed its attack on the trunk. The willow didn't have long to go.

Crouching in the shivering tree, Torak struggled to take aim. Branches hampered his draw arm – he couldn't get a clear shot . . .

He loosed an arrow. It thudded into one shoulder. The boar roared, but went on tusking the roots. That arrow had done as much damage as a gnat bite.

Clenching his teeth, Torak loosed another. It glanced harmlessly off the thick skull.

Use your wits, Torak. Hit a boar on the skull or the shoulder bone and you won't do any damage. Hit *behind* the shoulder, and you've got a chance at the heart.

Another splintering crunch – and the willow lurched wildly. Now Torak was barely out of reach.

The boar wheeled round for another attack. Just before it charged, Torak glimpsed paler fur behind its foreleg – took aim – and let fly.

The arrow stuck deep. The boar squealed – and crashed onto its side.

Silence.

All Torak could hear was his own gasping breath, and the rain pattering in the bracken.

The boar lay still.

Torak waited as long as he could bear. When it didn't move, he lowered himself down to the ground.

Standing on the torn earth with the willow dying behind him, he felt exposed. He had no arrows and no axe; only his knife.

It *must* be dead. Its foam-flecked sides weren't moving.

But he would take no chances. The carcass was three paces away. He wouldn't go near it till he was better armed.

Stealthily, he made his way behind the wreck of the willow, searching the bracken for his axe.

Behind him the boar staggered to its feet.

Desperately Torak scanned the bracken. It had to be somewhere . . .

The boar threw itself into a charge.

Torak saw his axe – lunged for it – whirled round, and sank it into the massive neck.

The boar fell dead.

Torak stood, his legs braced, his chest heaving; both hands clutching his axe.

Rain streamed down his cheeks like tears, and fell sadly on the leaves. He felt sick. Never in his life had he killed prey when he didn't need meat. Never had he killed a friend.

Letting go of the axe, he knelt and put a shaky hand on

the hot, bristly pelt. 'I'm sorry, my friend,' he told the boar. 'But I had to do it. May your souls – be at peace.'

The glazed eye met his sightlessly. The boar's souls had already left. Torak could feel them. Close. Angry.

'I will treat you with respect,' he said, caressing the sweat-soaked flank. 'I promise.'

In the matted fur his hand touched something hard.

He parted the hairs – and gasped. It was a dart of some kind, buried deep in the boar's ribs.

With his knife he dug it out, and washed it in the stream. He'd never seen anything like it. It was shaped like a leaf, but viciously barbed, and made of fire-hardened wood.

Behind him among the trees, he heard laughter. He spun round. The laughter faded into the Forest.

The meaning of what he'd found sank in. This was why the boar had attacked. It had not been sick. It had been wounded. Terribly wounded by someone so cruel, so evil, that they had not gone after it and finished it off, as they were bound to do by all the sacred laws of the hunt, but had left it mad with pain, to savage anyone it found.

And since Torak seemed to be the only one in this part of the Forest, whoever had shot the boar must have intended its first victim to be him.

TEN

Torak wrapped the slab of boar's liver in burdock leaves and tucked it into the fork of an oak tree.

'My thanks to the clan guardian for this meat,' he muttered as he'd done countless times before. For the first time in his life, he didn't feel thankful. All he could think about was the wise old boar snuffling in the leafmould, and keeping him company for the night. The fat, fluffy piglets who had lost a father.

He limped back to the carcass. It was enormous. After a struggle, he'd managed to roll it over and slit the belly to get at the innards, but that was as far as he'd got.

Until now, the biggest prey he'd ever killed had been a roe buck, and that had taken two exhausting days to deal with. The boar was many times bigger. It would take him a whole half-moon.

He didn't have a whole half-moon. He had to reach the Deep Forest and find the cure.

But he had no choice. It was the oldest law of all that when you made a kill, you had to treat the prey with respect, and use every part of it. That was the Pact which had been made long ago between the clans and the World Spirit. Torak had to honour it or risk untold bad luck.

He also had to tend to the wound in his calf. It was burning. Not even the rain cooled it down.

By the stream he found a clump of soapwort. Mashing some of the wet leaves to make a slippery froth, he washed his leg. The pain was so bad that it made his eyes water.

Now to sew up the wound. He found some bone needles in his pack – which hung unharmed on the holly tree – and chose the thinnest, and a length of deer-sinew thread. The thread he'd made from the roe buck had been lumpy and thick, and when Vedna had seen it she'd pursed her lips and given him some of hers. It was as fine as spider's gossamer, and he thanked her under his breath.

The first stab of the needle was agonising. Drawing the thread through his skin made him moan, and he had to hop in circles with the needle sticking out of his calf before he could work up the courage to make another stitch. When he'd finished, tears were streaming down his face.

Next, the dressing. He used some chewed green willow bark – at least there was plenty of that – although dabbing it on stung like fury. Then a soft pad peeled from the inside of a horsehoof mushroom, with a birch-bast binding to keep everything in place.

When it was over, he was trembling. The wound was still throbbing, but the pain had lessened a little.

He found his boots – muddy but undamaged – and pulled them on. He was glad they were summer ones, with a rawhide sole and soft buckskin sides which wouldn't chafe his calf. Lastly, he stowed the rest of the horsehoof mushroom in his pack, for changing the dressing in a few days.

A few days . . .

He would still be here, working on the carcass. If the Follower didn't get him first.

The rain had stopped. Water dripped off the ruined willow, and glistened on the carcass of the boar. A pair of ravens flew down, eyeing it hopefully. Torak shooed them away.

Black spots darted before his eyes, and he realised he was faint with hunger. Butchering the carcass would have to wait. He had to eat.

He'd finished the supplies he'd taken from the Ravens, but with the carcass, he had no shortage of meat. He'd never felt less like eating.

Watched by the ravens, he forced down the rest of the liver. Drinking the blood was harder. Most of it had drained into the mud – a mistake he couldn't now repair, and which, being against the Pact, would bring him bad luck. To make amends he took his birchwood cup from his pack and scooped up what remained in the body cavity. He tried not to think about Oslak whittling the cup for him one long winter's night; or that he was drinking the blood of a friend.

To take away the taste, he crunched up some young burdock stems. Then – at last – he made a start on the carcass.

Skinning it was back-straining, arm-wrenching work, and it was nearly dusk by the time he'd finished. He was covered in blood and shaking with tiredness, and the hide was a muddy, stinking mess. He still hadn't washed it or started scraping off the flesh and fat. After that there would be days spent curing it with wood-ash and mashed brains, and drying the meat, and splitting the bones for fish-hooks and arrowheads.

Not forgetting, of course, that he still had to build a shelter and a fire before it got dark . . .

'Wishing won't get it done,' said a voice behind him.

Torak gave a start.

He couldn't see anyone. The bracken was man-high, filled with shadow.

'Who are you?' he said. He took a step forward – then realised he'd left his weapons by the carcass.

That was when he saw it. A face in the bracken, staring at him.

A face of leaves.

ELEVEN

The creature with the face of leaves was not alone.

Another appeared close by. Then another and another. Torak was surrounded.

As more emerged from the trees, he saw that although their faces resembled that of the Follower, they were full-grown men and women – and they didn't have claws.

They wore their brown hair long, and braided with the tail-hairs of forest horses. The men's beards were dyed green, like the moss which hangs from spruce trees. The lips of both men and women were stained a darker green; but most startling of all were the leaves on their faces. Torak saw that these were dense greenish-brown tattoos: oak leaves for the women, holly for the men. The tattoos gave the disquieting impression that they were peering from the trees – even when, as now, they stood in the open.

They went barefoot, with knee-length leggings and sleeveless jerkins of wovenbark, although of a finer, suppler weave than Torak had ever seen. Each carried a magnificent, well-oiled bow; and each bow was nocked with a green slate arrow fletched with woodpecker feathers. All arrows were trained on him.

Swiftly he put his fists over his heart in token of friendship.

The arrows didn't move.

'You are – of the Deep Forest?' he said hoarsely. It was a guess. Something about them felt different from the Follower. He sensed wildness and danger – but not evil.

'And you,' said the woman who had first addressed him, 'you have reached its borders and must turn back.'

'I thought the Deep Forest was further east –'

'You were wrong,' said the woman in a voice as chill as a deep Forest pool. She had a narrow, distrustful face with hazel eyes set too close together, and she looked older than the others. Torak wondered if she was the leader.

'You have reached the True Forest,' she said. 'You may not pass.'

The 'True Forest'? In spite of himself, Torak was annoyed. What was wrong with the Forest where he'd grown up?

'I come as a friend,' he said, trying to sound friendly but not quite succeeding. 'My name is Torak. I have bone kin in the Deep Forest. Oak Clan and Red Deer by my mother. What clan are you?'

The woman drew herself up. 'Forest Horse,' she said haughtily. 'As you would know if you were telling the truth.'

'I am telling the truth,' said Torak.

'Prove it.'

Face flaming, Torak went to his pack and brought out his mother's medicine horn. It was made from the hollowed-

305

out tip of a red deer antler, fitted with a black oak base and stopper. Fin-Kedinn had told him to keep it hidden; but he couldn't think of any other proof.

'Here.' He held it out.

The Leader recoiled as if he'd threatened her. 'Put it down!' she cried. 'We never touch strangers! You might be a ghost or a demon!'

'I'm sorry,' Torak said hastily. 'I'll – put it here.'

He set it on the ground, and the Leader leaned forward to inspect it. Torak reflected that the Forest Horses seemed to have more in common with their clan-creatures than merely their horsetails.

'It is of Red Deer making,' declared the Leader.

A murmur of surprise rippled through her people.

Taking a step towards Torak, the Leader peered at his face. 'You have something of the True Forest in you, despite the evil you did here; but your clan-tattoos are unknown to us. You may not pass.'

'*What?*' said Torak. 'But I have to!'

'He cannot enter the True Forest!' said one of the clan. 'See how he treated the boar!'

'And the willow tree!' said another. 'Look at her lying in the mud! Dying with nothing to ease her pain!'

'How do you ease a tree's pain?' said Torak indignantly.

Seven pairs of hazel eyes glared at him through their leaf-tattoos.

'You have used our brother and sister very ill,' said the Leader. 'That you cannot deny.'

Torak glanced at the shattered tree and the muddy carcass. 'Take them,' he said.

'What?' said the Leader, her eyes narrowing.

'Take the boar and the willow,' said Torak. 'There's only one of me, but seven of you. You could deal with them much better than I could. And that way, we'd avoid the bad luck.'

The Leader hesitated, as if suspecting a trick. Then she turned to her people. To Torak's surprise, she didn't speak, but made a series of slight, subtle gestures with one hand.

Immediately, four of them stepped forwards, whipped out slender knives of green slate, and descended on the carcass. With astonishing speed and skill they cut it up, then packed it with the hide and innards in wovenbark nets drawn from their packs, and slung them over their shoulders.

'We will return for our sister,' said one, with a nod at the willow and a scornful glance at Torak. 'We will lay her to rest.' Then he was gone, melting into the Forest with his three companions.

All trace of the boar had vanished, apart from the tusks, which one of the Forest Horses now set before Torak. 'These you must keep,' she told him severely, 'to mark the great wrong you did to the prey. If you were of the True Forest, you would be forced to wear them for ever as a penance.'

Torak appealed to the Leader. 'I know I did wrong, but I didn't mean it.'

'That doesn't matter.'

He took a deep breath, and tried again. 'I came here because we need your help. There's a sickness in the Forest –'

'We know of this,' cut in the Leader.

'You do? Has it struck here too?'

The Leader raised her chin. 'We have no sickness in the True Forest. We guard our borders well. But the trees tell us many things. They tell of the evil that haunts their sisters in the west. They whisper whence it came.'

Torak thought about that. 'It's said that one of your Mages has the cure.'

'We have no cure,' said the Leader.

Torak's jaw dropped. 'I know I've angered you,' he said carefully, 'and I'm sorry. But if your own clan doesn't have the cure, then maybe another –'

'We have no cure!' insisted the Leader. 'There is no cure in the Deep Forest! The people of the Otter spoke too hastily! They are always too hasty, just like their clan-creature!'

'Can you really not help at all?' said Torak in disbelief. 'Not you or anyone else in the Deep Forest? People are dying.'

'I am grieved,' said the Leader, not sounding grieved at all, 'but I cannot alter the truth. What you seek is by the Sea.'

Torak stared at her. '*The Sea?*'

'You must head west. This is the message of the trees. Head west till you can go no further. There you shall find what you seek.'

'Why should I believe you?' said Torak. 'You're just trying to get rid of me.'

The Leader's green face closed. 'The trees never lie. If you had more than a splinter of the True Forest in your souls, you would know this. But you do not – or you would not have done the evil you did here!'

'I didn't want to kill the boar,' said Torak, 'but I had to. It attacked me. Someone had wounded it and left it to go mad.'

The remaining Forest Horses cried out in horror.

'This is a terrible evil!' said the Leader. 'Where is your proof? How could we be unaware of this, when not a twig may snap in our Forest that we do not hear?'

Torak stooped and picked up the dart he'd dug from the boar's side. Then he remembered the Forest Horses' reluctance to touch a stranger, and put it back on the ground.

He was unprepared for their reaction. The Leader snarled, revealing shockingly white teeth between her dark-green lips. 'You *dare* accuse us?'

'Of course not!' said Torak. Then he saw what he'd missed before: a clutch of dark wooden darts – exactly like the one that had wounded the boar – dangling from her belt.

'Then whom *do* you accuse?' demanded the Leader. 'Some other Deep Forest clan? Speak quickly, or you die!'

'I don't know!' cried Torak. 'I mean – I've seen it, but I don't know what it is! I only know that I found this dart in the boar's side!'

To his relief, the Forest Horses lowered their bows.

'I call it the Follower,' he said. 'It has a face like yours – no, no, I mean – a face tattooed with leaves, but smaller, like a child, and with claws on its hands and feet.'

The Leader backed away. Her green lips thinned, and beneath the leaf-tattoos her face went pale. 'You must leave at once,' she said, breathing hard. 'If you take one step into the True Forest, I swear by all the trees who gave me birth that you will not live to take another!'

Torak met her eyes, and saw the fear in them. 'You know what it is, don't you?' he said. 'The Follower. You know what it is.'

The Leader did not reply. She made another sign to her people, and they turned and melted into the trees.

'No!' shouted Torak, running after them. 'Tell me what it is! At least tell me that!'

An arrow whipped past his face.

'Tell me what it is!' he yelled.

Just before she vanished, the Leader turned. '*Tokoroth* . . .' she whispered.

'What does that mean?' said Torak.

'*Tokoroth . . .*'

The green face faded into the leaves.

Long after she had gone, the name hung on the air like an evil thought.

Tokoroth . . .

TWELVE

'*A tokoroth?*' said Renn, nursing her bandaged hand. 'What's that?'

'Not here,' snapped Saeunn.

Without another word she started through the camp. Though she was bent as an old tree battered by storms, she moved with surprising speed, clearing the way with her staff: past the people working at the smoking-racks, past the Guardian Rock, and into the shadow of the gorge. She did not look round. She simply assumed that Renn would follow.

Biting back her irritation, Renn did. As she went, people cast her the same wary glances they normally reserved for the Mage. More and more, they regarded her as Saeunn's apprentice. Renn hated that.

It was three days since the sickness had struck, and in that time, four more Ravens had fallen sick. To stop them harming others or themselves, Fin-Kedinn had taken drastic action, shutting them in a cave on the other side of the river, and setting a constant guard.

Renn could taste the fear in the air. She could see it in people's eyes. *Will I be next? Will you?*

She was horribly afraid that the bite on her hand meant it would be her. She needed to talk to someone; to be told she was wrong. But Saeunn had forbidden her to speak of it.

In the past, that wouldn't have stopped Renn; she'd been defying Saeunn all her life, and saw no reason to stop now. But everyone to whom she usually told her secrets was gone. Oslak was dead. Vedna had returned to her birth-clan, the Willows. Torak had disappeared.

Torak. It was two days since he'd left, and even thinking about him made her furious. He was no friend of hers. Friends do not run away without a word, leaving only a pebble, a painted pebble.

To work off her feelings, she'd been hunting every day; and since she was a good hunter, Fin-Kedinn had let her go. It was while she was hunting that she'd got bitten. So in a way, that was Torak's fault too.

It had happened that morning. She'd risen at dawn and started through the misty Forest to the hazel thicket on the south-east side of the valley, where she'd set some snares.

When she'd reached the thicket, she'd thought it was empty. Then, from deep within, had come a rustling of leaves.

That was when she'd forgotten one of the first rules Fin-Kedinn had ever taught her, and stuck in her hand without looking.

The pain was terrible. Her scream shook the Forest and sent woodpigeons bursting from the trees.

Howling, she yanked back her hand – but whatever had

bitten her clung on tight. She couldn't see it, the leaves were too dense, and she couldn't shake it off. Pulling out her knife, she plunged in – then jerked back in horror. It wasn't a viper or a weasel, it was a *child*. In a flash she took in a glitter of eyes in a mass of grimy hair; sharp brown teeth sunk deep in her palm.

She raised her knife to ward it off – and the creature shot her a look of pure malevolence, let go of her hand, and hissed at her – *hissed* like an angry wolverine – then fled.

That was when Thull and Fin-Kedinn had come running, axes at the ready.

For some reason Renn did not understand, she didn't tell them what had happened, but hid her hand behind her back and concealed how shaken she was by a show of embarrassment. 'Stupid of me not to look first! Lucky it was only a weasel!'

Thull had been relieved it was nothing worse, and had headed back for camp. Fin-Kedinn had given her a measuring look, which she'd returned in silence.

'What *was* it?' she said now as the Raven Mage halted twenty paces into the gorge. Uneasily, Renn glanced about. She didn't like the gorge, and seldom ventured in unless she had to.

Though it was midday, they were in deep shadow. The gorge was always in shadow, its looming sides shutting out all but a sliver of sky. The Widewater didn't like it any more than Renn. Angrily it thundered over a chaos of boulders.

Renn shivered. In here, a tokoroth could creep up behind you, and you'd never even hear it . . .

'Tokoroth,' muttered Saeunn, making her jump.

'But what does that mean?'

Saeunn didn't answer. Crouching on a patch of hard red earth by the river's edge, she tented her tunic over her bony knees. Her feet were bare, her toenails brown and hooked.

Once, Torak had told Renn that Saeunn reminded him of a raven. 'An old one, with no kind feelings left.' Renn thought she was more like scorched earth: dried up and very, very hard. But Torak was right about the feelings. Renn had known the Raven Mage all her life, and she'd never seen her smile.

'Why should I tell you about tokoroth?' said Saeunn in her rasping croak. 'You want to know this, yet you refuse to learn Magecraft.'

'Because I don't like Magecraft,' retorted Renn.

'But you're good at it. You know things before they happen.'

'I'm good at hunting too, but you –'

'You lose yourself in the hunt,' cut in Saeunn, 'to escape your destiny. To escape becoming a Mage.'

Renn took a deep breath and held onto her temper. Arguing with Saeunn was like trying to cut flint with a feather. And it didn't help that there might be some truth in what she said.

She resolved to be patient until she'd got what she wanted. 'Tell me about the tokoroth,' she said.

'A tokoroth,' said Saeunn, 'is a child raised alone and in darkness, as a host for a demon.'

As she spoke, the gloom deepened, and a thin rain began to fall, pocking the red earth.

'A tokoroth,' she went on, 'knows no good or evil. No right or wrong. It is utterly without mercy, for it has been taught to hate the world. It obeys no-one but its creator.' She stared at the black, rushing water. 'It is one of the most feared creatures in the Forest. I never thought to hear of one in my lifetime.'

Renn looked down at her injured hand. Beneath Saeunn's poultice of coltsfoot and cobwebs, the wound throbbed painfully. 'You said "its creator". What do you mean?'

Saeunn's claw-like hand gripped her staff. 'The one who captured the child. The one who caught the demon and trapped it in the body of the host.'

Renn shook her head. 'Why have I never heard of this before?'

'Few now know about tokoroth,' said Saeunn, 'and even fewer speak of them. Besides,' she added with an edge to her voice, 'you don't wish to learn Magecraft. Or had you forgotten?'

Renn flushed. 'How are they created?'

To her surprise, the corners of the lipless mouth went down in an approving grimace. 'You go to the roots of things, that's good. That's what a Mage does.'

Renn stayed silent.

Saeunn drew a mark in the earth which Renn couldn't see. 'The dark art of creating tokoroth,' she said, 'was lost long ago. Or so we thought. It seems that someone has learnt it afresh.' She took away her hand to reveal the three-pronged fork of the Soul-Eaters.

Renn had half expected that, but it was a shock to have her suspicion confirmed. 'But – *how* are they made?' she said, her voice barely audible above the roar of the Widewater.

Saeunn rested her chin on her knees and gazed into the water, and Renn followed her gaze – down, down, to the murky bottom of the river. 'First,' said the Mage, 'a child is taken. Maybe it goes missing when its kin turn away for a moment. They search, thinking it has wandered off into

315

the Forest. They never find it. They grieve, believing it lost, or taken by a lynx or a bear.'

Renn nodded. She knew people who'd lost children that way, everyone did, and she always felt a tearing pity for them. She too had lost kin. Her father had been missing for five moons before his body was found. She'd been seven summers old. She remembered the agony of not knowing.

'Better for the child,' Saeunn said grimly, 'if it *had* fallen prey to a bear. Better than being taken for a tokoroth.'

Renn frowned. 'Why? At least it's still alive.'

'Alive?' One bony hand clenched. 'Kept in darkness for moon after moon? No warmth but what will barely keep it alive? No food but rotting bat meat tossed into its own filth? Worst of all, no people. Not till it has forgotten the touch of its mother's hand; forgotten its very name.'

Renn felt the chill of evil seeping into her bones.

'Then,' said Saeunn, 'when it is nothing but an empty husk – only then does its creator summon the demon, and trap it in the body of the host.'

'You mean – the child,' mumbled Renn. 'It is still a child.'

'It is a host,' Saeunn said flatly. 'Its souls are in thrall to the demon for ever.'

'But –'

'Why do you doubt this?' said Saeunn.

'Because it's still a child, maybe it could be rescued –'

'Fool! Never let kindness get in your way! Now tell me. What *is* a demon? Quick! Tell!'

It was Renn's turn to be fierce. 'Everyone knows that. Why do you want me to say it?'

'Don't argue, girl, do as I say!'

Renn blew out. 'A demon,' she said, 'comes into being when something dies and its souls are scattered, so that it loses its clan-soul. With only the name-soul and world-soul

316

left, it doesn't have any clan feeling, so it can't know right or wrong. It hates the living.' She broke off, remembering the moment last autumn when she'd looked into the eyes of a demon, and seen nothing but hot, churning hatred. 'It lives to destroy all living things,' she faltered. 'Only to destroy.'

The Mage struck the ground with her staff and gave a croak almost like laughter. 'Good! Good!' She leaned forwards, and Renn saw the thick vein throbbing at her temple. 'You've just described a tokoroth. It may *look* like a child, but do not be deceived! That's only the body. The demon has won. The child's souls are buried too deep ever to escape.'

Renn hugged herself. 'How could anyone do that to a child?'

Saeunn lifted her shoulders in a shrug, as if the existence of evil was too obvious to need comment.

'And what is a tokoroth *for?*' said Renn. 'Why would you want to make one in the first place?'

'To do your bidding. To slink into shelters. To steal. To maim. To terrify. Why do you think Fin-Kedinn sets a watch every night?'

Renn gasped. 'You mean – you knew it was here?'

'Since the sickness came. We just didn't know why.'

Renn thought about that. 'So – you think the tokoroth is causing it?'

'The tokoroth does the bidding of its creator.'

'The Soul-Eaters.'

Saeunn nodded. 'The tokoroth is causing the sickness at the bidding of its masters – in some way we don't understand.'

Again Renn was silent. Then she said, 'I think Torak saw it. Before he left, he tried to warn me. But – he didn't know what it was.' A new thought struck her. 'Is there more than one?'

'Oh, I think we can be sure of that.'

Renn struggled to take that in. 'So there could be one here, and maybe another went after him?'

Saeunn spread her hands.

Suddenly the Forest Renn had grown up in seemed full of menace. 'But *why* are they causing the sickness? What do they *want*?'

'I don't know,' said Saeunn.

That frightened Renn more than anything. Saeunn was the Mage. She was supposed to know.

With a shiver, Renn stared at the thundering water. She thought of Torak heading east – maybe trailed by something far worse than he knew . . .

'You cannot go and warn him,' Saeunn said sternly. 'It is too late. You would never find him.'

'I know,' said Renn without turning her head.

To herself she added, But I've still got to try.

THIRTEEN

Wolf couldn't find Tall Tailless, but he knew that he had to keep trying.

Once, he'd caught the scent in a tangle of beech saplings where his pack-brother had dug a Den – but then he'd lost it again. The scent was chewed up with that of boar scat, and with the stink of the badness that haunted the Forest – and a troubling new smell: the smell of demon. Wolf had learnt that smell when he was a cub. The memory was very bad.

Once more he cast about, but in vain. And always the fear snapped at his hindpaws.

The Thunderer was angry with him for leaving the Mountain. Wolf felt it in his fur, and in the tingling of his pads. It was coming after him. Soon it would attack.

The Up had gone very dark, and the breath of the Thunderer was stirring the trees. Sounds were becoming louder, smells sharper, as they always did when it began to growl.

At last Wolf caught the scent of his pack-brother. He could have howled for joy. Filled with new purpose, he ran on, and the prey ran with him, desperate to escape, and sensing that Wolf wasn't hunting them. A beaver slid off a riverbank and swam for its den. A red deer doe raced with her fawn for the safety of the thickets.

Suddenly the Thunderer vent its fury. The wet burst upon the Forest, flattening bracken and bending trees like grass. A deafening crash – and down from the Up came the Bright Beast-that-Bites-Hot, missing Wolf by a pounce, and hitting a pine tree instead. The tree screamed. The Bright Beast swallowed it whole. Wolf swerved – but one of the Bright Beast's cubs fell in front of him and bit him on the forepaw. With a yelp he leapt high – then raced away with the stink of dying tree in his nose.

He felt as frightened as a cub. He wanted his mother. He wanted Tall Tailless. He was all alone, and very, very scared.

Renn was all alone in the Forest, and getting scared.

She'd slipped away from the camp two days before, and still hadn't found Torak. Twice she'd heard the demented shrieks of the sick echoing through the trees, and once she'd caught a rustling overhead. It felt as if every bush, every tree, concealed a tokoroth.

And now the storm was coming. The World Spirit was angry.

Through a gap in the branches she saw a heavy bank of wolf-grey cloud, and heard a rumble of thunder. She was already within striking range. She must take cover.

The valley she was crossing had granite crags on its

eastern side, and she saw some promising dots of darkness which might be caves. She ran, snatching up sticks of firewood as she went.

The storm burst with appalling suddenness. The World Spirit hammered at the clouds, splitting them open to let loose the rain, hurling dazzling arrows of lightning upon the Forest. In the distance, Renn caught the flare of a tree going up in flames. If she wasn't careful, she'd be next.

At last she found a cave – but wet as she was, she hung back. A cave can be a shelter or a death-trap, so she checked for signs of bear or boar, and that the roof was high enough: otherwise the lightning might find its way down a crack, and through her head. When she was sure it was safe, she plunged in.

She was shaking with cold and desperate for a fire, but first she saw to her bow. Pulling it out of its salmonskin wrapping, she hung it on a tree-root jutting from the cave wall. After that she propped up her arrows to dry, so that they wouldn't warp. Then she woke up a fire.

Out in the Forest, the storm raged. Renn wondered where Torak was, and if he'd found shelter.

Tracking him from the Raven camp had not been easy, and to begin with she'd had to guess. She'd reasoned that he'd stayed off the main clan trails, which left a number of choices. Bears and other hunters tend to stay down by the rivers where the prey comes to drink, which means that elk and deer trails are higher up the slopes. After what had happened last autumn, Renn had guessed that Torak would want to avoid bears, which meant he'd probably have taken the prey trails.

She'd been proven right when she'd found his shelter, but it had given her a shock to see it crushed beneath an ash tree. A huge relief to find no body inside; and she'd quickly located the remains of the new shelter beside it. She'd known it was his because he made his fires in a star pattern, which wasn't the Raven way.

Next morning she'd lost the trail again. A boar had obliterated the tracks.

The fire spat, jolting her back to the present.

Her wounded hand throbbed. As she huddled closer to the flames, she pictured the tokoroth's sharp brown teeth; heard again that malevolent hiss . . .

'Something to eat,' she said to chase away the thought.

Her pack contained dried elk meat, smoked salmon from the racks, and salmon cakes – although in a fit of mischief she hadn't taken fresh ones, but had raided Saeunn's private store: a neat stack of cakes packed into a length of dried auroch gut.

She took one, broke off a bit for the clan guardian, then ate the rest. It was from last summer's catch, but still good. It reminded her sharply of the clan.

Beside her lay the wickerwork quiver that Oslak had taught her to make. On two fingers of her left hand were the leather finger-guards that Vedna had sewn. Her right forearm bore the wrist-guard of polished green slate which Fin-Kedinn had made for her when he'd taught her to shoot. She rarely took it off, and her brother had often teased her about that. Her brother . . . He had died the previous winter. It hurt to think of him.

To cheer herself up, she took out the little grouse-bone whistle which Torak had given her the previous autumn. It didn't make any sound that she could hear, but she always kept it with her. Wolf seemed to hear it well enough, and once she'd used it to summon him, and it had saved her life.

Now she gave it a tentative blow.

Nothing happened.

Of course, she hadn't expected that it would. Wolf was far away on the Mountain.

Feeling lonely, she unrolled her sleeping-sack and curled up by the fire.

丰丰

She awoke to the prickling certainty that she was not alone.

The storm had passed, but the rain was still coming down in torrents, gurgling through secret channels in the cave walls. The fire had sunk to a smouldering glow. Beyond it – in the dark at the mouth of the cave – something was watching her.

She struggled upright and groped for her axe.

The thing in the cave mouth was big: too big for a tokoroth. A lynx? *A bear?*

But if it was a bear, she would hear it breathing. And it wouldn't stay outside.

Somehow that didn't make her feel any better.

'Who's there?' she said.

She sensed rather than heard the creature come forwards. Whatever it was, it moved as silently as breath.

Then she saw the gleam of eyes.

She cried out.

The creature backed away. Then it edged once more into the light.

Renn gasped.

It was a wolf. A big one, with a heavy coat of sodden grey fur. Its head was lowered to catch her scent, and it didn't look threatening or afraid. Just – wary.

Renn took in the thick mantle of black fur across its shoulders. The great amber eyes.

Those eyes . . .
It couldn't be.
Slowly she put down her axe.
'Wolf?'

FOURTEEN

'W olf?' Renn said again.

The wolf's tail was down but faintly wagging, his ears rammed forwards. He was watching her intently, but not meeting her eyes – and he was shivering, although whether from cold, fear or eagerness, she couldn't tell.

She leapt to her feet. '*Wolf!* It's me, Renn! Oh Wolf, it is you, isn't it?'

At her outburst the wolf backed away, giving short little grunt-whines that sounded aggrieved.

She couldn't remember how Torak had said 'hello' in wolf talk, so she got down on her hands and knees, grinning and trying to catch the wolf's eye.

That didn't seem right either. The wolf turned his head and backed even further away.

But was it really Wolf? When she'd known him he'd been a cub – but he'd grown so much! From nose to tail he was almost longer than she was; and if they'd stood side by side,

325

his head would have reached her waist.

As a cub his fur had been a fluffy light grey, with a sprinkling of black across the shoulders. Now it was rich and thick, the grey subtly blended with white, black, silver and foxy red. But he still had that black mantle across the shoulders, and those extraordinary amber eyes.

Thunder crashed directly overhead.

Renn ducked.

The wolf yelped and shot to the back of the cave. His ears were flattened, and he was trembling violently.

Whoever he is, thought Renn, he's not yet full-grown, even if he looks it. Inside, he's still part cub.

Out loud she said gently, 'It's all right. You're safe here.'

The wolf's ears flicked forward to listen.

'Wolf? It is you, isn't it?'

He put his head on one side.

She had an idea. From her food pouch she shook a handful of dried lingonberries into her palm. As a cub, Wolf had adored lingonberries.

The wolf drew close to her outstretched hand, and his black nose twitched. Then he delicately snuffled up the berries.

'Oh, *Wolf*,' cried Renn, 'it *is* you!'

He darted back into the shadows. She'd startled him.

She shook more lingonberries into her palm, and after some cajoling, he came forward and snuffled them up. Then he tried to nibble her finger-guards. To distract him, she put a salmon cake on the ground. Wolf patted it with one forepaw in a gesture she remembered – then gulped it down without even chewing.

Four more went the same way, and now Renn was sure. The Wolf she'd known had loved salmon cakes.

On hands and knees, she crawled towards him. 'It's me,'

she said, reaching out and stroking the pale fur on his throat.

Wolf leapt up and raced to the mouth of the cave, where he ran in circles, whining. She'd done something wrong. Again.

In dismay she retreated to the fire and sat down. 'Wolf, why are you here?' she said, although she knew he wouldn't understand. 'Are you trying to find Torak, too?'

Wolf licked crumbs of salmon off his chops, then trotted to the back of the cave and lay down with his muzzle between his paws.

Outside, the thunder faded into the north as the World Spirit strode back to its Mountain. The cave filled with the gurgle of rain, and the pungent smell of wet wolf.

Renn longed to tell Wolf how glad she was to see him, to ask if he'd found Torak; but she didn't know how. She'd never paid much attention when Torak spoke wolf, because she'd found it disturbing; it had made her feel as if she didn't really know him. Now she searched her memory.

Wolves, Torak had said once, *don't talk with their voices as much as we do, but more with their paws and tails, and ears and fur, and – um, with their whole bodies.*

But you haven't got a tail, Renn had pointed out. *Or fur. And you can't move your ears. So how do you do it?*

I leave bits out. It's not easy, but we get by.

If it was hard for Torak, how was she going to manage? How was Wolf going to help her find Torak if they couldn't even talk to each other?

Wolf did not *at all* understand the female tailless.

Her yip-and-yowls told him she was being friendly, but

the rest of her was all chewed up: sometimes threatening, sometimes saying sorry, and sometimes just – unsure.

At first she'd seemed glad to see him, although he'd sensed a lot of mistrust. Then she'd stared at him rudely, and made it worse by rearing on her hind legs. Then she'd tried to apologise. Then she'd given him lingonberries and the flat fish without eyes that smelt of juniper. Then she'd apologised *again* by scratching his throat. Wolf had been so confused that he'd run in circles.

Now the Dark was over, and he was bored with waiting for her to wake up, so he pounced on her and asked her to play.

She pushed him off, saying something in tailless talk that sounded like 'Way! Way!' Wolf remembered Tall Tailless doing that. It seemed to be tailless for a growl.

Leaving the female to get up and stumble out into the Light, he bounded off to explore the Den, and was soon digging a hole, enjoying the power of his paws and the feel of the earth against his pads.

He heard a mouse scurrying in a tunnel. He stomped on the earth and seized the mouse in his jaws, tossed it high, then crunched it in two. He ate some beetles and a worm, then trotted out to find the female.

The Hot Bright Eye was shining in the Up, and he smelt that the Thunderer was gone. Greatly relieved, he raced through the ferns, relishing their wetness on his fur. He heard a fledgling magpie exploring its nest, and a forest horse in the next valley, scratching its belly on a fallen spruce. He smelt the female down by the Fast Wet, and found her standing with the Long Claw-that-Flies in her forepaws, pointing it at the ducks.

Scaring ducks was one of Wolf's favourite games. It was how he'd learned to swim, when he'd leapt into what he'd *thought* was a little Wet covered in leaves, and gone under instead. Now he longed to crash into the Wet and send the ducks hurtling into the Up. Not to hunt them; only for fun.

First, though, he must check with the female.

Politely he waited, asking her with a flick of his ears if she was hunting the ducks.

She ignored him.

Wolf waited some more, knowing that taillesses hear and smell so poorly that you can be right in front of them and they don't know you're there.

At length he decided it must be all right, and crept through the ferns to where the ducks paddled, unaware.

He pounced. The ducks shot into the Up in a satisfying spray of indignant squawks.

To Wolf's astonishment, the female yowled at him angrily. 'Woof! Woof!' she howled, waving the Long Claw at him.

Offended, Wolf trotted away. She should have *told* him she was hunting. He had asked.

But he wasn't offended for long. And as he ran off to explore, he reflected that in some strange way, he needed the female to help him find Tall Tailless.

Wolf didn't know how he knew this; it was simply the sureness that came to him sometimes. And now it was telling him that he needed to stay close to the female.

The Hot Bright Eye rose in the Up, and at last she started along a deer trail to seek Tall Tailless. Being the leader, she went ahead and Wolf trotted behind – which was an effort, because she was as slow as a newborn cub.

After a while, they stopped at a little Wet, and the female shared some of the juniper fish. But when Wolf licked her muzzle and whined for more, she laughed and pushed him away.

He was still wondering why she'd laughed when the wind curled round, and the scent hit him full on the nose.

He stopped. He raised his muzzle and took long, deep sniffs. *Yes!* The best scent in the Forest! The scent of Tall Tailless!

Wolf turned and ran back to follow the scent trail, all the way to a pine tree where, some Lights before, Tall Tailless had rested his forepaw. Wolf raised his head to smell where the scent trail led.

Back there! *They were going the wrong way!* Tall Tailless *wasn't* heading for the deep Forest – he was heading *back*, to where the Hot Bright Eye sinks down to sleep!

The female was too far off for Wolf to see, but he could hear her crashing through the bracken, heading the wrong way.

He barked at her. *Wrong way! Back back back!*

He was frantic to follow his pack-brother, for he felt in his fur that Tall Tailless was many lopes away. But still the female refused to understand.

Snarling with frustration, Wolf ran to fetch her.

She stared at him.

He leapt at her, knocking her to the ground and standing on her chest, barking.

She was frightened. And she seemed to be finding it hard to breathe.

Leave her, then.

Wolf spun round on one forepaw and raced off to find Tall Tailless.

Winded, Renn got up and brushed herself off.

The Forest felt empty after Wolf had gone, but she was

too proud to use the grouse-bone whistle to call for him. He had left her. That was that.

In low spirits, she reached a fork in the trail, and stopped. She searched for some sign that Torak had come this way. Nothing. Just impenetrable holly trees and dripping bracken.

Wolf had been so excited. And he'd been heading *west* . . . West? But that would lead to the Sea. Why would Torak have turned away from the Deep Forest and headed for the Sea?

Suddenly, Wolf appeared on the trail before her.

Joy surged through her – but she repressed a cry of welcome. She'd made mistakes before. She wasn't going to repeat them.

Squatting on her haunches, she told him in a soft voice how pleased she was to see him: keeping her eyes averted, and only now and then letting her gaze graze his.

Wolf trotted up to her, wagging his tail. He nosed her cheek and gave her a ticklish grooming-nibble, followed by a lick.

Gently she scratched behind his ears, and he licked her hand, this time refraining from trying to eat her finger-guards.

Then he turned and trotted west.

'West,' she said. 'You're sure?'

Wolf glanced back at her, and she saw the certainty in his amber eyes.

'West,' she said again.

Wolf started along the trail, and Renn followed him at a run.

FIFTEEN

Torak caught a tang of salt on the air, and came to a halt. That smell brought back memories. He'd been to the seashore once, five summers ago. Once had been enough.

Above him the pines soughed in the breeze. North through the trees, the Widewater surged over boulders, eager to reach the Sea. Torak wasn't so eager. But the Forest Horse Leader had told him that what he sought was by the Sea. He wondered if he'd been a fool to believe her. He was bitterly aware that he was no nearer to finding the cure than when he'd left the Ravens. First he'd gone east, and now west. It was as if someone was playing with him, pushing him about like a bone on a gaming-stone.

It was two days since he'd left the edge of the Deep Forest. Two days and nights on the alert for the Follower. But though he sensed that it was still with him, it hadn't shown itself, or played one of its lethal tricks.

Then last night things had got abruptly worse – but for reasons that had nothing to do with the Follower.

Torak had been sitting by the fire, struggling to stay awake while he listened to a storm growling away in the eastern hills. Twice he heard a snatch of cruel laughter on the wind. Twice he ran out of the shelter – to find nothing but tossing branches and glinting stars.

Then – very far off – he heard the wolf.

Heart racing, he strained to catch the meaning of the howls. But they were too far away, the pines too loud. He couldn't make them out . . .

Desperate, he dropped to the ground and pressed both hands flat, trying to pick up the faint tremors which wolf howls sometimes send through the earth.

Nothing.

Had he really heard it? Or had he only heard what he'd wanted to hear?

He'd stayed up most of the night, but he didn't hear it again. It was if he'd dreamed it. But he knew that he hadn't.

The scream of a seabird wrenched him back to the present.

To his right the trees thinned, and he went to investigate – and nearly fell over a cliff. It wasn't high, but it was steep. He saw crumbly earth and tree-roots; heard a clamour of seabirds. They seemed to be nesting in it.

More cautiously, he continued west with the cliff to his right. Pine-needles deadened his footfalls. His breath sounded loud. The ground sloped down, and suddenly there were no more trees, and the sunlight blinded him. He had reached the edge of the Forest.

Before him the Widewater flowed into what appeared to be a very long, narrow lake – except that the lake had no end. To the west he saw a distant clutch of pine-covered islands. Maybe those were the Seal Islands, where his father's mother had been born. Beyond them lay the glittering haze of the open Sea.

As soon as he saw the Sea, memories flooded back.

He was seven summers old, and brimming with excitement. Until now, Fa had kept him away from people, but today they were going to the great gathering of the clans.

Fa didn't tell Torak *why* they were going, or why they had to disguise themselves by painting their faces with bearberry juice. He made a game of it, saying it was best if nobody knew their names.

Torak had thought it was fun. In his ignorance, he'd thought the people at the clan meet would think so, too.

By the time they got there, the shore at the mouth of the Fastwater was dotted with a bewildering number of shelters. Torak had never seen so many different kinds: of wood and bark, turf and hide. Or so many people . . .

His excitement didn't last long. The other children scented an outsider, and closed in for the attack.

A girl threw the first stone: a Viper with cheeks as plump as a squirrel's. 'Your Fa's *mad!*' she sneered. 'That's why he ran away from his clan, because he swallowed the breath of a ghost!' Willow and Salmon Clan children joined in. 'Mad! Mad!' they jeered. 'Painted faces! Addled souls!'

If Torak had been older, he would have realised that he couldn't win against so many, and beaten a retreat. Instead the red mist had descended. No-one insulted his father.

He'd snatched up a fistful of pebbles, and was on the point of letting fly when Fa had come along and hauled him off. To Torak's astonishment, Fa didn't seem to care about the insults. He was laughing as he swung Torak high in his arms and started back for the Forest.

He'd been laughing the night he'd died. Laughing at a joke Torak had made as they were pitching camp. That was when the bear had come.

It was nine moons since Fa had been killed, but there were still times when Torak couldn't believe that he was really gone. Some mornings when he'd just woken up, he would lie in his sleeping-sack and think, there's so much I've got to tell him. About Wolf and Renn and Fin-Kedinn . . .

Then it would hit him all over again. He was never going to tell Fa anything.

Don't think about it, he told himself.

But that hadn't worked in the past, and it didn't now.

Leaving the trees, he found himself on a narrow, curving beach of grey sand. At his feet, purple mounds of seaweed gave off a salty stink. To his left, great slabs of rock lay in chaos, as if shattered by a giant hammer. To his right, the Widewater flowed into the shimmering Sea.

Torak's spirits quailed. He didn't know this world. Seagulls screamed overhead, utterly unlike the tuneful singing of Forest birds. He saw unfamiliar tracks in the sand: a broad furrow flanked by five-clawed prints like half-eaten moons. He guessed they'd been made by some large, heavy creature dragging itself towards the water. But he didn't even know if it was hunter or prey.

He climbed onto the rocks, and tiny white shells crunched under his boots. They looked like some kind of snail, but he didn't know their name, or the name of the fleshy plants that grew in the cracks, their yellow flowers trembling in the breeze.

A few paces away, a black and white bird like a magpie, but with a long red beak, pecked at a shell stuck to the rock. The bird struck suddenly and hard, prised off the shell, and ate the innards. Then it flew off with a loud, piping call.

Torak watched it go. Then he knelt at the water's edge and peered into a strange, swaying world. He saw golden-brown fronds and thread-like green weeds. When he put in his hand, the fronds felt slimy as wet buckskin, and the weeds clung to his fingers like hair. A creature with a warty orange shell felt his shadow, and slid beneath a stone.

The salt stink was making his head throb, and the glare hurt his eyes. He was gripped by an overpowering urge to run back into the Forest: to hide, and never come out.

Then he thought of the clans battling the sickness. If he didn't find the cure . . .

He forced himself to stay – and went in search of food.

He didn't know what was good to eat on the shore, but to his relief he found a clump of goosefoot at the edge of the Forest, and picked handfuls of the succulent shoots. He made a driftwood fire, and heated some large pebbles in the embers. Then he half-filled his cooking-skin with seawater, hung it from a tripod of driftwood, and with a forked stick added the hot pebbles – followed by the goosefoot, and the remains of a hare he'd snared the night before. Soon he had a tasty if very salty stew.

He was tired, although too on edge to sleep. Instead he took off his clothes and had a wash. The seawater left him clean, but a bit sticky. He pulled on his leggings, and laid his boots and jerkin to air on the rocks.

At the bottom of his pack he found the boar's tusks.

Maybe the Forest Horse Leader had been right. Maybe he should make an amulet of the tusks, in memory of the friend he'd had to kill.

Taking them to a rock pool, he cleaned them, scraping the flesh from the insides with a stick. Then he put them on the rocks to dry.

Next he strung a line of bramble-thorn fishing-hooks

across an inlet where he guessed the fish might come to feed among the weeds. For bait he used the flesh from the tusks; but to keep the hooks below the surface, he would need sink-stones.

There were pebbles on the beach, but no more rawhide cords in his pack for tying them to the lines. He didn't like the idea of cutting strips from the slimy brown seaweed. There might be Hidden People in the water; maybe those weeds belonged to them.

A couple of split pine roots would do. Which meant going back into the Forest.

He felt safer among the trees, and he wanted a reason to stay. Maybe he should cut more pine roots; always useful to have some to spare. And that meant going further in, because you must never cut more than two roots from the same tree.

The sun was getting low by the time he got back to the Sea. His things lay on the rocks where he'd left them.

Almost.

Whoever had searched his gear had gone to some lengths to replace it, but Torak knew instantly that it had been moved. A patch of yellow flowers by his pack was slightly crushed: that was where he'd set down the pack in the first place. The boar tusks, too, had been rearranged: he made out the faint crescents of damp where they'd originally lain.

Noiselessly he slipped back into the Forest. Crouched low. Wished the undergrowth was higher.

Voices on the sand, thirty paces away. Two boys were climbing out from behind the rocks. Walking slowly, searching for tracks.

Both were bigger than Torak, and looked about a summer older than him. They had sun-darkened faces and long yellow hair beaded with shells. Bands of slitted grey hide tied across their eyes gave them a blank, mask-like look.

Torak didn't need to see their eyes to know that they meant him harm. Their weapons told him that: sturdy harpoons with barbed bone heads, and knives of blue flint. The smaller one carried a slingshot stuck in his belt.

They were barefoot, in knee-length breeches of some kind of supple grey hide, and sleeveless jerkins that revealed wavy blue clan-tattoos all over their arms. Their jerkins bore a strip of clan-creature skin: glossy grey fur marked with small dark rings. Whale? Seal? Torak didn't know.

But the oddest thing about them was that he could see their tattoos and their clan-creature skins at all, because over their jerkins each boy wore a long-sleeved parka of very light, yellowish hide: so light that Torak could see right through it. He wondered what kind of creature had skin that you could see through.

'He can't have gone far,' said the shorter of the two, his voice carrying in the evening air.

'He must have slunk back into the trees,' said the other. 'Like one of those – what d'you call them? Horses?'

His companion sniggered. 'Detlan, I don't think horses slink.'

'How would you know, Asrif?' said Detlan. 'You've never seen one either.'

'I've heard about them,' said Asrif. 'Come on, let's go. He's not coming back.'

'He'd better not,' said Detlan. 'Tainting the Sea with his filthy Forest gear . . .'

Holding his breath, Torak watched them make their way down to the rocks.

From beneath an overhang they pulled two long, slender hide canoes. The canoes were utterly different from those

Torak was used to: extremely shallow in the draught, and covered at prow and stern with tight-stretched grey hide. And they must be extraordinarily light, because each boy hoisted his boat on his head without difficulty, and carried it down to the water.

Torak watched them set the canoes in the shallows, then leap aboard. With narrow double-bladed paddles they began to row, and soon disappeared, gliding silently out of sight beyond the rocks.

But he knew that it was too soon to feel relieved. This felt like a trap. He would wait them out. And like all hunters, he knew how to wait.

The breeze fell to nothing, and the water became as smooth as polished slate. The only sounds were the suck and slap of wavelets, and a duck nibbling seaweed in the shallows.

The sun sank lower. The duck spread its wings and flew off. Dusk came on – although as it was the middle of the Moon of No Dark, night would be merely a brief interval of deep blue twilight.

Still Torak waited.

It was nearly dawn when he judged it safe to go out. Stiff from crouching so long, he made his way onto the rocks.

The dew had dampened his pack, but when he checked its contents, he found to his relief that nothing had been taken.

Hungry, he went to check the fish-hooks. Stooping to draw in the line, he brushed away piles of seaweed which the wind had blown across it.

Except – there had been no wind. So how had that seaweed got there?

He leapt back just as the rope snapped taut around his ankle and yanked him off his feet.

SIXTEEN

Torak fell, knocking his head on a rock. A tall figure blotted out the sun.

Against the glare, Torak glimpsed a dark face and a blaze of yellow hair; a knife in one hand and a rope in the other, pulled tight on the noose round his ankle.

'I've got him,' said his captor to someone Torak couldn't see. Then to Torak, 'Come quietly or I'll hurt you.' He spoke without malice, but clearly meant what he said.

Torak, however, was not about to come quietly. He didn't know many fighting tricks, but he knew about feints. As his captor leaned down to tie his hands, he whipped out his knife. His captor's head jerked to follow the blade – and with his free foot Torak kicked the boy's shin as hard as he could. With a howl of pain the boy crashed onto the rocks.

Torak cut the rope at his ankle and raced off into the Forest – keeping low, and zigzagging through the willowherb so that they wouldn't get a chance to take aim.

'You can't get away from us, Forest Boy!' called a voice some way behind him – and he recognised the small boy with the slingshot, the one named Asrif.

About sixty paces in, Torak threw himself beneath a fallen pine, biting his lips to keep his breath from betraying him. The Forest was deathly quiet. There was nothing to cover the noise of his escape.

'We've got you surrounded,' yelled another boy somewhere to his right; he recognised the big one, Detlan.

'Better come out,' urged the third boy, the tall one from the rocks.

Make me, Torak told him silently.

A stone smacked into the tree-trunk above his head.

'Oh, you're in trouble, Forest Boy!' taunted Asrif. By the sound of it, he was making no attempt at stealth.

'How could you do it?' cried Detlan.

'*Why* did you do it?' shouted the tall boy.

Why did I do what? wondered Torak. Then he realised what they were doing: talking to distract him while they closed in.

Quickly he looked about. Before him the ground sloped down into a long, lush hollow. He made out alders and willows; pale-green moss and fluffy white haregrass. If you knew the Forest, that told you one thing: a bog. But from what they'd said about horses, they didn't seem to know the Forest at all.

Staying low, Torak crept to the edge of the bog. It was big – about twenty paces long and fifteen wide – and by the smell of it, deep. No way around it. He'd have to get across, and noiselessly. Only when he was on the other side would he lure them in.

It might work. If he didn't fall in himself.

Quietly he climbed a willow overhanging the bog – first

making sure that it wasn't a crack willow. Then he made his way out onto a branch. There was an alder on the other side, if he could reach it . . .

He jumped, landing half in the alder, with his feet trailing in cold, stinking mud. A branch snapped as he hauled himself up, and he breathed an apology to the tree.

Shouts behind him. 'Down there!'

They crashed towards him, noisier than a herd of aurochs, and he fled up the slope, junipers scratching his shins.

Below him his pursuers bellowed with rage. Good. They'd blundered into the bog.

'Filthy Forest tricks!' yelled one.

'You're not getting away with this!' howled another.

But it sounded as if only two of them were down there. Where was the third one, the tall boy from the rocks?

No time to think about that. He reached the top of the slope – and would have tumbled off the cliff if he hadn't grabbed a sapling just in time.

He stifled a cry of frustration. He hadn't come nearly as far as he'd thought.

The bog wouldn't slow his pursuers for long; and even if he could scramble down the cliff, the river was too wide to swim, and in those canoes they'd easily catch him. He'd have to follow the Widewater upstream, and hope he could lose them in the Forest. Which would mean leaving his gear behind on the rocks; although at least he still had his knife . . .

His knife . . .

What he held in his hand was the knife Fin-Kedinn had made for him, but Fa's knife – his most precious possession – was in his pack.

Above him there was a tearing sound – and he glanced

up to see a large branch rushing towards him. He leapt aside – but not far enough. The branch caught him painfully on the elbow, and he cried out.

'Up there!' bayed his pursuers.

He heard a ripple of laughter – and looked up to see a face of leaves disappearing into the trees.

A stone struck him on the cheekbone, and he fell against the sapling.

'We've got him,' said a voice close by.

Through a blur of pain, Torak saw the tall boy from the rocks moving calmly towards him through the pines. 'Asrif,' he said to his companion, 'I've told you before, not the head. You could have killed him.'

Asrif tucked his slingshot in his belt and grinned. 'And then wouldn't I have been sorry.'

They were back on the rocks: Torak with his hands bound behind him, his captors prowling up and down. They no longer wore the strips of hide across their eyes, but it wasn't an improvement. He could see the violence in them; their fingers flexing on the hilts of their knives. Strange knives, with hilts made of something that was neither wood, antler nor bone.

The tall boy who'd caught him on the rocks came close. He had a clever, watchful face, and eyes as cold as blue flint. 'You shouldn't have run,' he said quietly. 'That's what a coward does.'

'I'm not a coward,' said Torak, meeting his gaze. His cheek was throbbing, his feet and shins burning with scratches.

Asrif gave a gleeful laugh. 'Oh, you're in trouble, Forest

Boy!' He had a weaselly look, and kept baring his teeth in an edgy grin. 'He is, isn't he, Bale?' he said to the tall boy.

The boy called Bale did not reply.

'I don't understand,' said Detlan, shaking his head. 'To taint the Sea with the Forest! Why would he do it?' His heavy brows made a deep crease on the bridge of his nose, and Torak guessed that he wasn't too bright, but very good at following orders.

Torak turned to Bale, who seemed to be the leader. 'I don't know what you think I've done, but I never –'

'Deerskin,' spat Bale, pacing up and down. 'Reindeer hide. Forest wood. Have you no respect?'

'For *what*?' said Torak.

Detlan's jaw dropped.

Asrif tapped his forehead. 'He's mad. He must be.'

Bale narrowed his eyes. 'No. He knew what he was doing.' Then to Torak, 'Bringing your unclean Forest skins right onto the shore! Setting your cowardly traps to snare our skinboats – trailing them in the Sea herself!'

'I was fishing,' said Torak.

'You broke the law!' roared Bale. '*You tainted the Sea with the Forest!*'

Torak took a breath. 'My name is Torak,' he said. 'I'm Wolf Clan. What clan are you?'

'Seal, of course.' Bale tapped the strip of grey fur on his chest. 'Don't you know sealskin when you see it?'

Torak shook his head. 'No, I've never seen one.'

'*Never seen a seal?*' said Detlan, aghast.

Asrif hooted. 'Told you he was mad!'

Torak's face grew hot. 'I'm Wolf Clan,' he said again. 'But I'm also –'

'Is that what this is?' sneered Asrif. With a piece of driftwood he jabbed at the strip of wolfskin on Torak's jerkin.

Bale's lip curled in scorn. 'So that's wolf hide. Looks a poor sort of creature to me.'

'You wouldn't say that if you'd ever seen one,' Torak said heatedly. Then to Asrif, 'Leave that alone!' Fa had prepared that skin for him last spring, from the carcass of a lone wolf they'd found in a cave. Since then it had been unpicked and sewn to his winter parka, and now to his summer jerkin. He was dreading the time when it would be worn to shreds.

Bale flicked Asrif a glance, and the smaller boy shrugged, and threw away the stick.

'I may be Wolf Clan,' Torak told Bale, 'but my father's mother was Seal. So whether you like it or not, we're bone kin.'

'That's a lie!' spat Bale. 'If you were kin, you'd know the law of the Sea.'

'Bale,' broke in Detlan, 'we should start back. She's getting restless.'

Bale glanced at the Sea. The waves had turned choppy. 'This is your doing,' he told Torak. 'Angering the Sea Mother. Tainting her waters with the Forest.'

Asrif snickered. 'Oh, Forest Boy, it'll be the Rock for you!'

'The Rock,' Torak said blankly.

Asrif's grin widened. 'A skerry near our island. You know what a skerry is, don't you?'

'It's a rock in the Sea,' put in Detlan, who seemed to be struggling to grasp the depths of Torak's ignorance.

'They give you a skin of water,' said Asrif, 'but no food, then they leave you on the Rock for a whole moon. Sometimes the Sea Mother lets you live; sometimes she washes you off.' His grin faltered, and in his pale-blue eyes Torak saw fear. 'Washes you off,' he repeated, 'into the jaws of the Hunters.'

'Asrif, that's enough,' said Bale. 'We'll have to take him with us, and let the Leader decide.'

'*No!*' protested Torak.

Bale wasn't listening. 'Asrif, load up the trade goods. Detlan, we need a fire to purify us, especially him. I'm going to repair my boat.' With that he jumped off the rocks and onto the beach.

Detlan seemed glad of something to do, and set about gathering armfuls of dried seaweed and driftwood. Soon he had a big fire blazing, giving off plumes of thick grey smoke.

'What are you going to do to me?' said Torak.

'Give you a taste of the Sea,' said Asrif with his weaselly grin.

'You can hardly go near our skinboats stinking of the Forest,' said Detlan, as if that was too obvious to need pointing out.

Before Torak could protest, Detlan had stripped him naked and pushed him into the fire.

He managed to leap clear of the flames – but Asrif was waiting on the other side, and forced him back with his harpoon – back through the acrid, choking smoke.

Again they pushed him through it until his eyes were streaming and his throat raw. Then they tossed him into the Sea.

The cold hit him like a punch in the chest, and he swallowed salt water. Kicking with all his might, he struggled to the surface, but couldn't break the bindings round his wrists.

Rough hands hauled him out and dragged him coughing onto the rocks. Then they cut the bindings at his wrists and bundled him into a grey hide jerkin and breeches that Asrif fetched from his boat. Torak felt naked without his knife and his clan-creature skin, and he hated having to wear someone else's clothes. 'Give me – back – my things!' he spluttered.

'Lucky for you the Salmon Clan didn't want to trade,' snorted Asrif, 'or you wouldn't have anything to wear!'

'He's so skinny!' said Detlan as he yanked Torak to his feet. 'Don't they have enough prey in the Forest?'

Half-pushing, half-pulling, they led him down to the sand. Swiftly Asrif loaded his canoe at prow and stern with large, lumpy bundles wrapped in hide. A short distance away, Bale crouched by his boat, smearing a patch on its side with what looked like fat from a small hide pouch. His hands moved tenderly, but when he saw Torak, he glowered. 'Take him with you, Detlan,' he growled. 'I don't want him near my boat.'

'In you go,' said Detlan, pushing Torak towards his craft. Like Asrif's, it was laden with bundles – including Torak's gear – but only at the prow end.

Torak hesitated. 'Your friend. Bale. Why is he so angry with me?'

It was Asrif who answered. 'One of your fish-hooks snagged his skinboat. It's as well for you that he can repair it.'

Torak was puzzled. 'But it's only a boat.'

Asrif and Detlan gaped.

'A skinboat is not just a *boat*!' said Detlan. 'It's a hunting partner! Don't ever let Bale hear you say that!'

Torak swallowed. 'I didn't mean to –'

'Just get in,' muttered Detlan. 'Sit in the stern, keep your feet on the cross-bar, and *don't move*. If you put your foot through the hide, we'll both go down.'

The skinboat was so shallow that it rocked with Torak's every move, and he had to grip the sides to keep from falling out. Detlan, although much heavier, leapt in without a wobble. Torak noticed that he braced his thighs against the sides of the craft for balance.

Bale led the way, skimming across the waves at amazing speed. With the wind at their backs they sped like seabirds over the water, and when Torak twisted round, he was dismayed to see how quickly the Forest was falling away.

Soon they reached the islands he'd seen from the shore – but to his alarm, they kept going. 'But – I thought we were going to your islands!'

'Oh, we are!' grinned Asrif.

'Then why have we gone past them?'

Detlan threw back his head and laughed. 'Not those islands! Much further! A whole day's rowing!'

'*What?*' cried Torak.

They cleared the last island, and suddenly there was no more land to right or left. There was nothing but Sea.

Torak clutched the sides and stared down into the murky water. 'I can't see the bottom,' he said.

'Of course you can't!' said Detlan. 'This is the Sea!'

Torak twisted round, and saw the Forest sinking beneath the waves – and with it, all hope of finding the cure.

Suddenly on the wind he caught the howl of a wolf. It wasn't just any wolf. It was *Wolf.*

Where are you? I am here! Where are you!

Wildly Torak staggered to his feet. '*Wolf!*'

'Get down!' bellowed Detlan.

'Too late to go back now!' mocked Asrif. 'And don't even think about jumping in, because then we'd have to shoot you!'

Too late . . .

Too late, Torak heard Wolf howling for him, as the Forest disappeared into the Sea.

'Wolf!' he yelled.

Wolf had heard his plea – had braved the wrath of the World Spirit to seek his pack-brother – but Torak had put himself utterly beyond his reach.

SEVENTEEN

The three skinboats flew over the waves as the sun sank towards the Sea, and hope died in Torak's heart.

In his mind he saw Wolf running up and down the shore: howling, unable to comprehend why his pack-brother had forsaken him.

Torak couldn't bear it. If only he'd howled a reply. But he'd been too stunned. And by the time it had occurred to him, he was far away, and Wolf's howls were nothing but memory.

Bitterly he berated himself for breaking the law of the Sea. If Renn had been with him this would never have happened; the Seals would never have got angry, and he'd be back there now with Wolf.

A gust of wind drenched him with spray, stinging his eyes and making the wound on his calf smart. He lurched and nearly went overboard.

'Keep still!' said Detlan over his shoulder. 'If you fall in, I'm not hauling you out.'

'Hear that, Forest boy?' shouted Asrif from his skinboat.

'Save your breath, Asrif,' cried Bale. 'Still a long way to go.'

Torak clutched the skinboat with numb fingers. Wherever he turned, he saw nothing but waves. The Sea had swallowed everything. Forest, Mountain, Raven, Wolf. He felt as insignificant as dust on the watery hide of this vast, endlessly heaving creature.

Peering over the edge, he stared into impenetrable dark. If he fell in, when would he reach the bottom? Or would he keep sinking down and down for ever?

A bird flew past. At first Torak thought it was a goose, but then he saw that it was black all over, and flying so low that its wingtips almost touched the Sea.

Some time later, they passed a flock of small, plump seabirds sitting on the water, talking to one another in mysterious, un-bird-like groans. They had black backs and white bellies, and very bright, triangular red and yellow beaks.

Detlan caught Torak staring at them. 'Puffins,' he said crossly, 'they're puffins. Don't you have puffins in the Forest?'

Torak shook his head. 'Are they hunter or prey?'

'Both,' said Detlan. 'But we never hunt them. Puffins are sacred to the Mages.' He paused, reluctant to talk, but unable to tolerate Torak's ignorance. 'They're not like other birds,' he said at last. 'They're the only creature that can fly through the air, *and* dive in the Sea, *and* burrow under the earth. That's why they're sacred. Because they can visit the spirits.'

Asrif brought his skinboat alongside theirs. 'I bet there's nothing like them in your Forest,' he jeered.

There wasn't, but Torak was not about to admit it. He gave Asrif a hostile stare.

The evening wore on, and still the sun hung low in the sky. Soon it would be Midsummer, the time of the white nights, when the sun didn't sleep at all.

Torak would have given a lot to go to sleep. His limbs were cramped, and he kept nodding off, then jolting awake again.

Then, from far beneath the waves, he heard singing.

Of one accord, all three Seals stopped paddling.

Bale whipped off his sun-visor and scanned the waves. Asrif bared his teeth in a grimace. Detlan muttered under his breath and clutched an amulet at his breast.

Torak leaned over the side, listening.

Such a remote, lonely song. Long, wavering cries that made ripples in his mind. Echoing groans as bottomless as the deeps. It was as if the Sea herself were singing a lament.

'The Hunters,' breathed Detlan.

'There,' Asrif said quietly, pointing to the north-west.

Bale turned his head, then nodded. 'They're after capelin. We must be careful not to disturb them.'

Torak squinted into the sun, but saw nothing. Then – ten paces away – he made out a large patch of calm water. It reminded him of the smoothness you see where a river flows over a rock just beneath the surface. 'What is it?' he whispered.

'A shoal of capelin,' murmured Detlan over his shoulder. 'They hide far below, and the Hunters chase them to the surface. That's why the gulls are coming.'

As if from nowhere, seabirds appeared, mewing excitedly. But according to Detlan, it was below the surface that the Hunters would make their kill. Torak pictured the terror among the fishes as they crowded together, seeking safety, but unable to get away from the Hunters who came at them from the dark . . .

But what *were* the Hunters?

'Watch the water,' whispered Detlan.

Torak shaded his eyes with his palm.

The Sea began to seethe. Bubbles broke the surface. The water turned pale green.

'That's the capelin rising,' hissed Detlan. 'The Hunters are beneath them, and all around. They've nowhere to go but up . . .'

More gulls came, till the sky was a screaming tumult. And now Torak saw a dense mass of fish rising to the surface: slender, twisting bodies packed so tight that they turned the Sea to silver and made the water boil. In their panic some leapt clear of the waves, desperate to escape. But the gulls were waiting for them.

A fish broke the surface right beside Torak: a silver dart no longer than his hand. A huge bird with a wingspan wider than a skinboat swept down, speared it in one sharp talon, and bore it skywards. Craning his neck, Torak recognised the broad, flicked-up wing-feathers of an eagle.

A gull flew after it, intent on stealing its prize. The sea-eagle gave a contemptuous twitch of its ash-coloured tail and flew away.

Down among the gulls, the fight for fish was savage. Torak saw one gull struggling to fly away with a half-swallowed capelin jutting from its gullet, while two more chased it, tugging at the fish's tail.

Then he saw something that made him forget the seabirds.

A black fin broke the surface.

He gasped.

The fin was as tall as a man, and moving faster than a skinboat.

'Ah,' breathed Detlan. 'The Hunters are come.'

Torak glanced at the Seals. All three were watching with awe – and in Bale's case, admiration.

Another towering fin broke the surface. Then another – this one with a notch bitten out of it just below the tip. It was moving fast and with deadly purpose, circling the capelin.

So that's a Hunter, thought Torak. His father had drawn him pictures of whales in the dust, but until now Torak had never grasped how huge they were. With a shiver he realised how vulnerable he was, bobbing about in a skinboat as fragile as an eggshell . . .

Suddenly he heard a splash – and turned to see a column of spray shooting high into the air. Then a great black tail lifted clear of the water and thrashed down again. More spray flew. The water became a chaos of flying foam and shattered sunlight. And this time when the Hunter with the notched fin turned to circle the capelin, it had a young one swimming beside it, its small fin just keeping up with the big one.

On and on the Hunters circled – dived – then surfaced again, taking their fill of the prey. Then – suddenly – they vanished.

Holding his breath, Torak scanned the Sea. They could be anywhere. They could be right beneath the skinboat . . .

A throaty 'kwssh!' behind him – and a jet of spray drenched the boat from prow to stern. And there was the one with the notched fin, so close that Torak could have reached out and touched the enormous blunt-nosed head – black on top and white underneath, with an oval patch of white behind the eye. For a moment the huge jaws gaped, and Torak saw sharp white teeth longer than his middle finger. For a moment a dark, shining eye met his. Then the Hunter arched its gleaming back and dived.

He braced himself, but it didn't come again. All that remained of the hunt were the gulls squabbling over scraps, and a glitter of silver fish-scales drifting down through the green water.

Bale bowed to the Sea where the Hunters had been, then took up his paddle and moved off. The others followed in silence.

Only after they were well clear of the hunting ground did Detlan turn to Torak. 'So now you've seen them,' he said.

Torak was silent for a moment. 'They hunt in a pack,' he said. 'Like wolves.'

Detlan scowled. 'The Hunters are like no Forest creature you've ever seen. They're the fastest creatures in the Sea. And the cleverest. And the deadliest.' He swallowed. 'A single Hunter can make a whirlpool that can sink the biggest skinboat. One flick of his tail can snap a man's backbone like a capelin's.'

Torak glanced over his shoulder. 'Do they hunt people?'

'Not unless we hunt them.'

'And do you?'

Detlan glared at him. 'Of course not! The Hunters are sacred to the Sea Mother! Besides,' he added, 'they always avenge harm done to their own.' His heavy face became thoughtful. 'There's a story that once, before the Great Wave, a boy from the Cormorant Clan caused the death of a young Hunter. He didn't mean to do it, it was an accident; the Hunter had become tangled in the boy's seal net, and he'd harpooned it before he could see what it was.' He shook his head. 'The boy was so terrified that he never went out in a skinboat again. All his life – his whole life – he stayed on the shore with the women. But many winters later, when he was an old, old man, he was seized with such a longing to be once more on the Sea that he told his son to take him out in his skinboat.' Detlan licked his lips. 'The Hunters were waiting for them. They were never seen again.'

Torak thought about that. 'But – he hadn't meant to kill the young one. Was there no way he could have appeased them?'

Again Detlan shook his head, and after that they didn't speak for a long time.

The wind dropped and they entered a fog bank. Bale and Asrif disappeared. Detlan's paddle cut noiselessly through the water.

A barren rock slid by to Torak's right, with a gull perched on top.

'There,' said Detlan with a nod. 'That's the Rock.'

Somewhere in the fog, Asrif sniggered. 'Soon that'll be you, Forest boy.'

Torak set his teeth, determined not to give them the satisfaction of seeing him flinch; but inside, his spirits quailed. The Rock was scarcely bigger than a skinboat, and even at its highest point it was no taller than he was. One big wave would wash him into the Sea. He couldn't imagine surviving on it for a day, let alone a whole moon.

On they went through the fog. Torak felt it settle on his skin, beading his strange new clothes with damp.

Up ahead, something bobbed in the water.

He blinked.

It was gone.

No – there it was again, bobbing up beside him. A head like a dog's: a grey dog with a blunt, whiskered muzzle and large, inquisitive black eyes.

Detlan saw it and smiled. 'Bale! Asrif!' he called. 'The guardian has come to show us the way home!'

The seal rolled over, showing a pale, spotted belly. Then it flipped round, scratched its muzzle with one hand-like flipper, shut its nostrils tight, and sank below the surface, where it swam alongside the skinboats.

So that's a seal, thought Torak. He thought it an odd blend of ungainliness and sleek beauty.

The guardian led them well, and the fog cleared as abruptly as it had descended. Suddenly they were out in sunlight again.

'We're home,' said Detlan. Laughing, he lifted his paddle high, scattering droplets.

Torak gasped. Before him lay an island like none he'd ever seen.

Three jagged peaks reared straight out of the Sea. There was no Forest. Just mountains and Sea. The mountains were almost sheer, their grim flanks speckled with seabirds and veined with waterfalls that cascaded from patches of ice mantling their shoulders. Only at their feet could Torak see a swathe of green – and below that, a wide, curving bay with a slash of sand stained pink by the setting sun.

Smoke rose from a cluster of humped grey shelters on the sand. Beside each shelter stood a rack on which were laid several skinboats. Below them on the beach, Torak saw that two saplings had been planted, and lashed together to form an arch. The saplings were bright scarlet. Uneasily he wondered what they were for.

From across the water came the murmur of voices and the clamour of birds. With a shock he saw that the cliffs were alive with seabirds: thousands of them – wheeling, crammed onto ledges. The shelters of the Seals, too, seemed precarious and cramped. He couldn't imagine how people could live like this: caught on a narrow strip of land between mountain and Sea.

'The Seal Islands,' said Bale, bringing his skinboat alongside Detlan's. There was no mistaking the pride in his voice.

'How many islands are there?' said Torak. He could only see one.

Bale looked at him suspiciously. 'This, and two smaller ones to the north. The Cormorant and the Kelp clans live on those, but this – this is the Seals' home. It's the biggest, which is why the whole group takes its name. The biggest and the best.'

Of course, thought Torak sourly. Everything the Seals did had to be the best.

But as they drew nearer, he forgot about that. There seemed to be something very wrong with the bay. Its waters were deep crimson: too deep to be coloured only by the setting sun.

Then he caught a familiar, salty-sweet stink, very strong in the windless air. It couldn't be . . .

It was.

The Bay of Seals was full of blood.

EIGHTEEN

The clamour of seagulls dinned in Torak's ears, and the smell of blood caught at his throat.

He saw children paddling in foaming red shallows, and women washing hide in crimson water. Men moved like shadows before a leaping fire, piling huge slabs of meat beside the sapling arch. Limbs, hands, faces: all were stained scarlet, like people in a dream.

'Someone's made a big kill,' said Asrif.

'First of the summer,' said Bale, 'and we missed it.' He made it sound as if that was Torak's fault.

Suddenly Torak realised that all this meat came from just a single kill. He saw a tail fin longer than a skinboat. What he'd taken for saplings were the jawbones of a whale.

At least – he guessed it was a whale, although it wasn't a Hunter. Instead of teeth, its jaws trailed a long fringe of coarse black hair, which a Seal man was chopping off with a knife. He'd cut off his own hair, too. It lay at his feet in the same pile as the whale's.

As Torak waded onto the slippery red pebbles, he saw how happy everyone was. The whole clan was bubbling with celebration. A kill this size would mean food for days to come.

Bale leapt out of his skinboat and told Torak to *stay there*. 'Islinn will decide what to do with you after the feast.'

Alone on the shingle, Torak was painfully aware of the Seals' stares. Among the Ravens he'd been an outsider, but this was worse. And these people were his bone kin.

He watched Bale unstrap his bundles and toss them to a weather-beaten man who'd come down to meet him. From the resemblance between them, Torak guessed they were father and son.

He saw Detlan setting his skinboat on a rack, flanked by a beaming woman and a small girl, clearly his sister, who was jumping up and down, clamouring for his attention. Detlan looked embarrassed, but pleased to see her.

Asrif, still in the shallows, was being scolded by a shrewish woman even shorter than he was. 'You were supposed to bring back *two* bundles of salmonskin!' she said, jabbing her finger in his chest. 'How could you leave one behind?'

'I don't *know*,' mumbled Asrif. 'I packed them both, I know I did. And now it's not there.'

Bale was speaking to his father and pointing at Torak. Then he ran up the beach to talk to a man by the fire.

Dusk came on, the Seals went to make ready for the feast, and still Torak waited. His cheek hurt. He was ravenous.

He saw now why nobody had bothered to tie him up. There was nowhere to run to: the mountains walled in the bay. At the south end, a waterfall pounded down from a cliff-face. At the north, a track climbed up towards an overhang which jutted over the Sea like an enormous skinboat. Unless the Seals let him go, he'd never get off the island. He would be trapped, while in the Forest the clans sickened and died . . .

The sky turned deep blue. Food smells wafted down to him. He saw cooking-skins hanging from supports of what looked like whale bones, and fair-haired women chatting as they stirred. Unlike the Seal men, their calves rather than their arms bore the wavy blue lines of their clan-tattoos.

Near them, a group of girls giggled as they dug into a steaming mound from which came the rich smell of baked meat. Torak knew this way of cooking from the Ravens, but he'd never seen it done quite like this. A hunk of meat as big as he was had been wrapped in seaweed, then buried in a pit of fire-heated stones, and covered with more seaweed and sand.

The women began sharing the food into bowls. Torak noticed that only they did the cooking, while the men had cut up the carcass. That struck him as bizarre. Didn't Seal girls hunt? He wondered what Renn would say about that.

Hungrily he watched the clan gather in a circle around the fire. Still no-one came to fetch him.

A murmuring began, like the sighing of the Sea, and the whole clan lifted its arms. A figure stepped from the circle, and Torak recognised the man who'd cut off his hair. Bearing a basket of capelin, the man approached the jawbone arch, and set the offering beneath it. Torak guessed he was thanking the whale for giving its life to the clan. But instead of returning to the feast, the man trudged into the gloom, towards a cave at the foot of the overhang.

When Torak had almost lost hope, Detlan came for him,

and they went to sit some distance from the fire, with Asrif and Bale.

A girl handed Torak a bowl. It was so heavy that he nearly dropped it, and to his astonishment he saw that it was made of stone. Why in the name of the Forest would anyone make bowls out of stone? How would you carry them when you moved camp?

A disturbing idea came to him. Perhaps the Seals *never* moved camp.

'Eat,' said Detlan, tossing him a spoon.

Torak glanced at his bowl. It contained a hunk of dark-pink meat topped by a thick slab of grey fat, and a smaller piece of purplish flesh. Around it swam a sludgy stew that stank of the Sea, half a capelin, and two long, pale things that looked like fingers.

'What's the matter,' said Bale, 'not good enough? You're lucky we're feeding you at all.'

'Haven't you ever eaten shellworms?' said Asrif.

'What's in it?' asked Torak.

'The red meat's whale,' said Detlan, 'and that's blubber on top.' With his knife he speared his own chunk of purple meat. 'Whale heart. Very special. We all get a piece, to take in its strength and courage.' He crammed it in his mouth and chewed.

'Bet you don't have anything this good in the Forest,' said Asrif.

Torak ignored him and ate. The whale meat was stringy, the blubber oily and bland, and the shellworms had no taste at all. But the capelin was good.

'Had you really never seen a seal?' said Detlan.

'Detlan, why waste your time?' said Bale.

But Detlan seemed to have taken Torak's ignorance as a personal affront. 'Seals give us *everything*,' he said earnestly.

'Clothes, shelters, skinboats. Food, harpoons, lamps.' He paused, clearly wondering if he'd left anything out.

'What about your parkas?' said Torak, curious despite himself. 'That thin hide you can see through. That can't be seal.'

'It is,' said Asrif. 'It's gutskin.'

'I told you,' said Detlan, 'the seals give us everything. We are the people of the seal.'

Torak frowned. 'But no-one's allowed to hunt their clan-creature. So why do you?'

All three of them looked horrified.

'We would *never* do that!' cried Detlan. Angrily he struck the spotted fur on his chest. '*This* is our clan-creature! This is *ring*-seal! What we hunt – what we eat – that's *grey* seal!'

Torak had never heard of such a distinction, and it struck him as slippery and false. Something must have shown in his face, because Detlan's brows lowered ominously.

'Told you it was a waste of time,' said Bale, rising to his feet. Then to Torak, 'Come on. Time to face the Leader.'

Islinn the Seal Clan Leader was old and shrunken. He looked as if the life were being sucked out of him.

His wispy white hair and beard were beaded with tiny blue slate beads, and his ears were pierced with twisted, spear-like shells whose weight had stretched his earlobes to his shoulders.

Bale forced Torak to his knees. Then he named the captive to the Seals, and told them how he'd broken the law.

At that, many people cried out and ran to lay placating hands on the whale's jawbone. The Leader stroked his beard with a shaky hand, but said nothing. His rheumy eyes moved constantly. Torak wondered if they hid intelligence, or the lack of it.

At last Islinn spoke. 'You *say* that you're kin,' he murmured in a reedy voice that sounded as if he barely had the strength to force it from his chest.

'My father's mother was a Seal,' said Torak.

'What was his name?'

'I can't name him. He died last autumn.'

The Leader pondered that, then murmured to the man beside him. The man's face was hidden by drifting smoke, but Torak could tell from the thick, sandy hair and the muscled limbs that he was much younger than Islinn. His jerkin and breeches were plain, but his belt was magnificent. Made of braided hide, it was two hands wide, and fringed with the red and yellow beaks of puffins.

Puffins, thought Torak. He must be the Mage.

'Name your father's mother,' said the Leader.

Torak did.

The Leader's lipless mouth tightened.

Among the Seals, someone caught their breath.

'I knew the woman,' wheezed the Leader. 'She mated with a Forest man. I never knew that she'd had a son.'

'How do we know that she did?' said the Mage without turning his head. 'How do we know that the boy is who he says he is?' He spoke quietly, but all the Seals leaned forward to listen.

It was a remarkable voice: smooth-flowing and low-pitched, but with an undertow of great power, like the Sea. It was a voice that anyone would want to hear. For a moment, Torak almost forgot that it had called him a liar.

The Leader was nodding. 'My thoughts too, Tenris.'

The smoke shifted, and Torak saw the Mage for the first time – or at least, he saw one side of his face, for Tenris was still turned away. He was handsome in a sharp-boned way: with a straight nose, a wide mouth flanked by deep laughter lines, and a dark-gold beard cut close to the strong line of his jaw.

Torak sensed that this was the man who wielded the real power among the Seals; the man who would decide his fate. For a moment, he was reminded of Fin-Kedinn. 'I am telling the truth,' he said. 'I am your bone kin.'

'We need more than your word,' said the Mage. He turned into the light, and Torak saw that the left side of his face was terribly burned. One grey eye peered from a lashless socket. His scalp had been scorched a mottled pink. Only his mouth was unscathed. He gave Torak a wry smile, as if daring him not to flinch.

Torak put his fists over his heart and bowed. 'I admit that I broke your law,' he said, 'but only because I didn't know. My father never taught me the ways of the Sea.'

Tenris the Seal Mage tilted his ruined head. 'Then what were you doing on the shore?'

'The Forest Horse Leader told me I'd find what I'm looking for by the Sea.'

'And what are you looking for?'

'A cure.'

'For what? Are you ill?'

Torak shook his head. Then he told Tenris about the sickness.

The effect on the Seals was startling.

The Leader threw up his wrinkled hands.

Many Seals shouted in alarm.

Bale leapt to his feet, his face thunderous. 'Why didn't you warn us?' he cried. 'What if you've brought it back?'

Torak stared at him. 'You know the sickness? You've seen it before?'

But Bale had turned away, his face etched with pain.

'It came three summers ago,' the Leader said grimly. 'His younger brother was the first to die. Then three more. My son among them.'

'But now you're free of it?' said Torak, biting back his excitement. 'You found a cure?'

'For the Seals,' snarled Bale, 'not for you.'

'But you must give it to me!' cried Torak.

Bale rounded on him. '*Must?* You break our law, you anger the Sea Mother, and now you say we *must?*'

'You don't know what it's like in the Forest!' said Torak. 'The Ravens are sick. And the Boars and the Otters and the Willows. Soon there won't be enough people to hunt –'

'Why should we care?' said the Leader.

The Seals murmured agreement.

'Merely because,' put in Tenris, 'you *say* that you're kin?'

'But I am!' insisted Torak. 'I can prove it! Where's my pack?'

At a glance from Tenris, Asrif ran to a shelter, returning moments later with Torak's pack.

Eagerly Torak pulled out the bundle which held his father's knife. 'Here,' he said, unwrapping it and holding it out to the Mage. 'The blade was made by the Seals. My father's mother gave it to him, and he made the hilt.'

Tenris went very quiet as he studied the knife. Torak saw that his left hand was a burnt and twisted claw, but his right was unharmed. The long brown fingers shook as they touched the blade.

With pounding heart, Torak waited for him to speak.

The Leader, too, was peering at the knife. He didn't seem to like what he saw. 'Tenris,' he breathed, 'how can this be?'

'Yes,' murmured Tenris. 'The hilt is red deer antler, mated to a blade of Sea slate.' He raised his head and fixed Torak with a gaze grown cold. 'You say your father made this. Who was he that he dared to mix the Forest with the Sea?'

Torak did not reply.

'My guess,' said Tenris, 'is that he was some kind of Mage.'

Belatedly Torak remembered Fin-Kedinn's warning, and shook his head.

To his surprise, a corner of Tenris's mouth twitched. 'Torak, you're not a very good liar.'

Torak hesitated. 'Fin-Kedinn told me not to talk of him.'

'Fin-Kedinn,' repeated Tenris. 'I've heard the name. Is he a Mage too?'

'No,' said Torak.

'But there are Mages among the Ravens.'

'Yes. Saeunn.'

'And did she teach you Magecraft?'

'No,' said Torak. 'I'm a hunter, like my father. He taught me hunting and tracking, not Magecraft.'

Again Tenris met his eyes – and this time Torak felt the full force of his intelligence, like a shaft of strong sunlight piercing clouds.

Suddenly the Mage's face softened. He spoke to the Leader. 'He's telling the truth. He is our bone kin.'

The Leader squinted at Torak.

Bale shook his head in disbelief.

'Then you will help me?' said Torak. 'You will give me the cure?'

Tenris deferred to Islinn. 'It's for you to decide, Leader.' But he leaned over and whispered in the old man's ear.

Aided by Tenris and Bale, the Leader rose to his feet. 'Since you are kin,' he wheezed, 'we will deal with you as one of our own.' He paused to catch his breath. 'If one of us had broken the law, he would be made to appease the Sea Mother. So must you. Tomorrow you will be taken to the Rock, and left there for a moon.'

NINETEEN

Torak is back at the edge of the Forest. The sun is shining, the Sea is a dazzling blue, and he's breathless with laughter as he rolls in the sand with Wolf.

An ecstasy of tail-wagging and flailing paws, of high twisting leaps! Wolf lands full on his chest and knocks him flat, covering his face with nibble-greetings; Torak grabs his scruff and licks his muzzle, telling him in low, fervent yip-and-yowls how much he's missed him.

Wolf has grown so much! His flanks and haunches are solid with muscle, and when he rears up and puts his forepaws on Torak's shoulders, they come head to head. But he's still the same Wolf. The same clear amber eyes and well-loved smell of sweet grass and warm, clean fur. The same mix of puppyish fun and mysterious wisdom.

Wolf gives him a rasping lick on the cheek, then races off across the sand; a moment later he's back, shaking a piece of seaweed in his jaws and daring Torak to snatch it . . .

. . . and now the seaweed is floating in the cold Sea, and they are both struggling to stay alive. Wolf is terrified of deep water. He tilts his muzzle above the waves – his ears flat back, his eyes black with terror. Torak tries to swim closer to reassure him, but his limbs are dream-heavy, and he only drifts further away.

Then, over Wolf's back, he sees the fin of the Hunter.

Wolf hasn't yet seen it; but he's closer, so it will take him first.

Torak tries to scream a warning – but no sound comes. There is no escape. No land. Just the pitiless Sea, and the Hunter closing in for the kill.

Torak will not let it take Wolf. That is a certainty: as sure as the icy waves buffeting his face; as sure as his own name. There is no hesitation. He knows what he must do.

Taking a deep breath, he dives. He moves with agonising slowness, but manages to swim beneath Wolf, then up again, putting himself in the path of the Hunter. Now Wolf is behind him. Now Wolf will have a chance.

There is nothing between Torak and the tall black fin. He sees the silver wave curling back. He sees the great blunt head racing towards him through the green water. His heart swells with terror.

The Hunter's jaws open wide to swallow him . . .

Torak awoke with a shudder.

He was lying in a Seal shelter surrounded by slumbering people. His cheeks were wet with tears. He dashed them away. He longed to be back in the dream with Wolf. But Wolf was far away. And he, Torak, was destined for the Rock.

For a moment he lay staring into the gloom. Above him he saw the arching whale ribs that made the frame of the shelter, their seal-hide covering heaving gently in and out. The whale had swallowed him, after all.

Quietly he got up and made his way between the sleepers. Bale turned on his side and opened a wary eye, but let him pass. They both knew why. Where could he run to?

Torak stumbled out into the grey light. High above him, clouds poured over the peaks and flowed slowly down the cliffs. In the Seal camp nothing stirred, not even a dog.

Thirsty, Torak made his way along the bay to where the waterfall tumbled down the cliff and over a bed of boulders towards the Sea. Here the Bay of Seals was more lush than it had appeared last night. The grass was studded with yellow suncups and purple cranesbill, and the lower slopes of the cliffs were bright with rowan and birch.

Torak thought it cruel that the Seals should allow him the freedom to enjoy all this. He felt like a fish caught in a net: swimming about, but knowing it was trapped.

Kneeling by the stream, he cupped freezing water in his palm.

The Follower crouched on a boulder on the other side of the stream, watching him.

Torak froze. Icy water trickled through his fingers.

'What do you want?' he said hoarsely.

The creature did not stir. Its tangled mane hid all but its claws, and the gleam of its eyes.

'Why are you following me?' cried Torak. 'What do you *want?*'

A shadow slid across the rocks towards him – and he glanced up to see a gull swooping low. When he looked again, the Follower was gone.

With a cry he splashed across the stream – but it had vanished among the boulders and juniper scrub.

He had not imagined it. When he stooped to examine the rock where it had been, he found scratch-marks in the lichen.

His thoughts raced. It had followed him across the Sea . . .

'Who were you talking to?' said a voice behind him, and he turned to see Bale staring suspiciously. 'You were talking to someone. Who?'

'Nobody,' said Torak. 'I was – talking to myself.'

Why had it followed him? And how had it got across the Sea?

Then he remembered Asrif's missing bundle of salmon skins. That must be it. While the Seal boys had been busy with their captive, the Follower had emptied one of the bundles and hidden inside. Torak hated to think of it so close, curled up in a skinboat . . .

'I don't believe you,' said Bale. 'If you were talking to yourself, why are you looking so guilty?'

Torak didn't answer. He looked guilty because he was. *What if you've brought it back?* Bale had said last night. He'd meant the sickness, not the Follower. But was there a difference?

Torak leapt to his feet and waded across the stream. 'Where's Tenris?' he said urgently. 'I've got to speak to him.'

Bale's blue eyes narrowed. 'Why? He's not going to help you.'

Torak ignored him. He'd had an idea. It was dangerous – dealing with Mages always was – but it might just keep him off the Rock. 'Where is he?' he said again.

Bale jerked his head towards the overhang that towered above the north end of the bay. 'On the Crag. But he won't want to talk to you.'

'Yes he will,' said Torak.

The track wound steeply up the flank of the mountain, and in places Torak had to scramble on hands and knees.

Breathless, he reached the top – and found himself on a narrow neck of rock which broadened into a flat, boat-shaped promontory jutting over the Sea. In the middle stood a low slab of granite, roughly shaped in the likeness of a fish. On this lay a pile of Sea eggs. Beside it squatted the Seal Mage, murmuring under his breath.

'Mage,' panted Torak, 'I must talk to you!'

'Not so loud,' warned Tenris without looking up. 'And take care not to tread on the lines.'

Glancing down, Torak saw that the whole surface of the Crag was webbed with fine silver lines: not hammer-etched, but polished into the grey rock, and so smooth that neither lichen nor weather could take hold. Torak saw Hunters and fishes, eagles and seals: some chasing each other, some overlaid, as if eating one another; all dancing the endless dance of hunter and prey.

The Seal Mage rose with three Sea eggs cradled in his burnt hand, and began laying them out on the Crag. 'You've come to bargain for your life,' he said.

'Yes,' said Torak.

'But you've offended the Sea Mother.'

'I didn't mean to –'

'She doesn't care,' said Tenris, setting down a stone. Without turning round he said, 'Here, help me with this. Hand me the Sea eggs one by one.'

Torak opened his mouth to protest, then shut it again. Together they moved about the Crag, Torak handing over the stones when the Mage held out his hand. Once, as they neared the edge, Torak caught a dizzying glimpse of the Sea far below.

'She looks calm today, doesn't she?' said Tenris,

following his gaze. 'But do you have any idea how powerful she is?'

Torak shook his head.

With easy grace the Mage set down another stone, and at his belt the puffin beaks clinked softly. 'The man who killed the whale we feasted on last night had to cut off his hair to make amends for taking one of her children. He must live alone for three days without eating, or touching his mate. Only when the whale's souls have returned to the Mother can he come back.' He gestured at the Sea eggs at his feet. 'That's what I'm doing with these. Making a path to guide the souls.' He paused. 'What you need to understand, Torak, is that the ways of the Mother are far harsher, less predictable, than the ways of your Forest.'

From down below came the distant sound of voices. Glancing over the edge, Torak saw that the Seal camp was waking up. Bale was talking to two men, and pointing up at the Crag.

'Mage,' said Torak, 'there's something I have to –'

Tenris silenced him with a raised hand. 'She lives in the very deep of the Sea,' he murmured, 'and she is stronger than the sun. If she is pleased, she sends the seals and the fishes and the seabirds to be hunted. If she is angry she keeps them with her, and thrashes her tail to make storms. When she breathes in, the Sea sinks. When she breathes out, the tide comes in.'

He paused, gazing at the figures moving on the beach. 'She kills without warning, malice or mercy. Many winters ago, the Great Wave came out of the west. Only those who climbed to this Crag survived.' He turned to Torak. 'The power of the wind is very great, Torak; but the power of the Sea is unimaginable.'

Torak wondered why Tenris was telling him all this.

'Because knowledge is power,' said the Mage as if he'd heard his thoughts.

Torak glanced about him. 'Is this where you made the cure?'

To his surprise, Tenris gave a wry smile. 'I was wondering when you'd bring that up.'

Moving back to the altar rock, he took up a crab claw that had been lying on top, put it to his lips, and blew out a thin stream of aromatic blue smoke. 'With the cure,' said Tenris between puffs, 'it isn't where, but *when*. It can only be made on one night of the year. The most potent night of all. Can you guess which one?'

Torak hesitated. 'Midsummer?'

Tenris shot him a keen glance. 'I thought you didn't know Magecraft.'

'I don't. But Midsummer's my birthnight, so it was in my mind. And it's also the night of greatest change, and everyone knows that Magecraft –'

'– is about change,' said Tenris. Again he smiled. 'As indeed is life. Wood into leaf. Prey into hunter. Boy into man. You have a quick mind, Torak. I could have taught you much. It's a pity you're for the Rock.'

Torak seized his chance. 'That's what I need to tell you. I'm not – I'm not going to the Rock.'

Tenris went still. In the bright morning light his burns were stark. 'What did you say?'

Torak caught his breath. 'I'm not going to the Rock. You're going to make the cure. And I'm going to take it back to –'

'*I* am going to make the cure?' repeated Tenris. The chill in his voice was like the sun going in. 'And why would I do that?'

'Because if you don't,' said Torak, 'your people will get sick too.'

He told Tenris about the Follower, and how it had reached the island. He told him of his belief that the Follower was a Soul-Eater spy, sent to cause the sickness. Tenris listened without saying a word, smoking his crab-claw pipe. It was impossible to tell what he felt, but Torak sensed the rapid current of his thoughts.

Apprehensively he watched the Mage circle the altar rock, then take up the final Sea egg and move towards him.

'Did you plan this?' said Tenris.

Torak was horrified. 'Of course not!'

'Because there's something you should know, Torak. I don't like tricks.'

'It wasn't a trick! I had no idea the Follower had crossed the Sea. Tenris, I'm only asking you to make the cure because –'

'"Only"?' Tenris cut in. 'This is not some potion I can simply ladle out of a pail! It took me three moons to perfect! I had to scale the Eagle Heights to find the selik root that grows nowhere else. I had to weave a spell on Midsummer night that no-one had attempted since the coming of the Wave!'

Torak licked his lips. 'Midsummer is only four days away.'

Tenris stared at him. 'You don't give up, do you?'

'I can't,' said Torak. 'The clans are sick.'

Tenris turned the Sea egg in his hand, and his eyes glinted dangerously. 'What's to stop me putting you on the Rock, and keeping the cure for the Seals?'

Torak opened his mouth, then shut it again. He hadn't thought of that.

'Learn from this, Torak,' warned Tenris. 'Never try to lock wills with a Mage. Especially not with me.'

Torak raised his chin. 'I thought Mages were supposed to help people.'

'What do you know about Mages? You're only a hunter.'

'The Ravens *need* you! So do the Otters and the Willows and the Boars, and for all I know, the other clans too! If you put me on the Rock, who will take the cure to the Forest?'

Tenris set down the final Sea egg at his feet. '*If* I made the cure, you'd have to help.'

Torak held his breath.

'Each summer,' said Tenris, 'the Sea clans celebrate the Midsummer rites on a different island. This time it's the turn of the Cormorants. Many of us leave today; more will follow. Soon the camp will be empty.'

'I'll do whatever it takes,' said Torak.

To his surprise, Tenris laughed. 'So hasty! You don't even know what it involves!'

'I'll do what it takes,' Torak said again.

Tenris stood looking down at him, and for a moment his ruined face contracted with pity. 'Poor little Torak,' he murmured. 'You don't know what you're agreeing to. You don't even know where you are.'

Torak glanced down, and at last he saw the pattern which Tenris had been making with the Sea eggs.

It was an enormous spiral, and they were standing at its centre; like two flies caught in a web.

TWENTY

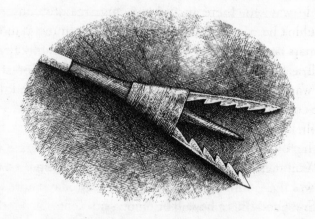

Renn had searched the shore, but she was no closer to discovering where Torak had gone.

Wolf had followed the scent for a day and a night, weaving tirelessly through the trees, but always running back for her so that she didn't get left behind.

When he'd reached the mouth of the Widewater, his eagerness had turned to agitation. Whimpering, he'd raced up and down the sand. Then he'd put back his head and howled. Such a terrible, wrenching howl.

Her search had revealed the remains of two fires: a big, messy one on the rocks, and a smaller one that was definitely Torak's, as well as a line of his double-barbed fish-hooks. But of Torak himself, she could find no trace. It was as if he'd vanished into the Sea.

That night she huddled in her sleeping-sack, listening to the sighing of the waves, wondering what had happened to him. The Sea Mother could have sent a storm to drown him within arrowshot of land. Her Hidden People could have dragged him under in their long green hair . . .

She fell into a troubled sleep. But all night long, Wolf ran up and down the shore.

He was still there in the morning. He wouldn't eat, wouldn't hunt, and showed only a fleeting interest in the fulmars nesting on the cliff – which was probably just as well, as fulmar chicks spit a foul-smelling oil, and Renn had no way of warning him. Now it was noon, and she knew she couldn't stay any longer. 'I have to find help,' she told Wolf, knowing he wouldn't understand, but needing to talk for her own sake. 'Are you coming?'

Wolf flicked his ears in her direction, but stayed where he was.

'Somebody may have seen him,' said Renn. 'A hunting party, or – someone. Come on, let's go!'

Wolf leapt onto the rocks and gazed out to Sea.

'Wolf. *Please*. I don't want to go without you.'

Wolf did not even turn his head.

She had her answer. She would be going alone. With a pang she shouldered her pack and headed towards the Forest.

Behind her, Wolf put up his muzzle and howled.

Wolf didn't know what to do.

He needed to stay in this terrible place and wait for his pack-brother; but he also needed to follow the female into the Forest.

He hated it here. The pale earth stung his eyes, the hot rocks bit his paws, and the fish-birds cawed at him to go away. But most of all he feared the huge, moaning creature who slumbered before him. She had a cold and ancient smell that he knew without ever having learnt. And if she woke up . . .

Wolf did not understand why Tall Tailless had gone where his pack-brother couldn't follow, or why his scent was so chewed up with that of three other taillesses. Wolf smelt that they were half-grown males, and angry, and not of the Forest; that they belonged to the Great Wet.

And now the female had gone too, blundering through the trees in the noisy way of the taillesses. Wolf didn't want her to go. At times she could be cross, but she could also be clever and kind. Should he follow her? But what if Tall Tailless came back and found nobody here?

Wolf ran in circles, wondering what to do.

Renn hadn't expected to miss Wolf quite so much.

She missed his warmth as he leaned against her, and his impatient little whine when he wanted a salmon cake. She even missed his enthusiasm for chasing ducks.

It hurt that he'd chosen not to follow her, and she felt lonely as she crossed the stepping stones over the Widewater, into the birch wood on the other side. Not for the first time, she asked herself what she was doing so far from her clan, in a Forest haunted by sickness. If Torak had wanted her with him, he would have asked. She was chasing a friend who didn't want her.

As she went deeper, the stillness began to trouble her. Not a thrush sang. Not a leaf stirred.

There should be people here, too. She knew this part of the Forest. When she was nine, Fin-Kedinn had put her to foster with the Whale Clan, to learn the ways of the Sea.

She knew that many other clans hunted along the coast: Sea-eagle, Salmon, Willow. They came for the cod in spring and the salmon in summer, and for the seals and the herring who sheltered here from the winter gales. But now the Forest felt eerily quiet.

Ahead, the trees thinned, and she glimpsed several large, untidy shelters made of branches. They resembled the eyries of eagles, and her spirits rose. The Sea-eagles were one of the more approachable Sea clans. They could be proud, but they always welcomed strangers; and they were fairly relaxed about mixing the Forest and the Sea, taking their lead from their clan-creature, who took its prey from both.

But the camp was deserted. The fires had been stamped out, leaving a bitter tang of woodsmoke. Renn knelt to touch the ashes. Still warm. She moved to the midden pile. Some of the mussel shells were wet. The Sea-eagles had only just left.

Behind her, something breathed.

She wheeled round.

It was coming from that shelter over there.

Drawing her knife, she moved towards it. 'Is anyone there?'

From the dark within came a guttural snarl.

She froze.

The darkness exploded.

With a cry she jumped back.

The creature sprang at her – then jerked to a halt. In a daze she saw that it was tethered at the wrists by sturdy bindings of braided rawhide.

'What are you *doing*?' shouted a voice behind her, and strong hands dragged her away. 'Are you sick too?' cried her captor, spinning her round. 'Answer! Are you sick? What's this on your hand?'

'A b–bite,' she stammered. 'It's a bite, I'm not sick . . . '

Ignoring her, he turned her head roughly to examine her face and scalp. Only when he found no sores did he release her.

'I'm not sick!' she repeated. 'What's *happened* here?'

'Same as everywhere,' he muttered.

'The sickness,' said Renn.

At the mouth of the shelter, the creature who had once been a man rocked back and forth, snarling and slobbering. Patches of his scalp glistened where he'd yanked out handfuls of hair. His eyes were gluey with pus.

The other man glanced at him, and pain tightened his face. 'He was my friend,' he said. 'I couldn't bring myself to kill him. It would've been better if I had.' He turned to Renn. 'Who are you? What are you doing here?'

'I'm Renn,' she said. 'Raven Clan. Who are you?'

'Tiu.' He held up his left hand, and on the back she saw his clan-tattoo: the four-clawed mark of the Sea-eagle.

'What will happen to your friend?' asked Renn.

Tiu went to retrieve a fishing spear propped against a tree. 'In a couple of days he'll chew through the ropes. He'll have as much chance as any of us.'

'But – he'll hurt someone.'

Tiu shook his head. 'We'll be long gone.'

'You're leaving the Forest?' said Renn.

With a last look at his friend, Tiu left the clearing, heading west.

Renn followed at a run.

'The island of the Cormorants,' he told her. 'It's their turn for the Midsummer rites; and unlike some, they're not afraid to let us come.'

'What about the other clans?' said Renn as they reached a sheltered bay where people hurried to load sturdy hide canoes.

'The Whales and the Salmons headed for the Cormorants' island a few days ago. The Willows went south.' Tiu threw her a sharp glance. 'And you? Why aren't you with your clan?'

'I'm looking for my friend. Have you seen him? His name's Torak. Thin, a little taller than me, with black hair and . . .'

'No,' said Tiu, turning away to help a woman with a bundle.

'I saw him,' called a young man loading rope into a canoe.

'When?' cried Renn. 'Where? Is he all right?'

'The Seals took him,' came the reply. 'You won't be seeing him again.'

'Three Seal boys came a few days ago,' said the young man, whose name was Kyo. 'They had flint and seal-hide clothes, but I was in no mood to trade, so I didn't show myself.' He frowned. 'The Whales made the trade. They were so desperate for Sea eggs they didn't tell the Seals about the sickness, in case it scared them off –'

'What about Torak?' broke in Renn. 'You said you saw them take him.'

'All I saw was a boy in a skinboat,' said Kyo. 'Dark, like you said. Thin, angry face. Lots of bruises. He didn't go without a fight.'

Renn's fists clenched. 'Why did they take him?'

Kyo shrugged. 'With the Seals, who knows? They're not like us, they've never learnt to live in peace with the Forest.'

'I've got to get to their island,' said Renn.

Tiu snorted. 'Not possible.'

'But you're going to the Cormorants,' she said, 'and their island isn't far from the Seals, is it?'

'You don't understand,' Tiu said angrily. 'We have no quarrel with the Seals, and we want to keep it that way!'

'But my friend is in danger!'

'We're all in danger!' snapped Tiu.

Renn looked at the worried faces around her, and wondered how to persuade them. 'There's something you need to know,' she said. 'My friend – Torak. He can do things that others can't. He might be able to find a cure.'

Tiu crossed his arms across his chest. 'You're making that up.'

'No. Listen to me. I need to tell you who he is.' By doing that, she would be going against Fin-Kedinn's orders; but Fin-Kedinn wasn't here. 'You all know what happened last winter,' she said. 'You know about the bear.'

People stopped what they were doing and drew nearer to listen.

'It killed some of our people,' Renn went on. 'It killed people here too, didn't it? Two from the Willow Clan. And we heard that among your clan it took a child.'

Tiu flinched. 'Why talk of this? What good does it do?'

'Because,' said Renn, 'my friend is the one who rid the Forest of the bear.'

Tiu stared at her. 'You said he's just a boy –'

'I said he's more than that. Fin-Kedinn would tell you if he was here. You know Fin-Kedinn?'

Tiu nodded. 'He has the respect of many clans.'

'He's my uncle. He'd tell you that what I'm saying is true.'

Anxiously Renn watched Tiu draw the others aside to talk. Moments later he returned. 'I'm sorry. We don't want to quarrel with the Seals.'

'Then don't take me to their camp,' she said. 'Leave me somewhere on their island, I'll find my own way.'

Kyo spoke to Tiu. 'There's that little bay to the southwest of their camp. We could put in there, and they'd never know.'

'And I could give her seaworthy clothes,' said a woman, 'and purify her for the journey. Tiu, she's just a girl, we can't leave her here on her own.'

Tiu sighed. 'You're asking a lot,' he told Renn.

'I know,' she replied.

She was about to go on, when – behind a juniper bush – she spotted a gleam of eyes. Amber eyes watching her.

Her heart leapt.

Excitedly she turned to Tiu. 'And I'm about to ask even more.'

'What?'

'There's someone else who needs to come too.'

The shore rang with laughter.

The Sea-eagles might be fleeing their camp, having left behind two dead and one mad with sickness, but the sight of a young wolf covered in fulmar spit made everyone smile.

'You won't need to purify him,' someone remarked. 'It looks as if he's done that by himself!'

Fulmar spit or no, Renn wanted to fling her arms around Wolf – but she contented herself with greeting him quietly, and scratching his flank.

Feebly, Wolf wagged his tail. He looked miserable. He'd taken a faceful of foul-smelling oil, then made it worse by trying to rub it off in the sand. He'd learned the hard way about not bothering fulmar chicks.

'I thought you *liked* strong smells,' Renn told him.

Wolf rubbed his face against her jerkin in a vain attempt to rid himself of the troublesome oil.

Tiu hurried past them with a bundle in his arms. 'If you can get him in my canoe,' he said over his shoulder, 'you can bring him. If not, you'll have to leave him behind.'

'I'm not leaving him,' said Renn.

'Then be quick! We're leaving!'

'Come on, Wolf,' said Renn, running down to the canoe.

Wolf didn't move. He stood with his big paws splayed and his hackles up, eyeing the canoe rocking in the shallows.

Renn's heart sank.

You didn't need to speak wolf talk to know what he was saying.

I am not going in that. Not ever, ever, ever.

TWENTY-ONE

Torak dreamed of Wolf again, but this time Wolf was warning him. *Uff! Uff! Danger! Shadow! Hunted!*

What shadow? asked Torak. Where?

But Wolf was getting further and further away – and Torak couldn't run after him, because someone was holding him back.

'Let me *go!*' he shouted, lashing out with his fists.

'Wake up!' said Bale.

'What?' Torak opened his eyes. He was in the Seal shelter, and daylight was streaming in through the door-flaps.

A day had passed since he'd spoken to Tenris on the Crag. A whole day of waiting, while the Seal Mage persuaded Islinn not to send him to the Rock, and Midsummer drew nearer, and in the Forest the sickness . . .

'Who's Wolf?' Bale said abruptly.

'What? No-one. I don't know what you mean.'

Bale wasn't fooled. 'You're not even awake and you're telling lies,' he said in disgust.

Torak did not reply. The dream lay heavy on him. *Shadow. Hunted.* What did that mean? Was it a warning against the Follower, or something else?

'Get up,' said Bale, kicking him in the thigh.

'Why? Are we setting off for the Heights?'

'That's tomorrow. Today I've got to teach you skinboating.'

'*You?* Why you?'

'Ask Tenris, it's his idea.' From his tone he didn't like it any more than Torak. 'Get some daymeal and meet me on the shore. I'll fetch the boats.'

'But why Bale?' Torak asked the Seal Mage when he found him on the rocks, gathering seaweed. 'Why can't it be someone else?' Anyone else, he thought.

The Seal Mage gave him a lopsided smile. 'And this is the thanks I get for keeping you off the Rock.'

'But Bale of all people, he –'

'– happens to be the best at skinboating,' said Tenris. 'Here, hold the basket and watch, you might learn something.'

'But –'

'This is kelp,' said Tenris, grasping a long stem of leathery brown weed. 'If you dry it, it goes hard, like this,' he tapped the hilt of his knife. 'If you wash it in sweet water, then soak it in seal oil, you can make rope. Did you see how I cut it? Always leave the holdfast on the rock so that it can grow back. That's important.'

When Torak stayed stubbornly silent, the Seal Mage paused. 'You're going to need Bale,' he said. 'And you'll need Asrif, too, he's the best at rock-climbing. Detlan will go along to lend some muscle.'

'All three of them?'

'Torak, you can't do this on your own.'

'I know. But I thought you'd be coming. You were the one who found the root before. Why not now?' He liked the Seal Mage. Tenris reminded him of Fin-Kedinn, only kinder and less remote.

With a sigh the Seal Mage touched the scarred side of his face. 'The fire that did this didn't only burn me on the outside. It scorched my lungs.' He tossed the kelp in the basket. 'I'd be no use to you on the Heights.'

Torak was abashed. 'I didn't know. I'm sorry.'

'So am I,' Tenris said mildly. 'But there's another reason I'm sending them. They're your kin, Torak. Whether you like it or not, you need to win their trust.'

'I don't care about that,' said Torak.

'Well you should.' The Mage's voice was gentle, but the undertow of strength was unmistakeable. 'Concentrate on Bale. If you win him over, the others will follow. And Torak.' His mouth twitched. 'It'll help if you're a quick learner.'

'No, no, *no!*' cried Bale, paddling closer to Torak's skinboat with infuriating ease. 'Brace your legs against the sides – you're tilting, shift your weight – no, not that much, you'll capsize!'

Reaching over, he yanked the skinboat upright. 'I *told* you! Don't use the paddle to steady yourself, that's not what it's for! You balance with your hips and your thighs, not your hands. If you're out hunting, you might need to drag a seal aboard, and then you'd need both hands free.'

'It'd help if it didn't wobble so much,' muttered Torak.

With its shallow draught and knife-edged hull, his skinboat was in constant danger of capsizing. He felt like a beetle struggling to stay afloat on a twig.

'That's not the boat's fault,' said Bale, 'it's yours.'

'Why does it have to be so shallow?'

'If the sides were any higher, you'd waste your strength fighting the wind. Try again. No! I *told* you! Don't slap the water, slice it! You need to be silent, completely silent!'

'I'm trying,' said Torak between clenched teeth.

'Try harder,' snapped Bale. 'Don't you have canoes in the Forest?'

'Of course we do!' Torak thought with longing of the dugouts of the Boars, and the Ravens' dependable deer-hide crafts. 'But they're good and solid, and we never –'

'Good and solid won't get you far on the Sea,' said Bale derisively. 'A round-bottomed boat would make bubbles that'd warn the seals you were coming from fifty harpoon throws away; and a hull that couldn't twist would break up in the first heavy swell. No, no, *over* the waves, not through them! You've got to skim the surface like a cormorant . . .'

A big wave buffeted Torak's prow, drenching him.

On the shore, children laughed. The smallest were playing at skinboats in holes in the sand lined with scraps of seal hide. The bigger ones were splashing about in beginners' crafts. Unlike Torak, they didn't have to worry about rolling over, as their boats were fitted with cross-bars that were steadied at either end by gutskin sacks filled with air.

When Bale had threatened Torak with a beginner's boat, he'd been outraged; but now after an exhausting day, he was tempted. Bale was an unforgiving teacher, driving him relentlessly. Clearly he was hoping to be able to tell Tenris that Torak was a failure.

It was beginning to look as if he'd get his wish. Torak was soaking wet, and his head was throbbing with sun-dazzle. His thighs and shoulders were screaming for rest, his arms shaking with fatigue. He could hardly hold his paddle, let alone keep his balance.

It didn't help that Bale handled his own skinboat superbly. He could bring it about with a flick of his wrist, and stand up in it as easily as if he were on dry land. He wasn't even showing off. He was simply so at home on the water that he didn't need to think about it.

Now, as the wind got up and Torak floundered to stay afloat, the older boy came alongside him, deftly steadying his own craft by sticking one end of his paddle in a cross-strap, which left the other blade in the Sea, and both hands free. 'You'll have to do better than this,' he said as he leaned over and started scooping out the water in Torak's boat with a baler.

'Or what?' said Torak. 'You'll leave me behind?'

'Yes, that's what I'm hoping.'

'Give me a chance. I've only had a day. You've been doing this since you were what, about six?'

'Five.' He glanced at the beginners in the shallows, and a shadow of sadness crossed his face. 'My brother started even younger.'

'Just give me a chance,' said Torak.

Bale thought for a moment. 'Head off over there,' he said, 'I'll follow. This time, don't think about each stroke. Just keep your eyes on the Sea, and go as fast as you can.'

Torak brought his boat about, and started to paddle.

For a while all he managed was his usual floundering, with the skinboat bucking like a hare in spring-time, and the waves slapping him stingingly in the face.

Then something happened. Almost without noticing, he

seemed to find a rhythm with the paddle. The blades cut the water without splashing, and with each stroke he felt the power of the Sea beneath him – *beneath* him, not against him. Faster and faster he went – and suddenly the skinboat gave a surge, and he was skimming over the waves, as fast and free as a seabird.

'I've got it!' he cried.

Bale came up beside him, watching with unsmiling concentration.

'Beautiful!' shouted Torak. 'It's beautiful!'

Bale nodded slowly. Now he was biting back a grin.

A gust of wind caught Torak's skinboat and spun him round, sending him straight towards the older boy.

'Turn away!' yelled Bale. 'Hard! Hard! You're going to ram me!'

Fighting the wind, Torak dug in his paddle – but it gave a jerk that nearly pitched him overboard – and when he brought it out of the water, he saw that the blade had snapped clean off.

'*Watch out!*' shouted Bale as Torak careened towards him.

'I can't turn it!'

Bale dug in his paddle and shot ahead – just in time to avoid a collision – while Torak's boat slewed round and capsized.

His clothes dragged him down, and it was a relief when Bale came about and caught him by the neck of his jerkin.

'What were you *doing?*' he yelled. 'You could have sunk us both!'

'It was an accident!' spluttered Torak.

'An accident? You tried to ram me!' Furious, he wrenched Torak's boat upright, then held its prow while Torak scrambled aboard.

'I said it was an accident!' panted Torak. 'My paddle broke!'

'That's impossible! They're made of the strongest driftwood –'

'Then what's this?' Torak brandished what remained of his paddle. 'If they're so strong, why did mine snap like a piece of kindling?' He fell silent, peering at the broken stem of the paddle. Someone had cut it. They'd only cut halfway through, leaving just enough to make it workable, but liable to snap at any time.

'What is it?' said Bale.

Torak's thoughts flew to the Follower. But it could have been anyone: Bale or Asrif or Detlan – or anyone else among the Seals.

Without a word he held out the broken paddle, and Bale took it. He was observant. Swiftly he spotted the cut edge of the stem. 'You think I did this,' he said.

'Well did you?'

'No!'

'But you want me to fail. You said so.'

'Because you'll slow us down, or get into trouble, and need rescuing.'

'No I won't,' said Torak with more conviction than he felt. 'Bale, we want the same thing. We want the cure.'

'And I'm supposed to believe that my clan is threatened,' Bale said sarcastically, 'just because you managed to talk your way off the Rock?'

Torak stared at him. 'What do you mean?'

'I don't know what story you told Tenris on the Crag,' said Bale, 'but I do know that you're a lying little coward who'd do anything to save your skin.' He tossed Torak the broken paddle. 'Maybe that's why you were so ready to believe I could play a trick like this. Because it's the sort of thing you'd do in the Forest.'

Bale's insults were ringing in Torak's ears as he made his way wearily back to shore. The older boy had gone on ahead, and carried his boat up to the racks. As far as he was concerned, there was nothing left to say.

You can't do this on your own, Tenris had said. *You need to win their trust. Concentrate on Bale . . . the others will follow.*

He was right, and Torak knew it. He had to prove to Bale that he hadn't tricked anyone.

He had an idea. If he could prove that the Follower was on the island, Bale would have to believe him.

Find the tracks, he told himself. Not even Bale could argue with that.

And it should be possible. Torak might not be any good at skinboating, but he knew how to find a trail.

As he reached the south end of the bay, dusk was coming on – or rather, the brief blue glow that counted for dusk this close to Midsummer. Leaving his skinboat on the beach, he crossed the stream, and started working his way along the bank. Terns hovered and dived above him, but he ignored them.

It was a good time for tracking: the low light would sharpen the shadows. He was glad, too, that the Seals were busy waking the fires for nightmeal, so that nobody saw him come ashore. He didn't feel like explaining what he was doing.

No prints in the soft mud. But there, on the grass: the merest hint where something small – the Follower? – had brushed off the damp as it passed.

It was hard to trace – dew trails always are – but Torak used the trick his father had taught him, turning his head to one side and looking at it from the corner of his eye.

After a few false starts, he tracked it to a stretch of limpet-crusted rocks that tilted into the Sea. Beyond the rocks, at the very edge of the bay, stood a clump of birch. To his surprise, the trail didn't lead towards them, but onto the rocks. He found a tiny piece of scuffed lichen, and a scent of rottenness where the Follower had scampered across a pile of dead seaweed.

Finally, in a patch of sand left by a previous tide, he saw it: a perfect, sharp-clawed print. Very fresh. No time for ants or sand-midges to blur the edges.

Look at this, Bale, he shouted in his head.

A cackle of laughter to his left – and there it was: a small humped figure shrouded in long hair like mouldy seaweed.

Torak was too elated to be scared. Here was the proof he needed. If he could catch it, Bale would have to admit defeat.

The creature turned and scuttled away.

Torak scrambled after it.

The seaweed was slimy under his bare feet, and a voice of caution sounded in his mind. The Follower would like nothing better than if he took a tumble into the Sea.

He reached a cleft in the rocks where the swirling Sea sent up jets of spray. The cleft was too wide to leap, but somehow the Follower had got across. There it was on the other side: eyes gleaming with malice, daring him to jump.

'Oh, no,' he panted, 'I'm not that stupid!'

The Follower bared its brown teeth in a hiss and sped into the gloom, its claws clicking on the rocks.

Torak raced round the edge of the cleft to where the seaweed was drier and less treacherous. It occurred to him to wonder how a patch of dry seaweed had come to be in the middle of all this wet . . .

Too late. The seaweed gave beneath him and he pitched into the Sea. Torak, you fool! A pitfall! The simplest trap of all!

Winded by the cold and covered in seaweed, he kicked to keep himself afloat as he sought a likely place to haul himself out. The swell was heavier than it had appeared from the rocks, but it should be easy enough, and the only harm done would be to his pride. The Follower, of course, would be long gone.

Clawing the seaweed off his face, he reached for a handhold. The seaweed was tougher than it looked. He couldn't seem to get it off his face – or push his hands through it to reach the rock.

Because it isn't seaweed, he realised in surprise. It's rope made of kelp, knotted kelp, and this is a seal net. You've fallen into a seal net. Which, presumably, was exactly what the Follower had intended.

The swell threw him against the rocks, knocking the breath from his chest. Treading water was becoming difficult, as the net clung to his legs, hampering movement. It seemed to be tied to the rocks at the top, and weighed down with something, maybe a stone, because he had to work to keep his head and shoulders above the water.

How Bale will laugh about this! he thought bitterly. How they'll all laugh when they find me floundering in a net within arrowshot of camp!

If he'd had his knife, he could have cut himself free, but the Seals hadn't trusted him with weapons. He'd have to call for help, and endure the inevitable taunts.

'Help!' he shouted. 'I'm over here! Somebody!'

The wind whistled across the bay. Terns screamed overhead. The Sea slapped noisily against the rocks.

Nobody came. Nobody could hear him.

Treading water was tiring. And strangely, the waves seemed to have risen: now they reached to just below his chin.

That was when the truth hit him, and he began to be frightened. He was trapped in a seal net, out of earshot of the camp, and the tide was coming in.

Fast.

TWENTY-TWO

The tide was creeping higher, and Torak had to fight to keep his chin above the waves.

The swell kept sucking him backwards, then smashing him against the rocks. The Sea was pounding the breath out of him. Her salt smell was thick in his throat, her restless moaning filled his head. She had taken him, and she wasn't letting go.

He tried to close his mind to her; to think what to do. There had to be some kind of opening in the net. After all, he'd fallen into it, so there must be a way out. But somehow he couldn't find it.

The mesh was small – he couldn't force his fist through – and the knots were hard as pebbles; a waste of time trying to unpick them with fingers grown numb. And the kelp was far too tough to rip apart with his hands, or bite through. 'They've got to be strong to hold a full-grown seal,' Detlan had told him at daymeal. 'And they are.'

If only he had his knife . . . What else could he use?

Again he smacked against the rocks, scraping painfully over the limpets.

Limpets. They had sharp edges, didn't they? If he could prise one off, maybe . . .

The swell drew him back, then battered him once more. As he kicked his way to the surface, the Sea's endless laughter rippled through him.

Don't listen to her, he told himself. Listen to yourself, listen to the blood drumming in your ears – anything but her . . .

Still kicking to stay above the waves, he pushed his thumb and two fingers through the meshing and grabbed the nearest limpet.

The creature clamped hard to the rock and refused to let go. Snarling, Torak clawed at its shell, but it stuck fast. It had become part of the rock.

Then he remembered the black and white bird he'd seen attacking a limpet on the shore. He'd spotted similar birds here on the Seals' island, Detlan called them oystercatchers. Torak remembered the way the bird had struck the limpet with its beak: abruptly, giving it no time to cling on.

He found another limpet and tried the same thing, striking a glancing blow with his fist. It worked. But the limpet slipped from his fingers and spiralled down, out of reach and through the net.

Again the Sea's vast laughter shuddered through him. *You cannot win,* she seemed to whisper. *Give up, give up!*

No! he shouted in his head. It's too soon!

The shout became a sob. Too *soon.* He had to find the cure, and make sure that the clans were safe. He had to see Wolf again, and Renn, and Fin-Kedinn . . .

If that stone weren't dragging down the net, he'd have a chance.

The thought woke him like a slap in the face. If he could get free of that stone, the tide would become his friend: he could make the Sea work against herself, make her lift him and carry him onto the rocks.

So why are you wasting time with limpets? he thought frantically. Get under the water and deal with that rock!

He took a deep breath and dived.

It was frightening being in her world, in a swirling chaos of black water and murky seaweed. He couldn't find the rope that tied the rock to the net, couldn't even tell up from down.

He surfaced again, gulping air. The waves were lapping higher. Now he had to strain to keep his mouth above them. Salt burned his lips, his throat, his eyes. His legs were heavy, his thoughts fogging with cold.

'Help!' he yelled. 'Somebody!' His cry ended in a gurgle that was horrible to hear.

The light was failing, and he couldn't see much: just the rock looming over him, and a deep blue sky pricked by faint stars that seemed to be sinking further and further away from him . . .

Drowning. The worst death of all. To feel the Sea Mother squeezing the life out of you, wrenching your souls apart. And without Death Marks, they would never find one another again. He would become a Sea demon, wandering for ever, hating and craving all living things, striving to snuff them out . . .

A wave washed over him, and he coughed seawater.

I am beyond pity or malice, the Sea Mother seemed to murmur in his ear, *beyond good and evil. I am stronger than the sun. I am eternal. I am the Sea.*

He was so tired. He couldn't keep treading water, he had to stop, just for a little while, to rest.

He sank, and the Sea Mother wrapped her arms about him – tight, tight, until his chest was bursting . . .

A silver flicker in the darkness.

A fish, he thought hazily. A small one, maybe a capelin?

And now there were more of them, a whole shimmering shoal, come to watch this big creature dying in their midst.

Down he sank, and the silver darts divided and flowed about him like a sparkling river, as the Sea crushed him in her arms . . .

A sickening jolt deep in his belly, as if his guts were being pulled loose. And now, quite suddenly, he was free of that crushing embrace; free of the cold and the darkness. He could no longer feel the net dragging him down, or the salt burning his throat. He couldn't even hear his own blood thumping in his head. He was light and nimble as a fish – and like a fish, he was neither cold nor warm, but part of the Sea.

And he could see so clearly! The murkiness was gone. The rocks, the floating weeds, the other capelin flowing about him – all were vivid and sharp, although strangely stretched at the edges. In some way that he didn't understand, he had *become* fish. He felt the tiny ripples in the water as each slender body flickered past; he felt the shoal's wary curiosity. He felt the stronger surges coming back from the rocks; and beneath them the vast sighs of the Mother.

Without warning, terror invaded the shoal. Panic coursed through them like lightning – and through Torak, too. Something was hunting them in the deep. Something huge . . .

What is it? asked Torak, fighting to master their terror,

which had become his own. *What is it that hunts us?*

The shoal didn't answer. Instead it whipped round and fled for the deep Sea – fleeing the Hunter prowling beneath them – leaving Torak behind. Another sickening jolt inside him . . .

. . . and he was Torak again, watching the capelin vanish into the dark.

His chest was bursting, the blood roaring in his ears. No time to wonder what had just happened. He was drowning.

Blindly he kicked out, fighting the Sea Mother's lethal embrace – and the net fought him, holding him back.

At that moment, a column of white water sent him spinning sideways, and something big plunged in beside him. Powerful teeth savaged the net – tearing him *free* . . .

Then hands were reaching down for him, trying to pull him out. They weren't strong enough – he was slipping back again, scraping his palms on limpets.

With his last shred of strength he gave a tremendous kick. It pushed him a little further out of the water: enough for the hands to grab him and wrench him out.

The Sea Mother gave a sigh, and let him go.

Torak lay gasping like a landed fish. He felt the roughness of limpets against his cheek, and the grittiness of seaweed between his teeth. He'd never tasted anything so good.

'What were you *doing?*' whispered a voice that was oddly familiar.

He rolled onto his side, then onto his knees, and spewed up what felt like half the Sea. 'D– drowning,' he gasped.

'I could see that!' said the voice, managing to sound both angry and shaken. 'But what were you *doing?* Why didn't you just climb out?'

Torak raised his head. '*Renn?* Is that you?'

'Sh! Someone might come! Can you stand? Come on! Follow me!'

Struggling to grasp what was happening, Torak staggered to his feet. He swayed, and would have toppled back into the water if Renn hadn't grabbed his wrist and dragged him towards the birch trees. 'Through here,' she whispered, 'there's a bay where we won't be seen!'

Together they scrambled between huge tumbled boulders and straggly birch, emerging at last onto a little white beach shadowed by a looming hillside.

Torak sank to his knees in the sand. 'How – did you find me?' he panted.

'It wasn't me,' said Renn, 'it was –'

A shadow bounded from behind a boulder and knocked Torak backwards into the sand, covering his face in hot, rasping licks.

'It was Wolf,' said Renn.

TWENTY-THREE

There was something fierce – almost desperate – about
the way they greeted each other. Wolf whimpering
and lashing his tail as he covered Torak's face in kisses;
Torak unnervingly like a wolf himself as he licked Wolf's
muzzle and buried his face in his fur, murmuring in the low,
fervent speech that Renn couldn't understand.

She felt like an intruder. And she was deeply shaken by
what had just happened. She kept seeing the body in the
water: face down, dark hair swirling. She'd thought he was
dead.

Her hands shook as she retrieved her quiver and bow
from where she'd hidden them behind a boulder, and
shouldered her wovengrass bag of limpets. 'Can you walk?'
she said more abruptly than she'd intended.

Still on his knees with Wolf, Torak turned and gazed at
her as if he'd no idea who she was. With his bruised face
and streaming hair he didn't look like her friend any more.

'I – I can't *believe* . . . ' His voice was rough with unshed tears.

'Torak, we've got to get out of here! We're too close to the camp, someone might come!'

But she could see that he wasn't taking it in.

'Come *on!*' she said, pulling him to his feet.

The hillside was steep, and the deep moss and crowberry made it tough to climb, but to her relief he managed it. Wolf pranced about them, swinging his tail and leaping up to nuzzle his face.

Just below the ridge, they had to stop for breath.

'How did you find me?' panted Torak, bent double with his hands on his knees.

'I was foraging on the shore,' said Renn. 'Suddenly Wolf gave that grunt he makes, and ran off.' She paused. 'Torak, what happened? Why couldn't you get onto the rocks?'

'I – was caught in a seal net.'

'A *net?*'

'I tried to get out, but I couldn't. Wolf bit through it. He saved my life.'

Renn thought about that: about the kind of love that had made Wolf brave the thing he feared the most. 'He hates the Sea,' she said. 'I had a terrible time getting him into a skinboat.'

'How did you manage?'

From inside her jerkin she drew out the thong on which hung the grouse-bone whistle.

Torak studied it. 'So if I hadn't given it to you all those moons ago, you wouldn't have been able to bring him with you. And I would have drowned.' He scratched Wolf's flank, and Wolf rubbed against him, wrinkling his muzzle in a grin.

Once again, Renn felt like an intruder. She realised that she knew nothing of what had happened to Torak since he'd left the Ravens. There was lots she had to tell him, too: about the sickness, and the tokoroth. 'Come on,' she said. 'My camp's not far.'

They crested the ridge, startling a pair of ravens who flew off with indignant caws. When Torak saw what lay before him, he cried out. 'But there's a *forest!*'

Below them lay a steep-sided valley like an axe cut through the mountains, with a long, narrow lake at the bottom. On all sides the slopes were darkened by willow, rowan and ash.

'They're not very tall,' said Renn, 'but at least they're trees. The Seals don't seem to come inland, so hiding's been easy. But yesterday I found someone's tracks down by the lake. A man's or a boy's, I think.'

'I miss the Forest so much,' said Torak, gazing at the trees.

'Me too,' said Renn. 'I miss salmon, and the taste of reindeer. And the nights are so *light* here. You don't notice it in the Forest, but here . . . I can't sleep.'

'Neither can I,' murmured Torak.

'There's my camp,' said Renn, leading him down to the hidden gully filled with ferns and meadowsweet and the frothy yellow flowers of bedstraw. A stream tumbled through, and in the east bank she'd dug herself a fox-hole, with a firepit in front. A rowan tree spread its arms protectively overhead.

'You can dry off by the fire,' she told him. 'I'll cook the limpets. They won't take long.'

Hanging up her quiver and bow, she knelt by the embers. They gave almost no smoke because she'd used ash, and peeled off the bark.

Before setting out, she'd placed a flat piece of slate over one end to heat up, and now she spat on it to check it was hot enough; it gave a satisfying sizzle. After rinsing the limpets in the stream, she set them on the slate to cook.

'What have you done for food?' asked Torak as he huddled by the fire, with Wolf leaning against him.

'Birds' eggs, mostly,' said Renn. 'A bit of hunting, but only small prey. There don't seem to be any elk or deer. There must be fish in the lake, but it's too exposed. That's why I went to the beach.' She paused. 'I'm all right, but I'm worried about Wolf. Those ravens led him to carrion, but it wasn't enough. And he won't go near seabirds, because he got spat at by a fulmar.' She gave a slight smile. 'He was so miserable. I had to find some soapwort and give him a wash. He hated that too.' She stopped, aware that she was talking too much.

Torak was frowning at the fire. 'Renn. I'm really glad you're here.'

Renn looked at him. 'Oh. Well, good.'

The limpets were cooked. With her knife she knocked them off the slate and onto a large goosefoot leaf. After tucking a limpet in a fork of the rowan tree for the clan guardian, she divided the rest into three. She put a third in the grass a short distance away for Wolf, then showed Torak how to cut away the black, blistered guts to get at the chewy orange meat. He eyed the limpets thoughtfully, then started to eat.

He'd pulled off his jerkin and hung it to dry on the rowan, and she saw that he was thinner, and that there was a wound on his calf which had been quite badly sewn up, and needed the stitches taken out. She said so, and he told her he'd do it later; then he asked about the scab on her hand.

'It's a bite,' she said, rubbing it against her thigh. She didn't want to mention the tokoroth just yet.

Wolf had already finished his limpets, and was eyeing Torak's. Torak let him have them. Then he rested his chin on his knees. 'What's it like in the Forest?' he said. 'How bad has it got?'

'Bad,' said Renn. She told him about the clans leaving, and the man in the Sea-eagles' camp.

Torak's frown deepened. 'I dreamed about Wolf, you know. He was warning me. "Shadow. Hunted." I think that's what he was saying.'

'Did he mean the sickness?' said Renn.

'I don't know. I'll ask him.' Torak lowered his head and gave a soft grunt-whine – and instantly Wolf leapt up, ears pricked. Then his tail rose, and he licked the corner of Torak's mouth, whining a reply.

'What's he saying?' asked Renn uneasily.

'Same as before. "Shadow. Hunted." I wonder what it means.'

Renn cleaned her knife in the ashes. 'Is that why you left? Because he warned you in a dream?'

'What?' said Torak.

'Is that why you left without telling anyone? Without telling me.' She couldn't keep the edge out of her voice.

'I left,' he said steadily, 'to find the cure. I didn't tell you because if you'd come with me you'd have been in danger.'

Renn stared at him. 'I was already in danger! We all were. Are! What could be worse than the sickness?'

He hesitated. 'The Follower.'

'What's that?'

'I don't know. It's small. Filthy. It's got claws.'

'The tokoroth,' Renn said in a low voice.

He sat up. 'That's what the Forest Horses said. Is that what it's called?'

408

She nodded. 'Saeunn told me after you left. That's why I came to find you. She says they're among the most feared creatures in the Forest.'

'*They*?' said Torak. 'You mean there's more than one?'

Again she nodded.

He considered that. 'It crossed the Sea hidden in Asrif's skinboat –'

'It's *here*?' cried Renn. 'Here on the island?'

'Like I said, it hid in Asrif's boat. And if one could do it –'

'– maybe others could too. They could have hidden in one of the Sea-eagles' canoes, or with the other clans.'

They were silent, thinking about that.

'But are you *sure* it's here?' said Renn.

'Oh, yes,' Torak said grimly. 'I saw it. It set the trap that nearly got me drowned.' He paused. 'I was trying to find proof – a track or something – to show the Seals.'

'To show the Seals? Why were you doing that?'

'They're helping me make the cure.'

'They're *helping* you? I don't understand. They beat you up, they took you prisoner –'

'Then they let me go.' He told her his story: about being followed through the Forest, and turned away from the Deep Forest; then being captured by the Seals, and talking his way out of punishment. 'I'm sure the tokoroth is causing the sickness,' he said, 'but the odd thing is, it hasn't given it to me. It's as if it's – testing me. I can't work out why.'

Renn was still trying to understand. 'And you say you're *not* their prisoner?'

'I told you, the Seals are helping me make the cure. They even taught me skinboating. Well. They tried. We're leaving for the Eagle Heights tomorrow.' He glanced east, where the light was growing. 'I mean, today.'

Renn reached for a stalk of goosefoot, and chewed. 'This

feels wrong. First they beat you up, and now they're *helping* you?'

'They need the cure too.'

She was unconvinced. 'This cure. I've heard of selik root, but never of its being used in Magecraft.'

'So?' Torak said sharply. 'Tenris knows what he's doing.'

'Who's Tenris?'

'Their Mage. Renn, they've had the sickness before, and he cured them! He can do it again.'

'Even if he can, what's to stop the Soul-Eaters sending more tokoroth?'

Torak stared at her. He got up and paced, then returned to the fire. 'The tokoroth,' he said. 'What *are* they?'

Renn winced. Then she took a deep breath and told him everything Saeunn had told her.

As he listened, his face drained of colour.

'Saeunn says they aren't children any more,' said Renn. 'They're demon. Utterly demon.'

'Like the bear that killed Fa,' said Torak.

Wolf got up and went to lean against him; he scratched the furry flank. Then he moved closer to the embers and knelt down. 'When I was in the net,' he said, 'something strange happened.'

Renn waited, wondering what was coming next.

'I got a sick feeling. Deep inside. I've had it before, at the healing rite. It felt – as if I was being pulled loose.' He swallowed. 'This time, in the net, I felt as if I was the fish.'

'*What?*' said Renn.

'I felt – I felt the shape of things in the water, like a fish would.' He gazed into the fire. 'Then something scared them. They felt a Hunter, somewhere in the deep water. And I felt it too, Renn. Just like a fish.'

Renn was bewildered. 'What fish? What are you talking about?'

Suddenly Wolf gave a grunt and trotted to the edge of the firelight, snuffing the air and standing with his tail extended. Even Renn knew that meant a possible threat.

She jumped up and reached for her bow.

Torak was already on his feet, pulling on his jerkin.

In the distance, a boy was calling Torak's name.

'It's Bale,' said Torak. 'I must go, or he'll get suspicious.'

'Who's Bale?' said Renn.

'He's – Bale,' said Torak, unhelpfully. 'He caught me in the Forest, but he –'

'And you want to go *back*?'

'Renn, I've got to. It's only three days till Midsummer.'

'But – you don't have to go by Sea to reach the Heights! We can go overland, I'm sure of it! Tiu's mother was a Seal, he knows the island; I got him to draw it in the sand. We could set off right now . . .'

Again that voice, calling for Torak.

'But you don't even trust them!' she cried.

'I trust – some of them,' he said. 'I think.'

'What does that mean?'

'What I do know,' he said, suddenly fierce, 'is that my friends get hurt – or killed – when they're with me. It happened to Oslak, and to the boar. You're better off staying here with Wolf.'

'Torak, no, I –'

'Keep him with you, and don't let the Seals see either of you.'

'So you're determined to go with them to the Heights.'

'Renn, I've got to.'

Her thoughts raced. 'Then we'll follow overland. Me and Wolf. You might need help.'

He met her eyes, saw that he couldn't dissuade her, and nodded once.

'Torak!' shouted Bale.

Swiftly, Torak went down on one knee and put his forehead against Wolf's, murmuring something Renn didn't understand. Wolf nosed his chin and whined.

Then Torak rose and started up the slope, heading back the way they'd come. 'Stay hidden,' he told Renn over his shoulder, 'and watch out for tokoroth.'

Uneasily, Renn glanced about her. She didn't want him to leave her here on this lonely hillside.

But he'd already gone, melting into the trees as silently as a wolf.

TWENTY-FOUR

'Torak!' shouted Bale. 'Torak! Where are you?'

Torak raced down the hill towards the little white beach. He couldn't see Bale, but he could hear him pushing through the birch trees.

Stumbling from tiredness, Torak crunched onto the sand and leaned against a boulder to catch his breath. He felt bruised and stiff and anxious. It had been wonderful seeing Wolf and Renn – but it was also terrifying. What if something happened to them?

In the ghostly twilight, the beach glowed faintly. He made out his own erratic tracks where he'd staggered from the birch trees – and then, to his horror, the tracks of Wolf and Renn. If Bale saw them . . .

Among the birches he caught a glimmer of torchlight. Bale was coming. He'd better move fast.

He was about to run forwards when two figures stepped from the trees, and Asrif said, 'I told you he'd run away. He couldn't face the Heights, so he scuttled off to hide in the woods.'

Torak drew back behind the boulder to listen.

'Maybe,' said Bale, 'or maybe he's in trouble.' To Torak's surprise, he sounded worried. 'I didn't see him get ashore.'

'So?' said Asrif. 'You don't have to look after him. I know you think you should because he's younger, but Bale, he's not your brother.'

'I know that,' snapped Bale. 'I just should've made sure he got back. It's not safe on the water for a beginner, especially not now. If the Cormorants are right –'

'Let's hope they're not,' said Asrif.

Torak stepped out from behind the boulder. 'Right about what?' he called, walking towards them and scuffing the tracks as he went.

'What *happened* to you?' cried Bale. Like Asrif, he was holding a torch of twisted kelp dipped in seal oil. In the flickering light his face was drawn. 'Where have you been?'

'Finding proof,' said Torak. 'Proof that I'm not a liar.'

Bale's face closed. 'Think of a better story. You've been gone most of the night.'

'I got caught in a seal net.'

'A seal net?' Asrif snorted. 'Now we know you're lying. We never lay them this close to camp, there aren't any seals!'

'Maybe not,' said Torak, 'but that's what happened. I'll show you.'

Praying that the tide hadn't carried it away, he led them through the birches and onto the main beach. Then he had an idea, and led them further up the sand.

'I thought you said there was a net,' said Bale.

'There is, but there's a track, too. I'll show you that first.'

He was in luck. The tide hadn't reached as far as the

tokoroth footprint, which was clearly visible in the torchlight.

Bale knelt over it. 'What made this?'

Torak hesitated. 'Something bad.'

'I think I've found the net,' shouted Asrif from the rocks. He hauled it out. 'But why would anyone put it here?' he said as they ran down to him. 'No seals come this close.'

'They weren't after seals,' said Torak, 'they were after me.'

Again Asrif snorted. 'You're making that up!'

'No, I don't think he is,' said Bale, kneeling to study the net. With his free hand he turned it over. 'Whoever did this knew what they were doing.'

'Why do you say that?' said Torak.

The older boy raised his head. 'The way to set a seal net is to fix the upper part to a line that you attach to the rocks, leaving the lower part hanging free in the water. And you've got to make sure that only one of the upper corners is firmly tied to the rock, so that when the seal swims in, it pulls the other side free, and the net collapses around it.'

'Well it worked,' said Torak with feeling. Suddenly he was back in the water, feeling the slippery kelp clinging to his legs . . .

'And look at this,' said Bale, pointing to two rows of barbed bone hooks that were set like fangs on opposite edges of the net. 'These make sure that when the net closes around the seal, it can't open again.'

Torak nodded. 'I wondered how I'd got in, but couldn't get out.'

Bale stood up. 'How *did* you get out?'

Again Torak hesitated. 'A limpet shell. I cut myself free with a limpet shell.'

Bale glanced from Torak to the ripped and tattered net, and raised his eyebrows.

Torak stared stubbornly back. He didn't like lying to Bale, but he didn't trust him enough to tell him the truth. The only way to keep Wolf and Renn safe was to keep them hidden.

'It doesn't matter how I got out,' he said. 'What matters is whether you believe me. There's something bad on the island, and it's brought the sickness. We've got to get the cure.'

Bale ran his thumb across his bottom lip. Then he said, 'All right, I was wrong. I think you are telling the truth. Or part of it. But tell me this. Why did someone want to trap you? Why you? Who *are* you?'

Torak dodged the question. 'I don't know what it wants any more than you do.'

'Are you sure about that?' said Bale.

'Quite sure.' He paused. 'So what were you and Asrif talking about just now? You said something about the Cormorants.'

Asrif and Bale exchanged glances.

Then Bale said, 'Something happened today in the strait between our island and theirs. A party of Cormorants were fishing. They were attacked.'

'Attacked?' said Torak.

'By a Hunter,' said Bale.

'A lone one,' said Asrif. 'With a notched fin.'

Torak thought of the black fins circling beneath a sky filled with seabirds; the towering fin with the notch in the tip. He thought of the terror of the capelin . . .

'Do you know how rare it is,' said Bale, 'for a Hunter to leave its pack? Males leave to seek a mate, but that's only in winter. And from what the Cormorants told us, this one wasn't seeking a mate.'

'Was anyone killed?' said Torak.

Bale shook his head. 'It smashed three skinboats, then dived. They didn't see it again. Their Mage thinks it let them live because they weren't who it was looking for.'

'Maybe it's after you, Forest boy,' said Asrif.

'Why?' said Torak with more defiance than he felt. 'Because I trailed some fish-hooks in the Sea?'

'Leave him alone, Asrif,' said Bale. He turned to Torak. 'Tenris doesn't think it's that. He says it must be something worse.' He peered at Torak. 'You haven't done anything else we need to know about, have you?'

Torak shook his head.

'Or to put it another way,' said Asrif, 'are you sure you want to come with us to the Heights?'

'I'm sure,' said Torak. But as he watched the dark waves sucking at the rocks, he wasn't sure at all. Maybe he'd done something wrong without even knowing it.

'If we haven't done anything wrong,' said Bale, 'we should be safe. We'll keep to the leads between the skerries and the coast; and to be certain, Tenris is making masking charms for the boats.' He gestured to the camp. 'Get something to eat. We're heading out soon.'

He and Asrif made for the camp, and Torak followed a few paces behind. Once again he was back in the water, watching the capelin flee. He remembered Wolf's warning in the dream. *Shadow. Hunted.*

Hunted – or *Hunter*?

Was that what Wolf had been trying to say?

Long after Torak had gone, Renn sat by the fire, thinking over everything he'd told her. That dream of his. She wished she'd asked him more.

Renn knew about dreams, because her own sometimes came true. When she was little, that had frightened her, so to dispel her fear, Fin-Kedinn had asked Saeunn to teach her about them. The Raven Mage had shown her how to find the hidden meaning. 'Dreams don't always mean what they seem to,' she'd said. 'You need to look at them sideways, as if you were searching for a dew trail.'

Shadow. Hunted.

Did that mean the sickness? Or the tokoroth? Or perhaps neither; perhaps it meant the Hunter Torak had mentioned.

The thought made her shiver. On the journey across the Sea, the Sea-eagles had been wary, having heard from the Kelp Clan that there was a lone Hunter roaming the Sea: an angry one. She should have told Torak, but there'd been so little time . . .

Wind stirred the rowan branches, and her hand crept to the hilt of her knife. It was a warm, blustery night, and the trees were moaning. Here and there she glimpsed a crouching boulder. Or maybe a tokoroth . . .

She sprang to her feet. It was no use staying here, scaring herself. It was at least a daywalk to the western tip of the island and the Eagle Heights; she should break camp now, and get a head start on the skinboats.

Feeling better for making a decision, she stamped out the fire and began gathering her things.

When she raised her head, she was startled to see that Wolf was already waiting for her on the trail. He had known what she was going to do almost before she'd known it herself.

This had happened a few times before; it was what Torak called 'the wolf sense', and usually Renn found it intriguing. Tonight she found it unnerving. It reminded her that there were some things about Wolf that would always remain hidden. And here, on this windy hillside haunted by tokoroth, that was not a comforting thought.

Shouldering her pack, she set off along a narrow hare trail that delved into gullies and gave the best cover. Wolf trotted before her, pausing now and then to catch the scents. His tail was relaxed and his hackles down, so Renn's fears began to ebb, and she let her mind drift.

I felt as if I was being pulled loose, Torak had said. *It felt as if I was the fish.*

That troubled her almost more than the tokoroth. And it had troubled Torak, too.

Suddenly she stopped. *It felt as if I was the fish.* That had nudged something in her memory – something just out of reach.

She knew it was connected to the sickness, but when she tried to grasp it, it sank beneath the surface . . .

Uff!

Wolf's warning dragged her back to the present.

He was standing motionless, gazing down at the lake.

Renn dropped to the ground and crawled behind a juniper bush.

There. Sliding through the water. A skinboat.

The light was too poor to make out who was in it. All Renn could see was that it was a man – or maybe a boy – with the long fair hair of the Sea clans. He was paddling silently east, in the direction of the Seal camp. Or almost silently. Now and then she heard the click of his paddle against the side of the boat.

Something in the turn of his head indicated stealth, and even though she was forty paces above him, Renn held her breath as she watched him reach the end of the lake and step into the shallows.

She knew that the lake drained into a stream which tumbled through a ravine and down into the Bay of Seals. The ravine was too steep and the stream too fast for anyone to pass through it – so what would the skinboater do now? The only means of reaching the bay was the way Tiu had shown her, by the little white beach.

She watched as the skinboater carried his craft ashore and hid it in a clump of birch. Then he disappeared into the trees – in the direction of the little white beach. Which meant that he was either a Seal, or someone who knew the island well.

Renn sucked in her cheeks, wondering what to do. She wanted to go after him and find out who he was and what he'd been doing; but she also needed to get a head start on Torak, or she'd never reach the Heights in time.

The thought of the Heights decided her. She didn't trust the Seals one bit; she couldn't let Torak go there alone. She would head west. And maybe when the light improved, she could pick up the skinboater's trail, and find out what he'd been doing.

As she stood up, she saw that Wolf had left her, in the noiseless way that wolves do. No doubt he'd simply gone off on one of his hunts, but she wished he'd stayed.

Treading as quietly as she could, and placing one hand on her clan-creature skin for protection, she started west.

Wolf was worried. As he loped towards the Den of the pale-pelted taillesses, he hardly smelt the voles scurrying on the other side of the Still Wet, or the female crashing through the brush. He would catch up with her once he'd made sure that his pack-brother was all right – and found something to eat.

The female had been generous with her kills, and yet a haunch of hare was nothing; he could happily have eaten a whole roe buck. But in this strange, light land where no wolf had run before, there weren't any roe buck. Or horses. Or elk. And the fish-birds were best left alone, because if you got too close, they spat.

Settling into the lope and trying to ignore the hunger gnawing his belly, Wolf raced up to the ridge, where the smells wafting from the valley were many and fascinating – then down the other side, past his friends the ravens, and on towards the Great Wet. The crunchy white ground scratched his pads, and the stink of the salt-grass made him sneeze, but Tall Tailless's scent was strong, and Wolf followed it easily to the Den.

Keeping to the shadows, he pricked his ears and snuffed the air. Tall Tailless was too far off to see, but Wolf smelt and heard him well enough – although of course his pack-brother and the other taillesses didn't even know he was there.

Taking long, deep sniffs, he sorted the different smells. Then he shook himself in frustration. Taillesses were so *complicated*. One of the pale-pelted ones spoke as a friend, but hid a terrible hunger. And Tall Tailless himself didn't say all that he felt, not even to his own pack-brother.

As Wolf stood uncertainly, a distant howling reached him – so far away that he could hardly hear it. In its feeling it was like a wolf, but not in the sound. Between the howls came many hard snapping noises, and high, swift squeaks.

Wolf had heard this howling before: once on that terrible journey in the floating hides; then again, the previous Light. It came from under the Great Wet. It came from the big black fish who hunted in packs, like wolves.

Wolf knew that the howling he could hear now was coming from the lone blackfish who had left its pack and was roaming the Great Wet alone, bitten by anger and sadness. Wolf dropped his ears in fear, and flicked his tail between his legs. He knew that against this blackfish he was as helpless as a tiny blind cub.

Tall Tailless, of course, was not helpless – but the strange thing was, he didn't know it.

Wolf had been astonished when he'd sensed this in his pack-brother as they'd sat together by the Bright Beast-That-Bites-Hot.

Tall Tailless didn't know what he was.

TWENTY-FIVE

'I told Bale you won't be taking any gear in your boat,' said Tenris as he helped Torak carry his craft down to the water. 'You'll need all your strength just to keep up.' He cast Torak a worried glance. 'You look tired. Didn't you sleep?'

Torak shook his head. He wanted to tell the Seal Mage about the net and the tokoroth, but there was no time. Already the others were loading their boats.

It was a hot day, and the Sea was deceptively smooth. But Torak kept thinking of the terror of the capelin; of black fins slicing the waves.

Tenris guessed his thoughts. 'I've put a masking charm on your hull. The Hunter won't even know you're there.'

'I wish you were coming,' said Torak.

Tenris smiled. 'So do I.' With his good hand he touched Torak's shoulder. 'Be careful.' Then he walked off up the beach.

Detlan approached, holding out a gutskin parka. 'You'll need this,' he said.

'Thanks,' said Torak. The gutskin felt stiff as he pulled it on over his jerkin, and it chafed his throat and wrists. But it would keep him dry.

'And tuck this inside your jerkin,' said Detlan, handing him a small roll of dried whale meat. 'But *don't* eat it.'

'What's it for?' said Torak.

'Always carry food on a Sea journey,' said Detlan, his brow creasing. 'Then if you go down, you don't go empty-handed.'

Torak stared at the whale meat, then tucked it in his jerkin.

On the beach, those Seals who hadn't yet left for the Cormorant island were waiting to see them off.

Detlan's little sister was trying not to cry. She was old enough to remember the last time the sickness had struck, and now, in her terror that her family would be taken, she was making a nuisance of herself by checking everyone's hands for sores.

Asrif's mother was subdued as she patted her son's chest, and told him for the tenth time to be careful.

Bale's father pressed something small into his son's hand. Bale murmured his thanks. His father's smile lit up his blue eyes.

Torak felt a pang, seeing them together. Then he thought of Wolf and Renn, and he didn't feel so bad.

'Is that an amulet?' he asked Bale when the older boy came over to check his skinboat.

Bale nodded. 'A rib from the first seal I ever caught. Fa's wound it with cormorant gullet, so if there's a storm, it'll help pull me to shore.' He glanced at Torak. 'What amulet do you carry?'

'I don't,' said Torak. 'But when I was in the Forest I had my father's knife and my mother's medicine horn.'

Bale looked thoughtful. Then he ran up the beach to the shelters, returning moments later with a slender rawhide bundle. 'Your amulets,' he said. 'Tenris says you can have them back.'

Torak unfolded the bundle. Inside were the blue slate knife, his medicine pouch, and the antler-tine horn. 'Thanks,' he muttered. But Bale had turned away, and didn't hear him.

Without ceremony they got under way. At first Torak had his hands full merely keeping his balance, but as they rounded the headland, he risked a glance over his shoulder. Tenris stood beneath the jawbone arch, watching them go. That gave Torak a twinge of unease. For a moment it looked as if the Seal Mage was being swallowed.

Heading west, they made good progress, accompanied by herring gulls and guillemots. A light breeze sprang up, shivering the surface of the Sea like the wrinkles on an old woman's face.

'She's at peace,' said Detlan, bringing his boat near Torak's.

Torak was unconvinced. Despite Tenris's masking charm, he couldn't stop scanning the water for tall black fins. Every time a fish darted beneath him or a gull's shadow slid across his bow, he jumped. Notched Fin could be anywhere. It could be under his skinboat right now.

All morning they paddled, as the sun beat down from a cloudless sky, and the coast slipped past. Torak surprised himself by keeping up, but soon the rhythm of the paddles sent him into a daze.

He was gazing blearily over the side when, almost

directly beneath him, he saw a small dark shape rising –
growing rapidly bigger.

He snapped awake, his skinboat rocking dangerously.
He tried to shout a warning, but it stuck in his throat.

A sleek grey head broke the surface beside his paddle,
and shook the droplets from its whiskers. Then the seal
yawned – baring lots of very sharp teeth – and gazed up at
him with mild, curious eyes.

Torak blew out a long, shaky breath.

The seal blew out too, opening its nostrils wide. Its
smooth grey fur was dotted with dark rings, which
explained why it was so friendly; it knew it wouldn't be
hunted.

Bale had seen it too. He was grinning as he brought his
boat about. 'The guardian! Now I know we'll be all right!'

The seal floated lazily on its back with its tail flippers
curled over its belly, watching him go by. Then with a soft
'oof' it shut its nostrils, and disappeared beneath the waves.

Maybe because of the guardian, they saw no sign of
Notched Fin, and made such good speed that in the mid-
afternoon they put in at a little bay to rest.

The tide was out, and the sand was webbed with
seaweed and the three-toed tracks of oystercatchers. Bale
and Asrif built a fire, then went to refill their waterskins,
while Detlan showed Torak how to catch shellworms.
Soon they had a pile of the long brown shells, which they
baked in the embers. Torak thought the shellworms tasted
slightly better than they had the first time. He must be
getting used to them.

With the shellworms they ate the crunchy stems of a sea-
plant which Asrif had gathered. It tasted like salty green
ice, and Torak only ate it because the others did; more to
his liking were the baked marshmallow roots that oozed a

gluey sweetness. Nobody spoke while they ate, and it struck Torak as odd that he should feel almost at ease with the same boys who'd hunted him only four days before.

The afternoon passed, and as they paddled west, Torak's arms and thighs began to ache. More than once he nodded off, jolting awake just when his paddle was about to slip from his hands. But still the Seals kept going, their fair hair streaming behind them.

He'd given up hope of ever stopping when he heard the distant din of seabirds. Narrowing his eyes against the glare, he saw a rockface rising sheer from the Sea towards a peak shaped like a Hunter's fin. At the very top he could just make out a few dark specks slowly circling.

Eagles, he thought.

'And you're really going up there?' said Torak, craning his neck at the Heights.

'I've done it before,' said Asrif with a shrug. But his face had gone the colour of wet sand.

'Once,' muttered Bale, 'you did it once. And never all the way to the eyries.'

They were standing right beneath the Heights, on a narrow stretch of rocks that followed the line of the cliffs, then reached out into the Sea like a claw. It was on this claw that they'd left the skinboats – so that, as Bale said, 'if he falls, he won't damage the boats.'

The Eagle Heights were the tallest cliffs Torak had ever seen. Scarred by the frosts of many winters, their gaunt flanks were the dark red of raw whale meat, and spattered with bird droppings. The stink caught at his throat; the din made his head throb.

And if he'd thought the cliffs at the Bay of Seals were crowded, this was far worse. You couldn't slip a feather between the cormorants huddled on the lowest rocks; further up, hordes of guillemots jostled for space, while kittiwakes and herring gulls squabbled above them. The highest crags of all held the huge, shapeless eyries of the eagles.

'Some of those eyries are hundreds of winters old,' murmured Bale, 'and some of the eagles are over fifty.' Despite the noise he spoke softly, and Torak understood why. It wasn't just the eagles they had to watch out for. The Heights themselves were awake, and would shrug off an unwanted intruder. At his feet lay fragments of shattered stone which meant only one thing. Rockfalls.

And yet according to Bale, the Seals did sometimes climb the Heights, if other prey was scarce, and they couldn't get enough eggs closer to camp. That explained the short stone pegs jutting at intervals from the rock all the way to the lowest eyrie, dizzyingly high above.

That was their target; but Torak couldn't see any plants growing around it, let alone the selik root Tenris had described. 'Small, about a hand high, with purple-grey leaves, and hooked roots, like the talons of an eagle.'

Torak's neck was getting sore, and he rubbed it. 'Who put in the climbing pegs?' he asked.

'My grandfather's grandfather,' said Bale. 'Although we have to replace them when the cliffs move.'

'And we don't usually go as far as the eyries,' said Asrif.

'And it's a bad time to be trying it,' said Detlan. 'They've got nestlings. They'll think Asrif's after them.'

'Let's hope they've got the wisdom to know that he's not,' said Bale. From a pouch at his belt he took a withered grey-green stalk which he broke into four. 'Here.' He handed out the pieces.

Detlan and Bale chewed theirs, but Torak eyed his suspiciously. 'What is it?'

'Cliffwort,' said Bale with his mouth full. 'Takes away giddiness.'

'I thought only Asrif was going up.'

'He is,' said Bale. 'But you can get just as giddy looking up as you can looking down.'

The stalk was bitter, but almost immediately Torak's head cleared.

He felt spare and useless as he watched Deltan help Asrif put on the heavy kelp-rope harness, and check the big wooden hook at its back; Bale slinging the coil of rope over his shoulder, and testing the hook at its end.

'What can I do?' he asked.

Asrif flashed him a grin that was more of a grimace. 'Catch me if I fall.'

'Just keep out of the way,' muttered Bale.

Torak ground his teeth. They wouldn't even let him help.

Stifling his frustration, he watched Bale draw back his arm and throw the rope. The hook floated high, then dropped neatly over a peg about ten paces up. Asrif caught the hook and fixed it to the one at his back, and Detlan took the other end of the rope and pulled it taut. Asrif began to climb, finding cracks and climbing pegs with his hands and feet, while Detlan braced himself to take his weight if he fell.

When he neared the peg over which the rope had been flung, he found a ledge beside it and balanced on his toes, clinging to the rockface with one hand while he unhooked the rope from his harness and tossed it down. It hit the ground with a thump – Torak had to jump smartly back – and Bale cast it again, this time over a higher peg, taking care to avoid knocking Asrif off. Asrif needed good balance to catch the swinging hook and attach it to his harness.

As he climbed higher, seabirds lifted off the cliff and fluttered indignantly about him. A couple of times he slipped and came off the rockface. Only the harness – and Detlan's muscle – stopped him plunging to his death.

While Detlan and Bale sweated at the rope, Torak stood by, hating his helplessness. Asrif made his way precariously up the cliff. For the last few lengths – which were out of Bale's reach – he cast the rope himself, choosing pegs that were close enough to allow him to do so without losing his balance. By now he was nearing the eyrie.

As Torak watched, shading his eyes with his palm, he saw a dark, hunched shape lift off a crag. It had the enormous, blunt–fingered wings of an eagle; and it was spiralling slowly down towards Asrif.

A solitary eagle circled the peak. Renn thought of Torak on the other side, and quickened her pace.

Although the sun was getting low, it was still hot on the trail, and the breeze wafting from the lake did little to cool her. She'd been walking since well before dawn. Wolf had returned soon after, to her great relief; but he'd been keen to head west, and it had been a struggle to keep up with him. Even now he was racing ahead – although always running back for her.

She wondered if he knew where Torak was, or if he'd picked up the trail of the skinboater she'd seen on the lake. She had found no trace of him, except for a second skinboat hidden under some brush at the edge of the lake. The boat had been empty. A spare, maybe. But that told her nothing about what the skinboater had been doing in this part of the island.

'These days, the Seals don't go inland,' Tiu had told her. 'They used to, but they've become much stricter about keeping Forest and Sea apart.'

'Doesn't anyone live on the west coast?' Renn had asked.

Tiu had shaken his head. 'It belongs to the eagles. You can see their home from far away: a great red peak shaped like a Hunter's fin.'

Renn had first glimpsed the peak at midday. Now, as she left the lake behind her, she stood directly beneath it.

From this side it was unscaleable: a treacherous scree slope on which not even crowberry could gain a hold. To her left, though, among some straggly rowan trees, there might be a way around its southern foot, and down to the Sea. She would need that if she was to find Torak.

But to her surprise, Wolf wasn't interested in that way. Instead he went north, disappearing into a birch thicket, then bursting out again, keen for her to follow. He didn't seem worried; simply excited. She decided to go after him.

Pushing through the thicket, she found herself climbing a rocky slope that soon had her breathless and scratched. It was a relief to come out on a windy ridge high above a beach of glittering black sand. To the north the beach came to an abrupt end where a cliff had fallen into the Sea, leaving a tumbled mass of boulders. In the midst of these, screaming flocks of birds squabbled over something large and dead.

Carrion, thought Renn, watching Wolf race down the slope to the beach. No wonder he's excited. Now he'll have enough to eat.

She'd come this far, so she decided to see what it was.

The wind changed, and she caught the stench of rottenness. As she reached the bottom and crunched through the charcoal-coloured sand, she saw Wolf at the other end of the beach, scattering the birds. Crows and gulls dived at him, but he fended them off with a few good snaps. The wiser ravens settled on the rocks to wait their turn.

Then she saw that someone else had been here before her. Beside Wolf's tracks were a man's. Walking, not running. Whatever the skinboater had been doing here, he'd taken his time.

As she drew nearer, the carrion stink grew so strong that she had to breathe through her mouth. In the glare of the sun she couldn't see much of whatever had died among the boulders. Just a big, humped shape splashed with bird droppings, and Wolf tearing hungrily at the dark-red flesh.

At her approach he moved round to the other side, to put more distance between them. That should have told her to give him more eating space, but what she saw made her forget about that. Oh no, she thought. It can't be.

Wolf raised his head and growled at her, then gave an uncertain whine and wagged his tail. He was telling her that he liked her, but she was getting too close to his meat.

She stumbled backwards. She'd seen enough.

The young Hunter had been trapped in a kelp net, and killed with an axe. Then its carcass had been left for the birds. Only its teeth had been hacked out.

Feeling sick, Renn sank to her knees in the sand, staring at the small black fin covered in peck-marks. Why would anyone do such a thing?

Then she remembered the Kelp Clan's warning about the lone Hunter.

No wonder it's angry, she thought.

TWENTY-SIX

On the Heights, Asrif was in trouble.

He'd reached a ledge just beneath the eyrie, but the back of his harness had caught on a rock, and he couldn't unsnag it.

'He could cut himself free,' said Detlan, craning his neck.

'Then what does he do for a harness?' said Bale.

Torak said, 'If he's really caught, then –'

'– then he can't get down,' snapped Bale. 'Yes, we've already thought of that.'

'What I mean,' said Torak, 'is I could go up and help him.'

'*What?*' said Detlan and Bale together.

'Those other pegs, a bit to the side? If I could reach them –'

'*If*,' said Bale.

Torak looked at him. 'You've got a spare harness and a spare coil of rope; and I'm lighter than Asrif. I saw how he did it.'

Bale was staring at him as if he'd never seen him before. 'You would do this?'

'We need that root,' Torak said simply. 'Besides,' he added, 'what else are we going to do?'

The first ten paces were easy. The harness crossed loosely over Torak's shoulders and round his waist, with the big wooden hook at the back linking to the hook at the end of the rope. A quick check reassured him that both hooks were well-made, of good hard spruce.

With Detlan holding Asrif's rope, Bale held Torak's while he climbed to the first ledge.

'Don't look down,' Bale warned him. 'And don't look too far up, either.'

Torak forgot that almost at once. As he waited to catch the hook after Bale tossed it over the next peg, he caught a glimpse of Asrif, impossibly high above; and above Asrif, a raft of branches jutting from a cleft. The eyrie. But where were the eagles?

At the second attempt he caught the hook, and after an awkward struggle, managed to link it to the one between his shoulder blades. Then, when he felt the tug on the rope that told him Bale was ready, he began to climb.

The pegs were sturdy, but too widely spaced for him, and twice he slipped, and the harness snapped taut, checking his fall.

The heat on the rockface was intense. Before starting, he'd taken off the gutskin parka, but even so, he quickly broke out in a sweat. Every ledge and cranny was smeared with bird-slime. The stink stung his eyes, and soon his hands and feet were grey and slippery.

Throwing the rope was a lot trickier than it had appeared when Asrif did it, but he managed it after several attempts. It reassured him to feel his father's knife bumping against his thigh, and the weight of his medicine pouch at his belt, with his mother's medicine horn inside.

Here and there he passed incongruous tufts of pink clover shivering in the breeze. A guillemot chick twisted its scrawny neck to watch him. Most birds fled at his coming, but some tried to chase him away. Kittiwakes fluttered screaming about him. As he climbed past a ledge crowded with fulmar chicks, he narrowly avoided a faceful of foul-smelling spit.

Just when he was beginning to wonder if he would ever get there, he heaved himself onto a ledge that brought him level with Asrif.

The Seal boy was a little over an arm's length away, on his hands and knees with his back to Torak, his shoulder strap hopelessly snagged on a jagged tongue of rock. No wonder he hadn't been able to free himself.

Asrif glanced awkwardly over his shoulder. 'Good to see you, Forest boy,' he said, trying for a grin that didn't work. His face was red, although whether from exhaustion or humiliation, Torak couldn't tell.

'I think I can unhook you,' said Torak. He began edging sideways along a narrow crack that led from his ledge to Asrif's.

'Watch out for the eagles,' warned Asrif.

Torak risked a glance up – and nearly fell off the cliff in shock. Directly above him, the eyrie blotted out the sky. A huge tangle of lichen-crusted branches, it was easily as big as a Raven's shelter. From deep inside he heard a faint 'chink chink' of nestlings. But of their parents he could see no sign.

'Where are they?' he murmured.

'Circling higher up,' said Asrif. 'I think they know I'm stuck. It won't be the same for you.'

Torak swallowed, and glanced back to the ledge he'd just left. His rope was securely looped over the final peg, a short way above it. If he missed his footing, that should stop him falling too far. If, of course, the rope didn't break, or his harness didn't snap, or the peg didn't crack . . .

If, if, if, he told himself impatiently. Get on with it.

He moved further along the crack. But even straining as far as he could, he couldn't reach Asrif's harness.

He tried to get closer – but his rope held him back. He tugged at it – the signal for Bale to feed him more slack – but nothing happened.

'He can't give you any more,' said Asrif. 'There's none left.'

Torak glanced down – a dizzying drop to the upturned faces far below – and saw Bale shaking his head.

He thought for a moment. Then he wriggled out of his harness, and let it swing free from the final peg. Now there would be nothing to hold him if he fell.

'What are you *doing*?' whispered Asrif in horror.

'Try to keep the birds off me,' said Torak as he edged closer.

Again he reached out for Asrif's harness – and this time his fingers brushed it.

A shadow slid across the rock – and he ducked as a herring gull flew at him with a strident 'kyow'. Asrif shouted and threw a stone. He missed, and the gull flew away, spattering them both. Foul white slime clogged Torak's hair and leaked down his face, narrowly missing one eye. He spat out the worst and tried again.

This time he grabbed Asrif's shoulder strap. His fingers

were slippery with bird-slime, and he couldn't pull the harness off the snag. 'Move back a bit,' he gasped, 'let it slacken.'

Asrif shuffled back.

With a jerk that nearly took him with it, Torak yanked the harness free of the rock.

Asrif was still on hands and knees, open-mouthed with shock. He turned and met Torak's eyes. 'Thanks,' he muttered.

Torak gave a curt nod. 'The root. Did you get the root?'

Asrif shook his head.

'*What?*'

'I couldn't reach.' His face puckered with shame. 'I chose the wrong pegs, climbed myself to a dead end. Should've taken your route instead.'

Torak risked another glance up, and saw that a short way to his right, a deep, slanting crack zigzagged up towards the nether part of the eyrie. At its top, in the very shadow of the eyrie, nestled a clump of glossy, dark-purple leaves. Selik root.

He thought about going back to the ledge he'd just come from, and putting on his harness. But there was no more slack in the rope; it wouldn't allow him to reach the eyrie. He would have to do without.

'I should be able to make it,' he said, with more confidence than he felt.

His arms and legs trembled with strain as he sought handholds and hoisted himself up the crack. He was hot and tired, and the stink of bird-slime was making him sick.

Beneath his foot, the crack gave. Just in time he climbed

further up – and watched part of the rim disintegrate, the fragments rolling and bouncing before shattering on the boulders, dangerously close to Detlan and Bale.

It occurred to him that he should have shouted a warning, but it was too late now. Besides, shouting would displease the cliff, which seemed to be waxing impatient with these interlopers on its flank.

He edged further up the crack towards the selik root.

'Look out!' whispered Asrif below him.

A menacing 'klek klek' echoed off the cliff – then a shadow sped towards him – and he looked round to see an eagle coming straight at him, its vicious talons reaching for his face. He needed both hands to cling on, he couldn't even shield his head, could only flatten himself against the rock. He caught a fleeting glimpse of fierce golden eyes and a sharp black tongue – heard the hiss of wings wider than a skinboat . . .

A stone struck the eagle on the breast, and it wheeled away with a screech.

Torak glanced down at Asrif, who'd found another pebble and was fitting it to his slingshot.

Torak couldn't see where the eagle had gone. Maybe it had been frightened off, but he didn't think so. More likely it was circling for another attack.

Above him, the cleft widened and became much easier to climb. When he reached the top, he found to his relief that it was deep enough to allow him to go down on his right knee, and by pressing himself against the sun-hot rock, reach down with his left and unsheath his knife.

The sky darkened. More wingbeats – more hammer-like alarm calls – this time from *two* eagles: the mated pair fighting to protect their nestlings.

'I'm not after your young!' cried Torak, forgetting to

lower his voice as he brandished his knife.

Not surprisingly, the eagles didn't listen. As he reached for a clump of the selik root and dug at it with his knife, he expected at any moment to be wrenched off the cliff.

Several well-aimed strikes from Asrif warded them back, but the eagles kept coming. The cliffs rang with their calls.

'Hurry *up!*' called Asrif.

Torak thought that too obvious to need a reply.

The selik root had taken hold in a sunbaked 'earth' of rotten wood and eagle pellets, and it didn't want to let go. Sweat poured down Torak's sides as he chipped away at the base of the plant with Fa's blue slate knife. The rim of the cleft on which he knelt was crumbly, and as he worked, more fragments broke off and bounced into nothingness. Desperately he grasped a clump of selik root by the stems, and rocked it loose.

'*Hurry!*' cried Asrif. 'I'm running out of stones!'

At last the plant came free. The root was small, no bigger than his forefinger: a pale, mottled green. For a moment Torak stared at it, unable to believe that so insignificant a thing could deliver the clans from the sickness.

'I've got it,' he called to Asrif. Tucking the root inside his jerkin and re-sheathing his knife, he started back down the cleft towards the ledge where his harness waited.

Beneath his foot, the rim cracked – and gave. He flung himself back, clutching at rock. '*Look out!*' he yelled, as a sheet of rock almost as big as he was broke off and hurtled down the cliff – taking his harness with it.

Torak clung to the rockface, watching in disbelief as the harness tangled with the rock – narrowly missed Asrif – and floated almost lazily down, striking the boulders with a distant thump a few paces from Detlan and Bale.

The noise of the seabirds fell away. All Torak could hear

was his own breath, and the trickle of pebbles.

Above him the eagles spiralled higher. They knew that he would trouble their nestlings no more.

Below him, Asrif raised his head and met his eyes.

Both knew what this meant, but neither wanted to say it. Torak now had no way off the cliff – except to attempt the long climb down without a harness, which would almost certainly kill him.

Asrif licked his lips. 'Climb down to my ledge,' he said.

Torak thought about that, and shook his head. 'No room,' he said.

'There might be. We could share my harness.'

'It'd never take the two of us. We'd both be killed.'

Asrif did not reply. He knew Torak was right.

'You take the root,' Torak said abruptly.

Asrif opened his mouth to protest, but Torak talked over him. 'It makes sense, you know it does. You can get down from there. You can take it to Tenris, he can make the cure. For everyone.'

He sounded very sure, but his heart was fluttering like a fledgling. Part of him could not believe what he was saying.

Leaning down as far as he could, he lowered his arm, then let fall the root. Asrif caught it and tucked it inside his jerkin. 'What will you do?' he said.

Torak felt surprisingly clear-headed as he thought over his choices. Maybe that was the cliffwort; or maybe he simply hadn't taken in what was happening.

The stretch of rocks where Bale and Detlan stood was directly beneath him. It was narrow, and behind it lay the Sea. If he jumped, he might hit that instead.

'You could *try* climbing down,' said Asrif, his face young and scared.

'With you below me?' said Torak. 'And what about Detlan and Bale? If I fell, I might kill you all.'

Asrif swallowed. 'But what else –'

'Watch your head,' said Torak, and launched himself off the cliff.

TWENTY-SEVEN

Torak was falling through glowing green water – through glowing green light – and he wasn't scared at all, just hugely relieved that he hadn't hit the rocks.

After the heat of the cliffs, the water was so cold it was a kick in the chest, but he hardly felt it, because now he was falling into a Forest.

Golden, sun-dappled kelp shimmered and swayed to the rhythms of the Sea. Its roots were lost in darkness, and through its undulating fronds the silver capelin sped like swallows.

And here through the kelp came the guardian, shooting towards him with one thrust of her flippers, then rolling over to gaze at him upside-down. With her big round eyes and bubble-beaded whiskers, she was so friendly and inquisitive that he wanted to laugh out loud.

The swell carried him sideways into colder water – and suddenly a sharp pain stabbed his gut. No time to wonder what was happening – no time to be afraid. Besides, the pain was fleeting, it had already gone. And now he wasn't cold any more, he was wonderfully *warm*, and weightless, and so at home in this beautiful, soft green world that he didn't ever want to leave.

And yet – he had to have air.

Reluctantly he kicked towards the surface. Up he spiralled, shooting through the water in a stream of silver bubbles. But when he put out his head, the world above the waves was so jagged and hard that he shut his nostrils tight, and flipped over again, back into the beautiful green light. Down he dived, faster than he'd ever thought possible, back into the kelp.

Something was floating down there in the kelp. Curious, he swam closer to take a look.

It was a boy: limp, unconscious, the current rolling him to and fro as the kelp entwined him. Torak wondered if Asrif had fallen in, or maybe Detlan or Bale. But the long, waving hair was darker than that of the Seal boys – and as it parted, he glimpsed a thin face with staring grey eyes; and on both cheekbones, the blue-black tattoos of the Wolf Clan.

With a surge of terror he realised that he was looking at himself.

His thoughts teemed like frightened fishes. What's happening? Am I dead? Is that why the guardian has come, to take me on the Death Journey?

Then he came to his senses. Don't be stupid, Torak, this guardian's a seal, and you're Wolf Clan! Your guardian would be a *wolf!*

But if I'm not dead, he thought as he stared in horrified fascination at the floating boy, *then what's happening?*

He dived closer towards himself, then came to a sudden

halt by spreading his front flippers to push back the water.

His flippers?

And they were *his* flippers, there was no doubt about it. He could open and close them like hands – and as he did so, he saw their short grey fur waving gently in the water.

He rolled over and swam upside-down, and found to his astonishment that he could see far down into the dark, to where purple starfish made their prickly way across the bottom. He could hear the tiny, hard, biting sounds of fish nibbling kelp; the brittle clink of crabs feeling their way over rocks.

But most of all, he could *feel* through his whiskers. His whiskers were so keen that they could pick up the rippling tracks of the smallest fish as it darted through the water. The Sea was webbed and criss-crossed with thousands of invisible fish trails. And he felt, too, the strong, slow tremors which the kelp sent back through the water; and the waves echoing off the rocks. He hung upside-down, trying to make sense of this bewilderment of trails.

Then – faint and far away, he heard singing.

Long, eerie shrieks; a furious hailstorm of clicks. A song of anger and loss, coming to him from the open Sea.

A shudder ran through him from the tips of his whiskers to the end of his stubby tail. And now he felt the huge disturbance in the water as the creature came closer at incredible speed . . .

His mind flooded with dreadful certainty.

The Hunter is coming.

Another sickening jolt – another sharp pain in his gut – and suddenly he was Torak. He was bitterly cold and desperate for air, and he couldn't see much at all, he was too far down – but out of the corner of his eye he saw a flash of silver flippers as the guardian fled for the shelter of the deeps.

The Hunter is coming!

With all his might, Torak kicked for the surface. His limbs were dream-heavy and he moved with infuriating slowness, but at last he broke free of the waves.

Gasping, coughing, he got a choppy view of limpet-crusted boulders – and saw with enormous relief that the current had carried him close to the claw of rock which jutted from the cliffs. Desperately he struck out for it. Maybe he could reach it before the Hunter . . .

Glancing over his shoulder, he saw that Asrif had managed to get down off the cliffs, and was jumping up and down, shouting frantically. Then, to Torak's horror, he saw Bale and Detlan setting out in their skinboats – setting out to rescue him. Didn't they know that they were far more at risk than he? He at least had a chance of reaching the claw – but in their boats they would be utterly exposed to the wrath of the Hunter.

'No!' he yelled. 'Get back! *Get out of the water!*'

They couldn't hear. Or did they think he was calling for help?

Swimming as fast as he could, he yelled again. 'Get out of the water! The Hunter's coming! *The Hunter's coming!*'

This time Bale heard him – but instead of turning his skinboat about, he paddled faster towards Torak, shaking his head in puzzlement. And Torak saw with consternation that the Sea around him was treacherously calm, with not a black fin in sight. Bale didn't understand the warning – *because he couldn't see the Hunter.* He didn't know it was coming.

'Get back!' yelled Torak again. 'The Hunter is coming!'

Now Bale understood – and plunged in his paddle and

brought his skinboat about, shouting at Detlan to do the same. 'Back! Back!'

The waves threw Torak against the claw, and he grabbed seaweed and hauled himself out – just as a loud, throaty 'kwoosh!' erupted behind him, and a shower of spray shot high into the air.

As he collapsed on the rocks he caught a fleeting glimpse of a great black back arching out of the water – then a towering, notched fin. He was so close that he saw the wave curling back from its edge; and as the huge blunt head powered past him, he met the dark, unknowable eye of the Hunter. Then it was gone, sweeping past him, making straight for the skinboats.

They had heeded his warning too late. Bale was nearly at the rocks, where Asrif was reaching out to him and yelling encouragement – but Detlan was further behind, and Notched Fin was gaining on him.

Torak scrambled to his feet and ran towards them, leaping over skinboats, slipping on seaweed. But the Hunter was many times faster than him, and he watched in horror as it closed in on Detlan – swerved, and slammed its enormous tail, catching the stern of the skinboat and sending it flying.

Detlan landed with a scream on the rocks, then slid back into the water. Asrif and Bale ran to his aid as the black fin raced towards him – then, at the last moment, twisted round and disappeared beneath the waves.

Asrif and Bale pulled Detlan's limp body from the water and laid him on the rocks.

Breathless and shaken, Torak scanned the Sea – but saw nothing. Only white foam rocking on the waves where the Hunter had been, moments before.

Then, far in the distance, he saw a black fin heading out

to Sea. Whatever – whoever – Notched Fin was seeking, it hadn't found them here. Torak turned and ran towards the others.

Asrif was on his knees, wrenching out the plug of a waterskin with his teeth. Bale was shaking the contents of a medicine pouch onto the rocks. Detlan lay with his eyes closed. His face was frighteningly pale, his lips blue with shock; but as Torak got nearer, he saw to his relief that the Seal boy was breathing.

Bale shot Torak a glance. 'You all right?' he said.

Torak nodded. Then to Asrif, 'Do you still have the root?'

Asrif touched his jerkin, but didn't speak.

Detlan's skinboat was shattered, and so was his leg. Torak could see the white gleam of shinbone poking through bloody flesh.

'Why me?' gasped Detlan. 'Why was it after me?'

Bale put his hand on his friend's shoulder. 'I don't think it was,' he said. 'If it had been, you'd be dead by now.'

'The Cormorants were right about one thing, though,' muttered Asrif, putting the waterskin to Detlan's lips. 'It's after someone.'

'But who?' said Bale.

Then he turned to Torak, and asked the question that Torak was already asking himself. 'And how in the name of the Sea Mother did you know it was coming?'

TWENTY-EIGHT

Renn thought Torak looked pale as he knelt by the injured boy.

Hiding among the boulders thirty paces away, she trilled her signal: the song of a redstart. She'd chosen a redstart because they are Forest birds, so he'd be sure to notice.

He didn't. That astonished her. For Torak not to notice something like that – he must be shaken indeed.

It was a hot, sticky night, with the breathless feel that comes before a storm, and she'd been sweating by the time she'd found her way through the rowans and boulders at the foot of the cliffs. She'd arrived just after the Hunter had attacked.

Neither Torak nor the Seal boys seemed to know *why* it had attacked; but she did. She could still smell the carrion stink, still hear Wolf's famished champing. He'd been so intent on his food that when she'd left the beach, he'd hardly glanced up.

As the sun sank lower and the blue midsummer glow

descended, she waited among the boulders, desperate to tell Torak about the slaughtered Hunter – but almost as desperate not to be seen by the Seals.

Then another Seal arrived in a skinboat: a man in a gutskin parka with a terribly burnt face, who took charge of everything. The short, slight Seal boy drew something from inside his jerkin, and the man put it carefully in a little pouch at his neck; Renn guessed it must be the selik root. Then, using pieces of the wrecked skinboat, the man splinted the wounded boy's leg, while giving orders to the others.

Renn was surprised at how Torak's face lit up when the burnt man came; and she felt a small stab of jealousy when the man told him to fetch wood for a fire, and he instantly obeyed.

'Is it all right if it's from ordinary trees instead of driftwood?' he asked, his voice carrying over the rocks.

The burnt man nodded, and Torak started moving across the rocks.

Renn forgot her jealousy. Maybe he'd heard her signal after all.

She watched him stoop for a stick of driftwood, then wander down to the Sea; then turn and start towards the boulders.

'Where are you?' he said softly.

'The rowan trees,' she whispered. 'Up here – no, further along.'

When he got within reach, she grabbed his jerkin and pulled him behind a spur which cut them off from the others. 'At last!' she breathed. 'I've been waiting and waiting –'

'Where's Wolf?' he said abruptly.

'In the next bay, feeding. That's what I –'

'You'd better gather some wood too,' he muttered, 'I can't go back empty-handed.'

'What? Oh. Yes, of course.' Close up, she saw that he was still pale, and not meeting her eyes. 'Torak, are you all right?'

He shook his head. 'What about you?'

She brushed that aside. 'Listen. I know why the Hunter attacked.' She told him about the murdered young one, and the tracks of the fair-haired skinboater. 'No wonder it's angry,' she said. 'That young one must have been its kin, and the skinboater trapped it and cut out its teeth, then left it to rot.'

'But – why would anyone do that?' said Torak.

'I don't know, but it's got to be some kind of spell. Although who would dare do anything that evil. To break clan law – to kill a *Hunter* . . .'

'Revenge,' murmured Torak to himself. 'Yes, that would be it.' He sounded sad as well as angry.

Renn was puzzled. 'Who did?'

His face contracted as if in pain. 'When I was in the water. It was so . . . I don't – I can't –'

'Torak, don't you see what this means?' she broke in. 'The skinboater who did this – *he was a Seal!*'

'What? What are you saying?'

'Something is terribly, terribly wrong – *and the Seals are part of it!* Who knows, maybe they're even causing the sickness! Maybe that's why he needed the teeth!'

Torak took a step back from her. In disbelief he shook his head.

'Haven't you ever wondered,' she went on, 'why none of them has fallen sick, and yet you've been on the island for days, and so has the tokoroth?'

'That doesn't mean anything,' he whispered.

'Then why did they send only boys to fetch the root? If they really thought they were threatened, why not send men?'

'Because Asrif is the best at climbing, and –'

'And you believe that?'

Torak hesitated, then shook himself. 'Ever since they knew about the sickness, the Seals have been trying to *help*.'

'Torak –'

He turned on her. 'Tenris kept me off the Rock! Asrif defended me from the eagles! Detlan and Bale were coming to *rescue* me when the Hunter attacked! Bale lost his *brother* to the sickness three summers ago!'

'Why are you so keen to defend them?'

'Why are you so keen to condemn them?'

'Because the skinboater had fair hair! Because his tracks show that he was the one who murdered the Hunter!'

'But almost everyone in the Sea clans has fair hair! Besides, you said yourself that you heard his paddle click against his skinboat! If you knew anything about Seals, you'd know they never *make* any noise! The man you saw could have been anyone. A Cormorant, or one of your friends the Sea-eagles –'

'But not one of your friends the Seals,' Renn said bitterly.

'They're not my friends,' he retorted. 'They're my kin.'

She flinched.

Stonily he took the firewood she'd gathered and added it to his own. 'I've got to go back,' he said without looking at her.

Renn was horrified. 'Haven't you been listening?'

'Renn, it's nearly Midsummer. We've only got a day to reach the camp.'

'By *Sea*? With a storm coming, and a vengeful Hunter –'

'Tenris has a masking charm, and he says –'

'And Tenris is never wrong.'

Torak did not reply.

'If I'm right about this,' said Renn, 'you're going back into

451

danger, and putting the clans at risk – because you won't listen.'

Torak turned on his heel and left.

It was much later, and on the cliffs, the seabirds were agitated. Many were leaving their roosts to fly inland. There was a storm on its way.

Torak had woken after a brief, unrefreshing sleep. Soon he would set off with Tenris and Bale. The plan was to leave Asrif and Detlan here, so that the three of them could return to camp at speed; with luck they would reach it before the bad weather hit, and in time for Midsummer night and the preparation of the cure.

On the other side of the fire, Detlan slept deeply, thanks to Tenris's sleeping-potion, Asrif and Bale through sheer exhaustion. Tenris sat by the fire, smoking his crab-claw pipe.

Blearily, Torak rubbed his face. He was tired, but he knew he wouldn't get any more sleep. The fight with Renn had left him churned up inside. They'd had quarrels before, but never one this bitter. He felt cut off from her – and not only because of what had been said between them, but because of what had happened in the water.

He had been a seal. He had heard things, felt things that only a seal could. But he had also been Torak . . .

Tenris tapped his pipe on a stone, making him jump.

A corner of the Mage's mouth lifted in a slight smile; Torak tried to smile back. Tenris had arrived without warning, saying simply that he'd 'felt he was needed'. Torak hadn't been able to say just how glad he was. Now he watched the Mage frown as he refilled his pipe, holding it in his twisted hand, while with his good one he tamped in another wad of aromatic leaves.

'Bale told me what happened out there in the water,' he said. Lighting the pipe with a glowing brand, he took a few puffs, narrowing his eyes against the smoke. 'Why don't you tell me the rest? How did you know the Hunter was coming?'

Torak hesitated. 'I can't explain. I don't understand it.'

Tenris raised an eyebrow. 'But you know more than you told Bale. Maybe I can help.'

Torak put his chin on his knees and stared into the fiery valleys of the embers. 'The seals,' he murmured. 'They feel it in their whiskers; the sounds coming through the water.'

From the corner of his eye, he saw Tenris tense.

'I was with the guardian,' Torak went on. 'She heard – no, she *felt* – the voice of the Hunter – from very far away.' He swallowed. 'That's how I knew it was coming.'

When Tenris still said nothing, Torak raised his head.

The Seal Mage sat with his pipe forgotten in his hand. His face was open and aghast.

'What does it mean?' whispered Torak.

The pipe slipped from the motionless fingers and rolled into the fire. Tenris made no move to retrieve it. Lurching to his feet, he staggered to the water's edge, and stood with his back to Torak. He stayed there for a long time. When he returned to the fire, he looked older, but also strangely excited. 'Tell me everything,' he said.

Torak took a deep breath – and did.

It was a relief to tell someone. He hadn't realised what a burden it had been, keeping it to himself. But the intensity in the Mage's face was frightening.

When he'd finished, there was silence between them.

Tenris ran his good hand shakily over his beard. 'Has this happened before?'

'I – think so.'

'You *think* so?' Tenris spoke with unusual sharpness. 'What do you mean?'

'I – I fell in a seal net. There were some capelin . . . But only for a moment.'

'For a moment? How long?'

'A few heartbeats, I don't know.'

The grey eyes pierced his: as if trying to see into his souls.

'What – what is it?' faltered Torak. 'What's wrong with me?'

Tenris did not reply at once. Then he said, 'Nothing is – wrong with you.' He glanced at the others to make sure they were still sleeping, then moved closer to Torak. 'It is . . . ' he broke off, shaking his head.

'It's what? Tell me!'

Tenris sighed. 'Ah, how to explain?' Picking up a stick, he probed the fire, sending sparks shooting skywards. 'Everything in the world,' he said at last, 'has a spirit. Hunter, prey, river, tree. Not all of them can talk, but all can hear and think. You know this, of course.'

Torak nodded, wondering what was coming next.

'The three souls of every creature – the souls which make the spirit – these are rooted in the body.' Again he probed the embers. 'Maybe the name-soul might slip out from time to time, if you're ill, or dreaming; but it rarely goes far, and it soon comes back.' He cast aside the stick and put out his hands to the fire, as if to draw something out of the flames. 'But once in every thousand winters, a creature is born who is – different.'

Despite the heat, Torak began to feel cold.

'This creature's souls,' Tenris went on, 'can leave its body – leave it for much longer than any Mage ever achieves

454

when he is curing the sick. This creature's souls can travel further.' He paused. 'They can enter the bodies of others. And when that happens, this creature sees, and hears, and feels, just as the body into which it has strayed – and yet remains himself.' His fists came to rest on his knees, and he turned and met Torak's horrified gaze. '*This creature*,' he whispered, '*is a spirit walker.*'

Torak couldn't breathe. 'No,' he said.

The grey gaze never wavered.

'No!' said Torak. 'It doesn't make sense! If the souls leave, then the body is dead! I would have been dead, that's what death is!'

Tenris gave him a look full of pity and understanding. 'But Torak. In spirit walking, not all the souls *do* leave the body. The Nanuak – the world-soul – always remains. It never leaves, not till the moment of death. It is only the name-soul and the clan-soul that walk.'

Torak had begun to shake. He'd never even heard of spirit walking. He didn't want to know anything about it.

Tenris put his good hand on his shoulder and gave him a little shake. 'You're right to be frightened. Spirit walking is the deepest of mysteries. All we know about it has been passed down from Mage to Mage; garbled, half-understood.' Again he paused, as if wondering how much more Torak could take. 'What we do know is that even for the spirit walker, it is very hard, and very dangerous.'

And it hurts, thought Torak, remembering the sickness and the pain. It had felt as if something deep inside him were being torn loose . . .

Then a thought occurred to him that gave him hope. 'But this can't be right!' he said eagerly. 'I'm not a spirit walker, I've got proof! In the Forest, I was treed by a boar. He nearly got me, and I was terrified – and *it didn't happen*! I didn't get the sick feeling, or the pain, and I never for one instant knew what he was feeling!'

The Seal Mage was shaking his head. 'Torak, Torak, that is not how it is. Think! You know enough about Magecraft to be aware that even for ordinary Mages, when they wish to cure the sick, they need help to free their own souls. There are many ways of doing this. A trance. A soul-loosening potion. Sometimes simply going without food, or holding your breath. It is the same for the spirit walker. Being merely afraid, as you were of that boar, would not have been enough to loosen your souls.'

Torak thought back to the other times when it had happened. At the healing rite, there had been Saeunn's soul-loosening smoke. In the seal net, he'd been close to drowning. With the guardian, too, he'd been drowning. It was beginning to make a terrible kind of sense.

'Besides,' said Tenris, and Torak was surprised to see that his half-smile was back, 'you were lucky you *didn't* spirit walk inside that boar. His souls would have been too strong for yours. You might have been trapped in there for good.'

Torak got to his feet, stumbled to the edge of the rocks, and stood there shivering. He didn't want to be different. And yet – wasn't this why his father had kept him separate from the clans? Why he'd said as he lay dying, *There's so much I haven't told you?*

'This is a curse,' he said, his teeth chattering. 'I don't want to be different. It's a curse!'

'No!' Tenris came to stand beside him. 'Not a curse, but a *gift!* You may not think so now, but in time, you will see this!'

'No,' said Torak. 'No.'

'*Listen* to me,' said the Seal Mage, his beautiful voice shaking with emotion. 'What you did so easily – without even trying – is something the cleverest Mages strive their whole lives to achieve! Why, once I knew a Mage – a good one – who tried for six winters on end. Six winters of trances and potions and fasting. Then finally, for a few heartbeats – he succeeded. And he counted himself the luckiest of men!'

'I don't want it,' said Torak. 'I never –'

'But Torak, this is the very *purpose* of Magecraft!' The handsome, ruined face was alight with fervour. 'We do not learn Magecraft merely to trick fools with coloured fire! We do it to delve deeper! To know the hearts of others!' He caught his breath. '*Think* what you could do if you learned to use this! You could discover such secrets! You could know the speech of hunters and prey. You could gain such power . . .'

'But I don't want it!' cried Torak – and on the other side of the fire, Bale stirred in his sleep.

'I don't want it,' said Torak more quietly. He had never felt so frightened and confused. All his life he had been Torak. Now Tenris was telling him he was someone else.

He stared out across the cold, heaving Sea. He longed for Wolf, so that he could tell him all about it. But how would he ever get Wolf to understand? He had no idea how to describe spirit walking in wolf talk. And that seemed to him to be the very worst of it: that in this he would be cut off from Wolf.

'What should I do now?' he said to the cold Sea.

Again Tenris put a hand on his shoulder. 'You should do what we planned to do,' he said calmly. 'I will waken Bale, and we will make ready to leave. We will take the selik root back to camp. And on Midsummer's night – this coming night – we will take it up to the Crag, and you will help me make the cure. That is what we shall do.'

His voice was as steady as an oak standing firm in a gale, and Torak took strength from it. 'Yes,' he said. 'Yes. This doesn't change what I have to do. Does it, Tenris?' He turned and looked up into the Mage's face.

'No,' said Tenris, 'it doesn't change anything.'

TWENTY-NINE

At last the hunger had been chased back into its Den,
and Wolf was free to seek the female and Tall Tailless.

But while he'd been gulping down delicious soft chunks
of rotting blackfish, the dark had come. Not the true Dark,
but the dark which covers the Up when the Thunderer is
angry. And this time it wasn't after Wolf. The taillesses
were the ones in danger.

Over the hot black earth he raced, then up the slope and
down again, to the boulders where the female had waited
for his pack-brother. He smelt that Tall Tailless had been
here too, and that he had fought with the female. *Fought!*
Wolf could not believe what he was smelling! The snarling,
the baring of teeth.

Swiftly he found the Bright Beast-That-Bites-Hot, with
the two pale-pelted half-growns sleeping beside it. Then to
his horror he smelt that his pack-brother had gone out on

the Great Wet, in one of the floating hides.

Mewing in distress, Wolf scrambled back up the boulders after the scent of the female. Ah, she was clever. She'd returned to the Still Wet, where there was less danger from the Thunderer, and there she'd dragged out a floating hide. She'd headed into the wind, so Wolf easily caught her scent. Now he knew what to do. He must follow her. She too was seeking Tall Tailless.

A roar from the Up. The wind began to howl through the valley, and the Wet came pouring down. Trees bent, fish-birds were tossed about like leaves. And still Wolf loped, flying over the rocks and the angry little Wets crashing down from the peaks.

As he ran, another scent hit him, and he skittered to a halt. Raising his muzzle, he took deep sniffs to make sure.

His claws tightened. His fur stood on end.

He smelt *demon*.

'Take my hand!' shouted Tenris, leaning perilously over the side of his skinboat and reaching for Torak.

Torak fought to keep his head above the waves, and strained to grasp the outstretched hand. He caught it – but another wall of water engulfed him, dragging him under.

Over and over he rolled in the crushing darkness. He couldn't see, couldn't breathe.

The Sea threw him above the waves, playing with him. His gutskin parka helped him stay afloat, and he bobbed up and down, gulping air.

Tenris was gone. Bale was gone. The sky was black as basalt. Crackling flares of lightning revealed nothing but raging Sea.

'Tenris!' he yelled. 'Bale!' The storm whipped his voice away.

Through the murk he glimpsed his overturned skinboat tossing about on the waves. He swam for it – the Sea dashed it against him – and he grabbed it with both hands. '*Tenris!*' he shouted.

But the Mage was gone.

Suddenly the skinboat gave a terrific jolt, and he was thrown against a rock. Winded, he reached for it with one hand, clutching the skinboat with the other. The Sea sucked at the boat, pulling him off the rock. He had a heartbeat to decide what to do.

He let go of the skinboat and hauled himself onto the rock. The boat was carried away into the gloom.

Shivering, storm-battered, he clung on.

He didn't know where he was. If he'd been thrown onto the shore, he had a chance. If not – if this was an isolated skerry somewhere in the Sea – he was in trouble.

A groping search of his haven soon told him that the rock was no bigger than a Seal's shelter, and surrounded by nothing but waves.

Panic gripped him.

Bale was gone. Tenris was gone. He was stranded on a rock in the middle of the Sea.

The storm blew over as abruptly as it had arisen.

By the time Renn reached the eastern end of the lake and laid down her paddle, the water was lapping the rocks, and scarcely stirring the reeds in the shallows.

She didn't want to think of how it must have been for Torak on the open Sea. *Why* hadn't he listened to her and come overland, instead of going with the Mage and the tall Seal boy?

Wearily she dragged her borrowed skinboat ashore, lifted out her pack and her sleeping-sack, then hid them behind a boulder. She didn't know what she would find at the Seal camp, but she doubted that she'd need anything but her quiver and bow.

Straightening up, she noticed that the sky wasn't clear, as it should be after a storm. Dirty white clouds were pouring down from the peaks, and tongues of mist were seeping towards her across the lake. Mist after a storm. She'd never seen that before.

At a run she started up the slope, making for the little white beach on the other side. She crested the ridge – and gasped. The Sea had disappeared behind a yellow wall of sea-mist that was rolling menacingly towards her.

This shouldn't *be*, she told herself. This *can't* be.

Then she remembered that it was Midsummer night. And on Midsummer night, anything is possible.

Exhausted, wet and scared, she half-slid, half-stumbled down the tussocky slope, and fell to her knees in the coarse white sand.

Anything is possible . . .

Maybe it's even possible that the Seal Mage is right: that Torak really is a spirit walker.

Back at the Heights as she'd crouched among the boulders, she'd flatly rejected what she'd heard the Mage telling Torak. It couldn't be true. It had to be some kind of trick.

But all through the long, hard journey on the lake, she'd been turning it over in her mind, and now she knew that it *was* true.

Torak was a spirit walker.

A spirit walker.

She had heard of such creatures, but only in the stories of long ago which Fin-Kedinn sometimes told on winter's nights: how Raven learned to hold onto the wind, how the First Tree came, and the first clans, and the first – spirit walker.

Now, as she crouched shivering on the little white beach, she sensed that in some way she didn't understand, Torak the spirit walker lay at the heart of everything. The tokoroth – the sickness – the cure. If only she could see the pattern.

Torak clung to the rock. He was cold, wet and hungry, and although the storm had passed with startling suddenness, he was trapped in the fog, with no idea where he was. The fog could take days to lift. He didn't have days.

Then he remembered the little roll of dried whale meat which Detlan had given him before they'd set off. It was smelly and salt-stained, and if he ate it, he'd have nothing for the Sea Mother. He ate it anyway.

The meat made him feel a bit better. Then another thought occurred to him which heartened him some more. He didn't have the selik root. Tenris did – and maybe Tenris had made it back to land; maybe the clans still had a chance . . .

A wave slapped into him, nearly knocking him off the rock.

Concentrate, he told himself. You've got to get off this rock and back to land.

He didn't have many choices. Sooner or later, he would have to swim for it. But he was exhausted, and he knew he wouldn't last long in the water. He'd need help to stay afloat.

The skinboat was gone, and so was his paddle. All he had were his clothes and Fa's knife, and his mother's medicine horn, safe in its pouch. It contained a small amount of earthblood: just enough for Death Marks. He wasn't ready for that yet.

More waves buffeted the rock. He crawled higher, drawing the gutskin parka closer about him.

The gutskin parka.

He remembered the way it had buoyed him up in the storm. He remembered the Seal children splashing in the shallows, their beginners' boats steadied by a cross-pole with an inflated gutskin sack at either end.

Yanking the parka over his head, he cut off the laces at the neck and used them to tie one wrist shut, and also the neck, and the waist. Then he put his mouth to the remaining wrist, and blew.

Blowing made him giddy, but after a sickeningly long time, he had a slightly squashy air-sack which floated when he tried it on the water. If he lashed it to his belt, it might help him stay afloat – or at least stop him sinking if he got too weak to swim.

Around him the Sea swirled and the fog billowed. Somewhere out there lay the Seal island. But which way?

All he could see was black water. No seabirds, no drifting seaweed; no silvery currents to indicate a headland. He couldn't see the sun, had no sense of the direction he should take. For all he knew, he might be making straight for the open Sea.

Far away, a wolf howled.

Torak caught his breath.

There it was again. A long howl, followed by several

short, sharp barks. *Where are you?* called Wolf.

Torak put his hands to his lips and howled a reply. *I'm here!* Again the answer – faint but clear, piercing the fog – floating to him across the Sea.

Again Torak howled. *Call to me, pack-brother! Call!*

Hunger, fatigue, cold – all were forgotten. He wasn't even scared of Notched Fin any more, because now Wolf was with him, showing him the way back. His guide would not let him down.

The water was freezing, but he didn't give himself time to think. With the air-sack lashed to his back, he slid off the rock and struck out through the fog and the whale-haunted Sea.

Alone in the fog on the little white beach, Renn heard wolf howls, and froze.

It sounded like – yes! Wolf! And Torak! She'd know his howl anywhere! That had to mean that he was all right!

He would be making for the Seal camp. That made her feel a bit braver about heading there too.

The fog was so thick that she couldn't see two paces in front. With her hands before her like a blind girl, she blundered through the birch trees and the boulders towards the Bay of Seals.

The trees ended. She still couldn't see. No camp. No Sea. No sounds except – somewhere nearby – the rush of wavelets on shingle. The howling had ceased.

She left the trees and stumbled towards where she hoped the Seal camp lay.

A scrape and a muffled gasp somewhere close. The sound of a skinboat being set down. Then – before she could draw back – a tall figure loomed out of the mist and ran straight into her.

With shouts of alarm they leapt apart.

'Who are you?' cried the boy.

'Where's Torak?' cried Renn.

Both were open-mouthed and staring with fright.

Renn recognised the tall Seal boy who'd set out with Torak from the Heights.

'Who *are* you?' he said, his eyes narrowing.

'I'm Renn,' she said with more assurance than she felt. 'Where's Torak? What have you done with him?'

His glance flicked to her bow, then back to her face. His shoulders slumped. 'The storm,' he muttered. 'We got separated. I – I saw his skinboat go over.'

'What do you mean?' she said.

He rubbed his eyes, and she saw how tired he was. 'Tenris tried to reach him. So did I. We couldn't . . . Tenris is still out looking for him.' He seemed genuinely distraught, and if he hadn't been a Seal, Renn would have felt sorry for him. 'I heard strange howls,' he said. 'I've never heard anything like it.'

She was tempted to tell him, but she hardened her heart. He was not to be trusted; let him go on thinking Torak was lost. She would not believe it. She'd heard Torak howling with Wolf; that had to mean they were safe.

Another skinboat slid out of the mist, and a man got out and lifted it onto the beach. It was the Seal Mage.

Full of concern, he ran to the Seal boy – saw Renn – recoiled in surprise – then turned back to the boy. 'I couldn't find him,' he said. Like the boy, he seemed devastated, and Renn began to wonder if she'd misjudged the Seals.

'And who is this?' said the Seal Mage, turning to her. His

expression was kind, his voice as quiet and strong as the Sea on a sunny day. But something about him put Renn on her guard.

'I'm Renn,' she said. 'I'm from the Raven Clan.'

'And what are you doing here, Renn from the Raven Clan?' he asked.

'I'm – looking for Torak.' She hadn't meant to say it. But his voice compelled obedience.

'So are we,' he said, looking grim. 'Come. We'll go up to the camp and decide what to do.'

As he walked, he pulled his gutskin parka over his head, and Renn saw for the first time his magnificent Mage's belt, and heard the soft clink of its puffin-beak fringe.

She stopped.

That sound sent ripples through her memory. It was the same sound she'd heard as she watched the skinboater gliding over the lake.

Sea-mist settled clammily on her skin. Her heart began to race. The pattern was coming together before her eyes. The tokoroth. The sickness. The Soul-Eaters . . .

The Seal Mage turned, and asked her what was wrong.

Blood thudded in her skull as she stared up into his handsome, terribly scarred face. She thought, *There is a Soul-Eater among the Seals. There is a Soul-Eater among the Seals, and his name is Tenris. And he is after Torak – Torak the spirit walker.*

'You've gone very pale,' said Tenris in his beautiful, gentle voice.

'I'm – I just need to find Torak,' she said.

'So do I,' he said, and a corner of his mouth lifted in a smile. It was a smile full of warmth, but as Renn met his calm grey gaze, she knew with a clutch of terror that he'd seen the knowledge in her face. He knew that she knew.

'Come,' he said, reaching out and taking her icy fingers

in his. 'Let's go and get something to eat.'

Then he saw the scab on her hand, and his face contracted in pity. 'Oh, my poor child, what's this?'

Before she could reply, he turned to the Seal boy. 'Look, Bale. The poor little thing has the sickness.'

Bale stared at her hand, then his own crept to his clan-creature skin.

'No I don't,' protested Renn, trying to pull her hand from the strong, steady grip. 'It's not the sickness, it's a –'

'You mustn't worry any more,' said the Seal Mage, taking both her hands in his. 'From now on, I will look after you.'

THIRTY

Torak was woken by Wolf licking his nose.

He was too tired to open his eyes. Instead he snuggled closer, pressing his face into soft wolf fur. He felt wonderfully warm and safe – and it was so *quiet*. No seabirds. No wind. Just the sighing of the Sea and the beat of Wolf's heart against his own.

Lick, lick, lick.

Hazily he remembered finding his way ashore. Wolf knocking him backwards into the sand, and keeping him there with a frenzy of snuffle-licks. Then curling up together and slipping down into sleep . . .

The licking turned to grooming-nibbles. Then a sharp, impatient nudge under his chin. *Wake up!*

He opened his eyes.

Crunchy sand under his cheek; Wolf's whiskers tickling his eyelids. Beyond that – nothing. The fog was so thick that he couldn't tell Sea from sky.

How long had he been asleep?

The cure.

He jerked upright, heart pounding. Where was he? Where was Tenris? It was Midsummer night – had they missed their chance? The fog blotted out the sun. He couldn't tell.

He got to his feet – and the blood soughed in his ears. He was stiff and sore all over. Thirst burned his throat.

Somewhere not far off, he heard a trickling sound. He stumbled through the fog, and splashed into a shallow stream choked with weeds. He knelt and gulped handfuls of gritty water.

Wolf trotted over to him, his paws making no noise on the sand. Still on his knees, Torak nuzzled his scruff and said a heartfelt *thank you*.

Wolf swung his tail and licked the corner of Torak's mouth. *My pack-brother.*

Feeling slightly better, Torak stood up and looked about. He still couldn't see two paces ahead, but this sand was familiar. White, coarsely crushed seashells. Maybe he was closer to the Seal camp than he'd dared hope . . .

To his right he heard the lapping of the Sea. He staggered across the beach – and suddenly birch trees and tumbled boulders loomed out of the mist. He ran towards them.

Behind him Wolf gave a low, shuddering growl.

Torak spun round.

Wolf's head was down, his lips peeled back in a snarl.

Whipping out his knife, Torak dropped to the ground and spoke in an urgent grunt-whine. *What is it?*

More growls. The fur on Wolf's hackles stood on end.

Torak felt the hairs on his own neck prickling. And yet – he couldn't see anything amiss. Up ahead, the birch trees were utterly still.

I have to go on, he told Wolf.

Again Wolf growled, warning him back.

Never before had Torak ignored his warnings, and it felt wrong to do so now. But he had to find Tenris. *I have to go on*, he said again. *Please. Come with me!*

To his dismay, Wolf backed away, growling.

Full of misgiving, Torak rose and entered the trees without him.

He was halfway through when a strong hand gripped his arm. 'There you are!' cried Tenris. 'Thank the Sea Mother you're safe!'

Torak glanced back over his shoulder – but Wolf was gone.

'We thought you'd drowned!' said Tenris, pulling him through the remaining trees.

'You frightened me,' said Torak.

'Sorry,' said Tenris. 'Come, let's go! Time's short, we've got to get up to the Crag.'

'You still have the selik root?' said Torak as they ran across the beach.

'Yes, of course!'

'And Bale? Did he make it ashore?'

'Yes, he's fine, he's guarding – he's fine.'

Torak stopped. 'Guarding who?'

Tenris's face became grave. 'She's sick, Torak. We had to lock her up.'

'Who?' said Torak. 'Who's sick?'

'It doesn't matter,' said Tenris. 'Come, we're wasting time.'

'Who is it?' Torak insisted. But a part of him already knew.

'Torak –'

'It's Renn, isn't it? Tenris, please. I need to see her.'

Tenris sighed. 'It'll have to be quick.' At a run he led
Torak through the deserted Seal camp and out to the cave
at the end of the bay, where the man who'd killed the whale
had spent his lonely vigil. 'We put her where we kept them
before,' he said as they drew near.

The cave mouth was all but sealed by a massive door of
whale bone and seal hide, and Bale stood on guard with a
harpoon. When he saw Torak, his face lit up. Torak pushed
past him without a word.

Through a gap between the door and the cave wall, he
saw Renn pacing up and down. It was too dark to see her
properly, but he made out her dishevelled hair and furious
expression, and the sore on the back of her hand. A cold
weight sank inside him like a stone.

When she saw him, her face cleared. '*Torak*! Oh, thank
the Spirit! Now get me out of here!'

'Renn – I can't,' he said. 'You're sick.'

Her mouth fell open. 'But – you don't believe them. Of
course I'm not sick!'

Behind him, Tenris put his hand on his shoulder. 'They
all say that,' he murmured under his breath. 'But don't
worry, Bale will look after her. And I've made sure she'll not
go hungry.'

When she saw the Mage, Renn shrank back. 'Get away
from me!' Then to Torak, 'I'm not sick!'

'Tenris is right,' said Bale, gripping the harpoon so hard
that his knuckles were white. 'My brother was just the
same.'

'Renn,' said Torak, putting both hands on the seal-hide
door. 'I'll bring you the cure, I promise. You will get –'

'I don't need the cure!' she spat. 'Why don't you
believe me?' She pointed at Tenris. 'It's him! *He's the
Soul-Eater*!'

'In the end they suspect everyone,' said Bale.

'Why won't you believe me?' cried Renn. 'Tell him to show you his mark! Make him show you his tattoo! He's a Soul-Eater!'

Tenris touched Torak's arm. 'Torak, we have to go – or it'll be too late for her or anyone else.'

'No – Torak – don't go!' shouted Renn. 'He'll kill you! *Torak!*' She threw herself against the door.

Bale braced it with his shoulder. 'Go,' he told Torak. 'I'll make sure she comes to no harm.'

'You will get better!' called Torak. 'I promise! You will get better!'

'Torak!' she screamed. '*Come back!*'

With her cries ringing in his ears, Torak followed Tenris into the fog.

'Quickly,' muttered the Seal Mage. 'The turn of the sun is close, I can feel it.'

With Renn's cries fading behind them, they started up the trail. Soon all Torak could hear was his own breathing and the sound of water trickling over the rocks. He felt oppressed by a choking sense of wrongness. In the space of a few heartbeats, he'd ignored warnings from both Wolf and Renn.

A clatter of claws behind him.

He swung round. *Wolf?*

He couldn't see anything in the swirling whiteness – except Tenris up ahead, disappearing into the fog. 'Tenris!' he called. 'Wait for me!'

More clattering claws – then a small humped figure scuttled across the trail. Not Wolf. The tokoroth.

Torak raced forwards. 'Tenris! *Look out!* The tokoroth!'

Pain exploded in his head, and the rocks rushed up to meet him.

Torak woke with a start.

His head was throbbing, his shoulders ached. Someone had taken off his jerkin and laid him on a cold stone slab. Someone had tied his wrists together, pulled his arms above his head, and hooked them over a horn of rock. The binding was tight – he couldn't wriggle out – although if he could push himself up with his heels, he might be able to unhook his wrists and . . .

Someone gripped his ankles, holding him back. Someone with sharp claws and a knife. When he tried to kick free, they pressed its point against his calf.

Mist swirled about him, tinged blue with woodsmoke. He heard the crackle of a fire, and caught the tang of juniper. He couldn't hear the Sea. He must be high up on the cliffs.

At his feet, two demon eyes glared at him from a face tattooed with leaves.

Fear settled on him like a second skin. He was on the Crag, laid out on the altar rock, guarded by the tokoroth.

Then a second tokoroth emerged from the smoke. A girl with matted hair falling to her knees, and stick limbs covered in bruises. Her fingernails and toenails were yellow, and filed to long, pointed claws.

In silence she leaned over him, and his skin crawled as her greasy locks brushed his belly. Her bony fingers drew his father's knife from the sheath at his belt.

'What do you want?' he whispered.

In silence she raised the knife in both hands.

'What do you *want?*'

In silence she laid the cold slate knife on his chest.

A soft clinking in the mist – and both tokoroth cowered on the ground.

A figure loomed out of the mist. With every step, the puffin beaks clinked at his belt.

Torak felt as if he were falling from a great height. All the kindness, the gentleness . . . All a lie. Wolf had been right. Renn had been right. And he had been wrong, wrong, wrong.

The Seal Mage had taken off his jerkin to reveal a lean, muscled body that was horribly burnt down the whole of the left side. His arms were smeared with wood-ash, obscuring his clan-tattoos. His face was an ashen mask – as if, thought Torak with a sick sense of dread – he were already mourning someone dead. He wore no amulet, except for a twist of something red and shrunken on a thong at his neck, and his naked chest was unmarked, save for a stark black tattoo over the heart. A three-pronged fork for snaring souls. The mark of the Soul-Eater.

'You,' said Torak. 'A Soul-Eater.'

'One of the seven, Torak.' His voice was the only thing that hadn't changed. Still beautiful, still as calm and powerful as the Sea on a sunlit day. 'But with your help,' he said quietly, 'I shall rise above the others. I shall become the greatest of them all.'

Slowly Torak shook his head. 'I won't help you do that.'

Tenris smiled. 'You don't have a choice.' Turning his head, he barked a command at the tokoroth, his voice suddenly harsh and cruel.

The boy raced to fetch a heavy basket almost as big as himself, while the girl scurried to the neck of the Crag. Torak saw that she was building a wall of driftwood across it, cutting them off from the trail.

The boy tokoroth hadn't finished the bindings round his

ankles. So if he could keep Tenris talking, maybe he could work his feet free. And maybe if he howled for Wolf . . .

But what then? Tenris had a spear and a harpoon lying ready by the fire, and both tokoroth had knives at their belts. Three against one. Against such odds, what could even Wolf achieve? 'Your friends can't help you,' said Tenris as if he'd read his thoughts. 'One of them is guarding the other. There's a kind of beauty in that, don't you think?' From the basket he took out several pale, cone-shaped objects and began laying them out around the altar rock. This time he didn't seem to care about treading on the silver lines polished in the stone.

Torak had to keep him talking, to give himself time to think. 'The sickness,' he said. 'You were the one who sent it.'

'I didn't *send* it,' said Tenris, standing back to study his work. 'I *created* it. My tokoroth have the demon skill for creeping into shelters. And I . . .Well, I'm very good at poisons.'

'But – *why*?'

'That's the interesting part,' said Tenris, resuming his task. 'When I began three summers ago, I had no idea how I'd use it; I simply knew that I needed a weapon.' He shook his head. 'Sometimes not even I can tell all that the future holds.'

Torak felt sick. 'So Bale's little brother . . . '

Tenris shrugged. 'I just wanted to know if it worked.'

'And this summer. The clans. *Why*?'

The Seal Mage raised his head, and his grey eyes glittered. 'To smoke you out. To find out what you can do.'

So Fin-Kedinn had been right, after all.

'And it worked,' said Tenris, 'although not in the way I expected. You see, I didn't know who you were. All I knew was that there was someone in the Forest with power. I thought that whoever it was would perform some great feat of Magecraft to rid his people of the sickness.' His lip curled. 'Instead what did you do? You came to me – *me*! Begging me to make the cure! Oh, it was meant to be!'

'And the cure,' said Torak. 'Was that a trick too?'

Tenris snorted. From the pouch at his belt he took the selik root and tossed it on the fire. 'There is no cure,' he said. 'I made it up.'

The flames flared a deep, throbbing purple. The two tokoroth drew closer and gazed at it in fascination.

Tenris eyed them with contempt. 'Sometimes being a Mage is almost too easy. All it takes is a little coloured fire.' He gave the girl a savage kick that sent her flying. Hissing, she scuttled back to her wood-pile.

To Torak's dismay, the boy rushed back to the bindings at his ankles. He kicked out sharply. The boy tokoroth jabbed his calf with the knife to make him hold still.

'So now that you've smoked me out,' he said to Tenris, 'what next?'

Tenris gazed down at him, and his face contracted with pain and longing. 'When I found out what you could do, I could not believe it. That a *boy* should have such power. Power to tame hunters and trammel prey. Power to rule the clans . . . ' He shook his head. 'What a waste.'

Then he leaned closer, and Torak smelt the bitterness of ash. 'Soon,' he murmured, 'that power will be *mine*. I will take it for myself, and become the spirit walker. *I* will be the greatest Mage who ever lived . . . '

'How?' Torak said hoarsely. 'What are you going to do?'

'Midsummer,' breathed the Seal Mage. 'The most potent night for Magecraft – and it's your birthnight! Oh, it is perfect! All the signs point to this, all telling me to do it!'

Gently he put out his hand and pushed back a lock of hair from Torak's forehead. 'Do you remember what I told you about Midsummer night? That it's all about change?'

Torak tried to swallow, but his mouth was dry.

'Tree into leaf,' murmured the Seal Mage, 'boy into man.' He leaned down, and his breath heated Torak's cheek as he whispered in his ear. *'I'm going to eat your heart.'*

THIRTY-ONE

Wolf had done what no wolf should ever do. He had abandoned his pack-brother.

He had been so astonished when Tall Tailless ignored his warnings – so astonished and so *cross* – that he had deserted him.

So while Tall Tailless went off alone to the Den of the pale-pelts, Wolf loped up the ridge and down to the Still Wet, where he snapped at the reeds in his anger, and chewed up a hunk of dead wood, until at last all the crossness had been spat out.

And now as he stood in the Wet to drink, he thought of the time when he'd been a lonely cub, and his pack-brother had found him. Tall Tailless had shared his kills, and given him the crunchy hooves to play with. When Wolf's pads had been hurting from the trail, Tall Tailless had carried him in his forepaws for many, many lopes.

A wolf does not abandon his pack-brother.

Wolf gave an anguished yelp, and raced back towards the Den. He loped over the ridge and down again; wove soundlessly between the birch trees and out onto the pebbles.

He couldn't see the Den, as it had been swallowed by the breath of the Great Wet – but he could smell it. And he could hear the female padding up and down in the smaller Den in the mountain. She was angry, worried and scared, and the pale-pelted tailless was growling at her; Wolf didn't know why. But apart from them, the Den was empty.

In fact, it was *too* still. He smelt the lemmings cowering in their burrows. He heard the fish-birds on the cliffs hiding their beaks under their wings. All were waiting. Frightened to move.

Wolf raised his muzzle to catch the smells. He smelt much fish, and the left-behind scents of many taillesses; he smelt the fat, friendly fish-dogs who swim in the Great Wet, and sometimes lumber up onto the rocks. And he smelt the other smell, too: the demon stink.

The stink grew stronger as he padded forwards, and his hackles rose. When he was a cub, that stink had frightened him. Now it awakened a strange hunger: deeper than the blood-urge, stronger even than the Pull of the Mountain . . .

But where was Tall Tailless? With all the smells whirling in the windless air, Wolf couldn't catch the one scent he longed to find.

And now the female and the pale-pelt were snarling at each other – and as Wolf ran towards them, he saw that the pale-pelt was carrying meat for the female in his forepaws: *meat which stank of demon!*

Wolf sensed that the female was hungry, and wanted to eat. He had to stop her! But what if she ignored his warning, just as Tall Tailless had done? What if she didn't even understand what he was telling her?

Wolf lowered his head and crept forwards, placing each paw with silent care. He had an idea. There was one thing the female always understood.

A snarl.

'I'm not hungry!' snarled Renn as the Seal boy set the bowl on the ground. 'And for the last time, *I'm not sick!*'

'Just eat,' said the boy. Backing out of the cave, he dragged the seal hide across the cave mouth, leaving a gap a couple of hands wide for air.

Renn didn't like the Seal boy, but she wished he hadn't gone. It was frightening being in here on her own. She could feel the suffering of the sick from three summers ago; the walls were dank with their despair.

But *you're* not sick, she reminded herself. You're just tired and hungry, and worried about Torak.

She decided to try again with the Seal boy. 'Do you know *why* the Hunter attacked?' she called out.

Silence.

'Because your Mage killed one of its young. I found the carcass. He trapped it in a seal net – the kind only your clan makes – and he took nothing but its teeth. Does that sound like something a good man would do?'

No reply.

She clenched her jaw. 'I know it was him,' she said. 'I heard his belt clink as he rowed across the lake.'

Still no answer, but she could tell that he was listening. She could hear him breathing on the other side of the door.

'The teeth of a Hunter?' she went on. 'Only a Mage

would have any use for those.' She paused. 'If I'm right, and he made the sickness – then he killed your brother.'

For a moment there was a stunned silence. 'How do you know about my brother?'

'Oh, I know many things,' said Renn. 'He killed your brother,' she said again. 'I know what it's like to lose a brother. I lost mine not long ago.'

'Be quiet,' said the Seal boy.

'Think back,' said Renn, 'to just before your brother fell sick. Tenris had been up on that clifftop, hadn't he? Doing Magecraft.'

'So?' came the reply. 'He's the Mage, that's what he does.'

'He did Magecraft, and then your brother got sick.'

It was a guess, but a good one. She heard a sharp intake of breath.

'He did it to bring the prey,' whispered the Seal boy. 'He did Magecraft to bring the prey . . . '

'That's what he told you,' said Renn.

She heard the crunch of sand as he walked up and down. 'No more talk,' he said abruptly. But there was doubt in his voice.

'You know I'm right,' she said.

'*I said no more talk!*' he shouted.

'Why won't you *listen!*' Renn shouted back.

The seal hide shuddered, and she knew that he'd punched it.

After that, neither of them spoke.

The smell of meat filled the cave. Renn hesitated – then went over to examine the bowl. Smoked whale meat with juniper berries. It smelt *really* good. But if she ate it, the Seal boy would think she was giving in. She put the bowl down. Paced the cave. Went back and picked it up.

She was just about to try a piece when the Seal boy gave

a cry, and in through the gap leapt Wolf – leapt straight at her – sending her flying, sending the meat spattering against the wall – flattening her beneath him. He was snarling, his black lips drawn back from his big white fangs. She tried to scream, but his forepaws were heavy on her chest. What was *wrong* with him?

'Wolf!' she gasped. 'Wolf – it's me!'

'I'm coming!' yelled the Seal boy, wrenching aside the hide and leaping in with his harpoon.

With astonishing speed, Wolf sprang off Renn and twisted round to face him.

'*No!*' screamed Renn. 'Don't hurt him! He must be sick – or – something!'

The Seal boy ignored her, and jabbed at Wolf with his harpoon.

Wolf sprang sideways, snapping at the shaft.

Renn saw her chance to escape – the cave mouth was wide open – but what about Wolf?

He was dodging the harpoon with ease.

She picked herself up and fled.

Behind her she heard another yell from the Seal boy – more in outrage than in pain – and glanced back to see Wolf leap from the cave and disappear.

Too shaken to make sense of it, she turned and raced off into the fog.

It was thicker than ever. She had no idea where she was; no idea how to find Torak.

She tripped over a pile of driftwood, then blundered into a rack full of whale meat. A shelter loomed out of the whiteness, and she clapped her hand to her mouth to keep from screaming. At any moment she dreaded to see the Seal boy leaping out at her – or the tokoroth – or the Soul-Eater.

Suddenly to the north, fire flared high in the sky.

She stopped.

Torak had said that the cure would be made in a rite on a clifftop. Although 'the cure' had to be a Soul-Eater trap.

She set off at a run towards the fire.

A noise behind her. She ducked. Too late. A hand grabbed her arm and yanked her back.

On the Crag, no trace remained of Tenris the kindly Seal Mage. That mask had been burned away, leaving nothing but ashes and bitterness.

Muttering spells under his breath, the Soul-Eater squatted by the altar rock, painting signs on Torak's chest. His brush was a bundle of seal's whiskers bound to the shinbone of an eagle; his paint was a dark, stinking sludge. Torak guessed it was the blood of the murdered Hunter; that the pale objects set in a ring around him were its teeth.

A scratching at his ankles told him that the boy tokoroth was back, to finish tightening the bindings. Torak kicked out hard, knowing his only hope lay in wriggling free when the time was right.

'Hold still,' snapped Tenris. He'd been chewing on a foul-smelling paste that had stained the whites of his eyes yellow, and turned his tongue black. He didn't look like a man any more.

Out of the corner of his vision, Torak caught a furtive movement.

There – beyond the wall of driftwood the girl tokoroth was building, and soaking in seal oil. *Wolf*.

Torak's heart tightened with dread. Three against one. If Wolf tried to help him, he'd get himself killed.

'Uff!' called Torak, warning him back. 'Uff! Uff!!'

Wolf pricked his ears, but did not retreat. He'd found a gap in the wall where the girl tokoroth hadn't yet piled the driftwood high. But it was right on the edge of the cliff.

Go back! Torak tried to tell him silently. *You can't help me!*

Fortunately, neither Tenris nor the tokoroth had spotted Wolf. All three were staring at Torak. '*What* did you say?' said Tenris.

Torak thought quickly. Jerking his head at the ring of teeth around him, he said, 'Those teeth, they're the Hunter's, aren't they? What are they for?'

Tenris regarded him narrowly. 'Spells,' he said, dipping his brush in the blood. 'When you showed me your father's knife, I suspected that you were the one. But I had to make sure.'

'And for that a Hunter had to die?'

'What do I care? They can't hurt me.' With his twisted claw he touched the amulet at his throat. 'A masking charm.'

Torak thought of Detlan, clenching his teeth in agony as Bale tended his shattered leg. If he lived, he would be a cripple. And all because Tenris had needed 'to make sure'.

Wolf was nosing his way through the gap, perilously close to the edge.

Quickly Torak spoke to Tenris. 'You said you thought I was "the one". What did you mean?'

The ruined face darkened. 'The one who destroyed the bear.'

Torak tensed. 'The bear.'

'*I* created it,' Tenris said between his teeth. '*I* caught the demon. *I* trapped it in the body of the bear. You destroyed it.'

For a moment, Torak forgot about Wolf. 'You're lying.

Whoever made the bear was crippled. A crippled wanderer.'

Tenris put back his head and laughed. Still laughing, he rose to his feet and circled the fire, limping piteously. 'Easy, isn't it? Although I confess I did get very bored.'

Tenris had created the bear – the bear that killed Fa . . .

Torak thought of the clearing where he and his father had camped on that final night. Fa's face, laughing at the joke Torak had made. Fa's face as he lay dying . . .

'What's this?' sneered Tenris. 'Tears?'

'You killed him,' whispered Torak. 'You killed Fa . . . '

At that moment the boy tokoroth touched his ankle. Torak lashed out savagely. *You killed Fa!* he screamed, fighting his bonds with all the rage and grief inside him. The rawhide held firm.

Just then, Wolf hurtled out of the mist and leapt at Tenris. The Seal Mage snatched up his harpoon – the tokoroth scuttled like spiders, drawing knives, seizing firebrands and lashing out at the attacker.

'Wolf!' shouted Torak, struggling to push himself off the horn of rock, but held back by the bindings round his ankles. 'Uff! Uff! Uff!'

Tenris lunged with the harpoon.

Wolf gave a great twisting leap – and the vicious barbs pierced empty fog.

Tenris barked a command, and the girl tokoroth set her firebrand to the driftwood wall. Flames shot up, licking at the sky. The tokoroth lashed out at Wolf with their torches – and he shrank back against the burning wall, snarling, cornered.

Just when Torak thought he was finished, Wolf spun round and scrambled over the last section of driftwood that had yet to catch light – pursued by the tokoroth with their flaming torches. The fire roared higher. The gap closed. The neck of the Crag was cut off by the blaze.

Tenris threw down his harpoon and turned to Torak. 'He's gone,' he said. 'Not even a wolf could get past that now.'

'Nor can your tokoroth,' said Torak. Both tokoroth were gone, clattering off down the mountain after Wolf.

Tenris shrugged. 'I don't need them any more,' he said as he took up the knife which lay on Torak's chest. 'I can manage this part on my own.'

Torak's heart was pounding. Wolf was gone. The wall of flames cut him off from all hope of rescue. He might be able to work his feet out of the bindings – he might even be able to push his wrists over the horn and roll off the altar – but what then? He was trapped on a clifftop, pitted against a grown man with a knife and a harpoon, who meant to kill him and eat his heart.

But there was one thing he had to find out first.

'Why did you do it?' he said as he stared up into the yellow eyes of the Soul-Eater. 'Why did you kill my father?'

Tenris shook his head in wonder. 'Ah, you're just like him! Always wanting to know *why*. Why, why, why.'

He circled the altar rock, fingers flexing on the knife, mouth twisting as he tasted bitter memories. 'He betrayed me,' he said. 'He was weak. Worthless. And yet he thought that he could –'

'He wasn't worthless,' said Torak.

'What do you know?' snarled Tenris.

'He was my father,' said Torak.

Tenris stood over him and bared his blackened teeth. 'He was my brother.'

THIRTY-TWO

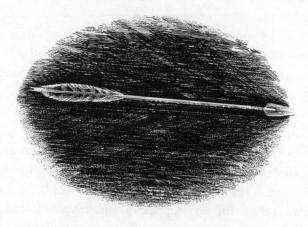

Renn craned her neck to see what was happening on the cliff, but the mist was too thick, and the overhang too deep. Only when the Soul-Eater moved right to the edge did she glimpse him: dark and stick-like against the flames.

'He's got a knife,' she said.

'It's too far up,' said the Seal boy beside her. 'We'd never get there in time.'

'But we can't just –'

'Look at that fire, it's right across the Neck! What are you going to do? Fly?'

Renn shot him a suspicious glance. Despite his professed change of heart, she still didn't trust him. But as she opened her mouth to protest, a wolf howled.

'What *is* that?' said the Seal boy.

'It's Wolf,' said Renn. She cupped her ear to listen. 'Oh, this is bad, he's somewhere in the west! *Why?* Why isn't he up there helping Torak? If not even Wolf can reach him . . .'

She thought quickly. 'You're right,' she told the Seal boy, 'we can't get up there in time. Fetch my bow.'

His jaw dropped. 'I won't let you shoot him! Whatever he's done –'

'How else do we save Torak?'

'But he's still our Mage!'

'Bale,' said Renn urgently, 'I don't want to kill him any more than you do, but we have to do something!'

Just then the Soul-Eater moved away from the edge, and disappeared. With a cry Renn ran backwards, desperate to catch sight of him again.

'The overhang's too deep,' said Bale. 'Quick. The skinboat.'

'What?' cried Renn.

Bale seized her wrist and dragged her after him. 'You can't see the altar rock from the land – only from the Sea!'

Down they raced towards the water. Bale ducked into a shelter, then came out again, and tossed Renn her quiver and bow. Grabbing his skinboat from a rack, he slid it into the shallows, practically threw her into the prow end, then vaulted in after her and snatched up his paddle. Renn had to grip the sides with both hands as they moved off faster than she would have thought possible.

A wind was getting up: an east wind from the Forest. As Renn turned to face the cliff, the fog blew apart to reveal the Soul-Eater – holding a knife high above his head, like an offering. At his feet lay a figure. It wasn't moving.

'I can see them!' shouted Renn.

With astonishing skill, Bale brought his craft about. Renn lurched and would have fallen overboard if he hadn't taken hold of her jerkin and yanked her back.

Her hands shook as she whipped out an arrow and nocked it to her bow. Despite Bale's best efforts, the skinboat rocked in the swell. She'd never be able to stand, she'd have to shoot from kneeling.

On the cliff, Torak still wasn't moving. A terrible fear seized her that they were too late.

'We're too far out,' muttered Bale, 'no-one could make that shot.'

Setting her teeth, Renn forced herself to ignore him – to think only of the target, as Fin-Kedinn had taught her.

Staring hard at the target, she took aim.

The arrow came arching out of the sky, and thudded deep into Tenris's palm. With a howl he fell to his knees, and the knife clattered away across the rock.

Torak seized his chance and wriggled out of the bindings around his ankles, then used his heels to launch himself forwards. His arms felt heavy and bloodless, but he managed to hook his wrists over the horn – and rolled off the altar.

On the opposite side, Tenris was still on his knees, clutching his wounded hand. Rising to his feet, he staggered away from the cliff edge – out of range of further arrows.

Torak struggled to stand, and circled out of reach. His shoulders were burning, his wrists throbbing from the bindings. They were on opposite sides of the altar; the edge of the cliff was directly behind him.

With a hiss, Tenris grasped the arrow and wrenched it from his palm. Sweat coursed down his face, scouring rivulets through the ash to reveal the scorched red flesh beneath. 'Give up, Torak,' he panted. 'It's over!'

More wolf howls. *The demons are gone!* called Wolf.

'He's far away,' said Tenris, snatching up his harpoon. 'He can't help you any more.'

'He's helped enough,' said Torak.

Tenris snorted. 'You're on your own now, Torak. Your friends can't try another shot at me, or they'd risk hitting you.'

Torak did not reply. He needed all his strength just to stay standing.

'Give up, Torak,' urged that beautiful, powerful voice. 'You've done well, but it's time to pass your power to one who knows how to use it.'

Torak glanced over his shoulder. The east wind was strengthening, blowing away the fog. A shaft of silver light was pouring down onto the Sea.

'I'll make it quick,' said Tenris. 'I promise.'

Far below him, Torak saw the restless, shimmering Sea. He felt the wind from the Forest on his face; he thought of Wolf and Renn and Fin-Kedinn, and of all the clans he'd never even met. If he let Tenris take his power – if he let the Soul-Eater become the spirit walker – then none of them would ever be safe.

'You have no choice,' murmured the Soul-Eater. 'You know that.'

Torak squared his shoulders, and met that intense grey gaze.

Too late, Tenris realised what he meant to do – and his eyes widened in disbelief.

'There's always a choice,' said Torak, and walked backwards off the cliff.

THIRTY-THREE

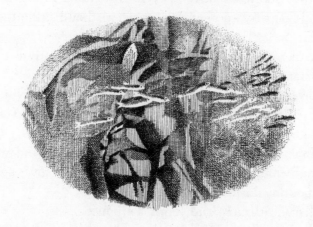

Down, down he fell – into the splintered Sea – into the golden forest of kelp – down into darkness.

Down he sank, kicking feebly at the water with what remained of his strength. It wasn't enough. His wrists were bound so tight that he couldn't slip free; his sodden leggings were dragging him down. He would never reach the surface.

But he had known that when he stepped off the cliff. He had known that this time there would be no friendly guardian; no Wolf leaping in to save him. This time there was only Torak and the hungry Sea. This time he was going to die.

He turned his face for a last look at the light – and saw, impossibly far above, a figure darkening the sun. It was swimming towards him, swimming faster than an eel.

Hope kindled. Was it Wolf? Renn? Bale?

Tenris seized him by the hair and yanked him upwards.

Torak struggled and kicked, but the Soul-Eater was too strong. With both hands, Torak grabbed the kelp around him – jerking Tenris backwards in a flurry of silver bubbles. Furiously they fought till their lungs were bursting, till the water flooded scarlet with blood from the Soul-Eater's wound.

The Seal Mage wrenched Torak's hands free of the kelp, and they rose again – locked together like vipers as they spiralled up towards the light.

Together they burst from the Sea.

'So you'd rather kill yourself, would you?' gasped Tenris. 'How noble! But I won't give you the chance!' Still gripping Torak by the hair, he struck out for the shore, swimming one-armed, but powering through the water with swift, sure strokes.

Torak tried to bite his hand – but Tenris lashed out with his free arm, landing him a savage blow on the temple.

Stunned, Torak went under. As he surfaced, he heard a deafening 'kwshsh!' – and saw an enormous black fin slicing towards them.

Terror turned his limbs to water.

Tenris hadn't seen the Hunter; he was bent on reaching the shore. Torak had an instant in which to act . . .

With one final burst of strength, he twisted round and lunged at the Soul-Eater, ripping the masking charm from his throat.

Tenris grunted in surprise, and lost his grip on Torak. Torak kicked with all his might, and swam out of reach.

Tenris turned to catch him – and saw the Hunter. His hand flew to his throat to grasp the masking charm, and clawed naked skin. He saw the charm in Torak's hand – he strained to grab it. Torak dodged, and hurled the masking charm across the waves. Tenris gave a shout of rage and plunged after it – but it had sunk.

Now they were both at the mercy of the Hunter, with no help in sight.

Torak saw Notched Fin bearing down upon them, shooting spray high into the air. At the edge of his vision he glimpsed a skinboat racing towards them – but it would never reach them in time . . .

And now Sea, sky, skinboat – were blotted out by the Hunter. Through the green water Torak saw the great blunt head looming closer . . .

At the last moment the Hunter swerved, showering him with spray as it made for Tenris.

A sudden stillness came over the Soul-Eater's ruined features as he watched his doom slicing towards him.

In the final heartbeat he turned his head and met Torak's eyes. 'Ask Fin-Kedinn about your father!' he shouted. 'Make him tell you the truth –'

Then he was lost in a flurry of silver water.

Torak heard one terrible scream, abruptly cut off – as the great jaws dragged the Soul-Eater down into the deep.

THIRTY-FOUR

The fire on the Crag was burning low, and grey smoke was rising into the sky as the skinboat reached the shore.

Bale hoisted his craft on his head and went to put it on the rack, leaving Renn and Torak in the shallows. Neither spoke as they trudged up the beach to the nearest shelter.

Renn wiped the spray off her bow and hung it from a rafter, then went inside to rummage for food.

Torak took driftwood from a pile and started waking up a fire. He felt shaky and cold, but at least the Sea had washed the markings from his chest. Inside his head, however, the marks would not so easily be washed away.

He wanted to tell Renn everything: about what had happened on the Crag; about being a spirit walker. But it was still too raw. Instead he said, 'I'm sorry. I really thought you were sick. You looked sick.'

Renn set a bowl on the ground, and sat down. 'Well,' she

said, 'I thought you were dead. Seems we were both wrong.' She pushed the bowl towards him. 'I found some whale meat. No juniper berries I'm afraid, but it tastes all right without.'

Both of them looked at the bowl, but neither made a move to eat.

Then Torak said, 'Renn. There is no cure. What he said about the selik root. He made it up.'

Renn clasped her arms about her knees and frowned.

'Did you hear what I said?' said Torak. '*There is no cure.*'

Suddenly Renn stopped frowning and straightened up. She stared at Torak, then at the meat. 'The juniper berries,' she said.

'What?' said Torak.

'When I was in the cave. Bale gave me some food, and Wolf leapt at me, and knocked it over. I thought he'd gone mad. But he was – Torak, he was *saving* me! Warning me off the juniper berries!'

She sprang to her feet and started to pace. 'That's how the Seal Mage caused the sickness! He sent the tokoroth to poison the juniper berries! And then the juniper berries went into the salmon cakes, and people got sick.' She stopped. 'That's why Wolf stopped me eating the food, because it was poisoned. And – that's why I *didn't* get sick before, even though I was eating salmon cakes, because I'd stolen Saeunn's, which were left over from last summer –'

'– and that's why I didn't get sick either,' put in Torak, 'because I didn't take any with me.'

They stared at one another.

'So if everyone gets rid of their juniper berries,' said Renn, '*and* their salmon cakes –'

'– maybe they'll get better –'

'–maybe we won't *need* a cure.'

This was the answer. Torak could feel it. It had the kind of elegance which would have appealed to Tenris. How he must have laughed as he watched them striving to find a cure which didn't exist! How clever he must have felt! How powerful.

And yet even now, Torak couldn't hate him. Tenris had been his bone kin. Torak had *liked* him. He'd wanted Tenris to like him back.

Bowing his head to his knees, he tried to shut out the pain. But that handsome, ruined face was still before him; that voice still rang in his ears. *Ask Fin-Kedinn about your father! Make him tell you the truth!*

What truth? What had he meant?

At that moment, Bale ran up. 'Come quickly!' he panted.

He led them to the south end of the bay and across the stream to the foot of the waterfall.

The tokoroth lay on the rocks where they had fallen. Spray misted their grimy faces and their broken stick-limbs.

Craning his neck, Torak gazed at the mountainside, and wondered what had made them scramble up there. Then he remembered Wolf's howls. *The demons are gone!*

'What *are* they?' whispered Bale.

'Tokoroth,' said Renn in a low voice.

Bale gasped. 'I thought those were only in stories. I thought –'

The girl tokoroth moaned, and a spasm convulsed her scrawny frame.

'She's still alive,' said Torak. He felt a twinge of pity.

They looked so young. No more than eight or nine summers.

'They're killers,' Bale said grimly. Drawing his knife, he moved forwards.

Wolf appeared from behind a boulder, warning him back with a growl.

Bale froze. 'What . . . '

Torak went down on one knee, and Wolf trotted over to him, snuffle-grunting and nuzzling his cheek. Torak glanced at Renn. 'He says he chased the demons away.'

'Where?' said Renn. 'Where did they go?'

Torak met Wolf's eyes for a moment, then shook his head. 'I'm not going to ask. They're gone. Let that be enough.'

Bale was staring at him in amazement. 'You can talk to it?'

'Him,' said Torak. 'Wolf is a him.'

'So that's a wolf,' said Bale. Placing one hand on his heart, he bowed. 'Beautiful.'

Again the tokoroth stirred.

Renn ran to kneel beside them. Her face became grave. 'Not long now,' she said. Then to Torak, 'Your medicine horn. Do you have any earthblood?'

Torak handed it to her, but Bale looked troubled. 'What are you doing?'

'Death Marks,' said Renn.

'They don't deserve them!' cried Bale.

Renn turned on him. 'They were children once! Their souls are still in there, deep inside! They'll need help to get free –'

'They're killers,' said Bale, unmoved.

'Let her do it,' said Torak. 'She knows about things like this.'

As they watched, Renn made the red ochre into a paste

with water, then daubed the Death Marks on both tokoroth: forehead, heart, heels.

Wolf came to sit beside her, whining softly and sweeping the grass with his tail. There was a light in his golden eyes. Torak wondered what he could see.

Renn's face became distant, and she began to murmur under her breath. Torak felt a flicker of unease. He guessed she was summoning the child souls from deep within; calling them out from their hiding-place.

Suddenly the boy tokoroth clenched his fists. The girl tokoroth twitched, then opened her eyes.

A tear rolled down Renn's cheek. 'Go in peace,' she whispered. 'You're free now. Free . . .'

The boy tokoroth shuddered, then lay still. The girl gave a long, rattling sigh that ended in – silence.

A breeze stirred the suncups. Wolf turned his head, as if to follow the passing of something swift.

'They're gone,' said Renn.

Next day the Seals returned from the Cormorants' island, and Torak, Renn and Bale spent a long time talking with the Clan Leader.

Surprisingly, Islinn was not as crushed by the news of his Mage's death as they had expected. In fact, the knowledge that he must now take charge seemed to imbue him with fresh vigour. He looked visibly younger as he dispatched his fleetest messengers to the Forest to warn the clans against the poison, and others to fetch Asrif and Detlan home. The bodies of the tokoroth were placed in a skinboat, taken out of sight of land, and given to the Sea Mother.

When all was done, Islinn ordered everyone out of his shelter, except for Torak. 'I'm sending Bale with you tomorrow,' he said. 'He will make sure that you get back safely.'

'Thank you, Leader,' Torak said tonelessly.

The Leader studied him. 'You are wrong to blame yourself. He tricked me too. And I have lived a good many more summers than you.'

Torak did not reply.

'You grieve for him,' stated the old man.

Torak was surprised that he should have perceived that. 'He was kind to me,' he said. 'I mean – before the end. Was it all a lie?'

The Seal Clan Leader regarded him with eyes that had witnessed every kind of wickedness and folly. 'I doubt if even he knew the answer to that.' He paused. 'Go back to the Forest, Torak. It's where you belong. But if you ever need a home, you have one here.'

Torak put his fists over his heart to show his thanks, but he didn't think he would ever take up Islinn's offer. For him this island was too full of ghosts.

They left the following morning. Wolf went in Torak's skinboat, and Renn in Bale's. It was a brilliantly sunny day, with a brisk west wind to speed them on their way. As they left the Bay of Seals, Torak looked back one last time. Smoke rose above the humped shelters, and children splashed in the shallows. Rowan trees and birches lapped the feet of the mountains, where white seabirds wheeled.

He knew that he didn't belong in this precarious, rocky world that was for ever at the mercy of the Sea. But in its way it was rich and beautiful, and at last he understood why Bale loved it so much.

Then his gaze travelled higher, and he saw the Crag, and

his spirits plunged. He hadn't been able to bring himself to return. Bale had gone up alone, and found Fa's knife, and brought it to him without a word.

They made good speed, with nothing but puffins and sea-eagles for company. Once in the distance, Torak thought he saw a tall, notched fin that followed them for a while. When he blinked, it was gone.

It was late in the day when Wolf gave a low bark, then stood up in the prow with his ears forwards, wagging his tail. Soon afterwards, Bale shouted something that Torak didn't catch, and Renn grinned and raised high her bow.

Then Torak turned and saw the Forest rising above the waves.

It was night by the time they reached the shore, although the huge amber sun still hung low over the Sea.

Swiftly, Torak changed into his old buckskin jerkin and leggings, and bundled up his seal-hide clothes. It felt good to have his clan-creature skin back, as well as his pack and bow and sleeping-sack. But as he helped Bale stow the borrowed clothes in his skinboat, he wondered when – or if – he would see the Seal boy again.

Bale had decided to head off at once. He was silent as they went down to the shallows, and Torak could see that he was thinking about the last time he and his friends had been on this beach, and the rough handling they'd meted out to the stranger from the Forest.

Torak said, 'I'll see you again, Bale. Some day I'll show you the Forest.'

Bale glanced at the tall pines fringing the beach. 'A few days ago, I wouldn't have thought that possible. But I suppose – I never thought I'd see a wolf in a skinboat. So –'

'– so why not a Seal in a forest?' said Torak with a smile.

Bale grinned. 'Why not indeed, kinsman?' Then with a nod to Renn and Wolf, he was back in his skinboat and heading off into the west, his fair hair flying behind him, and the Sea around him turning to gold in the sun.

That night, Torak and Renn built a real Forest shelter of living birch saplings in a glade filled with green ferns and the deep pink flowers of willowherb. They had a real Forest meal of stewed goosefoot leaves and baked hawkbit roots, with some early raspberries which Torak found by the bog where he'd decoyed Detlan and Asrif. 'And not a juniper berry in sight,' said Renn with a sigh of satisfaction.

Afterwards they sat by the fire, smelling the tang of pine-smoke and listening to the full-throated warbling of the Forest birds. For the first time in days, they were in half-darkness beneath whispering trees. They could even see a few pale stars between the branches.

Wolf trotted off on one of his nightly hunts, and Renn gave a huge yawn. 'Do you realise,' she said, 'it'll soon be the Cloudberry Moon? I like cloudberries.'

Torak did not reply. He couldn't put it off any longer. Ever since Bale had left, he'd been working up the courage to tell Renn about who – what – he was.

'Renn,' he said, frowning at the fire. 'There's something I've got to tell you.'

'What,' said Renn, rolling out her sleeping-sack.

He took a breath. 'When we were at the Eagle Heights, the Seal Mage told me something. Something about – me.'

Renn stopped what she was doing. 'You're a spirit walker,' she said quietly.

He stared at her. 'How long have you known?'

'Since he told you.' She picked at a loose stitch on her

leggings. 'That night after we had the fight, I was worried, so I followed you. I heard everything.'

He thought about that. Then he said, 'Do you mind?'

'What do you mean?'

'About – what I am.'

To his surprise, she grinned. 'Torak, you're a *who*, not a *what*! You're still a person.'

There was silence for a while. Then Renn said, 'When I found out, I wasn't really that surprised. I've always known you were different.'

Torak tried to smile, but couldn't manage it.

'Don't be sad,' she said. 'After all, maybe it's why you can talk to Wolf.'

'What do you mean?'

'Well it's always bothered me,' she said, renewing her attack on the stitching. 'You were just a baby when your father put you in the wolf den; much too small to learn person talk, let alone wolf talk. So how come you did?' She put her head on one side. 'Maybe your souls slipped into one of the wolves, or something. Don't you think?'

Torak chewed his lower lip. 'I never thought of that.'

Wolf came back from his hunt, his muzzle tinged with red. He wiped it off on the ferns, and sniffed the fire, then padded over to Torak and nosed his chin.

'Do you think he knows?' said Renn.

'About me?' said Torak, scratching behind Wolf's ears. 'How could he? And I couldn't begin to say it in wolf talk.'

Renn wriggled into her sleeping-sack and curled up. 'But he's still your friend,' she said.

Torak nodded. Somehow that didn't make him feel any less cut off.

Again Renn yawned. 'Get some sleep, Torak.'

Torak got into his sleeping-sack, and lay on his back. He

was tired, but he didn't think he would sleep.

Wolf slumped against him with a 'humph', and was soon twitching in his dreams.

Torak lay wide-eyed, staring at the fire.

Much later, Renn said, 'Torak? Are you awake?'

'Yes,' he said.

'At the end, when you were both in the water, the Seal Mage shouted something. What was it?'

Torak had been hoping she wouldn't ask. 'I can't tell you,' he said. 'At least, not yet. First I've got to talk to Fin-Kedinn.'

THIRTY-FIVE

'Tell me the truth,' Torak said to Fin-Kedinn seven days later.

It had taken him and Renn four days to reach the Raven camp, making their way through a Forest where the sickness was slowly ebbing, and the smell of burning juniper berries hung heavy in the air. Islinn's messengers had done their work swiftly. It was made easier by the fact that Fin-Kedinn had persuaded the Open Forest Clans to stay together, and help one another through the sickness. Many of the afflicted were now recovering. But the Ravens had lost five of their people.

For two days after they rejoined the clan, Torak couldn't get Fin-Kedinn alone. The Raven Leader was busy tending his clan, and making sure that every last hunting party in the Forest had been warned about the juniper berries.

But on the seventh day, things began to return to normal. Some of the Ravens went hunting, while others stayed by the river to spear trout. Renn sat with Saeunn, explaining how she'd freed the hidden souls of the tokoroth. Wolf, who had no liking for dogs, disappeared into the Forest.

Torak found the Raven Leader preparing lime bark on the banks of a stream which fed into the Widewater. It was a hot day, but the trees cast a cool green shade. The sweetness of late summer blossom filled the air, and the branches hummed with bees.

'So you want the truth,' said Fin-Kedinn, testing the edge of his axe with his thumb. 'About what?'

'Everything,' said Torak, seething with a frustration that had been building for days. 'Why didn't you *tell* me?'

With one stroke Fin-Kedinn cut a sucker from the base of a lime tree, and started peeling off the bark. 'What should I have told you?' he said.

'That I'm a spirit walker! That the Seal Mage was my father's brother! That the sickness was my fault!'

Fin-Kedinn stiffened. 'Don't ever say that.'

'He sent the sickness because of *me*,' said Torak. 'Because of *me* he killed Oslak and the others. It's my fault!'

'No!' The blue eyes blazed. 'You did nothing wrong! You cannot be blamed for the evil that man did. He was the one, Torak. Remember that.'

For a moment they faced each other, and the air crackled between them. Then the Raven Leader tossed the bark on a pile at his feet. 'And you're wrong. I did not know that you're a spirit walker, not till Renn told me last night. None of us knew.'

Torak frowned. 'But – I thought Fa must have told Saeunn. When I was little, at the clan meet by the Sea.'

Fin-Kedinn shook his head. 'He told her he'd put you in a wolf den when you were a baby; and that you might some day be the one to vanquish the Soul-Eaters. He didn't say why.'

'Why would he keep that from her?'

'Who knows? He'd been a hunted man for a long time. He'd grown wary.'

Wary towards his own son, too, thought Torak. That was the worst of it: that sometimes he was angry with Fa. For not telling him . . .

'He did what he thought was best,' said Fin-Kedinn. 'He didn't want your boyhood darkened by destiny.'

Torak threw himself down on the bank and began pulling up grass. 'You knew them both, didn't you? My father and his brother.'

Fin-Kedinn did not reply.

'Tell me about them. *Please.*'

The Raven Leader stroked his beard and sighed. 'I first met them twenty-eight summers ago,' he said. 'I was eleven, your father was nine. Wolf Clan, like his father. His brother – who was my age – was Seal Clan, like their mother. We spent five moons together, fostered with the Wolf Clan.'

'With the Wolf Clan?' Torak said, surprised. 'But I've never even seen them, so how –'

'They weren't always as elusive as they are now. Times change. People grow mistrustful.' With a length of withe he tied the pile of bark into a bundle. 'The three of us became friends,' he went on. 'I lived for hunting; but with the others it was always Magecraft. Your father was eager to learn the ways of trees, hunters, prey. His brother . . . ' He gave the knot a sharp tug. 'His brother wanted only to control. To dominate.'

Hoisting the bundle on his shoulder, he stepped down into the stream and set it to soak beneath a stone. 'Six winters came and went, and we stayed good friends. The seventh winter changed all that.' Water swirled round his calves as he bent to retrieve another bundle which had been soaking for days. 'Your father was named the Wolf Mage,' he said, tossing it on the bank. 'His brother – although the older and some said the more skilled – was not named the Seal Mage.' He shook his head. 'It was a bitter blow. None of us knew how bitter until it was too late. He left his clan, and wandered alone.'

'Where did he go?' asked Torak.

Sadness shadowed Fin-Kedinn's face. 'I don't know. I never saw him again. But later, I heard from your father that his brother had reappeared. Joined a group of Mages called the Healers.'

'But – he wasn't a Mage,' said Torak.

Fin-Kedinn's mouth curled. 'He was persuasive. You of all people should know that.' Climbing back onto the bank, he knelt by the bundle. 'I told you once how the Healers became the Soul-Eaters. How they brought terror to the Forest.' He paused. 'Then came the great fire that broke them. Some were terribly wounded. All were scattered, in hiding.'

'He was burned,' murmured Torak. 'On his face and down his side.'

'What none of us knew,' said Fin-Kedinn, 'was that he'd found his way back to his clan. All we knew was that the Seals had become – separate. Ceased their dealings with the Open Forest, traded only with the Sea clans. And they had a new Mage.'

Torak tossed the grass in the stream, and watched it sucked under by the current. He thought of Tenris, dragged down into the deep. He said, 'He was after me because I'm a spirit walker. Because he wanted that power.' He stared into the water. 'The other Soul-Eaters will want it too.'

Fin-Kedinn hesitated. 'They may not know about you yet. Maybe the Seal Mage acted alone.'

'And maybe he didn't,' said Torak. 'Maybe he had help.'

Suddenly the Forest seemed to close in around him. The buzzing of the bees became strangely menacing. In his mind, Torak saw again the yellow eyes of Tenris the Seal Mage. He thought of the other Soul-Eaters – the faceless ones whose names he didn't know, but who were out there somewhere. Waiting.

He said, 'They'll find out what I can do. They'll come after me.'

The Raven Leader nodded. 'You could make them more powerful than they ever dreamed. Or you could destroy them utterly.'

Torak met his eyes. 'Is that why you've never offered to foster me? Because I'm dangerous?'

Something flickered in the blue gaze. 'I must look to the safety of the clan, Torak. You could help us defeat them. Or you could be our ruin.'

'But I would never harm the Ravens!' cried Torak, leaping to his feet.

'You don't know that!' Fin-Kedinn said fiercely. 'You don't know what you will become. None of us does!'

'But –'

'Evil exists in us all, Torak. Some fight it. Some feed it. That's how it's always been.'

With a cry Torak turned away.

Fin-Kedinn made no move to comfort him. Instead he cut open the bundle, chose a strip of bark, and began peeling off the bast.

Torak felt giddy and frightened. He felt as if he stood at the edge of a cliff, about to jump off into the unknown.

Mustering his courage, he asked the question that had

been eating away at him ever since Tenris had met his end. 'Last winter, when you told me about the Soul-Eaters, you said there were seven. But you only described five.'

The Raven Leader's strong hands stilled.

'The Seal Mage was the sixth,' said Torak. 'I need to know about the seventh.' His fists clenched. 'My father had a scar on his chest. Here.' He touched his breastbone. 'That made it hard when I – when I put the Death Marks on him.' He tried to swallow. 'Something the Seal Mage said made me think that – the seventh Soul-Eater . . .'

Fin-Kedinn rubbed a hand over his face. Then he laid the lime bast in the grass.

'My father,' said Torak. 'It was my father.'

A gust of wind shivered the branches, hazing the air with drifting sweetness. The trees were trying to soften the blow.

'No,' said Torak, sinking to his knees. '*No.*'

He read his answer in the Raven Leader's eyes.

After a while, Fin-Kedinn came and sat beside him. 'Do you remember,' he said, 'when I told you that in the beginning they were not evil? Your father believed that. That's why he joined them. To heal the sick, to chase away demons.' His gaze became distant and full of pain. 'Your mother never believed it. She knew. But by the time he saw the truth, it was too late.' He spread his hands. 'He tried to leave. They wouldn't let him.'

'Is that why they killed him?' said Torak.

Slowly the Raven Leader nodded.

Torak sat with his head bowed to his knees, shaken by dry, wrenching sobs. Fin-Kedinn sat beside him: not touching, not speaking, but steadying by his presence alone.

At last the Raven Leader rose to his feet. 'I'm going back

to camp now. You stay here. Peel the rest of this bundle. Wash the bast in the stream. Hang it up to dry.'

Torak nodded, too numb to speak.

'Tomorrow,' said Fin-Kedinn, 'I'll teach you how to make rope.'

Torak had run till he could run no further, but his thoughts would not be stilled. Fa had been a Soul-Eater. Fa, his own Fa . . .

There was a tightness in his chest that made it hard to breathe. A storm of rage and grief and fear.

He came to a halt by a boisterous stream that tumbled over big, mossy boulders. A squirrel shot up a sycamore tree. An otter stopped eating a trout and fled into the ferns.

Torak knelt to drink, and his name-soul stared back at him. Torak of the Wolf Clan. Torak the spirit walker.

With a cry he snatched a clump of yellow suncups, and tore them to pieces. He didn't belong with the Ravens. He didn't belong anywhere . . .

After a while, the otter came back for its half-eaten trout, and settled down to finish its meal. In the sycamore, the squirrel started nibbling bark to get at the sweet, sticky tree-blood.

Torak sat with his back against the trunk, watching them – and some of his tumult eased. They didn't care that his father had been a Soul-Eater. They didn't care that he was a spirit walker. As long as he left them in peace, they were content for him to remain.

He placed his palm on the tree's rough bark, and felt its power coursing through him. The power of the Forest.

Deep within him, he felt a stirring of resolve. *This* was

where he belonged: here in the Forest. Through all the bad things that had happened, the Forest had given him strength. Strength to defeat the bear. Strength to survive Tenris and the Sea Mother. Strength to face his destiny. And maybe Fa's spirit – wherever it was – knew that, and was proud.

Above him the sycamore stirred in the breeze: spreading wide its arms, watching over him. Torak raised his head and stared at the glowing green leaves. With the help of the Forest, he would face his destiny. He would do whatever lay in his power to vanquish the Soul-Eaters.

'I will do this,' he said out loud. 'I *will* do this.'

Wolf found his pack-brother sitting by the little Fast Wet, tearing up shiny grey petals in his forepaws.

Wolf splashed into the wet to cool his pads, then ate some of the flowers to be companionable. He wagged his tail. Tall Tailless did not smile back. Wolf smelt his sadness, and was puzzled.

Wolf was feeling *very* happy. His confusion was gone. He knew what he was for. When he'd been a cub, he'd helped Tall Tailless fight the demon bear. Then on the island of the fish-birds, he'd chased the demons out of the half-grown taillesses. *This* was what he was for: to help Tall Tailless fight demons.

It meant never returning to his pack on the Mountain, but Wolf didn't mind too much, because he would be with his pack-brother. If only Tall Tailless wasn't so sad.

To make him feel better, Wolf leaned against him, and rubbed his scent into his pelt.

Tall Tailless turned to him and said, *Do you know what I am?*

Wolf was surprised. *My pack-brother.*

But do you know what creature I am? What I can do?

Yes, I know, Wolf replied a little impatiently. He'd always known.

To his surprise, Tall Tailless stared at him hard – which was scarcely polite. Then he began to smile. *You know?* he said.

Wolf wagged his tail.

He decided they'd had enough talk, and went down on his forepaws, barking and asking Tall Tailless to play. When his pack-brother still didn't move, Wolf pounced.

His pack-brother gave a startled yowl and toppled backwards onto the bank. Wolf nose-nudged him in the flanks. His pack-brother grabbed Wolf's scruff and play-bit him on the ear.

Soon they were rolling about in the grass, and Tall Tailless was making the odd, breathless yip-and-yowl that was his way of laughing.

SOUL
EATER

SEA
ICE

N

iced in
bay

OPEN
SEA

Mo
ice

ice edge

Sea ice

White Fox
* Camp

ice edge

WWWW shore

Eye of the Viper Mountain

NARWAL & WALRUS CLANS

ICE RIVER

ice cliffs

black ice

PTARMIGAN CLAN

THE FAR NORTH

snow hills

snow plains

Edge of the Forest

Mountain of the World Spirit

ONE

Torak did't want it to be an omen.

He didn't want it to be anything more than an owl feather lying in the snow. So he ignored it. That was his first mistake.

Quietly, he went back to the tracks they'd been following since dawn. They looked fresh. He slipped off his mitten and felt them. No ice in the bottom. Yes, fresh.

Turning to Renn, further uphill, he tapped his sleeve and raised his forefinger, then pointed down into the beech wood. *One reindeer, heading south.*

Renn gave a nod, whipped an arrow from her quiver, and nocked it to her bow. Like Torak, she was hard to see in a pale reindeer-hide parka and leggings, with wood-ash smeared on her face to mask her scent. Like him, she was hungry, having eaten nothing since a slip of dried boar meat for daymeal.

Unlike him, she hadn't seen the owl feather.

So don't tell her, he thought.

That was his second mistake.

A few paces below him, Wolf was sniffing at a patch where the reindeer had scraped away the snow to get at the lichen. His ears were pricked, his silver fur fluffed up with excitement. If he sensed Torak's unease, he didn't show it. Another sniff, then he raised his muzzle to catch the scent-laden breeze, and his amber gaze grazed Torak's. *Smells bad.*

Torak tilted his head. *What do you mean?* he asked in wolf talk.

Wolf twitched his whiskers. *Bad muzzle.*

Torak went to examine what he'd found, and spotted a tiny bead of yellow pus on the bare earth. Wolf was telling him that the reindeer was old, its teeth rotten after many winters of munching gritty lichen.

Torak wrinkled his nose in a brief wolf smile. *Thank you, pack-brother.* Then he glanced at Renn, and headed downhill as silently as his beaver-hide boots would allow.

Not silently enough for Wolf, who flicked a reproachful ear as he moved over the snow as soundlessly as smoke.

Together they crept between the sleeping trees. Black oaks and silvery beeches glittered with frost. Here and there, Torak saw the crimson blaze of holly berries; the deep green of a wakeful spruce standing guard over its slumbering sisters. The Forest was hushed. The rivers were frozen. Most of the birds had flown south.

Except for that owl, thought Torak.

He'd known it was an owl's feather as soon as he'd seen its furry upper side, which muffled the sound of flight when the owl was hunting. If it had been the dusky grey of a forest owl, he wouldn't have worried, he'd simply have given it to Renn, who used them to fletch her arrows. But this feather was barred with black and tawny; shadow and flame. That told Torak it belonged to the greatest, the fiercest of owls: the eagle owl. And to find one of those – that was bad.

Wolf's black nose twitched.

Torak was instantly alert.

Through the trees, he glimpsed the reindeer, nibbling beard-moss. He heard the crunch of its hooves, saw its misting breath. Good, they were still downwind. He forgot the feather, and thought of juicy meat and rich marrowfat.

Behind him, the faint creak of Renn's bow. He fitted an arrow to his own, then realized he was blocking her view, and dropped to one knee, since she was the better shot.

The reindeer moved behind a beech tree. They'd have to wait.

As Torak waited, he noticed a spruce, five paces below him. The way it spread its snowladen arms . . . warning him back.

Gripping his bow, he fixed his gaze on the prey.

A gust of wind stirred the beeches around him, and last summer's leaves rustled like dry, dead hands.

He swallowed. It felt as if the Forest were trying to tell him something.

Overhead, a branch shifted, and a flurry of snow hissed down. He glanced up. His heart jerked. An eagle owl. Tufted ears as sharp as spearpoints. Huge orange eyes like twin suns.

With a cry he leapt to his feet.

The reindeer fled.

Wolf raced off in pursuit.

Renn's arrow sped past Torak's hood.

The eagle owl spread its enormous wings and silently flew away.

'What were you *doing*?' shouted Renn furiously. 'Standing up like that? I might have killed you!'

Torak didn't reply. He was watching the eagle owl soar into the fierce blue of the noonday sky. But eagle owls, he thought, hunt by night.

Wolf came bounding through the trees and skittered to a halt beside him, shaking off snow and lashing his tail. He hadn't expected to catch the reindeer, but he'd enjoyed the chase.

Sensing Torak's unease, he rubbed against him. Torak knelt, burying his face in the deep, coarse scruff, breathing in Wolf's familiar, sweet-grass scent.

'What's wrong?' said Renn.

Torak raised his head. 'That owl, of course.'

'What owl?'

He blinked. 'But you must have seen it. The eagle owl, it was so close I could have touched it!'

When she still looked blank, he ran back up the hill, and found the feather. 'Here,' he panted, holding it out.

Wolf flattened his ears and growled.

Renn put her hand to her clan-creature feathers.

'What does it mean?' said Torak.

'I don't know, but it's bad. We should get back. Fin-Kedinn will know what to do. And Torak – ' She eyed the feather, 'leave it here.'

As he threw it in the snow, he wished he hadn't picked it up with his bare hand. A fine grey powder dusted his palm. He wiped it off on his parka, but his skin carried a whiff of rottenness that reminded him of the Raven bone-grounds.

Suddenly Wolf gave a grunt, and pricked his ears.

'What's he smelt?' said Renn. She didn't speak wolf talk, but she knew Wolf.

Torak frowned. 'I don't know.' Wolf's tail was high, but he wasn't giving any of the prey signals Torak recognized.

Strange prey, Wolf told him, and he realized that Wolf was puzzled, too.

An overwhelming sense of danger swept over Torak. He gave an urgent warning bark. 'Uff!' *Stay away!*

But Wolf was off, racing up the valley in his tireless lope. 'No!' shouted Torak, floundering after him.

'What's the matter?' cried Renn. 'What did he say?'

'"Strange prey",' said Torak.

With growing alarm, he watched Wolf crest the ridge and glance back at them. He looked magnificent: his thick winter pelt a rich blend of grey and black and foxy red, his bushy tail taut with the thrill of the hunt. *Follow me, pack-brother! Strange prey!*

Then he was gone.

They followed as fast as they could, but they were burdened with packs and sleeping-sacks, and the snow was deep, so they had to use their wicker snowshoes, which slowed them even more. When they reached the top, Wolf was nowhere to be seen.

'He'll be waiting for us,' said Renn, trying to be reassuring. She pointed to a thicket of aspen. 'Soon as we get down into that, he'll pounce.'

That made Torak feel a little better. Only yesterday, Wolf had hidden behind a juniper bush, then leapt out and knocked him into a snowdrift, growling and play-biting till Torak was helpless with laughter.

They reached the aspens. Wolf didn't pounce.

Torak uttered two short barks. *Where are you?*

No answer.

His tracks were plain enough, though. Several clans hunted here, and all used dogs, but there was no mistaking Wolf's tracks for a dog's. A dog runs haphazardly, because he knows his master will feed him, whereas a wolf runs with a purpose: he must find prey, or starve. And although Wolf had been with Torak and the Raven Clan for the past seven moons, Torak had never given him food, for fear of blunting his hunting skills.

The afternoon wore on, and still they followed his trail: a straight-line lope, in which the hindpaws trod in the prints of the forepaws. The crunch of their snowshoes and the rasp of their breath echoed through the Forest.

'We're getting quite far north,' said Renn. They were about a daywalk from the Raven camp, which lay to the south-west, by the Widewater river.

Again Torak barked. *Where are you?*

Snow drifted from a tree, pattering onto his hood. The stillness after it settled seemed deeper than before.

As he watched the gleam die on a cluster of holly berries, he sensed that the day was on the turn. Already the brightness was fading from the sky, and shadows were stealing out from under the trees. A chill crept into his heart, because he knew that the descent into darkness had begun.

The clans call this the demon time, because it's in winter, when the great bull Auroch rears high among the stars, that demons escape from the Otherworld, and flit through the Forest, to cause havoc and despair. It only takes one to taint a whole valley; and although the Mages keep watch, they can't trap them all. Demons are hard to see. You never catch more than a glimpse, and you can't be sure what they look like, because they change, the better to slip into sleeping mouths, and possess living bodies. There they crouch in the red darkness, sucking out courage and trust; leaving the seeds of malice and strife.

It was at this moment, at the demon time, that Torak knew the omens had come true. Wolf hadn't howled a reply because he could not. Because something had happened to him.

Nightmare visions flashed through Torak's mind. What if Wolf had tried to bring down an auroch or an elk on his own? He was only twenty moons old. A flying hoof can kill a foolhardy young wolf.

Maybe he'd been caught in a snare. Torak had taught him to avoid them, but what if he'd been careless? He'd be trapped. Unable to howl as the noose tightened round his neck.

The trees creaked. More snow pattered down. Torak put his hands to his lips and howled. *Where – are – you?*

No reply.

Renn gave him a worried smile; but in her dark eyes he saw his own anxiety. 'The sun's going down,' she said.

He swallowed. 'In a while the moon will be up. There'll be enough light to track.'

She gave a doubtful nod.

They'd gone another few paces when she turned aside. 'Torak! Over here!'

非丰

Whoever had caught Wolf had done it with the simplest of traps. They'd dug a pit, and hidden it with a flimsy screen of snow-covered branches.

That wouldn't have held him for long, but in the churned-up snow around the pit, Torak found shreds of braided rawhide. 'A net,' he said in disbelief. 'They had a net.'

'But – no spikes in the pit,' said Renn. 'They must have wanted him alive.'

This is a bad dream, thought Torak. I'm going to wake

up, and Wolf is going to come loping through the trees.

That was when he saw the blood. A shocking red spatter in the snow.

'Maybe he bit them,' muttered Renn. 'I hope he did, I hope he bit their hands off!'

Torak picked up a tuft of bloody fur. His fingers shook. He forced himself to read the snow.

Wolf had approached the pitfall warily, his tracks changing from a straight-line lope to a walk, in which front and hind prints showed side-by-side. But he'd approached just the same.

Oh Wolf, said Torak silently. Why weren't you more careful?

Then it struck him that maybe it was his friendship with Wolf that had made him more trusting of people. Maybe this was his fault.

He stared at the trampled trail that led north. Ice was forming in the tracks. Wolf's captors had a head start.

'How many sets of prints?' said Renn, staying well back, as Torak was by far the better tracker.

'Two. The bigger man's prints are deeper when he ran off.'

'So – he was carrying Wolf. But why take him at all? No-one would hurt Wolf. No-one would dare.' It was strict clan law that no harm should be done to any of the hunters in the Forest.

'Torak,' she called, crouching behind a clump of juniper. 'They hid over here. But I can't make out – '

'Don't move!' warned Torak.

'What?'

'There, by your boot!'

She froze. 'What – made *that*?'

He squatted to examine it.

526

His father had taught him tracking, and he thought he knew every print of every creature in the Forest; but these were the strangest he'd ever seen. Very light and small, like a bird's – but not. The hind tracks resembled tiny, crooked, five-clawed hands, but there were no front prints, only two pock-marks: as if the creature had been walking on stumps.

'"Strange prey",' murmured Torak.

Renn met his eyes. 'Bait. They used it as bait.'

He stood up. 'They went north, towards the valley of the Axehandle. Where could they go from there?'

She threw up her hands. 'Anywhere! They could've turned east for Lake Axehead, and kept going all the way to the High Mountains. Or doubled back south, for the Deep Forest. Or west, they could be halfway to the Sea by now –'

Voices, coming their way.

They ducked behind the junipers. Renn readied her bow, and Torak drew his black basalt axe from his belt.

Whoever it was, they were making no attempt at stealth. Torak saw a man and woman, followed by a large dog dragging a sled on which lolled a dead roe buck. A boy of about eight summers plunged eagerly ahead, and with him, a younger dog with a deerhide saddle-pack strapped to his belly.

The young dog caught Wolf's scent on Torak, gave a terrified yelp, and sped back to the boy, who halted. Torak saw the clan-tattoo between his eyebrows: three slender black ovals, like a permanent frown.

Renn breathed out. 'Willow Clan! Maybe they saw something!'

'No!' He pulled her back. 'We don't know if we can trust them!'

She stared at him. 'Torak, these are *Willows*! Of course we can!' Before he could stop her, she was running towards them, both fists over her heart in sign of friendship.

They saw her and broke into smiles. They were returning to their clan in the west, the woman explained. Her face was scarred, like birch canker, marking her as a survivor of last summer's sickness.

'Did you meet anyone?' said Renn. 'We're looking for –'

'"We"?' queried the man.

Torak stood up. 'You've come from the north. Did you see anyone?'

The man's eyes flicked to Torak's clan-tattoos, and his eyebrows rose. 'We don't meet many Wolf Clan these days.' Then to Renn, 'You're young to be hunting so far from your camp.'

Renn bridled. 'We're both thirteen summers old. And we have the Leader's leave – '

'Did you see anyone?' broke in Torak.

'I did,' said the boy.

'Who?' cried Torak. 'Who was it?'

The boy drew back, startled by his intensity. 'I – I'd gone to find Snapper.' He pointed at his dog, who gave a faint wag of his tail. 'He likes chasing squirrels, but he gets lost. Then I saw them. They had a net, it was struggling.'

So he's still alive, thought Torak. He'd been clenching his fists so hard that his nails were digging into his palms.

'What did they look like?' said Renn.

The boy stretched his arm above his head. 'A huge man. And another, big, with bandy legs.'

'What about their clan-tattoos?' said Torak. 'Clan-creature skins? Anything!'

The boy gulped. 'Their hoods were up, I didn't see their faces.'

528

Torak turned to the Willow man. 'Can you take a message to Fin-Kedinn?'

'Whatever it is,' said the man, 'you should tell him yourself. The Leader of the Ravens is wise, he'll know what to do.'

'There's no time,' said Torak. 'Tell him that someone has taken Wolf. Tell him we're going to get him back.'

Two

Night brought a bone-cracking frost that turned the trees white, and the snow-crust brittle underfoot.

It was past middle-night, and Torak was dizzy with tiredness. He forced himself to keep going. The trail of Wolf's captors lay like a snake in the moonlight. North, always north.

With heartstopping suddenness, seven Mages loomed before him. Lean, horned shadows cut across his path. *We will rule the Forest*, they whispered in voices colder than windblown snow. *All tremble before us. We are the Soul-Eaters . . .*

A hand touched his shoulder. He cried out.

'What's wrong?' said Renn.

He blinked. Before him, seven birch trees glittered with frost. 'A dream.'

'About what?' Renn knew something of dreams, because sometimes her own came true.

'Nothing,' said Torak.

She gave a disbelieving snort.

They trudged on, their breath smoking in the freezing air.

Torak wondered if the dream meant something. Could it be – was it possible that the *Soul-Eaters* were behind Wolf's disappearance?

But what would they want with Wolf?

Besides, no trace of them had been found. Since the sickness last summer, Fin-Kedinn had spoken to every clan in the Open Forest, and had sent word to the Deep Forest and the Sea and Mountain clans. Nothing. The Soul-Eaters had gone to ground like a bear in winter.

And yet – Wolf was still gone.

Torak felt as if he were walking in a blizzard of ignorance and fear. Raising his head, he saw the great bull Auroch high in the sky. He felt the malice of its cold red eye, and fought a rising tide of panic. First he'd lost his father. Now Wolf. What if he never saw Wolf again? What if he was already dead?

The trees thinned. Before them glimmered a frozen river, criss-crossed with hare tracks. On its banks, the dead umbels of hemlock reached spiked fingers towards the stars.

A herd of forest horses took fright and clattered off across the ice, then turned to stare. Their manes stood stiff as icicles, and in their moon-bright eyes, Torak glimpsed an echo of his own fear.

In his mind he saw Wolf as he'd looked before he vanished: magnificent and proud. Torak had known him since he was a cub. Most of the time he was simply Wolf: clever, inquisitive, and fiercely loyal. Sometimes he was the guide, with a mysterious certainty in his amber eyes. Always he was a pack-brother.

'What I don't understand,' said Renn, cutting across his thoughts, 'is why take Wolf at all?'

'Maybe it's a trap. Maybe they want me, not Wolf.'

'I thought of that, too.' Her voice dropped. 'Maybe – whoever took Wolf is after you because,' she hesitated. 'Because you're a spirit walker, and they want your power.'

He flinched. He hated being a spirit walker. And he hated that she'd said it out loud. It felt like a scab being torn off.

'But if they *were* after you,' she persisted, 'why not just take you? Two big strong men, we'd have been no match for them. So why – '

'I don't *know*!' snapped Torak. 'Why do you keep on? What good does it do?'

Renn stared at him.

'I don't *know* why they took him!' he cried. 'I don't *care* if it's a trap! I just want him back!'

After that, they didn't speak at all. The forest horses had trampled the trail, and for a while it was lost, which at least gave them an excuse to split up. When Torak found it again, it had changed. For the worse.

'They've made a sled,' he said. 'No dogs to pull it, but even without, they'll be able to go much faster downhill.'

Renn glanced at the sky. 'It's clouding over. We should build a shelter. Get some rest.'

'You can if you want, I'm going on.'

She put her hands on her hips. 'On your own?'

'If I have to.'

'Torak. He's my friend too.'

'He's not just my *friend*,' he retorted, 'he's my pack-brother!'

He could see that he'd hurt her.

'And how,' she said between her teeth, 'is blundering about missing things going to help him?'

He glared at her. 'I haven't missed anything!'

'Oh no? A few paces back, one of them turned aside to follow those otter tracks –'

'What otter tracks?'

'*That's what I mean*! You're exhausted! So am I!'

He knew she was right. But he didn't want to admit it.

In silence they found a storm-toppled spruce, and dug out the snow at its base to make a makeshift sleeping-space. They roofed it with spruce boughs, and used their snowshoes as shovels to pack on a thick layer of snow. Finally they dragged more boughs inside, and laid their reindeer-hide sleeping-sacks on top. When they'd finished, they were trembling with fatigue.

From his tinder pouch Torak took his strike-fire and some shredded birch bark, and woke up a fire. The only deadwood he'd found was spruce, so it smoked and spat. He was too exhausted to care.

Renn wrinkled her nose at the smoke, but didn't remark on it. She took a coil of elk-blood sausage from her pack and cut it in three, then put one piece on the roof of the shelter for the clan guardian, and tossed Torak another. Tucking her own share in her food pouch, she picked up her axe and waterskin. 'I'm going to the river. There's more meat in my pack, but *don't* touch the dried lingonberries.'

'Why not?'

'Because,' she said crossly, 'I'm saving them for Wolf!'

After she'd gone, Torak forced himself to eat. Then he crawled out of the shelter and made an offering.

Cutting a lock of his long dark hair, he tied it round a branch of the fallen spruce. Then he put his hand on his clan-creature skin: the tattered scrap of wolf fur sewn to the shoulder of his parka. 'Forest,' he said, 'hear me. I ask by each of my three souls – by my name-soul, my clan-soul, and my world-soul – I ask that you watch over Wolf, and keep him from harm.'

It was only when he'd finished that he noticed a lock of dark-red hair tied to another branch. Renn had made her own offering.

That made him feel guilty. He shouldn't have shouted at her.

Back in the shelter, he pulled off his boots, wriggled into his sleeping-sack, and lay watching the fire, smelling the mustiness of reindeer fur and the bitter tang of spruce.

Far away, an owl hooted. Not the familiar 'bvoo-bvoo' of a grey Forest owl, but the deep 'oo-hu, oo-hu, oo-hu' of an eagle owl.

Torak shivered.

He heard Renn's footsteps crunching through the snow, and called to her. 'You made an offering. So did I.'

When she didn't answer, he added, 'Sorry I snapped at you. It's just . . . Well. Sorry.'

Still no answer.

He heard her crunch towards the shelter – then circle *behind* it.

He sat up. 'Renn?'

The footsteps stopped.

His heart began to pound. It wasn't Renn.

As quietly as he could, he wriggled out of his sleeping-sack, pulled on his boots, and reached for his axe.

The footsteps came closer. Whoever it was stood only an arm's length away, separated by a flimsy wall of spruce.

For a moment there was silence. Then – very loud in the stillness – Torak heard wet, bubbling breath.

His skin prickled. He thought of the victims of last summer's sickness. The murderous light in their eyes; the slime catching in their throats . . .

He thought of Renn, alone by the river. He crawled towards the mouth of the shelter.

Clouds covered the moon, and the night was black. He caught a whiff of carrion. Heard again that bubbling breath.

'Who are you?' he called into the dark.

The breathing stopped. The stillness was absolute. The stillness of something waiting in the dark.

Torak scrambled out of the shelter and stood, clutching his axe with both hands. Smoke stung his eyes, but for a heartbeat he glimpsed a huge form melting into the shadows.

A cry rang out behind him – and he spun round to see Renn staggering through the trees. 'By the river!' she panted. 'It stank, it was horrible!'

'It was here,' he told her. 'It came close. I heard it.'

Back to back, they stared into the Forest. Whatever it was, it had gone, leaving only a whiff of carrion and a dread memory of bubbling breath.

Sleep was now impossible. They fed the fire, then sat up together, waiting for dawn.

'What do you think it was?' said Renn.

Torak shook his head. 'But I know one thing. If we'd had Wolf with us, it would never have got that close.'

They stared into the fire. With Wolf gone, they hadn't only lost a friend. They'd lost someone to keep them from harm.

THREE

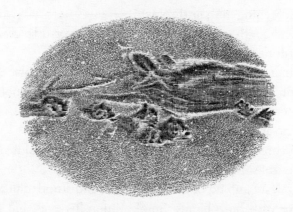

They heard nothing more that night, but in the morning they found tracks. Huge, man-like – but without any toes.

The tracks were nothing like the booted feet of the men who'd captured Wolf, but they headed the same way.

'Now there are three of them,' said Renn.

Torak didn't reply. They had no choice but to follow.

The sky was heavy with snow, and the Forest was full of shadows. With each step they dreaded seeing a figure lurching towards them. Demon? Soul-Eater? Or one of the Hidden People, whose backs are hollow as rotten trees . . .

The wind picked up. Torak watched the snow drifting across the tracks, and thought of Wolf. 'If this wind keeps up, the trail won't last much longer.'

Renn craned her neck to follow the flight of a raven. 'If only we could see what it can.'

Torak gave the bird a thoughtful stare.

They began their descent into the next valley through a silent birchwood. 'Look,' said Torak. 'Your otter's been here before us.' He pointed to a line of webbed prints and a long, smooth furrow in the snow. The otter had bounded down the slope, then slid on its belly, as otters love to do.

Renn smiled, and for a moment, they pictured a happy otter taking a snow-slide.

But the otter had never reached the frozen lake at the bottom of the hill. In the lee of a boulder twenty paces above the shore, Torak found a scattering of fish-scales and a shred of rawhide. 'They trapped it,' he said.

'*Why?*' said Renn. 'An otter's a hunter . . .'

Torak shook his head. It didn't make sense.

Suddenly, Renn tensed. '*Hide!*' she whispered, pulling him behind the boulder.

Through the trees, Torak caught movement on the lake. A creature snuffling, swaying, searching for something. It was very tall, with a shaggy pelt and a trailing, matted mane. Torak smelt carrion, and heard a wet bubbling of breath. Then it turned, and he saw a filthy one-eyed face as rough as bark. He gasped.

'It *can't* be!' whispered Renn.

They stared at one another. 'The Walker!'

The autumn before last, their paths had crossed with this terrifying, mad old man. They'd been lucky to escape with their lives.

'What's he doing so far from his valley?' breathed Torak as they shrank further behind the boulder.

'And how do we get past without being seen?' hissed Renn.

'Maybe – we don't.'

'*What?*'

'Maybe he saw who took Wolf!'

'Have you forgotten,' she said in a furious whisper, 'that he nearly killed us? That he threw my quiver in the stream, and threatened to *snap my bow*?' It was unclear which she considered worse: threatening them, or her bow.

'But he didn't, did he?' countered Torak. 'He let us go. And Renn. What if he saw something?'

'So you're just going to ask him, are you? Torak, he's *mad*! Whatever he says, we couldn't believe him!'

Torak opened his mouth to reply . . .

. . . and around them the snow exploded.

'*Give it back*!' roared the Walker, brandishing his green slate knife. 'She took his fire! She *tricked* him! The Walker wants it *back*!'

'The Walker has tricked the tricksters!' he bellowed, pinning them against the boulder. 'Now they must give it *back*!'

His mane was a tangle of beard-moss, his scrawny limbs as gnarled as roots. Loops of green slime swung like creepers from his shattered nose and his rotten, toothless mouth.

He'd left his cape on the ice to fool them, and was naked but for a hide loincloth stiff with filth, foot-bindings of mouldy wovenbark, and a rancid jerkin made from the skin of a red deer, which he'd ripped from the carcass, and then forgotten to clean. The tail, legs and hooves swung wildly as he waved his knife in their faces.

'She *took* it!' he shouted, spattering them with slime. 'She *tricked* him!'

'I – I didn't take anything,' stammered Renn, hiding her bow behind her back.

'Don't you remember us?' said Torak. 'We never stole anything!'

'Not she!' snarled the Walker. '*She!*' Quick as an eel, a grimy hand flashed out and seized Torak by the hair. His head was twisted back, his weapons tossed in the snow. 'The sideways one,' breathed the Walker, blasting him with an eye-watering stink. '*Her* fault that Narik is lost!'

'But *we* didn't do anything!' pleaded Renn. 'Let him go!'

'Axe!' spat the Walker, fixing her with his bloodshot eye. 'Knife! Arrows! Bow! In the snow, quick quick quick!'

Renn did as she was told.

The Walker pressed his knife against Torak's windpipe, cutting off his air. 'She gives him her fire,' he snarled, 'or he slits the wolf boy's throat! And he'll do it, oh yes!'

Black spots darted before Torak's eyes. 'Renn – ' he gasped, 'strike-fire – '

'Take it!' cried Renn, fumbling at her tinder pouch.

Deftly the old man caught the stone, and threw Torak to the ground. 'The Walker has *fire*!' he exulted. 'Beautiful *fire*! *Now* he can find Narik!'

That would have been the time to run. Torak knew it, and so did Renn. Neither of them moved.

'The sideways one,' panted Torak, rubbing his throat.

'Who is she?' said Renn.

The old man turned on her, and she dodged a flailing hoof. 'But the Walker is *mad*,' he sneered, 'so who can believe him?'

Seizing one of the deer legs, he sucked at the festering hide. 'The sideways one,' he mumbled. 'Not alone, oh no, oh no. Twisted legs and flying thoughts.' He hawked and spat, narrowly missing Torak. 'Big as as a tree, crushing the little creatures, the slitherers and scurriers too weak to fight back.' A spasm of pain twisted his ruined features. 'Worst,' he whispered, 'the Masked One. Cruellest of the cruel.'

Renn threw Torak a horrified look.

'But the Walker follows,' hissed the old man. 'Oh yes, oh yes, he listens in the cold!'

'Where are they going?' said Torak. 'Is Wolf still alive?'

'The Walker knows nothing of *wolves*! They seek the empty lands! The Far North!' He clawed the crusted tattoos on his throat. 'First you're cold, then you're not. Then you're hot, then you die.' His eye lit on Torak and he grinned. *'They are going to open the Door!'*

Torak swallowed. 'What door? Where?'

The old man cried out, and beat his forehead with his fists. *'But where is Narik?* They keep him and keep him, and Narik is *lost!'* He turned and blundered off towards the lake.

Torak and Renn exchanged glances – then snatched up their weapons, and raced after him.

Out on the ice, the Walker retrieved his shaggy cape, and resumed his snuffling search. One of his foot-bindings came loose and blew away.

Torak brought it back – and recoiled. The old man's foot was a blackened, frostbitten, toeless stump. 'What happened?'

The Walker shrugged. 'What always happens if you lose your fire. It bit his toes, so he cut them off.'

'What bit them?' said Renn.

'It! It!' He beat at the wind with his fists.

Suddenly his face changed, and for a moment Torak saw the man he'd been before the accident that had taken his eye and his wits. 'It can never rest, the wind, or it would cease to be. That's why it's angry. That's why it bit the Walker's toes.' He cackled. 'Ach, they tasted *bad*! Not even the Walker could eat them! He had to spit them out and leave them for the foxes!'

Torak's gorge rose. Renn clamped both hands over her mouth.

'So now the Walker keeps falling over. But still he searches for his Narik.' He ground his knuckle into his empty eye socket.

Narik, thought Torak. The mouse who'd been the old man's beloved companion. 'Did they take Narik too?' he said, determined to keep him talking.

The Walker shook his head sadly. 'Sometimes Narik goes away. He always comes back, in new fur. But not this time.'

'New fur?' queried Renn.

'Yes, yes!' the Walker said tetchily. 'Lemming. Vole. Mouse. Doesn't matter what, still the same Narik!'

'Oh,' said Renn. 'I see. New fur.'

'Only this time,' said the Walker, his mouth ragged with grief, 'Narik never came back!' He staggered away across the ice, howling for his fosterling.

Almost with reluctance, they left him, and made their way into the woods on the other side of the lake.

'He'll be better now that he has fire,' Renn said quietly.

'No he won't,' said Torak. 'Not without Narik.'

She sighed. 'Narik's dead. An owl probably ate him for nightmeal.'

'Another Narik, then.'

'He'll find one.' She tried to smile. 'One with new fur.'

'How? How can he track a mouse, with only one eye?'

'Come on. We'd better get going.'

Torak hesitated. The sun was getting low, the trail fast disappearing beneath windblown snow. And yet – he felt for the Walker. This stinking, angry, mad old man had found one spark of warmth in his life: his Narik, his fosterling. Now that spark was lost.

Before Renn could protest, Torak dropped his gear and ran back to the lake.

The old man didn't glance up, and Torak didn't speak to him. He put down his head and began looking for signs.

It didn't take long to find a lemming burrow. He spotted weasel tracks, and followed them to a clump of willow on the shore. There he crouched, listening for the small scratchings that told him where the lemmings were burrowing.

With its many knife-prick entrance holes, their winter shelter reminded him of an extremely small badger's sett. Peering at the snow, he found one hole rimed with tiny ice-arrows of frozen breath. That meant the occupant was at home.

He marked the spot with two crossed willow twigs, and ran to fetch the old man. 'Walker,' he said gently.

The old man swung round.

'Narik. He's over there.'

The Walker squinted at him. Then he followed Torak back to the crossed sticks.

As Torak watched, he knelt and began clearing the snow with feather-light gentleness, stooping to blow away the final flakes.

There, curled in its burrow on a neat bed of dried grass, lay a lemming about the size of Torak's palm: a soft, heaving ball of black and orange fur.

'Narik,' breathed the Walker.

The lemming woke with a start, sprang to its feet, and gave a fearsome hiss to frighten off the intruder.

The Walker grinned, and extended his big, grimy hand.

The lemming fluffed up its fur and hissed again.

The Walker didn't move.

The lemming sat down and scratched its ear vigorously with its hind paw. Then it waddled meekly onto the leathery palm, curled up, and went back to sleep.

Torak left them without a word.

Back on the shore, Renn handed him his weapons and pack. 'That was a good thing you did,' she said.

Torak shrugged. Then he grinned. 'Narik's grown a bit since we saw him. Now he's a lemming.'

She laughed.

They hadn't gone far when they heard the crunch of snow, and the Walker's angry muttering.

'Oh, *no!*' said Renn.

'But I *helped* him!' said Torak.

'*Giving?*' roared the Walker. In one hand he brandished his knife; the other clutched Narik to his chest. 'Do they think they can just *give*, and wander off? Do they think the Walker has *forgotten* the old ways?'

'Walker, we're sorry,' said Torak, 'but – '

'A gift looks for a *return! That* is the way of things! Now the Walker must give *back!*'

Torak and Renn wondered what was coming next.

'Black ice,' wheezed the Walker, 'white bears, red blood! They seek the eye of the viper!'

Torak caught his breath. 'What's that?'

'Oh, he'll find out,' said the Walker, 'the foxes will tell him.'

Suddenly he bent like a wind-snapped tree, and the look he gave Torak was wise, and fraught with such pain that it pierced Torak's souls. 'To enter the eye,' he breathed, 'is to enter the dark! You may find your way out again, Wolf boy; but once you've gone in, you'll never be whole. It'll keep a part of you down there. Down in the dark.'

FOUR

The Dark crept over the Forest, but Wolf didn't even notice. He was caught in a Dark of his own: of rage and pain and fear.

The tip of his tail ached where it had been stamped on in the fight, and his forepaw hurt from the bite of the big cold claw. He couldn't move at all, because he was squashed onto a strange, sliding tree, which the taillesses were dragging over the Bright Soft Cold. He couldn't even move to lick his wounds. He was flattened beneath a tangled deerhide that was pressing down on him hard. It was unlike any hide he'd ever encountered. It had lots of holes in it, but somehow it managed to be stronger than an auroch's leg-bone.

The growls inside him were fighting to get free, but *more* hide was tangled round his muzzle, so he couldn't let them out. That was the worst of it: that he couldn't growl or snap or howl. It hurt to hear Tall Tailless howling for him, and not be able to howl back.

Sharp and small inside his head, Wolf saw Tall Tailless and the female, running after him. They were coming. Wolf knew that as surely as he knew his own scent. Tall Tailless was his pack-brother, and a wolf never abandons his pack-brother.

But would Tall Tailless be able to *find* him? He was clever, but he wasn't at all good at finding, because he wasn't a normal wolf. Oh, he smelt of wolf (as well as lots of other things besides), and he talked like a wolf, even if he couldn't hit the highest yips. And he had the light silver eyes, and the spirit of a wolf. But he moved slowly on his hind legs, and was very bad at catching scents.

Suddenly the sliding tree shuddered to a halt. Wolf heard the harsh bark of tailless talk; then the crunch of the Bright Soft Cold as they began to dig their Den.

Behind him on the tree, the otter woke up, and started a piteous mewing. On and on she went, until Wolf wanted to shake her in his jaws to make her stop.

He heard a tailless approaching from behind. He was too squashed to turn and see, but he caught the smell of fish. The otter stopped mewing, and started making scrunching noises. That was a relief.

A few lopes ahead, the Bright Beast-that-Bites-Hot snarled into life. Wolf watched the taillesses gather round it.

They bewildered him. Until now, he'd thought he knew their kind. At least, he knew the pack that Tall Tailless ran with, the pack that smelt of ravens. But these – these were bad.

Why had they attacked him? Taillesses are not the enemies of wolves. The enemies of wolves are bears and lynxes, who sneak into Dens to kill wolf cubs. Not taillesses.

Of course, Wolf had met some bad ones before now, and even the good ones sometimes growled and waved their forepaws when he got too close to their meat. But to attack without warning? No true wolf would do this.

Straining ears and eyes and nose, Wolf watched the bad pack crouch round the Bright Beast. He swivelled his squashed ears to listen, and sniffed, trying to sort their tangled smells.

The slender female smelt of fresh leaves, but her tongue was black and pointed as a viper's, and her sideways smile was as empty as a carcass pecked by ravens.

The other female, the big one with the twisted hind legs, was clever, but Wolf sensed that she was unsure of her place in the pack, and unsure of herself. On her overpelt lay a patch of stinking fur. It was the fur of the strange prey which had lured him into the trap.

The last in the pack was a huge male with long, pale fur on his head and muzzle, and breath that reeked of spruce-blood. He was the worst, because he liked to hurt. He'd laughed as he'd trodden on Wolf's tail, and cut his pad with the big cold claw.

It was this pale-pelt who now rose on his hind legs and came towards Wolf.

Wolf gave a muffled growl.

Pale-Pelt bared his teeth, and brought his big claw close to Wolf's muzzle.

Wolf flinched.

Pale-Pelt laughed, lapping up Wolf's fear.

But what was this? Wolf's muzzle was *free*! Pale-Pelt had cut his muzzle free!

Wolf seized his chance and lunged – but the deerhide held him back, and he couldn't get his jaws around it to bite through it.

Here came the other one, the big twisted female with the stinking fur.

Pale-Pelt jabbed at Wolf again, but Stinkfur growled at him. Pale-Pelt stared hard, to let her know who was leader, then stalked off.

Crouching beside Wolf, Stinkfur pushed a scrap of elk meat through a hole in the deerhide.

Wolf ignored it. Did these taillesses think he was stupid? Did they think he was a dog, who would take meat from anyone?

Stinkfur threw up her forepaws, and walked away.

Now the viper-tongued female left the Bright Beast, and came over to Wolf. Squatting on her haunches, she talked softly to him.

Without wanting to, he listened. Her voice reminded him a little of the female who was Tall Tailless' pack-sister, whose talk was sharp and clever, but gentle underneath. As he listened to the viper-tongued female, he smelt that she was not afraid of him; that she was *curious*.

He flinched as she reached her forepaw towards him, but she didn't touch him. Instead he felt coldness on his flank. His whiskers quivered. She was smearing his pelt with elk blood!

The smell was so muzzle-wateringly delicious that it drove all else from his head. After much struggling, he twisted round and started to lick.

He knew it was odd that the female had done this, and something in her voice made him wary, but he couldn't stop. The blood-lust had him in its grip, and already the strength of the elk was loping through his limbs. He went on licking.

Wolf was becoming *very* tired. There was black fog in his head, and he could hardly keep his eyes open. He felt as if a great stone were crushing him.

Through the fog he heard the soft, sly laugh of the viper-tongued female, and knew that she had tricked him. The elk blood she'd fed him had been bad, and now he was sinking into the Dark.

The fog grew thicker. Fear seized him in its jaws. With the last twitch of his mind, he sent a silent howl to Tall Tailless.

FIVE

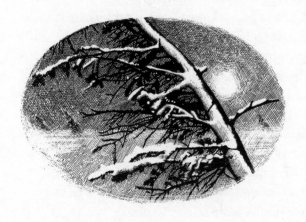

'Are you scared?' said Torak.

'Yes,' said Renn.

'Me too.'

They stood at the edge of the Forest, beneath the last – the very last – tree. Before them stretched an empty white land beneath an endless sky. Here and there, a stunted spruce withstood the onslaught of the wind, but that was the only sign of life.

They were now as far north as any of the Forest clans had been, except for Fin-Kedinn, who as a young man had journeyed into the frozen lands. In the two days since meeting the Walker, they'd crossed three valleys, and glimpsed the distant glare of the ice river at the roots of the High Mountains – where, the winter before last, the Ravens had camped, and Torak had gone in search of the Mountain of the World Spirit.

They stood with the north wind in their faces, staring at

the trail of Wolf's captors: a brutal knife-slash through the snow.

'I don't think we can do this on our own,' said Renn. 'We need help. We need Fin-Kedinn.'

'We can't go back now,' said Torak. 'There isn't time.'

She was silent. Since their encounter with the Walker, she'd been unusually subdued. Torak wondered if she too had been thinking about what the old man had said. *Twisted legs and flying thoughts . . . the sideways one . . . Big as a tree . . .* It had raised echoes in his mind: echoes of Fin-Kedinn, speaking of the Soul-Eaters. But he couldn't bring himself to mention them out loud. It couldn't be them. Why would they have taken Wolf, and not him?

So in the end, all he said was, 'Wolf needs us.'

Renn didn't reply.

Suddenly, he was gripped by the fear that she would turn round and leave him to carry on alone. The fear was so intense that it left him breathless.

He watched her brush the snow off her bow, and settle it on her shoulder. He braced himself for the worst.

'You're right,' she said abruptly. 'Let's go.' Without a backwards glance, she left the shelter of the trees.

He followed her into the empty lands.

As soon as they left the Forest, the sky pressed upon them, and the north wind scoured their faces with snow.

In the Forest, Torak had always been *aware* of the wind – as a hunter he had to be – but apart from storms, it was never a threat, because the power of the Forest kept it in check. Out here, nothing could hold it back. It was stronger, colder, wilder: a malevolent, unseen spirit, come to harass these puny intruders.

The trees became smaller and sparser, until they shrank to an occasional knee-high willow or birch. Then – nothing. No green thing. No hunters. No prey. Only snow.

Torak turned, and was shocked to see that the Forest had dwindled to a charcoal line on the horizon.

'It's the edge of the world,' said Renn, raising her voice above the wind. 'How far does it go on? What if we fall off?'

'If the edge of the world is out there,' he said, 'Wolf's captors will fall off first.'

To his surprise, she gave him a sharp-toothed grin.

The day wore on. The snow was firmer than in the Forest, so they didn't need their snowshoes, but the north wind blew it into low, hard ridges, which kept tripping them up.

Then, abruptly, the wind dropped. Now it was blowing softly from the north-east.

At first, it was a relief. Then Torak realized what was happening. He couldn't see his feet. He was standing in a river of snow. Around his calves, long, ghostly streams were flowing like smoke, obliterating the trail.

'The wind's covering the tracks!' he shouted. 'It knows we need them, so it's destroying them!'

Renn ran ahead to see if the trail was any clearer. She threw up her arms. 'Nothing! Not even you could find it!' As she ran back to him, he saw her expression, and his heart sank. He knew what she was going to say, because he'd been thinking it himself. 'Torak, this is wrong! We can't survive out here. We've got to go back.'

'But people do live here, don't they?' he insisted. 'The Ice clans? The Narwals, the Ptarmigans, the White Foxes? Isn't that what Fin-Kedinn said?'

'They know how. We don't.'

'But – we have dried meat and firewood. And we can find our way by the North Star. We can bind our eyes with wovenbark to keep out the glare, and – and there is prey out here. Willow grouse. Hare. That's how Fin-Kedinn managed.'

'And when the wood runs out?' said Renn.

'There's that willow he talked about, the kind that only grows ankle high, but you can still – '

'Can you *see* any willow out here? It's buried under snow!'

Her face was pale, and he knew that behind what she said lay a deeper dread. The clans whispered stories about the Far North. Blizzards so powerful they carried you screaming into the sky. Great white bears that were bigger and fiercer than any in the Forest. Snowfalls that buried you alive. And Renn knew about snowfalls. When she was seven summers old, her father had ventured onto the ice river east of Lake Axehead. He'd never come back.

'We can't do this on our own,' she said.

Torak rubbed a hand over his face. 'I agree. At least, for tonight. We should make camp.'

She looked relieved. 'There's a hill over there. We can dig a snow cave.'

He nodded. 'And then I'm going to do what it takes to find the trail.'

'What do you mean?' she said uneasily.

He hesitated. 'I'm going to spirit walk.'

Her mouth fell open. 'Torak. No.'

'Listen to me. Ever since we saw that raven, I've been thinking about it. I can spirit walk in a bird, I'm sure of it. I can go high in the sky, see far into the distance. I can see the trail!'

Renn folded her arms. 'Birds can fly. You can't.'

'I wouldn't have to,' he said. 'My souls would be inside

the bird's body – say it's a raven – I'd see what the raven sees, I'd feel what it feels. But I'd still be me.'

She walked in a circle, then faced him. 'Saeunn says you're not ready. She's the Clan Mage. She knows.'

'I did it last summer – '

'By accident! And it hurt! And you couldn't control it! Torak, your souls could get stuck inside, you might never get out! Then what happens to your body? The one that's lying on the snow, with only its world-soul keeping it alive?' Her voice was shrill, and there were two spots of colour on her cheeks. 'You'd die, that's what! I'd have to sit in the snow and watch you die!'

He couldn't argue with her, because everything she said was true. So he said, 'I need you to help me find a raven. I need you to help me loosen my souls. Are you going to help me or not?'

SIX

'First,' said Torak, 'we've got to attract a raven.'

He waited for Renn to comment, but she was hacking out the snow cave, making it plain that she wanted no part of this.

'I spotted a nest at the edge of the Forest,' he said.

Her axe struck, and chunks of snow flew.

'It's a daywalk away,' he added, 'but they may come foraging out here. And I brought bait.'

She stopped in mid-swing. 'What bait?'

From his pack he pulled a squirrel. 'I shot it yesterday. While I was filling the waterskins.'

'You planned this,' she said accusingly.

He glanced at the squirrel. 'Um. I thought I might need it.'

Renn resumed her attack on the snow, hitting harder than before.

Torak laid the squirrel twenty paces from where the

shelter would be – so that, once his name-soul and clan-soul had left his body, they wouldn't have far to go, to get into a raven. Well, that was the hope. He didn't know if it would work, because he didn't know anything about spirit walking. Nobody did.

Drawing his knife, he slit the squirrel's belly, and stood back to study the effect.

'That's not going to work,' called Renn.

'At least I'm trying,' he retorted.

She wiped her forehead on the back of her mitten. 'No, I mean, you're doing it wrong. Ravens are too clever to be fooled by that, they'll think it's a trap.'

'Oh,' said Torak. 'Yes, of course.'

'Make it like a wolf kill. That's what they look for, a kill.'

He nodded, and set to work.

Renn forgot about disapproving, and helped. They used her shoulder-bone scraper to chop up the squirrel's liver, mixed it with snow, and spattered this around to resemble blood. Then Torak cut off a hind leg and tossed it to one side, 'so that it'll look as if a wolf trotted away to eat in peace.'

Renn studied the "kill". 'Better,' she said.

The shadows were turning blue, and the wind had gone into the north, leaving a light breeze wafting snowflakes over the carcass. Torak said, 'The ravens will be flying home to roost. If they come, it won't be before first light.'

Renn shivered. 'It doesn't seem possible, but according to Fin-Kedinn, there are white foxes out here, so we'll have to stay awake to keep them off the carcass.'

'And we can't have a fire, or the ravens will smell it.'

Renn bit her lip. 'You do know that you can't have anything to eat? To go into a trance, you need to fast.'

Torak had forgotten that. 'What about you?'

'I'll eat when you're not looking. Then I'll make the paste for loosening your souls.'

'Do you have what you need?'

She patted her medicine pouch. 'I gathered a few things in the Forest.'

His lip curled. 'You planned this.'

She didn't smile back. 'I had a feeling I might need to.'

The sky was darkening, and a few stars were glinting. 'First light,' murmured Torak.

It was going to be a long night.

Torak huddled in his sleeping-sack, and tried to stop shivering. He'd been shivering all night, and he was sick of it. Peering throught the slit in the snow cave, he saw the half-eaten moon shining bright. Dawn wasn't far off. The sky was clear – and ravenless.

In one mitten, he clutched a scrap of birch bark containing Renn's soul-loosening paste: a mixture of deer fat and herbs which he was to smear on his face and hands when she gave the word. In the other, he held a small rawhide pouch fastened with sinew. What Renn called a "smoke-potion" smouldered inside. He'd asked what was in it, but she'd said it was better not to know, and he hadn't insisted. Renn had a talent for Magecraft, which for reasons she never went into, she tried to ignore. Practising it put her in a bad mood.

His belly rumbled, and she nudged him with her elbow. He refrained from nudging back. He was so hungry that if a raven didn't come soon, he'd eat the squirrel.

A thin scarlet line had just appeared in the east, when a black shape slid across the stars.

Again, Renn nudged him.

'I see it,' he whispered.

A smaller shape glided after the first: the raven's mate. Wingtip to wingtip, they wheeled over the kill – then flew away.

Some time later, they came back for another pass, flying a little lower. At the fifth pass, they flew so low that Torak heard their wingbeats: a strong, rhythmic 'wsh wsh wsh'.

He watched their heads turn from side to side, scanning the land below. He was glad he'd buried the gear beside the snow cave, which Renn had made into a featureless mound, with only a slit for air and observation. Ravens are the cleverest of birds, with senses sharp as grass.

Yellow fire spilled over the edge of the world, but still the ravens circled, spying out the "kill".

Suddenly, one folded its wings and dropped out of the sky.

Torak slipped off both mittens, to be ready.

Silently, the raven lit down on the snow. Its breath smoked as it stared at the shelter. Its wingspan was wider than Torak's outstretched arms, and it was utterly black. Eyes, feathers, legs, claws; like the First Raven herself, who woke the sun from its winter sleep, and was burnt black for her pains.

This raven, however, was more interested in the squirrel, which it approached at a cautious, stiff-legged walk.

'Now?' mouthed Torak.

Renn shook her head.

The raven gave the carcass a tentative peck. Then it hopped high in the air, landed – and flew off. It was checking that the squirrel was really dead.

When the carcass didn't move, both ravens flew down. Warily they walked towards it.

'*Now!*' mouthed Renn.

Torak smeared on the paste. It had a sour green smell that stung his eyes and made his skin prickle. Then he unfastened the pouch and sucked in the smoke-potion.

'Swallow it all,' Renn whispered in his ear, 'and *don't* cough!'

The smoke was bitter, the urge to cough almost overwhelming. He felt Renn's breath on his cheek. 'May the guardian fly with you!'

Feeling sick, he watched the big raven tug at the frozen innards. A sharp pain tugged at his own insides – and for a moment he felt a surge of panic. *No, no I don't want to . . .*

. . . and suddenly he was tugging at the squirrel's guts with his powerful beak, slicing off delicious tatters of frozen meat.

Swiftly he filled his throat-pouch, then pecked out an eye. Enjoying its slippery smoothness on his tongue, he hitched his wings and hopped onto the wind, and it bore him up, up into the light.

The wind was freezing and unimaginably strong, and his heart swelled with joy as it carried him higher. He loved the coldness rippling under his feathers, and the smell of ice in his nostrils, and the wind's wild laughter screaming through him. He loved the ease with which he rode upwards, twisting and turning with the merest tilt of his wings – he loved the power of his beautiful black wings!

A slippery 'wsh' – and his mate was at his side. As she folded her wings and rolled off the wind, she gave a graceful twitch of her tail, asking him to sky-dance. He slid after her and locked his icy talons in hers, and together they drew in their wings and dived.

Through the streaming cold they sped, through a blur of black feathers and splintered sun, exulting in their speed as the great white world rushed up to meet them.

Of one accord they unlocked their talons, and he snapped open his wings and struck the wind, and now he was soaring again, soaring towards the sun.

With his raven eyes he could see for ever. Far to the east, the tiny speck of a white fox trotted through the snow. To the south lay the dark rim of the Forest. To the west he saw the wrinkled ice of the frozen Sea. To the north: two figures in the snow.

With a cry he sped off in pursuit.

'Cark?' called his startled mate.

He left her, and the white land flowed beneath him.

As he drew nearer, he swooped, and in an instant that burned into his mind for ever, he took in every detail.

He saw two figures straining to haul a sled. He saw Wolf strapped to the sled, unable to move. As he strained to catch the least twitch of a paw, the smallest flicker which would tell him that Wolf was still alive, he saw the bigger man pause, pull his parka over his head, and loosen the neck of his jerkin to let out the heat. He saw the blue-black tattoo on the man's breastbone: the three-pronged fork for snaring souls. The mark of the Soul-Eater.

From his raven beak came a horrified croak. *The Soul-Eaters. The Soul-Eaters have taken Wolf.*

He flew higher, and the sun blinded him. The wind gave a furious twist, and threw him off.

His courage cracked like thin ice.

The wind screamed in triumph.

A sharp pain pierced his insides – and he was Torak again, and he was falling out of the sky.

SEVEN

Torak woke in the blue gloom of the snow cave with the wind's angry laughter ringing in his ears.

Renn was kneeling over him, looking scared. 'Oh, thank the Spirit! I've been trying to wake you all morning!'

'All – morning?' he mumbled. He felt like a piece of rawhide that had been pummelled and scraped.

'It's midday,' said Renn. 'What *happened*? You were breathing in snow, and your eyes had turned up inside your head. It was horrible!'

'Fell,' he said. With each breath, pain stabbed his ribs, and every joint screamed. But his limbs still obeyed him; so no broken bones. 'Do I – bruises?'

She shook her head. 'But souls get bruises too.'

He lay still, staring at a droplet about to fall from the roof. *The Soul-Eaters had taken Wolf.*

'Did you see the trail?' said Renn.

He swallowed. 'North. They headed north.'

She sensed that he was keeping something back. 'As soon as you went into a trance,' she said, 'the wind blew up. It sounded angry.'

'I was flying. I wasn't supposed to.'

The drop landed on Renn's parka and lost itself in the fur: like a soul falling to earth.

'You shouldn't have done it,' she said.

Raising himself painfully on one elbow, Torak peered through the slit. The wind was blowing softly, but the ghostly snow-fingers were back.

'I don't think it's finished with us,' said Renn.

Torak lay down again, and drew his sleeping-sack under his chin. *The Soul-Eaters had taken Wolf.*

He couldn't bring himself to tell her – at least, not yet. If she knew, she might insist that they went back to the Forest for help. She might leave.

He shut his eyes.

'But who *are* the Soul-Eaters?' he'd once asked Fin-Kedinn. 'I don't even know their names.'

'Few do,' Fin-Kedinn had replied, 'and they don't speak of them.'

'Do *you* know?' Torak had demanded. 'Why won't you tell me? It's my destiny to fight them!'

'In time,' was all the Raven Leader would say.

Torak couldn't make him out. Fin-Kedinn had taken him in when his father was killed; and long ago, Fa and he had been good friends. But he rarely spoke of the past, and only ever revealed what he thought Torak needed to know.

So now all Torak knew was that the Soul-Eaters had plotted to rule the Forest. Then their power had been shattered in a great fire, and they'd gone into hiding. Two of the seven had since met their deaths – and thus, under clan law, couldn't be mentioned by name for the next five

561

winters. One of them had been Torak's father.

Deep in his chest, Torak felt the familiar ache. Fa had joined them to do *good*; that was what Fin-Kedinn had told him. That was what Torak clung to. When they'd become evil, Fa had tried to leave, and they'd turned on him. For thirteen winters he'd been a hunted man, raising his son apart from the clans, never mentioning his past. Then, the autumn before last, the Soul-Eaters had sent the demon bear that killed him.

Now they'd taken Wolf.

But why Wolf, and not Torak? Why, why, why?

He fell asleep to the moaning of the wind.

Someone was shaking him, calling his name.

'Wha?' he mumbled into a mouthful of reindeer fur.

'Torak, wake *up!*' cried Renn. 'We can't get out!'

Awkwardly he sat up as far as the low roof would allow. Beside him, Renn was struggling not to panic.

The slit in the shelter was gone. In its place was a wall of hard-packed snow.

'I've been digging,' she said, 'but I can't break through. We're snowed in. It must have drifted in the night.'

Torak noticed that she said "it drifted", rather than "the wind did this, burying us while we slept".

'Where's my axe?' he said.

Her face worked. 'Outside. They're both outside, where we left them. With the rest of our gear.'

He took that in silence.

'I should have brought them inside,' said Renn.

'There wasn't room.'

'I should've made room. I should've thought.'

'You were looking after me, it's not your fault. We've got knives. We'll dig ourselves out.'

He drew his knife. Fin-Kedinn had made it for him last summer: a slender blade of reindeer shinbone, slotted with leaf-thin flakes of flint. It wasn't meant for digging in wind-hardened snow. Fa's blue slate knife would have been better, but Fin-Kedinn had warned Torak to keep it hidden in his pack. He regretted that now.

'Let's get started,' he said, trying to sound calm.

It was frightening, digging a tunnel with no idea how far they had to go. There was nowhere to put the hacked-out snow except behind them, so no matter how hard they worked, they remained trapped in the same cramped hole. The dripping walls pressed in, and their breath sounded panicky and loud.

After they'd moved about an arm's length, Torak put down his knife. 'This isn't working.'

Renn met his eyes. Her own were huge. 'You're right. A drift like this, it could go on for . . . We might never break out.'

He saw the effort she was making to stay calm, and guessed that she was thinking of her father. He said, 'We'll dig upwards instead.'

She nodded.

It was much harder, digging up. Chunks of snow fell in their eyes and down their necks, and their arms ached savagely. They worked back-to-back, trampling the snow beneath their boots. Torak clenched his jaw so hard that it hurt.

Gradually, the snow above him began to turn a warmer blue. 'Renn! Look!'

She'd seen it.

Feverishly they hammered with their knife-hilts. Suddenly it cracked like an eggshell – and they were through.

The glare was blinding, the cold burned their lungs. They stood with upturned faces, gaping like baby birds; then scrambled out and collapsed on the snow. A faint breeze chilled their sweat-soaked hair. The wind was gone.

Torak gave a shaky laugh.

Renn lay on her back, staring into nothingness.

Sitting up, Torak saw that their shelter had been buried beneath a long, sloping hill that hadn't existed the night before. 'Our gear,' he said. 'Where's our gear?'

Renn scrambled to her feet.

Apart from their knives and sleeping-sacks, everything they needed: bows, arrows, axes, food, firewood, waterskins, cooking-skins – *everything* – lay buried somewhere under the snow.

With exaggerated calm, Torak brushed off his leggings. 'We know where the shelter is. We'll dig a trench around it. Sooner or later, we'll find it.' But he knew as well as Renn that if they didn't find their gear before dark, they might not survive another night. This one mistake could be the death of them.

After so much effort digging *up*, it was a bitter blow to have to dig *down*; and as soon as they started, the wind returned, gusting snow about them in blinding, choking clouds.

Torak was beginning to lose hope when Renn gave a shout. 'My *bow*! I've found my bow!'

It was late afternoon by the time they found everything, and by then they were exhausted, drenched in sweat, and ragingly thirsty.

'We should dig in,' panted Renn, 'wait till dawn.'

'We can't,' said Torak. The need to go after Wolf was overwhelming.

'I know,' said Renn. 'I know.'

After eating a little dried meat and draining their waterskins, they tied strips of wovenbark over their eyes to keep out the glare – uncomfortably aware that they should have done this earlier – and set off, heading north by the sun, which was getting low.

Torak's head was throbbing, and he was stumbling with fatigue. He had an uneasy sense that they shouldn't be doing this – that they weren't thinking straight – but he was too tired to sort it out.

The wide plains gave way to steep hills and dizzying blue ridges of windblown snow. In places, these formed precarious overhangs that reared above them like monstrous, frozen waves. And always the north wind blew. Angry. Vengeful. Unappeased.

In the shifting snow, it became hard to judge distances. It didn't feel as if they'd walked far, but when Torak crested a hill and glanced back, he saw that the Forest was gone.

A savage gust punched him in the back and he fell, rolling all the way to the bottom.

Renn floundered after him. 'Should've used your axe to break your fall,' she mumbled as she helped him up. His axe had been stuck in his belt; there'd been no time to pull it out.

From then on, they walked with axes in hand.

They'd been tired when they set off, but now every step was an effort. Thirst returned, but they'd run out of wood for melting snow. They knew they shouldn't try eating it, but they did anyway. It blistered their mouths and gave them cramps. And still the wind blew: pelting their faces with tiny darts of ice until their cheeks cracked and their lips bled.

We don't belong here, Torak thought hazily. Everything's wrong. Nothing's as it should be.

Once, they heard the gobbling of willow grouse, startlingly close, but when they searched, the birds had vanished.

Another time, Renn saw a man in the distance; but when they reached him, he turned out to be a pile of rocks, with fluttering strands of hair and hide tied to his arms. Who had made him, and why?

Their sweat-soaked jerkins chilled them to the bone, and snow froze to their outer clothes, making them heavy and stiff. Their faces burned, then turned numb. Something the Walker had said surfaced in Torak's memory. *First you're cold, then you're not* . . . What came after that?

Renn was tugging his sleeve, pointing at the sky.

He swayed.

Purple-grey clouds were boiling up from the north.

'Storm!' she shouted. 'Keep together!' Already she was dragging a coil of rawhide rope from her pack. They'd been in a snowstorm before, and knew how easy it is to get separated.

'We've got to dig in!' she yelled as she struggled to tie one end of the frozen rope about her waist.

'Where?' he shouted, tying his end clumsily about him. The land had turned flat again.

'Down!' she shouted. 'Dig down! A snow hole!' She stamped up and down, feeling for firmer snow – and suddenly it broke beneath her, and she was gone.

'*Renn!*' shouted Torak.

The rope at his waist snapped taut, yanking him forwards. He threw himself back, dug in his heels. He couldn't see anything – just churning white chaos – but he could feel her weight on the rope, dragging him down.

Struggling, slipping, he slid inexorably forwards – and toppled . . . a few paces onto a pile of broken snow.

The snow heaved. It was Renn.

They sat up, badly shaken, but unhurt.

Craning his neck, Torak saw that they'd gone through an overhang. Without knowing it, they'd been walking on a fragile crust over thin air.

For Renn, this was the last arrow that brings down the auroch. 'I can't go on!' she cried, striking the snow with her fists.

'We have to dig in!' yelled Torak. But he knew it was hopeless. He barely had the strength to lift his axe.

With one final, wild burst of pride, he staggered to his feet and shouted at the wind. 'All right, you've won! I'm *sorry*! I'll never dare fly again! I'm *sorry*!'

The wind screamed. Terrible shapes flew at him through the snow. A twisting column whirled towards him, then blew apart . . .

Suddenly the snow seemed *not* to blow apart, but to draw *together*: thousands of tiny flakes meeting, coalescing, to form a creature unlike any he'd ever seen.

It had the staring eyes of an owl, and it flew towards him through the whiteness. Before it surged a silent pack of dogs.

Torak was too exhausted to be frightened. It's over, he thought numbly. I'm sorry, Wolf. Sorry I couldn't save you.

He sank to his knees as the owl-eyed creature bore down upon him.

EIGHT

The owl-eyed creature bellowed a command, and the dogs slewed to a halt. Whipping out a long curved knife, it started hacking a snow hole with astonishing speed. In moments, Torak and Renn were seized and thrown in, and a wall of snow was yanked down on top.

After the fury of the wind, the rasp of breath was loud in the gloom. Torak heard the creak of frozen hide; caught a rancid smell that was oddly familiar. He couldn't see Renn – the creature had leapt in between them – but he was too wretched to care.

To his surprise he found that he wasn't cold any more, he was hot. First you're cold, he thought, then you're not; then you're hot, and then you die.

He found that he liked death. It was beautifully warm and soft, like the pelt of a great white reindeer. He wanted to draw it over his head and snuggle down deep . . .

Someone was shaking him. He moaned. Owl eyes stared

into his, jolting him back from his lovely warm death.

He made out a ruff of snow-caked fur framing a round face purpled by frost. Ice crusted the brows and the short black beard. The flat nose had a dark band tattooed across it, which Torak didn't recognise. He just wanted to go back to death.

The creature snarled. Then it plucked out its eyes.

Torak saw that the owl eyes were thin bone discs on a strap. The man's real eyes were permanently slitted against the glare. Swiftly he yanked back the sleeve of his parka, took out a flint knife, and cut a vein in his stocky brown forearm. 'Drink!' he barked, pressing the wound to Torak's lips.

Salty-sweet heat filled Torak's mouth. He coughed, and swallowed blood. Strength and warmth coursed through him: real warmth, not the false heat of frostbite. With it came pain. His face was on fire. Burning needles pierced his joints.

In the gloom, he heard Renn. 'Leave me 'lone! Want to sleep!'

Now the man was chewing something. He spat a grey lump into his hand, and pushed it between Torak's teeth. 'Eat!'

It was rancid and oily, and he recognized the taste. Seal blubber. It was wonderful.

The man smeared more chewed blubber over Torak's face. At first it hurt – the man's palm was rough as granite – but amazingly soon, the pain faded to a bearable throb.

'Who are you?' mumbled Torak.

'Later,' grunted the man, 'when the wind's anger is spent.'

'How long will that be?' said Renn.

'One sleep, many, who knows? Now no more talk!'

Torak is twelve summers old, and Fa has been dead for nearly half a moon.

Torak has just killed his first roe buck, and to keep Wolf quiet while he's skinning it, he's given him the hooves; but the cub has tired of playing with them, and trots over to poke his muzzle into what Torak is doing.

Torak is washing deer gut in the stream. Wolf grabs the other end in his jaws and tugs. Torak tugs back. Wolf goes down on his forepaws and lashes his tail. A game!

Torak bites back a smile. 'No, it isn't a game.' Wolf persists. Torak tells him firmly in wolf talk to *let go* – and the cub obeys so promptly that Torak topples backwards into the water. Wolf pounces, and now they're splashing about, and Torak is laughing. His father is still dead; but he's no longer alone. He's found a pack-brother.

When he gets to his feet, the stream is frozen. Winter has the Forest in its grip. Wolf is full-grown, and trotting off through the glittering trees – trotting off with Fa.

'Come back!' shouts Torak, but the north wind carries his voice away. The wind is so strong that he can hardly stand, but it has no power to touch Wolf or Fa. Not a breath stirs Fa's long black hair; not a whisper ruffles Wolf's silver fur.

'*Come back!*' he cries. They can't hear him. Helplessly he watches them walk away through the trees.

He woke with a start. His chest ached with loss. His cheeks were stiff with frozen tears.

He was huddled in his sleeping-sack. His clothes were damp inside, and he was so cold that he was beyond shivering. Sitting up, he saw that he was no longer in the snowhole, but in a domed shelter made of blocks of snow.

On a flat stone lamp, a sludge of pounded blubber burned with a low orange flame. Above it hung a seal's bladder of melting ice. From the stillness outside, the storm had blown over. The strange man had gone.

'I had a *terrible* dream,' muttered Renn beside him. Her face was scabbed and blistered; there were dark smudges under her eyes.

'Me too,' he said. His face felt sore, and it hurt to talk. 'I dreamt that Wolf –'

The strange man crawled into the shelter. He was short and stocky, and his seal-hide parka made him look even stockier. Throwing back his hood, he revealed a flat face framed by short dark hair, with a fringe across his brow. His eyes were black slits of distrust. 'You're from the Far South,' he said accusingly.

'Who are you?' countered Torak.

'Inuktiluk. White Fox Clan. I was sent to find you.'

'Why?' said Renn.

The White Fox man tossed his head. 'Look at you! Your clothes are sopping wet! Don't you know it's not snow that kills, but wet? Here. Get out of them and into these.' He tossed them two hide bundles.

They were so cold that they didn't argue. Their limbs were as useless as sticks, and it took forever to get undressed. The bundles turned out to be sleeping-sacks of silvery seal fur, lined with an inner sack of soft birdskin, with the feathers on the inside. These were so warm that they felt better almost at once; but Torak realized with alarm that the White Fox man had disappeared, taking their clothes with him. Now they were completely in his power.

'He left us some food,' said Renn. She sniffed a strip of frozen seal meat.

Still in his sleeping-sack, Torak shuffled to the wall, and peered through a crack.

What he'd taken for the roof of the snow hole in which they'd sheltered overnight was in fact a large sled, which now stood upright. Its runners were the jawbones of a whale, its cross-bars the antlers of reindeer. A tangled harness disappeared into a smooth white hillock, and into five other hillocks a little further off. From the middle of each came a thin whisp of steam.

Inuktiluk whistled, and the hillocks erupted into six large dogs. They yawned and wagged their tails as they shook off the snow, and Inuktiluk batted away their noses as he untangled their harnesses and checked their paws for ice cuts.

With her thumbnail, Renn prised a shred of meat from between her teeth. 'The Walker said "the foxes" would tell us how to find the Eye of the Viper. Maybe he meant the White Foxes.'

Torak had thought of that too. 'But can we risk it?' he said. He wanted to trust Inuktiluk, but he'd learned the hard way that a man can do kind things, and still hide a rotten heart.

'You're right,' said Renn. 'We won't tell him anything. Not till we know we can trust him.'

Inuktiluk was turning their clothes inside out, and laying them on the sled. They froze in moments, and he beat the ice from them with the flat of his snow-knife. Then he fetched meat and tossed it to the dogs.

Five were full-grown, but the sixth was a puppy of about five moons. Its pads hadn't yet toughened, and it wore rawhide paw-boots; it squealed with pleasure as Inuktiluk flipped it onto its back, to check that they were securely fastened.

Torak thought of Wolf, and the dream returned to darken his spirit. He told Renn about it. Then he said, 'Wolf was with Fa, and Fa is dead. So was it Fa's spirit who sent the dream? Was he telling me that Wolf is dead too?'

'Or maybe,' said Renn, 'it wasn't your father's spirit that dreamed to you, but Wolf's. Maybe he's asking you for help.'

'But he must know that we're coming for him.'

She looked unhappy.

He was wondering if now was the time to tell her about the Soul-Eaters, when Inuktiluk returned.

'Get dressed,' he said sternly.

Their clothes were drier, but uncomfortably cold. It didn't help that Inuktiluk watched them with evident disapproval. 'You're much too thin. To survive on the ice, you need to be fat! Don't you even know that? Everything in the north is fat! Seals, bears, people!' Then he asked them what names they carried.

They exchanged glances. Renn told him their names and clans.

Inuktiluk seemed startled to learn that Torak was Wolf Clan. 'That makes it worse,' he murmured.

'What do you mean?' said Torak.

Inuktiluk frowned. 'We won't talk of it here.'

'I think we must,' said Torak. 'You saved our lives, and we're grateful. But please. Tell us why you were looking for us.'

The White Fox man hesitated. 'I'll tell you this. Three sleeps ago, one of our elders went into a trance to watch the night fires in the sky, and the spirits of the Dead sent her a vision. A girl with red willow hair, like the World Spirit in winter; and a boy with wolf eyes.' He paused. 'The boy was about to do a great evil. That's why I had to find you. To stop you bringing evil to the people of the ice.'

'I haven't done anything wrong,' Torak said hotly.

Inuktiluk ignored that. 'Who *are* you? What are you doing here, where you don't belong?'

When they didn't answer, he rolled up the sleeping-sacks and headed out. 'Rub more blubber on your faces, and bring the lamp. We're leaving.'

'Where?' said Torak and Renn together.

'Our camp.'

'Why?' said Renn. 'What are you going to do to us?'

Inuktiluk looked offended. 'We're not going to harm you, that's not our way! We'll just give you better gear, and send you home.'

'You can't make us go back,' said Torak.

To his surprise, Inuktiluk burst out laughing. 'Of course I can! I've got all your gear strapped to my sled!'

After that, they had no choice but to follow him outside. He'd already put on his owl-eyed visor, and now he tossed them both a pair. Then he snatched up a supple hide whip fully twenty paces long, and at once the dogs began howling and lashing their tails, eager to be off.

'Why is the sled pointing west?' said Renn uneasily.

'That's where our camp is,' said Inuktiluk. 'On the sea ice, where the seals are.'

'West?' cried Torak. 'But we've got to go *north*!'

Inuktiluk turned on him. 'North? Two children who know nothing of the ways of the ice? You'd be dead before the next sleep! Now get on the sled!'

NINE

The north wind howled over the white hills, and blasted the hunched spruce trees on the plains. It whistled through the northern reaches of the Forest, and whipped up the snow on the banks of the Axehandle, where the Raven Clan had pitched camp. It would have woken Fin-Kedinn – except that he was already awake. Since the Willows had given him Torak's message, he'd barely slept.

Someone has taken Wolf. We're going to get him back.

'But to rush off without thinking,' said the Raven Leader. With a stick he stabbed the fire that glowed at the entrance to his shelter. 'Why didn't he come back and seek help?'

'Why didn't the girl?' said Saeunn in her raven's croak. Without blinking, she met his look of pure blue anger. She was the only member of the clan who dared brave his displeasure.

They sat in silence, while above them the wind did its best to waken the Forest. The Raven Mage tented her robe over her bony knees, and stretched her shrunken claws to the fire.

Fin-Kedinn gave it another stab – and a dog, who'd been thinking about trying to slip inside, put back his ears and slunk off to find another shelter.

'I didn't think he'd be so reckless,' said Fin-Kedinn. 'To head for the Far North . . . '

'How do you know he has?' said Saeunn.

He hesitated. 'A Ptarmigan hunting party saw them in the distance. They told me this morning.'

Thoughtfully, Saeunn stroked her spiral amulet with a fingernail as ridged and yellow as horn. 'You want to go in search of them. You want to find your brother's child and bring her back.'

The Raven Leader rubbed a hand over his dark-red beard. 'I can't risk the safety of the clan by leading them into the Far North.'

Saeunn studied him with the icy dispassion of one who has never felt affection for any living creature. 'And yet you want to.'

'I've just said that I can't,' he replied. He threw away the stick, suppressing a wince. The wind had woken the old wound in his thigh.

'Then have done with it,' said Saeunn, shrugging her shoulders like a raven hitching its wings. 'The girl has shown herself to be wilful and stubborn, I can do no more with her. As for the boy, he has allowed his – *feelings*' – her lipless mouth puckered – 'to get in the way.'

'He's thirteen summers old,' said Fin-Kedinn.

'He has a destiny,' the Mage said coldly. 'His life is not his own, he may not risk it for a *friend*! He doesn't understand that, but he will. When he fails to find the wolf, he'll return, and you can punish them both.'

Fin-Kedinn stared into the embers. 'I was going to foster him,' he said. 'I should have told him. Maybe it would have made a difference. Maybe – he would have asked me for help.'

Saeunn spat into the fire. 'Why trouble yourself? Let him go! Let him go and seek his wolf!'

TEN

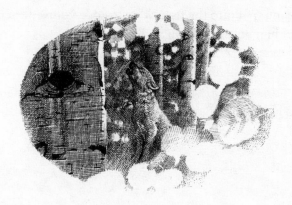

Wolf is in the other Now that he goes to in his sleeps. He can lope faster than the fastest deer, and bring down an auroch on his own; and *yet*, when he wakes up, he's just as hungry as if he hadn't killed at all.

This time, he is a cub again. He's cold and wet, and his mother and father and pack-brothers are lying still and Not-Breath in the mud. The Fast Wet did this. It came roaring through while Wolf was exploring on the rise.

He puts up his muzzle and howls.

On the other side of the Fast Wet, a wolf is coming, coming to rescue him!

Wolf bursts into a frenzied welcome. Then his welcome turns to puzzlement. This is such a strange wolf. Its scent is that of a half-grown male, but it smells of other creatures too, it walks on its hind legs, *and it has no tail!*

And yet – it has the light, bright eyes of a wolf; and something in its spirit calls to his. He has found a new pack-brother. A pack-brother who will never abandon him . . .

Wolf woke with a snap.

He was back on the sliding tree, squashed beneath the hated deerhide, jolting over the Bright Soft Cold. He longed for that other Now, in which he was a cub again, being rescued by Tall Tailless.

His head ached, and he'd been sick in his sleep, but he couldn't move to lick himself clean. His wounded pad hurt. His trodden-on tail hurt more.

Stinkfur came and pushed in another piece of meat – which Wolf ignored. On and on they dragged him, while the Light sank, and the Bright Soft Cold came drifting down from the Up.

After a while, Wolf smelt that they'd entered the range of a pack of stranger wolves. That meant danger.

The big pale-pelted male went off on his own, and hope leapt in Wolf's heart. Maybe Pale-Pelt would be foolish enough to attack the stranger wolves, and they would defend themselves, and he would be killed!

Much later, Pale-Pelt returned – unharmed. He was smiling his terrible smile, and carrying a small deerhide Den which wriggled and snarled. Wolf smelt the rank fury of a wolverine. A wolverine? What did this mean?

But he couldn't hold onto that for long, because he was getting tired again, sliding down into sleep.

A great owl hooted – and he woke. Without knowing why, his fur prickled with dread.

The owl fell silent. That was worse.

Wolf was now fully awake. While he'd slept, the Dark had come, and the sliding tree had stopped. The bad taillesses were some paces away, crouching round the Bright Beast-that-Bites-Hot. Wolf sensed that they were waiting for something. Something bad.

Around him the strange white land lay windless and still. He smelt a hare nibbling willow buds many lopes away. He heard the tiny scratchings of lemmings in their Dens, and the hiss of the Bright Soft Cold falling, falling.

Then through the Dark he heard a tailless approaching. His claws twitched with eagerness. Could it be Tall Tailless, come to rescue him?

His hope was swiftly torn to pieces. It wasn't his pack-brother. It was a female whom Wolf hadn't smelt before. He knew that she was part of the bad pack, for he saw the others rise on their hind legs to wait for her. He felt their dread as she came gliding through the hissing whiteness.

She was tall and very thin, and the pale fur of her head hung about her like worms. Her voice was as the rattle of dry bones, and her smell was of Not-Breath.

The others greeted her quietly in tailless talk; but although they hid it, Wolf smelt their fear. Even Pale-Pelt was afraid. So was Wolf.

Now she turned, and came towards him.

He cowered. His very spirit shrank from hers.

She came closer. He wanted to look away, but he couldn't. There was something terribly wrong with her face. It was blank as stone, and it didn't move at all, not even a twitch of her muzzle when she spoke. And her eyes were not eyes, but holes.

Wolf growled and tried to pull away, but the deerhide held him fast.

Now she was leaning over him, and her Not-Breath smell was dragging him down into a black fog of loneliness and loss.

Slowly she brought one forepaw close to his muzzle. She was holding something – he couldn't see what – but he caught the scent of that which has lain long in the deep of the earth. Through her pale flesh he glimpsed a grey light, and he knew, with the strange certainty that came to him sometimes, that what she held bit as fiercely as the Bright Beast-that-Bites-Hot. Except that it bit *cold*.

His growl became a terrified whimper. He shut his eyes and tried to think of Tall Tailless coming for him through the Bright Soft Cold: coming to rescue him, just as he'd done when Wolf was a cub.

ELEVEN

Inuktiluk's sled hurtled west, carrying Torak and Renn the wrong way. The only sounds were the panting of dogs and the scrape of runners on crusted snow; and an occasional gasp from Renn as they banked on a slope, and leaned in hard to avoid toppling over.

'You can't watch us all the time,' Torak told Inuktiluk when they'd stopped to rest by a wide, frozen lake. 'Sooner or later, we'll get away.'

'Where would you go?' retorted Inuktiluk. 'You'd never make it north, you'd never get round the ice river.'

They stared at him. 'What ice river?'

'It's about a sleep from here. No-one in the Ice clans has crossed it and lived.'

Torak set his teeth. 'We've crossed an ice river before.'

Inuktiluk snorted. 'Not one like this.'

'Then we'll go around it,' said Renn.

Inuktiluk threw up his hands. Whistling to his lead dog,

he started across the lake. 'We cross on foot,' he told them. 'Walk behind me, and do exactly as I say!'

Burning with frustration, they followed – and were soon absorbed in the difficult task of simply staying upright.

'Keep to the white ice,' called Inuktiluk.

'What's wrong with the grey ice?' said Renn, eyeing a patch to her right.

'That's new ice. Very dangerous! If you ever have to cross it, stay apart – and *keep moving*.'

Torak and Renn glanced at each other, and widened the gap between them.

Even the white ice was wind-polished to a treacherous slipperiness, and they slowed to an anxious shuffle. Inuktiluk's boots seemed to grip the ice, allowing him to stride ahead, and the dogs' sharp claws proved best of all; but the puppy slithered about in his seal-hide boots, reminding Torak painfully of Wolf. As a cub, he'd been forever tripping over his paws.

'How deep is the lake?' asked Renn.

Inuktiluk laughed. 'It doesn't matter! The cold will kill you before you can shout for help!'

It was a relief to reach the shore and climb onto solid snow. While Inuktiluk checked the dogs' paws, Torak drew Renn aside. 'There's more cover up ahead,' he whispered, 'we might be able to get away!'

'And go where?' she replied. 'How do we get round the ice river? How do we find the Eye of the Viper? Face it, Torak, we need him!'

The land became harder to cross, with jagged ridges and swooping declines. To help the dogs, they jumped off and ran up the slopes, leaping back on the sled as it sped downhill, while Inuktiluk slowed it by digging in the tines of a reindeer-antler brake.

The cold sapped their strength, but the White Fox man was tireless. Clearly he loved his strange, icy land, and he seemed troubled that they knew so little about it. He insisted that they drink often, even when they weren't thirsty, and he made them carry their waterskins *inside* their parkas, to stop them freezing. He also made them ration the amount of blubber they ate or smeared on their faces. 'You'll need it for melting ice,' he said. 'Remember, you only have as much water as you have blubber for melting ice!'

Seeing their puzzled expressions, he sighed. 'If you're to survive, you need to do as we do. Follow the ways of the creatures of the ice. The willow grouse burrows a shelter in the snow. We do too. The eider duck lines her nest with her feathers. We do the same with our sleeping-sacks. We eat our meat raw, like the ice bear. We borrow the strength and endurance of reindeer and seal, by making our clothes from their hides. This is the way of the ice.' He squinted at the sky. 'Above all, we pay heed to the wind, which rules our lives.'

As if in answer, it began blowing from the north. Torak felt its icy touch on his face, and knew that it was not appeased.

Inuktiluk must have guessed his thoughts, because he pointed to the far shore of the lake, where one of the stone men stood. 'We build those to honour it. Sooner or later, you'll have to make an offering.'

Torak worried about that. At the bottom of his pack lay Fa's blue slate knife, and in his medicine pouch, his mother's medicine horn. He couldn't imagine parting with either.

Around noon, they came to an eerie land where giant slabs of ice tilted crazily. From deep within came hollow groans and echoing cracks. The dogs flattened their ears, and Inuktiluk gripped an eagle-claw amulet sewn to his parka.

'This is the shore ice,' he said in a low voice, 'where land ice and sea ice fight for mastery. We must get through quickly.'

Renn craned her neck at a jagged spike looming overhead. 'It feels as if there are demons here.'

The White Fox looked at her sharply. 'This is one of the places where Sea demons get close to the skin of our world. They're restless. Trying to get out.'

'Can they?' said Torak.

'Sometimes one slips through a crack.'

'It's the same in the Forest,' said Renn. 'The Mages keep watch, but a few demons always escape.'

Inuktiluk nodded. 'This winter it's been worse than most. In the Dark Time, when the sun was dead, a demon sent a great island of ice surging inland. It crushed a Walrus Clan shelter, killing everyone inside. A little later, another demon sent a sickness that took the child of a woman of my clan. Then her older boy went onto the ice. We searched, but we never found him.' He paused. 'This is why we must send you south. You bring great evil.'

'We didn't bring it,' said Torak.

'We followed it,' said Renn.

'Tell me what you mean,' urged the White Fox.

They stayed silent. Torak felt bad, as he was growing to like Inuktiluk.

They pressed on through the broken mountains of ice. At last the shore ice gave way to flatter, crinkled ice. To Torak's surprise, Inuktiluk squared his shoulders and breathed deeply. 'Ah! Sea ice! *Much* better!'

Torak didn't share his ease. The ice before him seemed to be *bending*. Bewildered, he watched it gently rising and falling, like the hide of some enormous creature.

'Yes,' said Inuktiluk, 'it bends with the breath of the Sea Mother. Soon, in the Moon of Roaring Rivers, the thaw will begin, and this place will become deadly. Great cracks – tide cracks, we call them – appear beneath your feet, and swallow you up. But for now, it's a good place to hunt.'

'To hunt what?' said Torak. 'Back at the lake I saw hare tracks, but there's nothing here.'

For the first time, Inuktiluk looked at him with approval. 'So you noticed those? I hadn't thought a Forest boy would.' He pointed straight down. 'This prey is *under* the ice. We do as the ice bear. We hunt seal.'

Renn shivered. 'Do ice bears eat people?'

'The Great Wanderer eats anything,' said Inuktiluk, sticking the antler in the ice to tether the dogs. 'But he prefers seal. He's the best hunter there is. He can smell a seal through an arm's length of ice.'

'Why have you stopped?' said Torak.

'I'm going hunting,' said the White Fox.

'But – you can't! We can't stop to hunt!'

'Well what are you going to eat?' replied Inuktiluk. 'We need more blubber, and meat for the dogs!'

That shamed Torak into silence, but inside, he burned with impatience. It was six days since Wolf had been taken.

Inuktiluk unhitched his lead dog, and slowly paced the ice. Soon the dog found what it sought. 'A seal's breathing-hole,' Inuktiluk said quietly. It was tiny: a low molehill with a hole in the top about half a thumb wide, its edges grooved, where the seal had gnawed to keep it open.

From the sled, Inuktiluk took a piece of reindeer hide and laid it with the furry side on the ice, downwind of the hole. 'To muffle the sound of my boots, like the ice bear's furry pads.' He laid a swan's feather across the hole. 'Just before the seal surfaces, it breathes out – and the feather moves. That's when I've got to act fast. The seal only takes a few gulps of air before it's gone again.'

He motioned them back to the shelter of the sled. 'I must stand and wait, like the ice bear, but in those clothes you'd freeze. Stay out of the wind, and *stay still*! The slightest tremor will warn the seals.' He took up position, standing motionless, with his harpoon raised.

As Torak crouched behind the sled, he began to unpick the knots that fastened his pack to the runners.

'What are you doing?' whispered Renn.

'Getting out of here,' he said. 'Are you coming?'

She started untying her pack.

They were behind Inuktiluk, so they were able to shoulder their packs and sleeping-sacks without being seen; but as they rose, he turned his head. He didn't move or speak. He just looked.

Defiantly, Torak stared back. But he didn't stir. This man had opened a vein to save them. He was a hunter, like them. And they were about to spoil his hunt.

'We can't do this,' breathed Renn.

'I know,' replied Torak.

Slowly, they unhitched their packs.

Inuktiluk turned back to the breathing-hole.

Suddenly the feather twitched.

With the speed of a striking heron, Inuktiluk thrust in the harpoon. The harpoon head came off the shaft, and stuck like a toggle under the seal's hide. With one hand Inuktiluk hauled on the rope tied to the head, and with the other he used the shaft of the disarmed harpoon to enlarge the breathing-hole.

Dropping their packs, Torak and Renn ran to help. One tremendous pull – and the seal was out, and dead of a blow to the head before it hit the ice.

'Thanks!' panted Inuktiluk.

They helped him haul the streaming silver carcass away from the hole.

The dogs were in a frenzy to get at it, but Inuktiluk silenced them with a word. Easing the harpoon head from the wound, he stitched it shut with a slender bone that he called a "wound plug", so as not to waste blood. Then he rolled the seal onto its back, and tilted its snout into the hole. 'To send its souls down to the Sea Mother, to be born again.' Taking off his mitten, he stroked the pale, spotted belly. 'Thank you, my friend. May the Sea Mother give you a fine new body!'

'We do the same thing in the Forest,' said Renn.

Inuktiluk smiled. Slitting the seal at just the right place, he slipped in his hand and brought out the steaming, dark-red liver.

Behind them a bark rang out, and they saw a small white fox sitting on the ice. It was shorter and fatter than the red Forest foxes, and it was watching Inuktiluk with inquisitive golden-brown eyes.

He grinned. 'The guardian wants his share!' He threw it a piece, and the fox caught it neatly, and downed it in a gulp. Inuktiluk handed chunks of liver to Torak and Renn. It was firm and sweet, and slid down easily. The White Fox man tossed the lungs to the dogs, but Torak noticed that they only sniffed them, and seemed too restless to eat.

'We were lucky,' said Inuktiluk through a mouthful of liver. 'Sometimes I wait a whole day for a seal to come.' He raised an eyebrow. 'I wonder if you'd have the patience to wait that long.'

Torak thought for a moment. 'I want to tell you something.' He paused. Renn nodded. 'We came north to find our friend,' he went on. 'Please. You have to let us go.'

Inuktiluk sighed. 'I know now that you mean well. But you must understand, I can't do this.'

'Why not?' said Renn.

On the other side of the sled, the dogs were whining and tugging at their tethers.

Torak went to see what was troubling them.

'What is it?' said Renn.

He didn't reply. He was trying to make out the dogs' talk. Compared to wolf talk, it was much simpler, like the speech of puppies. 'They can smell something,' he said, 'but the wind's gusting, so they're not sure where it is.'

'What is it they smell?' said Renn, reaching for her bow.

Inuktiluk's jaw dropped. 'Do you – does he *understand* them?'

Torak never got the chance to reply. A ridge of ice to his left suddenly rose – and became a great white bear.

TWELVE

The ice bear raised its head on its long neck, and tasted Torak's scent.

With an effortless surge, it reared on its hind legs. It was taller than a tall man standing on the shoulders of another, and each paw was twice the size of Torak's head. One swat would snap his spine like a willow twig.

Swinging its head from side to side, it slitted its hard black eyes, and snuffed the air. It saw Torak standing alone on the ice; Renn and Inuktiluk moving to take cover behind the sled. It smelt the bloody snow beyond them, and the half-butchered carcass of the seal. It heard the dogs howling and straining at their tether in their foolish lust to attack. It took in everything with the unhurried ease of a creature who has never known fear. The power of winter was in its limbs, the savagery of the wind in its claws. It was invincible.

The blood roared in Torak's ears. The sled was ten paces

in front of him. It could have been a hundred.

In silence the ice bear dropped to all fours, and a ripple ran through its heavy, yellow-white pelt.

'Don't run,' Inuktiluk told Torak quietly. 'Walk. Towards us. Sideways. Don't show it your back.'

Out of the corner of his eye, Torak saw Renn nocking an arrow to her bow; Inuktiluk gripping a harpoon in either hand.

Don't run.

But his legs ached to run. He was back in the Forest, running from the wreck of the shelter where his father lay dying, running from the demon bear. *'Torak!'* shouted Fa with his final breath. *'Run!'*

Summoning every shred of will, Torak took a shaky step towards the sled.

The ice bear lowered its head and fixed its gaze upon him. Then – at a lazy, inturned walk – it ambled between him and the sled.

He swayed.

The ice bear made no sound as it set down each foot. Not a click of claws on ice. Not a whisper of breath.

Hardly knowing what he did, Torak slid his hand out of his mitten and felt for his knife. It wouldn't come free of its sheath. He pulled harder. No good. He should have heeded Inuktiluk's advice, and kept it inside his parka. The leather sheath had frozen solid.

'Torak!' called Inuktiluk softly. 'Catch!'

A harpoon flew through the air, and Torak caught it in one hand. The slender bone point looked feeble beyond measure. 'Will it be any use?' he said.

'Not much. But at least you'll die like a man.'

The ice bear breathed out with a rasping 'hssh' – and Torak caught a flash of yellow fangs, and knew with a cold clutch of terror that the harpoon had been a mistake. This bear would not be intimidated, but it could be goaded to attack.

He caught a flicker of movement. Renn pushing up her visor to take aim. 'Don't,' he warned. 'You'll only make it worse.'

She saw that he was right, and lowered her bow. But she kept the arrow nocked in readiness.

The dogs were barking and snapping at their traces. The bear twisted its head on its long neck, and snarled: a deep, reverberating thunder that shook the ice.

It locked eyes with Torak – and the world fell away. He couldn't hear the dogs, couldn't see Renn or Inuktiluk, couldn't even blink. Nothing existed but those eyes: blacker than basalt, stronger than hate. As he gazed into them he knew – he *knew* – that to the ice bear, all other creatures were prey.

His hand on the harpoon shaft was slippery with sweat. His legs wouldn't move.

The bear champed its great jaws, and slammed the ice with its paw. The force of the blow shuddered through Torak. Somehow he stood his ground.

A Forest bear snarls if it means only to threaten, but if it's hunting in earnest, it comes on in lethal silence. Did the same hold true on the ice?

No.

The ice bear leapt for him.

He saw the scarred black hide of its muzzle, the long, purple-grey tongue. He felt hot breath burning his cheek . . .

With fearsome agility the bear swerved – reared – and pounded the ice with both forepaws.

Torak's knees buckled and he nearly went down.

Now the ice bear was turning from him, rounding on the sled, clouting it out of the way as easily as if it were birch bark. Inuktiluk dived to one side, Renn to the other – but as the sled crashed down, it caught her on the shoulder and she fell with a cry, one arm trapped beneath a runner, directly in the path of the bear.

Torak launched himself forwards, waving his harpoon and yelling, 'Here I am! Not her, me! Me!'

Inuktiluk, too, was shouting and making stabbing feints with his harpoon – and in the instant the bear turned towards him, Torak wrenched the sled off Renn and grabbed her arm, half-dragging her out of its path. At that moment, one of the dogs snapped its trace and flew at the bear. A great paw batted it away, sending it flying through the air, to land with a sickening crack on the ice. As Torak and Renn threw themselves down, the bear leaped clean over them, bounded to the seal's carcass – and snatched its head in its jaws. Then it raced off across the ice, carrying the seal as easily as if it were a trout.

'The dogs!' shouted Renn. 'Hold them!'

The puppy was cowering under the sled, but the others were reckless in their blood-lust and hampered only by their traces – and now, as they strained together, they snapped them and hurtled off in pursuit, ignoring Inuktiluk's shouted commands. The trailing traces snagged his boot, and Torak and Renn watched in horror as he was dragged across the ice.

The dogs were strong and fast, too fast to catch. Torak put his hands to his lips and *barked*: the loud, sharp command that in wolf talk means: *STOP!*

His voice cut like a whiplash, and the dogs obeyed at once, cowering with their tails clamped between their legs.

Far away, the ice bear vanished among the blue hills.

Torak and Renn ran to where Inuktiluk was already sitting up, rubbing his forehead.

He recovered fast. Grabbing the traces in his fist, he drew his knife and with its hilt, dealt the dogs punishing blows that made them squeal. Then, breathing hard, he nodded his thanks to Torak.

'We should thank *you*,' Renn said shakily. 'If you hadn't distracted it . . .'

The White Fox shook his head. 'We only lived because it let us live.' He turned to Torak. The distrust was back in his face. 'My dogs. You *can* speak to them. Who are you? *What* are you?'

Torak wiped the sweat off his upper lip. 'We need to get going. That bear could be anywhere.'

Inuktiluk studied him for a moment. Then he gathered his remaining dogs, shouldered the body of the dead one, and limped back to the sled.

Torak dropped his harpoon with a clatter, and bent double with his hands on his knees.

Renn rubbed her shoulder.

He asked if she was all right.

'Hurts a bit,' she said. 'But at least it's not my draw arm. What about you?'

'Fine. I'm fine.' Then he sank to his knees and started to retch.

The sinking sun burned golden on the dark-blue ice as the dogs flew towards the White Fox camp.

Night fell. The slender moon rose. Torak kept glancing at the sky, but not once did he catch sight of the First Tree:

the vast, silent green fires that show themselves in winter. He longed for it as never before; he needed some link with the Forest. But it didn't come.

They passed dark, fanged ice hills, and heard distant cracks and groans. They thought of demons hammering to break free. At last, Torak spotted a speck of orange light. The weary dogs scented home, and picked up speed.

As they neared the White Fox camp, Torak saw a large, humped snow shelter with three smaller ones linked to it by short tunnels. All were honeycombed with light shining through the blocks. Around them, many little humps sprang to life, scattering snow and barking a noisy welcome.

Torak stepped stiffly from the sled. Renn winced and rubbed her shoulder. They were too numb with exhaustion to feel apprehensive of what lay ahead.

Inuktiluk insisted that they beat every flake of snow from their clothes and even pick the ice from their eyebrows, before crawling into the low entrance tunnel that was built like a dog-leg to keep out the wind. On hands and knees, Torak smelt the bitter stink of burning seal oil, and heard a murmur of voices, abruptly cut short.

In the smoky lamplight, he saw whalebone racks around the walls with many boots and mittens hung up to dry; a glittering haze of frozen breath; and a circle of round faces glistening with blubber.

Swiftly, Inuktiluk told his clan how he'd found the interlopers in the storm, and everything that had happened since. He was fair – he mentioned that Torak had saved him from being dragged across the ice – but his voice shook when he told how the "wolf boy" had spoken the tongue of dogs.

The White Foxes listened patiently, asking no questions, and studying Torak and Renn with inquisitive brown eyes not unlike those of their clan-creature. They didn't seem to have a leader, but four elders huddled close to the lamp, on a low sleeping-platform piled with reindeer hides.

'It's them,' shrilled one, a tiny woman, her face dark as a rosehip shrivelled by frost. 'These are the ones I saw in my vision.'

Torak heard Renn's sharp intake of breath. Placing both fists on his heart in sign of friendship, he bowed to the old woman. 'Inuktiluk said that in your vision, you saw me about to do evil. But I haven't. And I won't.'

To his surprise, laughter ran through the shelter, and all four elders gave toothless grins.

'Who among us,' said the old woman, 'knows what evil we will or won't do?' Her smile faded, and her brow furrowed with sadness. 'I saw you. You were about to break clan law.'

'He wouldn't do that,' said Renn.

The elder didn't seem annoyed at this interruption; she merely waited to see if Renn had finished, then turned back to Torak. 'The fires in the sky,' she said calmly, 'never lie.'

Torak was bewildered. 'I don't understand! What was I going to do?'

Pain tightened the ancient face. 'You were about to take an axe to a wolf.'

THIRTEEN

'*Attack Wolf?*' cried Torak. 'I'd never do that!'

'I saw it too,' Renn blurted out. 'In my dream, I saw it!'

She couldn't help herself. But as soon as she'd said it, she wished she hadn't.

Torak was staring at her as if he'd never seen her before. 'I could never hurt Wolf,' he said. 'It isn't possible.'

The White Fox elder spread her hands. 'The Dead don't lie.'

He opened his mouth to protest, but the old woman spoke first. 'Rest now, and eat. Tomorrow we send you south, and this evil will pass.'

Renn thought he'd fight back, but instead he went quiet, with that stubborn look which always meant trouble.

The White Foxes bustled about, taking food from niches cut in the walls. Now that their elders had spoken, they seemed happy to prepare a feast, as if Torak and Renn had simply happened by for a night of storytelling. Renn saw Inuktiluk regaling the others with the tale of how the ice bear had stolen his seal, which made everyone roar with laughter. 'Don't worry, little brother,' someone cried, 'I managed to hang onto mine, so we still get to eat!'

'Why didn't you *tell* me?' said Torak. His face was taut, but she could see that beneath his anger he was badly shaken.

'I was going to,' she said, 'but then you told me about *your* dream, and – '

'Do you really believe I could hurt Wolf?'

'Of course not! But I did see it. You had an axe. You were standing over him, you were going to strike.' All day she'd carried the dream inside her. And it wasn't the everyday kind which didn't always mean what it appeared to; it was the kind with the glaring colours, which she had maybe once every thirteen moons. The kind which came true.

Someone passed her a chunk of frozen seal meat, and she discovered that she was ravenous. As well as the seal, there was delicate whale skin with a chewy lining of blubber; sour pellets of ground-up willow buds from the gizzards of ptarmigans; and a delicious sweet mash of seal fat and cloudberries, her favourites. The shelter rang with talk and laughter. The White Foxes seemed extremely good at forgetting their worries and enjoying themselves. But it was disconcerting to have Torak sit beside her in glowering silence.

'Arguing won't help us find Wolf,' she said. 'I think we need to tell them about the Eye of the Viper – '

'Well I don't.'

'But if they knew, they might help.'

'They don't want to help. They want to get rid of us.'

'Torak, these are good people.'

He turned on her. 'Good people can smile, and be rotten inside! I know, I've seen it!'

She stared at him.

'I can't lose him again,' he said. 'It's different for you. You've got Fin-Kedinn and the rest of your clan. I've only got Wolf.'

Renn blinked. 'You've got me too.'

'That's not the same.'

She felt the heat rising to her ears. 'Sometimes,' she said, 'I wonder why I even like you!'

At that moment, a stout woman called her to come and try on her new clothes – and she left without a backwards glance.

His words were ringing in her ears as she crawled through a tunnel into a smaller shelter where four women sat sewing. *It's different for you.* No it isn't! she wanted to shout. Don't you know that you and Wolf are the first friends I've ever had?

'Sit by me,' said the woman, whose name was Tanugeak, 'and calm down.'

Renn threw herself onto a reindeer skin and started plucking out hairs.

'Anger,' Tanugeak said mildly, 'is a form of madness. And a waste of strength.'

'But sometimes you need it,' muttered Renn.

Tanugeak chuckled. 'You're just like your uncle! He was angry too, when he was young.'

Renn sat up. 'You know Fin-Kedinn?'

'He came here many summers ago.'

'Why? How did you meet him?'

Tanugeak patted her hand. 'You'll have to ask him.'

Renn sighed. She missed her uncle terribly. He would know what to do.

'These visions of yours,' said Tanugeak, examining Renn's wrist. 'They can be dangerous, you should have lightning marks for protection. I'm surprised your Mage hasn't seen to that.'

'She wanted to,' said Renn, 'but I never let her.'

'Let me. I'm a Mage too. And you'll need them, I think. You carry a lot of secrets.' Turning to a woman who sat apart from the others, she asked for her tattooing things. Then, without giving Renn time to protest, she laid her forearm on her ample lap, stretched the skin taut, and began swiftly pricking it with a bone needle, pausing to dip a scrap of gull hide in a cup of black dye, and rub it into the punctures.

It hurt at first, but Tanugeak kept up a stream of stories to keep Renn's mind off it. Soon her anger slipped away, leaving only the worry that Torak might do something stupid, like trying to escape without her.

She felt safe in here. On the sleeping-platform, three children slept in a heap, like puppies. Over the blubber lamp, a baby dangled in a seal's bladder snugly stuffed with moss. The women chatted and laughed, spangling the air with specks of frozen breath; only the one who sat apart, Akoomik, kept silent.

As the drowsy peace stole over her, Renn felt cared for in a way she'd never experienced before: as if the prickly shell she'd grown to protect herself were being gently peeled away.

Tanugeak started on the other wrist, and the women laid out Renn's new clothes, stroking them with weathered brown hands.

There were outer leggings and a parka of shimmering silver sealskin, to which someone had sewn her clan-creature feathers. There was a warm jerkin and inner leggings of eider duck hide, with the soft feathers worn against the skin. There were under-mittens of hare fur, and sturdy outer mittens; ptarmigan-down slippers, to be worn over fluffy stockings made from the pelts of young seals.

And to keep out the wet, there were magnificent boots of dehaired seal-hide, with criss-cross bindings of braided sinew, and finely pleated soles.

'Beautiful,' murmured Renn. 'But I've nothing to give you in return.'

The women looked astonished, then laughed. 'We don't want anything in return!' said one.

'Come back in the Dark Time,' said another, 'and we'll make you a set of winter clothes. These are just for spring!'

Akoomik didn't join in the laughter as she packed her needles in a little bone case. Renn noticed tiny toothmarks on it, and asked who'd made them.

'My baby,' replied Akoomik. 'When he was teething.'

Renn smiled. 'Is he over the worst?'

'Oh, yes,' said Akoomik in a voice that made Renn shiver. 'That's him over there.' She pointed to a ledge cut in the wall, on which lay a small, stiff bundle wrapped in hide.

'I'm sorry,' said Renn. She was scared, too. In the Forest, the clans carried their Dead far from their shelters, so that their souls couldn't trouble the living.

'We keep our Dead with us till spring,' said Akoomik, 'to save them from the foxes.'

'And to stop them feeling left out,' Tanugeak added comfortably. 'They like chatting just as much as we do. When you see a star travelling very fast, that's one of them setting off to visit their friends.'

Renn found that a comforting thought; but Akoomik pinched the bridge of her nose to hold back her grief. 'The demons took his breath a moon ago. Now they've taken my elder son, too.'

Renn remembered what Inuktiluk had said about the boy lost on the ice.

'My mate died of fever in the Moon of Long Dark,'

Akoomik went on. 'Then my mother felt death coming, and went out to meet it, so that she wouldn't take food from the young ones. If my son doesn't return, I'll have no-one.' Her eyes were dull: as if a light had gone out. Renn had seen that before, in people whose souls were sick.

If I lose Wolf, I'll have no-one.

At last she understood what Torak had meant. His mother had died when he was born. He'd lost his father to the bear. He'd never even met the rest of his clan. He was more alone than anyone she knew. And although she too had lost people, she realized that with Torak, as with Akoomik, the grief was still raw. If he lost Wolf . . .

Once again, she wondered how she could bring herself to tell him what she suspected.

'Finished,' said Tanugeak, making her jump.

Renn studied the neat black zigzags on the inside of her wrists. They made her feel stronger, better protected. 'Thank you,' she said. 'Now I need to find my friend.'

'First, take this.' Tanugeak gave her a small pouch made from the scaly skin of swans' feet, with the claws left on.

'What's in it?' asked Renn.

'Things you might need.' She leaned closer. 'Listen well,' she said under her breath. 'The elders saw something else in the sky that night. We're not sure what it means, but I have a feeling you might know.' She paused. 'It was a three-pronged fork, of the kind a healer might use for catching the souls of the sick. But this one felt bad.'

Renn's fingers tightened on the pouch.

'Ah,' said Tanugeak, 'I see that you've been dreading this.' She touched Renn's hand. 'Go. Find your friend. When the time is right, tell him the secrets you carry.'

When Renn got back to the main shelter, the White Foxes had settled down for the night. Most slept huddled together, while a few sat softening sinew between their teeth, or flexing stiff boots to make them wearable for the morning. Torak was fast asleep at one end of the sleeping-platform.

Renn got into her sleeping-sack, wondering what to do. The White Fox vision had confirmed the fear she'd been harbouring for days. The Soul-Eaters had taken Wolf.

She dreaded telling Torak. How much more could he bear?

She was woken by Inuktiluk shaking her shoulder.

Everyone else was asleep, but through a chink in the shelter she saw that the moon was low: it would be dawn soon. Torak was gone.

She shot upright.

'He's waiting outside,' mouthed Inuktiluk. 'Follow me!'

Quietly they made their way into the smaller shelter, where Renn exchanged her old clothes for the unfamiliar new ones.

The night air cut like a knife, but there was no wind. The snow glinted in the faint glow of the dying moon. The crust had frozen, so they had to tread carefully. A few dogs stirred, caught their scent, then slumped down again.

Torak was waiting. Like Renn, he had new clothes: she hardly recognized him in his silvery parka. 'They're helping us get away!' he whispered, his eyes glinting with excitement.

'Who's they?' hissed Renn. 'And *why*?'

Inuktiluk had vanished into the dark, and it was Torak who answered. 'I told him everything. You were right, they do know about the Eye of the Viper! And there's a woman –

Akoomik? She's going to tell us where it is!'

Renn was astonished. 'But – I thought you didn't trust them. What changed your mind?'

'You did.' He gave her one of his rare, wolfish grins. 'I do listen to you sometimes.'

Inuktiluk was beckoning, so they followed him west till they came to a rent in the ice. Renn saw the dark gleam of water, and caught the tang of the Sea.

They tracked the channel as it steadily broadened, then Torak touched her arm. 'Look.'

She gasped. 'A *skinboat*!'

It was ten paces long, sturdily built of dehaired seal-hide stretched over a whalebone frame. Their packs were neatly stowed at either end, and two double-bladed paddles lay on top.

'This channel leads to the open Sea,' said Inuktiluk. 'Once you reach it, keep the land in sight, but stay clear of the mouth of the ice river.'

'You told us that no-one had ever crossed it,' said Torak.

The round face split in a grin. 'But plenty have paddled *around* it!' Then his grin faded. 'Watch out for black ice. It's denser than white, and it'll sink you in moments. If you see a piece in the water, you've already passed several that you missed.'

Renn wondered how they were going to spot black ice in a black Sea.

Torak was hefting his paddle, keen to make a start. 'How do we find the Eye of the Viper?'

Akoomik emerged from the shadows, and with her knife began carving marks in the snow. 'Follow the North Star past the ice river,' she said, 'about a day's paddling from here. When you see a mountain shaped like three ravens perched on an ice floe, put in at the frozen bay below it, and head up the ridge that curls round its north-west flank.'

'But what *is* it?' said Renn. 'How will we know we've found it?'

Both White Foxes shivered, and made the sign of the hand. 'You'll know,' said Akoomik.

'And may the guardian save you,' said Inuktiluk, 'if you venture inside.' He helped them into the skinboat.

Torak handled his paddle confidently, but Renn was uneasy. She hadn't had as much practice in boats. 'Why are you helping us?' she asked the White Foxes.

'The elders don't know you as I do,' said Inuktiluk. 'When I explain, they won't be angry. Besides,' he added, 'if I don't help you, you'll go anyway!'

Akoomik peered into Torak's face. 'You've lost someone. So have I. If you find what you seek, maybe I will too.'

Torak thought for a moment, then rummaged in his pack, and pressed something into her mittens. 'Take these.'

She frowned. 'What are they?'

'Boar tusks. I'd forgotten I had them; but they're special. They belonged to a friend of mine. Offer them to the wind. For both of us.'

Inuktiluk grunted in approval, and Akoomik's white teeth showed in the first smile Renn had seen her give. '*Thank you!* May the guardian run with you!'

'And also with you!' whispered Renn.

Then they were off, slicing through the black water and heading for the open Sea, to find Wolf.

FOURTEEN

The stranger wolves were howling many lopes away, and as Wolf listened, he felt the bite of loneliness.

He heard that it was a big pack, and that each wolf was cleverly varying its howls to make it sound as if there were even more of them. Wolf knew that trick; he'd learned it when he'd run with the pack on the Mountain.

In his head he saw the wolves lifting their muzzles joyfully to the Bright White Eye. He longed to howl back. But he was squashed beneath the hated deerhide. Howling was only a memory.

The sliding tree lurched as the taillesses crested a ridge. Wolf forced himself to stay alert, to be ready for when his pack-brother came. But it was getting harder. Thirst scratched his throat. Pain gnawed his tail. When they'd been on the Great Wet in the terrible floating hides, he'd been sick. His belly still hurt.

The other creatures were feeling no better. The otter

had fallen into despairing silence, although Wolf smelt that she wasn't yet Not-Breath. The lynx and fox – whom Pale-Pelt had caught and crammed onto another sliding tree – hadn't yowled since the Light. Only the wolverine gave the occasional furious snarl.

The stranger pack ended its howl, and the white hills sang with silence. Wolf knew that now the wolves would be licking and snuffling each other in readiness for the hunt. Before he and Tall Tailless went hunting, they always snuffle-licked and touched noses, although of course only Wolf wagged his tail.

The sliding tree turned into the wind, and he smelt mountains drawing near. He sensed a shiver of excitement run through the taillesses, and guessed they were reaching the end of their long lope.

Stinkfur came to trot beside him, and thrust a chunk of the Bright Soft Cold through the deerhide. Awkwardly, Wolf took it in his cramped jaws, and crunched it up. He no longer had the will to refuse what he was given.

Up ahead, Pale-Pelt spoke to Viper-Tongue, and they glanced at him and broke into the yip-and-yowl of tailless laughter. Rage bit his belly. In his head he burst free of the deerhide and leapt at Pale-Pelt, tearing out his throat so that the hot blood gushed . . .

But only in his head. He was getting weaker. Even if he could break free, he wouldn't have the strength to bring down Pale-Pelt. He worried that when Tall Tailless and his pack-sister finally came, he would be too weak to fight alongside them.

As the Light fled, a mountain loomed. The wind dropped. Wolf smelt that there was little prey here, and no wolves. His pelt crawled with dread.

The sliding tree juddered to a halt.

607

There, against the flank of the mountain: a Bright Beast-that-Bites-Hot was snarling, and beside it – silent, unmoving – waited the Stone-Faced One.

She stood with her forepaws clenched at her sides, and Wolf sensed that in one she held the grey, glowing thing that bit cold. She was very still, and yet her shadow on the mountainflank leapt like tattered wings.

Wolf hadn't seen or smelt her since the time when she'd come through the hissing whiteness. Now, one glimpse of her terrible face made him a whimpering cub again.

In silence the other taillesses left the sliding trees, and went to join her. They were fearful, but as before, they hid their fear from each other.

The Stone-Faced One spoke in her rattling voice, and the whole pack crouched around the Bright Beast-that-Bites-Hot, and began to rock back and forth. Back and forth, back and forth. Watching them made Wolf dizzy, but he couldn't look away. Then they started a low, steady growling that thudded through Wolf like the hooves of reindeer galloping over hard ground. On and on it went, faster, louder, till his heart beat painfully in his chest.

And now from the mountain came a smell of Dark and demons, flowing over him like an unseen Fast Wet.

Suddenly Stone-Face raised her forepaw – the paw in which she held the grey thing that bit cold. Then – as Wolf watched in amazement – *she thrust her paw right into the jaws of the Bright Beast!*

Frozen with horror, he watched Stinkfur thrust in her forepaw, then Pale-Pelt, then Viper-Tongue. He watched them rocking back and forth, still growling that fast, stony growl, with their paws sunk deep in the crackling jaws of the Bright Beast.

All at once they gave a triumphant howl – and wrenched their paws out again.

Wolf could not believe what he was smelling! Their forepaws didn't stink of meat that has been bitten by the Bright Beast! They smelt cool and fresh! *What were these taillesses, whom even the Bright Beast feared to bite?*

Terror crushed Wolf: terror not only for himself but for his pack-brother.

Tall Tailless and the female were clever and brave, and they had Long Claws-that-Fly-Far. But if they attacked these strange, bad taillesses, they would be torn to pieces.

FIFTEEN

'What's that in the water?' hissed Renn.

'A seal,' said Torak over his shoulder.

'Are you sure?'

'– No.'

'It looked like an ice bear.'

'If it was an ice bear, we'd know it by now.'

But she had seen it. A great pale shape sliding through the dark water under the skinboat.

'Inuktiluk told me there are white whales,' said Torak. 'Maybe that's what you saw.'

To Renn's annoyance, he didn't seem frightened. But he was a better skinboater, and too intent on finding Wolf to be scared.

The swell lifted the boat and she dug in her paddle, trying not to think what lay beneath. The Sea Mother could drown them with one flick of her fin. Down they would sink into the bottomless black, their mouths open in a scream that had no end; and when the fishes had nibbled their bones bare, the Hidden People would roll them forever in their long green hair . . .

'Watch out,' said Torak, 'you're splashing me.'

'Sorry.'

Her arms ached, and despite her owl-eyed visor, her head was pounding from the glare. They'd reached the open Sea shortly after dawn, and were now in an eerie world of dark-green water and drifting blue ice mountains. To the east stretched the white expanse of the shore; to the north, the vast, shattered chaos of the ice river.

'Too slow,' muttered Torak. Picking up speed, he steered them behind a floating mountain.

'I don't think we should get so close,' said Renn.

'Why not? It keeps us out of the wind.'

She applied herself to her paddle. On the pale-green foot of the ice mountain, three seals lay basking. She fixed her eyes on them, and told herself not to worry.

It was no good. She *was* worried. Torak's need to find Wolf was all-consuming; she'd begun to wonder where it would lead. And she hadn't yet told him about the Soul-Eaters.

A smaller ice mountain slid past them on its mysterious journey. She felt its freezing breath, heard the slap and suck of the Sea carving a cavern in its flank. The cavern was a searing blue oval. Like an eye, she thought.

'The Eye of the Viper,' she said suddenly.

'I've been thinking about it too,' said Torak. 'It can't be anything to do with a real viper, there aren't any this far north –'

'– and Inuktiluk said, "if you venture *inside*".'

He turned to her, his owl eyes making him startlingly unfamiliar. 'I think I can guess what he meant.'

'Me too,' said Renn.

He shivered. 'I hope we're wrong. I *hate* caves.'

They paddled on in silence.

To keep up her spirits, Renn rummaged in her pack for food. The White Foxes had provisioned them well. Along with half a skin of blubber, she found frozen seal ribs and blood sausages. She cut two slices, and handed one to Torak. It tasted gritty, and she missed the tang of juniper berries. She missed the White Foxes more. 'I feel bad about them,' she said.

'Why?' said Torak, with his mouth full.

'They gave us so much, and we repaid them by running away.'

'They were going to send us south!'

'But all this gear. Snow-knives. Lamps. Better waterskins. A new strike-fire for me, and a beautiful case for my bow. There's even a repair kit for the boat.' She held up a pouch made from a seal's flipper.

Torak wasn't listening. He'd lowered his paddle, and was staring ahead.

'What is it?' said Renn.

Ahead of them on the ice mountain, the seals had woken up.

Renn was puzzled. 'But we've got enough food,' she whispered, 'we can't stop to hunt now!'

He ignored her.

Suddenly the seals slithered off the ice and into the water. At the same moment Torak plunged in his paddle and yelled, 'Turn! Turn!', swinging the skinboat hard to the left. A bewildered Renn did the same, and they shot sideways – out from the wake of the ice mountain – as a rending roar split the sky, and the mountain tilted and crashed into the Sea, sending a wall of water thundering over where they'd been a heartbeat before.

Panting, they bobbed up and down. In place of the ice mountain there was now a heaving white slush.

'How did you know that would happen?' said Renn.

'I didn't,' said Torak. 'The seals did.'

'How did you know they knew?'

He hesitated. 'They feel it in their whiskers. Last summer I spirit walked in a seal. Remember?'

Uneasily, Renn licked the salt from her lips. She'd forgotten; or she hadn't wanted to remember. She hated being reminded of how different he was.

He saw it in her face. 'Come on,' he said. 'Long way to go.'

They moved off, steering clear of ice mountains. Renn felt the distance between them of things unsaid. She'd have to tell him soon.

The wind picked up, blowing cold in their faces. But in her White Fox clothes, she hardly felt it. The seal hide cut out the wind, but was lighter than reindeer hide, while the eider-feather underclothes kept her snug, but let out the sweat, so that she didn't get chilled. The dog-fur ruff around the hood kept her face warm, but never became clogged with frozen breath; and her inner mittens had slits in the palms, so she could slide her fingers out for fiddly work like opening pouches. The clothes were beautiful, too, the silver fur shimmering in the sun. But they made her feel like someone else.

The zigzag tattoos on her wrists also made her feel different, and she wondered just why Tanugeak had given them to her. The White Fox Mage had seemed to know things about her that she thought only Saeunn and Fin-Kedinn knew; things that Renn kept hidden in a deep corner of her mind.

But it was Tanugeak's final gift which puzzled her most. The swansfoot pouch contained a dark powder that smelt of soot and seaweed. What was she supposed to do with that?

'Look,' said Torak, cutting across her thoughts.

He'd been steering them further out to Sea, and now she saw why.

To the east lay the glaring white of the ice river. Jagged peaks towered over dizzying cliffs riven with deep blue cracks. Renn heard a distant booming – and saw a great spur break away and crash into the Sea. Clouds of powdered ice shot into the sky. A green wave rolled towards them, rocking the skinboat.

If we'd been closer, she thought, we'd have been crushed. Like my father.

'Try not to think about it,' Torak said quietly.

She picked up her paddle and stabbed at the water.

The sun was low and the ice river far behind them when they finally glimpsed the mountain. From the dead white land it rose: three stark peaks piercing the sky, like ravens perching on ice.

Renn had never seen anything so lonely. Two winters ago, her clan had journeyed to the northern-most end of the High Mountains, and she'd felt as if she'd reached the edge of the world. Now she felt as if she'd fallen over it.

Torak sensed it too, and slipped one hand out of his mitten to touch his clan-creature skin.

South of the mountain's western flank, they found the iced-in bay which Akoomik had drawn in the snow. It was a relief to get out of the skinboat, although their legs were stiff. Once again, they were grateful to the White Foxes. The boat was easy to carry, and their boots' rough soles stopped them slipping on the ice.

Hiding the boat in the lee of a snow hill, they over-turned it and propped it up on four forked driftwood sticks. 'Inuktiluk called them shoresticks,' Torak told Renn. 'We can use them to make the boat into a shelter, too.'

Renn knew better than to suggest that they should do exactly that, right now, since it was mid-afternoon, and the shadows were turning purple. Already, Torak was scanning for tracks.

He soon found them: a broad swathe of churned-up snow. '*Two* sleds,' he said with a frown. 'Heavily laden, and heading for the mountain. Quite fresh.' He straightened up. 'Let's go.'

Renn shivered. All at once, the Soul-Eaters felt very close. 'Wait,' she said. 'We need to think about this.'

'Why?' he said impatiently.

She hesitated. 'One of the White Fox women told me something. I've been wanting to tell you all day.'

'Yes?'

She lowered her voice to a whisper. 'Torak. It's the Soul-Eaters. They're the ones who took Wolf.'

'I – know,' he said.

'*What?*'

He told her what he'd seen when he'd spirit walked in the raven.

'But – why didn't you *tell* me?' she cried. 'You've known for *days!*'

He scowled, and hacked at the snow with his heel. 'I know I should have, but I couldn't risk it. I thought you might go back to the Forest.' His scowl deepened. 'If you'd left . . . '

Suddenly she felt sorry for him. 'I've suspected for days, but I didn't leave. And I won't now.'

He met her eyes. 'So – we go on.'

She swallowed. 'Yes. We go on.'

They looked at the trail of the Soul-Eaters, winding up the mountain.

Renn said, 'What if this *is* some kind of trap?'

'I don't care,' he muttered.

'What if they've heard rumours of the Wolf Clan boy who's a spirit walker? If they catch you, if they take your power, it could endanger the whole Forest.'

'I don't *care*,' he repeated. 'I've got to find Wolf!'

She had an idea. 'What about a disguise?'

'What?'

'That'd throw them off the scent. And maybe Tanugeak had that in mind, too. At least, she gave me what we need.'

Torak took a few paces, then turned back to her. 'What do we do?'

It didn't take long to change their appearance. Their clan-tattoos weren't a problem, as their cheeks were still so blistered from the snowstorm that the fine marks hardly showed. Renn made a black stain by mixing Tanugeak's powder with water, then finger-painted a White Fox band across Torak's nose. She also cut his hair to shoulder length, with a fringe across the brow. He was too thin to make a truly convincing White Fox, but with luck, his clothes would conceal that.

She dyed her own hair black by combing in more of the stain, which she also used to darken her face. Then she got Torak to turn her into a Mountain Hare by painting her forehead with a zigzag band tinged with earthblood from his medicine horn.

He seemed disconcerted. 'You don't look like Renn any more.'

'Good,' she said. 'And you don't look like Torak.'

They stared at one another, both more unsettled than

they cared to admit. Then they set off on the trail of the Soul-Eaters.

The sleds had been dragged up a ridge that snaked round the western flank of the mountain, just as Akoomik had said. As they climbed higher, the shadows deepened from purple to charcoal. Often they paused to listen, but no living thing stirred. No eagles wheeled, no ravens cawed.

The air grew colder. The wind dropped. Their boots creaked in the stillness.

Then – with appalling suddenness – they came upon the sleds, casually piled at the side of the trail.

After so many days of following the faintest of clues, it was a shock to find solid structures of wood and hide. It made the Soul-Eaters solid, too.

Sensing they were nearing the end, they hid their packs and sleeping-sacks in the snow a few paces from the sleds. Renn saw what a wrench it was for Torak to leave behind his father's blue slate knife. 'But it's too dangerous,' she told him. 'They knew him, they might recognize it.'

They decided to take the waterskins the White Foxes had packed for them, a little food, and knives. Renn would also take her bow, and she wanted to take the axes as well, but Torak feared the White Fox vision too much to risk it.

Twenty paces beyond the sleds, the trail rounded a spur – and they halted.

Above them reared the gaunt mountain, lit crimson by the last rays of the sun. In its flank, a black hole gaped. Before it, like a warning, stood a tall grey pillar of stone.

White mist seeped from the darkness of the cave. Clammy tendrils reached for them, stinking of dread and demons. Hope fled. If the Soul-Eaters had taken Wolf in there . . .

Glancing over her shoulder, Renn saw the shape of the

whole mountain for the first time. She saw how it rose out of the snow like the head of some giant creature. She saw how the ice river uncoiled its sinuous bulk east, before twisting round to lose itself in the Sea.

Torak had seen it too. 'We've found the Viper,' he whispered.

'We're standing on it,' breathed Renn.

They turned back to the mountain: to the glaring black hole split by the standing stone.

'And there's the Eye,' she said.

Torak took off his owl visor and stowed it in his medicine pouch. 'They're in there,' he said, 'I can feel it. So is Wolf.'

Renn chewed her lower lip. 'We need to think about this.'

'I've done enough thinking,' he snapped.

Taking his arm, she drew him behind a rock, out of sight of the Eye. 'There's no sense going in,' she said, 'unless we know for sure that – that Wolf is still alive.'

He didn't reply. Then – to her horror – he put his hands to his mouth to howl.

She grabbed his wrist. *'Are you mad?* They'll hear you!'

'What if they do? They'll think I'm a wolf!'

'You don't know that! Torak, these are *Soul-Eaters!*'

'Then what?'

'There is another way.' Slipping her hand out of her mitten, she fumbled at the neck of her parka, and brought out the little grouse-bone whistle he'd given her once. She blew on it – and no sound came, as they had known it wouldn't; but if Wolf was alive, he would hear it.

Nothing. Not a breath of wind stirred the dead air.

'Try again,' said Torak.

She tried. And again. And again.

Still nothing. She couldn't meet his eyes.

Then – from deep inside the mountain – the faintest of howls.

Torak's face lit up. 'I told you! I *told* you!'

The howl was long and wavering, and even Renn could hear its misery and pain. It rose to a peak . . .

And cut off.

SIXTEEN

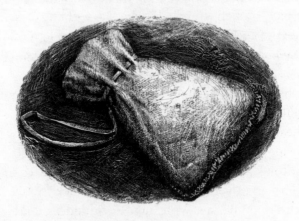

'Wolf!' cried Torak, throwing himself forwards.

Renn yanked him back. 'Torak, no! They'll hear you!'

'I don't care, let me go!' He pushed her away with such force that she went flying.

She landed on her back, and they stared at one another, both shocked by his violence.

He offered her his hand, but she got to her feet unaided. 'Don't you understand,' she hissed in a furious whisper, 'if you go into that cave, you might be walking right into their hands!'

'But he needs me!'

'And how does it help if you get yourself killed?' She dragged him down the trail, out of sight of the Eye. 'We have to *think*! He's down there. We know that. But if we blunder in, who knows what might happen?'

'You heard that howl,' he said through his teeth. 'If we don't go in now, he may die!'

Renn opened her mouth to protest – then froze.

Torak had heard it too. The crunch of footsteps coming up the slope.

Of one accord, they ducked behind the sleds.

Crunch, crunch, crunch. Unhurried. Coming closer.

Quietly, Torak drew his knife. Beside him, Renn slipped her hands out of her mittens and nocked an arrow to her bow.

A thickset man came into view. He was clad in mottled sealskin, and carried a grey hide pouch over one shoulder. His head was bowed. His hood concealed his face. He bore no weapons that they could see.

As Torak watched, rage choked him. His eyes misted red. This was one of them. This man had taken Wolf.

In his mind he saw Wolf standing proudly on the ridge above the Forest, his fur limned golden by the sun. He heard again that agonized howl. *Pack-brother! Help me!*

Crunch, crunch, crunch. The man was almost level with them. He stopped. Looked over his shoulder, as if reluctant to go on.

It was too much for Torak. Scarcely knowing what he did, he leapt forwards, head-butting the man in the belly, sending him crashing into the snow.

He lay winded, but then – with astonishing speed – rolled sideways, kicked Torak's knife from his hand, and grabbed his hood, twisting it backwards in a vicious choke-hold. Torak felt strong legs pinioning his arms, squeezing the breath from his chest; flint digging painfully into his throat.

'I wouldn't,' Renn said coldly. She took a step closer, her arrow aimed at the attacker's heart.

Torak felt the grip on his ribs loosen. His hood was released, the knife withdrawn.

'Please,' whined his attacker, 'don't hurt me!'

With her arrow still poised to shoot, Renn nudged Torak's knife towards him with her boot, then told her captive to get up.

'No, no!' whined the captive, cowering at her feet, 'I may not look upon the face of power!'

Torak and Renn exchanged startled glances.

The captive grovelled, scrabbling for the pouch he'd dropped in the attack. Torak was surprised to see that he wasn't a man, but a boy about his own age, although twice as heavy. He bore the black nose tattoo of the White Foxes, and his round face glistened with blubber and terror sweat.

'Where is he?' said Torak. 'What have you done with him?'

'Who?' bleated the boy. He saw Torak's tattoo, and his mouth fell open. 'You're not one of us. Who *are* you?'

'What are you doing here?' snapped Renn. 'You're no Soul-Eater!'

'But I will be!' retorted the boy with unexpected ferocity. 'They promised!'

'For the last time,' said Torak, advancing with his knife, 'what have you done with Wolf?'

'Get away from me!' squealed the boy, scrambling backwards like a crab. 'If – if I scream, they'll hear. They'll come to my rescue, all four of them! Is that what you want?'

Torak stared at Renn. *Four?*

'Get away from me!' The boy edged up the slope. 'I *chose* to do this! No-one can stop me!'

He sounded as if he were trying to convince himself. It gave Torak an idea. 'What have you got in that pouch?' he said, to keep the boy talking.

'A – an owl,' stammered the boy. 'They want it for sacrifice.'

'But an owl is a hunter,' said Renn accusingly.

'So is a wolf,' said Torak. 'And an otter. What are your masters doing in there? Tell us or we'll – '

'I don't *know*!' cried the boy, moving further up the slope. As they followed him, the Eye came into view.

'Your masters,' Renn said quietly, 'do they talk of the one who is a spirit walker? Tell the truth! I'll know if you lie!'

'A *spirit walker*?' The boy's eyes widened. 'Where?'

'Do they ever speak of this?' demanded Torak.

'No, no, I swear it!' He was sweating freely now, stinking of blubber. 'They came to make a sacrifice! That's all I know, I swear on my three souls!'

'And for this you'd break clan law by catching hunters for sacrifice?' said Renn. 'For an empty promise of a power that will never be yours?'

Sheathing his knife, Torak took a step towards the boy. 'Your mother wants you back,' he said.

He'd guessed right. The boy's body sagged.

Renn was puzzled, but Torak ignored her. If she got an inkling of what he meant to do, she'd try to stop him. 'Get out of here,' he told the boy. 'Go back to Akoomik while you still can.'

Terror and ambition fought in the blubbery face. 'I can't,' he whispered.

'If you don't go now,' said Torak, 'it'll be too late. Your clan will make you outcast. You'll never see them again.'

'I *can't*,' sobbed the boy.

From deep within the Eye, a voice boomed. 'Boy! It is time!'

'I'll make it easy for you,' snarled Torak. Wrenching the pouch from the boy's grip, he pushed him down the trail. 'Go on, go!' He hoisted the pouch over his shoulder. 'Renn, I'm sorry, but I've got to do this.'

Realization dawned in her face. 'Torak – no – it'll never work, they'll kill you!'

Turning his head, he shouted an answer to the Soul-Eaters. 'I'm coming!'

Then he raced up the trail and into the Eye of the Viper.

SEVENTEEN

After the twilit mountainside, the darkness hit Torak like a wall.

'Shut your eyes,' said a voice in front of him. 'Let the dark be your guide.'

Torak just had time to draw down his hood before a figure lurched towards him bearing a sputtering pine-pitch torch.

From the voice he expected a man, but when he stole a glimpse from under his hood, he was startled to see a woman.

She was heavy and squat, with legs so badly bowed that she rocked as she walked. Her features were at odds with the rest of her: small, darting eyes in a sharp-snouted face. Pointed ears that reminded Torak of a bat. He didn't recognize her clan; the spiky tattoo on her chin was unknown to him. What drew his gaze was the bone amulet on her breast: the three-pronged fork for snaring souls.

'You were a long time,' said the Soul-Eater. 'Did you get it?'

Hiding his face, Torak held up the pouch. Inside, the owl wriggled feebly.

The Soul-Eater grunted, then turned and hobbled further into the cave.

Glancing back, Torak saw that the last glimmer of daylight was far behind. He slung the pouch over his shoulder, and started after her.

The Soul-Eater moved fast, despite her bow legs, and in the swinging torchlight he caught only flashes as they went deeper. Ridged red walls like a gaping maw. A tunnel as pale and twisted as guts. Yellow hand-prints that flared, then faded in the gloom. And always the echoing drip, drip of water.

As he stumbled on, the folly of what he'd done sank in. When the Soul-Eaters saw his face, they would know he wasn't the White Fox boy. Maybe, too, they would detect some trace of his father in his features. Or maybe they already knew who he was, and this was all a trap.

Down, down they went. An unclean warmth seeped from the rocks and clung to his face like cobwebs. An acrid stink stole into his throat.

'Breathe through your mouth,' muttered the Soul-Eater.

Fa used to give him the same advice. It was terrible to hear it repeated by the enemy.

Above him, Torak saw thin sheets of reddish stone hanging down like flaps of bloody hide. In their folds, unseen creatures shrank from the light.

His head struck a rock and he fell, crying out in disgust as his fingers plunged into soft blackness seething with thin grey worms.

A strong hand grabbed his arm and hauled him to his

feet. 'Quiet!' said the Soul-Eater, 'you'll startle them!' Then to the darkness, 'There, there, my little ones.' As if in answer came the squeak and rustle of thousands of bats.

'The warmth makes them wakeful,' murmured the Soul-Eater. Laying her palm on the tunnel wall, she made Torak do the same.

He recoiled. The rock had the lingering warmth of a fresh carcass. He knew only one reason for that. The Otherworld.

'Yes, the Otherworld,' said the Soul-Eater, as if she'd heard his thoughts. 'Why do you think we came all this way?'

He didn't dare reply, which seemed to irritate her. 'Don't let the bats see your eyes,' she snarled. 'They go for the glitter.'

Abruptly, the tunnel widened into a long, low cavern the colour of dried blood. It had the eye-watering stink of a midden in high summer, and Torak's gorge rose.

Then he forgot about the smell. The walls were pitted with smaller hollows, some blocked with slabs of stone. From inside one he caught the hiss of a wolverine.

His heart quickened. Where there was a wolverine, maybe there was also a wolf.

He gave a low grunt-whine that Wolf would be sure to recognize. *It's me!*

No answer. Disappointment crashed over him like a wave. If Wolf was still alive, he wasn't here.

'Stop whining,' growled the Soul-Eater, 'and keep up! If you get lost down here, we'll never find you again.'

More tunnels, until Torak's head whirled. He wondered if the Soul-Eater had chosen a winding route on purpose, to make him lose his bearings. Behind that sharp face, he sensed a quick mind. *Twisted legs, flying thoughts.* That was what the Walker had said.

They emerged into a vast cavern – and Torak faltered. Before him loomed a forest. A forest of stone.

Shadowy thickets reached upwards, seeking sunlight they would never find. Stone waterfalls froze in an endless winter. As Torak followed the lurching torchlight, a sickly warmth made the sweat start out on his brow. He heard a furtive trickling; glimpsed still pools and twisted roots. He caught nightmare flashes of figures draped in stone: some crouching above him, some half-hidden in water. When he looked again, they were gone, but he felt their presence: the Hidden People of the Rocks.

The Soul-Eater led him to a massive trunk of greenish stone that looked as if it had been hacked to a stump by some act of unimaginable violence. He heard movement, and knew he was being watched.

His foot caught on a root, and he tripped and fell. Laughter rang through the cavern.

'What's this, Nef?' said a woman's mocking voice. 'Have you brought us your fosterling at last?'

Torak's heart began to pound. He'd managed to deceive one Soul-Eater. He'd need all his wits to deceive the others.

Grovelling where he lay, he began to whine. 'No, no, don't make me look upon the face of power!'

'Not that again!' grunted Nef. 'He won't even dare look at me!'

Torak felt a flicker of hope. If they hadn't seen the White Fox boy's face . . .

A cold finger slid down his cheek, making him flinch. 'If he daren't look at Nef the Bat Mage,' a woman whispered in his ear, 'dare he look upon Seshru, the Viper Mage?'

She drew back his hood, and he found himself staring into the most perfect face he'd ever seen. Slanting lynx eyes of fathomless blue; a mouth of daunting beauty. Dark hair, drawn back from a high white brow, revealed a stark black line of tattooed arrowheads, like the markings on a snake.

Fascinated yet repelled, he met the peerless gaze, while the Viper Mage studied him as a hunter regards its kill.

Her lovely features tightened with contempt – but nothing more. She didn't know who he was. 'He's thin for a White Fox,' she said. 'Nef, you disappoint me. You've found us a runt.' Her chill fingers slid inside the neck of his parka, and she smiled. 'What's this? He has a knife!'

'A knife?' said the Bat Mage.

The knife which Fin-Kedinn had made for him hung in its sheath from a thong about his neck. Now it was gone: lifted over his head and tossed to Nef.

'He has a *knife!*' jeered a man's voice as rich and deep as an oak wood. An enormous figure loomed from the darkness, and before Torak could resist, he was seized, and his arms twisted so viciously that he screamed.

More laughter, blasting him with the eye-stinging tang of spruce-blood. 'Should I be frightened, Seshru?' mocked the man. In his bulky reindeer-hide clothes, he seemed to fill the cavern. 'Does he mean to threaten the Oak Mage?'

Torak stared into a face as hard as sun-cracked earth. The beard was a twiggy thicket, the mane a russet tangle. The eyes that bore into his were a fierce leaf-green. 'Does he mean to threaten?' repeated the Oak Mage in a tone of menacing softness.

Torak felt as helpless as a lemming trapped by a lynx.

'Thiazzi, leave him!' snapped the Bat Mage. 'We need him alive, not dead of fright!'

The Viper Mage arched her white throat and laughed. 'Poor Nef! Always so eager to play the mother!'

'What would you know about mothering?' Nef threw back at her.

Seshru's beautiful lips thinned.

'Let's see what it's brought us, shall we?' said Thiazzi, grabbing the pouch from Torak's hand. He pulled out a small, half-grown white owl, and shook it until its eyes darkened with shock. From that moment, Torak hated Thiazzi the Oak Mage, who delighted in tormenting creatures weaker than himself.

The Bat Mage didn't seem to like it either. Shambling forwards, she snatched the owl from the Oak Mage and stuffed it back in the pouch. 'We need this one alive, too,' she muttered. Then she turned to Torak, indicated a birchbark bowl on the floor, and told him to eat.

To his surprise, he saw that the bowl contained a strip of dried horse meat and some hazelnuts.

'Go on,' urged Seshru with a curious sideways smile. 'Eat. You have to keep up your strength.' Her glance slid to Thiazzi, and Torak caught a flicker of amusement between them.

He pretended to eat, but his throat had closed. It seemed as if only a moment ago, he'd been out in the snow with Renn. Now he was in the bowels of the earth with the Soul-Eaters.

The Soul-Eaters. They had haunted his dreams. They had killed his father. Now, at last, here they were: mysterious, unknowable – and yet more *real* than he could ever have imagined.

Thiazzi the Oak Mage sprawled on the rocks, chewing spruce-blood, flecking his beard with golden crumbs. He could have been any hunter in the Forest, except that he tortured for pleasure.

Seshru the Viper Mage moved to lean against him:

slender, graceful, her supple seal-hide tunic shimmering like moonlight on a lake. The emptiness of her smile made Torak shudder. When she licked her lips, he glimpsed a little, pointed black tongue.

Nef the Bat Mage puzzled him most of all. Her small eyes darted suspiciously from Thiazzi to Seshru, and she seemed at odds with them both – and with herself.

Far away, an owl hooted.

Seshru's smile faltered.

Thiazzi went still.

Nef murmured under her breath, and put her hand to the dusky clan-creature fur on her shoulder.

The torchlight dipped.

With a start of terror, Torak saw that a *fourth* Soul-Eater sat in the deep of the cave – where before there had been only shadow.

'Behold,' whispered Seshru, 'the Masked One is come.'

'Eostra,' said Thiazzi hoarsely, 'the Eagle Owl Mage.'

Nef grasped a stone sapling and rose to her feet, hauling Torak with her.

The Masked One, thought Torak. He remembered the pain in the Walker's face. *Cruellest of the cruel.*

Through the gloom he made out a tall grey mask. From it glared the unblinking eyes of the greatest of owls. Owl feathers covered the head, from which rose two sharp owl ears. Long coils of ashen hair hung about a feathered robe. Only the hands could be seen. The nails were hooked, and tinged with blue, like those of a corpse. The flesh had the pale-green sheen of rotting meat.

'Bring it close,' said a voice as harsh as a death-rattle.

Torak was pushed nearer, and thrown to his knees. He caught a whiff of decay, like the smell of the Raven bone-grounds. Dread froze his heart.

With appalling slowness, the owl mask bent over him, and he felt a fierce and evil will beating at his mind.

Just when he could bear it no longer, the mask withdrew. 'It is well,' it said. 'Take it away.'

Torak breathed out shakily, and crawled back towards the light. The torches flared. When he dared look again, Eostra the Eagle Owl Mage was gone.

But the change in the cave was palpable. The Oak Mage and the Viper Mage moved with sharpened purpose among the stone trees, fetching baskets and pouches whose contents Torak couldn't see.

'Come, boy,' said Nef. 'Help me feed and water the offerings. Then you and I will make the first sacrifice.'

EIGHTEEN

The dread of Eostra's presence clung to Torak as he followed the Bat Mage through the forest of stone.

Nef handed him the pouch that held the owl. 'Put it there,' she said, indicating a ledge near the altar, 'and follow me.'

As he set down the pouch, Torak loosened the neck a little, to give the owl some air. Nef barked mirthlessly. 'It makes you uneasy to harm a hunter. You'll have to do worse if you want to be a Soul-Eater.' Snatching a torch, she set off through the twisting tunnels. 'You'll have to take on the burden of sin for the good of the many. Could you do that, boy?'

' – Yes,' Torak said doubtfully.

'We'll find out,' said Nef. 'Tell me. How old are you?'

He blinked. 'Thirteen summers.'

'Thirteen.' Her brow furrowed. 'My son would have been fifteen, if he'd lived.'

For a moment, Torak almost felt sorry for her.

'Thirteen summers,' repeated the Bat Mage. With a faraway look, she reached into a pouch at her belt and brought out a handful of dead flies. On her shoulder the clan-creature fur stirred – stretched its neck – and snapped them up. 'There, my beauty,' she murmured. She caught Torak staring. 'Well go on,' she said, 'let her sniff you!'

He offered it his finger. The bat's crumpled ears quivered, delicate as new leaves, and he felt the brief warmth of a tiny tongue tasting his skin. *Strange prey*, he thought. He pictured how the bat would move over snow: its claws digging in, its elbows making tiny stump-like tracks. With a pang he thought how the ever-curious Wolf would have raced to investigate.

'She likes you,' growled Nef. 'Odd.' Abruptly she headed off again, and Torak had to run to keep up.

'How did your son die?' he asked.

'He starved,' said Nef. 'The prey fled our part of the Forest. We must have done something to displease the World Spirit.' Her scowl deepened. 'I wanted to die too. I tried to, but the Wolf Mage saved me.'

At the mention of his father, Torak nearly fell over.

'He saved my life,' Nef said bitterly. 'Now he's dead, and I can never repay him. Gratitude is a terrible thing.'

Suddenly she seized Torak's hands and pressed them to the wall of the tunnel, crushing them under her own. 'That's why we're here, boy, to make things right with the World Spirit! Quick! Tell me what you feel!'

He struggled, but her hands imprisoned his. Beneath his palms the rock was clammy and warm. Deep within, he felt something squirm. 'It lives!' he whispered.

'What you feel,' said Nef, 'is the skin that separates our world from the Other. There are places under the earth where that skin has worn thin.'

Torak thought of a cave he'd once ventured into. He asked if there were such places in the Forest.

'There's one,' said Nef. 'We tried it, but the way was shut.'

'Why do you need it?' he said. 'Why are you here?'

The small eyes glinted. 'You know why.'

He licked his lips. 'But – I need to learn more if I'm to be a Soul-Eater.'

Nef leaned closer, engulfing him in the acrid smell of bat. 'First we must find the Door,' she said. 'The place where the skin is thinnest. Then we must make the charm to protect us from what will come forth. Last,' her voice sank to a whisper, 'in the dark of the moon – we must open the Door.'

Torak swallowed. Once again he heard the voice of the Walker. *They are going to open the Door!*

'But – why?' he breathed. 'Why do you –'

'No more questions!' snarled Nef. 'We've got work to do!'

They hurried on, emerging after a time into the stinking cavern where Torak had heard the wolverine. He saw a stream that he'd missed before, pooling in a hollow before vanishing down a crevice. Beside it stood a birchbark pail and a wovenbark sack of dried cod.

Nef told him to take them both and follow her. Shambling to the first of the hollows, she shifted the slab that blocked it by a hand's width. She tossed in a scrap of cod, drew out a small birchwood bowl, filled it, and pushed it in again.

Torak caught a gleam of eyes. An otter: the one whose joyful snow-slide he'd tracked in the Forest. Her sleek coat was matted, and she shrank from them. His pity for Nef drained away. If she could do this . . .

The Bat Mage pushed back the slab, leaving a narrow

gap for air, and limped to the next hollow. Slowly they made their way through the cavern. Torak glimpsed a white fox curled in exhausted slumber. An eagle: all ruffled feathers and glaring yellow rage. A lynx so cramped that it couldn't turn round. The spitting fury of a wolverine.

Finally, in a deep pit almost completely sealed by an enormous slab of stone, he glimpsed the awesome, unmistakeable bulk of an ice bear.

'That one gets only water,' said Nef, taking the pail and splashing some into the hole. 'We need to keep it starved, or it'll be too strong.'

The bear gave a thunderous growl, and hurled itself against the slab. The slab held firm. Not even the power of an ice bear could move it.

'How did you catch it?' said Torak.

Nef snorted. 'Seshru has some skill with sleeping-potions. Thiazzi's strength has its uses.'

Torak turned, and took in the length of the cavern. He'd begun to realize that what the Soul-Eaters were doing went far beyond threatening Wolf. 'Hunters,' he said. 'They're all hunters.'

'Yes,' said the Bat Mage.

'Where's the wolf?'

Nef went still. 'How do you know there is one?'

He thought quickly. 'I heard it. A howl.'

The Bat Mage lurched back the way they'd come. 'The wolf will be brought in tomorrow, in the dark of the moon. When it's time.'

Covertly, Torak glanced about him to see if some hollow remained unexplored.

Again Nef seemed to read his mind. 'He isn't here. We're keeping him apart from the others.'

'Why?'

That earned him a sharp glance. 'You ask a lot of questions.'

'I want to learn.'

The bat on Nef's shoulder squirmed, and she watched it lift off and flit away into the darkness. 'Because of Seshru,' she said. 'Last summer she received a strange message from our brother across the Sea. *The Wolf lives.* We don't know what it means. But that's why we keep the wolf separate.'

Torak's thoughts whirled. Did they know something? Maybe not enough to tip them off that he was a spirit walker, but something . . .

He realized that Nef was watching him keenly, so he asked the question to which he thought he already knew the answer. 'All these creatures. What are you going to do to them?'

'What do you think we're going to do?'

'Kill them,' he said.

The Bat Mage nodded. 'The blood of the nine hunters is the most dreadful – the most potent of sacrifices.'

His temples pounded. The cave walls pressed in on him.

'You say you want to be one of us,' said Nef. 'Well, that begins now.' She raised her torch, and Torak saw that she'd brought him full circle, back to the forest of stone. It was deserted. The other Soul-Eaters had gone. On the ledge at his shoulder, the owl in the pouch lay still. Awaiting sacrifice.

The breath caught in his throat. 'But – you said tomorrow. In the dark of the moon.'

'For the full charm, yes. But first we have the *finding* of the Door – and for that, too, we must protect ourselves. The blood of the owl will do that. And it will help us hear what lies within.'

Wedging the torch in a crevice, she reached for the pouch, and drew out the bird. With one hand she held it down. With the other she extended her knife-hilt to Torak. 'Take it,' she ordered. 'Cut off its head.'

Torak stared at the owl, and the owl stared back at him: bedraggled, limp with fright.

Nef jabbed the knife-hilt in his chest. 'Are you so weak that you fail at the first test?'

A test . . .

He saw now that everything the Bat Mage had done had been leading up to this. She meant to find out if he was who he pretended to be: a White Fox boy determined to step over into the murky world of the Soul-Eaters.

'But it isn't prey,' he said. 'We're not going to eat it. And we're not hunting. It hasn't had a chance to get away.'

The eyes of the Bat Mage were bright with a terrible certainty. 'Sometimes,' she said, 'the innocent must suffer for the good of the many.'

Good? thought Torak. What's this got to do with good?

'Take the knife,' commanded Nef.

He couldn't breathe. The air in his lungs was hot and heavy with sin.

'Come!' said Nef. 'We are the Soul-Eaters, we speak for the World Spirit! Are you with us or against us? There is no middle path!'

Torak took the knife. He knelt, and placed his free hand on the owl. He'd never felt anything so soft as those feathers; so delicate as the fragile bones that sheltered the small, racing heart.

If he refused to do this, Nef would kill him. And the Soul-Eaters would open the Door, and unleash who knew what horrors upon the world.

And Wolf would die.

He took a deep breath – silently begged the World Spirit for forgiveness – and brought down the knife.

NINETEEN

'It's done,' said the Bat Mage.

'Is that the blood?' said the Oak Mage.

'Of course.'

Hardly daring to breathe, Renn shrank deeper into her hiding-place: a dank fissure behind a thicket of stone saplings. Where was Torak? What had they done to him?

She watched the Soul-Eater bearing a sputtering torch in one hand and a horn cup in the other. In the flickering light, the bow-legged shadow was vast. Overhead, thousands of bats stirred.

'Where's the boy?' said the Oak Mage, taking his place before the altar.

'With the offerings,' said the Bat Mage. 'He seemed shaken. Seshru is watching him.'

Renn's skin crawled.

'So he's shaken, is he?' sneered the Oak Mage. 'Nef, he's a coward! I hope that won't affect the charm.'

'Why should it, Thiazzi?' retorted the Bat Mage. 'He came to *us*, he offered himself. He'll serve the purpose well enough.'

What purpose? thought Renn. From what she'd heard, Torak's disguise had succeeded; they didn't know who he was, or that he was a spirit walker. But why did they need him?

She wondered, too, how many Soul-Eaters there were in these caves. There had been seven when they'd banded together, and two were now dead, which left five; but the White Fox boy had mentioned only four. Where was the fifth?

Then she forgot about that. The Bat Mage set the torch in a cleft, dipped her forefinger in the cup, and daubed a streak of darkness on her brow. She did the same for the Oak Mage.

'*The blood of the owl,*' she chanted, '*for keenest hearing.*'

'*And to protect us from those who rage within,*' intoned the Oak Mage.

Renn stifled a gasp. *The blood of the owl* . . . So they'd killed it, just as the White Fox boy had said. But why? To kill a hunter angers the World Spirit, and brings bad luck on oneself and one's clan.

Resting her hand on a sapling, she was startled to feel a sickly warmth. She knew instantly what it was. The heat of the Otherworld.

To protect us from those who rage within . . . Did they mean demons? Demons from the Otherworld?

If only she'd followed Torak at once! But instead she'd paced the snow: furious with him, arguing with herself. By the time she'd made up her mind – had hidden her bow and found her courage – the cave had swallowed him.

That was when she'd heard the echoing tread of a man. She'd barely had time to slip inside before he'd loomed from the darkness: big as an auroch, his face hidden in a tangle of hair and beard. The Oak Clan tattoo had been plain on the back of his hand. The smell of spruce-blood had hung about him like mist in the Forest.

In awe she'd watched him put his shoulder to a slab of rock five times her size, and slide it across the cave mouth as if it had been a wicker screen. They were shut in. She'd had no choice but to follow him into the twisting tunnels: fearing to get too close, or worse – to be left behind in the dark.

At last they'd emerged into this forest of stone. Around her she felt the presence of shadowy figures watching, waiting. Even the drip, drip of water sounded stealthy. Worst of all was the flutter and squeak of thousands of bats. Did they know she was here? Would they tell the Soul-Eaters?

Peering between two stone saplings, she watched the Bat Mage take up her torch and touch it to others wedged around the altar. Firelight flared – then suddenly dipped, as if in homage. The bats fell silent. The air grew heavy with evil.

Renn jammed her knuckles in her mouth.

A *third* Soul-Eater sat at the head of the altar. In the gloom, Renn made out feathered robes that seemed to grow from the stone itself; the fearsome orange glare of an eagle owl.

Behind the mask, a chill voice spoke. 'The souls. Give me the souls.'

The Bat Mage placed something small on the altar – and the shadowy robes moved to cover it. Renn guessed that the Bat Mage had worked some kind of binding charm, and trapped the owl's souls in its feathers.

'It is well,' said the voice behind the mask.

Renn thought of the owl's souls, caught – perhaps for

ever – in the grip of the Eagle Owl Mage. She wondered if they would ever escape, to flutter into the sky, seeking the shelter of the First Tree . . .

Dread dragged at her heart as she watched the Mage place something dark and curved on the altar. It was the Walker's strike-fire: the stone claw that he'd taken from a cave in the Forest long ago.

Next, the Oak Mage reached into a pouch, and held up a small black pebble with the sheen and smoothness of an eye. *'This is the owl,'* he chanted as he laid it beside the strike-fire. *'The first of the nine hunters.'*

The nine hunters?

Renn's fingers closed about a slender twig of stone. Feeling sick, she watched the Oak Mage upend the pouch. More pebbles rattled onto the altar.

The Bat Mage chose one and laid it beside that which betokened the owl. *'This*, she chanted, *'is the eagle. For keenest sight.'*

'And to protect us from those who rage within,' chanted the others.

Another pebble was set beside the second. And another. And another. As Renn listened, the hideous extent of the impending sacrifice revealed itself.

'This is the fox. For cunning . . .

This is the otter. For water-skill . . .

This is the wolverine. For rage . . .

This is the bear. For strength . .

This is the lynx. For leaping . . .

This is the wolf . . .'

Renn shut her eyes.

' . . . For wisdom . . .'

A hush fell. The ninth pebble lay waiting to be set in its place: to close the ring of eyes encircling the strike-fire.

The Eagle Owl Mage extended a talon to grasp it. *'This,'* she chanted, *'is the man. For cruelty.'*

Man.

Renn's grip tightened on the stone. At last she knew why the Soul-Eaters had let the White Fox boy join them. And now Torak had taken his place . . .

The stone snapped. The bats exploded in a fluttering, squeaking cloud.

'Someone's there!' cried Nef, leaping to her feet.

'It's the boy!' boomed Thiazzi. 'He's been listening!'

Torchlight slid between the stone trees as the Soul-Eaters began to search the cave.

Wildly Renn cast about for an escape; but in choosing her hiding-place, she'd crept too far from the tunnel. She couldn't get back without being seen.

Nearer and nearer came the light, reaching for her. Nearer came the heavy tread of the Oak Mage.

She did the only thing she could. She climbed up.

The fissure was jagged as an axe-cut, and she skinned her palms as she groped for handholds. She raised her head – couldn't see anything – scrambled higher into the dark.

The footsteps were almost upon her.

Her fingers found a ledge. No time to think. She heaved herself onto it, praying that the rustling of the bats would mask the frantic scrabbling of her boots.

It wasn't a ledge, it was a tunnel, she'd found a tunnel! Too low to stand up – she bumped her head – dropped to all fours, and crawled in.

The tunnel bent to the right, good, if she could get inside, the light wouldn't find her. But it was so narrow that she could barely squeeze in, and the roof was getting lower – she had to crawl on her belly, and push herself ahead on her elbows.

Squirming like a lizard, she wriggled deeper. As she

twisted her head to look back, she saw the yellow light flickering closer, nearly touching her boots. She wasn't far enough in, it was going to find her . . .

With a tremendous heave she pulled herself round the bend – just as the light snapped at her heels.

Below her, a man's harsh breathing. The sharp tang of spruce-blood.

She bit down hard on her lower lip.

Then – from the other side of the cave – the thud of running feet.

'It wasn't the boy!' panted the Bat Mage. 'He's been with Seshru all the time!'

'Are you sure?' said the Oak Mage, his voice shockingly close.

'It must have been the bats,' said Nef.

'Well from now on,' growled Thiazzi, 'we'd better keep watch.'

His voice receded, taking the light with it. Darkness flooded back.

Weak with relief, Renn slumped on her belly. For a long time she lay in the blackness, listening to the Soul-Eaters moving about, talking in low voices.

At last, their voices faded. They had left the forest of stone. The bats fluttered, then sank into silence. Still Renn waited, fearing a trap.

When she was as certain as she could be that she was alone, she started to wriggle backwards out of the tunnel.

The hood of her parka snagged on the roof, and she kicked forwards to unhook it – but the tunnel was too low, she couldn't move far enough to free herself.

Irritated, she tried again. And again. She tried wriggling from side to side. The tunnel was too narrow, it didn't do any good.

She lay on her belly, struggling to take in what had happened. Her arms were folded awkwardly beneath her chest. Against her fists she felt the thunder of her heart.

The truth crashed upon her.

She was stuck.

TWENTY

She thought about screaming for help; but that would bring the Soul-Eaters. She thought about lying in this stinking weasel hole, dying of thirst. A quick death or a slow one. That was the choice.

She was soaked in sweat, and the tunnel walls blew back the smell of her fear. She could no longer hear the drip of water; only her ragged breath, and a strange, uneven 'drum-drum-drum' that was keeping pace with the thunder of her heart.

It *was* her heart, she realized: her heart echoing through the rock as it thumped against her ribs.

Suddenly she was horribly aware of the vast weight of stone that pressed upon her, of the utter impossibility of movement. The earth had swallowed her. It had only to give the slightest twitch to crush her like a louse.

No-one would ever know. No-one would find her bones and lay them to rest in the Raven bone-ground. No-one would put the Death Marks on her, to keep her souls together.

Darkness lay on her face like a second skin. She shut her eyes. Opened them. No difference. She dragged her hand from under her, held it before her nose. Couldn't see her fingers. They didn't exist. *She* didn't exist.

She couldn't get enough air. She took a great, shuddering breath – and the rock shrank tight around her.

She panicked. Clawing, kicking, moaning, drowning in a black sea of terror. She collapsed, exhausted, grinding her mouth into the unyielding stone to keep back the whimpers.

Deep in the earth, there is no time. No winter. No summer. No moon. No sun. There is only the dark. Renn lay for so long that she wasn't Renn anymore. Whole winters drifted over her. She became part of the rock.

She heard demons cackling on the other side. Lights flashed. Red eyes glared at her, coming nearer. She was dying. Soon her souls would be scattered, and she'd become a demon: squeaking and gibbering in the endless heat of the Otherworld, hating and desiring all living things.

But now more lights were coming: tiny, brilliant green needle-pricks that shimmered and danced, chasing the red eyes away. There was a humming in her ears, a humming of . . .

Bees?

She jerked awake. Bees? In winter, in a cave in the Far North?

The humming was nearer, and it was definitely bees. Although she couldn't see them, she could feel them, brushing against her cheeks. What were they? A message from her clan-guardian? The spirits of her ancestors? Or a trick of the demons, waiting behind the rock?

But they didn't feel evil. Shutting her eyes, she lay and listened to the humming of the bees . . .

It's the Moon of the Salmon Run, and the blackthorn trees are in bloom, and the bees are humming. Renn is eight summers old: hunting with Fin-Kedinn, eager to try out the beautiful new bow he has made for her. She pauses on the riverbank to admire its gleaming golden curve, and the blackthorn blossom drifts down like summer snow, and catches on the manes of the forest horses who stand in the shallows.

When she drags her eyes away from her bow, she's startled to see that Fin-Kedinn has crossed the river and gone on ahead. Hurriedly she tumbles down the bank and splashes after him.

The mares don't like her coming so close to their foals. They show the whites of their eyes, ready to kick.

Renn isn't frightened, but to avoid them she flounders deeper, and the mud sucks at her boots. She's stuck.

She panics. Since her father died, she's had nightmares about being trapped. What if the horses trample her? What if the Hidden People of the river pull her under?

Suddenly the sunlight is blotted out, and Fin-Kedinn is standing over her. His face is as impenetrable as ever, but in his blue eyes there's a glint of laughter.

'Renn,' he says calmly, 'there's an answer to this. But you won't find it if you don't use your head.'

She blinks. Glances down. Then – wobbling – she steps out of her boots.

Laughing, her uncle swings her high in his arms. And now she's laughing too, and squealing as he swings her down in a dizzying swoop to pluck her boots from the mud. Still laughing, he sets her on his shoulders, and wades to the bank, and around them the blossom is drifting, and the bees are humming . . .

The bees were still humming, but she couldn't see them any more because she was back in the weasel hole. The thought of Fin-Kedinn was like a beam of light in the dark. Her fingers touched the polished slate wrist-guard on her forearm. He'd made it for her when he'd taught her to shoot.

'There is an answer,' she whispered. 'Use your head . . .'

Her breathing slowed. Her chest was no longer heaving. The walls didn't seem to grip quite as tightly as before.

Of course! she thought. Don't breathe so deeply, and you won't take up so much space!

Keeping her breathing shallow was a small victory, and it cheered her greatly. She wasn't dead yet. If only there was some way of making herself narrower still.

Maybe it *was* possible. Yes! Why hadn't she thought of it before?

Slowly – painfully – she uncurled her right arm and stretched it forwards as far as she could. Then she tilted her left shoulder back. Now she really *was* narrower, because she wasn't blocking the tunnel face on, but tilting sideways.

The next bit would be harder. Bending her right arm back over her head, she clutched at her parka. Missed. Tried again, and grabbed the hood. Tugged. It was mercifully loose: Tanugeak had told her that the White Foxes made them like that because loose clothes are warmer. Like a snake sloughing off its skin, Renn wriggled and pulled, wriggled and pulled – and at last the parka slid over her head.

She lay panting, and the bees hummed giddily.

Now for the birdskin jerkin. This was harder – no hood to grab hold of – but without the parka she could move much more easily.

The relief when the jerkin came off was overwhelming. For a while she lay gasping, feeling the sweat chilling her skin, touching the clothes bunched up in front of her. But now she was resting with a purpose. In only her leggings, she was half the size she had been, and could slip through the tunnel like an eel. She could get back to the forest of stone, and find Torak and Wolf.

She started wriggling backwards, but her leggings snagged on a spur. It didn't stop her for long, but to her surprise, the buzzing of the bees turned as fierce as hornets. What did that mean? Didn't they want her to go back?

Stretching her hand into the darkness before her, she felt cool air stinging her raw fingers. It wasn't merely the chill of drying sweat, it was a current of cold air. And if it was cold, it must be coming from outside.

Pushing with her toes, she edged forwards through the tunnel. It sloped steeply up, but now that she had more room to squirm, it was easier, and she could grasp projections jutting from the rocks, and pull herself along.

Still she hesitated. If she went forwards – wherever that led – it would mean leaving Torak behind. She couldn't do that. She had to warn him that he was the ninth hunter in the sacrifice.

And yet – if she went back, she would find herself once again in the cavern of the Soul-Eaters; and even if she could evade them, and somehow find Torak – even if they could rescue Wolf, and make their way through the tunnels to the mouth of the cave – how would they get out, when it was blocked by that great slab which only Thiazzi could move?

She chewed her lip, wondering what to do.

Fin-Kedinn often said that when things went wrong, the worst you could do was nothing. 'Sometimes, Renn, you have to make a choice. Maybe it's a good one, maybe not.

But it's better than doing nothing.'

Renn thought for a moment. Then she started wriggling forwards.

TWENTY-ONE

In the forest of stone, the Soul-Eaters were making ready for the finding of the Door.

Nef hobbled about dipping torches in pitch and setting them in place, while her bat flitted overhead. The veins in Thiazzi's temples bulged as he hauled rocks into a circle about the altar. Seshru fitted three masks with gutskin eyes for seeing into the Otherworld. Of Eostra there was no sign.

Torak dreaded the return of the Eagle Owl Mage – and yet he needed it, too. He had to be certain that all four Soul-Eaters were here in this cave, before he could slip away and find Wolf. Until then, he had to be the apprentice Soul-Eater: grinding earthblood on a slab, while the blood of the owl stiffened on his forehead.

After he'd killed it, Nef had put her heavy hand on his shoulder. 'Well done. You've just taken the first step to becoming one of us.'

No I haven't, Torak had told her in his head.

But he knew what Renn would have said. 'Where will it end, Torak? How far will you go?'

He remembered an argument he'd had with Fin-Kedinn, when he'd begged the Raven Leader to let him go in search of the Soul-Eaters. In vain.

'Your father tried to fight them,' Fin-Kedinn had said, 'and they killed him! What makes you think you'd be any stronger?'

At the time, Torak had raged against the Raven Leader's refusal, but now he understood what lay behind it. It wasn't only the evil of the Soul-Eaters which Fin-Kedinn feared. It was that within Torak himself.

Once, the Raven Leader had told him the story of the first winter that ever was. 'The World Spirit fought a terrible battle with the Great Auroch, the most powerful of demons. At last the World Spirit flung the demon burning from the sky; but as it fell, the wind scattered its ashes, and a tiny speck settled in the marrow of every creature on earth. Evil exists in us all, Torak. Some fight it. Some feed it. That's how it's always been.'

Torak thought of that now: a tiny black seed in his marrow, waiting to burst into life.

'Bring me the earthblood,' said Seshru, startling him. 'Quickly. It's almost time.'

He lifted the heavy slab and carried it to the altar.

How long before he could escape and find Wolf?

The plan he'd come up with was dangerous – it might even kill him – but it was the only one he could think of. First he had to return to the stinking tunnel where the "offerings" were held; then he had to get as close to the ice bear as he dared, and then –

'Put it there,' ordered Seshru.

He did as he was told, and made to withdraw – but her cold hand clasped his wrist.

'Stay. Watch. Learn.'

He had no choice but to kneel beside her.

She'd painted the mask with lime, turning it glaring white. Now she dipped her forefinger in a paste of alder juice and earthblood, and reddened the mouth. Her finger worked in slow circles that made Torak dizzy. As he watched, the face began to live. The scarlet lips glistened with spittle. The mane of dead grass rustled and grew.

'Don't touch,' whispered the Viper Mage.

He jerked back with a cry.

Laughter rippled through the Soul-Eaters. They were playing with him, making him feel one of them for some purpose of their own.

'You want to know why we're doing this,' said Nef, guessing the question in his mind.

'Why are we going to open the Door?' murmured Seshru. 'Why are we going to let out the demons?'

'To rule,' said Thiazzi, coming to stand beside her. 'To unite the clans and rule.'

Torak licked his lips. 'But – the clans rule themselves.'

'Much good it does them,' growled Nef. 'Have you never asked yourself why the World Spirit is so fickle, so unpredictable? Why does it send the prey at some times, but not others? Why does it kill one child with sickness, but spare another? Because the clans don't live as they should!'

'They have different ways of sacrificing,' said Thiazzi, 'of sending their Dead on the Journey. This displeases the World Spirit.'

'There's no *order* to it,' said Nef.

Thiazzi drew himself up to his full height. '*We* know the

true way. We will show them.'

'But to do that,' said Seshru, fixing Torak with her unfathomable gaze, 'we must have power. The demons will give it to us.'

He tried to look away, but her eyes held his. 'No-one can control demons,' he said.

Thiazzi's laugh echoed through the cave. 'You're wrong. If only you knew how wrong!'

'The mistake others made in the past,' said Seshru, 'was to overreach themselves. Our brother who is lost summoned an elemental and trapped it in a great bear. Of course he couldn't control it. It was a magnificent madness.'

Magnificent? thought Torak. That madness had cost his father his life.

Nef hobbled towards him. 'The demons *we* summon,' she declared, 'will be as many as the bats that darken the moon – '

' – as many as the leaves in the Forest,' boomed the Oak Mage. 'We will flood the land with terror!'

'And after that . . . ' the Viper Mage stretched out her hands, then drew them towards her, as if grasping an invisible bounty, 'we will call them back, and the demons will do *our* bidding, because we – and only we – possess that which forces them to our will.'

Torak stared at her. 'What do you mean?'

The beautiful mouth curved. 'Ah. You'll see.'

Torak looked from Nef to Seshru to Thiazzi. Their faces were alight with fervour. While he had been plotting to rescue Wolf, they had been hatching a plan to gain dominion over the Forest.

'Soul-Eaters, they call us,' said Thiazzi. He spat out a crumb of spruce-blood.

'A foolish name,' said Nef.

'But useful,' murmured Seshru with her sideways smile, 'if it keeps them in fear.'

Torak rose uncertainly to his feet. 'I – should go,' he said. 'I should guard the offerings.'

'From what?' said Thiazzi, blocking his path. 'The Eye is shut. Nothing can get in.'

'Or out,' said Seshru.

Torak swallowed. 'One of them might escape.'

The Viper Mage slid him a mocking glance. 'He wants to get away from us.'

'I told you he was a coward,' sneered Thiazzi.

'Here.' Nef held out a length of shrivelled black root. 'Take it. Eat.'

'What is it?' said Torak.

Seshru licked her lips, showing her little pointed tongue. 'It'll send you into a trance.'

'This is part of being a Soul-Eater,' said Thiazzi. 'That is what you want. Isn't it?'

All three were watching him.

He took the root and put it in his mouth. It tasted sweet, but with an undertow of rottenness that made him gag.

They had trapped him. First the owl. Now this. Where would it end? How was he ever going to find Wolf?

TWENTY-TWO

There was black fog in Wolf's head, and it told him that Tall Tailless wasn't coming to rescue him, not ever ever ever.

Something had happened. He'd fallen prey to a Fast Wet, or been attacked by the bad taillesses. Otherwise he would have come by now.

As Wolf paced the tiny stinking Den, he shook his head to get rid of the fog, but only succeeded in bumping his nose on a rock. The Den was far away from all the other creatures, and so small that he could only take a single pace before he had to turn round and go back again. Pace, turn. Pace, turn.

He *ached* to run. In his sleeps, he loped up hills and down into valleys; he rolled about in ferns, waggling his paws and growling with delight. Sometimes he leapt so high that he soared into the Up, and snapped at the Bright White Eye. But always when he woke, he was back in the stinking Den.

He could have howled – if he'd had the spirit to howl. But what was the use? Nobody would hear him except the bad taillesses and the demons.

Pace, turn. Pace, turn.

Hunger gnawed at his belly. In the Forest, when he hadn't made a kill for a long time, hunger sharpened his nose and ears, and put a spring in his lope that sent him flying between the trees. But this hunger was so bad that it didn't even hurt.

All the pacing was making him giddy, but he couldn't stop, even though it got harder with every step. His tail was much, much worse. He'd tried licking it better, but it didn't taste like himself any more, and it didn't carry his scent. It smelt like Not-Breath prey that's lain in the Forest for many Lights and Darks. It tasted bad. The badness was making him sick. He could feel it seeping through him, eating up his strength.

Pace, turn. Pace, turn.

He was deep in the guts of the earth, and far from all other creatures. He missed the whimpering of the otter, and the fury of the wolverine; he even missed the stupid snarling of that stupid bear. And yet – he wasn't alone. His ears rang with the squeaking of bats and the gibber of demons. He could smell them behind the rocks, hear the scrabbling of their claws. There were so many. It was a torment not to be able to attack: to bite and snap and tear, as he was meant to do. Hunting demons was what he was *for*.

Pace, turn. Pace, turn.

It was demons that had put the badness in his tail; it was demons that were blowing black fog through his head. Because of them, he'd begun to see and hear things that weren't there. Sometimes he saw Tall Tailless crouching beside him. Once he'd heard the high, thin yowl that the female made when she put the grouse bone to her muzzle.

Now, beneath the bat-squeaks and the scratching of demons, he caught a new sound, a real one. Two taillesses coming closer: one small, one heavier.

For a moment, hope leapt. *Could it be Tall Tailless and the female?*

No. This wasn't his pack-brother coming to rescue him. It was the bad taillesses: Viper-Tongue and Pale-Pelt.

Knowing he was too weak to fight, Wolf cowered in the Den. He heard the covering being scraped back, and saw a lump of bark lowered onto the floor. He snapped up the wet. There was just enough to waken thirst, but not enough to send it back to sleep.

And yet – what was this? Another scent clung to Viper-Tongue's overpelt. A clean, well-loved scent: *the scent of Tall Tailless!*

Wolf's joy swiftly turned to horror as he realized that this could only mean one thing. The bad taillesses had caught his pack-brother!

He went wild. Yowling, hurling himself against the Den. He put up his muzzle to howl, but strong paws grabbed his head. He twisted – tried to bite – but he was too weak and they were too strong. Once again the hated tree bark was wound about his muzzle.

Once again he was unable to howl.

TWENTY-THREE

The forest of stone was growing before Torak's eyes.
Rocky trunks thrust upwards with splintering cracks.
Brittle branches spread with the jerky shudder of broken
fingers.

He shut his eyes, but still he saw it. He wondered if this
was the "inner eye" which Renn had told him about: the
one you used for Magecraft. He wished savagely that she
was with him now.

The black root was sweet and rotten in his mouth. He
could feel it tugging at his souls, although he'd only
chewed it for a moment, then hidden it under his tongue.
He felt dizzy and sick, but more alert than ever before in
his life.

He watched the Soul-Eaters circling the altar. Like the
forest of stone, they had changed beyond recognition. The
Bat Mage snarled through a wrinkled muzzle as she spread
her leathery wings to shadow the cave. The Oak Mage

towered over the stone trees, his gnarled bark crackling as he brandished twin rattles made of teeth and skulls. The Viper Mage glared with dead gutskin eyes through a hissing mane of serpents.

Only the Eagle Owl Mage remained unchanged, as if rooted in stone.

Forgotten in the shadows, Torak hung back. Now was the time to slip away: to go in search of Wolf. But the black root held him fast in an invisible web. He couldn't move.

Sounds came to him more keenly than ever before. He heard every drip from the stone trees; every bat-squeak, every flicker of wet snake tongues. He knew why, and the knowledge sickened him. The blood of the owl had sharpened his hearing.

Hating himself for doing nothing, he watched the Viper Mage whirl round and round, thrashing her snake head in dizzying circles. A serpent slithered past his face. He caught its split yellow stare, the black lightning of its tongue.

Suddenly the Viper Mage moved to the altar, and plunged both hands in a hollowed stone – then drew them out, spattering red. Thrashing, swaying, she glided to the back of the cavern, and planted her palms on the rock.

The Oak Mage and the Bat Mage bayed in ecstasy.

Torak gasped.

As the Viper Mage sprang away, her handprints smoked. The red stain was eating through the skin between this world and the Other.

At last he understood the meaning of the yellow handprints he'd glimpsed on his way into the caves. They'd been made by someone trying to find the Door.

And now, behind the serpent hiss and the rattle of tooth on bone – behind the groans of the earth itself – Torak heard a sound that made his knees give, and the back of his neck crawl as if a spider were scuttling across it. A sound to suck the hope from the marrow, and stop the heart with dread: harsh, malevolent, rasping *breath*.

Demons. Demons on the other side of the rock, lusting to be let loose.

In helpless horror he stared at the whirling, chanting Soul-Eaters. What should he do? He had to find Wolf. He had to stop them engulfing the world in terror.

The Viper Mage was clutching the Walker's strike-fire and tapping it over the rock, pausing now and then to listen. Faster went the rattles. Faster went the 'tap-tap-tap' of the black stone claw.

Torak's head swam. He tried to move, but the invisible web had him in its grip.

'Tap-tap-tap.'

Between the outstretched arms of the Viper Mage, *the rock began to move*.

Torak blinked. It had to be just a flicker of torchlight . . .

No. There it was again: like a hand pushing up beneath taut-stretched hide. Pushing up *beneath* the rock.

This time there was no mistaking it. Behind the rock – in the burning chaos of the Otherworld – the demons were straining to break through. Smooth, blind heads tented and stretched the stone. Cruel mouths gaped and sucked. Savage claws scrabbled. The wall of the cavern was buckling, fragile as a day-old leaf. Not for long could it withstand such terrible, insatiable hunger.

The Eagle Owl Mage rose and raised one arm, and Torak saw that she held a black oak mace surmounted by a fiery stone.

The Soul-Eaters paused in their dance. *'The fire-opal,'* they breathed.

Bewildered and fascinated, Torak sank to his knees – and the fire-opal filled the cavern with crimson light. It was the blistering heat at the heart of the fiercest ember. It was the clamorous scarlet of fresh blood on snow. It was the blaze of the angriest sunset, and the glare of the Great Auroch in the deep of winter. It was beauty and terror, ecstasy and pain – and the demons wanted it. Their howls shook the cavern as they hurled themselves at the rock, redoubling their onslaught in their frenzy.

Torak swayed. *This* was the secret power of the Soul-Eaters. With this they would bend the demons to their will.

'The fire-opal,' they whispered, as the Eagle Owl Mage held the mace on high, and around her the stone trees thrashed in a soundless wind.

As Torak watched, the Oak Mage and the Bat Mage gnashed their teeth until black spittle flew, and the Viper Mage planted her smoking palms against the rock – and threw up her head and cried, 'The Door – is – found!'

She staggered back, and Torak saw that on the rock she'd completed a great ring of handprints – and inside the ring, the demons were on the point of bursting through.

At that moment, the Eagle Owl Mage lowered the fire-opal, shrouding it in her robes – and its scarlet light was quenched. The taut-stretched rock sprang back. The howls of the demons sank to a furious panting.

'The Door is found,' hissed the Viper Mage, and slumped to the ground in a faint.

The invisible web holding Torak snapped.

He leapt to his feet and ran.

TWENTY-FOUR

Torak raced through the tunnels, skinning his knuckles and barking his shins. He stumbled, and the torch he'd snatched from the forest of stone lurched wildly. As he righted himself, a leathery wing fluttered past his face. He bit back a cry and staggered on.

Twice he thought he heard footsteps, but when he paused, he caught only his own echo. He doubted that the Soul-Eaters would follow him. They didn't need to. Where would he go? The Eye of the Viper was shut.

He closed his mind to that and ran on.

Fragments of what he'd witnessed flashed before his eyes. The thrusting snouts of the demons, fighting to break open the Door. The awful beauty of the fire-opal.

He couldn't believe that it had held him for so long. What spell had it cast, that had made him forget Wolf? Was this how it had been for his father? Drawn in by his curiosity, by his fatal need to know – until it was too late.

Too late. Terror seized him. Maybe it was already too late for Wolf.

As he ran, he spat out the black root, then bit it in two; crammed half in his medicine pouch, and chewed the other. The rotten undertaste made him gag, but he forced himself to swallow. No time for hesitation. He'd seen what the root had done to the Soul-Eaters. Now it had to work for him.

With alarming suddenness the first cramps gripped. Clutching his belly, he staggered into the tunnel of the offerings, jammed the torch in a crack, and fell on all fours.

He retched, spewing up a gobbet of black bile. His eyes were streaming, the tunnel was spinning. His souls were beginning to tug loose.

Still retching, he crawled to the pit that held the ice bear. He caught the sound of furred pads on stone.

Memory reached from the dark and pulled him down. A blue autumn dusk in the Forest. His father laughing at the joke he'd just made. Then, out of the shadows, the bear –

No! he told himself. Don't think about Fa, think about Wolf! *Find* Wolf.

Shivering, he crawled closer, and rested his burning forehead against the rock, peering through the chink between the floor and the slab that covered the pit.

Flinty eyes glared back at him. A growl shuddered through the rock. His spirit quailed. Even starved and weakened, the ice bear was all-powerful. Its souls would be too strong.

More cramps convulsed him. He retched . . .

. . . and suddenly he was trapped in the pit, slitting his eyes against the painful blur of light. He was so hot, so terribly hot. Above him the frail body of a boy taunted him with the maddening scent of fresh meat. The blood-smell was so strong that his claws ached as he paced and turned, and paced again.

He caught the distant murmur of man-voices, and for a moment his mind turned from the blood-smell, and he bared his teeth. He knew those voices. It was the evil ones who had taken him from the ice.

As he remembered his lost home, dull pain coursed through him. They had robbed him of his beautiful cold Sea, where the white whales sleep and the succulent seals swim; of the faithful wind which never failed to waft the blood-smell to his nose. They had stolen his ice, his never-ending ice, which hid him when he hunted, and carried him wherever he wished to go, which was all he'd ever known. They had brought him to this terrible, burning place where there was no ice; where the blood-smell was everywhere, but never within reach.

He growled as he thought how he would seize the heads of the evil ones and crush them in his jaws! He would slash their bellies and feast on their smoking guts and their sweet, slippery fat! Like the pounding of the Sea, the blood-urge thundered through him, and he roared till the rocks shook. He was the ice bear, he feared *nothing*! All, *all* was prey!

Deep inside the marrow of the ice bear, Torak's souls struggled to gain mastery. The bear's spirit was the strongest he'd ever encountered. Never had he been so engulfed by the feelings of another creature.

With a tremendous effort of will, he overcame – and the ice bear ceased to rage at the evil ones, and turned to the blood-smells: the tantalizing web of scent trails which led out into the dark, like the drag-marks after he'd hauled a walrus over the ice.

Close – maddeningly close – he smelt the blood of lynx

and otter, bat and boy; of wolverine and eagle. Further off, he smelt wolf.

Its scent was fainter than the others, and tainted with a badness he didn't understand – but for a bear who could scent a seal through the thickest ice, it was easy to trace.

The trail led down through the dark, and round to the side of his striking-paw – then up again, to where the air smelt cooler. They thought they were cunning to hide the wolf, but he would find it. And when he'd broken free and killed all the others, he would kill the wolf, too. He would catch it in his jaws and shake it till its spine cracked . . .

No! shouted Torak silently.

For a moment the great bear faltered, and in the pulsing marrow of its bones, Torak's souls struggled to escape. He'd smelt enough. His plan had worked. He knew where the Soul-Eaters had hidden Wolf.

The bear's souls were too strong.

He couldn't get out.

TWENTY-FIVE

Renn burst from the weasel hole and toppled headfirst into the snow.

After the heat of the caves, the cold was a knife in her lungs. She didn't care. She rolled onto her naked back and stared up into a blizzard of stars.

From high overhead came the caw of a raven. She gasped a fervent thanks – and her clan-guardian cawed back, warning her that it wasn't over yet.

Her teeth were chattering. She was losing heat fast. Getting to her feet, she discovered that she couldn't find her parka, jerkin or mittens, which she'd pushed before her out of the hole.

After an increasingly desperate search, she fell over them. She bundled them on, and they warmed her in moments. She blessed the skill of the White Fox women.

Above her the stars glimmered as clouds sped across the sky. No sign of the First Tree. And no moon, either.

No moon? But surely it couldn't be the dark of the moon already?

Yes it could. With a shiver she realized that she had no idea how long she'd been underground. She stared at the shadowy bulk of the mountain. Torak and Wolf were somewhere inside, bound for sacrifice in the dark of the moon. Which was now.

She had to find them. She had to go back inside.

As her eyes accustomed to the starlight, she realized that she didn't recognize her surroundings. Before her the weasel hole was a circle of blackness, but she couldn't see the standing stone, or the Eye of the Viper; only humped snow and charcoal rockfaces. For all she knew, she could be on the other side of the mountain.

Frantic, she felt her way forwards – tripped – and pitched into a snowdrift.

A very hard snowdrift, with something solid underneath.

She got to her knees and started to dig.

A skinboat. No. *Two* skinboats: both bigger than the one the White Foxes had given them, and stowed with paddles, harpoons, and rope. The Soul-Eaters had thought of everything. Drawing her knife, she slit the belly of each boat. There. See how far they got now!

From deep within the mountain came a roar.

She ran to the weasel hole. There it was again: the unmistakeable roar of an ice bear. She remembered the murderous chant of the Soul-Eaters. *A bear for strength.*

The roars fell silent. She strained to listen, but from the dark came only a warm uprush of bat-stink. She pictured Torak, alone against the might of the Soul-Eaters. She had to find him.

She thought fast. On her way through the weasel hole, she'd climbed steadily upwards. That must mean that she was now higher up the mountain than when she'd started.

'So head *down!*' she cried.

She ran, plunging into snowdrifts, pulling herself out, but heading down, always down.

With breathtaking suddenness she rounded a spur – and there was the standing stone and the Eye of the Viper. She never thought she'd be so glad to see them.

The Eye was shut, blocked by the slab which the Oak Mage had pushed across it. But maybe she could move it just enough to crawl in.

She put her shoulder against it and heaved. She might as well have tried to shift the mountain itself.

Steam misted from the bottom corner of the slab, where it didn't quite fit across the cave mouth. She tried to squeeze through the gap. It would be big enough for Wolf, but was just a few fingers too narrow for her.

As she stood before the Eye, the truth settled upon her as stealthily as snow. There was only one way back inside. The way she had come.

'I can't,' she whispered. Her breath swirled eerily in the gloom.

She ran back up the trail, and stood panting before the weasel hole. It was tiny. A tiny, cruel mouth waiting to swallow her.

She put back her head. 'I *can't!*'

Moonlight hit her smartly in the face.

She blinked. She'd got it wrong. It wasn't the dark of the moon. Not yet. There – riding above the clouds – was the thinnest of silver slivers: the very last bite that the Sky Bear hadn't yet caught. She still had one day left. And so did Torak and Wolf.

As she gazed up at the pure, steady white light, Renn felt new courage steal into her. The moon was the eternal prey:

eternally in flight across the sky, eternally caught and eaten, but always reborn, always faithfully lighting the way for hunters and prey – even in the very deep of winter, when the sun was dead. Whatever happened, the moon always came back. And so would she.

Before she could change her mind, she raced down the trail to the Soul-Eaters' sleds, where she and Torak had hidden their gear. Luckily there hadn't been any fresh snow, so she easily found her pack.

First she gobbled down a few mouthfuls of blubber, which steadied her a little. Then she packed more blubber in her food pouch for Wolf and Torak, stuck her axe in her belt, and crammed the rest of what she thought she might need in her medicine pouch. Then she raced back to the weasel hole.

The breath sawed painfully in her chest as she yanked her parka and jerkin over her head and rolled them up as small as they would go. The sweat on her skin froze instantly, but she ignored that as she tied her mitten strings round the bundled-up clothes, then fastened the other end to her ankle, so that she'd be dragging them behind her. She allowed herself one final glance at the moon, and muttered a quick prayer of thanks.

The wind burned like ice, but the unclean warmth of the weasel hole was worse. As she crawled into the blackness, panic rose in her throat. She choked it back down.

You did it once, she told herself. You can do it again.

She put down her head and began to crawl.

Ψ

She never knew how long it took her to find her way back inside. Back through the ever-shrinking weasel hole, back

671

through that final, heart-stopping narrowness – then out into the forest of stone, where – amazingly – the Soul-Eaters were nowhere to be found: only a flicker of torchlight, and a grim circle of red handprints on the wall that turned her sick with fear.

Something – maybe her clan-guardian wheeling far overhead – guided her through the twists and turns and sudden jolting drops, until she stumbled into a foetid stench, and the uncertain light of a guttering torch.

She was in a low tunnel with blood-coloured walls and smaller caves branching off it, blocked by slabs of stone. From behind the slabs she caught the scrabbling of claws, and guessed that this was where the "offerings" were confined.

'Torak?' she whispered.

No answer; but the scrabblings stilled.

'Wolf?'

Still nothing. Groping with her hands, she made her way through the gloom.

The torch went out, plunging her into blackness – and she tripped over something lying on the floor.

She lay winded, waiting for disaster to strike. When it didn't, she slipped off her mitten to investigate. Her hand touched the softness of seal-hide. It was a body in a seal-hide parka, lying on the floor.

'Torak?' she whispered.

Silence. He was either sleeping, or . . .

Dreading what she might find, she moved closer. *If he was dead.*

Her mind reeled. His souls might be thronging the dark: angry, bewildered, unable to stay together without Death Marks. His clan-soul might have got separated, leaving behind a demon. A terrible thought, that her friend might have turned against her.

No. She wouldn't believe it. Bringing her hand closer, she held it over where she guessed the face would be – and felt a faint warmth. Breath. He was alive!

Abruptly she drew back her hand. *Maybe it wasn't Torak. Maybe it was a Soul-Eater.*

Warily, she touched the hair. Thick, short, with a fringe across the forehead. A thin face, no beard; but scabbed, which could be snow-burn. It *felt* like Torak. But if she was wrong . . .

She had an idea. If it was Torak, she'd find a scar on his left calf. Last summer he'd been gashed by a boar, and had sewn it up quite badly, then forgotten to take out the stitches. In the end she'd had to do it for him, and he'd become impatient, and they'd bumped their heads, and burst out laughing.

Sliding her hand inside the boot, she ran it over the skin. *Yes*. Beneath her fingers she found the warm, smooth ridges of scarred flesh.

Trembling with relief, she grabbed him by the shoulders. 'Torak! Wake up!'

He was heavy and unresponsive.

She hissed in his ear. 'Stop it! Wake *up*!'

What was *wrong* with him? Had they given him a sleeping-potion?

'Who's there?' a woman called gruffly.

Renn froze.

A faint glow of torchlight appeared at the end of the tunnel.

'Boy?' called the woman. 'Where are you? Answer me!'

Wildly, Renn groped in the dark for a hiding-place. Her fingers found the edge of a slab blocking one of the hollows, but it was too heavy, she couldn't move it. Find another. Fast.

The footsteps came nearer. The torchlight grew brighter.

Renn found a slab that she could just move, pushed it back – quietly, *quietly* – crawled inside, and pulled it shut.

A thin line of light showed through the slit that remained. She held her breath.

The footsteps paused. Whoever it was, they were close.

She turned her head from the torchlight, in case they felt her staring, and fixed her gaze blindly on the dark.

From the back of the hiding-place, a pair of yellow eyes glared back at her.

TWENTY-SIX

In one horrified heartbeat, Renn glimpsed a beak sharp enough to slit a whale's belly; talons that could carry a reindeer calf to a clifftop eyrie.

Drawing in her legs, she shrank against the rock. The hollow was tiny: there was barely space for them both. Her weapons were useless. She pictured lightning-fast talons shredding her face and hands; the Soul-Eaters peering in at her ruined flesh, then finishing off what the eagle had begun.

'Boy!' called the Soul-Eater on the other side of the slab.

The eagle hunched its huge wings and fixed its eyes on Renn.

She heard the scrape of a torch being stuck in a crack; the thin squeak of a bat.

'There you are!' said the Bat Mage.

Renn froze.

'Boy! Wake up!'

'So you found him,' said another woman a little further off. Her voice was low and musical, like water rippling over stones. Renn's skin prickled.

'I can't wake him up,' said the Bat Mage. To Renn's surprise, she sounded concerned.

'He took too much root,' the other said scornfully. 'Leave him. We don't need him till tomorrow.'

The eagle spread its wings as far as it could, warding Renn back. Back where? She had nowhere to go. She tried to make herself even smaller, and an eagle pellet crunched beneath her palm.

The Soul-eaters went silent. Had they heard?

'What are you doing?' said the soft-voiced Soul-Eater.

'Turning him over,' replied the Bat Mage. 'Can't let him sleep on his back. If he's sick, he'll choke.'

'Oh Nef, why bother? He isn't worth – ' she broke off.

'What is it?' said Nef.

'I feel something,' said the other. 'Souls. I feel souls, in the air around us.'

Silence. Again that high, thin squeak.

Renn blinked. The stink of birdlime was making her eyes water and her nose run. She tried not to sniff.

'Your bat feels them too,' said the soft-voiced one.

'There, my beauty,' crooned the Bat Mage. 'But whose souls? Could one of the offerings be dead?'

'I don't think so,' murmured the other. 'It's more . . . No, it doesn't feel like one of them.'

'Still, we'd better check them.'

Terror settled on Renn like a covering of ice.

'Hold my torch,' said the Bat Mage, her voice receding as she moved away.

Renn heard the scrape of stone a few paces away, then the ferocious hiss of a wolverine.

'Well *he's* not dead yet!' laughed the soft-voiced one.

The Bat Mage grunted as she pushed back the stone.

Another slab was scraped aside, nearer Renn's hiding-place. She caught the squeak of an otter.

One by one, the Soul-Eaters checked the offerings, drawing steadily closer to where she huddled. Her mind raced. There was no way out. If she bolted, they'd see her. If she stayed where she was, she'd be caught like a weasel in a trap. She had to stop them looking inside. If she didn't, she was dead.

A fox barked in the hollow next to hers. They were almost upon her. *Think.*

Only one thing to do.

Screwing her eyes shut, she crossed her arms over her face – and kicked the eagle.

It lashed out with an ear-splitting 'klek-klek-klek' – and she felt a chill on her wrists as talons sliced a hair's breadth from her skin.

On the other side of the slab, the Soul-Eaters stopped.

The eagle shook itself angrily, and began preening its ruffled feathers.

Renn cowered with her arms over her face, unable to believe that she was unhurt.

'No point checking that one,' said the Bat Mage. 'Though it sounds like she's hungry again.'

'Oh, leave her!' cried the other impatiently. 'Leave the boy, leave them all! I need rest, and so do you! Let's *go!*'

Yes, go! Renn pleaded silently.

The Bat Mage hesitated. 'You're right,' she said. 'After all, they've only got to live one more day.'

Their footsteps receded down the tunnel.

Renn sagged with relief. With her fingertips she traced the zigzag tattoos on her wrists, and saw again Tanugeak's round, shrewd face. *You'll be needing them, I think.*

It was some time later, and the eagle was becoming restive again, before Renn dared to move. As she rubbed the feeling back into her legs, she heard someone stir on the other side of the slab.

'You can come out now,' whispered Torak.

ᚁ

He still couldn't believe it was really her.

'*Renn?*' he mumbled.

'Thank the Spirit, you're awake!' With her hair stained black, she looked eerily unfamiliar. But she was Renn all right: showing her small, sharp teeth in a wobbly smile, and giving him awkward little pats on the chest.

'Renn . . . ' he said again. The dizziness seized him, and he shut his eyes.

He wanted to tell her everything. About spirit walking in the ice bear, and getting trapped. About hearing Wolf howling – howling *inside* his head – and breaking free of the bear. Above all, he wanted to tell her how incredible, how wonderful it was that she'd made her way through the darkness, and found him.

But when he tried, the bitter bile rose in his throat, and all he managed was, 'I'm – going to be sick.'

He got on all fours and retched, and she knelt beside him, holding back his hair.

When it was over, she helped him stagger to his feet. As they moved into the torchlight, she saw his face for the first time. 'Torak, what *happened* to you? Your lips are black! There's blood on your forehead!'

He flinched from her touch. 'Don't, it's – tainted.'

'What happened?' she said again.

He couldn't bring himself to tell her. Instead he said, 'I know where they've got Wolf. Let's go.'

But as he staggered down the tunnel, she held him back. 'Wait. There's something I've got to tell you.' She paused. 'The Soul-Eaters. They're not only after Wolf. They want to sacrifice you, too!'

Then she told him a story that turned him sick all over again, about a chant she'd overheard in the forest of stone. 'It's a charm that will give them great power, and protect them from the demons.'

His knees buckled, and he leaned against the wall. 'The nine hunters. I heard them say it, but I never thought . . .' With a scowl, he snatched up the torch. 'Come on. Not much time.'

Renn looked puzzled. 'But – isn't Wolf here, with the others?'

'No. I'll tell you as we go.'

His head was clearing fast, and as he led her through the tunnels – trying to remember the scent trails smelt by the bear, and pausing to listen for sounds of pursuit – he told her of the message from across the Sea, which had prompted the Soul-Eaters to keep Wolf separate. Then he told her what he'd witnessed in the caves. The finding of the Door. The Soul-Eaters' plan for flooding the land with terror. The fire-opal.

Once again, Renn halted. 'The *fire-opal*? They've found the fire-opal?'

He stared at her. 'You know about it?'

'Well – yes. But not much.'

'Why haven't you told me?'

'I never thought . . .' She hesitated. 'It's something you hear about in stories, if – if you grow up in a clan.'

'Tell me now.'

She moved closer, and he felt her breath on his cheek. 'The fire-opal,' she whispered, 'is light from the eye of the Great Auroch. That's why the demons are drawn to it.'

He met her gaze, and in the fathomless black he saw two tiny, flickering torches. 'So whoever wields it,' he said, 'controls them.'

She nodded. 'As long as it touches neither earth nor stone, the demons are in thrall, and must do the bidding of the bearer.'

He remembered the crimson glow in the forest of stone. 'But it was so beautiful.'

'Evil can be beautiful,' said Renn with startling coldness. 'Didn't you know that?'

He was still trying to take it in. 'How old is it? When did it – '

'No-one knows.'

'But now it's found,' he murmured.

She licked her lips. 'Who has it?'

'Eostra, the Eagle Owl Mage. But after they found the Door, she disappeared.'

They fell silent, listening to the flutter of bats overhead, and a distant trickle of water, wondering what else thronged the dark.

It was Torak who spoke first. 'Come on. We're nearly there.'

Again, Renn was puzzled. 'How do you know where to go?'

He hesitated. 'I just do.'

ᚴ

They climbed higher, and eventually reached a dank little

cave where a dirty brown stream pooled before disappearing down an echoing hole. A birchbark pail stood beside it, with a wovenbark pouch containing a few scraps of mouldering cod. In a corner they found what appeared to be a pit, covered by a sturdy wattle screen weighted with rocks. Torak's heart raced. He knew – he *knew* – that Wolf was in the pit.

Handing the torch to Renn, he rolled the rocks away, and threw the screen aside.

Wolf lay in a tiny, filthy hole scarcely bigger than he was. He was painfully thin: the bones of his haunches jutted sharply. From his matted fur rose a stink of rottenness. He lay on his belly with his head on his paws, not moving at all, and for one terrible moment, Torak thought he was dead.

'*Wolf!*' he breathed.

The great silver head twitched – but the amber eyes were dull.

'His muzzle,' whispered Renn, 'look at his muzzle!'

It was bound with a length of rawhide, cruelly tight.

Rage burned in Torak's breast. 'I'll fix that,' he said between his teeth. 'Give me your knife.'

Jumping into the pit, he cut the binding. '*Pack-brother,*' he said in a shaky grunt-whine, '*it's me!*'

Wolf's tail didn't even twitch.

'Torak,' Renn said uneasily.

'*Pack-brother,*' Torak said again, more urgently.

'Torak!' cried Renn. '*Get out!*'

Wolf's lips drew back in a snarl, and he staggered to his feet. The instant before he sprang, Torak grabbed the edge of the pit and heaved himself up – while Renn seized his parka and pulled with all her might. He shot out, and they shoved the screen and the rocks back on top just as Wolf leapt, hitting it with a thud.

Renn clamped both hands over her mouth.

Torak stared at her, aghast. 'He doesn't know me,' he said.

TWENTY-SEVEN

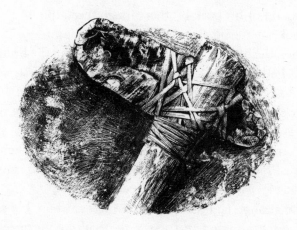

Wolf leapt at the strange, half-grown tailless – but the Den snapped shut, and he fell back onto the stone.

The badness in his tail wouldn't let him rest. He circled until his hind legs shook so much that he had to lie down. His pelt felt hot and tight, and there was a buzzing in his ears. The black fog was hurting his head.

From above him came the yip-and-yowl of the strange taillesses. He twitched his ears in bewilderment. He *knew* those voices. Or he thought he did. But although these taillesses *sounded* familiar, they smelt all wrong. The female smelt of fish-dog and eagle, and the male – who sounded so like Tall Tailless – stank of the bad ones and of the great white bear. Was it Tall Tailless, or wasn't it? Wolf didn't know. He couldn't untangle it in his head.

And yet, not long ago, he *had* caught the scent of his pack-brother, he was sure of it. He'd caught it on the overpelt of the Viper-tongued female; and even though she'd wound the hated deerhide about his muzzle, he had howled for his pack-brother, howled for him inside his head. And for a moment – the swiftest of snaps – he'd heard an answer; and the sound of his pack-brother's rough, beautiful howls had been like gentle breath whiffling through his fur.

Then the black fog had closed in again, and the beautiful howls had changed to the dull roar of a bear. *I am angry!* the bear had roared. *Angry! Angry!* Like all bears, this one was no good at talking, so it just kept saying the same thing over and over.

A scraping above him. Light stung his eyes. Then the lump of birch bark dangled before his nose, and came to rest. Listlessly, he lapped up the wet.

The strange taillesses were peering in at him. He smelt their confusion and fear. Now the half-grown male was leaning down almost within snapping range, giving soft grunt-whines. *'Pack-brother! It's me!'*

That voice . . . so familiar. So soothing to Wolf's aching head, like the feel of cool mud on sore pads.

But maybe Wolf was in the *other* Now, the one he went to in his sleeps. Maybe when he woke up, he would be alone again in this stinking Den.

Or maybe it was another trick of the bad taillesses.

Again the male was leaning in. Wolf saw the short fur on his head: much shorter than Tall Tailless. But he also saw a beloved, flat face, and bright wolf eyes.

Confused, Wolf sniffed the furless paw which reached towards him. It *smelt* a little like Tall Tailless – but was it? Should Wolf lick it? Or snap?

Wolf gave a warning growl, and Torak withdrew his hand.

'He doesn't recognize you,' said Renn.

Torak's fists clenched. 'But he will.' He stared into the tiny, squalid hole. The Soul-Eaters would pay for this. He didn't care if it took him the rest of his life, he would hunt them down and make them pay for what they'd done to Wolf.

'How much time do we have?' said Renn, wrenching him back to the present. 'Where are the Soul-Eaters?'

He shook his head. 'We're well out of earshot from the forest of stone; and from what Seshru said, they'll be resting. I don't think they'll come up here until – until tomorrow, when they open the Door. But that's just a guess.'

Renn nodded grimly. 'One thing's for sure. We won't get far with Wolf like this. He needs food and medicine. Fast.'

Opening her food pouch, she withdrew a slab of blubber, and dropped it into the pit. Wolf fell on it and gulped it down without even chewing.

'Good that you thought to bring food,' said Torak.

'I haven't finished,' muttered Renn. She pulled up the birchbark bowl on its cord, filled it with small, dark pellets from her food pouch, and lowered it into the pit. Wolf's black nose twitched. He heaved himself to his feet, and snuffled them up.

'Lingonberries,' said Renn.

For the first time in days, Torak grinned. Then his gaze returned to Wolf, and his grin faded. 'He will get better. Won't he?'

He saw her struggling to compose her face in an encouraging smile.

'But – Renn,' he faltered, 'it can't be that bad.'

Taking the sputtering torch, she held it over the pit. 'Look at his tail!'

Wolf gave a fierce growl. *Stay away!*

Torak went cold. The tip of Wolf's bushy silver tail was matted with dried blood; but it wasn't that which turned him ill with fear. It was the slimy greenish-black flesh which showed through in patches. Flesh which stank of rottenness.

'It's the blackening sickness,' said Renn. 'It's poisoning him. The worms of sickness are eating him up from inside.'

'But once we get him out into the snow, he'll be better – '

'No, Torak, no. We've got to stop this now, or it'll be too late.'

He knew what she meant, but he couldn't face it. 'There must be something you can do! After all, you know Magecraft!'

'If there was, don't you think I'd have done it? Torak, it's killing him! You know this!' She met his eyes. 'There's only one thing to do. We've got to cut it off.'

山

'You know I'm right,' Renn said again, but she could see that Torak wasn't listening.

Fearfully, she glanced over her shoulder. So far, there had been no sign of the Soul-Eaters.

She turned back to him. 'Do you trust me?' she said.

'What?'

'Do you trust me?'

'Of course I do!'

'Then you must know that I'm telling the truth! Now tell him. Tell Wolf what we have to do to make him better.'

He hesitated; then, slowly, he lowered himself into the pit, talking quietly in wolf talk.

Wolf raised his head and gave a warning growl. To

Renn's horror, Torak ignored it. He crouched, keeping his eyes steady but his gaze soft.

Wolf's hackles were stiff, his ears flat back.

Suddenly he lunged, snapping the air a hand's breadth from Torak's face. The clash of the great jaws rang through the cave.

Torak put his head still closer, and snuffled at the black lips.

Wolf went on growling, staring at Torak with eyes grown dark and threatening.

Torak drew back, and rose to his feet. 'He didn't understand,' he said dully.

'Why not?'

'I – I couldn't find a way to say it; to tell him this will make him better. Because in wolf talk there is no future.'

'Oh,' said Renn.

Slowly, she drew the axe from her belt: the axe she had known – with the knowledge which came to her some-times – that she would need. 'Take it.'

Torak didn't answer. He was staring at the axe.

'We'll only – cut off the tip,' she said. 'About the length of your thumb.' She swallowed. 'Torak. You've got to. He's your pack-brother.'

He took the axe. Weighed it in his hand.

Wolf raised his head, then slumped onto his side, his flanks heaving.

Torak braced his legs and raised the axe.

Renn felt sick. It was the vision of the White Fox elder.

Slowly, Torak lowered the axe. 'I *can't*,' he whispered. He glanced up at her, his eyes glistening. 'I can't.'

After a moment's hesitation, Renn let herself down into the pit. There was just enough room for her to stand beside him. She took the axe from his hand.

Wolf cast her a narrow glance, and drew back his lips to show his fearsome teeth.

'We should bind up his muzzle,' she breathed.

'No,' said Torak.

'He'll bite!'

'*No!*' he said fiercely. 'If I bind his muzzle now, he'll think I'm no better than the Soul-Eaters! If I don't – if I trust him not to hurt me – then maybe – *maybe* – he'll trust me to let us help him.'

For a moment they stared at one another. She saw the conviction in his face, and knew his mind was made up.

'I won't let him bite you,' he said, placing himself between her and Wolf's jaws. As he went down on his knees, Wolf raised his head and sniffed his fingers, then lay back again.

With his left hand, Torak stroked the fluffy fur behind Wolf's ears, whiffling and grunt-whining under his breath. His right hand passed gently over Wolf's flank, then over the haunch. When he reached the base of the tail, Wolf's muzzle wrinkled in a snarl.

Torak's hand continued – slowly – down the tail.

Wolf growled until his whole body shook.

Torak froze.

Then his fingers moved a little further, till they'd nearly reached the rottenness at the tip. His hand closed over the tail, holding it down.

With blinding speed, Wolf lunged – and seized Torak's other wrist in his jaws. His teeth clamped tight around the bone, denting the skin but not piercing it: poised to crush.

Renn held her breath. She'd once seen Wolf crack the thighbone of an elk. He could sever Torak's wrist as easily as snapping a twig.

Wolf's great amber eyes fixed on Torak's: waiting to see what he would do.

Torak's face glistened with sweat as he met Wolf's gaze. 'Get ready,' he told Renn.

She rearranged her icy fingers on the axe-hilt.

Torak never took his eyes from Wolf's. 'Do it,' he said.

TWENTY-EIGHT

Wolf's tail still hurt, but it was a clean hurt, and the badness was gone.

The black fog was gone too, and with it the last of his doubts. This half-grown male really was Tall Tailless.

It was the black fog which had made him glare at his pack-brother, and take his forepaw in his jaws. *If you harm me*, Wolf had told him with his eyes, *I bite*. But the gaze of Tall Tailless had been steady and true; and suddenly Wolf had remembered the time when he was a cub, and was choking on a duck bone, and Tall Tailless had grabbed his belly and squeezed. Wolf had been so outraged that he'd twisted round to bite, but Tall Tailless had kept squeezing, and the duck bone had shot out of Wolf's muzzle – and he'd understood. Tall Tailless had been *helping* him.

This was why Wolf had let the pack-sister cut his tail with the big stone claw. This was why he hadn't bitten his pack-brother's forepaw. Because they were helping him.

Now it was over, and the pack-sister was leaning against the side of the Den, panting, while Tall Tailless sat with his head in his forepaws, shaking all over.

Wolf went to sniff the bit of tail which lay upon the stone: the bit of tail which had been Wolf, but was now just a scrap of bad meat, not worth eating. Then he nose-nudged Tall Tailless under the chin to say sorry for glaring at him, and Tall Tailless made an odd gulping noise, and buried his muzzle in Wolf's scruff.

After that, things got better. The pack-sister gave Wolf more lingonberries, and delicious slithery chunks of fish-dog fat, and he felt his strength racing back. Tall Tailless sat beside him, scratching his flank, and the pack-sister dipped the bitten end of his tail in a thin mud that smelt of honey and wet ferns. Wolf let her do this, because he knew that she was making him better.

Putting his muzzle between his paws, he shut his eyes, and gave himself up to the scratching of his pack-brother, and the wonderful cool mud that was chasing away the last of the badness.

Wolf recovered with a speed that astonished and gratified Renn.

Already his fur seemed sleeker, and his nose had lost that dull, hot look. At the end of his tail – now a thumblength shorter than before – the wound smelt clean and fresh. To her surprise, Wolf had let her dress it with a salve of elder and meadowsweet in chewed blubber. He'd even let her bind it in wovenbark, which he'd made only a half-hearted attempt to eat.

It was Torak who couldn't watch; who seemed unable to

bear the sight of the wound, as if he felt the pain more than Wolf himself.

'He really is getting better,' said Renn, to reassure him. 'I think wolves heal faster than we do. Do you remember last autumn in the Moon of Roaring Stags, when he went after blackberries and tore his ear? Three days later, there wasn't even a scab.'

'I'd forgotten that.' He forced a smile. 'And your salve is helping, too.'

'He's getting stronger all the time,' she said, drawing her medicine pouch shut. 'I think we should – '

A bat fluttered overhead, and of one accord they paused to listen.

Nothing.

Three times during the day – this strange underground day that felt more like night – Torak had made his way back to the forest of stone, and stolen a freshly dipped torch, and checked that the Soul-Eaters were still sleeping off their trance. But they couldn't count on that for much longer.

'We should get him out of this pit,' said Renn. 'We can make a sling of our belts, and haul him out. If he'll let us.'

'He'll let us. You said Thiazzi's blocked the cave mouth?'

'Yes. We *might* be able to shift it.'

'We'll have to. It's the only way out.'

'No it isn't.' Reluctantly, she told him about the weasel hole.

Normally he would have wanted to know everything about it, including why she hadn't told him sooner; but instead he seemed distracted. She wondered if he was worrying about the same thing that had begun to trouble her.

She watched him nuzzle Wolf's scruff. Wolf flicked one

ear, and they exchanged one of those speaking glances that used to make her feel left out; but she didn't mind any more, she was just glad that Torak had his pack-brother back.

'The blood of the nine hunters,' he said suddenly. 'It's to protect them from the demons, isn't it, when they open the Door?'

She nodded. 'I've been thinking about that, too. Even for the Soul-Eaters, it's going to be incredibly hard to keep the Door open for more than a few heartbeats. But that'll be enough.'

They pictured demons spreading like a black flood over the snow. Across the ice. Towards the Forest.

'And the fire-opal,' said Torak, 'it will give them control once the demons are out.'

'Yes.'

He passed his hand over Wolf's flank, and Wolf stirred his tail in acknowlegement, taking care not to thump it.

'How can it be destroyed?' said Torak. 'Hammered? Thrown into the Sea?'

Her fingers tightened on her medicine pouch. 'Nothing so simple. You can only rob it of its power by burying it under earth or stone. And – ,' she hesitated. 'It needs a life. A life buried with it. Otherwise it won't be appeased.'

Torak rested his chin on his knees and frowned. 'When I put the Death Marks on my father,' he said, surprising her, 'I didn't do it very well. Especially not here, for the clan-soul.' He touched his breastbone. 'He had a scar, where he'd cut out the Soul-Eater tattoo.'

Renn swallowed.

'I couldn't go back and make things right for him,' he went on. 'Gather his bones, lay them to rest in the Wolf Clan bone-ground – wherever that is – because ever since then, in one way or another, I've been fighting the Soul-Eaters.' He paused. 'I left him because he told me to. Because he knew it was my destiny to fight the Soul-Eaters. I don't think I can turn my back on that destiny now.'

Renn didn't reply. This was what she'd feared.

She wished desperately that they could find their way out of these horrible caves, retrieve their skinboat, and get back to the White Foxes. Then Inuktiluk could take them on his dog sled to the Forest, and they would be with Fin-Kedinn again, and it would be over. But she knew this wasn't going to happen.

Torak raised his head, and his grey eyes were steady. 'This isn't about rescuing Wolf any more. I can't just run off and leave them to open the Door.'

'I know,' said Renn.

'Do you?' His face was open and vulnerable. 'Because I can't do this on my own. And I can't ask you to help. You've already done so much.'

That annoyed her. 'I know what we've got to do just as well as you do! We've got to make sure that Wolf is free, and then,' she caught her breath, 'then *we've* got to stop them opening the Door.'

TWENTY-NINE

After something of a struggle, they managed to haul
Wolf out of the pit, and headed off. Their way led
through the tunnel of the offerings, where they were
relieved to find no sign of the Soul-Eaters, although they'd
been there recently. The hole which had held the lynx was
empty.

Torak was wondering what this meant when Wolf gave a
low, urgent 'uff'!

'Hide!' he whispered – but Renn knew enough wolf talk
to recognize the warning, and was already scrambling into
the lynx's hollow. Torak pushed the slab across it, and an
instant later, Nef's bat flitted past his face.

'Boy?' called Nef from the end of the tunnel. 'Where are
you?'

Torak glanced behind him at Wolf, whose amber eyes
glowed in the torchlight. If Nef saw him . . .

As the Bat Mage limped towards them, Wolf turned and

melted into the dark. Torak breathed out in relief. He shouldn't have doubted Wolf. If he didn't want to be seen, it didn't happen.

'I'm here,' he said, struggling to keep his voice steady.

'Where have you been?' snapped Nef.

Rubbing his face, he tried to look bleary. 'I was asleep. That root . . . my head hurts.'

'Of course it hurts! You've got to be strong to be a Soul-Eater!'

To Torak's alarm, she stopped right outside Renn's hiding-place, and leaned her hand on the rock.

He edged away, in the hope that she would follow.

She didn't. Propping her torch against the wall, she squatted on her haunches. 'Strong,' she repeated, as if to herself, 'you've got to be *strong*.' She opened her hands and stared at them. They were dark with blood.

'The lynx,' said Torak. 'You've killed it. The sacrifice has begun.'

As Nef held her tainted hands before her, her fists clenched. 'It has to be done! The few *must* suffer for the good of the many!'

Torak licked his lips. He had to get rid of the Bat Mage before she discovered Renn. And yet . . .

'You don't have to do this,' he said.

Nef's head jerked up.

'The sacrifice. The Door.'

'*What?*' snarled the Bat Mage.

'These are demons!'

'That's the beauty of it! Demons don't *know* right from wrong! We can bend them to our will! Don't you see? This is our chance to make things right! To enforce the way of the World Spirit!'

'By breaking clan law?'

Nef stared at him. Suddenly she lurched to her feet, snatched the torch, and brought it close to his face: so close that he heard the sputtering hiss of pine-pitch. 'You were a coward,' she said, 'grovelling, whining – but not any more. Why did you hide your true nature?'

Torak did not reply.

She lowered the torch. 'Ah, but what does it matter now?'

A patch of darkness cut across the light, and dropped onto her shoulder. As Torak watched her stroke the soft bat fur, he wondered how she could caress her clan-creature, and yet stain her spirit with sin.

'The Opening of the Door is nearly upon us,' said Nef. 'You have work to do. Bring the offerings to the forest of stone.'

He stared at her. 'You mean – '

'We're going to kill them. We're going to kill them all!'

He swallowed. 'Where – where are you going?'

'Me?' barked Nef. 'I'm going to take care of the wolf.'

Ψ

'What were you *thinking*?' whispered Renn after the Bat Mage had gone. 'Arguing with a Soul-Eater? With me right there, waiting to be discovered?'

'I thought I might be able to change her mind,' said Torak.

'Torak, she's a Soul-Eater!'

She was right; but he didn't want to admit it.

'Come on,' he said brusquely. 'When she finds Wolf gone, she'll raise the alarm. We've got to free the offerings and get out of here!'

Swiftly, straining their ears for footsteps, they worked

their way down the tunnel, heaving rocks aside and setting the captives free. The fox and the otter fled the moment there was a gap big enough to wriggle through. The eagle gave them an outraged glare, hitched its bedraggled wings, and swept off into the dark. The wolverine was a spitting bundle of rage, and would have attacked them both if Wolf hadn't emerged from the shadows and seen it off.

'Phew!' panted Renn. 'That's gratitude!'

'Do you think they'll find their way out?' said Torak.

She nodded. 'That gap between the slab and the cave mouth. They'll get through.'

'And Wolf?'

'It's big enough for him. But not for us. And I don't think we should count on being able to shift that slab.'

'You mean – we'll have to use the weasel hole.'

The blood drained from her face. 'If we get the chance.'

They fell silent. They hadn't been able to come up with a plan for stopping the Soul-Eaters, other than making their way to the forest of stone, and doing – something.

Wolf's claws clicked as he trotted to the end of the tunnel, then abruptly stopped. He stared into the pit of the ice bear.

With a sense of foreboding, Torak went to investigate. What he saw made his knees give. 'We'll have a better chance than these two,' he said.

'What do you mean?' said Renn.

He moved aside to let her see.

The Soul-Eaters had slaughtered the ice bear and skinned it, leaving the reeking, steaming carcass in the pit. They'd done the same to the lynx, then tossed its corpse onto the bear's.

Renn sagged against the cave wall. 'How *could* they? They've just left them to rot.'

This is evil, thought Torak. This is what evil looks like.

In death the ice bear seemed pathetically smaller. Torak's heart twisted with pity. 'May your souls find their way back to the ice,' he murmured. 'May they be at peace.'

'Torak . . .' Renn's voice seemed to come to him from a distance. 'It's time. We've got to go. We've got to stop them opening the Door!'

�111

In the forest of stone, the rite of the Opening had already begun.

As Torak crouched in the shadows at the mouth of the cavern, his spirit faltered. Wolf trembled against him. Renn stood rigid.

The stone trees were spattered with scarlet. Acrid black smoke snaked from the altar, where the Soul-Eaters had made an offering of their hair. The Oak Mage and the Viper Mage prowled the shadows, jabbing at the dark with three-pronged forks, fending off the vengeful souls of the murdered hunters. Both were unrecognizable in their dead-eyed masks, their painted lips flecked with black foam. Both were stripped to the waist, clad only in a slimy, glistening hide.

The Viper Mage wore the lynx pelt: its gaping head set upon her own, its sleek hide rippling down her back as she brandished the Walker's strike-fire.

The Oak Mage had become the ice bear. With his hands thrust inside the forepaws, he wove between the stone saplings, hissing, slicing the air with his claws.

Only the Eagle Owl Mage was unchanged. Rooted to the stone, she faced the wall where the red handprints marked the Door. Her corpse hands covered the mace on which the fire-opal was set.

With a supreme effort, Torak shook himself free of the spell. Whatever they did, they had to act fast. Any moment now, and Nef would raise the alarm.

'The torches,' he breathed in Renn's ear. 'I can't see more than three. If we can put them out, then maybe . . .'

Renn didn't stir. She couldn't seem to take her eyes off the Soul-Eaters.

'Renn!' He shook her shoulder. 'The torches! We've got to do something!'

She dragged her gaze away. 'Here,' she whispered. 'Take my knife. I'll keep my axe.'

He nodded. 'The weasel hole. Where is it?'

'There, behind that greenish sapling. There's a big crack, you've got to climb up – '

'All right. We should be able to reach it, when the time comes.'

Suddenly he knelt, and pressed his face against Wolf's muzzle. Wolf gave a faint wag of his tail, and licked his ear.

'He'll find the other way out,' breathed Torak as he straightened up. 'He's got a better chance than we have.'

'And before then?' said Renn. 'How do we stop them?'

Torak stared at the circling, hissing Soul-Eaters. 'You see if you can douse the torches, while I keep them talking – '

'While you *what?*'

Before she could stop him, he'd risen to his feet, and stepped out into the light.

With startling speed the lynx and the ice bear spun round, and stared at him with dead gutskin eyes.

'The ninth hunter is come,' said the Oak Mage in a voice as deep as a bear's.

'But his hands are empty,' hissed the Viper Mage. 'He was to have brought the eagle, the wolverine, the otter, the fox.'

The talons of the Eagle Owl Mage tightened around the

700

head of the mace. 'Why has it failed?'

Torak opened his mouth to speak, but no sound came. What was Renn doing? Why were the torches still burning?

Desperately, he sought for some way of grabbing the fire-opal, and stopping them from opening the Door – of achieving the impossible.

A shout rang through the cavern – and Nef hobbled in. 'The wolf is gone!' she shouted. 'It's the boy, I know it is! He set the wolf free! He set them all free!'

Three masked heads turned towards Torak.

'Free?' said the Viper Mage with appalling gentleness.

Torak edged backwards.

The Bat Mage blocked his way.

The Oak Mage wiped the black froth from his painted lips and said, '"*The Wolf lives.*" That was the message from our brother across the Sea. What did it mean, we asked ourselves.'

'Then a boy came,' said the Viper Mage. 'A boy who wore the tattoos of the White Foxes, but didn't look like one. I felt souls in the air around me. What does this mean, I asked myself.'

Torak's hand tightened on his knife. And still the torches burned, and still the Soul-Eaters bore down on him.

'Who are you?' said the Oak Mage.

'*What* are you?' said the Viper Mage.

THIRTY

Tall Tailless was surrounded. Bravely he faced them, clutching the big claw; but against three full-grown taillesses, he didn't stand a chance.

Wolf lowered his head and crept forwards. The bad ones didn't hear him. They didn't know he was there.

Swivelling one ear, he heard the stealthy padding of the female, a few pounces away. A sizzling hiss, and that part of the Den went dark. Good. She was helping him. Wolf could see in the dark, but the bad ones couldn't.

Tall Tailless said something defiant in tailless talk, and the pale-pelt who stank of bear gave a cruel laugh. Then another part of the Den went dark. And another.

Suddenly, Stinkfur and Pale-Pelt leapt at Tall Tailless. He didn't dodge quickly enough – it didn't matter – Wolf was quicker than any of them. With a snarl he sprang at Pale-Pelt, knocking him to the ground and sinking his teeth into a forepaw. Pale-Pelt roared. Bones crunched. Wolf leapt away, gulping bloody flesh.

As he ran, his claws skittered on stone and he nearly went down, wobbling as he righted himself, because his newly shortened tail didn't give quite the balance it had before. He'd have to be careful, he thought as he raced through the dark to help his poor, blind pack-brother, who was still trying to get away from Stinkfur.

Not far off, the pack-sister held a glowing branch in one paw, narrowing her eyes as taillesses do when they cannot see.

Meanwhile, the Viper-Tongue had not been idle. She'd found her way through the silent trees, and past the Stone-Faced One to the end of the Den, where she was scraping a claw over the rock, hissing and whining in a way that made Wolf's pelt shrink with dread. He heard the clamour of demons. He didn't know what she meant to do, but he knew that he had to stop her.

And yet – Tall Tailless needed him! In his blindness, he was blundering towards Stinkfur!

Wolf faltered.

He decided in a snap – and leapt to the aid of his pack-brother, body-slamming him out of the path of the bad one. Tall Tailless slipped – steadied himself – and grabbed his pack-brother's scruff. Wolf led him to safety through the trees.

But it was too late to stop Viper-Tongue. Her whines rose to a hide-prickling scream as she spread her forepaws wide – and suddenly in the rock, a great mouth gaped.

Stone-Face gave a triumphant howl that pierced Wolf's ears like splintered bone. Then she lifted her forepaw high. The Den filled with the hard grey glare of the Bright Beast-that-Bites-Cold – *and the demons poured forth*.

Tall Tailless let go of Wolf's scruff and fell to his knees.

The pack-sister dropped the glowing branch and covered her ears with her forepaws. Wolf shrank trembling against Tall Tailless, as the terror of the demons blasted his fur.

He knew he had to attack them – it was what he was meant to do – but there were so many! Slithering, swooping, scrabbling over each other in their hunger for the cold grey light. Wolf saw their dripping fangs and their cruel, bright eyes. There were so *many* . . .

But suddenly, he smelt rage.

The female tailless had shaken off her fear, and was snarling with rage!

In amazement Wolf watched her snatch up the still-glowing branch, and hurl it at Viper-Tongue. It struck her full in the back – when she threw something, the female rarely missed – and Viper-Tongue howled with fury. Her forepaws lifted away from the rock, and the gaping Mouth crashed shut.

But even in so short a time, the demons had come pouring from it, and now the forest of stone thronged with them: swarming about the Bright Beast-that-Bites-Cold. And still Stone-Face held it high, forcing them to her will. And Wolf sensed that neither Tall Tailless nor the female – nor he himself – dared attack her, for they knew that she was the very evil of evils.

He was wrong.

The pack-sister's attack had roused Tall Tailless, and now he barked to her, and she turned and tossed him her great claw: the one that had bitten off part of Wolf's tail.

Tall Tailless caught it in one forepaw – then ran towards Stone-Face – towards the demons!

Terror dragged at Wolf's paws, but he loved his pack-brother too much to forsake him now. Together they ran through the fog of fear. Then Tall Tailless drew back his

704

forepaw and swung the great claw – not at Stone-Face, not at the demons – but at a thin stone sapling towering overhead.

Clever Tall Tailless! The trunk cracked – teetered – and crashed down. The demons screeched and skittered away like ants from an auroch's hooves, and Stone-Face was brought down, and the Bright Beast flew from her forepaw, clattering across the floor – and its cold light was swallowed by the Dark.

As one, the demons howled. They were free! And now they were spreading through the Den like a great Fast Wet, and Wolf hid with Tall Tailless in the thicket of stone, his heart bursting with terror and despair as they swept past him.

Already he could hear the bad taillesses fighting among themselves, blaming each other for the loss of the Bright Beast-that-Bites-Cold. Only Wolf saw the pack-sister stumble upon it and snatch it up, and hide it in the scrap of swan's hide that hung about her neck.

Then she grabbed Tall Tailless by the forepaw, and dragged him by the dim glow of the branch towards a smaller Den high in the side of the main Den; a narrow Den like a weasel's tunnel, through which flowed the clean, cold smell of the Up.

With a pang, Wolf realized what they meant to do. They meant to go by a path he couldn't take. His tail drooped as he watched them peel off their overpelts and make ready to go.

Tall Tailless knelt. *Go!* He told Wolf. *Find the other way out! Meet us in the Up!* And Wolf wagged his tail to reassure him, because he sensed his pack-brother's worry, his unwilling-ness to leave him.

Then they were gone, and Wolf turned on one paw and

raced from the Den, following the clean, cold scent pouring in from the Up.

Torak was lost in an endless tunnel of crawling and gasping, and more crawling. This terrible, terrible hole. How had Renn managed it, not once, but three times?

It was night when they dropped exhausted into the snow. A windy night in the dark of the moon, with only the glow of stars on snow to light the way – and no sign of Wolf.

At least, not yet, Torak told himself. But he'll make it out. If anyone can, it's Wolf.

After the warmth of the caves, the cold was merciless, and their teeth chattered too hard for speech as they struggled to untie their bundled-up clothes and yank them on.

'The fire-opal,' panted Torak at last. 'I saw it fall – it touched rock. That means the demons are free!'

Renn gave a terse nod. In the starlight her face was pale, and her black hair made her look like someone else.

'Did you see where it fell?' said Torak. 'Did one of them pick it up?'

She opened her mouth – then shook her head. 'Come on,' she muttered, 'we've got to reach the skinboat before they get out!'

He didn't know if she meant the Soul-Eaters or the demons. He didn't ask.

Floundering through the snow, they made their way round the spur. The Eye of the Viper was shut, but as they reached it, Torak glimpsed a small, pale shape slip through a gap and race away. His heart leapt. The white fox had found the way out!

706

He turned to Renn, and saw that she was smiling. At least someone had escaped.

As they watched, they saw the scuttling darkness of the wolverine – who for once was more intent on getting away than on biting anyone. Then the eagle emerged: ungainly in the snow, until she spread her wings and lifted into the sky.

'Go safely, my friend,' Renn said softly. 'May your guardian fly with you!'

Then came the otter: pausing for a moment to dart Torak a penetrating glance before streaking off down the mountain. And finally – when Torak was turning sick with dread – Wolf.

He had a struggle to squeeze through the hole, but once he was out, he simply shook himself and came bounding down to them with his tongue hanging out, as casually as if he fled demon-haunted caves every night of his life.

When he reached Torak, he rose lightly on his hind legs, put his forepaws on Torak's shoulders, and covered his face in wet wolf kisses.

Heedless of the Soul-Eaters – heedless of demons – Torak snuffle-licked him back. Then together they raced down to the sleds, and Wolf bounded about in circles while they hurriedly retrieved their packs.

Down the mountain they ran, with Wolf pausing to let them catch up. At the head of the iced-in bay, he helped them find their skinboat, buried beneath a fresh fall of snow.

But when the skinboat was in the water, and hastily loaded with their gear, when Renn and Torak had taken their places – Wolf refused to jump in.

'Can't you make him?' cried Renn.

With a sinking feeling, Torak took in the set of Wolf's

ears, and the stubborn spread of his paws. 'No,' he said. He heaved a sigh. 'He hates skinboats. And he's better off going overland. They'll never catch him.'

'Are you sure?' said Renn.

'No!' he snapped. 'But it's what he means to do!' Of course he wasn't sure. Even in the Forest, a lone wolf's life is a short one – but out here, on the ice?

There wasn't even time to say goodbye. As Wolf stood looking down at him, their eyes met briefly – but before Torak could speak, Wolf had turned and sped away, a silver streak racing over the snow.

The sun was just cresting the mountain as they brought the boat about and headed south, slicing the water with their paddles. Luckily, the wind was behind them, so they made good speed.

When they were out of arrowshot, Torak turned.

'Look,' said Renn.

The mountainside was still in shadow, but stark against the grey snow, Torak saw a darker shadow pouring down the slope.

'Demons,' he said.

Renn met his gaze, and in the gloom her eyes were blacker than the Sea.

'We failed,' she said. 'The demons are loose upon the world.'

THIRTY-ONE

Far away on the northernmost edge of the Forest, the sun rose over the High Mountains. Around the Raven camp, birch trees stirred uneasily as they dreamed.

'Demons,' said Saeunn, crouching on a willow mat to read the embers. 'I see demons coming from the Far North. A black flood, drowning all who stand in its path.'

Only Fin-Kedinn heard her. The hunting had been good, and the rest of the clan was asleep, their bellies full of baked red deer, and rowanberry mash; but the Raven Leader and his Mage had sat up all night at the entrance to his shelter, while the stars faded and the sky turned grey, and around them the Forest slept on in the hushed radiance of a heavy snowfall.

'And there can be no doubt?' said Fin-Kedinn. 'It is the work of the Soul-Eaters?'

As the Raven Mage stared into the embers, the veins on

her bald pate throbbed like tiny snakes. 'The fire spirit never lies.'

An ember cracked. Snow pattered down from the spruce tree overhead. Fin-Kedinn glanced up – and went very still.

'We've come too far north,' said Saeunn. 'If we stay here, there'll be nothing between us and the demons!'

'What about Renn and Torak?' said Fin-Kedinn, his eyes fixed on the spruce.

'What about the clan?' retorted Saeunn. 'Fin-Kedinn, we must go south! We must head for the Widewater, take refuge at the Guardian Rock! There I can weave spells to protect us, set lines of power about the camp.'

When Fin-Kedinn did not reply, she said, 'This must be the end to what you've been thinking.'

The Raven Leader dragged his gaze back to the Mage. 'And what have I been thinking?' he said in a quiet voice that would have made any other clan member blanch.

Saeunn was undaunted. 'You cannot lead us into the Far North.'

'Oh, I wouldn't lead *you*, Mage. I'd make sure that you stayed here, in the Forest – '

'I'm not thinking of myself, but of the clan, as you well know!'

'And so am I.'

'But – '

'Enough!' With a slicing motion of his palm, he cut short their talk. 'When I tell you how to do Magecraft, you may tell me how to lead!'

Again he raised his head, and this time he spoke not to Saeunn, but to the creature who stared down at him from the spruce tree: the eagle owl with the feathered ears and the fierce orange glare, who sat watching. Listening.

'I won't lead the clan out of the Forest,' said Fin-Kedinn

without dropping his gaze. 'I swear it on my souls.'

The eagle owl spread its enormous wings and glided north.

THIRTY-TWO

Torak and Renn made good speed, and for a while, relief at having escaped the caves raised their spirits. It was good to be out in the brilliance of ice and Sea and sky; to hear Wolf's brief, reassuring howls drifting from the east – *I'm here! I'm here!* – and to howl back an answer.

'They'll never catch us now!' yelled Renn.

She told Torak how she'd slashed the Soul-Eaters' skinboats, and he laughed. Wolf was free, and they were heading back to the Forest. Soul-Eaters and demons seemed very far away.

Then, quite suddenly, the day turned. Flinty clouds darkened the sun. Fog crept in from the Sea. Torak's head ached with fatigue. His paddle was heavy in his hands.

'We've got to rest,' said Renn. 'If we don't, we'll capsize, or crash into an ice mountain.'

He nodded, too exhausted to speak.

It took all their strength to haul the skinboat out of the

water, and drag it across the sea ice to the shelter of an ice hill; to prop it up on shoresticks, and pack snow over it for a makeshift shelter.

As he worked, Torak remembered the sudden stillness that had come over the Viper Mage. 'What are you?' she had said. She had sensed his souls in the tunnel of the offerings, as they were making their way back to his body; maybe she had guessed that he was a spirit walker.

From far away came the deep 'oo-hu, oo-hu' of an eagle owl.

Renn paused with her mittens full of snow. Her face was taut. 'They're after us.'

'I know,' said Torak.

'Oo-hu, oo-hu.'

He searched the sky, but saw only fog.

Renn had already gone inside the shelter, and he was alone on the ice. Sounds came to him unnaturally loud: the moaning of the wind, the distant boom of crashing ice. His head ached, his eyes stung. Even the shelter and the hill were strangely blurred.

Out of the corner of his vision, he caught movement.

He spun round.

Something small and dark, flitting from ridge to ridge.

His mouth went dry. A demon?

He wished Wolf were here. But he hadn't heard a howl since mid-afternoon.

Drawing his father's knife, he went to investigate.

Nothing behind the ice hill. But he *had* seen it.

He sheathed his knife and crawled into the shelter. Renn was already huddled in her sleeping-sack. He didn't tell her what he'd seen.

They were too exhausted to pound blubber for the lamp, or to force down more than a few bites of frozen seal meat.

Renn fell asleep instantly, but Torak lay awake, thinking about that dark shape flitting from ridge to ridge.

The demons were out there. He could feel them sapping his spirits, quenching courage and hope.

And it's your fault, he thought. You failed, and now they're loose. It was all for nothing.

He woke feeling stiff and sore. His eyes felt as if someone had rubbed sand in them. He couldn't think of a single reason for getting up. The demons were loose. It was no use fighting back.

Outside, Renn was moving about in the snow. *Why* did she have to make so much noise? Surely she knew that every crunch of her boots was ramming another icicle into his head.

To put off going outside, he checked what remained of his gear. In the rush to get away, he'd left behind his axe and bow, but his waterskin was still around his neck, his tinder pouch and medicine pouch on his belt, and Fa's knife safe in its sheath.

The hilt felt curiously hot. Maybe it was an omen. He should probably ask Renn. But that would only give her a chance to boast about how much more she knew than him. The thought filled him with unreasonable rage.

When he couldn't put it off any longer, he crawled outside.

Overnight, the breath of the World Spirit had swallowed the world. The ice – the Sea – it had taken it all. The wind had gone. Without it, the cold wasn't so biting; but the boom of breaking ice was closer.

That's all we need, thought Torak. The thaw is coming.

'You look terrible,' snapped Renn. 'Your eyes – you should've worn your snow-visor.'

'I *know*,' growled Torak.

'Then why didn't you?'

Her voice was so grating. She was always telling him what to do. And *she*, of course, had worn her visor all day, because *she* never forgot anything.

In prickly silence they dismantled the shelter, and carried the skinboat to the edge of the ice; then went back to fetch their gear.

'Just as well I thought to slash their boats,' boasted Renn, 'or they'd have caught up with us by now.'

'Boats can be mended,' Torak said nastily. 'You won't have slowed them down for long.'

She put her hands on her hips. 'I suppose you think I should've made a better job of it? Well I didn't have time, I had to go and rescue you!'

'You didn't *rescue* me!' spat Torak.

She snorted.

To give her something to snort about, he told her why the Soul-Eaters were coming after them: about the spirit walking, and Seshru sensing his souls.

Her jaw dropped. 'You were *spirit walking*? And you never told me?'

'So? I'm telling you now.'

She was silent. 'Anyway, you're wrong,' she said. 'They're not following us because of that.'

'Oh no? What makes you so sure?'

'It's the fire-opal. I took it. That's why they're after us.'

'Why didn't you *tell* me?' cried Torak.

'I'm telling you now. There wasn't time before.'

'There was plenty of time!' he shouted.

'Don't shout at me!' shouted Renn.

He was shaking his head. 'So it's not only the Soul-Eaters who are after us, it's the demons as well!'

'I did mask it,' she said defensively. 'I've got herbs, and I put it in a swansfoot pouch that Tanugeak gave me.'

He threw up his arms. 'Oh, well that makes it all right! How could you be such a fool?'

'How could *you*? You were the one who spirit walked!'

Her voice rang out across the ice. The silence that followed was louder. They stood glaring at each other, chests heaving.

Torak passed his hand over his face, as if he'd just woken up. 'What are we *doing*?' he said.

Renn shook her head to clear it. 'It's the demons. They're making us fight.' She hesitated. 'I think they can smell the fire-opal. Or – sense it.'

He nodded. 'That must be it.'

'No, no, I mean, I *know* they can.' She caught her lower lip in her teeth. 'I heard noises in the night.'

'What kind of noises?'

She shuddered. 'I stayed awake to keep watch. Then I heard Wolf. He was howling, the way he does before he goes hunting. After that they were gone.'

He took a few paces, then turned back to her. 'We've got to get rid of it.'

'How? We'd have to bury it in earth or stone – and there isn't any out here, there's only ice!'

They stared bleakly at each other.

Renn opened her mouth to speak . . .

. . . and an ear-splitting crack split the air, as a fine black line zigzagged across the ice a hand's breadth from her boots.

She stared at her feet.

The sea ice gave a sudden heave, and she staggered back.

The black line was now a channel of water as wide as a paddle blade.

'A tide crack,' said Torak in disbelief.

Time seemed to slow. He saw that he stood on the landfast ice – the side that held the boat and their provisions – while Renn stood on the other side: the side that was breaking away.

'Jump,' he told her.

The floe lurched. She braced her legs to keep from falling.

'*Jump!*' he cried.

Her face was blank with shock. 'I can't. It's too late.'

She was right. The crack was already more than two paces wide.

'I'll get the boat,' he said. He raced over the ice towards the skinboat – stumbled – staggered upright again. Why couldn't he see properly? Why was everything taking so long?

He'd nearly reached the boat when it rocked – teetered – and slid gracefully off the ice, into the Sea. With a cry he lunged for it – but the waves sucked it just out of reach. He howled with rage – and the Sea Mother splashed saltwater in his eyes, laughing at him.

'Torak!' Renn's voice was muffled by the fog.

He got to his feet – and was horrified to see how far she'd drifted.

'*Torak!*'

He ran to the edge of the ice – but he was powerless, he could only watch as the Sea bore her away, and the breath of the World Spirit closed in around her.

Then there was nothing left but silence.

THIRTY-THREE

The ice gave another lurch, jolting Torak to his senses. He had to get away from the edge, or he'd be next.

The fog was so thick that he could hardly see; or were his eyes getting worse? Even this weak light felt like hot needles drilling into his skull.

In a blur he cast about for their remaining gear. Apart from what he had on him, there was a snow-knife, the sleeping-sacks, and no food. He *thought* he remembered seeing Renn stowing a food pouch in the skinboat, and hoped he was wrong, hoped she had it with her –

The sleeping-sacks? He had *both*?

Oh, Renn.

At least she had her bow with her, but . . .

He stopped short. She had the fire-opal. The demons would be after her.

As he recalled how he'd shouted at her, he burned with shame. Taking the fire-opal had been the bravest thing she could have done. Then she'd stayed awake all night, keeping watch. 'And all you could do was shout,' he said in disgust.

The fog whirled before his eyes, melting into a searing red blur. He squinted. Put his hand before his face. The red blur didn't change. He couldn't see.

'Snow-blind,' he said aloud – and the fog reached icy fingers down his throat. He'd never felt so vulnerable.

He did the only thing he could. He put his hands to his lips and howled.

Wolf didn't come. Nor did he send back an answering howl. Which must mean that he was out of earshot – and knowing Wolf's ears, that was a long way away off, indeed.

Again Torak howled. And again.

Silence. No wind. Just the insidious lapping of the Sea, and a horrible, waiting stillness. He pictured dark shapes flitting from ridge to ridge. He sensed that he was not alone.

'Get away from me,' he whispered to the demons.

He thought he heard laughter.

'Get away!' he shouted, waving his arms.

More laughter.

With a sob, he sank to his knees. Tears stung his eyes. Angrily he dashed them away.

If Renn were here, she'd be reaching for her medicine pouch.

That kindled a tiny spark of courage. Slipping off his mittens, he fumbled for his own pouch, found some elder leaves by their smell, and chewed them. They stung terribly when he pressed them to his eyes, but he told himself they were doing him good.

Then he had another idea. He found his mother's medicine horn, and shook a little powdered earthblood into his palm.

Suddenly, the air around him crackled with tension. Maybe the demons didn't like earthblood.

Mixing the red powder to a paste with spit, he daubed what he hoped was the sign of the hand on his forehead – remembering too late that he should have rubbed off the owl blood first. He didn't know if that would stop it working. He only knew that you made the sign of the hand to protect yourself, and he needed all the protection he could get.

He struggled to his feet – and this time he heard a hiss, and the scrabble of claws. Maybe they were shrinking back from the mark of power.

'Get away from me,' he told them shakily. 'I'm not dead yet. Neither is Renn.'

Silence. He didn't know if they were listening or mocking.

On hands and knees, he found the sleeping-sacks and strapped them on his back; then stuck the snow-knife in his belt. He forced himself to think. The thaw was coming, so he had to get further inland. Then head off and find Renn.

The day before, the current and the wind had carried them south. The ice floe, too, had carried Renn south.

'Head south,' he said out loud. And maybe the floe would get stuck in landfast ice, and she'd find her way ashore.

But where *was* south?

He took a few steps, but kept stumbling. The ice was so uneven, all these little ridges . . .

Ridges. The wind blowing the snow into ridges. Blowing mainly from the *north*!

'Thank you!' he shouted. He thanked Inuktiluk, too, for advising him to make an offering. The wind must have liked those boar tusks, or it wouldn't be helping him now.

Groping with his mittens, he felt the shape of the ridges.

Then he stood up, and squared his shoulders. 'Not dead yet,' he told the demons. 'Not dead yet!' he shouted.

He started south.

It was agonisingly slow going. At times he heard a juddering crunch, and the sea ice bucked beneath him. He probed the way ahead with the snow-knife. But if he did hit a patch of thin ice, it would probably be too late.

What had Inuktiluk said? *Grey ice is new ice, very dangerous . . . keep to the white ice.* Not much use when he couldn't see; when his next step might take him onto thin ice, or down a tide crack.

He struggled on. The cold sapped his strength, and he began to feel weak with hunger. How he was going to find food when he had neither harpoon, bow, nor sight, was beyond him.

After a while, he heard the sound of approaching wings. The sky was a pinkish blur, he couldn't even make out a darker blur flying towards him.

Owls fly silently, so it couldn't be the eagle owl; and these wingbeats had a strong, steady rustle that he recognized.

'Wsh, wsh, wsh.' The raven flew lower to inspect him. Then, with a short, deep caw, it flew away.

His belly tightened. That caw had sounded muffled, as if the raven had food in its beak. Maybe it had found a carcass, and was flying off to hide its cache. Maybe it would be back for more.

Not long afterwards, he heard it return. He strained to listen. He ran towards it.

Just when he was giving up hope, he heard the bark of a

white fox, and the sonorous caws of ravens at a kill-site. *Meat!* From the clamour, there were lots of them, so it must be a big carcass. Maybe a seal.

His foot struck something solid, and he fell. The ravens erupted into the sky in a wild clatter of wings, and the white fox uttered short barks that sounded suspiciously like laughter.

Torak groped for what had tripped him. It wasn't a wind ridge, but a smooth hummock of ice, twice the size of his head. Puzzled, he found another, a little further off. Then more of them, in a curving double line.

His heart began to thud. These weren't hummocks. They were tracks. The tracks of an ice bear. Inuktiluk had told him how the bear's weight packed the snow hard, then the wind blew away the surrounding snow, leaving perfect, raised paw-prints.

In his mind, Torak saw the seal basking in the sun beside its breathing-hole, oblivious of the ice bear stalking it downwind. Noiselessly the bear creeps closer, hiding behind every ridge and hummock. It is patient. It knows how to wait. At last the seal slips into a doze. The bear gathers itself for the silent charge . . . The seal is dead before it knows what struck.

At the carcass, the ravens had noisily resumed their feast, having apparently decided that Torak posed no threat.

They wouldn't be feeding if the bear was still close – would they? He was desperate to believe that. And by the sound of it, there were a great many ravens, as well as that fox, which must mean that the bear had left plenty of meat. Inuktiluk had said that when the hunting was good, ice bears take only the blubber, and leave the rest.

But what if it was hungry again? *What if it was stalking him right now?*

Suddenly the ravens burst skywards. Something had frightened them.

Torak's breath hammered in his chest. Reaching inside his parka, he drew his father's knife.

He pictured the great bear hunting him: placing its huge, furred paws soundlessly on the ice.

He got to his feet. The silence was deafening. He braced himself, and waited for the White Death to come for him.

Wolf knocked him backwards into the snow, and covered his face in snuffle-licks.

Wolf *loved* surprising his pack-brother. No matter how often he did it, Tall Tailless never knew he was coming, and Wolf never tired of it: the stalk – the pounce – the head-over-paws tumble.

Now, in an ecstasy of play-biting and tail-lashing – with his newly shortened tail, that he was fast getting used to – he clambered over his pack-brother. He was so happy he could howl! All thought of demons and bad taillesses and stranger wolves was chased away. After being crushed and cramped for so long, he was free to stretch and leap and lope! To feel the Bright Soft Cold beneath his pads, and clean wind in his fur! To play with his pack-brother!

As often happened when Wolf ambushed him, Tall Tailless was both cross and delighted. But Wolf sensed that this time, he was also in pain.

Where was the pack-sister? She'd been with Tall Tailless when they'd set off in the floating hide. Had she got lost on the Great Wet?

And Tall Tailless was being strangely clumsy. After his first joyful greeting, he'd made an awkward lunge at Wolf's muzzle, missed, and tried to lick his ear. Which was odd. Now his forepaw swung out and biffed Wolf hard on the nose. Wolf was startled. He hadn't done anything wrong.

Going down on his forelegs, he asked Tall Tailless to play.

Tall Tailless ignored him.

Wolf gave an aggrieved whine, and cast his pack-brother a questioning glance.

Tall Tailless stared – he actually *stared* – right past Wolf.

Wolf began to be worried. To stare like that must mean that Tall Tailless was extremely displeased. Perhaps Wolf had done something wrong without knowing it.

Then he had an idea. Loping over to the fish-dog kill and scattering the ravens, he bit off a scrap of hide, raced back with it, and tossed it at Tall Tailless' feet, looking at him expectantly. *There! Let's play toss-and-catch!*

Tall Tailless did nothing. He didn't even seem to know the hide was there.

Wolf padded closer.

Tall Tailless reached out a forepaw, and clumsily touched his muzzle.

Wolf studied the beloved, furless face. The beautiful wolf eyes were crumpled shut, and streaming wet. Delicately, Wolf sniffed them. They smelt wrong. He gave them a tentative lick.

Tall Tailless gulped, and buried his face in Wolf's scruff.

Suddenly, Wolf understood. Poor, poor Tall Tailless. He couldn't see.

To reassure him, Wolf rubbed himself against his shoulder, covering his overpelt in comforting Wolf smell. Then he nudged his head under Tall Tailless' furry forepaw.

Tailless rose unsteadily to his hind legs, and Wolf waited

until he was ready, then walked forwards as slowly as a newborn cub.

He would look after Tall Tailless. He would lead him to the fish-dog kill, and wait patiently while he ate – because he was still the lead wolf, so he got to eat first. Then, when Wolf had also eaten, he would lead Tall Taillesss in search of the pack-sister.

THIRTY-FOUR

In the Forest, the coming of spring is welcomed; in the Far North, it's feared. Now Renn understood why.

An ice mountain floated towards her out of the fog – tilted, and crashed into the Sea, sending out a wave that rocked the floe on which she huddled. She threw herself flat, and waited till the lurching eased.

Up ahead, two huge slabs smashed into each other: the larger grinding over the smaller, forcing it under.

That could have been me, thought Renn.

She had no idea where the Sea was taking her. She couldn't see any land. Only fog and looming ice in lethal black water. The din of the thaw was all around her. The trickle and gurgle of meltwater. The crunch and grind of ice.

Her floe was about twenty paces across, and she crouched in the middle, staring at the edge which the Sea Mother was gradually gnawing away. The wind moaned, and despite the White Fox visor, her eyes watered with cold. In the distance, but getting closer, she heard the thunderous voice of the ice river.

She wondered what she would do without a sleeping-sack, when night came. She remembered a story Tanugeak had told her of how her grandmother had survived a blizzard. 'She took off her mittens and sat on them, to stop the cold coming up from below; then she drew her arms inside her parka and hunched forward with her chin on her knees, so that if she fell asleep, she wouldn't topple over.'

Renn did as Tanugeak's grandmother had done, and felt warmer; but she was in no danger of falling asleep. She had to keep watch in case the fog cleared, and she got a glimpse of the shore. She had to stay on guard against Soul-Eaters in skinboats. And demons.

Hunger and thirst tormented her, but she was deter-mined not to touch her provisions. Provisions! A morsel of frozen seal meat, and a bladder of water on a thong around her neck. She tried not to think of the food pouch she'd stowed in the skinboat, moments before it happened; just as she tried not to think about the demon.

It was here on the ice floe, she could feel it. But she only ever caught a flicker of darkness, a clatter of claws.

It would have come closer if she hadn't scrubbed off the Mountain Hare "tattoo" on her forehead, and daubed on the sign of the hand, remembering to add the lines of power emanating from the middle finger. She'd thought about adding Death Marks, too; but not yet.

In the swansfoot pouch, the fire-opal throbbed with cold fire against her breastbone. Casting it into the Sea would be the coward's way out. Who knew what evil it might do down there. And there was no earth or stone in which to bury it.

A sudden honking of geese overhead. Thrusting her arms into her sleeves, she drew her bow from its seal-hide carrier.

Too late. They were out of range.

'Stupid!' she berated herself. 'You should've been ready! You should always be *ready*!'

She sat and waited for more prey. She watched till her eyes hurt. At last, her head began to nod.

The demon was so close she could smell it. Its tongue flickered out to taste her breath. Its glare drew her down into seething black flame . . .

With a cry she jolted awake. 'Get away from me!' she shouted.

A flock of gulls lifted off from a nearby ice mountain. She fumbled for her bow – but the gulls were gone.

Somewhere behind her, the demon cackled.

'There will be more gulls,' she told it. There would have to be more gulls.

None came.

Her hand crept to her medicine pouch. Inside, nestling in her dwindling supply of herbs, lay the pebble on which Torak had painted his clan-tattoo last summer; she wondered if he even knew she'd kept it. And here was the grouse-bone whistle for calling Wolf. She longed to blow it. But even if he heard, he couldn't swim out this far. She'd only be endangering him.

Her thoughts drifted to the previous autumn, when Torak had tried to teach her to howl, in case she ever lost the whistle. She hadn't been able to keep a straight face, and he'd got cross and stalked off; but when she'd tried to summon him back with a howl, she'd sounded so odd that he'd laughed till he cried.

Now she attempted a wobbly howl. It wasn't loud

enough to summon Wolf, but it made her feel a bit better.

If any more gulls came, she ought to be ready. She checked the fletching on her best flint arrow, then took all the lengths of sinew thread from her sewing pouch, knotted them together, and tied the line to the arrowshaft. Next she oiled her bow and bowstring by rubbing them with the seal meat, resisting the temptation to gobble the lot. As she worked, she seemed to see Fin-Kedinn's rough hands overlaying her own. He'd made this bow for her, and it held not only the endurance of the yew from which it came, but some of his strength, too. It wouldn't let her down.

With the arrow nocked in readiness, she pushed up her visor, and settled down to wait.

Behind her the demon clawed the ice to distract her. Her lip curled. Let it try! Fin-Kedinn had taught her to concentrate. When she was hunting, nothing could distract her, like Torak when he was tracking.

In the distance, she heard the strange, neighing cries of guillemots. They were coming her way.

Doubts flooded her mind. *They're too far away, the line isn't long enough. Your hands are frozen, you can't shoot straight . . .* She ignored the demon, and concentrated on the prey.

They were flying low, as guillemots do, beating the air with their stubby black wings. Renn chose one, and fixed her eye on it, waiting out the gusts of wind.

The arrow flew straight, and the guillemot plopped into the Sea. With a shout of triumph, Renn hauled it in on the line.

Her shot had only caught the tail, and the bird was struggling. Murmuring thanks and praise, she slipped her hand beneath its wing and held its heart between her fingers, to still it. Then she cut off the wings, and gave one to the Sea Mother and one to the wind, to thank them for not killing her yet. The head she threw to the end of the floe for her clan-guardian, and she thanked her bow by smoothing on a little of the fat.

Finally, she slit the belly, drew out the warm purple breast, and crammed it in her mouth. It tasted oily and wonderful. The guillemot's strength became hers.

She plucked the carcass, keeping the feathers for fletching, and tied it to her belt. The demon had fled. She spat out a fleck of guillemot down, and grinned. Clearly it preferred her hungry and miserable to well-fed and defiant.

A raven swooped low, snatched the guillemot's head, and flew away. Renn felt a surge of pride. Ravens are one of the few birds tough enough to winter in the Far North. She was proud to be its descendant, a member of its clan.

Drawing back her hood, she rubbed snow on her hair to wipe away the last traces of Tanugeak's black stain. She was herself again. Renn of the Raven Clan.

She was trying so hard to spot the coast that she nearly missed it.

One moment the ice floe was slowly turning, and the next there was a crunch that nearly tipped her into the Sea, and it ground to a halt.

Back on her feet, she saw that she'd been looking the wrong way. Her floe had crashed into a jumble of pack ice. Then the fog parted – and the ice river towered above her.

The floe had become stuck at its northern edge. Before her stretched a glaring expanse of landfast ice, and beyond that, a swathe of jagged, shadowy hills which cowered beneath the vast blue cliffs of the ice river.

If she could get across the pack ice, if she could reach that landfast ice . . .

But what then? The ice river had only to twitch, and those cliffs would fall on her and crush her like a beetle.

She'd think about that later. Right now, she had to get ashore.

Shouldering her bow, she clambered off the floe and onto the pack ice. It rocked alarmingly, and she had to leap to the next bit, and the next, keeping always to the white ice, and never pausing, as Inuktiluk had taught her. The pack ice was riven with gaps – one misplaced step, and she'd be in the Sea. She was sweating by the time she reached what felt like landfast ice.

She bent double, too dazed to feel relief. It was hard to stay upright, as her legs still swayed to the rhythms of the Sea.

To the south, from deep within the ice river, she heard pounding. Eerie, grinding groans. She straightened up.

The wind hissed over the ice. The cold was so intense that her eyelashes stuck together. Her hand crept to her clan-creature feathers. This place didn't feel right. This dead cold. Those fanged hills at the foot of the cliffs, so sunk in gloom that they looked almost black.

With a start she realized that it wasn't shadow that was making them look black, it couldn't be, the cliffs faced west, and the low sun shone directly onto them. Those hills *were* black. And at their heart yawned a chasm. A chasm of black ice.

She felt strangely drawn to it.

Stumbling over the landfast ice, she made her way towards the black hills. As she got nearer, the ice beneath her boots turned black: brittle black ice that crackled at every step.

731

She stooped for a shard, and crushed it in her mitten. It melted, leaving nothing but black specks. She stared at her palm. Those black specks . . . they weren't ice, but *stone*. Stone from some buried mountain, crushed fine by the might of the ice river.

Her hand dropped to her side, and water dripped sadly from her mitten. Now she understood why the Sea had carried her here, to the dark underbelly of the ice river. She'd done the impossible. She'd found a way of burying the fire-opal in stone.

But the only life she could give it was her own.

THIRTY-FIVE

Beneath his mitten, Torak felt Wolf becoming restless.

He hoped desperately that the scent trail Wolf had caught was Renn's, but he couldn't be sure. So much wolf talk isn't in the voice but in gestures: a glance, a tilt of the head, a flick of the ears. Being blind made it much harder to know what Wolf was saying. And although Torak's sight was slowly coming back, Wolf was still only a dark-grey blur.

The wind was restless too, moaning in his ears and tugging at his parka. High, thin voices reached him, just at the edge of hearing. Demons? Soul-Eater spies? Or Renn, calling for help?

Wolf stopped so abruptly that Torak nearly fell over him. He felt the tension in Wolf's shoulders; the dip of his head as he sniffed the ice. His heart sank. Another tide crack. They'd crossed three already, and it wasn't getting any easier.

Without further ado, Wolf wriggled out of Torak's grip – and leapt. Torak heard the whisper of paws landing on snow, then an encouraging bark. *Come!*

Torak unslung the sleeping-sacks and the side of seal ribs which he'd cut from the carcass, and threw them towards the shadow that was Wolf. He was reassured to hear a thud rather than a splash.

Now for the hardest part. He couldn't make out the crack, it could be anything from a hand's breadth to two paces wide. Too risky to kneel and feel its edge with his mittens; his weight might break it. He'd just have to jump, and trust that Wolf – who could leap three paces with ease – would remember that his pack-brother couldn't.

Another bark, and an impatient whine. *Come!*

Torak took a deep breath – and jumped.

He landed on solid ice, wobbling wildly. Wolf was there to steady him. He retrieved his gear, then put his hand on Wolf's scruff, and they headed off.

By mid-afternoon, and despite Wolf's impatient nudgings, he had to rest. While Wolf ran in anxious circles, he huddled on the ice, sawing meat from the seal ribs. His sight was improving all the time, and he could see the meat now. Well, he could make out a dark-red blur against the pinkish blur of the ice. He fumbled for his owl-eyed visor, and put it on.

To his surprise, Wolf gave a low growl.

Maybe he didn't like the visors.

'What's wrong?' mumbled Torak, too tired to speak wolf.

Another growl: not hostile, but uneasy. Maybe it wasn't the visor. Maybe he didn't like it that Torak had brought the meat: a draw for any ice bear within two daywalks. But he had no choice. Unlike Wolf, he couldn't devour half a seal, then go hungry for days.

An impatient nose-nudge. *Come on!*

Torak sighed, and heaved himself to his feet.

The day wore on, and he felt the cold deepening as the sun went down. Suddenly he couldn't take another step. He found a snow hill and hacked out a rough shelter, lined it with one of the sleeping-sacks, and crawled into the other.

Wolf crawled in too, and lay against him: heavy and beautifully warm. For the first time in days, Torak felt safe. With Wolf beside him, no demon or Soul-Eater or ice bear could get near. He fell asleep to the mothwing tickle of whiskers on his face.

He woke to darkness – and no Wolf.

He knew he hadn't slept long, and when he crawled outside, he saw a vast black sky glittering with stars.

He saw! The snow-blindness was gone!

He stood with upturned face, drinking in the stars.

As he watched, a great spear of green light streaked across the sky. Then a shower of arrows streamed upwards, and suddenly, rays of green light were rippling across the darkness: shimmering, melting, silently reappearing.

Torak smiled. At last. The First Tree. From the dark of the Beginning it had grown, bringing life to all things: river and rock, hunter and prey. Often in the deep of winter it returned, to lighten hearts and kindle courage. Torak thought of Fa, and wondered if he'd completed the Death Journey, and found his way safely into its boughs. Maybe even now, he was looking down on him.

Far in the distance, an eagle owl called.

Torak's skin prickled.

Then – much closer – he heard a slithering on the ice.

Crouching, he drew his knife.

'Drop it,' said Thiazzi.

4

'Where is the fire-opal?'

'I haven't got it.'

A blow to the head sent him flying. As he landed, his chest struck an ice ridge with winding force.

'Where is it?' bellowed the Oak Mage, yanking him upright.

'I haven't – got it!'

The huge fist drew back again – but Nef hobbled forwards and grabbed his arm. 'We need him alive, or we'll never find it!'

'I'll beat it out of him!' roared the Oak Mage.

'Thiazzi!' cried Seshru. 'You don't know your own strength! You'll kill him!'

The Oak Mage snarled at her – but lowered his fist, and let Torak fall.

He lay panting, trying to take in what was happening. With Wolf unaccountably gone, they must have crept up on him in the night. A few paces away, he saw two skinboats lying on the ice, their hulls patched with seal-hide. He couldn't see Eostra; but ten paces away, an eagle owl perched on a fang of ice, fixing him with fierce orange eyes.

As he stared at the murky forms of the three Soul-Eaters, he sensed the discord between them: threads of tension stretched between them like a spider's web.

Of course, he thought. They didn't complete the sacrifice, so they're not fully protected from the demons. He wondered if he could make use of that.

'Search him,' said the Viper Mage. 'It's got to be somewhere.'

Thiazzi and Nef seized Torak's parka and dragged it over his head, then ripped off his jerkin and the rest of his clothes, till he stood naked and shuddering on the ice.

The Oak Mage took malicious pleasure in making the search a slow one: shaking out mittens and boots, snapping the snow-knife in two, emptying Torak's medicine horn, so that its precious earthblood blew away on the wind.

'It isn't here,' said Nef in surprise.

'He's hidden it,' said Seshru. Drawing closer, she studied Torak's face, and her pointed tongue flickered out to moisten her lips. 'Those are Wolf Clan tattoos. *"The Wolf lives"*. Who *are* you?'

'I t-told you,' he stammered, 'I haven't got the fire-opal!'

Nef stooped for Fa's knife. 'Get dressed,' she told Torak without looking at him.

Clumsy with cold, he pulled on his clothes, then scrambled for what remained of his gear. His tinder pouch had been emptied, and his mother's medicine horn had lost its stopper; but in a corner of his medicine pouch, he found the remaining fragment of the Soul-Eaters' black root. He slipped it inside his mitten, closing his fist around it. He didn't know why, but he sensed that he might need it.

Just in time. Thiazzi seized his wrists and bound them behind him with a length of rawhide rope. The binding was cruelly tight, and Torak cried out. The Oak Mage laughed. Nef flinched, but made no move to stop him.

Torak noticed that Thiazzi's left hand was heavily bandaged in bloodstained buckskin, and missing two fingers. Good, he thought savagely. At least Wolf got his revenge.

'Where did you get this?' Nef said in an altered voice. She was standing very still, staring at the knife in her hands. Fa's knife.

Torak lifted his chin. 'It was my father's,' he said proudly.

A hush fell upon the Soul-Eaters. The eagle owl swivelled its head and stared.

'Your – father,' said Nef, aghast. 'He was – the Wolf Mage?'

'Yes,' said Torak. 'The man who saved your life.'

'The man who betrayed us!' spat Thiazzi.

Torak shot him a look of pure hatred. 'The man who discovered what you were! The man you murdered!'

'His *son*,' whispered Nef. Her brow creased. 'What – what's your name?'

'Torak.'

'Torak,' repeated the Bat Mage. Her eyes sought his, and Torak could tell that for the first time she was seeing him not merely as "boy", the ninth hunter in the sacrifice, but as Torak, the son of the Wolf Mage.

'"*The Wolf lives*"', the Viper Mage said again. Her lips curved in her sideways smile. 'So that's what it means. What a disappointment.'

The Oak Mage had reached the limits of his patience. Pushing past Seshru, he seized Torak by the hair and twisted back his head, pressing a blade against his throat. 'Tell us where you hid the fire-opal, or I'll slit your throat!'

Torak stared into the green eyes, and saw that he meant it. He thought fast. 'The girl has it,' he panted. 'The spirit walker.'

ᛙ

'What girl?' sneered Thiazzi.

'A *spirit walker*?' Nef said hoarsely.

Torak flicked Seshru a glance. 'She knows,' he said. 'She knows, and she hasn't told you!'

Thiazzi and Nef stared at the Viper Mage.

'You *knew?*' said Thiazzi accusingly, releasing Torak with such force that he fell to his knees.

'He's making it up,' said Seshru. 'Can't you see? He's trying to set us against each other.'

'I'm telling the truth!' cried Torak. Then to Nef and Thiazzi, 'You know there was a girl with me, you must have seen the tracks!'

They had. He could tell from their faces.

Nef turned to Seshru. 'There was a moment in the caves, when you sensed souls. But you never told us what.'

'She knew,' said Torak. 'She sensed the spirit walker, she sensed souls walking free, between bodies.' A plan was forming. A desperate, deadly plan that would put both him and Renn in danger. But he couldn't think of any other way.

Out loud he said, 'The girl is the spirit walker. She's got the fire-opal.'

'Take us to her,' said Nef.

'It's a trick!' cried Seshru. 'He's tricking us!'

'What can he do to us?' growled Thiazzi.

'If you let me live,' said Torak, 'I'll take you to the fire-opal. I swear it on my three souls.'

Silently, Seshru glided towards him, and brought her face close to his. Her breath heated his skin. He felt himself drowning in her peerless gaze.

Slowly she took off her mitten and raised her hand.

He flinched.

The perfect lips curved in a smile. Her chill fingers smoothed the sign of the hand from his forehead, 'You won't need that any more,' she murmured. One long forefinger caressed his cheek: gently, but letting him feel the edge of her nail.

'Your father tried to trick us,' she breathed, 'and we killed him.' She leaned closer, and whispered in his ear. 'If you trick me, I shall make sure that you will never be free of me.'

Torak swallowed. 'I will take you to the fire-opal. I swear.'

Nef thrust Fa's knife into her belt, and stared at Torak with a strange, unreadable expression. 'How?'

'The wolf,' said Torak, jerking his head at the paw-prints that wound south across the ice. 'We must follow the tracks of the wolf.'

THIRTY-SIX

Wolf felt as if he was being torn in pieces.

He had to find the pack-sister. He had to save Tall Tailless from the bad ones. *And* he had to chase the demons back into the Underneath. But he couldn't do it alone, he needed help. He could think of only one way of finding it. That way would be dangerous: the most dangerous thing a lone wolf could attempt. But he had to try.

On and on he loped through the glittering Dark. In the Up, the Bright White Eye was hiding, but her many little cubs shed their light upon the land.

As Wolf ran, he thought of Tall Tailless, and felt a fresh snap of worry. Would his pack-brother understand why he'd gone? Would he wait for his return, or blunder off and fall prey to the Great Wet?

It was too terrible to think about, so Wolf tried to lose himself in the sounds and smells carried on the wind. The furtive scratchings of a white grouse snuggling deeper into her burrow. The growls of the Great White Cold up ahead. The sharp, familiar scent of the pack-sister.

On Wolf went, following her scent. He knew that he had to find her *before* he went for help against the demons, although he didn't know why; he just felt it in his fur, with the sureness that came to him at times.

He raced up a long, sparkling slope, and paused at the top. Down there. She was sleeping down there in the dark.

A new scent assailed his nose, tightening his pelt and making his claws tingle. Demons. The urge to hunt them ran hot in his limbs. But not yet. And not alone.

Turning on one paw, he raced down the slope, the same way he'd come – then struck out to seek help.

The Dark wore on, and tirelessly he flew over the Bright Soft Cold. He came to a broken land where stunted willows rattled dry leaves in the wind. He slowed to a trot.

The scent-markings of the lead wolf were fresh, strong, and rich. This told Wolf that the stranger wolves had recently made a kill, and that the pack wasn't far away.

He kept close to the scent-markings, which would tell the stranger wolves that he'd entered their range on purpose, and was here because he wanted to be. He hoped this would make them curious rather than angry, but he didn't know. He didn't know what manner of wolves they were, or – most importantly – what kind of wolf their leader was. Wolves guard their ranges fiercely, seldom permitting a lone wolf to enter; and it's only rarely that a pack will allow a stranger to run with them, as Wolf had run with the pack on the Mountain, and Tall Tailless with the tailless pack that smelt of ravens.

The scent-markings were getting stronger, closer together. It wouldn't be long now.

It wasn't.

The white wolves came racing through the willows at a speed that took even Wolf by surprise. They were a big pack, and like Forest wolves, they ran in a line in the tracks of the leader; but they were slightly shorter than Forest wolves, and stockier. Wolf thought they looked very, very strong.

He stood absolutely still, waiting for them to approach. His heart tumbled in his chest, but he held his head and tail high. He must not look scared.

On they came over the Bright Soft Cold.

The leader glanced over his shoulder – and the pack spread out, forming a ring around Wolf.

In silence they halted. Their pelts glowed, their breath drifted like mist. Their eyes glinted silver.

Wolf stilled his own breathing, so that he would appear calm.

Stiffly the lead wolf walked towards him. His ears were pricked, his tail high, and his fur was fluffed out to the full.

Wolf dropped his own ears, but only slightly. His fur was fluffed up, but not as much as the leader's, and his tail was very slightly lower. Too high, and he'd seem disrespectful; too low, and he'd appear weak.

Sternly, the leader stared past him: too proud to meet his eyes.

Wolf turned his head a whisker to one side, and slid his gaze down and away.

The lead wolf moved closer, till he stood within pawing distance of Wolf's nose.

Hardly daring to breathe, Wolf stood his ground. He saw the scars on the leader's muzzle, and the bitten edge of one ear. This was a wolf who had fought many fights, and won.

The lead wolf took another step, and sniffed under

Wolf's tail, then at the bark binding the tip. He drew back sharply, twitching his ears in puzzlement. Then he brought his muzzle close to Wolf's. Close, but not touching, breathing in his scent.

Wolf, too, took deep breaths, tasting the strong, sweet scent of the leader, while around them the white wolves waited in silence.

The leader raised his forepaw – and touched Wolf's shoulder.

Wolf tensed.

The next moment would decide it. Either they would help him – or tear him to pieces.

THIRTY-SEVEN

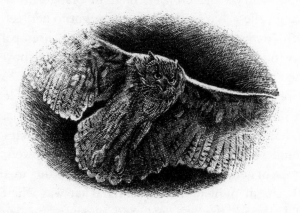

After a wretched night in a hastily hacked-out snow shelter, Renn sat waiting for dawn to come. Her last dawn. She kept saying it in her head, to make it real.

She knew she should have had the courage to end it last night, but she hadn't. She needed to see the sun one final time.

The night was quiet. Nothing but the restless wind, and an occasional rumble as the ice river shifted in its sleep. The stars had never looked so distant or so cold. She longed for voices. People, foxes, anyone. "Voice hunger" is what the clans of the north call it: when you're alone on the ice, and you crave voices more than warmth or meat; because you don't want to die alone.

It wasn't fair. Why *should* she go down into the ice with the demons? She wanted to see Torak again, and Fin-Kedinn, and Wolf.

'What you want doesn't matter,' she said out loud, 'this

is how it is.' Her voice sounded old and cracked, like Saeunn's.

Above the ice river, a slash of deep crimson appeared: a wound in the sky.

She watched the crimson melt to orange, then to a blazing yellow. No more excuses. She got to her feet. The Death Marks were stiff on her skin. The fire-opal was heavy on her breast. Shouldering her faithful bow, she started for the cliffs.

It began to snow. White flakes speckling black ice, an eerie reversal of how things should be. The ice was jagged. She had to fight her way over towering ridges and bottomless cracks. One slip, and she'd be swallowed, with no hope of getting out. And she had to get further in, to the black chasm right under the cliffs. That was where she would unmask the fire-opal, and summon the demons. That was where she would lead them down into the dark.

An ear-splitting groan – and to the south, part of the cliff-face collapsed. Billowing clouds of ice blasted her face. Nothing could withstand the might of the ice river. Not even demons.

She brushed off her parka, and pressed on.

It was noon by the time she neared the darkness under the cliffs. In the driving snow she stood on a ridge, staring down at the slash in the belly of the ice river.

There, she thought. In there it will be buried for good.

4

Torak had been walking all night, following Wolf's tracks by the glimmer of the Soul-Eaters' rushlight. Behind him Nef and Thiazzi trudged with the skinboats on their shoulders; in front went Seshru, the rushlight in one hand, the rope that bound his wrists in the other. At times, he sensed the sinister presence of Eostra, although he never saw her; but when he glanced up, there was the shadowy form of an eagle owl, wheeling against the stars.

His chest ached, his feet dragged. He forced himself to keep going. Nothing mattered, except finding Renn. Gritting his teeth against the pain, he twisted his wrists so that the rawhide bit into his flesh. He had to leave a blood trail. That was part of the plan.

Dawn came. In the ashen light, the land was humped and menacing. He sensed they were being followed. Either Wolf had come back, or his plan was working – but far too soon.

Seshru jerked at the rope, yanking him forwards.

Pretending to stumble, Torak fell to his knees, rubbing his bloody wrists in the snow.

'Up!' snapped Seshru, giving a tug that made him cry out.

'Listen to him whine,' sneered Thiazzi. 'Like that wolf when I stamped on his tail. Whining like a cub.'

You'll pay for that, thought Torak as he staggered to his feet. I don't know how, but you will pay.

Noon approached. It began to snow. Through the flying whiteness, Torak made out a long, low hill. Beyond it he heard the boom of the ice river; far to the south, on the very edge of hearing, the howling of wolves.

Seshru had reached the top of the hill. Her face was blank as a mask in its slit-eyed visor, and her black tongue flicked out to taste the air. She smiled. 'The demons are coming.'

Nef dropped the skinboat and hobbled up the slope. As she whipped off her visor, Torak was shocked to see how she'd aged in the course of one night. 'There,' said the Bat Mage. 'She's down there in the shadow of the cliffs.'

Renn halted twenty paces from the chasm, in the lee of a ridge of black ice.

Slipping her hands out of her mittens, she drew the swansfoot pouch from inside her parka. Her fingers were shaking so badly that it took several attempts to loosen the neck of the pouch, but at last she managed, and the fire-opal rolled onto her palm. It lay dull and lifeless, strangely heavier than when she'd carried it in the pouch, and so cold that it burned her skin.

You couldn't stop this now, she thought. Even if you wanted to.

Snow fell thickly, chilling her palm, but the fire-opal remained untouched.

Deep within the stone, a crimson spark flickered. The spark flared to a flame. Pure. Steady. Beautiful . . .

Shutting her eyes, Renn made a cage around it with her fingers. When she looked again, it was still glowing: crimson light bleeding through her flesh.

Snow swirled in her face. Beneath her boots the black ice shuddered. She raised her hand, and held up the fire-opal.

The ice river fell silent. The wind dropped to a whisper. Waiting to see what would come.

At first it was only a distant rustling: a murmur of hunger and hatred on the wind. Then it swelled to a raucous clamour that pierced her skull and beat at her spirit. The demons were coming.

An arrow shattered the ice a hand's breadth from her head.

'Don't move!' A man's voice shouted.

ᛃ

Torak scarcely recognized Renn.

Her red hair floated like flame in the whirling snow, and her white face was severely beautiful as she held up the fire-opal. She didn't look like his friend any more, she looked like the World Spirit in winter: a woman with bare red willow branches for hair, who walks the snow alone, striking terror in all she meets.

'Don't move!' bellowed the Oak Mage again.

'We will shoot!' warned the Bat Mage.

'You can't escape!' cried the Viper Mage, nocking another arrow to her bow.

'Get back!' shouted Renn – and took a step towards the edge of the chasm, ten paces behind her. 'There are cracks all around me, if you shoot, you'll lose it for ever!'

The Soul-Eaters froze. She was thirty paces away from them, well within arrowshot; but the risk was too great.

Desperately, Torak tugged at the rope that bound his wrists behind him, but he couldn't break free of the tether; Thiazzi had hammered the stake deep into the ice.

Thinking fast, he slipped his hand out of his mitten, opened his fist, and dropped the black root onto the ice, then twisted round to reach it with his teeth. He prayed that he hadn't left it too late, that his plan would work against the odds, and –

A shadow flew over him. 'Renn!' he shouted. 'Above you!'

She'd already seen it. As the eagle owl swooped towards her with talons outstretched, she lashed out with her knife, and sent it screeching skywards. 'Stay back!' she warned the Soul-Eaters sternly. 'You can't stop me!'

'Renn, don't do it!' yelled Torak. '*Don't jump!*'

She seemed to see him for the first time. Her face crumpled, and she was Renn again. 'Torak! I can't – '

Her eyes widened with horror as she stared at something

behind him – and he turned, and saw, through the whirling whiteness, a black tide racing like cloudshadow over the ice.

Demons.

For a moment he could only watch the darkness sweeping towards him. Then he bent his head, caught the root in his mouth, and chewed – gagging, forcing himself to swallow.

'Renn!' he shouted. *'Don't jump!'*

'Don't jump!' shouted Torak – and Renn hesitated.

Through the snow she saw him kneeling on the black ice: tied to a stake, his hood thrown back from his bruised face. The Soul-Eaters stood on either side of him, he didn't stand a chance – and yet for a moment, hope made her falter. He sounded so certain.

But the demons were sweeping closer, and the Soul-Eaters were moving forwards, bearing down on her.

She saw Torak sway – and watched in horror as the blood left his face, his eyes rolled up into his head, and he pitched forwards onto the ice.

Get up! she told him silently. Do something, anything, just let me know you're still alive!

He lay still.

It's over, she thought in disbelief. I'm the only one left.

Her fingers tightened about the fire-opal, and she edged backwards, closer to the chasm.

THIRTY-EIGHT

The bile was bitter in Torak's mouth as he lay face down in the snow.

With the last of his strength he turned his head, and saw Renn backing towards the chasm, and the Soul-Eaters advancing on her. Then the demons came roaring over him. He sensed their hunger for the fire-opal, and their terror of the wolves who hunted them: the white wolves of the north and the grey wolf of the Forest, who'd sought them tirelessly through the snow, and now came streaking across the ice, driving all before them.

'*Wolf* . . .' Torak tried to say, but his lips wouldn't move. Cramps twisted his guts. The sickness came at him in waves.

Just before he slid into darkness, he saw the Viper Mage turn, her mouth slack with horror. There, at the edge of the pack-ice: a great white bear exploded from the Sea . . .

. . . and now he was surging onto the ice, shaking the

751

water from his fur. He was leaping towards the evil ones, and they quailed before him, their terror rank on the wind.

The Viper Mage faltered with an arrow nocked to her bow. She glanced from the bear to Torak's slumped body, and her face contorted with fury. 'The boy! The *boy* is the spirit walker!'

With one sweep of his paw, the bear sent her screaming through the air, to land in a limp huddle on the ice. Over the crackling blackness he bounded, drinking in the scents streaming towards him on the wind. The fury of the Oak Mage, the terror of Renn. Before him the Bat Mage fled, the demons parted like a river. His growl filled the sky, his roar shattered ice. He was invincible!

Torak felt the fury of the ice bear as his own; he felt its blood-urge drowning him in a crimson flood. He fought to conquer it . . .

He lost.

The killing hunger roared through him, the hunger which had led him as he'd followed the blood trail over the snow. He would slaughter this prey: the evil ones who dared invade his ice, the girl with the flaming hair! He would feast on their hot, tender hearts, he would kill them *all*!

Before him the evil one with the pale hair brandished a feeble weapon. Scornfully he swatted it aside, delighting in the anguished howl of the fallen.

The prey whimpered and squirmed. He moved in for the kill . . .

. . . and a great grey wolf leapt in front of him. It stood facing him, its lips drawn back from its fangs in a snarl.

The bear bellowed his rage. He reared and pounded the ice with his forepaws, twisting his head, roaring at the wolf.

The wolf stood its ground, unafraid. Its amber eyes were fixed on the bear's: steady and strong as the sun. They pierced the darkness of the bear's souls, and found Torak. They saw his souls, they called to him. With an agonising jolt he shook himself free of the blood-urge – he knew Wolf, and he knew himself again. He wrenched the souls of the ice bear to his will.

Thiazzi still cowered before him: his arm broken, his weapons lost.

Torak faltered. Here was a Soul-Eater at his mercy: to be killed with a single shake of his terrible jaws. But now it wasn't the blood-urge of the bear which drove him, it was his own. *He* would do the killing – with the might of the greatest of hunters at his command. And he *wanted* to kill. The Oak Mage had tortured Wolf, and tried to kill Renn, and hunted his father to death. Oh, how he wanted to kill!

But Wolf's amber eyes were fixed on him; and suddenly he knew that if he killed the Soul-Eater now, then, truly, he would become as one of them.

With a deafening roar he rose once more on his hind legs, looming over the Oak Mage. With a roar he crashed down, pounding the ice so that black shards flew. He – would – not – kill!

In the instant that he turned from killing, he saw Renn stagger to the chasm, poised to jump. He saw the Bat Mage hobble after her, snatch the fire-opal from her hand, and push her away from the edge with such force that she went flying.

Then the Bat Mage turned with a look of bitter triumph, and called to Torak's body lying on the ice: 'The debt is repaid! Tell your father when you meet him! *The debt is repaid!*'

She threw herself in – and the demons gave a rending

howl, and leapt after her. The ice river groaned, the black ice collapsed, shutting the chasm for ever – and the light of the fire-opal was quenched.

THIRTY-NINE

Torak awoke on the ice, lying on his back.

His head was spinning, and he felt sick. But the last snowflakes were drifting gently onto his face, and the sky had a lightness to it that told him the demons were gone.

Renn sat beside him, her head on her knees. She was shaking.

'You all right?' he mumbled.

She straightened up. She was very pale, and there was a Death Mark on her forehead that he hadn't noticed before. 'Mm,' she said. 'What about you?'

'Mm,' he lied. He shut his eyes, and visions whirled in his head. The Bat Mage on the brink of the chasm. The Oak Mage cowering before him: *him*, the ice bear, bent on killing . . .

'The Soul-Eaters are gone,' said Renn. 'They took the skinboats and fled. At least, I think they did.' She told him how she'd scrambled to safety just before the ice crashed down, and how, when the snow clouds had cleared, the Viper Mage and the Oak Mage were gone. So was the eagle owl, and the white wolves.

Torak opened his eyes. 'Where's Wolf?'

'He hasn't gone far.' She plucked at the fur of her mitten. 'He helped me find you. I couldn't see for the snow, then I heard him howling. It was horrible. I thought he was mourning you.'

'Sorry,' muttered Torak.

'The Viper Mage,' she said with a catch in her voice. 'She knows you're a spirit walker.'

'Yes.'

'So now they all know.'

'Yes.'

She stared across the ice and shivered. 'What did the Bat Mage mean, "The debt is repaid"?'

He told her how his father had once stopped the Bat Mage from killing herself.

'Ah,' said Renn. Then she put something heavy into his hand. 'Here. This is for you.'

It was Fa's blue slate knife.

'When she pushed me aside,' said Renn, 'she must have stuck it in my belt. I didn't find it till afterwards.'

Torak's fingers closed over the hilt. 'She wasn't wholly bad,' he murmured. 'Not all the way through.'

Renn stared at him. 'She was a Soul-Eater!'

'But she did her best to repair what she'd done.'

He thought about the souls of the Bat Mage, trapped in the black ice with the demons. And he thought about the small dark shadow he'd seen lifting off from Nef's shoulder just before she jumped. She'd sent her beloved bat away so that it wouldn't perish with her.

'It was you, wasn't it,' said Renn in a low voice. 'The ice

bear. You spirit walked in the ice bear.'

He met her eyes, but didn't say anything.

'Torak, you might never have got out! You might have been trapped in it for good!'

Painfully he raised himself on one elbow. 'There was nothing else I could do.'

'But – '

'You were the one who risked everything, who was prepared to give your life to keep the fire-opal buried. That was so brave . . . I can't imagine doing that.'

She scowled, and plucked more fur off her mitten. Then she shrugged. 'There was nothing else I could do.'

Silence between them. Renn took a handful of snow and scrubbed the Death Mark off her forehead. Then she set about cleaning the wounds on Torak's wrists.

'What if no ice bear had come?' she said. 'What would you have done then?'

'I'd have spirit walked in Thiazzi,' he said without hesitation, 'or Seshru. I wasn't going to let you die.'

She blinked. 'You saved my life. If you hadn't – '

'Wolf saved us,' said Torak. 'He hunted down the demons. He stopped me killing Thiazzi. He saved us all.'

As if they'd summoned him, Wolf came loping over the ice, slipped, righted himself with a deft twirl of his shortened tail, and skittered to a halt in a shower of snow. Then he pounced on Torak and gave him a thorough face-licking.

Suddenly Torak wanted to bury his head in Wolf's scruff and cry till his heart broke: for the Bat Mage, for himself, and in a tangled way, for his father.

'Here,' said Renn, holding out a scrap of seal meat.

He sniffed, took the meat, and tried to sit up, but the pain in his chest made him wince.

'Are you hurt?' said Renn.

'No, I just fell. Bruised my chest.'

'Do you want me to take a look?'

'No,' he said quickly, 'I'm fine.'

She looked puzzled. Then she gave another shrug, and went off to leave a piece of meat for the clan guardian. When she came back, she gave another piece to Wolf, keeping the last for herself.

They ate in silence, watching the sun sink towards the Sea. The wind had gone, and the ice river was asleep. The afternoon was still. Torak watched a solitary raven rowing across the vast white sky – and was suddenly sharply aware of how far they were from the Forest.

He glanced at Renn, and saw that she'd had the same thought.

She said, 'We've got no food, no blubber, and no skinboat. How in the name of the Spirit are we going to get home?'

That was how Fin-Kedinn and Inuktiluk found them when they came up from the south in their skinboats: Torak and Renn huddled together on the ice, with Wolf standing guard beside them.

FORTY

After that first stunned moment, Renn had given a strangled sob and thrown herself at her uncle. He'd stood on the ice and held her, and she'd breathed in his smell of reindeer hide and Forest.

He'd borrowed a skin-boat from the Sea-eagle Clan, he told her, and kept to the leads between the skerries and the coast until he'd reached the camp of his old friends, the White Foxes.

'And the rest of the clan?' she said, wiping her nose on her sleeve.

'Back in the Forest.'

'In the Forest? So you – '

' – came alone. I thought you needed me more.'

Now she lay curled in his skinboat, wonderfully warm beneath a sleeping-sack of white winter reindeer hide. Torak was in Inuktiluk's boat, and Wolf was keeping level with them on the ice.

After a while, she said to Fin-Kedinn's back, 'I still don't understand. The Soul-Eaters. Torak says they want to make all the clans the same; but we *are* the same. We all live by the same laws.'

Fin-Kedinn turned his head. 'Do we? Tell me. Since you've been in the Far North, what have you lived on? Seal?'

She nodded.

'And what do seals eat?'

She gasped. 'Fish! They're hunters. I never thought.'

Fin-Kedinn swerved to avoid a chunk of black ice. 'The Ice clans live as the ice bear does. They have to, or they wouldn't survive. Some Sea clans do too. In the Forest, it's different. That's what the Soul-Eaters want to change.'

Renn was thoughtful. 'They told Torak that they speak for the World Spirit. But –'

'Nobody speaks for the World Spirit,' said Fin-Kedinn.

After that, they didn't talk again.

It was an overcast day, and the sky was heavy with snow. Gulls wheeled overhead. A fox trotted over the ice, scented Wolf, and fled. Renn watched Fin-Kedinn's paddle slicing the water, and began to feel drowsy.

The spirit bees were back. She reached out to touch them, laughing as they brushed her fingers. Then they were gone, and she was alone on a high mountain, and red eyes were coming at her from the dark . . .

She cried out.

'Renn,' Fin-Kedinn said softly. 'Wake up.'

She screwed up her eyes against the light. 'I had a dream.'

The Raven Leader steadied the boat by sticking one end of his paddle in a cross-strap, then twisted round to look at her. 'The Soul-Eaters,' he said quietly. 'You got close to them, didn't you?'

She caught her breath. 'Before, they were just shadows, but now I've seen them. Thiazzi. Eostra. The Bat Mage . . . Seshru.'

They exchanged glances. Then Fin-Kedinn said, 'When we reach the Forest, tell me everything. Not here.'

She nodded, comforted. She didn't want to talk about it yet. She didn't want to bring it back.

Fin-Kedinn took up his paddle, and they moved off again.

Inuktiluk steered his boat alongside them. Torak sat behind him, and Renn tried to catch his eye, but he didn't see her. With his short hair and fringe he looked disturbingly unfamiliar.

He'd been very subdued since the battle on the ice. At first she'd thought it was because of what he must have witnessed in the caves. Now she wondered if there was something more; something he wasn't telling her.

A little later, she said to Fin-Kedinn, 'It isn't over, is it?'

Again, the Raven Leader turned to look at her. 'It's never over,' he said.

Wolf was troubled because Tall Tailless was troubled. So now, in the deep of the Dark, Wolf decided to brave the great white Den of the taillesses who smelt like foxes, and make sure that his pack-brother was safe.

Luckily, all the dogs had been taken off to hunt, and Wolf was able to crawl into the Den un-smelt. A tangle of scents hit his nose: reindeer, fish-dog, tailless, fox, lingonberry; but it wasn't hard to find his pack-brother among them.

Tall Tailless slept curled in his reindeer hide, back to

back with his pack-sister. He was frowning and twitching; Wolf sensed the depth of his trouble. Tall Tailless was trying to make a choice about something. He was frightened. He didn't know what to do. More than that, Wolf didn't understand.

For the present, though, his pack-brother seemed safe with the other taillesses, so Wolf turned his attention to the interesting smells in the Den. The bladder of a fish-dog was intriguing – until he bit it, and it spurted him with wet. Then he found a hanging ball of hide, and patted it with his paw. It gurgled. Looking inside, he was startled to see a small tailless cub gazing up at him. Wolf licked its nose, and it gave a happy squeal.

Next, Wolf went to sniff the fish-dog meat that hung from a branch in the middle of the Den. Around him the taillesses were whiffling in their sleeps. Stretching his neck, he took the meat delicately in his jaws, and lifted it down. He was just about to leave when he caught a gleam of eyes.

Of all the taillesses, the lead wolf of the raven pack was the one Wolf respected the most. Only this tailless slept as lightly and woke as often as a normal wolf. He was awake now.

Wolf dropped his ears and wagged his tail, hoping the lead wolf hadn't noticed the meat in his jaws.

The lead wolf had. He didn't growl. He didn't need to. He simply crossed his forepaws on his chest, and regarded Wolf.

Wolf understood, put down the meat, and left the Den.

Out in the Dark again, he found himself a place in the Bright Soft Cold, and curled up. Now he was sure that Tall Tailless was safe, at least for the moment, because the leader of the raven pack was watching over him.

The clearing in the Forest was aglow with firelight, and heady with the smells of woodsmoke and roasting meat. Fat sizzled on the fire – 'The first real fire,' said Renn, 'that we've had in half a moon!'

After the dim flicker of the White Fox blubber lamps, it was wonderful to be able to scorch themselves before a proper Raven long-fire. An entire pine tree lay ablaze in the middle of the clearing, its flames leaping higher than a man could jump, its embers hot enough to singe your eyebrows if you got too close.

Many people from other clans had joined the Ravens on the banks of the Axehandle, to celebrate the return of the travellers from the Far North, and the vanquishing of the demons. All had brought food. The Boars had brought a whole side of forest horse, which they'd baked in a pit, to much good-natured argument about whether spruce boughs or pine gave a better flavour. The Otters brought delicious sticky cakes of cranberry and reed flour, as well as a strange-tasting stew of dried bog-mushrooms and frogs' legs, which nobody much liked, except them. The Willows brought piles of salted herring, and several skins of their famously potent rowanberry brew; and the Ravens provided great coils of auroch-gut sausage stuffed with a delicious mix of blood, marrowfat, and pounded hazelnuts.

As the night wore on, everyone became flushed and voluble. Dogs raced about excitedly, and those trees that remained awake leaned closer to the fire, warming their branches and listening to the talk.

Torak hadn't drunk as much as the others, because he didn't want his souls to wander. He'd done his best to take part in the jokes and the hunting stories, but he knew he wasn't very good at it. Even before the Far North, he hadn't really belonged, and now it was harder. People kept looking at him and whispering.

'They say he was with the Soul-Eaters for *days*,' breathed a Boar girl to her mother.

'Sh!' hissed the mother. 'He'll hear!'

Torak pretended he hadn't. He sat on a log by the fire, watching Fin-Kedinn cutting chunks of horse and putting them in bowls; Renn wrinkling her nose as she fished a frog's leg from her bowl, and surreptitiously fed it to a waiting dog. He felt cut off from them. They didn't know what he was concealing; and he didn't know how to tell them.

Of everyone, only Inuktiluk had seemed to have some idea of what was tormenting him. As they'd stood together on the ice on their last morning in the Far North, the White Fox hunter had turned to him and said, 'You have good friends among the Ravens. Don't be in a hurry to leave them when you're back in the Forest.'

Torak had been startled. How much did Inuktiluk know, or guess?

The round face had creased in a smile tinged with sadness. 'It seems to me that you're like the black ice bear, who comes once in a thousand winters. You may never find peace. But you will make friends along the way. And many lands will know your name.' Then he'd put both fists to his chest and bowed. 'Hunt well, Torak. And may your guardian run with you.'

In the clearing, food had given way to singing and story-telling. Suddenly, Torak couldn't bear it any longer. When no-one was looking, he slipped off to his shelter.

Throwing himself onto the willow mat, he stared into

the fire at the mouth of the shelter, wondering what to do.

'What's the matter?' said Renn, making him jump.

She stood on the other side of the fire. He thought she looked as frightened as he felt. 'You're not thinking of leaving?' she said.

He hesitated. 'If I did, I'd tell you first.'

Picking up a stick, she poked the fire. 'What is it you're afraid of?'

'What do you mean?'

'There is something, I can feel it.'

He didn't reply.

'All right,' she said, throwing away the stick, 'I'll guess. In the caves, you had blood on your forehead. You said it was tainted. Was it – did they make you take part in the sacrifice?'

It was a good guess, though not the right one. But he decided to go along with it. 'Yes,' he said. 'The owl. The first of the nine hunters. I killed it.'

Renn's face drained of colour.

Torak's heart sank. How would she feel if she knew the rest?

But she recovered fast, and forced a shrug. 'After all, I fletch my arrows with owl feathers. Though I don't actually kill for them, I wait till I find a dead one, or someone brings me one.' She realized she was talking too fast, and sucked in her lips. 'We can make this right, Torak. There are ways of purifying you.'

'Renn –'

'You don't have to leave,' she said urgently. 'That won't solve anything.'

When he didn't answer, she persisted. 'At least wait till you've talked to Fin-Kedinn. Swear you won't leave till you've talked to Fin-Kedinn.'

Her face was so open and hopeful. He swore.

When she'd gone, he bowed his head to his knees. Suddenly he was back on ice, with his hands tied behind his back. Seshru was running her finger down his cheek. 'You will never be free of me,' she whispered in his ear. Then he felt Thiazzi's strong grip on his shoulders, holding him down, and Seshru was pricking his chest with a bone needle, rubbing in the stinking black stain made from the bones of murdered hunters and the blood of the Soul-Eaters.

'This mark,' she breathed, 'will be like the harpoon head beneath the skin of the seal. One twitch, and it will draw you, no matter how hard you struggle . . .'

Opening the neck of his jerkin, Torak put his finger to the crusted scab on his breastbone. He wondered if he could ever bring himself to show the Ravens – the Ravens who trusted him – this mark on his chest. The three-pronged fork for snaring souls.

The mark of the Soul-Eater.

FORTY-ONE

Fin-Kedinn woke Torak before dawn, and told him to come and help check the fishing-lines. When Torak emerged from the shelter, he found Renn waiting with her uncle. He knew from their faces that she'd told the Raven Leader of their talk the night before.

Nothing was said as they made their way through the sleeping Forest. Fog lay thick in the valley; along the riverbank, the bare branches of the alders made a delicate purple haze. Torak glimpsed Wolf, weaving between the trees. The only sound was the Axehandle, which was bubbling noisily under the ice that still crusted its banks.

They reached the flat, boggy part of the valley where the river broadened into pools. It was across these pools that wovenbark ropes had been strung, with baited lines trailing in the water.

The catch was good, and soon they had small piles of perch and bream. Fin-Kedinn thanked the spirits of the prey, then stuck a fish head in the fork of a spruce for the clan guardian. After that they woke up a fire beneath a battered old oak, and began the finger-numbing work of gutting, and scraping off the scales. As each fish was cleaned, they threaded it by the gills on a line which they hung from the oak, well out of Wolf's reach.

A breeze sprang up. The oak was slumbering too deeply to feel it, but the beech trees sighed, and the alders rattled their tiny black cones, chattering even in their sleep.

A weasel in its white winter coat rose on its hind legs to snuff the wind. Wolf pricked his ears, and shot off in pursuit.

Fin-Kedinn watched him go. Then he turned to Torak and said, 'I told you once of the great fire that broke up the Soul-Eaters.'

Renn froze with a fish in one hand.

Torak stiffened. 'I remember,' he said carefully.

Scrape, scrape, scrape went Fin-Kedinn's antler knife, scattering fish-scales. 'Your father caused it,' he said.

Torak's mouth went dry.

'The fire-opal,' said the Raven Leader, 'was the heart of Soul-Eater power. Your father took it. He shattered it into pieces.'

Renn put down the fish. 'He *shattered* the fire-opal?'

'Then he started the great fire,' said Fin-Kedinn. He paused. 'One Soul-Eater was killed in that fire. Killed trying to reach a fragment of the fire-opal.'

'The seventh Soul-Eater,' murmured Renn. 'I wondered about that.'

Torak stared into the red heart of the embers, and thought of his father. His father, who had started the great fire. 'So he didn't just run away,' he said.

'Oh, he was no coward,' said the Raven Leader. 'He was

clever, too. He made it appear that he and his mate had also perished in the fire. Then they fled to the Deep Forest.'

'The Deep Forest,' said Torak. The previous summer, he'd reached its borders. He remembered the dense shadows beneath the secretive, watchful trees. 'They should have stayed there. They would have been safe.'

With his knife, Fin-Kedinn woke up the fire. In the flaring light, his features seemed carved in granite. 'They should have stayed with your mother's people, yes. Leaving was their undoing.' He looked at Torak. 'But they were betrayed. Your father's brother learned that they still lived. From then on, they were hunted. And your mother – ,' he drew a sharp breath, 'your mother wouldn't endanger her people by staying. So they left.' Again he stirred the embers. 'The following summer, you were born.'

'And she died,' said Torak.

The Raven Leader did not reply. He was gazing into the past, his blue eyes bright with pain.

Torak turned his head and stared at the birch trees that stretched their naked branches to the cold sky.

Wolf returned, with a hare's front leg dangling from his jaws. He splashed into the shallows, tossed the hare's leg high, then made a spectacular leap and caught it in mid-air.

'The fire-opal,' said Renn. 'You said it was broken into pieces.'

Fin-Kedinn fed more wood to the fire. 'Tell me, Renn. When you held it in your hand, how big was it?'

Torak twitched in irritation. What did that matter now?

'About the size of a duck's egg,' said Renn. She caught her breath. 'It was only a fragment!'

The Raven Leader nodded. 'That from which it came was almost the size of your fist.'

There was a silence. Wolf lay on the bank, quietly

demolishing the hare's leg. Even the alders had stopped talking.

Torak said, 'So the stone that went down with the Bat Mage was only one piece. There may be more?'

'There are more,' said the Raven Leader. 'Think, Torak. There was at least one other that we know of. The Soul-Eater across the Sea must have had one, to have made the demon bear that killed your father.'

Torak struggled to take it in. 'How many in all?'

'I don't know,' said Fin-Kedinn.

'Three,' said Renn in a low voice. 'There were three.'

They stared at her.

'Three red eyes in the dark. I saw them in my dream. One taken by the Sea. One by the Bat Mage. And one . . . ' she broke off. 'Where's the third?'

Fin-Kedinn spread his hands. 'We don't know.'

Torak raised his head and stared into the gnarled branches above him. High up – so high that he hadn't spotted it till now – he saw a ball of mistletoe. The oak wasn't asleep after all, he realized. There above him was its small, green, ever-wakeful heart. He wondered what secrets it knew. Did it know about him? Did it see the mark on his chest?

Slipping his hand inside his parka, he touched the scab. This mark by itself endangered those around him, just as Renn's lightning tattoos protected her. And somewhere in the Forest, or in the Far North, or beyond the Sea, the three remaining Soul-Eaters were plotting: to find the final fragment of the fire-opal; to find him, Torak the spirit walker . . .

'Renn,' said Fin-Kedinn, making him start. 'Go back to camp, and tell Saeunn about the fire-opal.'

'But I want to stay here,' protested Renn.

'Go. I need to talk to Torak alone.'

Renn sighed, and got to her feet.

Suddenly, Torak felt that it was terribly important to speak to her before she left. 'Renn,' he said, drawing her aside and talking under his breath so that Fin-Kedinn wouldn't hear, 'I need you to know something.'

'What?' she said crossly.

'There are things I haven't told you yet. But I will.'

To his surprise, she didn't roll her eyes impatiently. She fiddled with her quiver-strap and scowled. 'Oh well,' she muttered, 'everybody has secrets. Even me.' Then she brightened up. 'Does this mean you're staying?'

'I don't know.'

'You should stay. Stay with us.'

'I don't fit in.'

She snorted. 'I know that! But you don't fit in anywhere else either, do you?' Then she flashed him her sharp-toothed grin, hoisted her bow on her shoulder, and walked off through the trees.

For a while after she'd gone, neither Torak nor Fin-Kedinn spoke. The Raven Leader skewered a big bream on a stick, and set it to roast in the embers, while Torak sat brooding.

'Eat,' said Fin-Kedinn at last.

'I'm not hungry.'

'Eat.'

Torak ate – and discovered that he was ravenous. He'd finished off most of the bream before he realized that the Raven Leader had eaten little.

It was the first time they'd been alone together since Fin-Kedinn had rescued them on the ice. Torak wiped his mouth on his sleeve, and said, 'Are you angry with me?'

Fin-Kedinn cleaned his knife in the snow. 'Why should I be angry?'

'Because I went off to seek Wolf without your leave.'

'You don't need my leave. You're nearly a man.' He paused, then added drily, 'You'd better start acting like one.'

That stung. 'What was I supposed to do, let the Soul-Eaters sacrifice Wolf? Let them overrun the Forest with demons?'

'You should have come back and sought my help.'

Torak opened his mouth to protest, but the Raven Leader silenced him with a glance. 'You survived by luck, Torak. And because the World Spirit wanted you to. But luck runs out. The World Spirit turns its favour elsewhere. You need to stay with the clan.'

Torak remained stubbornly silent.

'Tell me,' said Fin-Kedinn. 'What tracks can you see around you?'

Torak stared at him. 'What?'

'You heard me.'

Puzzled, Torak told him. The deep, dragging hoof-prints of an auroch. A few raggedly bitten-off twigs left by a red deer. A cluster of barely visible hollows, each with a tiny pile of frozen droppings at the bottom, where some willow grouse had huddled together for company.

Fin-Kedinn nodded. 'Your father taught you well. He taught you tracking because it teaches you to listen: to stay open to what the Forest is telling you. But when he was a young man, he never listened to anyone. He was convinced he was right. Tracking, listening – that was your mother's gift.' He paused. 'Maybe by teaching you tracking, your father was trying to prevent you making the same mistakes he did.'

Torak thought about that.

'If you left now,' Fin-Kedinn went on, 'it would be you against three Mages of enormous power. You wouldn't stand a chance.'

On the riverbank, Wolf had finished the hare's leg, and now stood wagging his tail at his name-soul in the water.

Fin-Kedinn watched him. 'A young wolf,' he said, 'can be foolhardy. He may think he can bring down an elk on his own, but he forgets that it only takes one kick to kill him. And yet if he has the sense to wait, he'll live to bring down many.' He turned to Torak. 'I'm not telling you to stay. I'm asking you.'

Torak swallowed. Fin-Kedinn had never asked him anything before.

Leaning towards him, the Raven Leader spoke with unaccustomed gentleness. 'Something's troubling you. Tell me what it is.'

Torak wanted to. But he couldn't. At last he mumbled, 'The knife that you made for me. I lost it. I'm sorry.'

Fin-Kedinn read the evasion in his face, and sighed. 'I'll make you another,' he said. With the aid of his staff, he rose to his feet. 'Watch the catch. I'm going up the hill to check the snares. And Torak ... Whatever it is that's wrong, you're better off here, with people who – with your friends.'

When he'd gone, Torak remained by the fire. He could feel the Soul-Eater tattoo burning through his parka. *You will never be free of us . . .*

In the shallows, Wolf had found fresh prey: the battered carcass of a roe buck which had drowned further upstream, and was now drifting slowly past. He pounced on it, and it sank beneath his weight, taking him with it. He surfaced, scrambled onto the bank, shook the water from his fur, and tried again. Again the buck sank. After the third attempt,

Wolf sat down, whining softly. A raven alighted on the carcass, and laughed at him.

Maybe the Viper Mage was right, thought Torak. Maybe I will never be free of her.

He sat up straighter. But *she* will never be free of *me*.

You know who I am now, he told the Soul-Eaters silently, but *I* know *you*, too. I know who I'm fighting. And I'm not alone. I can tell the Ravens what's happened. I will tell them. Not today, but soon. I can trust them. Fin-Kedinn will know what to do.

The breeze loosed a flurry of snow from the branches overhead, and at the same moment, the sun came out, and turned the falling flakes to tiny slivers of rainbow.

Wolf came loping up the bank, bringing the fresh, cold smell of the river. They touched muzzles. On impulse, Torak pulled down the neck of his parka, and showed Wolf the Soul-Eater tattoo. Wolf gave it a sniff and a lick, then wandered off to snuffle up the fish-scales around the fire.

He doesn't mind, thought Torak in surprise.

With a new sense of hope, he glanced about him. Signs of spring were everywhere. Fluffy silver catkins bursting out on the willow trees. Sunlight gleaming on the sharp buds of beechlings pushing through the snow around their parents.

He remembered the offering he'd made on the night that Wolf was taken. He'd asked the Forest to watch over Wolf. It had heard him. Maybe now it would watch over him, too.

Around mid-afternoon, Fin-Kedinn returned, carrying three woodgrouse and a hare. He didn't look at Torak, but Torak could see the tension in his face as he went to the oak tree and began untying the lines of fish.

Torak stood up and started to help. 'I want to stay,' he said.

Fin-Kedinn's blue eyes glinted. He pressed his lips together in a smile. 'Good,' he said. 'That's good.' Then he put his hand on Torak's shoulder and gave it a shake, and together they started back for camp.

AUTHOR'S NOTE

Torak's world is the world of six thousand years ago: after the Ice Age, but before farming spread to his part of north-west Europe. The mammoths and sabre-toothed tigers had gone, and the land was one vast Forest. Most of the trees, plants and animals were pretty much the same as they are now, although the forest horses were a little sturdier, and you might be astonished at your first sight of an auroch: an enormous wild ox with forward-pointing horns, which stood about six feet high at the shoulder.

The people of Torak's world looked like you or me, but their way of life was very different, as they lived by hunting and gathering what they wanted. They hadn't yet thought of farming, and they didn't have writing, metals, or the wheel. They didn't need them. They were superb survivors. They knew all about the animals, trees, plants and rocks around them. When they wanted something, they knew where to find it, or how to make it.

Hunter-gatherers lived in small clans, and they tended to move from place to place: sometimes only staying in a campsite for a few days, like Torak and Fa of the Wolf Clan; sometimes for a whole moon or a season, like the Raven and Boar Clans; while others stayed put all year round, like the Seal Clan. (Thus the map of Torak's world in this book shows where the clans happen to be during the events in *Wolf Brother*; thereafter, in *Spirit Walker* and *Soul Eater*, some of them have moved a bit.)

I've learned much of all this from archaeology: that is,

from the study of traces left behind of the clans' weapons, food, clothes and shelters. But how did they *think*? What did they believe about life and death, and where they came from? For that, I've looked at the lives of more recent hunter-gatherers, including many American Indian tribes, the Inuit (Eskimo), the San of southern Africa, and the Ainu of Japan.

This still leaves the question of how it *feels* to be a hunter-gatherer. Is reindeer heart good to eat? What is it like to sleep on skins in an open-fronted shelter, to swim with killer whales, or track wolves in the snow? I've tried to find out.

To research *Wolf Brother*, I learned about the traditional ways of the Sami people, and camped in the forests of Finland, where – among other things – I picked up hunting tips, tasted lingonberries and spruce resin, and learned how to carry fire in a piece of smouldering fungus rolled in birch bark.

For *Spirit Walker*, I gained inspiration for the Seal Islands by visiting the Lofoten Islands, and the ancient rock carvings at Leiknes, both in north-west Norway. In Greenland I studied traditional Inuit ways of life, including boat-building and seal-hunting. Most memorably, I went to Tysfjord in north Norway, and swam with wild killer whales. I couldn't have written about Torak's experiences in the water without being there too; and like Torak, swimming in the sea with killer whales altered for ever my perception of these amazing creatures.

To research *Soul Eater*, I wandered through a snowy forest in the foothills of the Carpathian mountains in Romania, finding the tracks of wolves, boar, deer, lynx, badger and many more (although to my relief, the bears were still hibernating). I also watched ravens at a carcass, and learned how to fake a kill in order to attract these most intelligent of birds. To learn about husky-sledding, I met huskies in Finland and Greenland, where they took me on several exhilarating (and freezing) races across the ice. To understand the lives of the Ice clans, I studied the traditional skills of the Inuit of Greenland and northern Canada, particularly their snow-houses and their superbly made hide clothes. It was in Greenland that I experienced the might of wind and ice, and – on one memorable solo hike – the terror of glimpsing a polar bear in the distance. To get even closer to polar bears, I went to Churchill in northern Canada, where I watched them at rest and at play, by day and night. It's a privilege to come face to face with a wild polar bear, and to meet the gaze of the creature whom the Inuit of north-west Greenland call *pisugtooq*, the Great Wanderer. I'll always be haunted by the look in those fearsome, yet strangely innocent, dark eyes.

For all the books, a crucial part of my research has been getting close to wolves. The times I've spent watching them as they investigate their surroundings, squabble over food and their position in the pack, and communicate with each other in ways which only Torak could truly understand, has given me precious insights into how Wolf perceives his world. Above all, it has allowed me to do justice to these intelligent, endearing, and endlessly fascinating creatures.

Ψ

I'd like to thank all those who helped me when I was researching *Wolf Brother*, including Jorma Patosalmi for guiding me through the forest of northern Finland, and Mr Derrick Coyle, the Yeoman Ravenmaster of the Tower of

London, for sharing his extensive knowledge of some very special ravens. For *Spirit Walker*, my thanks go to the people at the Polaria in Tromso for helping me understand what it's like to be a seal, and the people of Tysfjord for helping me get close to killer whales and white-tailed eagles. For *Soul Eater*, my thanks to Christoph Promberger of the Carpathian Large Carnivore Project in Transylvania for sharing his knowledge of tracking, wolves and ravens; the people of Churchill, Manitoba, for helping me get closer to wild polar bears; and the people of east Greenland for their hospitality, openness and good humour.

Lastly, and as always, I want to thank the UK Wolf Conservation Trust for providing me with so many unforgettable times with some wonderful wolves; my agent, Peter Cox, for his unfailing enthusiasm and support; and my wonderful editor and publisher, Fiona Kennedy, for her imagination, commitment and understanding.

Michelle Paver

A WORD ABOUT WOLF

At the start of *Wolf Brother*, Wolf was three moons old. By the beginning of *Soul Eater*, he's twenty moons old, and he looks like a full-grown wolf – but he isn't, not in terms of experience.

When he ran with the pack on the Mountain of the World Spirit, he picked up some of the hunting skills he'll need if he's to survive, but he's still got a lot to learn.

And although he'll soon be physically capable of fathering cubs, he won't be doing that for a while. Many wolves are three years old or more before they find a mate and start a family. Until then, they often act as baby-sitters for their younger brothers and sisters, looking after them while the rest of the pack is out hunting.

Because Wolf's chest is narrow, and his legs are long and slender, he can plough through deep snow quickly and easily. His big paws act like snowshoes, letting him run over the top of crusted snow, where the sharp hooves of deer might sink right in.

Because it's winter, Wolf's fur is much thicker than it was in *Spirit Walker*, which makes him look even bigger. His pelt has two layers: the short, fluffy **underfur**, which traps air to insulate him from the cold; and the long, coarse **guard hairs** which protect him from rain, snow, and scratchy juniper bushes. It's because of his superb winter pelt that Wolf can brave the Far North without feeling the cold like Torak and Renn.

Unlike them, Wolf has incredible endurance. Even his walk is twice as fast as Torak's (unless he's deliberately slowing down to let Torak keep up), but most of the time he prefers to trot: a beautiful, fluid, floating gait which he can keep up for hours. And his run, of course, is *much* faster than Torak's.

Some of Wolf's senses are much better than Torak's, while others are about the same. We don't know very much about a wolf's sense of **taste**, although we know that their tongues can sense the same kinds of taste as us: salty, sweet, bitter and sour. But we don't know how meat tastes to Wolf; or water, or blood.

It's thought that wolves' **eyesight** is roughly similar to ours, although they're better at distinguishing shades of grey, and seeing in the dark. They also seem to be better at spotting movement – which is useful for hunting in the Forest – and it's thought that they don't see in colour, at least, not as well as we do.

Wolf's sense of **hearing** is better than Torak's. He can

hear sounds that are too high for Torak to catch, and his large ears help him pick up very faint sounds. This partly explains why not even Torak will ever be able to grasp all the subtleties of wolf talk, or express himself as well as a real wolf: because he can't make or hear the highest yips and whines, as Wolf can.

Wolf's sense of **smell** is *much* more sensitive than Torak's. It's not known for sure exactly *how* much, but judging from the number of smell receptors in his long nose, it's been estimated at between a thousand to a million times better.

Like all wolves, Wolf communicates by means of **wolf talk**: a highly complex combination of sounds, movements, and smells. Torak knows more about this than we do, but wolf scientists and observers are learning more all the time.

When Wolf uses his **voice**, he doesn't only howl. He can make all sorts of other noises, including yips, grunts, wheezes, whines, growls, and snarls.

He also uses **movement**: from big gestures like body-slamming or waggling his paws, to more subtle twitches of his eyes, muzzle, ears, hackles, paws, body, tail, and fur.

He uses his **scent** to communicate, too, by spilling it, or rubbing against a marking-point (or Torak) – in ways which not even Torak fully understands.

And of course, when Wolf wants to say something, he may not use only *one* such sound, movement or smell, but a complex **combination** of several, which changes depending on who he's

talking to, and the mood he's in. Thus if he wants to smile at Torak, he might bow his head and flatten his ears, wrinkling his muzzle and wagging his tail, while whining, nose-pushing, and giving Torak's face and hands tickly little nibbles. All just to say hello!

Michelle Paver
2006

THE WAYS OF THE SEA

The clans of Torak's world had many beliefs and customs to do with the Sea, and traces of these still exist today.

The Hunters

Many sea-going peoples such as the Tlinglit and the Kwak-iutl (Kwakwa'ka'wakw) of North-West America revered killer whales, and believed that you should never harm one, because then the whale's family would seek revenge. Elsewhere in the world, other cultures have similar taboos against killing different animals. The Cherokee believed it was wrong to kill a wolf; the Dyaks of Borneo would never kill a crocodile; while in England, many people still believe it's very bad luck to kill a robin or a wren.

The Sea Mother

Among the Inuit of Greenland, the Sea Mother, sometimes known as Sedna or Sassuma Arnaa, was believed to live in the deeps, and to rule the seals, fishes and whales upon which the people depended for survival. Great care had to be taken not to offend her. If a hunter wasted any part of a carcass, or if he didn't keep his hide clothing clean and in good repair, the Sea Mother would be angry, and would keep the prey below, rather than sending it up to the surface to be hunted. In northern Scotland until well into last century, the Mither o' the Sea was invoked by Shetland fishermen as protection against the Devil.

Torak's crime: tainting the Sea with the Forest

Some Inuit people believed that the Sea Mother hated to

see her sea creatures tainted by contact with land creatures, particularly reindeer. To avoid offending her, the people made sure to hunt reindeer and work their hides well *before* they went after seals; and when they did set out on a seal hunt, hunters purified their gear and their reindeer-hide clothing over seaweed fires. In more recent times, all sorts of different things have been thought to bring bad luck to fishermen. In parts of Scotland, it was believed that even to mention hares or red-haired women near a boat would bring bad luck; and it was a grave mistake to let a cat near the bait or the fishing-tackle, as the smell was thought to keep the fish away.

Making an offering to the spirit of the whale

Many hunting peoples honoured their prey after it was killed, and held rites and sacrifices to thank its spirit for allowing its body to be eaten. By doing so, they hoped to appease it, and thus avoid bad luck, while ensuring that they would catch more prey in the future. For instance, the Nootka of Vancouver Island honoured a whale when it was brought in, as did the Koryak of Siberia; while the Tlinglit of Alaska and the Ainu of Japan honoured the first catch of the fishing season. Even today, among the more traditional of the Inuit of Greenland, a hunter who has killed a seal will taste a small piece of its raw liver, to honour the prey, and ensure hunting luck.

Tenris' belt of puffin beaks

In some cultures, shamans, or medicine men (and women) wore ceremonial belts which helped them contact the spirit world, heal the sick, and predict the weather and the movements of the prey. Until recently among the Inuit, the *angakkuq*, or shaman, wore a belt to which might be attached all kinds of powerful objects: the foot-bones of foxes and wolves, the beaks of puffins and auklets, miniature knives to help fight evil spirits, and small gifts from people whom the *angakkuq* had helped in the past. Today, some people in the West wear charm bracelets. Could this be a distant legacy of such traditions?

The Great Wave
Only a few thousand years before Torak's time, a massive landslide occurred in the Arctic Ocean, somewhere between the coast of Norway and Iceland. Archaeologists call this the Storrega slide. It created a huge tidal wave, or tsunami, which drowned many thousands of kilometres of coastline. It's this tsunami which is remembered by the clans of Torak's world as "the Great Wave".

Bale's amulet: a rib from the first seal he ever caught, wound with cormorant gullet
An amulet is a small object or piece of jewellery which is carried as a good-luck charm, or to protect against evil. Bale's amulet is of a kind used by many Inuit in the recent past. Other such amulets included seal claws (for speed), polar bear claws (for strength), or a wooden carving of a bird (to peck at evil spirits). The use of amulets remains widespread today. In Scotland, some people carry a slip of white heather for luck, while in North America, a rabbit's foot is considered lucky; and of course, children the world over take a lucky toy or a special pencil-case into an exam, to help them do well.

Michelle Paver, 2006

Outcast

Torak crouched on a beach of black sand, his clothes in tatters, his face wild and hopeless as he lashed out with a flaming brand — lashed out at Wolf.

For two moons Torak has hidden a dreadful secret. Now it is revealed. He bears the mark of the Soul-Eater, and must pay the price. Cast out from the clans, he is alone and on the run: cut off from his best friend Renn and his beloved pack-brother, Wolf.

In the haunted reedbeds of Lake Axehead, he is hunted by the Otter Clan, taunted by the Hidden People and, as soul-sickness claims him, he falls prey to an even greater menace. Tormented by secrets and broken trust, he uncovers a deception which will turn his world upside down.

Outcast is an enthralling story of friendship, survival and of the need to belong. It draws you into the distant past, and takes you further on Torak's quest to vanquish the Soul-Eaters, which began with *Wolf Brother*, *Spirit Walker* and *Soul Eater*.

OATH BREAKER

*Torak circled the fire and Thiazzi came after him:
slowly, cracking his whip, playing with his prey as a
lynx plays with a lemming. Torak was exhausted.
He wasn't going to last much longer.*

When he was outcast, Torak was the hunted one.
Nine moons later he becomes the hunter, when
he vows to avenge the killing of one of his
closest friends.

Racked by guilt and grief, he follows the killer
into the Deep Forest, where the World Spirit stalks the
hidden valleys as a tall man with the antlers of a stag.
But there is a rottenness at the heart of the Forest, for its
clans have succumbed to the lies of the Soul-Eaters.
Here Torak must face fire, war and overwhelming evil.

Oath Breaker is a story about keeping promises,
and the true cost of vengeance. It leads you
back into the distant past, and further on the
adventure which began in *Wolf Brother,
Spirit Walker, Soul Eater* and *Outcast.*

FAR NORTH ↑

NARWAL,
WALRUS CLANS

MOUNTAIN OF
THE WORLD
SPIRIT

RAVEN
CAMP

RAVINE

ICE
CLIFFS

SLOPES

HILLS

MOUNTAIN
HARE CLAN

ICE
RIVER

SWAN
CLAN

THE HIGH MOUNTAINS

THE
DEEP
FOREST

AUROCH, LYNX,
FOREST HORSE,
RED DEER,
BAT CLANS

ROWAN
CLAN

ROCK

ORS